THE SHAKESPEARE STEALER SERIES

THE SHAKESPEARE STEALER

SHAKESPEARE'S SCRIBE

SHAKESPEARE'S SPY

Gary Blackwood

DUTTON CHILDREN'S BOOKS
New York

Published in the United States by Dutton Children's Books,
a division of Penguin Young Readers Group
345 Hudson Street, New York, New York 10014
www.penguin.com

Printed in USA First Edition
ISBN 0-525-47320-3
1 3 5 7 9 10 8 6 4 2

THE SHAKESPEARE STEALER

Gary Blackwood

DUTTON CHILDREN'S BOOKS
New York

Library of Congress Cataloging-in-Publication Data
Blackwood, Gary L.
The Shakespeare stealer / by Gary Blackwood.—1st ed. p. cm.
Summary: A young orphan boy is ordered by his master to infiltrate
Shakespeare's acting troupe in order to steal the script of "Hamlet,"
but he discovers instead the meaning of friendship and loyalty.
ISBN 0-525-45863-8
[1. Theater—Fiction. 2. Orphans—Fiction.
3. Actors and actresses—Fiction. 4. Great Britain—History—Elizabeth,
1558–1603—Fiction. 5. Shakespeare, William, 1558–1603—Fiction.]
I. Title.
PZ7.B5338Sh 1998 [Fic]—dc21 97-42987 CIP AC

Published in the United States by Dutton Children's Books,
a member of Penguin Putnam Inc.
375 Hudson Street, New York, New York 10014
Designed by Amy Berniker
Printed in USA
First Edition
20 19 18 17 16 15 14 13 12 11

For Tegan,
my only collaboration—
and a masterpiece

THE
SHAKESPEARE
STEALER

I never knew my mother or my father. As reliably as I can learn, my mother died the same year I was born, the year of our Lord 1587, the twenty-ninth of Queen Elizabeth's reign.

The name I carried with me throughout my youth was attached to me, more or less accidentally, by Mistress MacGregor of the orphanage. I was placed in her care by some neighbor. When she saw how small and frail I was, she exclaimed "*Och*, the poor little pigwidgeon!" From that unfortunate expression came the appellation of Widge, which stuck to me for years, like pitch. It might have been worse, of course. They might have called me Pig.

Of my life at the orphanage, I have made it a habit to recall as little as possible. The long and short of it is, it was an institution, and institutions are governed by expediency. Mistress MacGregor was not a bad woman, just an overburdened one. Occasionally she lost her temper and beat one of us, but for the most part we were not mistreated so much as neglected.

The money given us by the parish was not enough to keep one child properly clothed and fed, let alone six or seven. We depended mostly upon charity. When someone felt charitable, our bellies were relatively full. Otherwise, we dined on barley mush and wild greens. When times were hard for others, they were doubly so for us.

It was the dream of each child within those dreary walls that someday a real family would come and claim him. Preferably it would be his true parents—who were, of course, royalty—but any set would do. Or so we thought.

When I was seven years of age, my prospects changed, as some say they do every seven years of a person's life—the grand climateric, I have heard it called. That orphan's dream suddenly became a reality for me.

The rector from the nearby hamlet of Berwick came looking for an apprentice and, thanks to Mistress MacGregor's praise, settled on me. The man's name was Dr. Timothy Bright. His title was not a religious one but a medical one. He had studied physick at Cambridge and practiced in the city of London before coming north to Yorkshire.

Naturally I was grateful and eager to please. I did readily whatever was asked of me, and at first it seemed I had been very fortunate. Dr. Bright and his wife were not affectionate toward me—nor, indeed, toward their own children. But they gave me a comfortable place to sleep at one end of the apothecary, the room where the doctor prepared his medicines and infusions.

There was always some potion simmering over a pot of burning pitch, and one of my duties was to tend to these. The pitch fire kept the room reasonably warm. I took my meals in the kitchen. Though the situation was hardly what we orphans had secretly hoped for, it was more or less what I had expected—with one exception. I was to be taught to read and write, not only in English but in Latin, and not only in Latin but also in a curious abbreviated language of Dr. Bright's own devising. *Charactery*, he called it. It was, to use his own words, "an art of short, swift, and secret writing, by the which one may transcribe the spoken word as rapidly as it issues from the tongue."

His object, I soon learned, was not to offer me an education so much as to prepare me to be his assistant. I was to keep his scientific notes for him, and to transcribe his weekly sermons.

I had always been a quick student, but I was never quick enough to suit the doctor. He had some idea that his method of stenography could be learned in a matter of mere months, and he meant to use me to prove it.

I was a sore disappointment to him. It was an awkward system, and it took me a full year to become reasonably adept, and another year before I could set down every word without begging him to speak more slowly. This vexed him, for once his ample mouth was set in motion, he did not like to stop it. To his mind, of course, the fault lay not with his system but with me, for being so thickheaded.

I never saw him write anything in this short hand himself. I am inclined to think he never mastered it. As I grew confident with the system, I began to make my own small improvements in it—without the doctor's knowledge, of course. He was a vain man. Because he had once written a book, a dry treatise on melancholy, he felt the world should ever after make special allowances for him. He had written nothing since, so far as I knew, except his weekly sermons. And, as I was soon to discover, not always those.

When I was twelve, and could handle a horse as well as a plumbago pencil, the doctor set me off to neighboring parishes each Sabbath to copy other rectors' sermons. He meant, he said, to compile a book of the best ones. I believed him until one Sunday when the weather kept me home. I sat in on Dr. Bright's service and heard the very sermon I had transcribed at Dewsbury a fortnight before.

It did not prick my conscience to know that I had been doing something wrong. We were not given much instruction in right and wrong at the orphanage. As nearly as I could tell, Right was what benefited you, and anything which did you harm was Wrong.

My main concern was that I might be caught. I had never asked for any special consideration, but now I asked Dr. Bright, as humbly as I could, to be excused from the task. He blinked at me owlishly, as if not certain he had heard me properly. Then he scratched his long, red-veined nose and said, "You are my boy, and you will do exactly as I tell you."

He said it as though it were an unarguable fact of life. That discouraged me far more than any threat or show of anger could have done. And he was right. According to law, I was his property. I had to obey or be sent back to the orphanage. As Mistress Bright was fond of reminding me, prentices were easily come by and easily replaced. In truth, he had too much invested in me to dismiss me lightly. But he would not have hesitated to beat me, and heavily.

There was a popular saying to the effect that England is a paradise for women, a prison for servants, and a hell for horses. Prentices were too lowly to even deserve mention.

Eventually our sermon stealing was discovered. The wily old rector at Leeds noticed my feverish scribbling, and a small scandal ensued. Though Dr. Bright received only a mild reprimand from the church, he behaved as though his reputation were ruined. As usual, the blame fell squarely on my thin shoulders. My existence there, which had never been so much to begin with, went steadily downhill.

As I had so often done in my orphanage days, I began to wish for some savior to come by and, seeing at a glance my superior qualities, take me away.

In my more desperate moments, I even considered running away on my own. As I learned to read and transcribe such books as Holinshed's *Chronicles* and Ralegh's *Discov-*

ery of Guiana, I discovered that there was a whole world out there beyond Yorkshire, beyond England, and I longed to see it with my own eyes.

Up to now, my life had been bleak and limited, and it showed no sign of changing. In a new country such as Guiana, I imagined, or a city the size of London, there would be opportunities for a lad with a bit of wherewithal to make something of himself, something more than an orphan and a drudge. And yet I held no real hope of ever seeing anything beyond the bounds of Berwick. Indeed, the thought of leaving rather frightened me.

I was so ill-equipped to set out into that world alone. I could read and write, but I knew none of the skills needed to survive in the unfamiliar, perhaps hostile lands that lay beyond the fields and folds of our little parish. And so I waited, and worked, and wished.

If I had had any notion of what actually lay in store for me, I might not have wished so hard for it.

When I was fourteen, the grand climateric struck again, and my fortunes took a turn that made me actually long for the safety and security of the Brights' home.

In March, a stranger paid a visit to the rectory, but it was not some gentleman come to claim me as his heir. He was, in fact, no gentleman at all.

The doctor and I were in the apothecary when the housekeeper showed the stranger in. Though dark was almost upon us, we had not yet lighted the rush lights. The frugal doctor put that off as long as possible. The flickering flames of a pitch pot threw wavering, grotesque shadows upon the walls.

The stranger stood just inside the doorway, motionless and silent. He might have been taken for one of the shadows, or for some spectral figure—Death, or the devil—come to claim one of us. He was well over average height; a long, dark cloak of coarse fabric masked all his clothing save his high-heeled leather boots. He kept the hood of the cloak pulled forward, and it cast his face in shadow. The only feature I could make out was an unruly black beard, which curled over his collar. A bulge under the left side of his cloak hinted at some concealed object—a rapier, I guessed.

We all stood a long moment in a silence broken only by the sound of the potion boiling over its pot of flame. Dr. Bright blinked rapidly, as if coming awake, and snatched the clay vessel from the flame with a pair of tongs. Then he turned to the cloaked figure and said, with forced heartiness, "Now, then. How may I serve you, sir?"

The stranger stepped forward and reached under his cloak—for the rapier, I feared. But instead he drew out a small book bound in red leather. When he spoke, his voice was deep and hollow-sounding, befitting a spectre. "This is yours, is it not?"

Hesitantly, the doctor moved nearer and glanced at the volume. "Why, yes. Yes it is." I recognized it as well now. It was one of a small edition Dr. Bright had printed up the year before, with the abundant title, *Charactery: An Art of Short, Swift, and Secret Writing.*

"Does it work?"

"I beg your pardon?"

"The system," the man said irritably. "Does it work?"

"Of course it works," Dr. Bright replied indignantly. "With my system, one may without effort transcribe the written or the spoken word—"

"How long does it take?" the man interrupted.

Dr. Bright blinked at him. "Why, as I was about to say, one may set down speech as rapidly as it is spoken."

The man gestured impatiently, as if waving the doctor's words aside. "How long to *learn* it?"

The doctor glanced at me and cleared his throat. "Well, that depends on the aptitude of the—"

"How *long*?"

The doctor shrugged. "Two months, perhaps. Perhaps more." Perhaps a lot more, I thought.

The stranger flung the book onto the trestle table, which held the doctor's equipment. A glass vessel fell to the floor and shattered.

"Now see here—" Dr. Bright began. But the man had turned away, his long cloak swirling so violently that the flame in the pitch pot guttered and smoked. He stood facing away a moment, as if deep in thought. I busied myself cleaning up the broken beaker, content for once to be a lowly prentice with no hand in this business.

The black-bearded stranger turned back, his face still shadowed and unreadable. "To how many have you taught this system of yours?"

"Let me see . . . There's my boy, Widge, here, and then—"

"How many?

"Well . . . one, actually."

The hooded countenance turned on me. "How well has he learned it?"

Dr. Bright assumed his false heartiness again. "Oh, perfectly," he said, to my surprise. He had never before allowed that I was anything more than adequate.

"Show me," the man said, whether to me or the doctor I could not tell. I stood holding the shards of glass in my hand.

"Are you quite deaf?" the doctor demanded. "The gentleman wishes a demonstration of your skill."

I set the glass in a heap on the table, then picked up my small table-book and plumbago pencil. "What must I write?"

"Write this," the stranger said. "I hereby convey to the bearer of this paper the services of my former apprentice—" The man paused.

"Go on," I said. "I've kept up wi' you." I was so intent on transcribing correctly and speedily that I'd paid no attention to the sense of the words.

"Your name," the man said.

"Eh?"

"What is your *name*?"

"It's Widge," the doctor answered for me, then laughed nervously, as if suddenly aware how odd was the name he had been calling me for seven years.

The stranger did not share his amusement. "—my former apprentice, Widge, in consideration of which I have accepted the amount of ten pounds sterling." He paused again, and I looked up. For some reason, Dr. Bright was staring openmouthed, seemingly struck dumb.

"Is that all?" I asked.

The man held out an unexpectedly soft and well-manicured hand. "Let me see it." I handed him the table-book. He turned it toward the light. "You have copied down every word?" I could not see the expression on his face, but I fancied his voice held a hint of surprise.

"Aye."

He thrust the table-book into my hand. "Read it back to me."

To the unschooled eye, the scribbles would have been wholly mysterious and indecipherable:

Yet I read it back to him without pause, and this time I was struck by the import of the words. "Do you—does this mean—?" I looked to Dr. Bright for an explanation, but he avoided my gaze.

"Copy it out now in a normal hand," the stranger said.

"But I—"

"Go on!" the doctor snapped. "Do as he says."

It was useless to protest. What feeble objection of mine could carry the weight of ten pounds of currency? I doubted the doctor earned that much in a year. Swallowing hard, I copied out the message in my best hand, as slowly as I reasonably might. Meantime my brain raced, searching for some way to avoid being handed over to this cold and menacing stranger.

Whatever the miseries of my life with the Brights, they were at least familiar miseries. To go off with this man was to be dragged into the unknown. A part of me longed for new places, new experiences. But a larger part clung to the security of the familiar, as a sailor cast adrift might cling fast to any rock, no matter how small or barren.

Briefly, I considered fleeing, but that was pointless. Even if I could escape them, where would I go? At last I came to the end of the message and gave it up to Dr. Bright, who appended his signature, then stood folding the paper carefully. I knew him well enough to know that he was waiting to see the color of the man's money.

In truth, I suppose I knew him better than I knew anyone in the world. It was a sad thought, and even sadder to think that, after seven years, he could just hand me over to someone he had never before met, someone whose name he did not know, someone whose face he had never even seen.

The stranger drew out a leather pouch and shook ten gold sovereigns from it onto the table. As he bent nearer the light of the pitch pot, I caught my first glimpse of his features. Dark, heavy brows met at the bridge of a long, hooked nose. On his left cheek, an ugly raised scar ran all the way from the corner of his eye into the depths of his dark beard. I must have gasped at the sight of it, for he turned toward me, throwing his face into shadow again.

He thrust the signed paper into the wallet at his belt, revealing for an instant the ornate handle of his rapier. "If you have anything to take along, you'd best fetch it now, boy."

It took even less time to gather up my belongings than it had for my life to be signed away. All I owned was the small dagger I used for eating; a linen tunic and woollen stockings I wore only on the Sabbath; a worn leather wallet containing money received each year on the anniversary of my birth—or as near it as could be determined; and an ill-fitting sheepskin doublet handed down from Dr. Bright's son. It was little enough to show for fourteen years on this Earth.

Yet, all in all, I was more fortunate than many of my fellow orphans. Those who were unsound of mind or body were still at the orphanage. Others had died there.

I tied up my possessions with a length of cord and returned to where the men waited. Dr. Bright fidgeted with the sovereigns, as though worried that they might be taken back. The stranger stood as still and silent as a figure carved of wood.

When he moved, it was to take me roughly by the arm and usher me toward the door. "Keep a close eye on him, now," the doctor called after us. I thought it was his way of expressing concern for my welfare. Then he added, "He can be sluggish if you don't stir him from time to time with a stick."

The stranger pushed me out the front door and closed it behind him. A thin rain had begun to fall. I hunched my shoulders against it and looked about for a wagon or carriage. There was none, only a single horse at the snubbing post. The stranger untied the animal and swung into the saddle. "I've only the one mount. You'll have to walk." He pulled the horse's head about and started off down the road.

I lingered a moment and turned to look back at the rectory. The windows were lighted now against the gathering dark. I half hoped someone from the household might be watching my departure, and might wish me Godspeed, and I could bid farewell in return before I left this place behind forever. There was no one, only the placid tabby cat gazing at me from under the shelter of the eaves.

"God buy you, then," I told the cat and, slinging my bundle over my shoulder, turned and hurried off after my new master.

I had no notion of where I was being taken. We headed south out of Berwick, past the slate-roofed house of Mr. Cheyney, the wool merchant, past the old mill, past the common fields. I had been south as far as Wakefield; beyond that, my geography was unreliable. I knew that if one continued south a week or so, one would end up in the vicinity of London. But I was sure this man was no Londoner.

Judging from Dr. Bright's accounts, the men of London dressed in splendid clothing, all ornamented and embroidered, and spoke in a civil and cultured manner. They lived in houses ten times larger and grander than Mr. Cheyney's and consorted with ladies of elegance and beauty.

I had a hard time matching the stranger's pace. He never

looked back to see whether I was keeping up, or whether I was following at all. Yet I was sure that, if I took it into my head to slip off into the dark woods, he would know at once. Besides, there were the woods themselves to be reckoned with.

About Berwick, the woods were tame. The trees were broad and widely spaced; sheep and pigs grazed on the swards among them, and on my rare free afternoon, I had walked there without fear.

These woods were dense and dark and dreadful. To run there would be like jumping into the fire to escape the cooking pot. Those trees, I had heard, concealed every unsavory brigand and every ravenous beast of prey in the shire—until nightfall, when they ventured out upon roads such as this, in search of victims.

I shuddered and, breaking into a trot, closed the gap between myself and the stranger's horse. When I grasped the frame of his saddle, I could shuffle along with less effort. Still, I was not used to physical exertion, and the pace took its toll on me. I summoned enough breath to say, "Will we be stopping for the night, then?"

The man twisted in his saddle and glanced down at my hand clutching the frame. I was afraid he might push me away, but he faced front again. "Speak when you are spoken to," he said in a low voice.

We pushed on long after the last light was gone from the watery sky. I hoped that we might put up at the King's Head in Wakefield, but we passed by without pausing.

From there, the road was unfamiliar to me, though its ruts and rocks felt all too familiar. The bottoms of my shoes, which were thin as paper, grew ragged. At last I trod on a sharp stone that pierced the leather sole, and the sole of my foot as well. "Gog's blood!" Losing my grip on the saddle, I fell to my knees on the hard dirt.

The stranger wheeled his horse about. "Silence!" he hissed. "You'll have every cutpurse within a league down upon us!"

"Sorry!" I whispered. "I've hurt meself."

He sighed in disgust. "Can you walk?"

I tried to place my weight on the injured foot. It was like stepping on a knife. "I wis not."

"If I give you the flat of my blade, can you?"

I considered a moment, then took a sharp breath. "Nay, I still wis not."

He reached out for me, and instinctively, I ducked. "Give me your hand!" His voice was harsh and impatient. Hesitantly, I put my hand in his. Despite the clammy air, his palm was hot and dry, like that of a man with a fever, and his grip was painfully strong. He lifted me bodily and dragged me across the horse's flank until I could swing one leg over the animal's haunches. I had scarcely settled in before we were off again, at a quicker gait than before. I dropped my bundle in my lap and clung desperately to the saddle frame.

After a time, I relaxed a bit, and even felt drowsy. My head drooped forward and came to rest on the stranger's damp cloak. He jerked violently, as though bitten, and I sat abruptly erect again. Despite all my care, this happened several more times. Finally, the man snapped, "Either ride properly, or go back to shank's mare"—meaning, of course, my feet.

As the night advanced, the air grew more chill, which helped keep me uncomfortably awake. In the small hours, we came upon an inn. My master took a room; I was given a pallet on the floor and was wakened long before I was ready the following morning. A loaf of bread and some cheese served as both breakfast and dinner. Each was eaten unceremoniously upon the back of the horse.

We paused once in the afternoon, to allow the animal to drink from a stream. I barely had time to soak my swollen foot before we were again on our way. When night fell, we were once more beset by woods on either hand, and no settlement in sight before or behind. What drove this man so, I wondered, to risk his life—and mine—on the high road after dark? Were we too near the end of our journey to stop?

All the preceding night and day, I had been in a sort of daze, brought on by the abrupt change in my circumstances. Now I was beginning to come out of it, and a hundred thoughts and questions rose in me, none of which I dared give voice to. All I could do was what I had always done: wait and watch and hope for the best.

The trees edged in and threatened to claim the very road. In places, their branches met above our heads and interlaced, nearly blocking out the light of the half moon. In one such dismal spot we got our first taste of trouble. There was no warning; one moment the road was deserted, dappled with moonlight, the next, half a dozen shadowy figures stood before us. I stiffened, and a gasp escaped me.

Instead of turning back or spurring the horse in a bid for escape, the stranger reined in and slowly approached the bandits, who stood in a crescent, blocking the path. Most were armed only with staves and short swords, but one man of imposing stature held a crossbow leveled at us. "Hold!"

The stranger let his horse advance until we were nearly abreast of the big man. "God rest you, gentlemen," he said, in a surprisingly amiable tone.

The big man, crowded by our horse, let his crossbow drift to one side. "Don't tell me you're a parson."

"Far from it."

"Good. I don't like doing business with parsons. They're too parsimonious." He guffawed at his own joke. "Well, let's have it, then."

"Have what?" the stranger asked innocently.

The big man laughed again, and this time his companions joined in. "Have what? 'a says. Have what? Why have a pot of ale wi' us, of course." More soberly, the man said, "Come now, enough pleasantries. Let's have your purse."

The stranger reached inside his cloak and drew out the

purse with which he had bought me. It was still heavy with coins. "Forgive me for not taking your meaning."

"Oh, aye," the big man said. "An you forgive us for taking your money."

The stranger leaned down, as if to surrender the pouch. But instead he swung it in a sudden arc and struck the bandit full in the face. The man staggered backward; his crossbow loosed its bolt, which flew wild. I gave a cry of dismay as the other thieves sprang forward.

But the stranger was ready. The hand that had held the purse an instant before now grasped his rapier. He kicked the nearest man's stave aside and give him a quick thrust to the throat. A second man's sword he deflected with his cloak, and sent the man reeling away, clutching at his bloody face. He seized the blade of a third man's weapon in his cloak-wrapped hand and yanked it away.

I, meantime, was struggling with a one-armed ruffian who had latched on to my tunic and was trying to pull me to the ground. I clung tenaciously to the saddle frame and kicked at my assailant, but it was no use. My small strength gave out, and I toppled like a wounded bird from my perch.

Flailing about for something to break my fall, I fastened on the neck of the one-armed man. He cursed and stumbled backward, and we both crashed to the ground. A rock struck my elbow, numbing my arm. It did even more damage to the bandit's head, and he lay suddenly still.

I dragged my limp arm free and got to my feet to see the

stranger dispatch the last of the outlaws with a sweeping blow that knocked the man into the road, where his companions lay in various attitudes and degrees of unconsciousness.

The stranger guided the horse to where the crossbow lay. With a flick of his blade, he severed its string, then lifted his fallen purse with the point of the sword. He shook a single coin from it and tossed it at the feet of the big man, who sat ruefully holding his jaw. "If this is a toll road, you might simply have tolled me."

The big man let out an abrupt laugh, then groaned with pain. "Would that you had been a parson after all."

Several of the bandits had begun to come around now. "Could we go on?" I pleaded. The stranger twisted about impatiently and, grasping the back of my tunic, hoisted me up behind him. Though I kept a wary eye on the thieves, he did not deign to glance back even once. Only when they were well out of sight did I breathe easily again. "What you did back there—I've never seen the like."

The stranger was silent a long moment, then he said gruffly, "You were told not to speak unless spoken to."

We rode on until at last, dew damp and bone weary, we came upon a small inn, where we took a room for what remained of the night. In the morning, after breaking fast with cold beef and ale, we set out once more, still heading south. My thighs were chafed raw from the constant motion of the horse, and every sinew and muscle ached fiercely.

About midday, I got up enough courage to ask, "When will we be there?"

The stranger gave me a glowering glance. "We will be there when we get there." Even in daylight, I saw little of his face, for he never pulled back the hood, except by accident. I did, however, memorize every square inch of the back of his cloak.

I despaired of that day ever reaching its end, but of course it did, and with it our journey. Just as the sun rounded the corners of the Earth, we came around a bend in the road and before us lay a landscape of stark steeples and thatched roofs glowing golden in the last rays of the sun—more buildings than I had ever seen in one place. "Is this London, then?" I asked, forgetting in my astonishment the commandment to hold my tongue.

Unexpectedly, the stranger laughed. "Hardly. It's only Leicester."

"I've heard of that," I said, feeling like an ignorant lumpkin.

Before we quite entered the town, we turned off the road and down a narrow lane to a substantial house surrounded by a high hedge. The stranger guided our horse down a cobbled walk to a stable nearly as imposing as the house.

I was scarcely able to believe that we had reached our destination, but the stranger dismounted and snapped, "Don't sit there like a dolt; get down!" My legs were in such a condition that they buckled under me. The stranger seized my arm and all but dragged me to the rear of the house.

As we came around the corner, we nearly collided with a husky youth who was headed for the stable. He stepped aside quickly and bobbed his head apologetically. "You're back, then. I'll see to your horse, sir."

"Give her an extra ration of oats. She's had a hard trip."

"Right, sir." The boy tried to be on his way, but the master stopped him.

"Adam."

"Yes, sir?"

"Your place is in the stable. Stay out of the kitchen."

"I will, sir." He hurried off.

"Lazy swad," the man muttered. We entered a spacious kitchen, lit not by rush lights but by actual candles. A plain young woman in a linen apron and cap was busy at the fireplace. "We'll be wanting supper, Libby," the man told her. "The boy will have his in his room."

"The garret?" the girl asked.

The man nodded brusquely, turned, and was gone.

The girl looked me over curiously. "Where are you from?"

"Berwick-in-Elmet."

She raised her eyebrows as though I'd said I came from the Antipodes. "Where's *that*?"

"Up Yorkshire way. Near Leeds."

"I see," she said, as if that explained something—my appearance, perhaps, or my speech. "Well, come. Best get you to your room."

"I'm to have a room of me own?"

"It looks that way, don't it?" She picked up a candle and led me through the pantry and up a set of steps, which in my exhaustion I was hard put to climb, to a small attic room. "Here you are. It's not much."

It could have been a pit full of snakes for all I cared. The moment she was gone, I blew out the candle and collapsed on the bed. I expected to be shaken awake at the crack of dawn, but when I finally woke, the sun was streaming through the gabled windows. I leaped up, hardly knowing where I was, struck my head on the low ceiling, and sat down again. For several minutes I remained there, holding my head and letting my mind adjust to these new and strange surroundings.

A pewter bowl of cold meat, carrots, and potatoes sat beside the bed. I gobbled it in a trice, then tried standing again. My legs felt uncertain, and my foot still pained me. Hearing footfalls on the stairs, I straightened myself and tried to look as though I had been up for hours and awaiting my master's call. But my visitor was only the stableboy. He thrust my bundle of clothing into my arms. "I'd put on something clean if I was you," he said. "You smell."

It seemed wicked to don my Sunday garb on an ordinary day, but it was all I had. The bundle had been tampered with, untied and hastily retied. I spread the clothing out on my bed and found my wallet, which had contained my meager savings. The money was gone, every farthing.

Though I was sure it was the stableboy's doing, I knew better than to say so. I was the new boy here, and I had long since learned that new boys have no rights. I would have to content myself with cursing him roundly and silently.

When I carried my dirty clothing downstairs, the girl

called Libby took them and gingerly dropped them in a basket. "The master said to bring you to him as soon as you were up, but I expect you'll want to be fed first."

"I've eaten. What was in the bowl."

She clucked her tongue. "That was last night's supper, you ninny. You were asleep when I brought it up."

I shrugged. "It served well enough as breakfast."

"Dinner, more like. It's nearly noon. Come, then."

As we passed from the kitchen into a great open room, I said, "Will 'a be cross wi' me, do you wis?"

She cast me the same doubtful glance she'd given when I told her where I hailed from. *"Wis?"*

"Aye," I said, wondering what she found so strange in a word I'd used all my life.

Libby led me up a wide staircase, to a large gallery with a dozen windows, and tapestries hung between them. "I can't say whether he'll be cross or no. He's a queer one, the master is." She turned and whispered, "Not to tell him I said so, now."

I made a cross over my heart as proof that I would not. We stopped before a paneled door, on which the girl knocked lightly. "Enter!" called a voice from within. The girl motioned me inside. As Libby pushed the door shut, she sent me an encouraging wink.

The room in which I found myself was so foreign that I might have stepped into another land. A soft carpet covered the floor; two of the paneled walls were hung with pictures; the other two were obscured top to bottom by more books than I would have suspected existed in all of England. If this is but Leicester, I thought, what must London be like?

So awed was I that it was a moment before my eyes fell on the figure at the writing desk, bent over some close task. "Widge?" he said, without turning.

I swallowed nervously. "Aye."

"Come, sit down." I was almost at the man's side before he looked up from his papers. I stared dumbly at him. This was not the fearsome stranger who had brought me here. This was a mild-looking man with a well-trimmed beard and a balding head of hair of an odd, reddish hue. He smiled slightly at my obvious bewilderment. "My name is Simon Bass," he said. "I am your new master."

"You might sit down," Simon Bass said, "before you fall down."

I sank into an upholstered chair. "But—but I thought—"

"You thought the one who brought you here was to be your master." Bass shrugged. "Falconer is not the most communicative of men, nor the most genial. But he is reliable, and effective. I could not go to Yorkshire myself because . . . well, for various reasons. He got you here in one piece, at any rate."

"Aye . . . mostly."

Bass chuckled. "Neither is Falconer the most considerate of traveling companions, I warrant. Have you eaten?"

"Aye."

"Good. Good." He shoved his papers aside, took up a

pipe, and filled the bowl of it with tobacco from an earthenware jar. "Then we can get right down to business. You'll be wanting to know what's expected of you."

"Aye." Though my seat was comfortable, I shifted about nervously.

"Very well." He went to the fireplace, touched a taper to a live coal, and lit the pipe. "The first thing I expect is that you say 'yes' rather than 'aye.' Your task will not require you to speak overmuch, but I'd as soon you did not brand yourself as a complete rustic. Understood?"

"Aye—I mean, yes."

"Excellent." His manner, which had become prickly, turned cordial again. "Now. When you go to London—"

"London?"

"Yes, yes, London. It's a large city to the south of here."

"I ken that, but—"

"Let me finish, then ask questions. When you go to London, you will attend a performance of a play called *The Tragedy of Hamlet, Prince of Denmark*. You will copy it in Dr. Bright's 'charactery' and you will deliver it to me. Now. Any questions?"

I scarcely knew where to begin. "I—well, how—that is—they will not object? The men who present the play?"

"Only if they discover you. Naturally you will be as surreptitious as possible."

"And an they do discover me?" I asked, thinking of the sermon-copying affair.

Bass blew out a cloud of smoke which made me cough.

"The Globe's audience is customarily between five hundred and one thousand. Do you suppose they can watch over every member of it?"

"I wis not."

"You *wis* not. Of course they can't. You will use a small table-book, easily concealed." He rummaged through the riot of papers on his writing desk. "You see how easily it is concealed? Even I can't find it." Finally he came up with a bound pad of paper the size of his hand. "There. Keep it in your wallet. You have a plumbago pencil?"

"Ay—yes."

"Any further questions?"

"An I might ask . . . for what purpose am I to do this?"

Bass turned a penetrating look on me. "Does it matter?"

"Nay, I wis not. I was only curious."

He nodded and scratched the balding top of his head. "You'll know sooner or later, I suppose." He puffed thoughtfully at his pipe, then continued. "I am a man of business, Widge, and one of my more profitable ventures is a company of players. They are not nearly so successful as the Lord Chamberlain's or the Admiral's Men, but they do a respectable business here in the Midlands. As they have no competent poet of their own, they make do with hand-me-downs, so well used as to be threadbare. If they could stage a current work, by a poet of some reputation, they could double their box."

"Box?"

"The money they take in. And my profit would also double. Now someone, sooner or later, will pry this *Tragedy of Hamlet* from the hands of its poet, Mr. Shakespeare, just as they did *Romeo and Juliet* and *Titus Andronicus.*" He jabbed his pipe stem at me for emphasis. "I would like it to be us, and I would like it to be now, while it is new enough to be a novelty. Besides, if we wait for others to obtain it, they will do a botched job, patched together from various sources, none of them reliable. Mr. Shakespeare deserves better; he is a poet of quality, perhaps of genius, and if his work is to be appropriated, it ought to be done well. That is your mission. If you fulfill it satisfactorily, the rewards will be considerable. If you do not—" He gave a wry smile. "Well, Falconer will make certain that you do."

The anticipation that had been growing in me turned suddenly sour. "I—I did not ken 'a would go wi' me."

Bass laughed. "Did you suppose I would send you off to London on your own? You can't even speak the language properly. I might just as well send you to Guiana." He patted one of my sagging shoulders. "Don't look so inconsolable. Falconer will take good care of you, and you can learn a lot from him. Besides, looking on the bright side, this time you'll have a horse of your own."

So the room that was to be mine was mine for two nights only. The following morning, we set out for London.

Though my legs had not quite recovered, by shortening my stirrups and leaning back in the saddle, I could ride without too much discomfort.

Naturally, Falconer set a brisk pace. Mr. Bass had no doubt instructed him not to delay, and he, in his fanatical fashion, took this to mean that we should drive our mounts and ourselves to exhaustion.

I was better fed this time, for Libby had provided me with all manner of victuals—fruit, meat pies, clapbread. She had also found time to wash and mend my workaday clothing, and patch my torn shoe. When I thanked her, she had waved my words away. "Tush, it's no more than is expected of me. Don't you go getting yourself into trouble in the city, now."

Trouble? I thought. In London? Ever since I could remember, I had heard Dr. Bright and others speak of London in tones usually reserved for talk of the Heavenly City. As the Earth was the center of the greater universe, so London was the center of our miniature universe. And I, Widge, orphan and lowly apprentice, was moving toward that center.

Sore legs be damned. I dug my heels into my horse's ribs and urged her into a gait that, for a short time, outstripped even Falconer. I had gone no more than a mile when a hare scampered from the brush and across the roadway. My mount reared, nearly spilling me from the saddle. Falconer came abreast of me. "What's the trouble?" he demanded.

"A hare," I said, shaken. " 'A ran across me path."

"That's all? From your face, anyone would guess it was a dragon at least."

"Do you not ken it's a bad omen?"

"I take no stock in omens. Men make their own fates."

"Not prentices," I muttered. I urged my horse forward, but not with quite the same eagerness as before.

Despite our haste, it took us two full days to reach London. Our passage was uneventful, and our conversation limited. We slept the night in Bedford, and in late afteroon of the following day, I first caught sight of the rooftops of the great city on the Thames.

The volume of traffic had swelled threefold. We passed carts and wagons of every size and description—full ones on their way into the city, empty ones coming back. Apparently, London had an enormous appetite for goods of every kind, from livestock and vegetables to timber and stone. In my poor parish, most of what we used came from the farms roundabout. It was curious to think of carting in food and materials from all over the country.

We approached the city on Aldersgate Street. All around

us lay fields and orchards; I might have imagined I had never left home had I not looked dead ahead, where the thousand buildings of the city, with their red tile roofs, lay ranged in rows within the ancient stone wall, so densely packed that those which lined the river seemed about to be nudged into it by those on the hill above.

"Close your mouth," Falconer said, "before your soul flies out."

Embarrassed, I clamped my mouth shut and urged my horse forward. By the time we passed through the wall at Aldersgate, the sun had set, and the streets were growing dark. There was much less bustle and clamor than I had expected. I was, in truth, a bit disappointed.

We had gone no more than a hundred yards before a man carrying a pikestaff and a bell and leading a mastiff on a leash stalked up to us. "You're to lead your horses within the walls!"

Falconer reined in. I watched him anxiously, wondering how he would respond to this order. To my surprise, he swung from his saddle without a word, though his bearing spoke of resentment and disdain, and walked on, leading his mount. I dropped to the cobblestones and hurried after.

My eyes were on Falconer, not on my footing. I stumbled into a deep depression in the ground and landed painfully on one knee. The watchman burst out laughing. "You're a green one, an't you?"

I was tempted to reply that, where I came from, we did

not leave holes in the street for people to fall into. But I thought better of it and limped off with my horse in tow. Now I saw that the depression was in fact a ditch that ran the length of the street. I also became aware of the noisome stench arising from it.

Falconer growled, "Must I watch you every moment, like an errant sheep?"

"I couldn't help it. I fell in that ditch."

"Then you have reason to act sheepish. That's the sewer." He waved a hand at me, as though to keep me at a distance. "Be sure you walk downwind of me from here on."

I saw at once that Falconer was no stranger to London. He made his way through the streets with such an air of assurance, indeed of arrogance, that those few townfolk still abroad gave him a wide berth—or perhaps it was due to the air about *me*.

Even in the dark, the buildings that towered over us were impressive. Some were a full four storeys high; in one block, the fronts of the buildings were decorated with beaten gold. To our right, a huge cathedral was silhouetted against the rising moon. As I stared at it, the bells in its square steeple rang the hour of compline.

"Stop gawking, and move your pins!" Falconer called. "That's the curfew bell!"

"London has a curfew?" I asked incredulously. The largest and most cosmopolitan city in England, the symbol of freedom to thousands upon thousands of country youths, compelled its citizens to be off the streets at nine o'clock?

Falconer strode on without replying. We passed the public stocks, which were empty, then came upon a spot where three streets diverged, like a trident. Falconer took the right-hand prong, and we walked another several blocks before we stopped under a sign which depicted St. George slaying a rather pitiful-looking dragon. "This will be our lodgings," Falconer said. "If we should become separated, find your way here. Just ask anyone for The George, near the Four Corners. Understood?"

"Aye. The George, near the Four Corners."

"Otherwise you are to talk to no one. Is *that* understood?"

"Aye."

He handed me the reins of his mount. "Take the horses through that archway to the stable." I started off, but his voice made me turn back. "One more thing."

"Aye?"

"Stop saying aye."

"I will," I promised. *Yes*, I told myself as I led the horses into the courtyard. Not aye, yes. Yes, yes, yes. Anything that would make me appear more like a Londoner and less like a green country woodcock, I was more than willing to adopt. But if I truly did not wish to be sniggered at, my first task would have to be to change my reeking clothing.

The main room of the inn, where we supped, was enormous, with a wide fireplace and half a dozen massive tables. At each sat four or five patrons, some eating, some drinking, some playing at dice.

As I sat opposite Falconer, gobbling my bread and herring, a quarrel kindled among the dice players. Two men sprang to their feet, their hands reaching for their rapiers, but a third man stepped between them. There was a moment's heated discussion, then one of the antagonists stalked from the room, wearing a grim look. Falconer seemed to take no notice of the scene. "There was nearly a fight!" I whispered.

"There will be one yet," he said. "They've merely chosen another time and place."

"You mean a duel? Over a game of dice?"

He shrugged, and his hood moved a little, revealing the long scar that traversed his cheek. "Some men will fight over nearly anything."

We finished our supper in silence. When Falconer started up to his room, I hastened after him. He waved me away with an impatient gesture, as if I still stank, though I had done my best to wash thoroughly. "You will make your bed in the stables, boy."

I backed away, surprised and a bit hurt. Simon Bass had led me to believe that my part in this "mission," as he had called it, was an important one. But to Falconer I was apparently no more than an unskilled and incompetent prentice, not fit to converse with or share a room with. In truth I was, except perhaps for my diet, no better than his horses.

For three days we sat idle at the inn, waiting for the

Lord Chamberlain's men to perform *The Tragedy of Hamlet*. There was a different play each afternoon, and *Hamlet* would not be presented until Tuesday. I spent much of the time watching the traffic that thronged the streets. Every conceivable conveyance passed by, from rude carts to fine coaches, and every conceivable class of person: ragged street urchins begging for farthings; fat merchants in sensible clothing; young dandies in doublets so extravagantly slit and slashed as to appear ready to fall off; dozens of prentices my age or younger, all wearing the same style of woollen cap.

The cries of street vendors mingled in a kind of exotic music: "Quick periwinkles, quick, quick!" "Fine Seville oranges, fine lemons." "I ha' ripe cowcumbers, ripe!" "Sweep! Chimbly sweep, mistress, from bottom to top. No soot shall then fall in your porridge pot!" "Ha' you any rats, mice, polecats, or weasels, or any old cows sick o' the measles?" I occupied several hours transcribing these cries, partly because thcy were so colorful, partly to exercise my stenography.

I had never witnessed a play, except for a few short interludes played on the bed of a wagon in the town square at May festival, so I had little idea of what to expect. How long would the performance last? Half an hour? Six hours? How rapidly would the players speak? What about their actions; should I transcribe them as well? What if they recited in Latin, or Greek?

I longed to ask Falconer all these things, but I knew

what his reply would be. He would glare at me and tell me to wait and see. So I sat about the courtyard and the stable, and like a good prentice, I waited.

On Tuesday, after a midday meal of fried fish and oysters, we set out for the theatre. We followed a narrow, unpaved street downhill to the Thames, and I was suddenly presented with a whole different aspect of the city.

Here were no gold-plated buildings or great cathedrals, only shabby rows of houses, cheek by jowl. With no space to spread sidewise, they had arched over the street, like the trees on that desolate stretch of road where we had met the outlaws, nearly meeting above our heads, shutting out the sun.

There were no street vendors here, nor prosperous merchants, only sullen wives emptying their slop jars into the street, sometimes missing the scrawny, shoeless children playing there, sometimes not. Falconer strode heedlessly along, as if daring anyone to empty a chamber pot on his head. No one did. One house had been boarded up, and a crude wooden cross nailed to its front door. Beneath the cross were scrawled the words LORD HAVE MERCY UPON US.

"Is that a church?" I said.

Falconer gave a derisive laugh. "That's a plague house, boy."

I shuddered. Though the plague had not been widespread in our parish, Dr. Bright had treated enough cases for me to know why that plea for mercy had been painted upon the door.

Ever since we left the inn, my stomach had been growing distressed, and the stench that hung in the stagnant air of that street did nothing to improve it. I laid the blame on the fried fish and oysters I had eaten, but it might have been due to nervousness. Suddenly I was unsure that I was up to the task of copying a whole play. And if I failed, Falconer would not be pleased. I would have pleaded illness, but I knew that Falconer would brook no excuse short of my writing hand being lopped off—and even then he would probably insist that I transcribe left-handed.

At the end of the street, a set of narrow stone steps led to the water's edge. Falconer took them two at a time. I followed more cautiously and caught up just as he was handing several pennies to a waterman with a small wherry-boat.

"Get in," Falconer said.

"In the boat?" I had never imagined the theatre would lie across the river.

"No, in the water," he said acidly and, I hoped, sarcastically.

It was no use protesting that I had never set foot in a boat in my life, and did not care to now, or that if the craft were to capsize I would be lost, for I had never learned to swim. There was nothing to do but to swallow my fear and step into the insubstantial bottom of the boat, which was all that lay between me and the Land of Rumbelow, that is to say a watery grave.

I took my place in the stern and sat gripping the gunwales with white-knuckled hands while Falconer climbed in, rocking the boat sickeningly, and the wherryman cast off.

Without the solid earth beneath my feet, my stomach grew even queasier. Before we were halfway across, I felt my dinner coming up. I tried to hold it back and, failing, thrust my head over the side of the boat and threw my fish back into the Thames, whence it had come. Unfortunately, I leancd out a bit too far. The boat listed suddenly, and I toppled over the side.

My head broke the surface of the water. But I had submerged only as far as my neck before something snatched the belt of my tunic and yanked me back aboard. It was Falconer. He set me forcibly in my seat and there I remained, sick and shamefaced, with water coursing from my hair, for the rest of the trip.

As we disembarked on the south bank, I said, "Thank you."

"For what?"

"For saving me life."

"I saved your master's investment, that's all." He headed down a wide road away from the river, and I trotted after.

"I'm sorry to have heaved up in the river."

Falconer snorted derisively. "There's enough garbage floating there already; a bit more will scarcely matter."

We were walking now in the company of a dozen or more theatregoers. The nearer we drew to the theatre, the more dense the crowd became. The people were of all positions and persuasions, from court ladies with coiffures that rivaled their skirts in volume to rank-smelling tanners' prentices. A number of the crowd turned down the lane that led to what I assumed was the theatre, but Falconer kept on straight ahead. "Is that not the theatre?"

"No. It's the bearbaiting."

I'd heard tell of bearbaitings but never witnessed one. Folk said it was a sport in which a bear, with its teeth broken off deliberately, was chained to a post and set upon by a pack of dogs. It did not sound very sporting to me.

A building that resembled an overgrown saltcellar lay ahead of us. I thought it circular at first, but it proved to be eight-sided, a good thirty feet in height, and three times that in breadth. I wondered that the ground here could support such a large structure. It was soft, swampy land, drained by half a dozen deep ditches, which we crossed on wooden footbridges.

The well-dressed patrons paid their admission to money gatherers, and mounted steps leading to upper galleries. The less elegant crowded through the main entrance and into a kind of courtyard. Above the entrance was a carving depicting Atlas with a globe of the world atop his shoulders—hence the theatre's name, the Globe. Under his feet was the legend *Totus mundus agit histrionem.*

I translated haltingly. "The whole world . . . practices theatrics?"

Falconer shook his head at my ignorance. "All the world's a stage. A line from *As You Like It.*"

"Oh," I said. "The play will not be in Latin, I trust?"

"No." Falconer made no move to approach the entrance but stood on the very fringes of the crowd, looking thoughtful. Finally he dug a penny from his purse and handed it to me. "Go on in."

"By *meself*?"

"Yes, yes, by yourself." He grasped my wrist and thrust the penny into my palm.

"But what an they—what an they catch me?"

"Whist!" Falconer held up a cautioning hand. "Softly!" In a low voice, he went on. "Just be certain they don't. And be certain you put down every word. Understood?"

"Aye," I said, forgetting in my anxiety the correct response.

"Go on, then!"

I felt in my wallet for the pad and pencil, then slipped into the stream of people which bore me, like a stick on the flood, through the entrance. A gatherer took my penny and I shuffled on, jostled from this side and that, until I bumped up against an unmoving mass of spectators. God help us, I thought, should the playhouse catch fire or collapse. We would all be trapped as surely as coneys in a snare.

The Globe's stage was a raised platform some ten yards across and equally as deep. Its boards were strewn with rushes. On the back wall were two curtained doorways, with a larger curtained space between them. Above these was a small balcony backed by a curtain and, above that, a thatched roof which covered the rear half of the stage.

A vendor with a basket of fruit and another selling leather bottles of beer wove through the crowd. The roar of voices and the smell of closely packed bodies were overpowering and unremitting. Even after a trumpeter appeared on a tiny balcony at the peak of the playhouse and blew a fanfare, the babble scarcely diminished. Nor did it leave off when two men in leather jerkins and helmets strode onto the stage.

At first, I thought they had been sent out to calm the crowd—or was it to apprehend would-be play pirates? I thrust my table-book and pencil into my wallet. As the chatter at last abated, the two men's words became audible, and I realized they were the players.

"Have you had a quiet guard?" one said, at the top of his voice.

"Not a mouse stirring," said the other, fairly shouting.

"Well, good night. If you do meet Horatio and Marcellus, the rivals of my watch, bid them make haste."

I fumbled frantically with the paper and pencil. Falconer had warned me to get down every word. Two more men entered, and I began to transcribe:

It was obvious at once that this would be no leisurely task, as copying those sermons back in Yorkshire had been. The players attacked their lines as though afraid that, if they did not keep their words in close order, the audience might throw comments of their own into the breach. And in fact, they often did.

My most pressing problem, however, was not the pell-mell flow of words, but how to identify each speaker on the page. All I could think of was to assign each a number, but that soon led to further confusion, as I forgot what number I'd given to which man. When half a dozen new players trooped out upon the stage, my heart sank into my shoes.

Gradually I learned the names of the major characters and labeled their lines accordingly. But then a new complication presented itself. I was caught up in the action of the play. I began to think of these people not as players mouthing speeches but as actual persons, living out a part of their lives before me.

Simon Bass had informed me that, because many considered the world of the theatre immoral, women were forbidden by law to act upon the stage. All women's roles were played by men and boys. That fact did not occur to me now. I was totally convinced that the Queen and Ophelia were what they seemed to be. In fact, Ophelia was quite fetching. So drawn in was I by the events on the stage that it seemed less important to me to copy down the lines than to find out what these people would say or do next.

When the ghost of Hamlet's father appeared upon the balcony and beckoned him, I gasped and shuddered but kept on writing. When Hamlet thrust his sword through the draperies, slaying Polonius, who was concealed there, I was lost. I no longer noticed the press of the crowd, nor its unwashed smell for I was no longer there among them, but in a castle in Denmark.

My petty mission no longer seemed to matter. All that mattered was whether or not Hamlet would take action to avenge his father. I wanted to call out to him, to tell him to stop delaying and debating, to go ahead and do what must be done. And yet I understood why he did not. I knew how it was to be swept along on the tide of events, and to feel you had no control over any of it, not even your own fate.

Every now and again, there was a passage of much talk and little action, and then I came to myself and began copying feverishly. But eventually I was drawn into the world of the play again, forgetting the world about me and the world outside, where Falconer waited.

From the onset of the fencing match between Hamlet and Laertes until Hamlet's death, I believe I did not commit to paper more than ten lines. I did get down every syllable of the final few speeches, but that was small comfort.

I had gone into the theatre fearful of being discovered and punished for writing down the play. I left with a dread of being punished for *not* having written it down. I need not have worried about the former; no one in the audience or on the stage had paid the least attention to my jottings.

Falconer, I knew, would not be so easy to fool. I hung back, trying to buy a little time in which to think. I could simply lie to Falconer, assure him that I'd transcribed the entire performance. Lying was one skill I'd acquired at the orphanage and polished during my apprenticeship to Dr. Bright. And of course there was no way Falconer could determine from looking at my scribbles whether or not I spoke the truth.

But eventually I was going to have to translate the play into ordinary script, and then the gaps would be as ostentatious as the slashes in the clothing of those young dandies I'd seen. To patch them in with a matching fabric would require an ability far greater than mine.

What to do, then? I would have to come up with some reasonable explanation very soon, for the theatre was rapidly emptying out. In a matter of minutes, I would be left standing in the arena all alone, like that toothless bear waiting to be savaged by the dogs.

The only thing I could think of to do was to admit that I'd overlooked a few lines, but lie about just how many, and hope that I'd be allowed a second chance. When I emerged on the tag end of the crowd, Falconer stood where I had left him, a dozen yards from the playhouse, his face turned toward the river, as though watching the slow progress of the coal barges. I considered bolting, losing myself in the crowd and thence in the streets of the city. But something made me hesitate. Perhaps it was the reward promised me by Simon Bass, perhaps it was the thought of having to fend for myself in this unfamiliar territory, perhaps it was both. Then Falconer turned and saw me, and it was too late. Gloomily, I approached him.

"Well?" he said.

"I got down most of it."

"*Most* of it?"

"Aye. Yes. The greater part. Nearly all, in fact. Save for a few wee bits here and there."

He smacked his fist into his palm so violently that I shrank back. "Why not all of it?"

"I—I couldn't hear well from where I stood. It was a very noisy crowd."

Falconer cursed under his breath. "How much is missing, exactly?"

"I don't ken, exactly."

"Twenty lines? Fifty? A hundred?"

I tried to choose a figure that would not sound too drastic yet would necessitate my coming back to fill in the gaps. "Not a hundred," I ventured. "Closer to fifty, I wis."

"You *wis*." He sighed heavily and stood watching the barges a moment. "When is the next performance of this play?"

"Friday, I wi—I think."

"Friday." Abruptly he turned to glare at me. "You'd best clean out your ears before then. Understood?"

"Aye. Yes. I will."

He stalked off, and I hastened after. As we neared the first of the footbridges, a man appeared from the rear of the playhouse and stepped onto the bridge. Falconer brushed past him so brusquely that he knocked the man off balance. The man stumbled sideways, tripped on the edge of the bridge, and splashed into the drainage ditch. He sprang up dripping wet, strode after Falconer, and snatched the back of Falconer's cloak, pulling the hood away from his head.

Falconer whirled about, his rapier already sweeping free of its hanger. The other man halted. His hand, too, went to his weapon. But before he could fully draw it, Falconer's sword point leaped forward. The move was so swift I am not certain I saw it clearly, but I believe he thrust his point through the guard of the other's weapon, then jerked upward. The man's rapier took flight and came to earth in the water of the ditch. With equal quickness, Falconer pulled the hood of his cloak forward again.

"Well," said the disarmed man, with surprising calm. "You have the advantage of me." Now that I heard his voice, I knew who he was—the first gravedigger in the play. Small wonder I did not recognize him at first; his appearance and speech were radically changed. Within the world of the play, he had been a shabby, half-drunk clown. Outside the playhouse walls, he cut quite a different figure. He was well built, well dressed, and well mannered, with nothing foolish or humble about him, despite the fact that he had just fallen into a ditch and been relieved of his weapon.

Falconer was putting away his sword. The player held up a hand to stay him. "Will you not allow me to salvage my weapon, sir, and with it my honor?"

Without replying, Falconer thrust his rapier into its hanger and turned away.

"May I at least know your name, then? One does not often meet a man with so disarming a manner."

I guessed that Falconer would not be able to resist a bit of wordplay, and I was right. "You know my arms. You need not know my name." It took me a moment to grasp the pun—if you recognized a man's coat of arms, then you knew his family name—but the player laughed appreciatively at once.

"It does seem to me that there is something familiar about you. Have we met before?"

"In another life, perhaps." Falconer strode away. The player gazed after him thoughtfully. I hastened after Falconer, not wishing to be left behind, but the player took hold of the sleeve of my tunic.

"What is your master's name?"

"Me master? Why, Dr. Bright," I said, perhaps out of old habit, perhaps as a deliberate lie—I was not sure which.

"*That* is Dr. Bright?" the player said incredulously, nodding after Falconer's departing figure.

"*That* is not me master. I don't ken that wight, and I'm as glad of it."

The man laughed. "He is an unmannerly lout, isn't he?" He let go of my sleeve. "You're merely a playgoer, then? Tell me, how did you like the play, a country lad like yourself?"

"Oh, very much," I said earnestly, trying not to seem anxious as Falconer faded from me.

"Did you indeed?" He stroked his short beard with a trace of amusement. "And what parts did you fancy most?"

"The fencing bout," I said instantly. "It looked so real!"

The man laughed. "Excellent!" He waded into the ditch and fished out his rapier. "I am the company's fencing master, you see." He looked ruefully at the muddy sword. "Though you would hardly guess it from that display just now."

"You are?" I was torn between catching up with Falconer and hearing more about the play.

"Aye." He climbed from the ditch and wiped his weapon in the grass.

I frowned. "You mock me speech."

"Not at all," he assured me. "I fell into it out of old habit. I'm a country wight meself, born and bred in Yorkshire. Judging from your speech, your master must be a South County man."

"Aye."

"But surely he's not the same Dr. Bright who authored the *Treatise on Melancholy*?"

"Aye. You don't mean you ken his work?"

"Oh, we do indeed ken it. In fact you might tell him that our Mr. Shakespeare has found his book invaluable. As you may have noticed, Hamlet is a very master of melancholy." He clapped me on the shoulder. "I'll be off now, or my colleagues will be several beers ahead of me, and I'll have trouble catching up." Laughing, he shook his head and licked his lips. "Performing works up a thirst like nothing else—save dueling, perhaps. Adieu, my young friend. Come see us again."

Unused to such civility, I let him get a dozen paces

down the road before I thought to reply. "Aye!" I called. "Thank you! I'll surely do that!"

After all, I thought, what choice did I have?

I found my way back to the bank of the Thames, but Falconer was nowhere in sight. Since I had no penny for passage—and did not care to risk my life in another boat, in any case—I would have to find another way of crossing the river. The only bridge was a formidable one of wood and stone several hundred yards downstream. In truth, it seemed less like a bridge than like a crowded city street, so heavily laden with shops that I feared the whole affair might collapse under the rumbling wheels of the carts and the pounding hooves of the horses.

Once safely on the north bank, I asked a cheerful fish-wife the way to The George, where I found Falconer eating his supper—fish, again.

"So, you finally found your way," he said.

"The player—'a held me back."

"And what did you tell him?"

"Naught. Just as you said I should."

He stared at me a long moment with his shadowed eyes, as if trying to see into my soul. Then he devoured the last of his meal and rose. "I don't like liars," he said, his voice low and harsh. "I hope you are not one."

I shook my head emphatically, too intimidated to speak. I don't believe he noticed, for he was already on his way upstairs.

I saw little of Falconer over the next two days. Around midday on Friday, he came to the stable where, to pass the time, I was helping the stableboy curry horses. He neither spoke nor beckoned to me, only stepped back out into the courtyard, knowing I would follow.

He was even less talkative than usual, but finally, as we walked down a deserted alley, he said, "Be sure you complete your work today. We've lost our lodgings."

"Lost them?"

"I killed one of the other lodgers. In a duel."

It was several minutes before I recovered from this news enough to ask, "What—what was it about, then? The duel?"

I was certain he would reprimand me for talking too

much. But he did not. Instead he replied, "The man called me a filthy Jew."

Something possessed me to ask, "Are you?"

"Filthy? Or a Jew?" He sounded almost amused.

"A Jew."

He gave a short, bitter laugh. "There are no Jews in England. Only former Jews."

The sky scowled down upon us, threatening rain as we boated over to Southwark and joined the throng of bear-baiters and playgoers. At the Globe, Falconer drew me aside. "We must find a better vantage point for you, one where you will hear *every* word."

"The galleries?" I suggested.

"Among those overdressed fops and their painted doxys? You might as well go right up on stage. No, I've a better spot for you. Come." He led me to the rear of the playhouse, to the players' entrance. The door stood ajar, and through the crack, I could just make out lines being spoken on the stage.

"This is no better," I whispered.

"Not here. Up there." He pointed to the stairs beside us. "Through that door. Conceal yourself behind the curtains at the rear of the small balcony."

I gaped upward. "Up *there*? But—"

His hand closed painfully around my upper arm. "And mark me! No excuses this time. I want every word set down. Understood?"

Wincing, I nodded. His grip relaxed, and he pushed me roughly toward the stairs. "Go on, then."

I reluctantly mounted the stairs, wondering how it was that Falconer knew this playhouse so intimately. I cracked the door, listened a moment, then peered in. The interior was dim and deserted. Apparently the ghost had already done his turn on the balcony and departed. I slipped through the entrance and pulled the door carefully closed. From that spot, I could hear clearly every word spoken by Hamlet, for his voice carried well. But the speeches of the less forceful players were still lost.

I tiptoed to the draperies that hung at the rear of the balcony. When I pulled back the edge of the drape slightly, I could hear well enough; I could also see the front half of the stage. Hamlet stood there, conversing with the ghost of his father. The ghost's hollow, haunting voice—a voice not unlike Falconer's—sent a shiver up my spine.

I clenched my teeth resolutely, determined not to be caught up in the play again, and set to work transcribing all that had slipped by me before. Now that I knew how the story came out, I could concentrate better on my task. But I was still nervous about being discovered, and jumped at every sound.

Halfway through the performance, my writing hand grew cramped, but otherwise there were no problems. I believe I still lost a line or two during the riveting fencing match, but no one would miss them. As the end neared, I congratulated myself silently—and, as it turned out, prematurely.

At Hamlet's death, my work was done; I had copied the rest on my previous visit. Greatly relieved and, at the same time, a little sorry because I might never have a chance to see a play again, I closed the table-book and backed away, meaning to slip out as quietly as I had come in.

It was then that I heard footfalls on the stairs—not the outside steps I had used, but a steep, narrow flight rising from behind the stage. I choked back a gasp and desperately glanced about for a place of concealment. Seeing none, I ducked between the end of the drapery and the wall. There was just enough room for me to stand there without being seen by the audience, provided I did not move so much as a finger.

The footsteps drew near. The drapes parted in the center, and a man in soldier's garb stepped onto the balcony, where a small cannon stood bolted to the floor. He dumped a charge of powder down the bore of the cannon, rammed in a wad of cloth, and set a fuse in the fuse-hole. As he lifted his smouldering stick of touchwood and blew on it, he caught sight of me for the first time.

His eyes widened. He took a step toward me, then hesitated and glanced back at the cannon, obviously torn between apprehending me and being faithful to his cue. I started to slip away, but to my dismay, the point of the dagger in my belt snagged on the edge of the drape.

I fought desperately with the fabric, struggling to free myself. The audience had now spotted me and were tittering and pointing. As the cannoneer started for me again, his cue was spoken on the stage: "Go, bid the soldiers shoot."

Glaring at me, he rushed to the cannon, knocking it askew in his haste, and thrust the touchwood against the fuse. Nothing happened. Furious, he blew on the wood and touched the fuse again. The cannon went off, a full thirty seconds late, and the man descended on me.

I gave the drapery a prodigious yank and was free. As I stumbled for the door, the cannoneer burst through the center of the curtain and blocked my path. I looked about frantically. The only other route of escape was the inside stairs. I scrambled for them and, clinging to the rickety railing, half-ran, half-fell down them, with the soldier hard upon my heels.

I was not quite halfway to the bottom when the burly, greybearded man who had played the second gravedigger suddenly appeared at the foot of the stairs. I was trapped.

My only chance for escape lay in jumping off the stairs to the floor below, a fall of some six or eight feet—risky, but better to sprain an ankle than to be whipped or put in the stocks. I ducked under the railing and was about to leap when a cry rang through the theatre that stopped every one of us dead in his tracks. "Fire! Fire!"

The stocky greybeard at the foot of the stairs shook a finger at me, as if to say he'd deal with me later, then hastened away. The cannoneer came thundering down the steps, but I scrambled faster than he and ran for the rear door. When I burst through it, Falconer was gone. I ran on, around the side of the playhouse.

People were streaming out of the main entrance in panic. The elegant ladies from the gallery scurried fearfully down the steps, hoisting their vast skirts above their ankles in an unseemly way. One was sobbing, and the tears made tracks through her heavy white makeup.

I was mostly afraid of being pursued. I pushed into the center of the noisy, milling mob. Some were staring at the roof of the theatre. When I followed their gaze, I saw a thick cloud of grey smoke rising from the thatch, to become lost in the darker grey of the sky.

The players had set a ladder on the uppermost landing of the outside stairs, and several of them were now on the roof, beating at the smouldering thatch with their capes. A line of men, comprised of players and audience alike, formed between the playhouse and the nearest drainage ditch. They dipped up buckets of water and passed them from hand to hand along the line, up the stairs and the ladder to the men on the roof, who tossed the water onto the spreading flames.

In the middle of the line, passing buckets with the rest, stood the slim boy who had played Ophelia. He was wigless now but still in his stage makeup. Above the waist, he wore the bodice of his lady-like costume; below it, he wore men's breeches and hose.

"What set it off?" said a man next to me.

"The wad from the cannon, is my guess," said another.

My stomach twisted. If that was so, then I was partly to blame, for I had distracted the cannoneer and caused him to misdirect the shot. I had seen buildings burn before. In fact, it was not uncommon, even in a village as small as Berwick. But I had never before been the cause. Furthermore, I felt as though it were something more than a mere building at stake. It was an entire world, one into which I had been privileged to look briefly, and which was now in danger of crumbling.

So distressed was I that I was on the verge of lending my efforts to the fire fighters, even at the risk of being recognized. Then someone jostled me from behind, bringing me to my senses. I whirled about, expecting to see Falconer at my elbow, demanding the completed script. But it was only a thin fellow with a red nose and a scraggly beard, smiling apologetically. "Begging your pardon, my young friend," he said and moved off through the crowd.

Now that my thoughts were on Falconer, I cast my eyes about for him, but my stature was so small and the throng so dense that I stood no hope of spotting him. I turned back to the drama being played out atop the theatre.

The men on the roof were making little headway against the flames. They would, I believe, have lost their livelihood had not the gloomy sky chosen that moment to open up, dousing the burning thatch with more water than the poor players could have carried to it in a week. A cheer went up from the line of water bearers, then from the crowd. I joined in.

I was so relieved that I scarcely minded the soaking rain. I turned my face up to it and laughed appreciatively. The timing of the deluge had been so perfect, I could almost believe it was some grand theatrical effect produced by the company for our amazement. The whole world practices theatrics, I thought, and laughed again.

Then, as the crowd dispersed, I caught a glimpse of a sinister figure standing at a distance, looking out over the river as before. Sighing, I moved toward him. I laid one hand on my wallet, to reassure myself that the hard-won script was still safely tucked within. The pouch seemed flat and empty. My heart suddenly felt the same. I halted, yanked up the flap of the wallet, and plunged my hand inside. My fingers closed on the pencil, but the table-book was unquestionably, inexplicably gone.

For a moment, I stood unmoving and unthinking, feeling as though I'd been struck soundly on the brain-pan. Then my mind began to react. How could the table-book be gone? I clearly remembered putting it in my wallet back on the balcony of the theatre. I turned the wallet upside down and shook it vigorously, as if hoping the book was lodged in some out-of-the-way corner. It was not, of course.

I glanced fearfully at Falconer. He was still gazing out over the Thames. Cautiously, I backed toward the playhouse. When I had put several groups of lingering theatregoers between him and me, I retraced the course I had taken when I emerged so hastily from the playhouse a short time before. I wiped the rain from my eyes and scanned every inch of the soggy ground. If I didn't find the table-book soon, it would be a useless mass of pulp.

But already I was halfway around the building and had seen nothing but orange peels and apple cores, discarded playbills and ballad-sheets. To proceed was to risk encountering the men from whom I'd just escaped. Yet, if it came down to it, I might be better off with them than facing Falconer without the script in my hands. After all, he had killed a man just for calling him a Jew. Though I doubted my fate would be so drastic, the man was unpredictable. Even if all he did was abandon me, that in itself was a frightening prospect. How would I survive in this strange city on my own?

I went on, keeping my eyes open both for the table-book and for trouble. I came to within a few yards of the rear door and still saw no sign of either. "The devil take me," I breathed. "It must be inside, then."

It took me some time to muster the nerve required to pull the door open an inch or two and peer inside. Just as I stuck my face up to the crack, the door flew open, knocking me on the forehead and sending me flying backward, to land on my huckle bones in the mud.

Before I could scramble away, a strong hand took my arm and pulled me to my feet. "Well, now," a hearty voice said. "What have we here?"

Groaning, I held my hand to my afflicted head and squinted at my captor. It was the second gravedigger, the hefty old man who had blocked my way on the stair. "You've brast me costard!" I complained.

He laughed at my Upland speech. "Brast your costard, have I? Well, it serves you right, for all your mischief. What are you up to, scuttling about behind the stage like a great rat?"

"Me?" I tried to sound as innocent as I might while moaning in pain. "Behind the stage?"

The old man laughed again. "Ho, quite the actor, aren't you? Perhaps you belong *on* the stage and not behind it, eh? Yes, my lad, you're the only one going about in a pudding-basin hair style and a skirt, I'm afraid." He referred to my knee-length tunic and the bowl-shaped haircut common among country lads. He gently pulled my hand away from my head. "Hmm. That is a nasty bump you've suffered, though. Come. No use getting drenched into the bargain." Keeping a firm hold on my arm, he led me inside.

I considered breaking free and making a run for it. He was, after all, an old man, and I, though slow to sprout, was fleet of foot. But he was also a brawny man, and his grip was as inescapable as Falconer's. My brain, which had always been as fleet as my feet, began to race instead, looking for a way out. What was it the man had said—that I belonged on the stage rather than behind it? Perhaps my salvation lay that way.

The old player ushered me through the cluttered area behind the stage and into a large, windowed room where most of the company stood or sat about in various stages of undress. Several were grimy with soot from the fire, and one man had a large part of his beard singed away. All were rain soaked. Yet they did not appear miserable in the least; instead, they were laughing and joking, as though they had just played a game of bowls and not fought a potentially disastrous fire.

The cannoneer, who was cleaning mud from his costume, was the first to notice our entrance. "So!" he called, over the uproar. "You've caught the dirty dastard, Mr. Pope!"

My captor set me down on a stool. "Yes, he made the classic mistake of all criminals; he returned to the scene of the crime."

I tried to rise, but he pushed me down. "I'm no criminal!" I protested, wondering if someone had come across my lost table-book.

A tall, kindly looking man who had been Polonius in thc play said, "Of c-course you're not." I did not recall him stuttering on stage, but he did so now. He bent and looked closely at my bruised forehead. "Wh-what did you hit him with, T-Thomas? Your sh-shovel?"

My captor, whose name, I gathered, was Thomas Pope, looked hurt. "I am not a violent man. The fact is, I opened a door into his head."

"A d-door into his head, eh? I hope his b-brains didn't spill out."

"I'll spill his brains," the cannoneer threatened. "This is the hoddypeak who caused me to miss my aim, Mr. Heminges, and shoot that wad into the thatch."

"I hardly think he is to b-blame for that," Mr. Heminges said. "However, it is t-true that you disrupted our performance. Would you c-care to explain why?"

Though the throbbing in my head had subsided, I went on holding it and grimacing pitifully but bravely, to play on their sympathies. "I meant no harm. I only wished to see the play."

"The usual method," Mr. Pope said, "is to pay your penny and stand in *front* of the stage."

"I ken that. But I ha' no penny."

Mr. Pope clucked his tongue incredulously. "What sort of master would refuse his prentice a penny to see a play?"

"Well, the truth is . . . I ha' no master."

"You've c-come to London on your own?" said Mr. Heminges.

"Aye."

"For what purpose?"

It was time to bring into play the strategy that had been forming in my mind. But not too quickly. "You'll laugh at me."

"Not I," Mr. Heminges assured me.

Hesitantly, I said, "I want . . . I want to be a player."

True to his word, Mr. Heminges did not laugh—but several of the others did, and he gave them an exasperated glance. "You t-truly believe you would want to t-turn Turk and become like these disreputable wights?"

"Aye, by these bones, I would," I lied earnestly. In truth, aside from wanting to escape a beating, or wanting a meal, I had scarcely ever given any thought to what I wanted. No one had ever asked.

"Ahh, he's as full of lies as an egg is of meat," Jack, the cannoneer, said.

"I believe him," a voice beside me said. It was the first gravedigger, the man who had crossed swords so briefly with Falconer a few days before. "Though you did lie about not having a master," he reprimanded me. "You told me Dr. Bright was your master. Come, the truth now. You've run off, haven't you?"

I hung my head in mock remorse. "Aye."

"There, now," said the cannoneer. "If he lied about that, how do you know he's telling the truth about wanting to be a player?"

"Well," the other man said, "for one thing, he's seen the play before, and talked to me with some enthusiasm about it. Why risk a thrashing in order to see it a second time? And why desert his master and come to London alone unless he has a strong hunger for some food to be found nowhere else?" He looked about at the other players. "You've felt that hunger, every mother's son of you. Would you refuse to let him satisfy it?"

Mr. Heminges scratched his beard thoughtfully. "As

f-far as that g-goes, we could use another b-boy. Nick's golden voice threatens to turn b-bass any day now, and his b-beard to betray him." There was general merriment over this, and the strapping boy who had played the queen flushed and kicked the shin of the laughing youth next to him.

"This is a democratic c-company. Let us p-put the matter to a vote. All who favor t-taking on—What is your name, my young friend?"

With no time to concoct a lie, I said, "Widge."

Mr. Heminges's eyebrows raised skeptically. "All who favor taking on *W-Widge* as our new p-prentice." Most of the hands in the room went up. The cannoneer and the boy named Nick were the sole objectors. "That settles it. Widge, allow me to w-welcome you to the Lord Chamberlain's c-company."

11

Though I had been transported by the magic of these players, I had no thought in the world that I could become one of them. I thought only of doing what I had been hired to do. I meant to retrieve my table-book or, failing that, to seek an opportunity to transcribe the play again. Better yet, I might manage to make off with the theatre's copy, saving myself a good deal of toil and trouble.

"Now," Mr. Heminges said. "Who would like to b-be responsible for this b-boy?"

Mr. Pope clapped a heavy hand on my shoulder. "I suppose I can make room for one more. He's not very large. You don't eat much, do you, lad?"

"I hardly ken, sir. I've never had the chance to find out." This, said in all seriousness, earned me a laugh from the players. I had been laughed at for being a fool, but never for being witty. I found it pleased me.

"Well answered," Mr. Pope said. "Come then. Goodwife Willingson will be waiting supper for us." As he ushered me through the door, he called over his shoulder, "Sander!"

"Coming!" a voice from the far side of the room replied. As we passed behind the stage, I glanced furtively about for the incriminating table-book. The boy Mr. Pope had called Sander caught up with us just outside the rear door. He was of an age with me, but nearly a head taller, and as thin as Banbury cheese.

"Widge," said Mr. Pope, "shake hands with Alexander Cooke, known familiarly as Sander."

The boy pumped my hand as though he expected me to spout water. "Welcome to the company, Widge. It's a lot of work, but it's fun as well."

Work? I thought. What could be so difficult about dressing up in fine clothing and saying witty and poetic things already written out for you?

The rain had dwindled to a fine drizzle—what we in Yorkshire called a cobweb day. We were soaked by the time we reached Mr. Pope's home, though it lay a mere five minutes' walk from the Globe. All the way there, I cast my eyes about furtively, wondering if Falconer would return to find me.

"Sander," said Mr. Pope, "see if you can hunt up a change of clothing for Widge. He looks as though he's been wrestling pigs."

Sander led me upstairs to a small dormer room. The walls were papered with hundreds of broadsides and ballad-sheets, plus playbills for half a dozen theatres. While I looked them over, Sander rummaged through an ironbound chest and tossed me a short kersey tunic and a pair of plain breeches. "Try those. I've grown out of them."

As we changed, I glanced about the room. "You ha' this all to yourself?"

"Until now."

"Oh. I'm sorry."

He shrugged. "I don't mind. It'll give me somebody to talk to—and to study lines with."

"They let you perform in the plays?"

"Sometimes. Not the one today. Usually I play a serving maid or some such."

"So you ha' no copy of *Hamlet*?"

Sander laughed. "No one gets a copy of the whole play."

"But then how do you con your speeches?"

"Learn the lines, you mean? Oh, you get a little sheaf of paper we call a *side*, with just your part on it. You'll see."

"But there has to be a copy of the whole play somewhere," I insisted.

"Of course. The book keeper keeps it under lock and key. People filch them sometimes, you know. Do their own version. It hurts our box, then."

"Box. That's the money you take in," I said, recalling Simon Bass's words.

"Right. But the worst of it is, they don't give Mr. Shakespeare a farthing for it. And it is his work, after all." He gave my new attire a critical glance. "That looks well enough. A bit loose, but clean and dry at least. Let's go now, or we'll have Goody Willingson angry with us. She's the housekeeper."

"Does she beat you, then?" I asked softly as we descended the stairs.

Sander laughed. "Mistress Willingson? She can hardly bear to beat the carpets."

"And Mr. Pope? Does he beat you?"

Sander turned to me with a puzzled look. "Say, what sort of family are you used to?"

"Family?" I said.

Mr. Pope was already at the table, along with half a dozen young boys who, I later learned, were orphans Mr. Pope had taken in. The housekeeper showed no sign of exasperation at our lateness. She merely filled plates and set them before us.

The other boys were well behaved, except for staring at me, the newcomer. I kept my attention on my plate and tried to ignore them.

"So," Mr. Pope said. "You've run off from your master."

I choked down a piece of beef. "Aye."

"Will he be content to let you go, or will he come after you?"

"I can't say." In truth, I was certain that, should I really desert, Simon Bass would not let me go lightly. He was a man of business, and I suspected he would not like losing the ten pounds sterling he had invested in me. To such a man, I would not be a runaway prentice but an uncollected debt. And Falconer would be the collector.

"Well, I can sympathize with you," Mr. Pope was saying. "I was apprenticed to a weaver myself, before I heard the theatre's siren call. Most of the members of our company, in fact, were destined for some more respectable trade. Mr. Heminges was to be a goldsmith, Mr. Shakespeare a glover." He looked sternly about at the young children. "That is not to say that I condone prentices running off willy-nilly from their masters. You will all be prentices one day, and I expect each of you to work hard at learning your trade—just as I expect Widge, here, to work hard at becoming a player." He turned his gaze on me again. I gave what I hoped would pass for an eager look and turned my attention to my plate once more.

How had I gotten myself into this? Until today, there had been but one set of demands upon me. Now two threats hung over me, like the buildings in that narrow, stinking alley. Sooner or later, they were sure to meet, and I would be caught squarely in the middle, up to my ears in muck-water.

The bed I shared with Sander was the softest I had known, and Sander neither tossed nor snored unduly. Yet I slept fitfully. Once I even rose and began to dress, thinking that the most prudent course might be to run away. But I could not think of anywhere to run. I crept back into bed and lay there, contemplating the terrible sorts of fates that seem possible only in the small hours, until matins rang.

Though it was not fully light, Sander and I dressed, breakfasted, and set out for the Globe. I glanced into each alley we passed, half expecting to spy a cloaked figure waiting to spring on me. But of course Falconer had no way of knowing where I was, and I didn't think he would haunt the vicinity of the theatre; for some reason he had seemed reluctant to show himself there. Probably he feared that someone would guess his purpose. One thing I was sure of—he was still in London somewhere and still determined to have the script. The thought made me newly determined to have it as a shield against his wrath when he caught up with me, as he surely would.

We were far from the first arrivals at the playhouse. Men were busy re-thatching the roof. Behind the stage, others were carrying pieces of scenery and furniture upstairs, and carrying new ones down.

Gone was any hope I had harbored of searching for my table-book. Players stood or sat in odd corners, talking to themselves, making curious faces and sudden gestures, for all the world like residents of a madhouse.

A ruddy-faced young man gave an unexpected sweep of his arm, striking me on the side of the head. I backed away, ready to apologize for getting in the way. To my surprise, the man was the one to offer an apology. "Sorry. Didn't see you."

He turned to Sander, waving his script. "Mr. Jonson has

kindly provided me with thirty new lines to learn before today's performance. I had difficulty enough recalling the old ones."

Sander patted him on the shoulder. "You'll learn them, Will. You always do. And if you don't, you'll make something up." In a confidential voice, he added, "Something better, no doubt."

The man named Will gave a grudging smile. "I suppose so."

"So, the performance is on for today? I thought it looked like rain again."

"You know how they are." Will rolled his eyes upward, as though referring to the gods, but I presumed he meant the men who held shares in the company. "We'll go on unless the stage is under water, and even then they'd likely haul out boats and do *The Spanish Armada*."

Sander laughed. "They'll be wanting the stage cleared, then. I'll tell you what; I'll learn your lines for you if you'll clear the stage for me."

Will waved him away. Sander picked up two brooms and handed one to me. I glanced back at Will, who was mumbling and gesturing again. "Surely that was not Mr. Shakespeare?"

Sander gave a laugh that held no disdain, only amusement. "Hardly. That's Will Sly. He was a prentice like us a few years ago. Now he's a hired man. You won't see much of Mr. Shakespeare. He's a private man, and a very busy one. But no—you have seen him."

"I have?"

"He was the ghost in *Hamlet.*" He pulled back the curtain and let me precede him onto the stage. Bereft of players and properties, it bore no resemblance to a castle in Denmark. It was a mere platform of boards, covered with damp and dirty rushes.

On the ground, two boys of about nine or ten years of age were gathering discarded beer bottles and mashed fruit. "Samuel and James," Sander told me. "Our hopefuls."

"Hopeful of what?"

"Of staying on as prentices." He rolled up his sleeves. "Well, let's have at it."

We spent the next hour sweeping the heavy mat of soiled and soggy rushes onto the ground, spreading a fresh supply from a wagon over the boards, then loading the old ones on the wagon. By the time we finished, I was as limp and wet as the rushes. I sank down on the edge of the stage. "No one told me a player's life would be like this."

Sander gave another good-humored laugh. How could he be so cheerful in the face of such drudgery? "We don't do this every day. Some days we clean out the jakes and pile it on the dung heap."

I shook my head wearily and silently prayed that I might find the missing table-book very soon. "When does a wight get to be a hired man?"

"When your voice changes. If you're a good prentice, meantime." Sander picked up his broom. "Come. Time for lessons."

"I already ken how to read and write," I pointed out as we climbed the narrow stairs I had scrambled down the day before. Even as I spoke, my eyes were casting about for some sign of my table-book.

"That will be useful," Sander said, "but these are lessons of a different sort."

Behind us as we came up the stairs was a large room in which a group of players were rehearsing some scene. We proceeded past the drapes on which I had snagged myself; I saw no table-book there, either. I would have to return later and search more carefully.

We stopped outside the door to another room. From within the room came the sound of blows, and an occasional cry. I felt a wrenching in my stomach. Whatever lessons lay ahead, they were obviously being driven home with the aid of a willow switch. First hard labor, now beatings. I should have known the theatre would prove to be as heartless and harsh as any other institution.

I hung back, very nearly resolved to flee and take my chances with Falconer—had I known where he was—or even on my own in that unknown city.

But just then Sander turned and beckoned to me with such a cheerful and friendly countenance that I swallowed my misgivings and followed him inside the lesson room.

The scene within was not at all what I had expected. There were no sullen students lined up on benches with slates in their hands. Nor was there any sign of anyone being beaten. The sounds had apparently come from two boys mock sword fighting with wooden singlesticks. One was Nick, the fellow who had been the butt of the players' jokes the day before, and who had played the queen in *Hamlet*. The other was the play's Ophelia, a slender boy no taller than I, and far better suited to playing girls' parts than the swaggering Nick, who seemed too husky in voice and in build to portray anything but older women.

On the other side of the room, two players were dancing a jig to a tune played on an hautboy. Nearby, Samuel and James, the two hopefuls, were turning somersets atop a row of rush mats, under the eye of a small, athletic-looking man.

"Mr. Phillips," Sander informed me. "He's our stage manager, among other things. Mr. Armin you already know." He gestured toward the man who had run afoul of Falconer, and who had stood up for me before the other players. He was demonstrating sword positions to Nick and his partner. He nodded in our direction, and Sander approached him. "Where shall I start our new boy?"

"Stramazone!" Mr. Armin shouted, and I shrank back, believing we were being cursed in some foreign tongue. The two students made slicing motions with their sticks. "He may as well begin here," Mr. Armin said, in a perfectly civil tone. Then he shouted, *"Riversa!"* The two boys cut with their sticks from the other side. "Get him a single-stick."

For the next hour I stood in a rank with Sander and the others, facing Mr. Armin and attempting to duplicate his stance and movements. I had never had anything to do with weapons, beyond the mock skirmishes with elder sticks at the orphanage. Before long, my limbs began to ache. I could sense that the others were secretly laughing at my bumbling efforts, and I longed to throw the stick aside—preferably at them—and show them my skill with a pen. But to do so, of course, would be to give myself away.

I would have to continue to seem a willing prentice until I could complete my real mission here. And when I did, when I had stolen the script from under their very noses, then I would be the one to laugh.

At last Mr. Armin called a halt, and he and Nick paired off. Nick was armed with a real rapier, now—blunted, of course. They saluted with their swords, their faces smiling and cordial. Then Mr. Armin said "Have at you!" and the two transformed before our eyes into deadly enemies. Their blades clashed and parted and met again with such rapidity that my eye could scarcely follow.

Sander and Ophelia cheered them on. Their sentiments were obviously with Mr. Armin, but they shouted encouragement to Nick as well. Even with my ignorance of fencing, I could see that Mr. Armin was holding back, giving Nick time to ward and counter. The fencing scene in the play had displayed this same measured pace. As with the play, I was drawn into the drama. Just as I was tempted to shout a word of encouragement myself, Mr. Armin effortlessly caught Nick's sideways blow on the guard of his rapier, flung his arm outward, and delivered a quick but gentle *stocatta* to Nick's unguarded chest. "Touch," he said.

Nick's face, already red from exertion, grew redder. He peevishly flung down the rapier and stalked off. Mr. Armin ignored his outburst and approached us. "Do you three feel you're ready for a real weapon?"

"No, sir!" we said, almost as one person.

"Then go practice your *passatas*," he said. "We have an audience who pays to see us; we don't need you lot standing about gawking."

As we moved away, Sander said, "Widge is going to need a bit of coaching, I think. Do you want to do it, Julian, or shall I?"

Ophelia, whose name was apparently Julian, shrugged. "We could take turns."

"All right with you, Widge?" Sander asked.

Unused as I was to being asked my preferences, I took a moment to reply. "Oh, aye. I don't mind. But Mr. Armin said—"

"Fie on what Mr. Armin said," Sander replied, but softly. "I've done so many *passatas* I could do them in my sleep."

"Just be sure you do them on your side of the bed."

He laughed. "We'll soon have you doing them in your sleep as well. Now, the first thing we'll have to show you is the three wards."

"Three words?"

"No, wards." He held the singlestick at the height of his forehead. "This is high ward." I copied his stance. He moved the stick to his waist. "Broad ward." His hand went down near his knee. "Base ward."

"You might just as well show him the right way,

Cooke," a voice said. I turned to see Nick standing close by. "Here, let me have that stick." Sander gave it up reluctantly. Nick planted himself in front of me, a distinctly unpleasant smile on his face. "I'll learn you properly."

"Let him be," Sander said, not as forcefully as he might have.

"I'm only going to see that he learns his lesson," Nick said innocently. "Now then. Widge, is it? You know what a widge is where I come from?"

My throat felt too tight to speak. I shook my head.

"A horse. I think I'll call you Horse, though you look more like an ass to me. Hold your stick like this, Horse—the hand close to the knee, and the tip pointing at your opponent's throat-bole."

With a shaking hand, I tried to mirror his position.

"Get your point up," he commanded. I was slow to respond, and he whacked my stick sharply. "Get the point up, I said. Get the point?"

"Aye."

"Aye? Do I look like the captain of a ship?"

"Nay."

"Ah, you can neigh like a horse as well. Now, bring your hoof—I mean your *hand*—in closer to your leg, else your opponent might do *this*." He brought his stick swiftly down on my knuckles. With a gasp, I let my stick fall. "And if you do that, he'll certainly do *this*." He lunged, and his stick struck my breastbone painfully.

My fear gave way to anger, and I scrambled for the

fallen weapon. Laughing, Nick knocked it out of my reach. When I was young at the orphanage, and the bigger boys taunted me, I invariably burst into tears. But finding that it was an invitation to further abuse, I had learned to refrain from tears, whatever the provocation. I even prided myself on it. Now, facing Nick, I trembled with shame and frustration, but I was dry-eyed.

"Pick it up, Horse," Nick ordered me. With his foot, he sent it skating across the floor at me.

As I hesitated, unsure whether I would look more like a fool by picking it up or by letting it lie, Julian suddenly stepped between us, his stick at broad ward. "That's enough, Nick. We can all see he's no match for you."

"And you are, I suppose."

"No," the boy replied evenly. "But Sander and I together may be."

Nick scowled at Sander, who had taken the cue and come up behind him. "That's unfair odds."

"So is you against Widge," Sander said. "Give him a few months of practice, and he'll go a round with you, won't you, Widge?"

Though in truth I meant to be gone long before that, I nodded. "Aye."

Nick pointed his stick threateningly at me. "Study your footwork well, then, Hobbyhorse, for I mean to hobble you." He gave a token thrust toward Sander, who jumped back. Laughing, Nick tossed the stick aside and swaggered off.

Only then did I notice Mr. Armin watching from across the room. "Why did 'a not put a stop to 't?"

"I suppose," Julian said, "he believes a man should fight his own battles."

"Then why did you step in?" I said crossly.

"I beg your humble pardon! Next time I'll let him put a dent in your stupid pudding basin!" Julian stomped away.

"A bit of a hothead, isn't 'a?" I observed.

"And you're a bit of a muttonhead," Sander said mildly. "He was only trying to help."

"I don't need any help," I said sullenly.

"Yes, you do. Now why don't you take up that stick, and we'll start over. High ward." As I grudgingly strove to mimic his movements, he said, "Nick isn't really such a bad sort, you know. He was just testing your mettle. Broad ward. I don't think Nick is truly mean at heart. He's just going through a bad time. He's been a prentice for six or seven years, and now he'll have to begin playing a man's part."

"On the stage, or in life?"

"Both, I suppose. Low ward."

"That's as may be," I said. "But we can scarcely judge a person by what 'a's like inside. It's th' outside we ha' to do wi'."

Sander lowered his singlestick and sighed. "Well, on the inside you may be a very good fencer, but on the outside you stink."

"I washed but last week," I protested.

Sander laughed. "I didn't mean it literally, you goose. It means you're terrible. Come. We'll try some *passatas*."

It was a long morning. When Mr. Armin finally tired of trying to make us into some semblance of "scrimers"—his word for swordsmen—he passed us on to Mr. Phillips, who worked on our diction—mostly mine—and something called projection, which meant, as nearly as I could tell, shouting more loudly than the audience.

To my relief, the afternoon was less taxing. The company was presenting a play called *Every Man Out of His Humour*, which fit my mood exactly. As the book keeper was ill, Sander was given the task of holding the play book and throwing out lines to players who were floundering.

I was posted, along with Samuel, one of the hopefuls, in the tiring-room to help the players change costume. In my ignorance, I did more to hinder than to help, yet none complained—except Nick. When I stepped on the hem of his gown, he aimed a blow at me. I ducked it easily; ducking was one athletic skill I had long since mastered. Before he could try it again, his cue came. "I'll see to you later, Horse," he growled, and swept out. His voice was so much at odds with his feminine appearance that I could not help snickering.

"Such a lady," Sam said, and set us both laughing.

Julian came into the tiring-room, greeted us, and retreated into the wardrobe to change. I stared after him. "Feels 'a's too good for us, does 'a?"

"Oh, it's nothing against us," Sam said. "He's a modest

one, is all. Mr. Shakespeare's the same, and Mr. Burbage. Don't like others pawing them, I guess."

The mention of Mr. Shakespeare brought to mind something that the day's constant activity had pushed aside—the lost script. If I did not find it soon, someone else would. Leaving Sam to take care of matters in the tiring-room, I crept up the stairs to the balcony.

My luck was good that day; the balcony was not in use. I drew back the drapery and inspected the spot where I'd concealed myself the day before.

So much for luck. The notebook was not there. Where in heaven's name was it, then? Had some member of the company found it?

Then it came to me: the man in the crowd who had jostled me from behind. He had smiled so sincerely. It never occurred to me that he had dipped his thieving fingers in my wallet. "Gog's bread!" I murmured. "'A's stolen me script!"

The thief must have been upset to discover that he had filched not a purse but a book full of scribbles. He could hardly return it, though. And however great his frustration, it could not have held a candle to the dismay that I felt at that moment, knowing that all my work and worry was for naught.

Despite my exhaustion, I lay awake a long time that night, wondering how I could possibly survive another week of lessons until such time as *Hamlet* came around again. And how would I manage to transcribe it unobserved? I tried hard to think of some alternative.

Perhaps I could copy out the players' individual parts from their "sides." The problem with that was that they had all learned their parts and seldom used the sides. What about the book used to prompt the players, then? But I had seen how diligently Sander guarded it, never letting it out of his hands, let alone his sight. At last my battered brain succumbed to sleep.

The following day, Sunday, the theatre was closed. I was grateful for the day off, and for the chance to sleep late. In truth, I slept only an hour or so past matins; then several of Mr. Pope's orphans invaded our room, begging for stories and horseback rides.

At first I refused. Bad enough to be called Horse by Nick; now I was expected to behave as one. But when the boys pleaded with me, tugging eagerly at my sleeve, it brought to my mind a picture of myself at that age, tugging at Mistress MacGregor's skirts as she handed out the contents of some charity basket. Grudgingly I let myself be pulled down onto all fours, straddled, and spurred by bare feet into a sluggish gait.

Sander, burdened with a pair of riders, glanced at me and grinned broadly. I shook my head in exasperation. "Make horsie noises!" my rider commanded gleefully.

"Nay!" I protested.

The boy burst out in giggles. "That's not how horsies say it!"

After church, Sander said, "We have the whole day and the whole city at our disposal. Where shall we go?"

"You decide."

"Well, there's a zoo in the Tower, with lions and tigers and a porpentine, even a camel. But all they do is sleep. We could go to Paul's instead."

"Who is Paul?"

"*Saint* Paul's. It's a cathedral. I'll pay for the crossing."

Though a cathedral did not sound like the height of excitement to me, I had no better suggestion. It was another cobweb day, and by the time we crossed the Thames we looked as though we had swum it. Sander's spirits were not dampened in the least. His long legs carried him so swiftly up the hill that I had to fairly trot to keep up. At last we came to the huge cathedral which had attracted my awe the night of my arrival.

"St. Paul's," Sander said. "The center of things."

So now I stood in the center of the center of the universe. I stared about, openmouthed, like the greenest plowboy. The chaotic courtyard of the cathedral was packed with people and vendors' booths. Voices hung in the air as densely as the misty rain. I felt the urge to hold my breath as we plunged into the sea of bodies.

"Keep a firm hold on your wallet," Sander called over the clamor.

I laughed mirthlessly. "I've naught left to steal," I said.

"You want to go up in the tower? I'll pay."

"What's there?"

"A good view of the city. And a few bats." The view from the top of Paul's was, indeed, a good one. Sander pointed out the roofs of the queen's London residence far off to the west, and the Tower prison to the east. Between the two lay more buildings than a man could count. The streets were as crooked and wayward as country streams, dissecting the city not into square blocks but into convoluted shapes of all sizes.

"Beautiful, isn't it?" said Sander.

"It's like a maze. How in heaven's name do you find your way about?"

Sander laughed. "It's easy, when you've grown up in it."

"And you like it?"

"Of course. Don't you?"

"Perhaps I'm just not used to it yet."

"You'll come to like it." He put a hand on my shoulder. I was not used to being touched in a comradely way either, and I flinched. "Sorry," he said. "I forget that the height makes people nervous."

"Aye," I said. "Let's go back down."

The courtyard was no place for a person who was shy of being touched. I lost sight of Sander temporarily but caught up with him again at a bookseller's stall. "Here," he said. "Have a look at this."

Displayed prominently were a number of plays and poems written by "Wm. Shaksper." "Is that our Mr. Shakespeare?"

"Of course."

Eagerly I searched for a copy of *The Tragedy of Hamlet*, then realized that of course if it were bound and printed like these Simon Bass would never have gone to the trouble to send me and Falconer here; he would simply have bought one.

They say that if you mention the devil's name, he is likely to appear. As I turned away from the bookstall, I found that, by thinking his name, I had somehow conjured up Falconer, and to my dismay, he was headed directly for us.

I could not have said whether or not he saw me. As always, his hood sheltered his face. He was pushing his way impatiently through the crowd, but then he always did that. Perhaps it was not too late to avoid him. I plunged into the shifting maze of people. Sander shouted after me, "Widge! Where are you going?"

I did not bother to reply; I only pressed on, burrowing through the tangle of arms and legs like a hare through briars. At last I found daylight at the edge of the courtyard and turned to look back.

Falconer was a tall man, and I could see the tip of his hood bobbing through the crowd. "Gog's blood!" I murmured. He was onto me for certain, and he'd want the script, and perhaps my blood as well. No excuses, he'd said. There was nothing for me to do but run, and no way to run but through the cathedral graveyard.

Though I did not care for the company of dead folk, it was easier to make my way through them. I slipped as quietly as I could between headstones and crypts. The earth was soft from the rain and, in places, from being recently turned up. It gave way slightly under my feet, making me fear that if I did not move quickly, I would sink down into the realm of the dead.

Shuddering, I broke into a trot, never pausing until I reached solid ground. When I peered back through the drizzle, I thought I spied a dark figure weaving among the tombstones. I began to run again, with no goal but to get away. I trotted down one unknown street, then another, sending up sprays of water with each step.

Finally I sank exhausted onto a doorstep. If I hadn't lost Falconer by now, I never would. Unfortunately, I had lost myself as well. I had no idea in which direction Southwark lay. South, of course, but with the sun so well concealed, who could say where that was?

It stood to reason, though, that if I followed the water in the gutters and kept a downhill course, I would eventually run into the Thames as well. How I would get to the far side was another matter. I would have to cross that bridge, or lack of one, when I came to it.

As it turned out, my reasoning was seriously flawed. After only a few minutes' walk, I came to the massive wall that encircled the city. Even I knew that the wall did not run between St. Paul's and the Thames. But by now I was so disoriented that I kept on that street, which was at least broad and well traveled.

Finally I found the good sense to ask an old farmer to point me in the right direction. "Turn left at the next chance," he said, "and follow your nose 'til you wets your toes." I thanked him and hurried on.

The thoroughfare onto which I turned seemed innocuous enough at first, but after a time I noticed that each block was a bit more dismal-looking than the last. Before long the street began to seem less like the path to the river than like a descent into hell.

The prosperous merchants and busy tradesmen had disappeared, and in their place were coarse women and menacing men, bands of noisy, grimy children and scores of beggars.

Lining both sides of the street were ramshackle booths and huts constructed of any material that would keep out the weather—hides, sticks, mud. My impulse was to turn and retrace my steps, but I told myself that I could not possibly be far from the river now, so I kept on, dodging piles of muck.

I did not see the two youths until they were directly before me, blocking my path. My immediate impression was that they were large—large of body, with large grinning mouths and large daggers at their belts. Separately, each would have been daunting; together they were terrifying. I stepped back. They stepped forward. I stepped aside. They followed.

"Wh-what do you want?"

"What have you got?" one of them said.

"Naught but the clothes on me back."

He fingered the hilt of his dagger. "We'll have that, then."

I took a few more backward steps, preparing to run. "You won't get far," the boy said. "There's not a man or woman in sight that won't help catch you. We're all one big family here, you see. And we don't like strangers."

"I was—I was just passing through."

"Well, then you've got to pay a passing-through fee." He drew his dagger. "Now, what will it be? Your clothing? Or your ears?"

"Neither," said a voice behind them. The large boys turned, and I took immediate advantage of the distraction. For the second time that day I was on the run, and this time I was far from fresh. Hands reached out to stay me, but I was a confirmed Master of Dodging, and left them with a handful of air.

I expected at any moment to hear the boys thundering after me. Instead I heard my name being called. "Widge! Wait, Widge!"

I raced on, nearly blind with panic and fatigue. How had they learned my name?

"Widge!" the voice called again, high and clear. "Wait! It's me!"

I slowed and half-turned. The two bully boys were nowhere in sight. Instead a slighter and far more welcome figure was chasing after me. "Julian?" I gasped. I stumbled over some obstacle and fell to my knees, struggling for breath. Julian reached me and held out a hand. I pushed it away. "I can manage."

"Yes, well, you wouldn't have managed if I hadn't happened to show up just then, would you? Come." He guided me to a booth with grain sacks piled against it. "Mind if we rest here a bit, Hugh?" he asked the man within the booth.

"Anyfing you axe, m'dear," the man said.

"You seem to be kenned here," I observed when my breath had caught up with me.

"Known, you mean? I should hope so. It's where I was born and raised. Alsatia, we call it."

"You grew up *here*?" I looked at our squalid surroundings, then at Julian, whose appearance and manner spoke of better things.

He shrugged. "There's worse places."

"None that I've seen."

"Watch what you say, or you may never leave—not standing up at any rate."

I glanced about nervously and got to my feet. "I'll leave now, then, I wis." I pointed down the street. "The river's that way?"

"I may as well go with you. It's only an hour or so until curfew anyway."

"But you said you lived here."

"No longer. Not since I began my prenticeship three years ago. I live with Mr. Phillips and his wife, now."

"And your parents . . . they don't mind?"

Julian gave a humorless laugh, but said nothing.

I looked back over my shoulder. "How is it you escaped those two back there so easily?"

"They wouldn't dare touch a hair of my head. I've got friends here that would cut their ears off, and they know it."

I rubbed at my own ears instinctively. "They came near to cutting mine off. I should thank you."

"Yes," he said. "You should."

"Well," I said. "Thanks, then."

"You're welcome."

I truly was thankful, but at the same time I resented the fact that he'd had to rescue me. Ever since I'd come to London, I'd been getting into situations from which someone else had had to extract me. I was weary of feeling foolish and helpless and useless. I had failed even to make fruitful use of the one skill I did possess—the art of charactery.

When we descended the rain-slick stairs to the water, Julian asked, "Do you have passage money?"

"Nay," I said, feeling helpless yet again.

He handed a wherryman two pennies and four farthings. As we pushed out into the river, he said, "You can repay me when you get your wages."

"You mean—I'm to be paid?"

"When you get through your trial period. It's only three shillings a week, but it's better than nothing. Although, come to that, I suppose I'd do it for nothing."

"You would? Why?"

"Why?" he repeated, with a puzzlement equal to my own. "If you don't know, you won't make much of a prentice, much less a player."

"I won't in any case."

"Not with that attitude. The only ones who succeed are the ones who want it so badly that nothing will keep them from it."

That was hard for me to imagine. I had never bothered to want anything that badly, for I knew it was no use. In the past few days, I'd gotten glimpses of a world very different from the one I was used to, a world I might have wished to be a part of but knew I never could. What was the good in longing for something you could not have? Life was full enough of disappointments, without making more.

Once on the south bank, Julian said, "You can find your way to Mr. Pope's from here?"

"I'm not wholly helpless," I said indignantly.

"I'm glad to hear that."

At Mr. Pope's house, everyone was seated at supper. Mr. Pope lifted his shaggy eyebrows in surprise as I entered. "Well. I supposed we had seen the last of you."

"Why?"

"You wouldn't be the first prentice who's run off. Sander said you'd found your first day not quite to your liking."

"That may be. But I'm not one to quit."

He nodded and smiled slightly. "Good, good. Perhaps you'd best change before you come to the table. You look like a drowned cat."

As I climbed the stairs to our room, Sander came up behind me. "Why did you run off like that? Is something wrong?"

"Nay," I said. "It's naught."

"You can tell me, Widge. I can keep a secret."

For a fleeting moment, I was tempted to open up to him. But how could I? If I did, I would be burning both my bridges. I could never finish my mission for Simon Bass, but neither could I go on being a prentice, once they had learned the truth about me. I shook my head. "It's naught."

He sighed. "I can't be your friend if you won't talk to me."

"I never asked you to be my friend. I never asked for anything." The moment I spoke the words, I regretted them, but I could hardly take them back. Besides, they carried a certain truth. I didn't want him, or any of the players, to be my friend, for I would only have to betray them. And yet some part of me wondered how it would be to have a friend, and to be one.

Blinking, Sander backed away, down the stairs. "Very well," he said in a hurt voice. "I was only trying to help."

I spent as much time as I reasonably could drying off and donning my old clothing, which had been washed without my knowing. When I came downstairs, everyone had left the dining room except Mistress Willingson, who cheerfully set before me a plate of food she had kept warm on the back of the stove.

My day of rest had proved far from restful, nor did I get much rest that night. Each time I fell asleep, I dreamed of a hooded figure pursuing me, and woke in a sweat. As we started for the Globe in the morning, I was heartened to see that, for a change, the sky was clear. But my small delight vanished when we arrived to find that our morning's task was to whitewash the roof thatch.

"Gog's bread!" I grumbled as we climbed the ladder. "Why does the thatch ha' to be made *white*?"

Sander laughed. "It's to keep it from catching fire again."

"Would that it had burned to the ground," I muttered.

Sander pulled up the bucket of whitewash. "What's that?"

"I said, would that we could do this from the ground."

I stuck my long-handled brush in the bucket and made a

few grudging passes at the thatch, then paused and looked out over the plain of red-tiled roofs below me. "Why did they not make this one of tile?"

"Too much of an expense."

"Aye, and it won't cost them a thing if we breaks our necks." As I made another careless swipe at the rough reeds, I spotted on the road below a cloaked figure that I momentarily took to be Falconer. So startled was I that I lost my hold on the brush. It skittered across the thatch and plummeted to the yard three storeys below. "Oh, Holy Mother."

"What's wrong now?"

"I've lost me brush." I stared gloomily after it. Half the yard was eclipsed from my view. Into the half I could see stepped a man with a large white splotch on one shoulder of his dark brown doublet.

"Who is that up there?" the man called.

"It's Widge!" I replied, in a voice as high and unsteady as my perch.

"Who?"

"Widge! The new boy!"

"Well, we don't need the yard whitewashed, Widge, nor the players."

"Aye, sir." I turned to Sander, who was holding a hand over his mouth to stifle his laughter. "It's not funny! It struck someone."

"Who was it? Not Mr. Burbage, I hope?"

"I don't ken. A wight wi' long, dark hair and a pointy beard."

Sander bit his lip and raised his eyebrows. "Mr. Shakespeare."

"Oh, gis. Will 'a ha' me dismissed, do you wis?"

"Not very like. He's a bit prickly at times, but not mean-spirited. Best go fetch your brush."

Before I climbed down, I took another look toward the road. Falconer—if indeed it had been he—was not in sight.

We whitewashed no more than the fourth part of the roof before the church bells rang terce, the hour for our lessons to begin. There were fencing exercises, made slightly more tolerable by the fact that Nick was gone—no one seemed to know where or why. After fencing, one of the hired men, a former apothecary's apprentice named Richard, instructed us in the art of painting our faces. As I sat before the looking glass brushing cochineal on my cheeks, a gypsyish-looking man with a high forehead and a mane of curly black hair came up behind me.

"A likely looking lot of lissome ladies, eh, Mr. Shakespeare?"

"Very fetching." Mr. Shakespeare glanced down at me. "Have a care, now. You don't want that brush to escape you." I flushed with embarrassment. "There, you see, you've reddened your whole face."

"I'm sorry about the whitewash," I murmured.

"It will wash," he said. "A pity it did not fall a bit to the left. You'd have saved me the trouble of whiting my face for today's performance." His words puzzled me until I recalled his role as the ghost. So *Hamlet* was scheduled for this very afternoon, and here was I with no table-book in which to set it down. "That was meant to be a jest," Mr. Shakespeare said.

"Sorry."

He shook his head. "Thank heaven my audience is not made up of such sobersides. Sander, see that this lad is given instructions in laughing."

Sander grinned. "Yes, sir."

When Mr. Shakespeare had gone, Richard looked us over critically. "Very good, Julian. Sander, too much black about the eyes. You look as though you're consumptive. Widge, a little less whitewash next time, and smooth it out under your chin. Clean up now; it's nearly dinner time." As we wiped our faces, he said, "It's sunny today, so wear a hat outside, else we'll be having to put a pound of white on, to hide the freckles. Remember, it's easier to tan a hide than to hide a tan."

Sander elbowed me in the ribs. "Laugh," he said.

As it happened, Sander would have done well to leave his face made up. When the time came for the performance, Nick failed to appear. Mr. Heminges came back and took the book from Sander's hands. "G-go and g-et yourself up in Nick's costume. D-do you know his lines?"

"I've a nodding acquaintance with them," Sander said, his voice sounding uncharacteristically nervous.

"Have the p-property master give you his side, and read from it if you m-must."

"Yes, sir." Sander hurried off.

Mr. Heminges looked after him, rubbing his forehead as though it pained him. Then he glanced over at me and, to my astonishment, thrust the book into my hands. "Widge, you'll hold the b-book. If anyone seems l-lost for a line, f-feed them a few words. Not a whole m-mouthful, mind you, just a t-taste, to start their chawbones m-moving. Can you do that?"

I closed my gaping mouth and said "Aye," and he strode off to deal with some other crisis. For a moment all I could do was stare at the book in disbelief. All the fretting and scheming I'd done over how I would copy the play, and suddenly here it was, handed over to me in one piece, without the slightest effort on my part. All I had to do was tuck it under my arm and turn and walk out of the theatre.

Everyone else in the company was occupied with some task. No one would notice. And yet, what if they *did* notice? My intentions would be obvious, and all chance of completing my mission would be lost. I turned toward the door, hesitated, turned back, started for the door again—and encountered Sander sweeping from the tiring-room, dressed as Hamlet's mother.

"How do I look?" he asked anxiously, pushing at his voluminous wig.

Far from calm myself, I gave him a cursory look up and down. "Well enough, I wis. Wait. Your sleeve's coming off."

"Pin it on, would you?"

"Yes, very well," I said irritably. The task required both

hands, and I glanced about, wondering what to do with the play book. "Here." I handed it to Sander.

"Make haste," he begged. "I'm due on the stage."

"I'm trying!" I snapped, fumbling with the pins. "Why don't they just sew these on?"

"You can change the dress about this way, put different sleeves on. Have you got it?"

"Almost."

There was a flourish of trumpets above the stage. "It'll have to do. There's my cue." He started for the stage entrance.

"The book!" I whispered urgently.

He shoved it into my hands and dashed for the doorway, tripped himself up in his hem, recovered, hoisted the skirts in a very unladylike fashion, and burst through the curtain onto the stage.

"Ah, Gertrude," the king said. "So glad you could join us." The audience guffawed at this spontaneous addition to the script. The king then launched into a speech that promised to be lengthy. Time to go, I thought.

Suddenly the king broke off, his arm upraised, as though frozen in place. I froze, too, aware that something was amiss, but not quite sure what. A few snickers arose from the audience. The king cast a perturbed glance in my direction, and I realized he had forgotten his line.

I yanked the book open. Before I could locate the proper passage, Laertes closed the breach: "Sorry to interrupt, my lord, but I beg your leave and favor to return to France."

I looked about anxiously, certain that someone would swoop down to snatch the book from my incompetent hands. But everyone was too busy to notice. If I had had the sense that God gave sheep, I would have made my escape at that moment. But the king had another attack of forgetfulness. This time I had the book open to the place. "Take thy fair hour!" I called out, too loudly, drawing another snicker from the audience. The king snatched up the cue and ran with it. Behind his back, Sander made a gesture of approval at me. I couldn't help smiling.

Ah, well, I thought; I can just as easily stay and help out here, and still slip away before the finish of the play.

When the scene was over, Sander came to where I stood. "How did I do?"

"Whist!" I said. "You'll make me lose me place!"

"It wouldn't be the first time," he teased. "Come now, truly. How was I?"

"You were magnificent," I said dryly. "You fairly lit up the stage."

He delivered a most unqueenly swat to my arm. "You dolt!"

"Ouch! Will you go faddle wi' your pins or something, and let me do me job?"

"All right, then. It's plain I'll get no useful criticism from you."

"You don't want criticism. You want praise."

"Suppose I do. It would scarcely kill you." His voice had lost some of its jesting tone.

"What do you care what I think?"

"I thought we were friends."

"Oh." I thought of how my words had stung him the day before. "Aye." I dropped my gaze to the script, as though it might provide my next line, but it was of no help.

Just then, the rear door of the playhouse flew open, and Nick burst in, disheveled and panting. "Am I late?" he gasped.

"By about half an act," Sander said.

Nick glared at him. "What are you doing in my costume?"

"Playing your part, actually."

"Well, take it off!" When Sander made no move to comply, Nick tugged at the bodice. "Did you hear me, Cooke? Get out of my costume!"

"Soft!" I said. "You'll be heard out there!"

"Go eat hay, Horse." He turned back to Sander. "Do I have to shake you out of it?"

"You're in no shape to go on," Sander said, calmly. "You've got a bit of a beard, for one thing. And, from the smell of your breath, I'd say a bit of beer as well."

"I'll beard you," Nick growled. He yanked at the bodice, pulling loose the hooks at the side. Sander stumbled backward and tripped on the hem. His head struck the edge of the stage doorway with an audible thump.

I had been doing foolish things with great frequency the past few days—and most of my life, for that matter—and I now did another. I swung the heavy bound book into the small of Nick's back. He let out a grunt of pain and turned on me, like a baited bear turning on the hounds. He lashed out at me, and the blow would have caught me full in the face had I not been so adept at ducking. Instead, it glanced off the top of my pate.

Before he could swing again, he was seized from behind by Jack, the cannoneer. "What's going on here?" Jack demanded in a loud whisper.

Nick shook loose from him. "He's trying to steal my part."

Jack scowled at me. "You, eh? I knew you was up to no good."

Sander got to his feet, rubbing the back of his head. "It's me he's accusing, Jack. Nick, if you're not here, somebody has to go on for you, you know that."

Mr. Armin hurried up. "What are you boys doing? Your clamor carried all the way to the tiring-room. Nick, where have you been?"

"I overslept," Nick said sullenly.

"Until nones?" He looked the boy over distastefully. "Go home. You're obviously not fit to perform. We'll discuss your fine later."

"I've nothing to pay a fine with. I lost it all at dice."

"We'll take it out of your future wages, then—if there are any. Go on, now." Mr. Armin waved a hand at us. "Back to work, boys. You're doing well, Sander. You too, Widge."

Though it was small enough praise, it took me off

guard. I was as unaccustomed to praise as I was to having a friend, or being one. The pleasant feeling it gave me was unaccustomed, too, and gave me a small hint of what the players must experience when the audience applauded their efforts.

For the first time, Jack noticed that I was holding the play book. He snatched it from my hands. "What are *you* doing with that?"

"Mr. Heminges gave it to me."

"Well, I'm taking it back. I don't trust you."

"But you can't—!" I started to protest. Sander pulled me away.

"Let it be. No point in making another commotion."

"But that was me job!"

"Don't worry, you'll have it back soon enough." With a grin, he whispered, "Jack can scarcely read his own name."

I made no reply. There was no way I could tell him how important that book was to me, or why. As I headed for the tiring-room, I cursed myself for having hesitated and lost my best chance to hand the book of the play over to Falconer. I would have to keep him waiting yet a while, and he was not the sort who would relish it. Nor, I thought, was he the sort, when I finally did deliver, to praise me for a job well done.

In the tiring-room, Mr. Heminges was putting more white in his beard for his part as Polonius, and Mr. Shakespeare, dressed all in armor, was touching up his ghostly white makeup. Mr. Heminges gave me a startled look. "Wh-where is the b-book?"

"Jack insisted on taking it over," Sander answered for me.

"Lord h-help us."

"Still," said Mr. Shakespeare, "it's better than I feared. In view of his habit of dropping things, I expected that Widge had let it fall into Hell."

"Hell?" I echoed.

"Our word for the cellar beneath the stage." Sander

leaned close to me. "Don't listen to him. He's just heckling you."

"I ken that."

Mr. Heminges sighed. "I'm due on the stage. We'll settle this later." He dusted the excess powder from his beard and started for the door, pausing long enough to say to Mr. Shakespeare, "You wouldn't care to t-trade duties for a t-time, would you, Will? I'll write the p-plays, and you run the c-company?"

Mr. Shakespeare considered a moment. "I suppose that's no more absurd than letting Jack hold the book." He turned his gaze back to the looking glass. The man who played Laertes came into the room and struck up a conversation with Sander. I let my thoughts wander, and my eyes with them.

Because of his helmet, I could not see Mr. Shakespeare's face directly, only his reflection in the glass. He had finished repairing his ghostly pallor and now sat staring at his reflection, not as if assessing his appearance, but as though the looking glass were a scrying glass and, like the gypsies he resembled, he was seeing into another time or place. And perhaps he was. Perhaps he was preparing his next play in his mind, even as he prepared himself physically for this one.

Before I could look away, his gaze caught mine in the glass. He frowned. "Do you have nothing better to do than lounge about in the tiring-room?"

"Well, I was to hold the book, sir."

"Then you should have held it more firmly." He rose and strode from the room, his armor clanking.

"What was that about?" said Sander.

"I hardly ken. Was 'a truly cross wi' me, do you wis?"

"You can't tell sometimes, with him."

"That's so," said the man who played Laertes. "He's a hard one to know. They say that, in his younger days, he was a good companion—and he still can be on occasion. But much of the time he's withdrawn and pensive. If having a touch of genius also means having so strong a dose of melancholy, I'll settle for merely being extremely talented."

"And extremely conceited," Sander said. "By the by, you two haven't met, have you? Widge, this is Chris Beeston. Not so long ago he was a lowly prentice like us."

Beeston held out a hand, which I took hesitantly. "Widge, eh? You're the one who made me do a little jig to cover for Henry when he dropped his lines? How is it you're not out there now, holding the book?"

"It's not me fault!" I said. "Why does everyone fret so about the book?"

"Because," Beeston said, "they have a way of ending up in the wrong hands if we're not careful."

"What do you mean?" I said, though I knew well enough.

"He means sometimes they get stolen," Sander said.

"Oh?" I did not care for the direction this conversation was taking. "Who would want to steal a play?"

"Other theatre companies." Beeston leaned forward and lowered his voice. "I've heard it said that's why Will Kempe left the company. They say he made off with the book of *As You Like It*, and sold it to a touring company in Leicester."

"Leicester?" I said, my voice sounding strained.

Beeston nodded. "The man who runs the Leicester company was with the Chamberlain's Men for a time, back when I was still doing girls' parts—a fellow named Simon Bass." I had feared this was coming, and had my face ready so that it did not betray me—or so I hoped. "He gave me my first fencing lessons." Beeston held out his right hand. "I've still got a scar there, where he struck me. I never knew him well, but there was always something about him that didn't go down right. I never quite trusted him. One thing I will admit, he knew more about makeup than anyone else in the company. His Shylock in *Merchant of Venice* is one of the most astounding transformations I've ever seen. But then, perhaps it wasn't all acting." His voice became even softer. "They say his name is really Simon Bashevi, and he's a Jew himself."

"A jewel?" I echoed. The others burst out laughing. "What?"

"A *Jew*," Beeston said. "Don't you know what a Jew is?"

"Of course. I heard you wrong, that's all." In truth, the concept was hazy in my mind. I knew that Falconer had killed a man for calling him one. To mask my ignorance, I repeated what Falconer had said. "There are no Jews in England. Only former Jews."

"Well, that's so," Beeston said. "After what Lopez did."

Though I had no notion who Lopez was, I nodded knowingly. It was not until a month or two later that I learned how Dr. Lopez had tried to poison the queen and been executed, and how all other Jews had been forced to renounce their religion or be banished.

Sander jumped up from the bench then, as suddenly as if stuck by one of his dress pins. "The cock crow!"

"The what?"

"The cock crow! Come!" I followed him from the tiring-room. "I missed the first one while I was dressing, and Jack is sure to forget this one." Jack stood by the stage entrance, peering at the book as though he'd lost his place long ago.

He gave us a sullen glance. "I don't need no help."

"I wasn't offering any," Sander told him. "I've come to do the cock crow."

"I can do it well enough," Jack said. "Where is it?" He ran a finger down the page. "Cock crows. There. Off with you, now."

"I've practiced it," Sander insisted. "I'll do it."

"I know how to crow!" Jack said.

On the stage, Mr. Shakespeare gave the cue in his hollow ghost's voice: "Adieu, adieu, adieu. Remember me." Both Jack and Sander opened their mouths. One let out a sound reminiscent of a squalling baby; the other sounded uncannily like a stuck pig. Either by itself would have been startling; together they were positively unnerving.

I shook a finger in the ear that had borne the brunt of the noise. "Do you truly wis that's how a cock sounds?"

"I suppose you can do it better," Sander said.

"I'm a country wight, remember? I ken what a cock sounds like, and that's not it."

Jack scowled at me. "As it so happens," he said, "this was a *Danish* cock."

Sander and I looked at one another, then broke into fits of laughter. We had to stagger back to the tiring-room holding our hands over our mouths and close the door, lest we infect the audience. It had been a long while since I'd laughed so freely, if indeed I ever had.

By all accounts, Jack did not furnish a single word to assist the poor players, who were forced to invent or to omit whole passages. He was not permitted to hold the book again. Neither, unfortunately, was I—not because I was not trusted, but because our book keeper recovered and resumed his duties. So I had no further chance to carry off the script.

I could not honestly say that I regretted it. The longer I stayed with the company, and the longer I was away from Falconer, the less incentive I felt to complete my mission. I had not forgotten the reward promised me, but that, too, prompted me less and less. All I had was Bass's word in the matter, and judging from what Chris Beeston had said, his word was not worth much. One thing I did know from hard experience: a master's promise to a prentice is likely to be redeemed only at the last Lammas, as they say—which is to say never.

When a week went by, and Falconer had made no attempt to contact me, I convinced myself that he had lost patience and returned to Leicester, to report to Simon Bass. Still, I stuck close to the theatre and, in my free hours, to Mr. Pope's. Though Falconer was impatient, I had the feeling he was used to getting what he wanted, one way or another.

I applied myself to my daily tasks and lessons at the theatre and, to my surprise, began to actually enjoy them. Dr. Bright had trained me as a man might train a dumb beast, through repetition, reinforced by beatings. Here the method was different. We were given credit for some intelligence. We were expected to learn each technique quickly and to practice what we had learned on our own until it became second nature.

At the end of that week, I was, to my astonishment, given a small part to play, that of the Messenger in *The Spanish Tragedy*. "I have a letter to your lordship," I was to say, and "From Pedringano that's imprisoned," and then "Aye, my good lord." That was the extent of my role. I swear by Saint Pintle that I practiced those lines a thousand times at the very least. I believe I may have repeated them in my sleep.

Sander bore with me and the infinite variations I employed in saying my lines, and my inability to say the name Pedringano properly, until he could bear it no longer. One morning as I stood before the looking glass in our room saying, "Perigando. Predinago. Pedigango," he reached the limits of his tolerance.

"Widge! For all the loves on Earth! What will you do when they give you an entire speech?"

I stared at him in dismay. "Oh, gis! Do you think they will?"

Sander began to laugh. "What did you just say?"

"I said, will they give me a whole speech?"

"No, you didn't. You said, 'Do you *think* they will?' Not do you *wis*, but do you *think*." He slapped me on the back, and for a change, I did not flinch. "My boy, I believe you're turning into a Londoner."

"Gog's bread," I muttered, not knowing whether to be pleased or alarmed. "I hope not."

The play was to be put before an audience on Wednesday. Tuesday night I scarcely slept. Toward daybreak, as I sat up, reading in the half-light one of the ballad-sheets on the walls, Sander woke and peered drowsily at me. "What are you doing?"

"Fretting, mostly."

He clucked his tongue. "It's only three lines, Widge."

"All the more cause to fret. An I say them wrong, I'll ha' no chance to redeem meself."

Sander sighed. "Do you want me to play the lines for you?"

"You've a part of your own."

"I can play more than one. It's done all the time."

"Nay. Nay, I'm not one to quit. I'll do it—somehow."

He yawned and lay back down. After a moment, I said, "It gets easier, doesn't it? Playing a part?"

Sander did not reply. He had fallen asleep.

Eventually I succumbed to sleep myself and woke with the sun on my face. I shook my head to dispel the dream that had filled it. In the dream, I made my maiden entrance upon the stage, and the audience at once broke into gales of applause and laughter. Pleased at having created such a sensation without opening my mouth, I smiled and bowed deeply—to discover that I stood before them *in puris naturalibus*, that is to say naked as a worm.

"Oh, Sander, what a dream!" I said. But Sander was not in bed, nor in the room. Then it came to me that if the sun was up, I should be too, long since. I scrambled into my clothing and hurried downstairs. Goodwife Willingson was feeding the smaller children. "Good morning, Widge!" the boys chorused.

I gulped a bowl of porridge, burning my mouth in my haste, and excused myself. "God buy, Widge!" the boys called after me. I paused long enough to wave to them.

Their enthusiasm made me smile as I closed the door and set out for the theatre.

A hundred yards or so from the house I became aware of another set of footsteps behind me, even swifter than my brisk pace—some fellow player late for morning rehearsal, I guessed.

As I turned to see, a hand seized the neck of my tunic. I was dragged to the side of the road, hoisted like a sack of grain over a low hedge, and flung on my back in the grass.

I sat up, dazed and frightened, to find the dark, hooded figure of Falconer crouching over me like some rough beast over its prey. "Where is it?" he demanded, in that harsh and hollow voice.

I tried to rise. "I—I—I've been having trouble—"

He shoved me back. "Trouble? You haven't begun to learn what trouble is! Where is the script?"

"It was—it was stolen from me wallet. By a thief."

"The devil take your lying tongue!" He snatched his dagger from his belt and thrust it under my chin. "The truth, now!"

"It's true!" I cried frantically. "As true as steel, I swear it!"

"Then you've made a new copy for me?"

"I'm trying."

"Trying? You think I haven't watched your comings and goings? You've been at the Globe every day, and you've nothing to show for it!"

"I can't do 't wi'out being seen!"

He let out a hiss of disgust and let the tip of the dagger drop an inch or two. Gasping, I rubbed at the spot where it had pricked my skin. "Well," he said, "there's nothing left to do, then, but to take the book."

"I meant to, but they keep such a close watch on it."

"Take it from the trunk. It'll be kept in the property room."

"Suppose it's locked?"

"Break the lock! I want that script, and I am accustomed to getting what I want. Have it for me tonight. I'll be waiting. Understood?"

I nodded, very carefully in view of the dagger so near my chin. Falconer suddenly lifted the point again and pressed it against my chin. "And mark me, boy. Breathe no word of this to anyone, or I'll cut out your wagging tongue." With that he stood, stepped over the hedge, and was gone.

I lay in the grass for some time, my heart clamoring in my chest and my limbs weak as water, before I could compose myself enough to continue on to the playhouse.

When I came through the rear door, Mr. Pope was just making an exit from the stage, his face set in the jolly grin required by his role. When he saw me, he resumed his usual gruff expression. "Ah, Widge, you've decided to join us." He shook his head in mock exasperation. "Give a boy a few lines to say, and he thinks he owns the theatre." As he came nearer, his face took on a look of concern. "Are you well, boy? You look as if you'd eaten a batch of bad oysters. Sander said you'd been upset, but—"

"It's naught," I said. "I ran too hard getting here, that's all."

"There was no need. We can manage without you for an hour or two."

"I ken that. I don't like it thought that I'm shirking me duties."

"No one thought that." He lifted my chin. "What have you done to yourself? You're bleeding."

"Oh, that. I—ah—I stumbled and fell into a hedge."

Mr. Pope pulled his kerchief from his sleeve. "Hold that on it. Now, will you need the morning free to study your daunting part, do you think?"

I flushed. "Nay, I can speak it well enough."

In the practice room, Mr. Armin was strapping a metal plate to Sander's waist. "Just in time, Widge." Mr. Armin tossed a short sword to me. So shaken was I that I dropped it, drawing a derisive laugh from Nick. "We'll have to practice that," Mr. Armin said. "But for the moment, you will all be learning how to die properly."

I had come as close to dying as I cared to for one day, but I kept silent and tried to attend to Mr. Armin's words. "We'll be enlisting you prentices for battle scenes soon.

Your weapons will be blunted, but there will be no protective tips. So, lest you die *too* convincingly, you'll wear a metal plate." He tapped the one at Sander's waist. "It is the responsibility of your adversary to see that he strikes this, and not your gut. Of course, in Nick's case, it may be difficult to avoid." He gave a wry glance at the pronounced belly Nick had begun to develop as a result of his regular carousing.

"Now, you've all seen the small bladders full of sheep's blood which we use. They are tied flat to the plate, and the point of the sword bursts them. We'll try that another time. For now, pair off and take turns being killer and victim." He handed Julian a metal plate. "You and Widge trade blows. Carefully."

"Are you sure he's ready for this, Mr. Armin?" Julian asked anxiously as he strapped on the plate.

"He'll do well enough. Now. Low ward. *Dritta. Riversa. Incartata.*" I thrust under Julian's singlestick; the sword hit the protective plate, but to my astonishment, the plate did not stop it. My momentum carried the hilt forward six inches.

"Oh, God!" I cried. "I've stuck him!"

But Julian did not appear to be stuck. Indeed, he was laughing. "It's your sword. It collapses into the hilt!"

I gaped at him, then at the sword. "It's a trick sword? Why didn't you tell me?"

"And miss the look on your face?"

"I was afeared I'd slain you," I said sulkily.

Julian laid an arm upon my shoulder. I shrugged it off. "Come now, no hard feelings, eh? It was a jest."

We took up our positions again. When I struck Julian this time, he gave a halfhearted groan and clutched at his belly. "You look as though you'd eaten too many sweets, not suffered a mortal wound," Mr. Armin said. "Trade roles, now."

I handed my sword to Julian and strapped on the protective plate. In the school of hard knocks where I had become a Master of Dodging, I had also learned to feign injury, as a way of lessening the severity of a beating. The experience stood me in good stead now. When Julian struck me, I gave a howl of agony and crumpled to the floor, my face a very picture of pain and terror.

"Mother Mary!" Julian breathed. "Are you wounded?" I grinned up at him. He gave me an exasperated nudge with one foot. "You sot!"

"Very dramatic," Mr. Armin said dryly. "No one will even notice the principals, they'll be so busy looking at you."

During our rest time, Julian and I sat against the wall, sipping cups of water. "Well," he said casually, "perhaps you're not such a bad sort after all, for a country wight."

I stared at him. "Is that the London way of giving a compliment?"

He smiled. "I suppose it is."

"In that case, I suppose you're not such a bad sort, either. For a city wight."

"Touch. Your point. So, how do you come to be in London?"

"That's something of a long tale."

"Just give me a brief summary."

"I ran away from me master, that's the long and short of it."

"And your parents?"

"Me mother's long since dead. Me father . . ." I hesitated and then, seeing Julian's sympathetic look, went on. "I don't ken who me father was."

Julian nodded. "We're birds of a feather, then. I lost my mum when I was small, to the plague. And my da is—" He shrugged. "Well, my da will die of the dropsy one day, I've no doubt."

"The dropsy?"

"One of the words we use to mean hanging from Tyburn Tree."

"Hanging? Why? What has 'a done?"

"What *hasn't* he done, you might as well ask. As far as I know, he's never murdered anyone, and I don't suppose he's ever betrayed one of his fellows. Anything else he'll do, if there's money in it. That's why he lets me prentice here—they pay him a small sum yearly."

"Aye? Do you think that—"

"What?"

"Oh, I was just wondering whether me master might be willing to do the same—let me stay on an they paid him a bit."

"You think he'll come after you, then?"

"Aye, I'm afeard 'a will."

"I hope he doesn't," Julian said. "You're just beginning to show some promise."

I felt myself flush. "Do you truly think so?"

Julian grinned. "Well, if you can feign love or compassion half so well as you can feign an agonizing death, you'll be as famous as Burbage."

"I've had no experience in such things," I said. "But I'm willing to learn."

We were kept so busy through the morning that I scarcely had time to dread the afternoon, when I would step onstage and say my three lines. Yet the threat of it hung over my head, along with the more dire threat of Falconer out there, waiting for me to deliver the script.

An hour before the performance I was in costume, not wishing to see my dream come true. I paced about behind the stage muttering "Pedringano, Pedringano" like an incantation.

"Widge," Sander said, "sit somewhere and practice breathing deeply. I'll call you when you're due on the stage."

"An you forget, what then?"

"I won't forget."

Nonetheless, I was unable to sit still. I went on stomping about, repeating my lines and getting in everyone's way until at last Julian took me by the arm. "Come. You're going to help me with my lines for *Satiromastix*."

It did calm me a bit, having something to do, and Sander was as good as his word, though he got me to the stage with a scant half-minute to spare. "Gives you less time to fret," he said. When my cue came, I froze, and he was forced to propel me onto the stage.

My actual moment of glory is a blank in my memory. I must have gotten out my lines, Pedringano and all, without disgracing myself or the company, for afterward, in the tiring-room, I was congratulated by the other players as though I had passed through fire—which, in a sense, I had.

"I remember well my first faltering steps upon the boards," Mr. Pope said.

"I'd no idea they had boards so long ago," Mr. Armin said.

"Oh, we knew how to make boards well enough. It wasn't until your time that we learned how to make an *audience* bored." There was much laughter. "To return to my story, I was given the part of gluttony in a play called *Nature*. I was not so well upholstered in those days, so they strapped a sack of buckram about my waist. Halfway through the play it came loose and descended about my knees, so that I resembled not a glutton so much as a pear with legs."

"I had much the same experience," Mr. Phillips said, "save that I was playing a woman, and it was my bosom which migrated south."

I was enjoying the players' tales so much that I neglected to undress and remove my makeup. When everyone else was ready to leave, I was still wiping off my face paint.

"Want us to wait for you?" Sander asked.

I hesitated. If I was in their company, Falconer could not accost me again. Yet I could not avoid him forever. He had said I must have the script for him that very night, or—well, he had not made it clear what the alternative was, but I knew it would not be pleasant. "Nay," I said, trying to sound casual. "Go on wi'out me. I'll be along."

When they were gone, I sat staring into the looking glass as I had seen Mr. Shakespeare do, pondering my dilemma. All my life I had done what I was told to do without question, without thinking about the right or the wrong of it. This time I couldn't help questioning.

I had no doubt that what Falconer and my master, Simon Bass, were asking me to do was wrong. Even a thief, Julian had said, would not betray his fellows. And if I took the script, I would indeed have betrayed my fellows. I had no desire to do so. They had taken me in and shown me kindness and trust and friendship. I had been alone and friendless a long time and had accepted it as my lot. But in the past weeks, I had learned something of what it meant to have friends, and to be a real prentice, not a mere slave. It was a piece of knowledge late to come and hard-won, and one I did not wish to forget.

Yet I had learned what it means to have an enemy, too. As I scrubbed the makeup from my chin, I wiped the spot where Falconer's dagger had pricked the skin. I flinched.

Another piece of hard-won knowledge I did not care to forget, lest it be impressed upon me again, more forcefully and more permanently.

I turned away from the looking glass. I had been contemplating the matter as if I had a choice. The truth was, if I hoped to save my own skin, I had no choice.

By the time I shed my costume and hung it in the wardrobe and dressed in my customary clothing, the light coming through the high windows had faded. I stepped from the tiring-room and looked about and listened. The area behind the stage was deserted.

Cautiously I moved across to the door of the property room. It was unlocked. I stepped inside and pushed it closed behind me, leaving a gap of a hand's breadth to let a bit of light into the windowless room.

It contained half a dozen trunks, several of them secured with locks. There was no way of knowing which one contained the play books. I had long since learned to look for the easiest way of pursuing a task. It would be far easier to look in the unlocked chests first, on the slight chance that one of them might hold the treasure.

I raised the lid of the nearest one. The hinges protested feebly and I halted, fearing someone might still be in the theatre. Hearing nothing, I yanked the lid open and peered inside. Small weapons of all sorts, from bucklers to broadswords, were piled within. I went on to the next trunk.

The light was so far gone that I had to lay the lid back and bend close in order to see. I gasped and stumbled backward in horror. The trunk was packed with parts of human bodies—bloody arms, hands cut off at the wrist, severed heads with staring, sightless eyes.

I knocked against another chest and sat heavily down upon it. Holding a hand over my mouth to muffle my frantic breathing, I gaped at the trunk as though the awful contents might crawl from it. Slowly it came to me that these were mere stage properties, made of plaster and paint, and then I had to keep my hand over my mouth to stifle the relieved laughter that rose in me.

I was suddenly sobered by the sound of footfalls close by. I rolled off the trunk and crouched behind it. The footsteps approached and halted before the door of the property room. For a moment there was utter silence. I held my breath. Then I heard the door swing on its hinges—not open, but closed. The thin shaft of light was eclipsed. The latch clicked; a key rattled in the lock; the bolt slid into place. Then the footsteps retreated. Finally there was a distant, muffled thump—the rear door of the theatre being closed and locked.

I crawled out from behind the trunk and felt my way across the black room, banging painfully against racks of weapons and corners of trunks. As I expected, the door was locked as surely and securely as those locked trunks. If I groped about in the dark long enough, I might manage eventually to break into the book keeper's trunk and liberate the script. But what good would it do me if I was still a prisoner?

In the end, I made no attempt to force the trunks or locate the play book. If discovered here in the morning, I could contrive some explanation of how I came to be shut up in the property room. But even with my skill at lying I would have a hard time explaining broken locks and a missing script.

There was one advantage, at least, in being locked up so securely: Falconer could not get to me. There were also several distinct disadvantages: I had no food, no water, no place to relieve myself, and no bed to sleep in. Such discomforts were not new to me, but lately I had become accustomed to regular meals and soft bedding.

I found by touch a helmet to relieve myself in, and a pile of carpets in one corner of the room to lie down upon and sleep the untroubled sleep of the prisoner who is resigned to his prison.

I woke in the morning to the sound of footsteps, and the property room door being unlocked. Like a mouse, I scrambled for a hiding place, but I need not have bothered. The door was not opened. When I heard the footsteps climb the stairs, I stole across the room and out the door, and thence out of the theatre.

The sun had not yet shown itself, and I hoped I might be at Mr. Pope's in time for breakfast. Fearing that Falconer might lie in wait, I took a roundabout route and came upon Mr. Pope and Sander as they were leaving the house.

"And where have you been the whole night long, my lad?" Mr. Pope demanded.

"Well," I replied, to buy a bit of time, "it's rather a long tale."

"Then you'd best begin at once."

"Well, sir, the truth is, it's . . . it's me old master. 'A hunted me down here—'a kenned how I had me heart set on being a player, you see—and 'a tried to force me to return to Yorkshire wi' him. I went along as far as St. Albans"—such details add credibility to a lie—"where I slipped away, and I've spent the night walking back."

"Saints' mercy," said Sander. "You must be exhausted."

Mr. Pope was more skeptical. "You walked all the way from St. Albans? That's upwards of twenty miles."

"Nay, nay," I said quickly. "I never walked the whole time. A farmer brought me half that way on his cart. I even slept a bit on his load of straw." I brushed imaginary chaff from my tunic.

This seemed to satisfy him, and he grew more solicitous. "Have you eaten, then?"

"Aye," I said, not wishing to try his patience. "The good farmer shared his bread and cheese wi' me." Would that I could have lied so convincingly to my complaining stomach.

As we walked on, Sander hung back and whispered, "I didn't tell him you were gone. He just noticed. He was anxious about you."

"About me? Truly?"

Sander nodded. "He takes the welfare of his boys very seriously."

I was accustomed to being called someone's "boy." Like the term "his man," it can mean you are the servant, or chattel, of that person. But the way Sander used the word, it implied something more, something better—that I was not merely part of a household, but part of a family.

My empty belly made the morning's lessons seem interminable. We were well into them before Nick appeared, looking as though he'd slept in his clothing, and at the same time as though he hadn't slept at all. Mr. Armin left us to perform our *passatas*, and drew Nick into a corner, where they had a lengthy conversation. As their tempers mounted, so did their voices.

"I'm not a child!" Nick was saying. "When will you stop treating me as one?"

"When you stop behaving as one! Drinking and gaming until all hours is not the mark of a man!"

"Neither is wearing skirts and prancing about the stage like a woman!"

"Ah, that's it, is it? You feel you're ready for men's roles, do you?"

"Well, I—" Nick hesitated. "I'm sick of playing a girl, that's all." He rubbed at the stubble on his cheeks. "And I'm sick of being thought a callow boy wherever I go, because I'm forced to shave my beard."

"So you feel you're ready to move from prentice to hired man. Are you quite certain you've learned everything you need to know?"

Nick's voice faltered. "Perhaps . . . perhaps not everything."

"No, I think not. Come. Let's try to fill in what you lack, so that when the time comes for you to play a man's part, you'll be ready." Mr. Armin glanced at the three of us, who had been eavesdropping. "You lot have far more to learn than he does," he called. "Get back to work. Fifty more *passatas*."

As we thrust over and over at the unyielding wall, I whispered to Sander, "An Nick is so much of a trouble, why do you not give him the chuck?"

Sander gave me a puzzled look. "The chuck?"

"Aye. Throw him out."

Sander stopped to wipe his brow. "Would you throw out your brother, if you had one?"

"I don't have one."

"But if you did?"

"That's different."

"Not really. Don't you see? The theatre is a sort of family and, like him or no, Nick is a part of it." A few weeks before, I would not have understood his meaning, but now I felt I did. "Besides," Sander went on, "he's having a bad time just now, that's all. He'll come around."

"Perhaps," I said doubtfully. "I'd just prefer 'a didn't come around me."

Later, as we were on our way downstairs, Will Sly stopped me. "Mr. Heminges wants to see you."

"Me?"

"Do you know another Widge? He's in the property room."

"The—the property room?"

"Has anyone checked this boy's ears? I believe he's a trifle deaf."

"Perhaps you're not saying things properly," Julian countered. "You haven't been drinking, have you?"

Will grinned. "No more than usual."

"Ah, that's the problem, then. You've not lubricated your chawbones."

I was not in a mood to appreciate their jests. What business could Mr. Heminges have with me, particularly in the property room? I could think of but one possible topic, and it was not one I was eager to discuss.

I considered walking on past the property room and out the rear door. What kept me from it was the thought of Falconer. If I had to answer to someone, I preferred that it be the person least likely to cut my throat.

I halted before the property room door, like a condemned man at the foot of the gallows. Mr. Heminges sat within at a table, writing figures in a ledger. He looked up and beckoned to me. "C-come in, Widge. I'm just d-doing accounts. My least favorite d-duty, but a n-necessary one." He sprinkled sand on the fresh ink, blew it off, and closed the ledger. "N-now. I understand you were in a b-bit of t-trouble last night."

My stomach knotted up. "Aye. But it wasn't me own fault—"

"I know that. T-Thomas gave me a full account."

"Thomas?"

"Mr. Pope."

"Oh." How could Mr. Pope have known about my attempted theft? Had he been the one who locked me in the room?

"This is a serious p-problem, but not an unusual one."

"It's not?"

"N-no. In f-fact several of our prentices have done the same."

"Truly? What did you do to them?"

"D-do to them?" Now it was Mr. Heminges's turn to sound bewildered.

"Were they not punished?"

Mr. Heminges laughed. "For running off from their m-masters? If we t-took on only those b-boys whose masters have agreed to hand them over, we'd b-be rather short on p-prentices. M-most would as soon hand them over to the d-Devil."

It came to me then, almost too late, that we were talking of two entirely different matters. I was concerned with what I'd actually done, and he with the lie I'd concocted to cover it. I hastened to scramble out of the hole I'd dug for myself. I shook my head glumly. "Me master seemed bent on having me back."

"This is England, not China. A man has the right to choose his own p-path. If you truly wish to stay on here, and p-prove yourself able, we will stand with you. If your m-master comes for you, we will offer him the usual f-fee to b-buy off your obligation, and he may take or l-leave it. But we'll see that he leaves *you*, in any c-case. Does that suit you?"

I nodded, so taken aback by this offer of kindness where I had looked for wrath that I could scarcely speak. "Aye. It does indeed."

"Good. G-go back to your lessons, then." I turned to go. "Oh, by the by. They tell me you m-managed to deliver your three lines without f-fainting yesterday. We'll have to try you with four or f-five next time, eh?"

"I don't ken, sir. I'm not sure I could bear it."

He laughed, taking this for a jest, and I let him. "One more th-thing, Widge. I've f-fancied all morning that I smelled something r-rotten, as Mr. Shakespeare says, but my n-nose isn't what it was. Do you smell anything?"

I did indeed, but it took me a moment to recall what it was—the helmet I had used as a chamber pot. I felt my face go red. "A dead rat, most like," I said, and quickly turned away.

For the second time that day, I had been made to feel that I was among people who cared about me and my welfare. My guilt at the thought of betraying him and the rest of the company came back, stronger than ever.

They would stand with me, Mr. Heminges had said. But he said it without knowing the true source of my troubles.

If anyone came after me, it would not be Dr. Bright nor my current master, Simon Bass, who might be willing to listen to reason. It would be the formidable and unreasonable Falconer.

I did not wish to endanger anyone in the company, yet my only means of keeping Falconer at bay was to stick close to Mr. Pope's or to the theatre, where Falconer seemed reluctant to set foot. For the next week I saw no sign of that dread hooded figure, but this time I did not fool myself into thinking that he had gone away. I kept a vigilant watch, sometimes rising in the small hours of the night to gaze out at the moonlit lanes and hedgerows.

"Widge," Sander said one day on our way to the Globe. "We're friends, aren't we?"

"Aye," I said, and felt I spoke the truth.

"Then will you tell me please why you always glance about so nervously? You look like a dickey bird in a yard full of cats, as Mr. Pope would say."

"It's naught. I'm not used to the city yet, that's all." There was some truth in that, too. But it was also true that I no longer found the landscape of church spires and grimy tenements so strange. London speech no longer felt so foreign on my ear or on my tongue, and I'd learned to ignore the clamor of its streets.

"You know, five minutes' walk in that direction"—he pointed south—"brings you into the country. And tomorrow is our idle day."

The prospect of an afternoon in the fields and woods

was tempting—until I thought of Falconer. "I don't suppose you'd care to come along."

"I don't mind. I've nothing against the country."

To my relief, Julian agreed to join us. The larger the company, the safer I would be. I stopped short of inviting Nick, though. Not that he would have gone anyway. It was obvious that he no longer considered himself a prentice. He avoided our company, preferring to spend his time with his drinking companions, mostly hired men from the less reputable theatre companies. When forced to rub elbows with us boys, he put on superior airs.

That morning, during fencing instruction, Mr. Armin and Mr. Phillips were wanted downstairs, and Nick interpreted this to mean that he was in charge. "All right now, line up here and let's see what sort of scrimers you are."

"Take a walk in the Thames," Julian told him and turned away.

Nick stepped in front of him. "I said we'll see what you've learned. Would you prefer to demonstrate against the wall, or against me?"

Julian considered a moment. "Well, I'd say the wall has more wits."

"It's too bad you're not as quick with your sword as with your tongue. I think you've all been playing at girls too long. That's what you look like, with your mincing steps and your polite little cuts and thrusts. And you—" He gave Julian's stick a blow with his own. "You're the worst of the lot. You'd best stick to dancing."

Julian's face, always pale, had gone white, and his eyes narrowed. "I'll dance on your grave, you sot," he said, and came on guard.

Nick smiled nastily, as though this was what he had been waiting for. He brought his stick to high ward, seeming to invite a thrust from Julian. When it came, he stepped aside and struck Julian on the collarbone. Julian staggered, his face drawn with pain.

Nick stood calmly waiting for the next move. Julian feigned another *stocatta*, then performed one of the *passatas* we had practiced so interminably. His stick caught Nick beneath the breastbone. He let out a grunt of surprise and pain.

His mood changed suddenly. He set upon Julian like a Tom 'a Bedlam, striking edgeblows, downright blows, blows which had no name. "You'll hurt him!" I shouted and flung my stick at Nick's legs. It served only to anger him more. "Do something!" I told Sander.

Sander stepped forward with his stick raised. "Nick! Stop now!" He might as well have told the wall to stop standing there.

Being small, I had never been one to solve a problem by a physical attack. I preferred to talk my way out of things or to perform Cobbe's Traverse, that is to run. But Nick would not listen to reason, and running would only leave Julian to his fate. He had rescued me, and now he needed my help. My fencing skills were no match for Nick's, so I fell back on the method of defense that every child of the orphanage learns—catch-as-catch-can wrestling.

I at least had the advantage of surprise. I threw myself at Nick's legs, and all his weight collapsed on me. The first principle of wrestling is to hang on to your opponent come what may, so I clung to Nick's breeches like a leech, though he kicked madly and pummeled my back with his fists.

I felt his struggles suddenly grow more desperate and lifted my face to see why. Julian had his stick pressed against Nick's throat-bole. The more fiercely Nick struggled and clawed, the more pressure Julian applied, yet Nick refused to yield.

"That will do!" a voice rang out. "Let him up!"

Julian cautiously removed the stick, and I disentangled myself. Mr. Armin stood scowling at us, but under the mask of disapproval I detected a hint of amusement. I wondered how long he had stood observing before he interfered.

He offered a hand to Nick, who ignored it and got unsteadily to his feet, rubbing his windpipe and glaring at us like some trapped and wounded beast.

"If you're quite done trying to kill one another," Mr. Armin said, "we'll continue with our lessons. Not you, Nick," he added as Nick retrieved his singlestick. "They'll be wanting you downstairs, to rehearse *Love's Labour's*."

"What part?" Nick growled, his voice sounding choked and weak.

"Dumaine."

Nick stared at him. "A man's part?"

"Do you imagine you can pass for a girl with that voice? It sounds as though Julian squeezed the last drop of sweetness from it."

Certainly there was no sweetness in the glance Nick threw us as he left the room.

"If Nick is to take on men's roles," Mr. Armin said, "that will change things for you boys as well. Sander, you and Julian will begin studying Nick's old roles. Widge, you'll be given some of Sander's duties, and his smaller parts. Can you manage that?"

"Yes, sir." I tried to sound confident.

He raised his eyebrows. "What happened to 'aye'?"

"I'm trying to civilize me speech—*my* speech."

He nodded thoughtfully. "A pity, though. Soon you'll sound the same as all the rest of us."

As we returned to our lessons, Julian said, "That was a brave thing you did."

I shrugged. "You were no coward yourself. I was afeard you'd thropple him."

"It'd be no more than he deserves."

"That's so, saying we fight like girls. I daresay 'a's never had a girl do such as that to him."

Julian gave me a curious look and seemed about to say something, but Mr. Armin interrupted. "We're not doing voice lessons, you two! Lay on!"

. . .

Our country outing next day was more in the nature of a rehearsal at first. Sander and Julian brought along the sides they needed in order to learn Nick's old roles. The brief bits I inherited were not worth the bother of a separate side. I merely jotted them down as Sander recited them.

Without thinking, I wrote them in Dr. Bright's charactery. Julian peered over my shoulder. "What sort of writing is *that*? I thought Mr. Shakespeare's hand was hard to read."

"Ah . . . it's just . . . something of me own invention." I tried to tuck the paper into my wallet, but Sander plucked it from my grasp.

"Let me see." He turned the paper this way and that, frowning. "Can you actually read this?"

"When it's right side up." I tried to retrieve the paper, but he kept it from me—an easy task, considering our relative heights.

"No, no. Wait a bit. This is amazing, you know. You can write out anything in this fashion?"

"Well, no," I lied. "It's rather slow going, in truth."

"Slow?" Julian said. "You wrote out those lines as quickly as Sander said them. A trick like that could be really useful. Why, you could copy down the plays of the Lord Admiral's men, word for word!"

"*Steal* them?" I said.

Julian shrugged. "They do it to us."

"That's because our plays are better than theirs," Sander said. "Not much point in our copying their weak stuff, is there?"

"I suppose not. All the same, there should be some use for that writing of yours, Widge. You should show it to Mr. Heminges."

"What?" I said, disguising my real dismay with mock dismay. "And saddle meself wi' yet another duty?"

Sander laughed. "He's right. We'll keep mum about it. Right, Julian?"

"I'm not one to give away others' secrets," Julian said.

The day was too fine to spend it all on lines. Goodwife Willingson had packed a cold meal for us, and we chose an inviting spot in the shade of an ancient oak. When I had had my fill, I stretched out and watched the clouds, as I had so often done in the meadows about Berwick.

"Look at him," Sander said. "He's in his element. We'll have to truss him up and carry him back to the city like a captured deer."

I turned my head to make some lazy reply, but it was stopped in my throat by the sight of a dark-clothed figure coming down the road. My face must have reflected my alarm, for Julian said, "What's wrong, Widge?"

"Someone's coming," I breathed.

The others turned to see who was approaching. "It's only Mr. Shakespeare," Julian said. I gave a sigh of relief. "Who did you think it was?"

"I was afeared it was—it was me master."

"He must be a harsh one, for you to fear him so."

"Aye. He is that." So pensive and self-absorbed was Mr. Shakespeare that he walked by without even noting our presence. "Should we not at least greet him?" I asked.

Julian shook his head. "Better not. If he's mulling over some problem in a play, he won't welcome the interruption."

"Why is 'a so glum and gloomy, do you think?"

Julian slid closer to me and said confidentially, "I've heard it said he's brooding on a thwarted love affair."

Sander gave him an indignant look. "The man has a wife and two daughters in Stratford."

Julian grinned. "When did that ever prevent a man from having a love affair?"

"You clod. If you want to know what I think, I think it's his son that's the cause of it."

"I didn't know he had a son."

"He doesn't, any longer. The boy grew ill and died while Mr. Shakespeare was here in London. I doubt that he's ever forgiven himself."

"Perhaps," I said, " 'a's simply ruled by a melancholy humour."

"A what?" said Sander.

"Me old master says we're all ruled by the four humours, and when we're ill or out of sorts, it's because we ha' too much of one. Now, Nick, 'a's choleric—hot and dry. Dr. Bright would prescribe something cold and wet, to offset it."

"All the beer he drinks doesn't seem to help much."

"Perhaps Julian had it right," I said. " 'A should take a walk in the Thames."

Julian laughed. "What would your master make of me?"

"Sanguine, I'd say."

"And me?" said Sander.

I considered a moment. "For you, they would ha' to think up a whole new category."

Sander aimed a good-natured swat at me, which I

dodged. He grabbed me, and laughing, we rolled about in the grass like two pups. "You're daft, the both of you," Julian said. Then, apparently feeling left out, he pulled up tufts of grass and flung them at us.

Sander spat out a few blades and whispered, "Let's get him!"

"Aye!" We sprang for Julian. He backed up against the tree, calling "No! No!" between fits of laughter. But when we took hold of his arms and tried to drag him down, he turned suddenly serious, indeed angry. "No! I don't want to wrestle!"

We teased him a moment longer, but he remained stiff and stern, so we left off. For some time afterward, a melancholy humour seemed to rule us as well. A gloominess was cast over our day, as though a cloud had come across the sun. But gradually we warmed to one another again and spent several hours poking about a stagnant pond and playing a game of nineholes with stones, and in other pursuits too trivial to recount. When we heard the bells in Southwark ringing vespers, we were reluctant to return—not just the country boy, I think, but all of us.

The week that followed was mostly uneventful, if days which begin with two hours of manual labor, proceed to four hours of lessons and rehearsals, and conclude with performing in or assisting with a different play each afternoon can be called uneventful. Compared to the preceding perilous weeks, this was a veritable holiday. I was not locked in any rooms, nor were any daggers held to my throat. I did not wander into any dangerous parts of the city, nor risk my life crossing the Thames.

Though I was never quite able to put Falconer out of my mind, I saw no sign of him. Surely, I thought, even he must have given up by now. I did not even quarrel with Nick, for he no longer took lessons with us mere prentices. He still played a few of his old parts, but most of the time he was downstairs, rehearsing men's roles.

Or at least he was supposed to be. In truth, he was still up to his old tricks, throwing his money away on dice and drink all night long, then coming to rehearsal half-drunk or late, or both. It was as though he had taken on a role he was not prepared to play, not only on stage but in life, and was looking for someone who would tell him what to do next. Yet, though he received advice from all quarters, he heeded none of it.

Before his second week was out, the part in *Love's Labour's* was given to Chris Beeston, and Nick was back upstairs with us, practicing his swordsmanship. "What he needs," Julian said, "is not fencing lessons but lessons in manners."

"Would you like to be the one to learn them to him?" I said.

Julian rolled his eyes. "And you could use a few lessons in grammar."

Nick's attitude toward us was even more hostile than before, especially toward Sander, who had taken over several of Nick's roles. With the demotion of Nick to our ranks, the peaceful interlude began to slip away, and my life once more became complicated, filled with anxiety and finally danger.

The first complication cropped up soon after Nick's return. The moment we arrived at the Globe that morning, we sensed that something was in the air. The sharers were in the property room, discussing some matter so intently that none of them so much as raised a hand to greet us. Halfway through the morning, we discovered what the matter was.

For a change, Nick was on time for fencing practice, and Mr. Armin was late. When he finally arrived, he beckoned to us, cleared his throat comically, and proclaimed with exaggerated formality, "Oyez, oyez! Be it known that the Lord Chamberlain's Men have been asked, or commanded if you will, to present the play *The Tragedy of Hamlet* at Whitehall a fortnight from this day!"

The other prentices looked at one another in surprise—or was it alarm? "What is Whitehall?" I whispered to Julian.

"The royal court."

"You mean the palace? Where the queen lives?"

"No," he said sarcastically, "the royal *tennis* court, you sot."

Two weeks seemed to me ample time to prepare, but the company behaved as though Judgment Day were almost upon them and they must put not only their parts but their entire lives in order. Our property men spent most of their day at the office of the queen's master of revels, preparing elaborate scenery for the great event, so the task of seeing to the properties for the regular performances fell to us prentices. It was not unusual in those next weeks for a player to cry "Behold!" and open the curtains of the rear alcove to reveal two frantic prentices struggling with some unwieldy piece of scenery or furniture. Our tire man, too, deserted us, leaving us to clean our costumes and hold our split seams together as best we might.

The principal players, meantime, rehearsed *Hamlet* endlessly, employing a slightly different version each day, as Mr. Shakespeare deleted or added passages to suit the fancy of the master of revels.

Even Julian and Sander, who ordinarily took things as they came, seemed to breathe in the air of anxiety that hung about the place. "Why is everyone in such a dither?" I asked Julian. "You've played at the court before, ha' you not?"

"Not I. The company has, many times. But this time is different. I don't know quite all that's behind it, but I do know the company got on Her Majesty's bad side a few months ago by giving a private performance of *Richard II* for the earl of Essex."

"What's wrong in that?"

"The queen had said that no one should perform the play, because it shows a ruler being deposed. I suppose she didn't want it giving anyone any ideas. But apparently that's just what Essex meant to do, for the day after the performance, he tried to gather an army to storm the palace."

"What happened?"

Julian shrugged. "She made him king." He let me puzzle over that a moment, then laughed. "He didn't succeed, of course, you ninny. The queen's guard threw him in the Tower, and a few days later they chopped off his head. Because of the play, the queen suspected our players of being in league with Essex. They weren't, of course. But they're all walking very carefully now, to avoid treading on the queen's toes."

"I can see why," I said. "If Essex was the queen's favorite and she chopped his costard off, who kens what she might do to someone she doesn't care for?"

Julian nodded soberly, as thought contemplating what dreadful fate the queen might devise if she were truly displeased.

Our lessons were all but suspended for a time, but Mr. Armin insisted on an hour's fencing practice each day. We worked frequently with blunted rapiers and protective plates. We were even permitted one day to strap on a bag of sheep's blood, which gave an added luster to our mock death throes.

Nick and Julian were again paired. Julian wore the protective plate and the bladder of blood. Nick wielded a blunted rapier. He was having trouble piercing the blood bag with the dull point and, growing angry, he thrust harder than was necessary and without the necessary control. His point struck the bag high and, deflected by the metal plate, caught Julian squarely in the center of the chest.

Julian gave a sharp gasp and went down on one knee, holding his chest and biting his lip against the pain. Sander laughed, obviously thinking it was all a sham. "Good acting!"

"He's not acting." Mr. Armin strode over to Julian. "What is it? What's happened?"

Nick stood white-faced, his sword hanging at his side. "I—it was an accident. I—I stuck him—"

Mr. Armin supported Julian with one arm and helped him sit on the floor. "Let me see," he said, and began unhooking the front of Julian's doublet.

"No, no," Julian protested. "It's nothing." But his strained voice and drawn face gave the lie to this.

"I'll decide that," Mr. Armin said.

"I didn't mean to do it," Nick put in, sullenly. When Mr. Armin ignored him, he turned away and began pacing irritably back and forth.

Mr. Armin tried to pull open the doublet, but Julian pushed his hand away and struggled to rise. "I'm all right, I tell you."

"Stop fighting me. This is not time for false pride or false courage." When Mr. Armin yanked the doublet open, I could see the red stain on Julian's linen shirt. "You see, you're bleeding." He drew out the kerchief from his sleeve.

"Please," Julian begged, pulling at the gaping front of his doublet. "I'll see to it myself."

"Yes, and bleed to death by yourself, most like." Mr. Armin forced Julian's hands away and pulled at the neck of the shirt, laying Julian's torso bare.

In truth, though, it was not bare. A cloth was wound tightly about his chest. "What is this?" Mr. Armin demanded. Then his puzzled scowl transformed into a look of disbelief. "The devil take me!" he breathed.

Julian was fairly frantic now, clutching at the front of his shirt, while tears streamed down his cheeks. "Let me alone! Please, let me alone!"

Mr. Armin recovered and shook his head. "We have to stop the bleeding. Just let me put this on the wound, and you can hold it in place. All right?"

Julian nodded shortly and turned his head aside in an attempt to hide his tears. Sharing his embarrassment, we hung our heads and moved back a few paces.

"Come, now." Mr. Armin lifted Julian's slight body easily in his arms. "We'll get you downstairs where you can lie down, and then we'll find someone who can bandage that properly."

"But why—?" Nick started to ask. Mr. Armin shot him a warning glance, and carried Julian from the room.

When they were gone, Nick said, "Why can't he bandage it himself? Surely it's not so bad as to require a doctor. Though from the way the boy carried on, you'd think I'd gutted him. It couldn't be that bad. Could it?"

I glanced at Sander and knew from the stunned look on his face that, like me, he had guessed the truth that Nick was either too slow-witted or too unobservant to see. "I don't believe the wound is what concerns Mr. Armin, or Julian," Sander said.

"What, then?"

Sander looked to me and shrugged. "It may as well be said. It'll be no secret soon."

I shook my head. "I'll not be the one to tell it."

"Tell *what*?" Nick demanded.

Sander gave a sigh of resignation. "It would seem," he said, "that Julian is a girl."

I had rarely seen Nick at a loss for words, but he was now. He gaped at us, then at the door through which Julian had been carried. "A girl," he said finally, as though unsure of the meaning of the word. "That's impossible."

Certainly it seemed impossible that such a fact could have escaped our notice all this time. But of course, looking backward, I could see a dozen clues that, had I bothered to add them together, would have led me to that very conclusion.

"Impossible or not," Sander said, "I'm afraid it's true."

Nick's astonishment gave way to anger. "It can't be true! You can't tell me I've been fencing with a girl for most of a year, and never knew it!"

"I won't tell you, then, but it's so all the same."

Nick stalked back and forth, scowling and slicing the air with his blade, as though to fend off the truth that was attempting to seize him. At last he cried, "God's blood! A girl!" and, flinging the sword aside, stormed out of the room.

Sander clucked his tongue in sympathy. "It's a hard morsel for him to swallow. But even harder for Julian. They'll never let him go on performing."

"Her," I reminded him.

"Yes," he said. "Her."

Mr. Phillips's wife was sent for to bandage the wound, which was not so grave, aside from the damage it had done to Julian's pride and to her future as a player. Julia, I should now call her, for that was her given name.

Mistress Phillips tried to coax Julia to come home with her, but Julia refused. "I have never yet missed a performance, and I do not intend to miss this one."

After much discussion, the sharers concluded that it was better to let a girl play the part than to assign it to a prentice who would have to read the lines from a side.

Besides, it began to look as though one of us might be needed to take Nick's place. He had left the theatre and not returned, and there was little more than an hour until performance. "We could go seek him out," Sander suggested to Mr. Heminges. "No doubt we'll find him in his usual haunts."

"M-meaning an ale house," Mr. Heminges said sourly. "Perhaps you'd b-best do that. Just be sure the t-two of you are b-back in time, else I'll be out there m-myself, clean-shaven and speaking f-falsetto."

Despite the circumstances, we could not help laughing at the picture this conjured up. "You may well laugh," Mr. Heminges said, "but I served my t-time in skirts, and by all accounts I was quite f-fetching. More so than N-Nick, certainly. But though Nick may not be fetching, still he must be f-fetched."

"And though 'a be not comely, yet 'a must come," I added, drawing an appreciative laugh from the others.

"Very good, Widge," said Mr. Heminges. "You've the wit of a true p-player."

As Sander and I walked toward the river, I said, "Do you think that I could actually be a player?"

He gave me a puzzled look. "You say that as though the idea had just struck you. Isn't that what you came here for?"

"Oh. Aye, of course it is." Once again, I was sorely tempted to tell him the truth. I was weary of carrying the baggage of that secret about with me, always having to be careful not to let it slip. I tried to imagine how Julia must have felt, guarding her secret for years, wanting so badly to belong to the company of players that she would risk such a desperate device and yet, because of that very device, never being able to truly belong.

We were, as she had said, birds of a feather, for I had never belonged anywhere, either. Now there was a chance that I might, and I could not bring myself to endanger that chance by revealing my original purpose here, even though I had abandoned that purpose and, to all appearances, so had Falconer.

The south bank of the Thames was like a poor reflection of the north bank, a sort of lesser London. Across the river the great houses of great gentlemen lined the embankment. Here on the lower ground the buildings were nearly as imposing in size but housed a separate family behind each of their many grimy windows. Scattered among these tenements were smaller dwellings that had given over their ground floors to some business, usually a tavern.

"How in heaven's name will we ken which one Nick is in?"

"Any which looks prosperous or reputable," Sander said, "we can surely pass by."

We found him in a place with a sagging roof and the customary ivy growing up the front wall. Nick sat at one of the stained, scarred tables, in the company of two fellows I took to be university students, a species we all knew well, as they had more money and leisure for playgoing than the working class.

Sander and I stood just inside the door and tried to attract Nick's attention, but he was too absorbed in his ale, or had absorbed too much of it, to notice. Finally we approached his table. "Nick," Sander said.

Nick glanced up. "What are you doing here? They don't serve boys."

"Oh, they serve them occasionally," one of the students put in. "Well roasted, with an apple in their mouth."

Nick laughed harder than the jest deserved. Sander said, "They're wanting you back at the Globe. It's nearly performance time."

"I don't need you to tell me that. I'll be along—when it suits me."

"I thought you'd want to know, too, that Julian isn't badly hurt."

"What's this?" the student said eagerly. "You've been dueling?"

"A trifle," Nick said with a pale smile, then turned on us. "Out of here with you now, before I give the same to you, and worse!"

Sander backed away. "I just thought perhaps you were . . . well, reluctant to come back and face her." I could tell as soon as the final word left his mouth that he would have liked to call it back. But the student had already seized upon it.

"Her?" he echoed, laughing. "Don't tell me you've taken to fighting women, Nick?"

Nick clapped his mug on the table so fiercely that it cracked the earthenware. "I take that as an insult!"

"Take it however you like," the student said casually. "It was offered as a jest, nothing more." He gave his companion a sidelong glance of amusement. "Unless of course it's true."

Nick got unsteadily to his feet and reached across to tap the student on the front of his embroidered doublet. "Be careful what you say, or I'll show you that steel is true."

"Quite a boast for a man without a sword," the student said.

"Swords are easily come by, as are university asses."

The student leaped up to face him, knocking his chair to the floor. "Your jest has the bitter taste of an insult!"

"Here now, here now!" the tavern keeper called. "No quarreling inside! Take your dispute into the street!"

Sander snatched at Nick's sleeve. "Let's go, Nick, before it comes to blows."

Nick pushed him away. "I've no fear of blows. They're braver than words." But I could see how his hand trembled.

"No more do I fear them," the student replied, though his face had gone white as *Hamlet*'s ghost.

"I'll give you cause to, then!" Nick raised a hand as if to strike the other.

The student's hand went to the hilt of his rapier. "I am no woman, to be silenced with a slap!"

This was more than Nick's pride could bear. He lunged across the table, seized the weapon of the second student, and yanked it free of its hanger. "Enough of words!"

The student sprang away from the table and drew his sword as well. The tavern keeper shouted a curse, and Sander called out, "No!" but both protests were lost in the sudden clash of steel upon steel.

It was obvious at once that Nick was overmatched, and I believe he recognized it. The look on his face was that of a man who has stepped into a stream and found that the water is over his head.

He beat away the student's first two blows, but the third stung his leg and made him shuffle backward. The student followed step for step, like his partner in a deadly dance.

All the techniques Nick had learned at Mr. Armin's hands seemed to desert him. He hardly tried to strike an offensive blow; it was all he could do to ward off those of his opponent. In desperation, he drew his dagger and held it before him as an added defense. The student did the same.

As much as I disliked Nick, I felt something like sympathy for him. Though he was no friend, yet he was a fellow prentice, and I had no desire to see him run through. "What will we do?" I asked Sander above the din.

He shook his head despondently. "There's nothing we can do. It's a matter of honor."

"Honor? 'A'll be spitted like a pigeon an we don't help him. Where's the honor in that?"

"It's his fight, not ours."

"Then I'll make it ours!" I hoisted a three-legged stool, meaning to launch it at Nick's opponent. Before I could, the student moved in and feinted an edge blow at Nick's legs. When Nick lowered his dagger to ward it, the student delivered a quick *stocatta* to Nick's throat.

Nick gave a strangled cry and staggered backward. Both his weapons fell from his grasp as he clutched at the wound. He collided with a bench and toppled to the floor.

"The devil take you!" I shouted at the student. "You've killed him!"

I let fly with the stool. It knocked the student's rapier from his hand and struck him on the shoulder. Without waiting to see what he would do, I knelt beside Nick and pulled his hands away from the wound. It was a serious one, but the knowledge of medicine and anatomy I'd absorbed willy-nilly in Dr. Bright's service told me that no artery had been severed. The thrust had struck next to his throat-bole and been stopped by his jaw. Still, there was a copious flow of blood. Using Nick's dagger, I cut off the sleeve of his linen shirt and pressed it into a ball over the wound.

Nick's eyes were wide, darting about as though searching for something. He tried to rise, and I put a knee on his chest. "Lie still, now. We've got to stop the bleeding."

When the first compress was dyed red, I had Sander cut another and pressed it to the wound until at last the bleeding slowed enough to allow me to bind it in place.

"Stay there a bit, yet," I told Nick. When I rose and looked about, the two students were gone.

"How bad is he?" Sander asked, his voice anxious and unsteady.

" 'A'll live, most like. What do we do wi' him now?"

"The tavern keeper's sent for a constable—which is why those two fled. You can go to prison for dueling."

"That doesn't seem to keep anyone from it."

"No. Some men's honor is easily insulted."

"Not mine," I said. "There's little in this world worth fighting over, as far as I can see."

"Then why did you take Nick's part?"

"Did you not once say he was a part of the family?"

"So I did. All the same, it was a brave thing."

I shrugged. " 'A'd have done as much for me."

Sander looked down at Nick, who lay staring at the rotted ceiling. "I doubt it."

The authorities seemed to feel that Nick had suffered enough. Instead of taking him to prison, they took him to a hospital. Within a fortnight, he was on his feet again—too late to be of any use in our command performance at Whitehall.

We could have dealt with his absence alone, for Sander had been studying the part of Hamlet's mother, but we were deprived of our Ophelia as well. Had the decision been left to Julia, I feel sure she would have taken the risk, for she had gone on playing her old roles on the stage of the Globe, despite the fact that her secret was out. Though I didn't expect anyone would deliberately give her away, someone might let the truth slip, as Sander himself had done at the tavern.

I knew that, were my own secret revealed, I would not have had the nerve to face Mr. Pope or Mr. Heminges or Mr. Shakespeare or Sander. Julia was the only one I felt might understand. Yet I wasn't sure. When I believed her to be a boy, I had begun to think of her as a friend. Now suddenly I felt as though she were a stranger. Before, I had talked freely with her, more freely than I ever had with anyone, even Sander. Now, when we were thrown together, I scarcely knew what to say.

During a performance of *A Larum for London* I was assisting in the tiring-room when she came into the room to change costume. "You don't mind if I forgo your help, do you?" she said dryly.

"No, no," I said, embarrassed. She disappeared into the wardrobe. It took me some time to think of how best to ask what I wanted to ask her. Finally, concluding that there was no good way, I said it straight out. "Why did you do it?"

After a long pause, her voice came from the other room. "Do what?"

"You ken."

She emerged, still hooking her bodice together. "Disguise myself?" She shrugged. "For the same reason we all do it. To give others what they expect of us."

"I don't ken what you mean."

"Yes, you do. You do the same yourself."

"Disguise meself?"

"Of course. Why do you speak so politely to Mr. Armin and Mr. Pope and the other sharers, and do as they tell you without complaint?"

I laughed. "Because they'd box me ears an I did not."

"I doubt that. Anyway, you don't act that way with Sander and me."

"You'd think me daft an I did."

"You see? We play the roles others expect of us. If I'd come here as a girl and said I wished to be a player, they'd have laughed and turned me away. Girls are not permitted on the stage; it corrupts them." She shook her head and smiled bitterly. "If I was not corrupted long since, growing up in Alsatia among thieves and beggars, then I must be incorruptible." She hoisted herself up on the table next to me so casually that I had to remind myself that this was no boy made up to resemble a girl, but the actual thing.

"It was nothing new to me," she went on, "dressing and acting as a boy does. My da wanted a boy, and made no secret of it—to carry on the family trade, you might say. He didn't provide me with much girl's clothing. 'You can't outrun the law wearing skirts, he always said." She laughed and flapped the hem of her elegant costume. "In truth, I wore skirts and bodices regularly only after I began masquerading as a boy."

"Will they let you go on wi' it?"

Her face grew solemn, and she shook her head. "They can't, now that they know. If the queen gets wind of it, we're all in the soup."

"What will you do, then?"

"Would that I knew," she said, with something nearer to despair than I had ever heard from her. "I've never wanted anything but to be a player, ever since the day I crept into the theatre at Blackfriars and watched *The Lady of May* through the crack of the door." She stared into space, as though seeing that performance once more. A tear welled in her eye and coursed down her rouged cheek. She raised a sleeve to dash it impatiently away and forced a smile. "Perhaps I'll take up my da's trade after all. As I said, it's best to be what people expect of you."

"It's not fair," I said.

"No," she said. "It's not." She jumped down from the table. "I'll miss my cue."

"Does it matter, now?"

She shrugged and gave an ironic smile. "It does to me."

Of course what she said was perfectly true. The company could not let her go on performing for long. No matter how loyal or how closemouthed the other players were, sooner or later someone was sure to let the truth slip out, and this time the company might not be let off lightly as they had been in the Essex affair.

Even if we could have carried the deceit off successfully at the Globe, we dared not risk it under the very nose of the queen. The part of Ophelia would have to go to a boy. Sander was out of the question, being occupied with Nick's part. Sam and James, the hopefuls, were neither old enough nor experienced enough.

So the company was left with a clear choice: either they must hire a boy from some other company, someone who would be unfamiliar with the role and with the methods of the Chamberlain's Men, or they must settle for me.

They settled for me.

To the company's credit, they did not simply thrust the part upon me. Mr. Heminges asked me if I wanted it. I was not used to being asked my opinion on anything, and it confused me. Did I truly have a choice, or was this an offer, like Simon Bass's offer, that I was not permitted to refuse? "I don't suppose I could think on it."

"We have less than a w-week left until the p-performance."

"Aye," I said mournfully. "I ken that."

"Julia has offered to g-go over the p-part with you."

"That would help," I admitted. "But I'm just not certain. I mean, do you really think I'm ready to play so important a role? Before so important an audience?"

"If we didn't feel you c-could do it, we would not have offered it to you. Whether or n-no you have the ability is not the question, but whether or n-not you have the c-courage."

If this was calculated to prick my pride, it worked, and that surprised me. I was sure that what small pride I had was buried deep, for it seldom bothered me. I had never been much of a hand for courage, either. When two paths were open to me—which is not often in the life of a prentice—I took the one easiest to travel, without regard to where it led. I had never deliberately chosen the perilous or demanding path.

But I had done many things recently that I had never done before, and never dreamed I would do. "Well," I said with a sigh, "I suppose if Julian could be a boy for three years, I can be a girl for an hour or two."

23

Without Julia's help, I could never have hoped to be ready. Each afternoon, long after the others had gone, we sat and went over the lines again and again. She taught me not only the words but their proper reading and what gestures to use. As difficult as this was for me, it must have been doubly difficult for her, having to tutor me in a role she had worked so hard to make her own, a role she had gone through years of disguise and deception to be able to play.

And here was I, with no real notion of being a player until a few weeks before, having the part handed to me. Yet she made no complaint. In fact, she was so generous as to tell me that, if she had to surrender the part to someone, she was glad it was me. I feel sure, though, that her cheerful acceptance was itself a disguise. Something in her eyes spoke of sorrow, and in unguarded moments they sometimes shone with tears. I determined then to put every ounce of effort and ability I had into playing the part, so that she would not be disappointed in me.

I had no time for a prentice's lessons, or a prentice's tasks. Every available moment was spent rehearsing, sometimes under the eye of Mr. Shakespeare or Mr. Phillips, who pointed out my many flaws. For an hour or two each day, I worked with the other players. Only twice did I share the stage with our Hamlet, Mr. Burbage, and then only to work out where I was to move and on what line. He was patient enough with me and my blunders, but he seldom displayed any real warmth or friendliness.

That week was a paradoxical one. Because I trod the same ground over and over, repeating my lines until they threatened to choke me, each day seemed endless. Yet taken as a whole, the week passed with astounding speed. On Wednesday evening, we ferried across the river to rehearse before the queen's master of revels. The performance was a nightmare.

The stage was half the size of the Globe's, which drove us to distraction. To add to the confusion, there were all the new properties and painted backdrops our hired men had constructed. Whatever way I turned, I came up against another player or a piece of scenery. My lines, which were not yet securely seated in my brain, flew from it like startled birds.

To our tiny audience, it must have looked as though we were playing not *The Tragedy of Hamlet* but *The Comedy of Errors*. When at long last we came to the end of it, I had made up my mind that my best course would be to share Ophelia's fate—that is, to throw myself over the side of the wherryboat into the Thames and join the rest of the offal there, none of which could be any more putrid than my performance had been.

No one else seemed upset, either with the rehearsal or with my part in it. "You needn't look so glum, Widge," Mr. Armin said. "A bad rehearsal means a good performance."

"That makes no sense at all. You may as well say a bad cook makes a good meal."

He laughed. "It's true, though. You'll see. Besides, we still have three days before the performance."

I tried to take some hope from this, but secretly I was wondering how far I could get from London in three days.

Saturday dawned grey and gloomy, in keeping with my mood. Julia and Sander tried to cheer me, but the only thing that might have done the trick was to hear that the queen had changed her mind and would have the Lord Admiral's men instead.

Immediately after the performance of *Satiromastix*, the company set out for Whitehall, on a barge provided by Her Majesty—a gesture not unlike providing the cart to haul a condemned man to the scaffold.

Julia was asked to come along and assist behind the

scenes, on the condition that she dress as a girl. She refused. But as we were climbing onto the barge, she came running down the landing stairs, clothed in her costume from *Love's Labour's Lost*, her skirts lifted so high we could see her ankles. She sprang onto the barge and took a place on the railing next to me, flushed and scant of breath and—something I had somehow failed to notice before—quite pretty.

"I'm glad you decided to come," I said. "I can do wi' a bit of support."

She shrugged casually. "You'll be all right without me. Actually I came along in order to meet the queen."

"You lie," I said, and she laughed.

I had always thought of Whitehall as being just that—a large hall, painted white. But what lay before us was more in the nature of a small, walled town. I gawked about me like the greenest country lad as we were escorted to a massive square hall with a lead roof and high, arched windows. Within, the hall was as grand as the grandest cathedral.

"Where is the stage?" I asked Sander.

"There is none. Only the floor."

"Gog's malt!" I murmured. We would not be set apart from our distinguished audience at all; instead, we would be playing practically in their royal laps.

It was fortunate that my entrance came well into the play, for I spent the first quarter hour of the performance in the jakes, emptying my stomach of what little supper I had been able to force down. Julia found me there and pulled me like a balky sheep to the stage entrance. "Wait! Wait!" I whispered urgently.

"What is it?"

"I can't recall me first line!"

"Do you doubt that?" she said.

"What?"

"That's your line, Widge. 'Do you doubt that?' "

"Oh." The cue line came to my ears. Chris Beeston took me by the arm and strode onto the stage with me in tow. Ah, well, I told myself, there's no turning back now.

Sometimes in dreams we do things we could never do in everyday life. The moment I stood before that glittering crowd of sumptuously dressed courtiers, I lapsed into a sort of dream. Through some miraculous process, I ceased to be Widge and became Ophelia, except for some small part of myself that seemed to hover overhead, observing my transformation with amazement.

The lines flowed from me as though they had just occurred to my brain and not been penned by Mr. Shakespeare a year earlier. The audience seemed vague and distant. Only when I had spoken my final line in the scene and swept off the stage did I come to myself again, to find Julia grasping my hands and fairly jumping up and down with delight. "You were wonderful! You didn't miss a single word!"

I grinned back at her. "I did so. I forgot to say 'So please you' to Polonius."

She gave me an exasperated shove. "You sot. Admit it; you were good, very good."

I shrugged, embarrassed. "An I was, I owe it to you. I'm only sorry you couldn't do the part yourself."

Her gaze fell. "It can't be helped." Then she put on something of a smile again and pulled at my wig. "You're all askew. Come sit down, I'll repair you."

So in the end it was not courage that got me through; it was a trick of the mind. As I had survived my orphanage days by pretending I was someone else, someone whose parents still lived and were great and wealthy and would someday come for him, so I survived my hour or so upon the stage by pretending I was a wistful Danish girl, driven mad by love.

After the play, we were presented to the queen and her court, and I was compelled to be Widge again. "What do I say?" I whispered to Sander as we stood in line like soldiers awaiting inspection—or execution.

"Don't say anything," Sander advised me. "Just smile and bow, and kiss her hand."

I practiced my smile. It felt as though I had painted it on, and the paint was cracking. By the time the queen approached, my dry lips were stuck so fast to my teeth that I feared if I pressed my mouth to her hand, I would draw blood.

Mr. Heminges introduced each member of the company in turn. Even had I not known the queen's countenance from the likeness of her that hung in every inn and shop, I could not have mistaken her. Among all those elegant lords and ladies, she was the most elegant of all, in her bearing and in her appearance. She looked far too young and sprightly to have worn the crown for over forty years.

Or so I thought, seeing her at a distance. When she stood before me, her face not three feet from mine, I saw that the fair complexion was a layer of white paint, a ghastly mask, through which her age clearly showed, and the red hair the result of dye. When she smiled, her teeth were black with decay.

"This is our Ophelia," Mr. Heminges was saying. "Widge has been with us but a few months."

I bowed quickly, as much to hide my shock as to do homage to her. She held out her gloved hand, and I touched my lips to it. Now I thought, she will move on. But to my horror, she spoke to me. "What sort of name is that?"

Pretend you're someone else, I told myself—someone charming and witty, someone whose voice works. "It's a—a sort of nickname, Your Majesty," I said, and the voice certainly sounded like someone else's.

"What is your Christian name, then?" She spoke with kindness and, it seemed, genuine interest.

"I don't ken. It's the only name I've got."

"Well, Widge, if you go on performing as admirably as you did for us, you'll make a name for yourself."

"Thank you, mum—I mean, Your Majesty." I bowed again, and when I came erect, she had moved on.

That night in bed, the evening's events replayed themselves over and over in my head. In the space of a few hours, I had done more than transform temporarily into Ophelia. I had undergone a more dramatic change, from a shabby impostor, a thief and orphan who had been given a task far beyond his abilities, into a reliable, valued member of an acting company who performed daily at the center of the universe.

The queen herself had said I would make a name for myself. A name? Yes, I needed a real name. I would not be plain Widge any longer. I would be . . . Pedringano. I said it aloud, grandly. "Pedringano!"

Sander stirred next to me. "What?"

"My name," I said, "is Pedringano!"

He hit me with a pillow. "Go to sleep, Widge. We have to haul scenery first thing in the morning."

24

Though the company had survived the command performance, our troubles were far from over. We were still desperately short of bodies to fill roles. When Julia gave up the role of Ophelia, she seemed to give up as well all hope of being a player.

Mr. Heminges offered her a position gathering money at one of the theatre entrances. Though I knew he meant well, Julia behaved as though she'd been offered a job as a dung collector. I understood her feelings, the more so because I'd now succumbed myself to what Mr. Pope called "the siren call."

The position of gatherer paid well, and carried a certain amount of responsibility, but it was not the same as being a player. Still, Julia admitted that she would have to make a living somehow. She stuck with it for one week.

From the stage, I could see her standing just inside the second-level entrance, her shoulders sagging under the weight of the money box, her eyes fixed on the stage, saying silently that she would give any amount of money to be up there with us. I would have given mine as well, had I had any.

When Monday's performance came around, she was not in her place. Mr. Phillips said that she had disappeared sometime during the night, taking the few articles of woman's clothing she owned, and leaving behind all her boy's garb.

I tried to understand that, too, but it was difficult. I had been persuaded that she and I were friends, and though I knew little as yet about what friendship entailed, I felt that surely a friend would wish to say farewell.

Nick seemed to have deserted us, too. Though some of the players had seen him up and about and looking well enough, save for a bandage on his throat, he did not return to the theatre. Sander went on substituting for him in *Hamlet*, and I for Julia, but the two of us could not hope to fill all the roles both of them had been playing.

A hired boy took on a few, and Chris Beeston reluctantly agreed to don women's costume again, and for a time the sharers scheduled the plays with the fewest female roles. But these were only temporary measures. If Nick did not rejoin us soon, a replacement would have to be found. Sander and I were dispatched once again to try and surprise him at one of his customary watering holes.

I doubted that he would show his face again at the tavern where he had fought the duel, and I was right. The only sign of Nick there was the blood stain he had left on the floorboards. We stopped at three other taverns before we finally discovered him at the sign of the Dagger, and then I had cause to wish we had not.

As soon as we stepped inside the door, Sander spotted him. "There he is, with a pot of ale in his hand as usual."

My eyes had not quite grown used to the dim interior. "Where?" Sander pointed. Nick sat at the far side of the room, gripping a pewter pot as if it were the only stable thing in the room. Across from him sat another familiar figure. His upper body was bent forward, as though to discuss some private matter. His face was shrouded in a dark hood, leaving only a hooked nose and a black, curly beard by which to identify him.

"Gog's blood!" I breathed. I backed through the door as noiselessly as I could and ducked into a narrow space between the tavern and the building next to it. There I stood, pressed to the wall, trying to recover my breath, which seemed to have been squeezed from my chest.

After a moment, Sander came into view, looking about in a bewildered fashion. "Whist!" I called softly. "Over here!" He turned in my direction. "No! Don't look at me!" I cried, and he turned away again, more bewildered than ever. "Is anyone coming out of the tavern?"

He glanced toward the door. "No."

Fearfully, I emerged from my hiding place and pulled at his arm. "Let's go."

"Where?"

"Back to the theatre."

"But—but what about Nick?"

"I'll explain later. Just come."

Good friend that he was, he did not waste time arguing. But when we had put several blocks behind us, he said, "Could you explain, now?"

How could I? What could I tell him? Would I be a better friend if I revealed the truth to him, or if I concocted another lie? Once again, two paths had opened before me, and I could take the expedient one, or the one that required courage.

"That man wi' Nick," I said. "I ken him."

"From the way you bolted, I'd guess you're not on the best of terms."

I couldn't help smiling grimly at this understatement. "You might say so." I paused, still considering the other path, then sighed and went on. " 'A's called Falconer. 'A's been sent here by Simon Bass to steal the book of *Hamlet*."

"Bass? The same Simon Bass who was with the Chamberlain's Men?"

"Aye, the very same." I knew what his next question would be, and I dreaded it.

"What has that to do with you?"

"I . . . I was sent wi' him. To copy the play."

Sander stared at me, his face a very picture of astonishment. "Copy it? How do you mean?"

"In the writing I showed you," I said, unable to meet his eyes.

"The devil take me!" He walked on in silence for a bit, trying, I guessed, to come to terms with this idea. "Have you done it?" he asked finally.

"Of course not! I made up me mind not to, long ago! Well, some time ago, anyway."

He shook his head in disbelief. "What a dunce I've been! I truly believed you wanted to be a player!"

"I do, Sander! As God's me witness, I do now!" He stared at me, and the look of mistrust in his eyes, where I had never seen it, pained me deeply. "I didn't think of it as wrong at first. I thought of it only as a job given me by me master. That was before I kenned any of you. Don't you see, an I'd meant to carry it out, I had ample chance. Gog's bread, I had the book in me hands!"

He blinked thoughtfully. "That's so," he admitted. But the look of mistrust lingered. "All the same, you made fools of us. You and Julia."

"I'm sorry." The words felt strange and foreign upon my tongue. It felt strange, too, to have told the harsh truth for once, rather than an easy lie, yet I did not regret it. "You won't tell the others?"

"How can I not? If that fellow is still planning to steal the book, they need to know."

" 'A won't come near the Globe himself. 'A's too canny for that."

"Then how—" He paused as the answer came to him. "You don't think Nick would—?"

"Aye. I've no doubt of it. An Falconer offers him enough money, 'a'll recite every line 'a recalls, and make up what 'a doesn't, and we've no way of preventing him."

"We could tell the sharers."

"And what good would that do? They can't stop him, either, short of locking him up, or cutting out his tongue. All it will do is bring out me own part in this matter."

"I suppose so." Sander shook his head. "I can't believe that Nick would really betray the company," he said, though the look on his face said that he found the idea all too likely. "But then," he added, "I'd never have believed it of you, either."

The fact that I had elected to tell the truth one time did not diminish my ability to lie accurately when the occasion demanded it. Upon our return, I told Mr. Heminges that we had failed to find Nick. For a moment, I feared that Sander might contradict me, but he let it go. That, I assumed, would be the end of the matter. Nick and Falconer would come to some mutually satisfactory agreement, and with any luck, we would never see either of them again.

Knowing Falconer as I did, I should have known better. I should have realized that he would not be content to take to Simon Bass a secondhand version of the play.

The following afternoon, we were performing *Tamburlaine*. I was playing several small roles, my most dramatic being that of a soldier who dies a bloody death in one of the battle scenes. I had just finished strapping on my blood bag and rapier and dressing myself and was about to step from the tiring-room, when the rear door of the theatre opened and Nick stepped inside. He let the door close softly behind him and stood gazing about, as if to see whether anything had changed in his absence.

I ducked back into the tiring-room, my mind in confusion. How could he have the nerve to come here, after selling us out to Falconer? Then, for the first time, it occurred to me that perhaps he had not. Perhaps he had refused Falconer's offer. Or perhaps there had been no such offer. What if, instead, Falconer had hired Nick to bring me to him? Or what if I had misjudged Nick altogether? What if, in spite of everything, he still felt some loyalty to his theatre family and, learning of my association with Falconer, he had come to expose me?

I stood against the wall for several long minutes, overcome with anxiety and indecision. The reflection staring back at me from the looking glass appeared grotesque and strange. What was I doing dressed in soldier's garb, with an oversized sword dragging the floor at my side? What had ever made me imagine that I could impersonate someone else, that I could be anything other than Widge, the orphan, the unwilling prentice of some unsympathetic master in some unbearable trade?

My heart sank, and I turned from the glass. I did not have the courage Julian had. If Nick was here to reveal my secret, I could not bear to witness it. I moved to the tiring-room door and peered out. To my surprise, Nick was gone. If I meant to make good my escape, now was the moment.

I slipped across the area behind the stage to the rear door without attracting anyone's attention. In another moment I would have been out of the theatre had not my notice been attracted by something out of the ordinary. The door of the property room, which always stood open during performances to give the players quick access to their properties, was now firmly closed. In the perpetual gloom that prevailed behind the stage, I could see a faint light issuing through the crack at the bottom of the door.

I hesitated. Was Nick within, searching for the book? Or was it some member of the company—Mr. Heminges, perhaps, seeking a moment of solitude in which to balance his accounts? A faint grating noise came from within the room, and it was not, I was certain, the sound of someone writing in a ledger.

Knowing full well that I might be sorry, I stepped away from the exit. Carefully lifting the latch on the property room door, I eased it open.

Inside, in the light of a candle, I could make out a figure crouched over one of the property trunks, lifting some object from it. As the figure stood and turned to the light, I saw that it was Nick, and that the object he held was a play book.

Before I could retreat from the doorway, Nick lifted his gaze and spied me. His hand went to his rapier, and he drew it from its hanger in one swift motion. "Hold!" he commanded, his voice as faint and rasping as the sound I had heard moments before—the sound of the trunk being forced open.

I could likely have pulled the door closed before his sword point reached me, but I did not. If I ran, even to bring help, I would be letting Nick go, and the play book with him, and betraying the company as surely as if I had taken it myself.

He beckoned with his blade. "Inside! And keep quiet!" I did as he said, but when he gestured for me to move to the rear of the room, I shook my head.

"I won't let you leave wi' that," I said in a voice nearly as faint and faltering as his.

"You can't stop me, Horse."

"I can call for help."

"I'll gut you if you do."

"I don't think so," I said, trying to sound confident. "If it hadn't been for me, you'd have bled to death on that tavern floor."

I had not expected his gratitude, but neither did I expect the response he gave. He shrugged contemptuously, as if to say he would as soon have been left to die. "No matter. Step aside."

"Nay," I said, gambling that he would not strike me. "Leave the book and go."

"Stand aside!" His voice broke like glass under the strain. His face reddened with anger and shame, and he swung his blade at me. I stumbled back against the wall and crashed painfully into a rack of weapons. Rolling aside, I yanked my stage sword awkwardly from its hanger and brought it to broad ward.

"Fool!" Nick swung at me again. I should have cried out for help, but I still feared that, if cornered by the company, Nick would reveal my connection with Falconer. Poor swordsman that I was, I would have to stop him myself.

I beat his blade aside and, from long habit, replied with a thrust. Nick warded it effortlessly, then aimed a swift cut at my head. Instead of warding it, I ducked and came up under his blade with my own. The blunted tip glanced off his ribs and knocked the play book from his grasp. With a growl of rage and pain, he set upon me in earnest, battering aside my defenses until he found a breach and delivered a quick, angry thrust. His point was not blunted, as mine was. It struck me just above the belt.

I staggered back, clutching the spot, staring in dismay at the blood welling from between my fingers and coursing down the front of my breeches. Nick was as stunned as I. His face went white, and he backed up a few steps, his eyes wide with surprise and alarm. In the next instant, he recovered enough to scoop up the play book and bolt from the room.

I collapsed on the lid of a trunk, gasping for breath but feeling no real pain yet, only a kind of numb panic flooding through my body. Footsteps pounded outside the room and Sander appeared in the doorway. "Holy Mother!" he breathed as he saw me slumped there, drenched in blood. "What happened?"

"Nick stuck me. 'A's getting away!"

"Let him." Sander crouched before me and tore open my doublet.

"But 'a's got the book!"

"Your life is more important—" Sander started to say. Then he halted, staring at my bloody belly.

"Is it that bad?" I asked. "Am I going to die?"

To my astonishment, he began to laugh. "You sot! He stuck your blood bag!"

"Me what?" And then it came to me. Nick's point had been stopped by the protective plate, and the only blood that had been spilled was that of an unfortunate sheep. Feeling sheepish myself, I struggled to my feet. "Come! We've got to catch Nick before 'a delivers that to Falconer!" I stumbled from the property room and ran headlong into Mr. Armin.

"Widge!" He stared at my gory costume. "What in heaven's name—?"

"It's naught," I interrupted. "Can you come wi' me, sir? Nick's stolen the book of *Hamlet*."

As I suspected, he was not the sort to waste time on words when action was wanted. "You're due on stage, Sander," he said, and we were out the door.

When we rounded the playhouse, I saw Nick, far ahead of us, heading for the river. So desperate was his flight that he had dropped his sword and not bothered to retrieve it. Mr. Armin paused long enough to snatch it up, thrust it in his belt, then set off again in pursuit.

I did my best to keep up, but I was hampered by the metal plate, which pinched my skin with every step. Mr. Armin glanced over at me. "Shouldn't you stay here? You're wounded."

I shook my head. "Sheep's blood," I said breathlessly, and he laughed in understanding.

By the time we reached the bank of the Thames, Nick had hired a wherryboat and was well out into the river. Mr. Armin sprang into a second boat, and swallowing my fear, I climbed in after him. "Catch that craft, and you'll have a shilling," Mr. Armin told the startled wherryman.

Had there been a choice, I'd have picked someone more muscular and less sickly-looking than the old sailor who propelled us into the current. When the play let out, the bank would be thick with boats, but at the moment, his was the only one.

To my surprise, our wiry wherryman, spurred on by the promise of more money, slowly closed the gap between Nick's boat and ours. When Nick turned and saw that we were gaining, he called something to his boatman and pointed. The boat abruptly changed course; instead of heading for the opposite bank, it swung downstream, in the direction of the bridge.

"A pest upon him!" Mr. Armin muttered. "He's going to shoot the bridge!"

"Oh, gis! 'A must ha' maggots in his brain!"

"Shall I go after?" our wherryman asked, not very eagerly.

"There's another shilling in it," Mr. Armin said.

I clutched frantically at my seat as the boat dipped and swayed. Then, catching the current, it surged downstream. Ahead, the river churned through the dozen stone arches of the bridge, as water in a smaller stream will boil between the fingers of one's hand, but with a volume and force a thousand times greater.

Nick's boatman steered toward one of the narrow archways. The boat was swept through like a leaf on a flood, bobbing wildly as the water beneath it struck the bridge supports and was flung away. One side of their boat banged and scraped sickeningly against the stone arches, but it emerged in one piece on the far side of the bridge.

" 'A made it!" I said, hardly knowing whether to be relieved or disappointed. In the next moment, I was neither; I was merely terrified, for our turn had come to shoot the bridge. Our boatman was either less skillful than Nick's, or less favored by the Fates. As the foaming mouth of the archway swallowed us, the stern of the boat swung sideways. Though the boatman thrust out his pole to try and keep us clear, we smashed against the stone support. The boat careened, and water poured over the gunwales, overturning it and spilling us into the rushing river.

The feeling of being flung into that whirling world of water is one I fervently hope never to experience again. Everything familiar and secure was snatched away and replaced by a single, suffocating element that robbed me of sight and hearing, of my very breath.

The seething water tossed me this way and that. I fought it madly, but it was as much use as fighting the wind. There was nothing to take hold of, nothing to kick out at. It took hold of me; it wrapped itself about me, dragging me deeper. When I gasped for air, it filled my lungs.

Curiously, even in my panic, a portion of my mind stood apart, observing my plight, as it had done during the performance at Whitehall. I'm going to die now, it said; how strange.

And then my flailing arms struck something solid. I had no idea what it was and cared less. My hands clutched it. Something grasped my chin and lifted it above the surface. I spewed out a pigginful of water and began to breathe again.

"Don't struggle, now," a voice said, sounding distant and muffled to my water-filled ears. "Try to relax." The voice was Mr. Armin's. "Kick your legs gently." I was accustomed to obeying his instructions, and I obeyed now. "Good, keep kicking that way."

There were more voices, then, and hands and boathooks snatched at our clothing and dragged us over the side of another wherryboat, which had apparently seen our plight and come to the rescue. When I had coughed up a portion of the river, I sat up and looked about. Mr. Armin sat next to me, breathing heavily, water streaming from his hair and clothing. In the bottom of the boat, our wherryman was stretched out, unmoving.

"Is 'a drownded?" I asked fearfully.

"No," said one of our rescuers. "More's the pity. It's swads like him give us rivermen a bad name."

"Well, he won't any longer," Mr. Armin said, "for his boat's gone to the bottom." He pulled his purse from inside his drenched doublet, took out two shillings, and pressed them into the unconscious man's hand. "As agreed," he said.

When our feet were on firm ground again on the north bank, we stood looking up and down, wondering what to do next. "Have you any notion of where Nick is likely to take the book?"

"I ken who 'a's taking it to, I just don't ken where."

Mr. Armin stared at me sternly. "I'll ask you to explain all this later. For now, I'll be content to get back the book. You think someone hired him to steal it?"

"Aye. A man named Falconer. The man you quarrelled wi' outside the Globe that day."

Mr. Armin nodded. "He's not a Londoner, is he?"

"Nay, sir. 'A hails from Leicester."

He frowned thoughtfully. "Leicester, is it? And you think he'll go there now?"

"Most like. 'A's not the sort to linger once 'a's got what 'a wants."

"He'll be leaving by way of Aldersgate, then. Perhaps we can head him off. Come." He shifted Nick's rapier, which he had somehow retained through our ducking in the river, and strode off. I had been in the process of unstrapping the protective plate. I yanked it off and hurried after.

Though I was free of that discomfort, I had a suit of clammy clothing to hinder me. In addition, I was close to exhaustion from my struggle with the river. Still, I trotted along in silence, not wishing to do or say anything irksome; my position was precarious enough already. "I'm sorry to be missing me part in the play," I said at length.

"They'll manage without you. This is more important."

"Does it matter so much an one company besides—besides yours puts on the play?" Besides *ours*, I was about to say, but I did not know whether or not they would still count me as part of the company after this.

"Of course it matters. It's wrong. No one has the right to the fruits of another's labor."

"Oh," I said. "I never thought of it that way."

"Besides, there are other concerns. Suppose this—What did you call him?"

"Falconer."

"Suppose this Falconer sells the play to a printer, who publishes it and has it registered. Then the Chamberlain's Men lose all legal right to perform it ourselves."

"Oh. I didn't ken."

"We generally delay publication as long as possible.

Some companies care little for registrations or rights, and to print the play is the same as saying 'Here it is, and welcome to it.' Yet if we *don't* publish it ourselves, someone will sell a pirated version. It's a tricky and an unfair business."

"Aye, I see that now." I felt more ashamed than ever of the part I'd played in the whole affair. I wanted to believe that we still might retrieve the play book, but knowing Falconer, I did not hold out much hope. Even if we did catch up with him, he was not likely to just apologize and hand it over.

By the time we reached St. Paul's and turned on to Aldersgate Street, I was sweating and trembling as if in the grip of the ague. But with the gate in sight, I managed to push myself yet a little farther. A ragged, legless beggar sat by the gate. Mr. Armin crouched and dropped a shilling into the man's filthy hat. "We want to know if you've seen a certain man pass by here. Describe him, Widge."

" 'A's tall and swarthy, wi' a black, unruly beard and a long scar on one cheek. 'A wears a dark cloak wi' the hood drawn up, and will have a brown horse, most like."

The beggar squinted thoughtfully, then shook his shaggy head. "Not as I recall, and I've a good eye and a good memory."

"We'll keep you company a bit, then," Mr. Armin said.

The beggar waved us away. "You'll have to sit somewheres else. No one gives aught to a beggar with well-dressed friends."

We sat on the far side of the gate, in the shade of an overhanging tree. I was grateful for the chance to rest at last, but I did not rest for long. Before five minutes went by, the beggar tossed a pebble at us to draw our attention and jerked his head down the street.

The beggar did indeed have a good eye. It was several moments before I saw the dark, cloaked figure leading a horse—the very figure I had been hoping, yet dreading, to see. I scrambled up, prepared to run. "It's him!"

Mr. Armin held out a hand to stay me. "Patience. Let's not frighten him off." He sat there, seemingly calm, until Falconer was nearly to the gate. Then he rose quickly to his feet and blocked Falconer's path.

Falconer did not appear in the least surprised or alarmed. "I thought we might meet again," he said, in that deep, rough voice.

"Really?" Mr. Armin replied. "I rather hoped we might not."

"Oh? I did not take you for a coward, sir."

"Nor am I, sir. It's not that I fear you, simply that I don't like you."

"You scarcely know me."

"That may or may not be. In any case, I have never liked thieves, and I suspect you are one."

Falconer dropped his horse's rein and pulled his cloak aside to reveal the hilt of his rapier. "No man calls me a thief—not more than once, at any rate."

"I did not say you were a thief. I said I suspected it. If I am wrong, I'll gladly tender an apology." He stepped casually to Falconer's horse and began to unlace the saddlebag.

Falconer drew his rapier. "Take your hands off that or I'll take them off for you—at the wrists."

Mr. Armin went on calmly unlacing the pouch. "I'll just have a look, and that will be that."

"Look well, then, for it will be the last thing you see in this world!" Falconer lifted his blade and brought it down, not upon Mr. Armin's head, as I feared, but upon the flank of the horse. The animal bolted. Just as suddenly, Mr. Armin's rapier left his side and came to low ward before him.

To my surprise, Falconer did not set upon him in the fierce and ruthless manner he had used to dispatch the band of outlaws. In truth, he seemed almost cautious. He tossed back the right edge of his cloak so it would not obstruct his sword arm, then grasped the other edge in his left hand and, with one deft movement, wrapped the hem of it twice around his forearm.

Mr. Armin seemed cautious, too, recalling no doubt their previous encounter, in which he had been so easily outdone. I know that I was recalling it. Though Mr. Armin was unquestionably an excellent fencing master, when it came to a duel fought in deadly earnest, I feared that he was no match for Falconer.

In such a situation, I had come to Julia's aid, and even Nick's, but this time there was nothing I could do, short of throwing myself upon Falconer's sword. Or was there?

What if I were to retrieve the play book? That was, after all, the reason behind the fight.

I dashed through the gate and looked about. Falconer's horse stood alongside the road a dozen yards off, grazing blithely, with no interest in his master's quarrels. But the moment I approached and reached for the saddlebag, he shied away, making me miss my footing and nearly fall on my face.

"Whist, now!" I called and moved in close again. Again he moved away. "The devil take you!" I muttered and approached once more. This time I got a firm purchase upon the saddle, and when the horse moved he pulled me with him.

He lashed at me irritably with his tail, then seeing he could not dislodge me, broke into a trot, dragging me along. Clutching the saddle frame with one hand, I plunged the other into the saddlebag, yanked out the play book, then dropped off onto the hard ground.

I limped hurriedly back to the gate, to find Mr. Armin and Falconer engaged in heated combat. "Stop!" I shouted above the clamor of blade upon blade. "Mr. Armin! I've got the book! Let's go!"

Mr. Armin stepped back and disengaged. "You go, Widge. I've unfinished business here."

"But there's no need for it now! I've got the book!"

Falconer pointed his sword at me. "Put it down, boy! I've enough of a score to settle with you as it is!"

"One score at a time," said Mr. Armin, and he closed in again.

"Stop!" I cried, more desperately. "Please! It's not worth it!" Neither man heeded me, if indeed they heard me above the din of their weapons.

I could not begin to describe their movements or strategies, so rapidly did they follow one upon the other. Their blades struck and warded and struck again with such speed that the eye could scarcely see them. Had it not been for their frantic clashing, I might have imagined they were not solid metal at all, but something thin and insubstantial, like the elder sticks we fought with as boys. If only it could have been so. If only they could have fought, as we did, until one adversary's weapon broke.

But this was a grown man's game, and the winner would not be the one whose weapon survived but the one who lived. And, I thought, clutching the play book to my chest, if that one proved to be Falconer, then what would become of me?

Mr. Armin had taught us in fencing class never to retreat from an opponent, for it is a defensive and not an offensive posture. He seemed to have forgotten his own advice. He was in almost constant retreat before Falconer's attack. I wanted to shout encouragement and instructions to him, as he had so often done to us. But even had my tight throat been able to form the words, I feared distracting him, so I watched in anxious silence.

Falconer grew more confident as the duel went on, pressing his advantage, driving Mr. Armin backward first one step, then another. Mr. Armin warded the blows easily enough but often failed to return them. Finally he found an opening and delivered an edge blow that would have sorely wounded Falconer except that he absorbed its force with the hem of his cloak.

In the same instant, Falconer stepped forward and thrust at Mr. Armin's unprotected chest. Mr. Armin spun aside, but not quickly enough. The point pierced his doublet and passed along his ribs, making him gasp in pain and stumble back. Falconer withdrew and thrust again, meaning to catch Mr. Armin unprepared.

But Mr. Armin was better prepared than he seemed. Instead of beating the blade aside, he performed a maneuver I had never before seen, and have not seen since. In truth, I thought it was a blunder. He fell forward, under Falconer's blade, and landed on his outstretched left hand, at the same time thrusting his sword before him, parallel to the ground. It took Falconer squarely in the belly and drove in halfway to the hilt.

Falconer gave a gasp of surprise and drew back. His hood fell away from his face, revealing his startled and scowling countenance. The skin of his face looked tight and twisted, as though something were pulling it askew.

He seized the blade of Mr. Armin's sword in his cloak-wrapped hand and, with a contemptuous gesture, jerked it free and flung it aside. For a moment, it seemed as though he had not been wounded at all. It was a trick, I thought, a collapsible sword. I half expected him to laugh and come at Mr. Armin again.

Then the blood began to well from the wound, spreading across his doublet, dyeing it red, and I realized with a shock that this was no illusion. This was not sheep's blood spurting from a bag, but his own life's blood draining away, and no amount of bandaging would staunch it.

Yet we had to try. Though Mr. Armin was bleeding himself from the gash under his arm, he stripped off his doublet and his linen shirt. We knelt next to Falconer, who had sunk onto the stones of the street, and tried to wrap the cloth about him.

He pushed it impatiently aside. "Let it be," he said in a voice so unlike his usual growl that I blinked in surprise. "It's no use."

Mr. Armin let the shirt drop and put an arm under Falconer's head as he sighed heavily and lay back. He seemed less like a man in pain than one who is simply unutterably weary. His face was weary, too. In full daylight, there was something curiously mask-like about his features.

He pressed a hand to his face, as though trying to hide it from our view, but his words said the opposite. "I suppose you have a right to see the true face of the man you've slain." As I watched in astonishment, he plucked at the dark skin of his cheek with his fingernails, and pulled away a great chunk of it. Where the repulsive scar had been there was now a smooth, pale patch of skin. Again his fingers dug at his face, and this time pulled away a portion of his hooked nose, leaving it straight and similarly pale-skinned. His eyes turned to me, and the look in them was almost amused. "You know me now?"

I swallowed hard. "Aye. Mr. Bass."

"And you?" he said to Mr. Armin. "But you knew before, did you not?"

"I suspected it."

"Still it was a good disguise, was it not? My masterpiece. Everyone's idea of what a Jew looks like, eh?"

"An excellent disguise," Mr. Armin said. "Such a talent should not be wasted."

"I agree. The very reason I left the Chamberlain's Men. There were too many fools in it to suit me."

"Better a company of fools than the company of thieves."

Mr. Bass coughed, and wiped the corner of his mouth. A bit of red smeared the back of his hand. "Perhaps so. But you must allow that I had the good taste to steal only from the best." Those were the last words he spoke, in this life at any rate.

Though death had taken my fellow orphans, and Dr. Bright's patients, I had never seen a man die at the hand of another, and had no notion of how I should react. I glanced at Mr. Armin, as if for a cue. He avoided my gaze and busied himself folding his doublet to prop up Mr. Bass's black-dyed head.

I had not shed tears in a long time, nor did I shed them now. All the same, I was overcome with a strange sadness, at odds with the relief I had expected to feel, now that the threat which had hung over me for so long was removed. The sensation was something like what I'd felt for Julia, when she had been forced to relinquish her position as a player. I could give no name to it, unless perhaps it was the word Julia had once tried to acquaint me with—compassion.

We sat with the dead man, ignoring the gawking crowd that had gathered, until a constable came and summoned a cart to bear the body away. The constable knew Mr. Armin, and when he was satisfied that the duel had arisen over stolen property, he let us go free.

We both had had our fill of the Thames, and so walked back to the Globe by way of the bridge. "How is it you kenned Mr. Bass?" I asked.

"I might ask the same of you. But I'd rather you told your story to the company as a whole, and let them judge you."

"Will they—will they turn me out, do you think?"

"I can't speak for them. As for how I knew Simon Bass—the truth is, I was with his company a short while before I came here. They were a sorry lot. Not only did they steal scripts, they often borrowed the name and reputation of some respectable company. They would give a single performance, then depart in the dead of night, often with the contents of the town's treasury. They seldom played the same town twice. There were scores of places where Bass dared not even go on legitimate business without disguising himself."

"But why bother to disguise himself from me?"

"I suppose he didn't want to risk your giving him away.

Or it may be he believed you'd follow orders better if they came from Falconer."

" 'A was right about that." I shook my head, still unable to quite understand. "But how could 'a bear to play a part for so long a time, and never reveal his true self?"

"Perhaps," Mr. Armin said, "it *was* his true self."

The Chamberlain's Men were more lenient than I expected or deserved. Both Mr. Pope and Mr. Armin argued on my behalf. Even Mr. Shakespeare, who had most cause to call for my dismissal, seemed inclined to forgive me. Only Jack spoke out against me, and not very vehemently.

So it was that I was permitted to stay on as a prentice with the company, and I was very grateful for it. I recognized now that I was being offered something more than just a career as a player, acting out a variety of roles. I was also being offered a chance at a real-life role, as a valued member of the Globe family.

My only cause for regret was that Julia had not been so fortunate as I. What had become of her no one seemed to know. Neither had we heard any news of Nick, but in his case no one cared much.

When several weeks went by with no word from Julia, Sander and I persuaded Mr. Armin to accompany us into the grimy depths of Alsatia, where we made a few inquiries. The man named Hugh recalled hearing that she was working as a serving maid for a household in Petty France, that colony of French émigrés just outside the walls of the city. Sander and I tried to track her down there, but neither of us knew enough French to make much headway.

All through the summer and into the fall, my schedule at the Globe remained hectic. In addition to all my new roles, I was given the task of copying out the individual sides from the book of each new play. Still I doubt that a day went by in which I did not think of Julia and wonder how she fared. I began to fear that she had joined her father at his unsavory trade and disappeared into the city's underworld, in which case we might despair of ever seeing her again.

Then, a week before Christmas, as we were preparing *Twelfth Night* for presentation at the court, Julia entered our lives again briefly, like the well-known Messenger I had so often played, who delivers his message and then departs.

Mr. Pope and Sander and I were on our way home after a trying performance, at which three so-called gentlemen took seats upon the very stage, thrust their feet in the players' paths, and distracted us with their "witty" comments. So busy were we venting our irritation that we scarcely noticed the serving maid who approached us until she spoke our names. "Widge? Sander?"

We halted and stared at her. "Julia?" I said.

She laughed at our looks of surprise. "Yes, it's me, disguised as a serving maid. Good day, Mr. Pope," she added, not very cordially.

Mr. Pope bowed slightly, as if to a lady—which, I had to

remind myself, Julia now was. "We've all been wondering what became of you."

"Nothing of any consequence, I'm afraid."

"That is unfortunate," Mr. Pope said, and I could tell that his words were sincere. "I truly wish that . . . that things could have worked out differently."

"So do I." Her tone was still far from friendly.

Mr. Pope cleared his throat uncomfortably. "Well. You'll want to talk with your friends, I expect. I'll bid you good morrow."

She made him a curtsy that was neither very graceful nor very gracious. When Mr. Pope was out of hearing, Sander said, "You might have been more kind. It wasn't his fault you had to go."

"I know that. It's no one's fault, really—or everyone's. It's just that I haven't quite gotten over it." She tossed her hair, which had grown long, and went on more cheerfully. "But I didn't come to open up old wounds. I came to tell you some good news, actually. It seems I may have the chance to be a player after all."

"Truly?" I said eagerly. "They've changed the rule?"

"No. No, I'm afraid not. But you see, Mr. Heminges once told me that in France women are permitted to act on the stage. So I've been working in the household of a French wine merchant, saving up my wages for passage money, and learning the language and—well, the long and short of it is, I sail for France in the morning."

"That's the good news?" I asked.

"Yes. Aren't you happy for me?"

"Oh. Aye. Of course."

"That's as happy as Widge gets, I think," Sander said, and shook his head. "Gog's bread, Julia, it's hard enough learning lines in English. How are you going to do it in French?"

She gave him an indignant look. *"Je parle français très bien, monsieur."*

He laughed and held up his hands in surrender. "Very well, *mademoiselle*. If anyone can do it, it's you. Best of luck. I mean, *bonne chance*."

"Merci." She curtsied again, less awkwardly. "Widge? Aren't you going to wish me luck?"

"Aye," I said glumly. "Good luck."

She reached out and took my hand. "You needn't look so forlorn. Come, now, smile a little. For me?"

This business of friendship was a curious thing, I thought, almost as difficult to learn as the business of acting. Sometimes you were expected to tell the truth, to express your thoughts and your feelings, and then other times what was wanted was a lie, a bit of disguise. I was still but a prentice in the art, but slowly and painfully I was learning. Though in truth I felt more like crying, I put on the smile she asked for, or as near to it as I could come. "Up Yorkshire, we say 'Fair 'chieve you.' "

She squeezed my hand. "Fair 'chieve you, then." She backed away, as though compelled to leave, yet reluctant to let us from her sight. At last, she turned and hurried off in the direction of the Thames, which tomorrow would carry her to the sea.

As I watched her go, tears welled in my eyes, and for the first time since I was a child, I let them come. Now I understood why she had left us before without any farewell. Parting was not, as I had heard one of Mr. Shakespeare's characters say, a sweet sorrow. It was bitter as gall.

Behind us, Mr. Pope cleared his throat again. "She's a plucky girl."

Embarrassed, I wiped at my eyes. "She is that."

He put a hand on Sander's shoulder and mine. "We'd best be heading home now, boys. Goody Willingson has promised us toad-in-the-hole for tonight's repast."

"Toad-in-the-hole?" I said, laughing a little despite myself.

"Don't laugh," Sander said. "It's good. Almost as good as bubble and squeak."

"It certainly doesn't sound very good. But I can rely on your judgment, I suppose."

"You can that."

As the three of us—Mr. Pope and his boys—walked home, I reflected on these new terms and all the others I had learned—and unlearned—since my arrival here but a few months before. Though I hadn't quite learned a new language, as Julia was doing, I felt almost as though I had.

For every *ken* and *wis* and *aye* I had dropped from my vocabulary, I had picked up a dozen new and useful terms. Some were fencing terms, some were peculiar to London, some were the jargon of the players' trade. But the ones that had made the most difference to me were the words I had heard before and never fully understood their import—words such as honesty and trust, loyalty and friendship.

And family.

And home.

SHAKESPEARE'S SCRIBE

ALSO BY GARY BLACKWOOD
The Shakespeare Stealer

SHAKESPEARE'S SCRIBE

Gary Blackwood

DUTTON CHILDREN'S BOOKS
New York

For Lucia,

who gave poor Widge a home at last

Library of Congress Cataloging-in-Publication Data
Blackwood, Gary L.
Shakespeare's scribe / Gary Blackwood.—1st ed.
p. cm.
Sequel to: The Shakespeare stealer.
Summary: In plague-ridden 1602 England, a fifteen-year-old orphan boy, who has become an apprentice actor, goes on the road with Shakespeare's troupe and finds out more about his parents along the way.
ISBN 0-525-46444-1
[1. Theater—Fiction. 2. Orphans—Fiction. 3. Actors and actresses—Fiction. 4. Plague—England—Fiction. 5. Shakespeare, William, 1564–1616—Fiction. 6. Great Britain—History—Elizabeth, 1558–1603—Fiction.] I. Title.
PZ7.B5338 Sk 2000 [Fic]—dc21 00-034603

Published in the United States by Dutton Children's Books,
a division of Penguin Putnam Books for Young Readers
345 Hudson Street, New York, New York 10014
www.penguinputnam.com
Designed by Amy Berniker
Printed in USA
First Edition
5 7 9 10 8 6

AUTHOR'S NOTE

Several readers of *The Shakespeare Stealer*, the book to which this is a sequel, have mentioned that they had some trouble sorting out what was fact from what was fiction. (I hope that means I made everything in the book seem real and not that it all sounded totally made up!) This time I'll try to make things easier by giving you, the reader, a better notion before you begin of which parts are a result of research and which are a product of the imagination.

There really was a Dr. Timothy Bright, and he really did devise a system of "swift writing." In fact, that bit of information, stumbled upon purely by accident, was the seed from which *The Shakespeare Stealer* and its sequel grew. The passages of charactery in the books are as much like Dr. Bright's shorthand as I can make them.

With the exception of Widge and Jamie Redshaw, nearly all the characters who make up the Lord Chamberlain's Men are based on William Shakespeare's actual fellow players. Some, such as Alexander Cooke, we know nothing about except the name. Others, such as Richard Burbage and Robert Armin, were so well known that it's possible to get some idea from sixteenth-century sources of what they were like, at least onstage. William Shakespeare did have a younger brother, Edmund.

Salathiel Pavy was a member of the Children of the Chapel in reality, too, and was known for his ability to play old men's parts convincingly. All the plays mentioned in the book, whether written by Shakespeare or by someone else, were actual works of the period.

The bubonic plague was, of course, all too real. Spread in two ways—by fleas that fed on infected rats, then on humans, and by bacteria in the air—it had wiped out, by various estimates, one-fourth to one-half of the population of Europe in the fourteenth century, and regularly made a comeback. During the worst outbreaks, all public gatherings were banned. The epidemic described here actually reached its peak in the following year, 1603.

SHAKESPEARE'S SCRIBE

Acting seems, on the face of it, a simple enough matter. It is, after all, but an elaborate form of lying—pretending to be someone you are not, committing to memory words set down by someone else and passing them off as your own.

I was an admirable liar. I had even lied myself into the most successful company of players in London, the Lord Chamberlain's Men. It stood to reason that I would be an admirable actor as well.

But I had since discovered that there is far more to performing than merely mouthing words in a lifelike fashion. A lad who aspires to be a player must be able to sing as sweetly as a nightingale, dance as gracefully as the Queen, change garments as swiftly as the wind changes, sword-fight as skillfully as a soldier, die as satisfyingly as a martyr, and learn an astonishingly large number of lines in a distressingly short time. And if he is less than competent at any of these skills, then he must be adept at dodging a variety of missiles aimed at him by an audience that is as easily displeased as it is pleased.

I have also heard it said that, to be a successful player, one must be at least partly insane. I have no doubt that this is true. What person in his right mind would willingly endure so many demands for so little reward?

Certainly anyone who found himself behind the stage at the Globe Theatre just before a performance would have readily subscribed to the insanity theory. In fact, a first-time visitor might well imagine that, rather than entering a playhouse, he had stumbled by mistake into Bedlam, London's asylum for the mentally deranged.

In my early days at the Globe, all the hurly-burly that preceded a performance had been overwhelming for a country boy like me. And even after a year's apprenticeship, it could still be unnerving if the level of activity was frantic enough—as it was, for example, on the afternoon when we opened a new production of *Richard III*, one of Mr. Shakespeare's early plays.

Several of the players were pacing about like caged cats, muttering their lines ferociously and somehow managing to avoid colliding with one another or with our dancing and singing master, who was practicing an intricate dance step. Mr. Pope, my mentor, was berating the man who was trying desperately to strap the old fellow into a boiled-leather breastplate that seemed to have grown too small to contain Mr. Pope's ample belly.

Mr. Heminges, the company's manager, was hastily repairing the curtain that concealed the alcove at the rear of the stage. It had been torn nearly from its hooks by our clod-footed hired man, Jack, as he struggled to put one of the heavy wooden royal thrones in its proper place. Meanwhile he and Sam, one of our apprentices, were attempting to wrestle the other throne down the stairs; the throne appeared to be winning.

"C-careful, gentlemen!" called Mr. Heminges. "D-don't d-damage the arms!"

"Which ones?" groaned Sam. "Ours or the throne's?"

I and my fellow prentice and closest companion, Sander Cooke, were in the relatively calm reaches of the tiring-room, getting into our costumes. The chaos outside did not concern me overly. I had learned that, like Mr. Heminges's stuttering, all trace of it would vanish once we were upon the stage. Then Mr. Shakespeare strode into the room, bearing a fistful of crumpled papers, which he held out to me. "Can you copy these out in the form of sides, Widge?"

Because of my skill with a pen, it was my job to copy out the sides, or partial scripts from which each actor learned his lines. I smoothed out one of the pages and peered at Mr. Shakespeare's deformed handwriting. "Aye," I said. Under my breath I added, "An I can manage to decipher them." The others in the company were fond of poking fun at the system of swift writing I had learned from my first master, Dr. Timothy Bright, calling it "scribble-hand," but in truth it was scarcely more difficult to read than Mr. Shakespeare's scrawl.

I was about to tuck the pages inside my wallet, but Mr. Shakespeare waved an urgent hand at me. "No, no, it's to be done at once."

I blinked at him in disbelief. "What, *now,* do you mean? But—but we've no more than a quarter hour before the performance begins."

Mr. Shakespeare shrugged. "Not to worry. They're not needed until Act Four."

"Ah, well," I said sarcastically, "wi' that much time at me disposal, I could copy out all of *The Faerie Queene.*"

The moment Mr. Shakespeare was gone, I unfolded the sheets and stared at them, feeling dazed. "Does 'a truly expect me to copy all these lines, and the actors to con them, before the fourth act?"

"He didn't seem to me to be jesting," Sander said. "Did he to you?"

"Nay." I sighed. "I'll ha' to use Mr. Heminges's desk."

"I'll come with you and deliver the sides as you complete them."

"Thanks." As we headed for the property room, I said, "I sometimes get the feeling that I'm of more value to the company as a scribe than as a player."

"Oh, I'd hardly say that."

"I'm not complaining, mind you. Not exactly. I mean . . ." I lowered my voice. "In truth, I'd volunteer to clean out the jakes and haul the contents to the dung heap an that's what it took to belong to the company."

Sander grinned. "So would I. But let's not make it known, shall we? We've enough to do already."

There was no denying that. Our every morning was occupied with learning the essential skills of a player, our afternoons with demonstrating them upon the stage. And when we were not practicing or performing, we were engaged in some menial task—cleaning up the yard of the theatre, whitewashing the walls, polishing stage armor and weapons.

In return for all our work, we received three shillings a week, Sunday afternoons free, and, if we performed well enough, the applause of the audience. It was not an easy life. Yet I would not have traded it for any other.

Part of the attraction, of course, was the performing. Odd as it may seem, there is a satisfaction unlike any other in creating an imaginary world and in pretending to be someone you are not. That in itself may be a sign of insanity. In the world at large, after all, a wight who goes about trying to convince others that he is a woman, or a faerie, or a famous historical personage, is ordinarily shut up somewhere safe.

But the opportunity to act before an audience was not my only reason, or perhaps even my primary one, for relishing my position with the Chamberlain's Men. I had grown up an orphan, and they were the nearest thing to a family I had ever known, partly mad though they might be.

As I set to work copying out the sides, trying to strike a balance between writing speedily and writing legibly, I became aware of a sort of murmuring or rustling coming from the yard of the theatre. At first it was very like the way the wind sounds, soughing through treetops. But as it grew in intensity, it came to resemble more the grumbling of some great beast, impatient to be fed.

It was our audience, impatient to be entertained. To soothe them, our trio of hired musicians struck up a tune, and some players came on to dance a jig for them. When the music ended, there was a moment of relative silence, followed by a ripple of laughter. Mr. Armin, one of our best actors, was on the stage now, doing his comical turn, perhaps trading gibes with the audience, perhaps impersonating one of the foolish fops who turned up at nearly every performance and sat on stools upon the very stage so they might be seen and admired by the groundlings.

These dandies seemed not to mind being mocked by Mr. Armin, whose antics included tripping over the fashionably elongated toes of his shoes or getting his ostentatious jewelry caught in his cloak; pretending to doze off, then slipping from his stool and landing on his hucklebones; or dropping his rapier and, as he bent to retrieve it, revealing a wide rip in the seat of his breeches.

The audience responded, as usual, with uproarious laughter. Mr. Armin's exit was accompanied by an explosion of applause, whistles, and cheers so enthusiastic that I looked up from my work. He came capering off the stage, wearing a broad smile that vanished the moment he was out of the audience's sight, to be replaced by an expression that, while still pleasant enough, was businesslike. "How are you progressing?" he asked.

"Nearly done," I replied—not much of an exaggeration.

"Excellent. I knew we could depend on you."

I nodded. As much as I appreciated the praise, it seemed faint compared to the boisterous acclaim Mr. Armin himself had just received. "Do you suppose," I said wistfully, "that I can ever hope for a response like that?"

Mr. Armin raised his eyebrows, as though taken aback by my question. "What? The applause? The laughter? Anyone can do that. All it takes is a few pratfalls, a few jests. You want more than that, Widge. You want their silence. You want their tears."

And how, I wondered, did I go about earning that? In my year's apprenticeship I had worked as hard as any other player or prentice, I was sure, and had been awarded ever more substantial parts—Maria in *Twelfth Night*, Rosaline in *Love's Labour's Lost*, Hero in *Much Ado About Nothing*.

But for all my seeming success, in my idle moments—of which there were few—I sometimes felt an anxious something worrying at the back of my brain. At first I could not give a name to it, but in time I recognized it for what it was—a lack of confidence in my skills, the nagging feeling that I was an impostor, a sham. Secretly I suspected that, beneath all the trappings, behind all the grand lines I spoke, I was not a real actor but only a rootless, feckless orphan acting the part of an actor, and I feared that one day someone in the audience or in the company would expose me.

It was not an unreasonable fear. Just in the year I had been with the company, they had dismissed my friend Julia and another apprentice named Nick, who could not be considered a friend. Of course, there had been compelling reasons: Nick had stolen a play script; Julia had had the misfortune to be a girl in a profession that admitted only boys and men.

Though I had not gotten off to a very good start with the Chamberlain's Men—in fact, I had joined them initially only in order to copy down *Hamlet* for a rival company—my transgressions since then had been minor: missed cues, forgotten lines, and the like. Still, I did not feel entirely secure. If the company did decide they could do without me, God only knew what would become of me. Aside from my dubious skills as a player and a scribe, I had no means of supporting myself. Even more unpleasant than the prospect of being out on the streets was the thought of losing the only family I had ever known and being an orphan again.

Perhaps it was just as well that I had little leisure to dwell on my fears. The sharers of the company, for reasons they did not feel compelled to explain to us prentices, had not bothered to replace Nick or Julia. That meant that Sander and Sam and I had to double up frequently—that is, play several parts apiece.

Our only respite came when the weather made it impossible to perform. During the winter months, the weather was not a factor, for we played indoors, usually at the Cross Keys Inn. But when spring came, the company moved to the open-air Globe Theatre.

That spring of 1602 was warmer than usual, so we began our outdoor season early in May. Unfortunately, it was also wetter than usual. Only when there was a distinct downpour did the sharers call off a performance. This did not mean that we did not work. They might simply call a rehearsal instead, in one of the practice rooms. Or they might send us out to spy on some rival company, such as the Lord Admiral's Men or the Children of the Chapel Royal, who had begun to get a reputation for their lively comedies and satires.

Though we did not regard a company of children as a serious threat, neither did we wish to underestimate them. So it was that, one sodden day in June, Sander and I were dispatched to the Blackfriars Theatre to see how much of the young upstarts' reputation was deserved. Since the essence of spying is to go unnoticed, we prentices were the logical choice for the mission, for our faces were not likely to be recognized, unadorned as they were with wigs or face paint.

Blackfriars, which lay just across the Thames from the Globe, was so called because it had once been home to a brotherhood of monks called the Black Friars. The building that housed the theatre had formerly been a guest house. The walls had been removed to create a spacious hall that was lighted, on this gloomy afternoon, by dozens of candles in sconces. While Sander pursued a vendor hawking apples, nuts, and candies, I found us a seat a few rows back from the stage. My neighbor was a burly, sunburned man dressed in the wide-legged trousers and conical wool cap of a seaman. He was chewing as noisily as any cow at some substance that gave off a smell so acrid and spicy it made me screw up my nose.

The sailor grinned, showing teeth that had been brown to begin with and were made more so by the substance he was chewing. "Angelica root," he said, and a bit of it came flying forth to land upon my sleeve. " 'Tis a sovereign protection against the plague." He tapped the side of his red, prominent nose. "But just to be certain, I've stuffed my nose holes with rue and wormwood."

I felt a chill run up my back. "Why . . . ?" I began, but my throat was thick, and I had to clear it to continue. "Why take such measures now, though? The plague is no particular threat."

"That may be true here, but . . ." The man leaned down close to me, as if not wishing all to hear. "I've just come from Yarmouth, and they're dying by the dozens there. The city fathers have taken to shooting dogs, and setting off gunpowder in the streets to clear the air. It's but a matter of time before the contagion spreads to London—if it hasn't already."

I shrank back from the man and his foul, angelica-scented breath. I had known the smell was familiar, but until that moment I had not known why. Now the answer came to me in a flash of memory. I saw myself at the age of seven, standing by my old master, Dr. Bright, as he treated a plague victim. I was heating over a candle flame some concoction of grease and herbs, which the doctor then plastered on the patient's open sores. The reek of the medicine alone was enough to nauseate; added to it was the putrid stench of the sores themselves and, underneath it all, the bitter presence of the angelica root that lay like a tumor beneath my tongue, gagging me.

Now, with the same scent strong in my nostrils, I felt

nausea rising in me again, accompanied by a sickening feeling of dread. Most folk believed that the plague was caused by corrupted air. But according to Dr. Bright's theory, the contagion spread by means of tiny plague seeds, invisible to the eye, which entered our orifices and took root inside us. When they matured, they bore more seeds that went wafting, like the seeds of a dandelion, on the wind of our breath until they found fertile ground.

I sprang from my seat and made for the rear of the room, meaning to put as much distance between myself and the sailor as I possibly could. As I swam against the incoming tide of playgoers, I collided with Sander, who carried a paper cone filled with roasted hazelnuts. "Why did you not save our spot, Widge?" he asked. "It would have given us a good view of the stage."

"Too close," I muttered. "The players' spittle rains down upon you when they say their *t*'s and *p*'s. Let's move back." Before he could protest, I struggled on to the very last row of benches and plopped down. "This is good," I said. "An there's a fire, we'll be the first ones out." Agreeable as always, Sander took a seat next to me.

The play was a fairly challenging one—Jonson's satire *The Poetaster*—and the Children of the Chapel, who ranged in age from about ten to fourteen or fifteen, were sadly inadequate to the challenge. Though they tried hard to please, mugging and gesturing in an effort to coax laughs from the audience, the whole thing was more in the nature of a pageant than a performance, all surface and no depth.

I leaned over to Sander, meaning to say that I had seen enough. Then the boy who played Horace strode out upon the stage and sang,

"Swell me a bowl with lusty wine,
Till I may see the plump Lyaeus swim
Above the brim:
I drink, as I would write,
In flowing measure, filled with flame, and spright."

I sat up in surprise. Could it be that there was a real performer among them? The newcomer was tall and thin, with a head of blond curls that would have let him play any of our young ladies' parts without benefit of a wig. Though he was likely a year or two younger than Sander or me, he had the assurance of an adult actor. His voice was not mature, and it had a rough edge to it, as though he was straining a bit to be heard. Yet he spoke his lines with such authority, such conviction, as to give the feeling not only that he understood them, but that he *meant* them.

When the boy took his bow, the applause and cheers were not quite as raucous as they had been for Mr. Armin, but they were enough to make me envious. As we left the theatre, Sander said, "Was the blond fellow truly that good, or did he only seem so put up against the others?"

" 'A was truly that good," I replied. "I'm glad 'a's wi' the Chapel Children and not the Chamberlain's Men."

Sander gave me a look of surprise. "Why?"

"Because, an 'a were wi' our company, 'a'd have all the

meaty parts, and you and I would ha' to be content wi' scraps."

Sander laughed. "Don't price yourself so cheaply, Widge. You're as capable an actor as he is."

"Liar," I said, but I couldn't help feeling grateful for his loyalty. I said nothing about the sailor and his talk of the plague, for I was trying hard not to think about it. Instead, I said, "Did not the fellow who played Tibullus put you in mind of our old friend Nick?"

Sander considered this. "Now that you say it, he did bear a certain resemblance, though I think that Nick, for all his faults, was a better actor. I wonder what's become of him?"

" 'A's drunk himself to death, most like, or been gutted by someone in a duel."

Sander nodded soberly. "It would scarcely surprise me. I never knew anyone so determined to make himself miserable."

"Not to mention those around him."

Sander clucked his tongue. "We shouldn't speak so uncharitably of him. Perhaps he's learned the error of his ways."

"Oh, aye," I replied, "and perhaps a dunghill can learn not to stink."

The look of disapproval Sander gave me was severely undermined by the snort of laughter that escaped him. We would not have been so quick to laugh had we known how near the mark our jabs had struck.

A few days later, as we were dressing for a performance

of *What You Will,* Sam rushed in, wide-eyed and breathless. "You'll not believe what I just learned!"

Had I been wearing hose and not a dress, my heart would have sunk into them, for I expected him to reveal that there had been an outbreak of the contagion in the city. Instead, he said, "I've just been at the Swan playhouse, talking with a prentice from the Earl of Pembroke's Men. It seems they lately took Nick on as hired man."

"What, *our* Nick?" Sander said.

"The very same. But that's not the news. He says that Nick had a falling-out with one of the other members of the company, and the man challenged him to a duel."

"Gog's blood," I muttered. "It's just as I said."

"This prentice, he served as a second in the duel, and the weapon of choice was not swords but pistols."

"I doubt that Nick has ever fired a pistol before," said Sander.

"Apparently not," said Sam, "for it was loaded wrong—they put in too much powder, perhaps—and blew up in his face."

Sander drew in a sharp, sympathetic breath. "He's all right, though?" he said hopefully.

Sam shook his head. "This fellow says not. He and his man made a hasty departure to avoid arrest, but he seemed to think Nick was a gone goose."

Sander and I glanced guiltily at one another. "It's as if we wished it upon him," Sander said softly.

"Nay, don't think that," I protested. "Though I'm sorry

for him, it was none of our doing. 'A brought it upon himself."

"Widge is right," said Sam. "You know as well as I what a hothead Nick was."

"I know. But he wasn't a bad fellow. He didn't deserve to die."

We relayed the sad news to the sharers. They made inquiries but could learn nothing more of the matter. This was no surprise. Though dueling was a common enough practice in London, it was also against the law. Pembroke's Men would naturally make every effort to protect the player who had been involved, as any company worth the name would do. We could only hope that poor Nick had been delivered into the hands of the church or the coroner's office and given a proper burial.

As the second act of a play follows without intermission upon the heels of the first, the warm, wet spring gave way without a break to a sultry summer. We at the Globe were, as usual, too busy to notice. Though our company was smaller than normal, the size of our audience was, the sharers said, at an all-time high. A portion of the profits went toward having the roof rethatched, purchasing properties and costumes, and buying new plays for our repertoire. But much of the money was paid to the temporary players.

It was hard for us prentices, always having to work with someone new. But I made no complaint; I had no wish to be but a temporary player myself. It could not have been easy for the sharers, either, constantly having to seek competent actors. If a player was not already attached to some company, there was usually a reason. Perhaps he drank too much, or was a thief, or was at that awkward age when his voice could not decide between treble and bass. The situation put a strain on Mr. Shakespeare especially. He could hardly tailor a play to suit the players when the players changed from week to week or day to day.

The only member of the company I heard complain, though, was Sam, and he was not being quarrelous so much as just speaking his mind—something that, as with the lines he spoke on the stage, he did with little or no prompting. Though he lodged with Mr. Phillips, Sam often dined at Mr. Pope's, where Sander and I lived, along with a small troupe of young orphans Mr. Pope had generously taken in. Over dinner one evening, Sam said, "I hope we never hire that Thomas fellow again. He's got two left feet, or perhaps three. Did you see him step on the hem of my gown?"

"Nay, but I heard it," I said, and imitated the ripping sound.

"Is that what it was?" said Mr. Pope innocently. "I thought it was Sam passing wind."

"Very funny," Sam said. "In fact, the gown is in stitches over it."

"Well, we will not be likely to use him again," Mr. Pope said, "unless we're desperate. He tore his lines up rather badly, too, I noticed. It's fortunate you two are so adept at thribbling."

I couldn't help feeling pleased, for thribbling—that is, improvising when another player falters—was something I'd only lately learned to do with any degree of skill. But Sam was in no mood for compliments.

"Why do we put up with such ninnies?" he asked. "Why does the company not take on more prentices or hired men?"

Mr. Pope stroked his beard thoughtfully, looking not as though he was unsure of the answer but as though he was unwilling to divulge it. "There are . . . a number of reasons," he said finally. We waited, but he did not seem inclined to tell us what those reasons were.

We were not long in finding out.

When we arrived at the Globe in the morning, we found a notice tacked to the rear door announcing that, beginning Monday next, all public performances would be banned, by order of the Queen's physicians. A familiar thrill of dread went through me. "Oh, gis," I murmured. "It's the plague."

Sander stared at the paper incredulously. "No, surely that can't be it. The rule has always been that they close the theatres when the weekly death toll reaches thirty." He turned to Mr. Pope. "It's been nowhere near that, has it?"

Mr. Pope pulled the notice from the door and carefully rolled it up. He did not seem particularly upset over finding it there. He looked, in fact, as though he'd expected it. "That has been the rule in the past," he said. "But the Queen has a new chief physician, a Dr. Gilbert, and from what Mr. Tilney, the Master of Revels, tells us, this Dr. Gilbert has advised Her Majesty to ban all public gatherings *before* the plague becomes a problem."

"Oh, what does he know?" said Sam. "I've heard he also claims that the earth is a giant magnet."

"Anyway," put in Sander, "what makes him think there'll be a problem at all? There can't be more than a dozen cases a month. That's fewer than the number of murders."

Mr. Pope spread his hands in a gesture of helplessness. "Apparently this doctor of hers is predicting a bad year for the plague, based on certain signs and portents."

Sam sniffed skeptically. "What, the alignment of the planets, I suppose? Or has a comet been spied?"

"No, he's no astrologer." Mr. Pope unrolled the paper and, holding it at arm's length, peered at the print. "Judging from this, he's more concerned with conditions closer to home, such as . . . quote, 'the unusually warm and rainy weather, the abundance of fog and vapors, the prevailing southerly winds, the great number of worms, frogs, flies, and other creatures engendered of putrefaction, rats and moles running rampant in the streets, birds falling from the skies, et cetera, et cetera.' "

"Birds falling from the skies?" Sam echoed. "When was the last time you saw birds falling from the skies?" He pointed up in the air and exclaimed in a comical old man's voice, "God's blood, Maude, look—it's raining pigeons!"

No one laughed. "What does this mean for us, then?" I said glumly.

Mr. Pope carefully rolled up the paper again. "That remains to be seen. We've been expecting this; that's why we've not taken on any new prentices or hired men. But we haven't yet decided what to do about it."

They decided that very morning. The sharers gathered in the dining room of the theatre, behind closed doors, to discuss the matter while the prentices and hired men sat about, silent and gloomy, like prisoners waiting to be sentenced.

Mercifully, we had not long to wait. After no more than half an hour Mr. Heminges called us in. "G-good news. We've decided to g-go on performing."

I stared at him, not certain I'd heard him properly. "Truly?" I said eagerly. "But—how can we do that?"

"By turning gypsy," said Mr. Shakespeare.

"Traveling, you mean?" asked Sander.

"Exactly. We've done it before, eight or nine years ago, when the plague last hit London in earnest. It was . . ." He paused and, toying thoughtfully with his earring, glanced about at the other sharers with a curious, almost amused expression. "How shall I describe it, gentlemen?"

"Unconventional?" suggested Mr. Armin.

"Uncomfortable," said Mr. Pope.

"Unprofitable," said Mr. Burbage.

Mr. Heminges gave them all a disapproving look. "It was n-not so bad."

Of course not, I thought optimistically. How bad could it be, a summer spent traveling from town to town in the company of my friends and fellow players, bringing the magic of theatre to poor country wights starved for entertainment?

"Now n-naturally," Mr. Heminges went on, "the smaller

the t-troupe, the m-more economically we can travel. So, you see, n-not everyone in the company will be able to g-go."

The hope that had risen in me at the prospect of a reprieve abruptly subsided.

"Mr. P-Pope has begged off, on the g-grounds that his orphan b-boys need him—also on the g-grounds that he's getting t-too old to go g-gadding all over the country. Mr. B-Burbage will stay in London as well, t-to see to his many b-business affairs."

I could not bring myself to ask the question that was uppermost in my mind: What would become of us prentices? But as we were on our way home, Sam asked it for me. "What about us?"

"Us?" said Mr. Pope.

"Us prentices. Are we to stay or go?"

Mr. Pope gave him a look of reproach, which I took to mean that we were foolish to imagine there would be room for us in a company that was pared down to the core. My heart felt as heavy as barley bread. "Boys, boys," said Mr. Pope. "How could the Chamberlain's Men ever hope to manage without its bevy of beauteous ladies?"

His answer so filled me with relief that I was able to ignore for the moment all the other unanswered questions: How would we ever put on a play with only nine or ten actors? What would we do for properties and costumes? Where would we perform? Where would we lodge? How would we get from town to town? I told myself that I would find it all out in due time.

One thing I did learn was how long we were likely to lead the gypsy life. In past plague years, Mr. Heminges said, the theatres had been allowed to reopen in late September or early October, for the coming of cold weather, it seemed, reduced drastically the number of deaths.

That meant we would be on the road perhaps four months at most. I suspected I would not miss London overmuch. After all, I had lived most of my life in small country towns. What I would miss, though, were the things I had at Mr. Pope's: Goody Willingson's savory meals and kind heart, Mr. Pope's endless stock of theatre tales, the antics and affection of the orphan boys who boarded with us.

I made it a point to play longer than usual with the boys that evening, while I still might. To their number Mr. Pope had lately added a sober-faced girl of seven or eight who had lost both parents to the plague the summer before. Few households would have taken in such a child, but Mr. Pope reasoned that, if she had shown no symptoms of the plague by now, she never would.

I knew from my years of assisting Dr. Bright that this was probably so. But I also knew how capricious—and how deadly—the plague could be. Though I was a little ashamed of myself for it, I carefully avoided any close contact with the girl, whose name was Tetty. Sometimes I felt her solemn, dark eyes upon me and turned to see her gazing at me from across the room. Though she seldom spoke, I fancied that those eyes were saying, "You of all people should understand; you're an orphan, too."

Sander and the rest of Mr. Pope's boys seemed to have no

such qualms as I did. Her fellow orphans included her in their games and made room for her at the table without a second thought—or, I expect, even a first.

The sad prospect of leaving Mr. Pope and the others behind was made bearable by the knowledge that at least I would have Sander along. Or so I imagined.

Long after we were abed I lay sleepless, with my head full of all that had happened lately. I assumed that Sander had long since dropped off; he seemed able to lose himself in the arms of Morpheus anytime and anywhere—the sign of a clear conscience, I supposed.

But to my surprise I heard him whisper, "Widge? Are you awake?"

"As awake as a fish," I said.

"I've thought it over," he said, "and I'm not going."

"Not going where?"

"On the tour."

I sat up as if bitten by a bedbug and stared at him. In the moonlight that came through our small window, I could see that his eyes were closed, and his face had a peaceful look, as though he were perfectly at ease with his decision. I was not. "What possible reason could you have for not going?" I demanded.

"Whist! You'll wake the boys."

"Well," I said more softly, "what's your reason?"

"I'm needed here. With the company gone, there'll be no money coming in. Someone will have to provide for the boys and Tetty, and at Mr. Pope's age, it will be difficult for him to find work."

"It will hardly be easy for you. What will you do?"

"I don't know. Something."

"But surely the company will send Mr. Pope's share of the box to him."

"Perhaps. But the sixth part of nothing is nothing."

"You think it's possible we'll make no profit at all?"

"I think it's probable. I've heard the sharers talk of what such tours are like. Mr. Phillips was with Derby's Men in 1594. They were stranded in Sheffield and had to sell their costumes to pay their way home."

"But ours is the most noted company in England," I protested, "wi' the best plays. Folk will flock to see us. Won't they?"

"I hope so. But I won't risk these boys' welfare on it. Besides, if the plague does strike, as Dr. Gilbert predicts, I'll be needed even more here."

I swung my legs off the bed and sat with my head in my hands. "A lot of good you'll be, an the plague strikes you."

"I was hoping you'd know of some preventative."

"Me? What do I ken about it?"

"You prenticed with a doctor for seven years. What methods did he use?"

"Mostly a method known as Staying Away From Anyone

Who's Ill. An 'a could not avoid treating someone, 'a tied a cloth soaked in wine over his face."

Sander laughed. "Is that like washing your face in an ale clout?" Londoners, I had learned, used this phrase to mean getting drunk.

" 'A said it killed the plague seeds. 'A also advocated chewing angelica root and drinking plague water."

"Plague water?" Sander said with apparent alarm.

"Nay, it's not like it sounds. You make it by steeping various herbs in wine."

"Wine again, eh?"

I smiled, despite myself. "Dr. Bright prescribed wine for nearly anything—a sore throat, aching joints, a paper cut—and followed his own advice religiously." I sighed heavily and held my head again. "I can't see how we'll get by wi'out you, Sander. Who'll play the tall women?"

"They'll hire someone. The children's companies have plenty of capable actors, and they'll all be out of work, too."

That was true enough—with the theatres closed, players would be easy to come by. It was friends that were in short supply. "Well," I said glumly, "I suppose there's no changing your mind."

"No. I'm sorry."

"Well, that's a comfort to ken that you're sorry," I said. A feeling of emptiness had settled into me. Though I knew well enough that it was not hunger, I lit a candle and headed for the stairs.

"Where are you going?" Sander asked.

"To the kitchen. Want to come?"

"No, thanks. I'll stay here."

I scowled. "Don't remind me."

As I was slicing bread and beef left over from supper, I heard a curious sort of scuffling noise from one corner of the room. Suspecting a rat, I raised the carving knife and the candle and crept across the kitchen. To my surprise, I discovered a figure considerably larger than a rat huddled in the corner next to the fireplace.

It wore a white nightshirt, and at first I thought it was one of the boys. But then it lifted its head and I saw the dark eyes glistening with tears. I took an involuntary step backward. "Tetty? What are you doing down here so late?"

She did not answer with words, only shook her head sharply and put her hand over her eyes, whether to hide the tears there or to shade them from the sudden light I could not tell. "Goody Willingson will be cross wi' you an you smudge your nightshirt," I said, though we both knew that our housekeeper's wrath was to be preferred to most people's good humor. "Why don't you go on up to bed, now?"

She made no move and no reply. I stuck the knife in the chopping block and crouched down on a level with her, but still at a distance. "Is there aught amiss?" I asked, though it was plain as Dunstable highway that something was wrong. "Tetty? Tell me."

When she spoke, her voice was as soft, nearly, as the rustle of the nightshirt she gathered about her bare ankles. "I'm afeared."

"Afeared? Of what?" No answer. "The dark?" I asked. She shook her head. "What, then?"

She raised her eyes to mine. I nodded to her, to encourage her to say what was on her mind, then almost wished I had not, for she said, so softly I had to strain to hear, "Of the Black Death."

I wanted to confess to Tetty that I, like her, had seen the ravages of the plague and that she was right to fear it, that I feared it, too, so much that I shunned anyone who had come in contact with it, including her. But I knew that what she wanted, what she needed, was for someone to allay her fears, not confirm them. Had I been Sander or Goody Willingson, I would have folded her in my arms and comforted her. But I was not, and could not. All I could offer was words, and they sounded as unconvincing to my ears as the prating of the Chapel Children. "There's no danger. You're safe here."

"That's what my ma used to tell me," she whispered. "But there's nowhere safe."

"Nay, that's not so. You've naught to fear as long as you don't get too close to someone who has it."

"But I have done," she said, her voice faint and hoarse, "and now—" She bit her lip, and tears welled in her eyes again. "And now I've a pain . . . here." She put a hand to her throat. "That's how it began for my da."

My chest grew tight, so that I had trouble catching my breath. I was reluctant to take a breath, anyway, for fear of what was in the air between us. Shakily, I put a hand up before my mouth and cleared my throat. "Perhaps . . ." I ventured, "perhaps it's not . . . what you think. Do you have a fever? Is your forehead warm?"

She put a palm to her brow. "A little."

I nodded thoughtfully. "Will you do something else for me?"

"What?"

"Will you raise the hem of your nightshirt a bit, so I can examine your limbs?"

She gave me a puzzled look but did as I asked. I held the candle at arm's length and peered at her legs. The skin was smooth, pale, unblemished. "Well," I said. "That's a good sign."

"What is?"

"No red spots. Me old master told me that's one of the early signals of the plague—red marks, like pox or flea bites, on the limbs. Do you notice any soreness or swelling of the kernels just below your ears or in the hollow beneath your arm?"

She pressed her fingers to those places. "No," she said hopefully.

"You've not been vomiting or sweating—a cold sweat, I mean?"

"No."

"And you've a good appetite?"

She nodded. "I'm starved," she said, and unexpectedly giggled.

I stood and breathed a sigh of relief. "Well, you've come to the right place, then." I took up the knife and returned to slicing the roast. From the corner of my eye, I saw Tetty crawl cautiously from her hidey-hole.

"You don't think it's the plague, then?"

"Well, I'm no doctor of physic, but from what you've told me, I'd say you're suffering from that dread disease known as a sore throat." I set before her two slices of bread with beef packed between them. "It's not too sore to swallow that, is it?" She shook her head. "Good. After we've eaten, I'll make you up some swish water to gargle with."

She blinked her dark eyes quizzically. "What's *that*?"

"Warm water wi' honeycomb, pepper, and cloves. Mr. Phillips has me use it to sweeten me voice for singing. It has yet to work. But it does soothe a person's pipes."

Around a prodigious mouthful of bread and beef, Tetty said, "You know a lot about medicine."

I laughed. "Nay, I only act as though I do."

"Then you're a good actor."

"I hope so. I mean to make it me trade."

She gazed at me appraisingly a moment. "Do you no longer dislike me, then, or is that just more acting?"

"Dislike you? I never disliked you. I only—" I paused. No matter how many times I resolved not to lie, it seemed I always ended up needing to. "I'm not much good at making friends yet, that's all," I said, which was true enough.

Tetty nodded soberly. "Nor am I. I'm afeared—" She lowered her eyes and her voice. "I'm afeared that if I come to like someone, they'll . . ."

"They'll die?" I said.

She nodded again. "Like my ma and da."

"Don't think that way. It was none of your doing. It was the contagion."

"Then why did it not take me as well?"

I shrugged helplessly. "I don't ken th' answer to that. I doubt that anyone does."

"Was it the contagion that took your ma and da, then?" she asked.

I hesitated. This was not a subject I liked to speak of. "Nay," I said simply, "me mother died borning me." Though I had meant to leave it at that, I found myself going on. "For a passing while, like you I . . . I held meself somehow responsible for 't."

"But you no longer do?"

"Nay," I said, though it was not entirely true. There were still times, late at night, when I was tormented by the thought that, had it not been for me, she would certainly be alive yet. Of course, I still would not have known her.

"And your da?" said Tetty.

I sighed. Why was this lass so full of questions that I was so unprepared to answer? Impatient, I said the first thing that came into my head—prompted, no doubt, by the fact that we had performed *Henry VI, Part I* that afternoon. " 'A was a soldier; 'a was killed in battle, skewered by an enemy lance."

Tetty gave a slight shudder, whether from the cold or from picturing my supposed father's supposed death, I could not tell. "I'm sorry."

"Aye, so am I," I said, and I was, for having deceived her. "You'd best go on up to bed now, before that sore throat turns into something more severe."

That Saturday we gave our farewell performance at the Globe. The yard and the galleries were crammed to overflowing with folk who well knew that it would likely be their last chance to see a play until cold weather came around again and, with it, the end of the plague season.

The days that followed were every bit as hectic as if we had gone on performing. But instead of learning lessons and playing roles, we occupied our hours by packing wooden chests full of properties and costumes and taking them down to the yard, where we loaded them into one of the two carewares, or play wagons, that the sharers had had specially constructed for the tour.

Mr. Burbage, who had learned the skills of a joiner, or carpenter, from his father, had designed the carewares so that the sides could be taken down and laid across the wagon beds to form a makeshift stage. The wagons were equipped with canvas tops to keep the rain off—not off the players, I mean, but off the properties and costumes, which, unlike us, could not be easily replaced.

In addition to the paraphernalia necessary for staging our plays, we would be carrying with us wool-filled ticks and bedding, for, as Mr. Heminges pointed out, we could not always be certain of finding an inn—or, if we did, of having the money to lodge there.

Meanwhile, the sharers were attending to more subtle and less muscular matters, such as purchasing horses and supplies, obtaining our playing license, and auditioning boys to take Sander's place in the company—as if anyone could.

Though I knew I would be wise to make the most of our last days together for some time to come, I spent much of the time stupidly sulking. Sander pretended not to notice my resentful manner and went on being his usual cheerful self.

As we were carrying a heavy trunk filled with stage armor and weapons along the second-floor gallery, I spotted Mr. Armin entering the yard, accompanied by a youth who, though I had seen him but once before, I recognized immediately by his head of blond curls. I set my end of the trunk on the gallery railing and clapped a hand to my head. "Oh, Law," I groaned, "they've hired the boy from the Chapel Children."

Sander glanced over the railing at the boy, who was being introduced around to the company, and then looked back to me. "You need not look so stricken, Widge. Surely it's better to have a capable actor like him than one of those dolts we've had to put up with lately."

"Oh, aye. Well may you say that. You'll not ha' to compete wi' him for parts. You'll be *here,* playing horsey and wiping noses."

Sander smiled patiently. "Did I not tell you that you're every bit as good an actor as he is?"

"Aye, but it's not me you ha' to convince; it's the sharers."

"No," said Sander. "I think it's you."

"Let's get this down to the careware," I muttered, "before me arms fall off and they pack them i' the chest wi' the fake plaster limbs."

As we wrestled the trunk down the gallery stairs, I kept one eye on the new boy. His manner was agreeable enough. He smiled in a charming way and greeted each member of the company with what seemed sincere pleasure. When he was introduced to Mr. Burbage, he was almost reverential and, from what I could overhear, lavish in praising the man's portrayal of Hamlet, which the boy apparently had seen no less than twelve times. He seemed equally honored to make the acquaintance of Mr. Shakespeare.

As we loaded the chest in the careware, Mr. Armin called, "Widge, Sander! Come and meet our new prentice! You, too, Sam!"

Sam, who was in the bed of the wagon arranging boxes and bundles, jumped down next to me. "Looks like a bit of a lickspittle to me," he whispered.

"A what?"

"You know—a bootlicker, a flatterer."

"Whist!" scolded Sander. "Be nice, now! 'It hurts not the tongue to give fair words.' "

"Just don't ask me to hold my tongue," Sam said. "That does hurt."

We strolled over to Mr. Armin. "Boys," he said, "I'd like you to make welcome your new colleague, Salathiel Pavy."

"Salathiel?" Sam echoed. I would have sworn he was set to snicker, but he somehow restrained himself. "Very pleased to meet you." He held out a hand to Salathiel Pavy, who took it very genially—but very briefly. In a trice his charming smile had transformed to a look of horror. He jumped as if he'd been bitten, and flung to the ground the hand that Sam had offered him—for it was one of the plaster models that represented Lavinia's severed hands in *Titus Andronicus*.

Sam doubled over with laughter and Sander and I could not help following suit. Even Mr. Armin had trouble keeping a sober face. "As you can see," he said, "our boys are always willing to give a new member of the company a hand."

I expected Salathiel Pavy, once he had recovered from the initial shock, to join in the laughter and perhaps make a jest of his own in return. Instead, he turned on his heel indignantly and stalked out of the yard. "Well," Sam said, "I trust you were not counting on him to play comic parts. Clearly he has no sense of humor."

"And you," said Mr. Armin, "clearly have no sense of

tact. You've had your fun. Now I expect you to make him welcome, boys, just as you were made welcome when you joined the company. Is that clear?"

We wiped off our foolish grins and nodded and tried to look properly chastened. As Mr. Armin walked away, he called over his shoulder, "Sam, you need to work on your remorseful look. Have the others coach you."

When he was gone, Sander said, "He's right, you know."

"What was wrong with the way I looked?" Sam demanded.

"I mean about making the new boy welcome. I doubt he's ever played in an adult company before. It's bound to be hard for him."

I thought back on how difficult it had been for me during my early weeks as a prentice, learning what was expected of me, and delivering it. If Sander and Julia had not given me help and encouragement, I would not still have been with the company. It was, I supposed, my turn to do the same. "I'll fetch him," I said, "and we'll start over."

"Sam?" prompted Sander.

Sam sighed and rolled his eyes. "Yes, all right, I'll try." He screwed his face up into a grimace. "How's that? Do I look remorseful now?"

"You look as though you've swallowed a fish bone," I said. "Just look normal."

"Ooh," said Sam, "that's even harder."

Salathiel Pavy was sitting on the edge of a wooden footbridge that crossed one of the many drainage ditches around the theatre. He was looking glumly out over the Thames toward Blackfriars, as though wishing he'd never left it. I came up behind him, clearing my throat so as not to startle him. "Salathiel? Or do they call you Sal?" He did not answer, or even acknowledge my presence. Undaunted, I went on. "It seems we started off on the wrong foot." I couldn't help adding, "Or hand, as it were."

He gave me a sidewise glance that was anything but amused. Perhaps Sam was right; perhaps he just did not appreciate a jest. Knowing he must be feeling like an outsider, I looked for a way to include him. "We'd all appreciate it an you'd give us a"—I'd almost said "a hand" —"an you'd help us wi' loading the carewares for the tour."

He turned to look at me directly at last, and his expression was less hostile than wary. "Would you?"

"Aye. Those trunks get heavy," I said, flexing my aching arms.

He gave me a thin smile that was totally unlike the one he had displayed when greeting the company; it held no charm nor warmth but was cold as a key. "You'll excuse me if I do not oblige you. I was hired to be an actor, not a stagehand."

For a moment I was struck dumb by the unexpected and unwarranted rudeness of his reply. Then I felt a flush of anger. I could scarcely keep myself from giving him a slight shove, which was all that would be required to topple him into the drainage ditch. But I reminded myself of Mr. Armin's instructions to make him feel welcome. I tried again.

"I saw you perform, some two weeks ago, in *The Poet-*

aster. You were . . ." I paused. I did not wish to overrate him. "You were noticeably better than the others."

"Is that supposed to be a compliment?"

"Aye."

He tilted his head in a way that, had he been a lesser actor, might have seemed merely quizzical. He managed somehow to make it clear that he was mocking my speech. "I beg your pardon?"

"*Yes,*" I said peevishly. "It was meant to be, yes."

"Well, I'm afraid it did not succeed. If I were only 'noticeably better' than those wretches, I'd begin looking for a new career."

I was sorely tempted to suggest some possibilities—perhaps something in the hermiting line—but again I restrained myself, not without effort. When I returned to the yard, Sander asked, "Did you find him?"

"Aye," I said. "I found him a conceited ass."

"Really?" said Sam. "That's good."

I frowned at him. "Why's that?"

"Well, don't you see? We can take turns riding him."

Though Sam's comment was made in jest, it had teeth in it. The truth was, the company could not afford mounts for all of us, so only the sharers would ride. We prentices and hired men would, as usual, have to rely on shank's mare. The company had purchased teams of horses to pull the wagons, of course, but these were plodding draft animals; even if they could have borne the extra weight of a rider, we could not have stood their jolting gait for long.

The day we had set for our departure proved a dismal one, but we could not put it off, for Mr. Heminges had booked an appearance for us in Reading two days hence. It would have been hard enough in the best of weather to leave the comfortable, familiar surroundings and the folk I knew and loved best, for an uncertain existence on the road. The rain that leaked from the smudged sky made the prospect even less appealing.

My leavc-taking was as different from the way I had left Dr. Bright's home a year earlier as Berwick is different from London. Back then, not a soul had seemed to care a rush what became of me. Now the young boys vowed noisily not to let me go, and clung to my clothing like burrs until Mr. Pope pulled them off. Tetty, meanwhile, stood apart and gazed at me, unblinking, as though memorizing me.

Goody Willingson tearfully embraced me as though I had been her own son. Mr. Pope left me with a litany of advice nearly as extensive as that given by Polonius to Laertes in Mr. Shakespeare's *Hamlet*. But, whereas Polonius's ultimate admonition was "To thine own self be true," Mr. Pope stressed that, above all, I should not whistle in the tiring-room, lest I bring ill luck down upon the company.

I reminded him that we would not have a tiring-room. He dismissed this and went on to tell me of a wight he had known who whistled behind the stage during a performance.

"What befell him?" I asked.

"One of his fellow players chucked a pot of face paint at

him to shut him up. It struck him in the temple and killed him dead as a duck."

"Well," I said, "that certainly was ill luck." I donned my cloak. "I must go. We're to meet at nine o'clock outside Newgate."

"I'll walk with you a way," said Sander.

Just as we were going out the door Tetty rushed up to me, pressed something into my hand, and quickly retreated. I glanced down at the object. It was a sheet of paper folded into a tiny square. I looked around for Tetty, but she had vanished. "Move your bones!" called Sander. "I'm getting soaked!" I thrust the square of paper into my wallet and caught up with him.

"You'll write me now and again, I hope," said Sander as we traversed the muddy slope to the river. "Mr. Pope says that most carriers who travel to and from the city will also handle letters."

"Aye, but how will you ever reply?"

"They've told me some of the towns you'll be playing in. I can send letters ahead, to be held for you."

"I wish you were coming."

"No more than I do. But sometimes wishes must yield to duty." He put a hand upon my shoulder. "Cheer up. Autumn will be here before you know it, and everything will be the way it was. Perhaps better."

"I would that I could believe that."

"Have I ever lied to you?"

"Nay, not that I ken."

"Go on, then." We shook hands, then he urged me toward the waiting wherry boat. As it pulled away from shore, he called after me, "Cheer up!"

I waved and feigned a smile that did no credit to my acting skills. The boat had a small canopy that shielded me from the rain. Remembering the paper Tetty had given me, I drew it from my wallet and unfolded it carefully.

It was a crudely drawn picture of a group of human figures: two fat ones—Goody Willingson and Mr. Pope, I imagined; a tall, thin one—Sander, no doubt; and half a dozen small ones wearing wide grins. Standing apart from the others was a small figure with dark hair and eyes. Beneath the picture, printed in crooked, uncertain letters, were the words SO YOU'LL NOT FORGET US.

I reached Newgate, drenched and downhearted, just as the bells at St. Paul's rang tierce. The carewares, each with a pair of draft horses hitched to it, sat by the road. A sheet of canvas was stretched between the wagons, and under this the rest of the company were gathered, looking more like a forlorn band of vagabonds than one of London's premier theatre troupes.

We had all been issued navy blue hats and cloaks embroidered with our badge, a rampant swan. This livery marked us as the Lord Chamberlain's Men, licensed to perform anywhere in the realm. But no one wished to soil this fine livery by wearing it in such unpleasant weather, so we made a rather motley company, and a dismayingly small one. As Mr. Heminges had said, Mr. Burbage chose not to make the tour. That left us with the following cast, in order of importance, as it were:

MR. WILLIAM SHAKESPEARE, *ordinary playwright of the company*
MR. JOHN HEMINGES, *business manager*
MR. ROBERT ARMIN, *clown and fencing master*
MR. AUGUSTINE PHILLIPS, *player of villains and dancing and singing instructor*
MR. WILLIAM SLY, *hired man*
MR. JACK GRYMES, *hired man*
MASTER SALATHIEL PAVY, *prentice*
MASTER SAMUEL CROSSE, *prentice*
MASTER WIDGE (NO SURNAME), *prentice*

There was, in addition, an unfamiliar face in the group. Though he was well past the age of a prentice, he had not let his beard grow. His head of black hair was worn longer than most men's and, in deference to the weather, pulled into a horse tail. He slouched indolently against one of the carewares, with a pained look upon his face, as though he would much rather have been somewhere else, somewhere warm and dry.

"Have you met my brother Ned?" asked Mr. Shakespeare. "He'll be joining us on the tour."

"Though God knows why anyone would want to," put in Will Sly.

Ned shrugged. "It seemed to me preferable to starving or dying of the plague."

I offered my hand to him. "I'm Widge." Without changing position he languidly held out his left hand to me. I gave it an awkward shake.

Mr. Shakespeare said, "Ned has been a player in London for—how long, now?"

"Nearly a year."

"The same as I," I said. "Wi' what company?"

"The Admiral's Men." Before I could remark upon this, he went on. "Lord Pembroke's Men. Leicester's Men, for a time."

I reacted with surprise. "All in less than a year?"

He shrugged again and scowled up at the slaty sky. "None was quite to my liking."

I glanced past him at Sam, who was making a wry face as if to say, "That's *his* version of it."

"I b-believe the rain is l-letting up," Mr. Heminges said hopefully.

"If by 'letting up' you mean coming down harder," said Will Sly, "I'd agree."

"Well," said Mr. Shakespeare, "whether it's coming or going, we can delay no longer if we're to make Reading by nightfall tomorrow."

As soon as we prentices had stowed the canvas shect in the rear of one of the already overloaded wagons, the company set off, the sharers riding horseback at the head of the procession, the teams and wagons slogging along behind them through six inches of mud, the hired men and prentices bringing up the rear, wading through the wet grass alongside the highway.

The rain went on coming down—or, as Mr. Heminges would have it, letting up—steadily all day long. By the time we reached Slough we were exhausted from dragging our waterlogged limbs along. The inn where we lodged was small, so there were but two rooms available to us. The four sharers took one; we prentices and hired men were left to crowd into the other.

We set about making ourselves as comfortable as we might—all except Sal Pavy, who merely stood in the doorway, looking about with obvious distaste at the spartan accommodations. I was not a little surprised at his attitude, for, all during the day, despite the wearisome weather, he had not uttered a word of complaint; in fact, he had put on quite a cheerful face. Apparently the face had been a false one, which he could don and doff at will.

"I was never informed that I would have to share sleeping quarters with half a dozen . . . others," he said.

"Oh, you don't have to," said Sam.

"I don't?" said Sal Pavy hopefully.

"No. Half a dozen means six, you see, and there are only five of us . . . *others.*"

As usual, Sal Pavy was not amused. "I am not at all accustomed to this sort of arrangement. At Blackfriars I had a room to myself, with a feather bed." Disdainfully he prodded one of the straw mattresses furnished by the inn. "This is worse than sleeping in a stable."

"Well," said Jack grumpily, "why don't you sleep in the stable, then?"

Sal Pavy flushed. "Perhaps I will." He disappeared from the doorway.

As we stretched out upon the lumpy mattresses, I said, "A room to himself and a feather bed. Do you suppose that's so?"

"I never heard of a prentice having it that soft," said Sam. "Of course, they may have given him a separate room just to be rid of him."

"I hope he does sleep in the stable," growled Jack. "Him and his airs. Thinks he's better than the rest of us."

"And perhaps," said Sam, "being an ass, he'll feel more at home with the horses."

By the time morning came, I heartily wished I had slept in the stable. What with Jack's vigorous snoring and the bedbugs and other vermin that infested the straw mattress, I spent a restless night. The sharers evidently fared little better, for when we sat down to breakfast in the main hall of the inn, Mr. Heminges proclaimed, while scratching irritably at his bug bites, "F-from now on, we use our own m-mattresses and bedclothes."

When Sal Pavy entered the room, Sam called out to him, "Well, how were the horses?"

Sal Pavy pretended not to have heard. He looked well rested and had taken care to put on his cordial face again.

"The horses?" said Mr. Armin.

Sam nodded emphatically. "He slept in the stable, didn't you, Sal?"

"I did," Sal Pavy admitted blithely. "I don't care for crowded rooms. I believe them to be unhealthy."

Out of the corner of his mouth, Will Sly murmured to me, "Particularly when they're filled with wights who would very much like to strangle you."

I snickered. "Well, 'a does have a point, though."

"How's that?"

I nodded in Sal Pavy's direction. "You don't see him scratching, do you?"

The rain truly had let up now, but the surface of the road still resembled porridge more than earth. We made such slow progress that, by the time we reached the outskirts of Reading, its church bells were ringing compline.

Weary though we were, upon our arrival at the George & Dragon we retrieved our wool mattresses and bedclothes from the carewares and spread them on our bed frames, having deposited the inn's bedding in a pile in the hall. Though we had the luxury of a larger room this time, and no bedbugs, Sal Pavy still did not deign to bunk with us. No one seemed to mind. Though he was amiable and cooperative in the presence of the sharers, when he was in the company of hired men and prentices alone he showed his true colors, and they were not attractive ones.

In the morning, after breakfast, we cleaned the mud from ourselves as best we could, given the limited washing facilities—a ewer of lukewarm water and a bowl—and dressed in doublets and breeches taken from our costume trunk, for these were the only unmuddied garments we had. Then we donned the blue caps and capes that distinguished us as the Chamberlain's Men, and set out for the town hall.

We were forced to wait half an hour outside the mayor's chambers before he could see us, but the time passed quickly, for we were once again in good spirits with the prospect of a performance ahead of us, the first one in over a week. We occupied the time with jests and with stories of past triumphs and debacles, such as players like to tell.

Mr. Shakespeare's brother Ned held the floor longer than anyone, recalling the circumstances that had led him to leave his family home in Stratford. It seems he was caught by Sir Thomas Lucy's gamekeeper in the act of dispatching one of the lord's deer. He hinted that, in addition, he had gotten a prominent landowner's daughter with child. As a result of these trespasses, he no longer felt welcome in Stratford and had come to try his luck in London, only to be kicked out into the countryside again.

His monologue was cut short by the arrival of the mayor, a heavyset fellow dressed in gaudy scarlet clothing and adorned with gold chains of office so numerous and weighty that they would surely have brought a less brawny man to his knees. Mr. Heminges stepped forward and gave a slight bow. Just as it did when he was upon the stage, the stutter that ordinarily plagued him disappeared. "The Lord Chamberlain's Men at your service, sir."

The mayor shook hands with him and the other sharers, smiling broadly as though delighted to have a company of such renown in his city. He seemed especially honored to greet Mr. Shakespeare. "Your reputation has preceded you, sir," he boomed.

"Has it?" said Mr. Shakespeare. "Would that it had secured us better lodgings, then, and perhaps tacked a few handbills up around town." The mayor laughed, but it sounded more dutiful than amused.

"We'd like to begin setting up as soon as possible," Mr. Heminges said, "if you can direct us to where we are to perform."

The mayor's smile grew a trifle stiff, and he rubbed his beefy hands together in a way that, had a player performed the gesture on stage, would have demonstrated obvious unease. "Well, the fact is, there's been a . . . a change of plans, you might say."

"Oh?" said Mr. Heminges.

"Yes," the mayor went on uncomfortably. "You see, we've had some . . . problems. Illness, you know. In point of fact, the plague. Twelve deaths in the past week alone. In view of this, I—that is, we—that is, the town council have decided to ban all public gatherings."

"Including plays," said Mr. Heminges.

The mayor nodded emphatically, setting his wealth of chains jangling. Unexpectedly, the sound set a shiver through me, for it called to mind the clanging of a bell heard long ago in the streets of Berwick, a doleful sound that was always accompanied by the cry of "Bring out your dead! Bring out your dead!"

Our brief stay in Reading was not a total disappointment. The town councillors had authorized the sum of eighty shillings to be given the company—a reward, as it were, for *not* performing our plays. Mr. Heminges was obviously insulted and would, I believe, have turned the money down had not Mr. Shakespeare's practical sense prevailed. "John," he said, "I'm afraid we cannot afford to be overly scrupulous. This will pay for a week's lodging."

So we took the money, but, like a coin tested with the teeth for its gold content, it left a bitter taste in our mouths. We moved on to Basingstoke, where, to our dismay, we found the situation much the same. The mayor here seemed less concerned about spreading the plague, though, than about offending the church. The clergy of the city, he said, were preaching that the source of the plague deaths was not corrupted air but corrupted morals, and were singling out the bands of traveling players as a particularly evil influence.

Apparently the Earl of Sussex's Men had performed at the Guild Hall a few weeks prior; handbills advertising a matinee of *The Malcontent* were still stuck to buildings and trees. The mayor said that shortly after their departure the number of plague deaths had begun to rise.

"But that doesn't m-mean that Sussex's Men were *responsible* for the p-plague!" protested Mr. Heminges, so upset that his stutter was surfacing.

The mayor refused to listen to reason. Again we were offered money to move on; this time the bribe was only sixty shillings. "Well," sniffed Will Sly indignantly, "I should certainly have thought we had amongst us at least five pounds' worth of corruption."

Two days later, in Newbury, we encountered the same attitude, and with even less reason. There had been no plague to speak of, and the authorities were determined to keep it that way. This time Mr. Heminges refused to accept the paltry sum offered us not to play. "F-fie on them! We've a license to p-perform, and perform we will, whether they l-like it or no." I had seldom seen him so cross. Normally he was as tolerant and even-tempered as Sander. He turned to the rest of the sharers with a look that dared them to challenge him. "Are you w-with me?"

Mr. Armin held up his hands as if in surrender. Mr. Phillips nodded quickly. Mr. Shakespeare toyed thoughtfully with his earring and then smiled slightly. "You're right, John. We are not beggars; we are players. Let us not play according to someone else's script."

"They'll never let us use the town hall," Mr. Phillips said.

"Then we'll s-set up our stage in the street," Mr. Heminges declared.

While the hired men unloaded most of our equipment from the carewares and stored it in the granary of the inn, we three prentices were sent through the town with preprinted handbills announcing a performance of Mr. Shakespeare's *Love's Labour's Lost*. On each sheet we had printed in ink 2 O'CLOCK TODAY ON THE SQUARE. Some we handed out to shopkeepers and passersby; others we tacked to trees and fences and the sides of buildings.

We spent most of the morning getting our lines fixed in our heads. Though we had performed the play many times at the Globe, this was a special gypsy players' version, with all the excess parts trimmed away to make it suitable for traveling.

Even though Mr. Shakespeare had reduced the number of speaking roles from nineteen to thirteen, there were but ten of us in the company, so some of us had to double up. Sam, for example, donned a wig and dress to play Maria, then doffed them to play Moth. I played both Jaquenetta, my usual role, and Rosaline, the part usually played by Sander. Luckily for me, the two of them never appeared in the same scene.

I believe Sal Pavy's lot was the hardest. Though Ned

Shakespeare was new to the company, he had at least acted with an adult company before. Sal Pavy had not. Nor had he ever had a part in one of Mr. Shakespeare's plays. Worse, he had been given but two scant weeks to con half a dozen different roles.

In my early days with the company, when I was coaxed into playing the part of Ophelia in *Hamlet* before I was truly ready, my friend Julia had made certain that I did not disgrace myself; she had gone over and over my lines with me until they stuck in my head. Though I did not care for Sal Pavy's company, I felt it would be right for me to follow Julia's example.

I found Sal Pavy sitting alone in a corner of the courtyard with his eyes closed. He was silently mouthing his lines. "Excuse me," I said. "I thought perhaps you could use some help."

His eyes opened slowly. The look he turned on me was distracted, irritable. "Help?" he said. "With what?"

I gestured at the partial script he held in one hand. "Why wi' your part, of course."

"Oh. No, I need no help." He closed his eyes again. "And if I ever did, I would certainly ask someone more competent to give it."

I had not truly expected him to be grateful, but neither had I anticipated that he would insult me. "How would you ken," I demanded, "how competent I am or am not? You've never even seen me perform!"

"You're quite wrong," he replied calmly. "I saw you only

last month, in *Titus Andronicus*. You were . . . how can I put it kindly? . . . *dreary.*"

I was not a violent person, but if I had had a sword in my hand at that moment, I would surely have thrust it through his heart—or at least considered it. When I recounted the scene for Sam, he shook his head in disgust. "The lad has a bad case of swollen head, all right. I recommend we give him a dose of the same medicine we give to Jack."

Several times in the past, when Jack had gone beyond the bounds of his duties as a hired man and insisted on pointing out our shortcomings, we had retaliated during a performance by replacing some crucial cue line with a line of our own invention. It was like throwing a lead weight to a wight who could not swim. We always rescued him eventually, but not until he had gone under a time or two.

The notion of giving Sal Pavy the same treatment was appealing; there was no doubt that he deserved it. But I reluctantly shook my head.

"Why not?" protested Sam. "It'll be great fun!"

"Because. Mr. Armin said we should make him welcome."

"Yes, well, that doesn't mean we're obliged to cheerfully accept his insults."

" 'A never insulted you. Let it pass, all right? It's not worth creating ill will over."

Sam rolled his eyes. "You sound like Sander."

"Good," I said. "I meant to."

As two o'clock approached, we set up our makeshift

stage atop the wagon beds and then returned to the inn to get into our costumes. As usual, Sal Pavy was not among us. "I expect he has a nasty case of stage stomach," said Mr. Armin, "and is somewhere vomiting his victuals."

"A little fear is good for a fellow," said Mr. Phillips. "It keeps him from getting over confident."

As we headed for the town square, Sal Pavy caught up with us. He certainly did not look as though he had spent the last hour or so puking and agonizing. He looked, in fact, as cool as a cowcumber.

"Don't tell me," Sam said. "You got dressed in the stable."

"Yes. I'm accustomed to having a modicum of privacy."

"Weren't you afraid the horses would look at you?" Sam teased. Sal Pavy ignored him. "I suppose at Blackfriars you had your own private tiring-room?"

Sal Pavy smiled smugly. "As a matter of fact, I did."

A crowd of a hundred or more townfolk had gathered before the wagon-stage, drawn by the notes of Mr. Phillips's pennywhistle. While the rest of the company went behind the striped curtain we had suspended at the rear of the stage, we prentices passed among the audience with our caps in our hands, calling "One penny, please"—or rather Sam and I did. Sal Pavy stood off to one side, silent and unmoving, with his cap held in both hands as though he found the prospect of actually soliciting money too demeaning. "Another thing he's not accustomed to, I expect," Sam muttered.

As I reached the rear of the crowd, I heard a commotion

from down the street and glanced up to see a body of eight or nine men striding purposefully toward us, wearing grim looks on their faces and carrying cudgels in their hands.

"Gog's blood!" I breathed. "They've come to run us off!" I pushed back through the crowd, raising cries of indignation, and scrambled around to the rear of the stage, where the players were waiting to make their entrances. "There's a bunch of wights wi' wasters coming!" I blurted between gasps. "I think it's the catchpolls!"

"C-constables, you mean?" said Mr. Heminges calmly. "I'll s-speak to them." He stepped through the curtain. I peered over the edge of the stage. The band of constables were dispersing the crowd, yelling, "Go home!" and brandishing their clubs.

"Gentlemen!" Mr. Heminges called in his best Pilate's voice over the clamor of the audience. "This is a lawful assembly! We are a licensed theatrical company! If you question that, we have here a decree issued by our patron, Lord Cobham!" He withdrew a paper from his wallet and began to read in a voice as mellifluous and dramatic as though he were reading the player's speech from *Hamlet*.

"To all justices, mayors, sheriffs, constables, headboroughs, and other officers, greeting. Know ye that I have licensed these my servants and their associates to freely exercise the art of playing comedies, tragedies, and histories—"

He got no further, for two of the catchpolls had climbed onto the stage and seized him by the arms. Despite his protests and those of the audience, they dragged him to the edge of the stage—not an easy task, for Mr. Heminges was not nearly as old nor as frail as he appeared in his guise of Ferdinand, King of Navarre.

One of the constables cried, "Stop struggling, old man!" and raised his cudgel. Before it could descend, Mr. Armin was through the curtains and across the boards. As quick as a dog can lick a dish, he had Mr. Heminges's rapier out of its sheath and pointing at the constable's throat-bole.

Though the sword was blunted, it would have gone badly for the man had he not let his cudgel drop. His fellow officer, taken aback by this turn of events, had loosened his grip. Mr. Heminges elbowed him sharply in the stomach and he toppled from the platform, waving his arms wildly.

Now the rest of the catchpolls were swarming onto the stage, scowling and shouting in anger. Mr. Armin booted his adversary off the apron, and he and Mr. Heminges backed away, into the ranks of the other players, who had now made an entrance en masse, with their stage swords drawn. The battle was joined.

The fight that ensued was nothing like scriming on the stage. There was no elegant, choreographed swordplay, no dramatic cries of "Have at you, now!" or "Yield, cur!"—only blows and grunts and curses. At first our men held their own, but when the officers discovered that our stage swords were more dull than deadly, the tide quickly turned.

Ned Shakespeare was the first to fall. He was struck in the ribs by a constable's cudgel and doubled up, gasping for air. His brother rushed stage left to come to his aid, but was in turn felled by a blow to his forearm that made a sickening crack, audible even over the sounds of the struggle. Mr. Shakespeare gave a bellow of pain, dropped his weapon, and sank to his knees, clutching his arm to his chest.

As I was in ladies' attire, I had no weapon save the stones

at my feet. I scooped up a handful and let one fly at Mr. Shakespeare's attacker. The man staggered downstage, holding his neck and howling. I loosed more stones whenever there was no danger of my hitting one of my fellows, and a few of them hit their mark, but it made no difference in the outcome.

Within five minutes' time, all our company were sprawled upon the stage, holding their bruised limbs and pates—all save Mr. Armin. He was backed up against the curtain with a dagger in one hand and a rapier in the other. But the look on his face, a sort of gleeful menace, was far more daunting than those dull weapons were.

The clump of catchpolls backed off, all breathing heavily, and many of them nursing wounds of their own. The largest of the men, who seemed to be their leader, took a moment to get his wind, then growled, "If it was up to me, I'd throw the lot of you in jail, but the mayor says only to make sure you leave town—as speedily as possible." He glanced up at the clock on the town hall; it read a quarter past two. "You've got until three o'clock. Then we come back." He nodded to his men. They swung to the ground—more gingerly, for the most part, than they had ascended—and departed the square.

One by one our men got to their feet, wincing and groaning. Mr. Heminges's doublet was torn; Mr. Phillips's head was bleeding; Will Sly was holding a red-stained kerchief to his mouth and muttering muffled curses; Mr. Shakespeare was cradling his right arm against his body, his face drawn and white with pain.

I glanced around for Sam. He emerged from beneath the stage. In one hand he held the cudgel that one of the constables had dropped; in the other he clutched my cap and his, which sagged under the weight of the coins we had collected. "Sorry I didn't join the fray," he told the others. "I thought I'd do better to guard the box."

Mr. Heminges smiled wanly. "G-good lad. But we m-mustn't keep the m-money, for we've not earned it."

"Not earned it?" Sam protested. "I'd say the audience got treated to quite a stirring performance."

"But more like t-two minutes' traffic upon the stage than two hours."

"Well, we can't just give it back, though, can we?" Sam gestured at the empty square. "They've all gone home."

"We'll l-leave it with the innkeeper, then."

"He's got enough of our money already—"

"That will do, Sam," said Mr. Heminges sharply.

Sam hung his head, and thrust the caps full of money at me. "You do it," he murmured. "I can't bear to."

"Have you seen Sal Pavy?" I asked him.

"Not since the excitement began. Try looking in the stable."

As we headed back to the inn, I said to Sam, "I don't think it's wise to speak back to the sharers, as you did just then."

Sam gave me a curious look. "I seem to recall you speaking back a time or two yourself. When did you become so cautious?"

I did not reply.

We were hard-pressed to take down the stage and get the carewares reloaded before the specified time. Sal Pavy turned up and, to my surprise, worked as hard as anyone. For once, all the sharers lent a hand with the labor as well, including Mr. Shakespeare, though his right arm was obviously causing him considerable pain.

The granary of the inn, where we had stored our equipment, was the center of activity. As I was dragging a property chest from the room, Mr. Shakespeare came in, his arm still clamped to his chest, his face as white as when he had played the ghost in *Hamlet.* "Where's Ned?" he demanded of the company at large. "Has anyone seen him?"

The other players glanced at one another uncertainly, and then Jack volunteered, "I seen him a quarter of an hour ago, in the kitchen, dallying with one of the maids."

Mr. Shakespeare scowled. "A plague on him! We need all the hands we have." He reached down with his uninjured arm and hefted one end of the property trunk I was struggling with. "Let me help with that." He got halfway to the careware before his legs buckled beneath him and he collapsed in a heap on the cobbles of the inn yard.

Alarmed, I called to Mr. Armin, who was hitching up the horses. "Come quickly!"

Mr. Armin knelt next to the playwright's limp body. "He's passed out. His injury must be worse than we thought." Carefully he lifted Mr. Shakespeare's right arm and gently probed the lower limb with his fingertips. Even in his unconscious state, Mr. Shakespeare cried out. "It's badly swollen," said Mr. Armin, "and I think I can feel the bone shifting. I'd say it's broken, but I can't be sure. My specialty is sword wounds. See what you think."

"Me?" I said. "Can we not find a surgeon?"

"We haven't time. You were apprenticed to a physician, Widge. Surely you must have seen him deal with broken bones."

"Seeing is one thing," I said. "Doing is another." Mr. Armin did not reply, only gazed at me expectantly. Sighing, I put my fingers very tentatively on the arm, then jerked back as Mr. Shakespeare groaned. But even that brief touch had confirmed the fracture. "Aye, it's a bad break. It'll need a splint."

"Do it quickly, then. I'd just as soon not have to face the mayor's men again, even with a sharp sword."

"But I don't—" I started to say, to no avail. He had already gone back to his task. "I don't ken what I'm doing," I muttered, and then, because there was no one else to do it, I went about setting the arm as best I might, using soft cloth for padding and two stage daggers from the property trunk for splints, binding them in place with a scarlet sash from the costume chest. Then, with Jack's reluctant help, I hoisted Mr. Shakespeare, still unconscious, and laid him out atop the supplies in one of the carewares.

The company rolled out of the inn yard just as the church bells rang nones. Mr. Armin guided his fine black mare up alongside me. "Climb on," he said. "You've earned a ride."

Gratefully, I grabbed hold of his saddle and swung up behind him. "That splint will do for now," I said. "Perhaps there'll be a surgeon in the next place we stop, who can do the job right."

"Perhaps. But you know, no matter how well it's fixed, Will's going to be unhappy with it."

"Why? 'A'll still be able to act, will 'a not?"

"No doubt. But I expect he'll have some difficulty writing."

"Oh. I hadn't thought of that. 'A's working on a new play, then?"

Mr. Armin nodded. "He's trying. I don't think it's going very well."

I wasn't surprised, considering how hectic the past several weeks had been for us. "But . . . when could 'a possibly find time the time to write?"

Mr. Armin laughed a little, as though he found my question naive. "When the rest of us are abed."

We did not attempt to account for many miles that day, for we were all of us spent, and most were sore and aching from the afternoon's skirmish. We put up at a small inn on the outskirts of Hungerford. Mr. Armin rode into the town to search for a surgeon, but without success. The best we could do for poor Mr. Shakespeare was to fortify him against the pain with brandy and put him to bed.

Over supper the rest of the sharers discussed what our next move should be. Back at the Globe, the prentices and hired men ordinarily would not have been privy to such matters, but here on the road the distance between owners and mere players seemed to have narrowed. There was an unexpressed sense of shared destiny, a feeling that we were all cooking at the same fire—or perhaps over it.

"Obviously," said Mr. Heminges, "we c-cannot go on this way. If we are n-not to be allowed t-to perform, we m-might as well have stayed in London."

Mr. Phillips tapped the side of his ale mug thoughtfully with his fingers. "I believe the problem may be that we're still too near to London. The towns here are the very ones that, during the last outbreak of the plague, were deluged with folk fleeing the city. They have not forgotten, and they're wary of travelers. I think we'll find that, farther north, or west or east, for that matter, we'll be more welcome."

"I agree," said Mr. Armin. "Northern towns especially, such as Sheffield and York, do not have dozens of theatre troupes passing through, as the towns here do. They'll be starved for a show. Isn't that so, Widge?"

So seldom did anyone ask my opinion of anything, it took me a moment to come up with a reply. "Aye," I said, feeling myself go red from all the sharers' eyes upon me. It was like being thrust upon a stage but without being told what to say. "Those few times when a company came to Berwick or even York, it was like a holiday. Shops closed, prentices were given the day off." I scratched my head and shrugged wryly. "At least *most* prentices were."

The company laughed—except, of course, for Sal Pavy.

The matter was put to a vote. To my surprise, the opinion of us prentices counted as one vote, as did that of the three hired men. With the exception of Ned Shakespeare, who felt we would find the pickings even leaner the farther we got from London, and Jack, who was generally opposed to everything, we all voted to proceed directly to the northern shires.

"I feel certain that M-Mr. Shakespeare will v-vote the same way," said Mr. Heminges.

"He may vote as he will," said Mr. Armin, "for the will of the company outweighs the will of Will, will he or nil he."

"And the weal of the company," added Mr. Phillips, "outweighs the weal of Will as well."

Mr. Armin rose from the table and picked up one of the candles. "Well, we'll see if all's well with Will. Widge?"

As we went upstairs to the room he and Mr. Shakespeare shared, I said, "I've been trying to think of a way to keep Mr. Shakespeare's bones in place while they heal, wi'out using such a bulky bandage. 'A needs something 'a can wear beneath his costume."

"And have you come up with something?"

"I believe I have." I hesitated, unsure whether my idea would sound clever or crack-brained. "You . . . you ken how we make fake limbs wi' gauze and plaster of Paris?"

Mr. Armin nodded.

"Well, why could we not do the same wi' a real limb?"

Mr. Armin stopped on the stairs, looking thoughtful. "I don't think that's a good idea."

My heart sank into my hose. "You don't?"

His face broke into a smile. "I think it's a brilliant one. Go get what you need from the wagons."

When I removed the splint, I found Mr. Shakespeare's arm still badly swollen. I wrapped a layer of plain gauze around it as tightly as I might, though it made him squirm with pain even as he slept his drugged sleep. Over that we wound layer upon layer of gauze laden with wet plaster, to a thickness of half an inch or so. "Do you suppose that will suffice?" I asked.

"Surely. You don't want to make it so heavy he can't lift it."

We bound the plastered arm to Mr. Shakespeare's chest so he could not move it until it dried. Then I sat back and heaved a long sigh of weariness and relief. "I hope it works."

"It will." Mr. Armin accompanied me into the hall. "I expect you're looking forward to making a triumphant return to Yorkshire."

"Triumphant?" I said.

"Well, you're a member of—if I may say so—the most renowned theatre company in the kingdom. Surely that will impress all your old friends and your kin."

I shrugged. "I've no kin there that I'm aware of—and no friends, either, save Mistress MacGregor at the orphanage, who gave me a name."

"She had no notion who your parents might be?"

"Not a hint. She once said me mother died in the poorhouse, giving birth to me, and that's th' extent of it."

"It must be a sad thing, always having to wonder."

"Not sad so much as frustrating. I mean . . ." I hesitated. I had never spoken of this to anyone before, not even Sander. But I was weary, and my guard was down. "I mean, wi'out any sense of who they were I've only half a sense of who *I* am. It's not just that I don't ken me proper name. It's that I don't ken what . . . what I'm made of, you might say."

Mr. Armin nodded. "Well, I've always thought that what you're made of is not as important as what you do with it."

"Aye," I said halfheartedly. "I suppose that's so." I knew he meant well, but I did not think he truly understood.

As I turned to go, he patted my shoulder in a way that put me in mind of Sander. With a sharpness and a suddenness that startled me, I found myself wishing that Sander were here. The days since we left London had been so exhausting and eventful, I had scarcely given a thought to him or to the rest of Mr. Pope's household.

Recalling Tetty's picture, I fished it from my wallet, unfolded it carefully, and gazed at it for a long while. Then, even though I was even more exhausted than usual, thanks to the nerve-racking business of binding the broken arm, I shuffled past the room where the prentices and hired men were sleeping and on down the stairs. I borrowed pen and paper from the innkeeper's wife and managed to put down nearly a page to my friend about the company's fortunes before Morpheus made my nodding head droop onto the paper. Not wishing Sander to fret, I did not write how sorely I missed him.

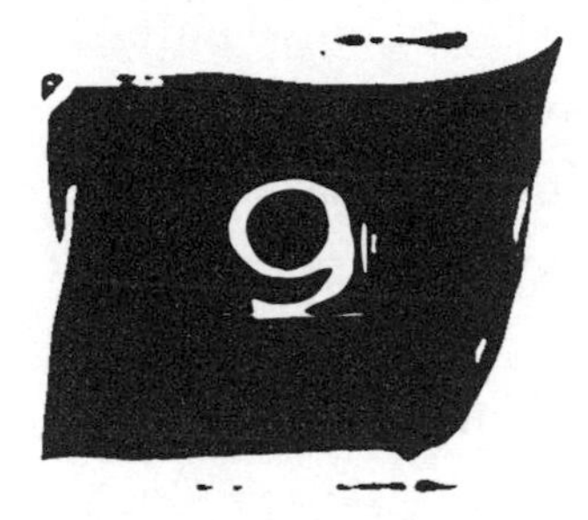

By the time we set out from Hungerford the next morning, Mr. Shakespeare was strong enough to ride, though he had to have a bit of help in mounting. The effects of the alcohol he had consumed the night before seemed to bother him as much as the arm did. Though he pronounced my plaster bandage satisfactory, I was not satisfied, for I could see how hard his swollen flesh pressed against it, and I knew it must be painful. He dismissed my concern. "The swelling will go down in a day or two," he said.

But that evening, when Mr. Shakespeare summoned me to his room at the King's Head in Wantage, I found the arm as swollen as ever. Mr. Shakespeare was clearly suffering; he had a glass of brandy at hand to ease the pain. "Perhaps I did something wrong," I said anxiously. "Perhaps I should cut the bandage off again."

"No," Mr. Shakespeare insisted. "But there is something you might do for me."

"Name it," I said, assuming he meant for me to fetch him more brandy or the like.

"Have you ever taken dictation?"

"Dictation? You mean, writing down the spoken word?"

"Exactly."

"Well . . . aye. Dr. Bright often asked me . . ." I paused. Now that I had a clearer sense of right and wrong, it embarrassed me to admit my past transgressions. " 'A was a clergyman as well as a doctor, you ken, and 'a had me visit neighboring churches and copy down the sermons of other rectors."

Mr. Shakespeare seemed more amused than disapproving. "Steal them, in other words?"

"Aye."

"And then Simon Bass had you steal my play." He shook his head. "You've had ill luck in masters."

"Until now," I said.

"Well put. What I'm asking is not dishonest, but it may be difficult. I have promised the Queen I would write a new comedy for her, to be performed upon our return to London. Her Majesty finds that such fare as *Hamlet* and *Caesar* puts her in a melancholy humor. She prefers something more . . . lightweight." The pained expression Mr. Shakespeare now wore was, I fancied, due to more than just the swollen arm.

"So," he went on, "it is my duty as a loyal subject to

concoct something her appetite finds more digestible—a trifle, as it were, and not the more substantial fare I am inclined to prepare." He gestured impatiently at his plaster-bound right arm with his left one. "And, since I cannot possibly put pen to paper for myself, I must have someone do it for me, or else fail in my duty to my Queen. If you think you're up to the task, I am prepared to give you an extra shilling a week . . . presuming I have it to give—which, in view of our singular lack of success so far, may be in doubt. So, what do you say? Will you do it?"

The offer came so unexpectedly that I found my tongue temporarily tied. "I . . . I . . ."

"Good," said Mr. Shakespeare, apparently mistaking an "I" for an "aye." He picked up a leather-bound portfolio and opened it upon the small folding desk he had brought along. The portfolio was cleverly and compactly designed, with a pocket for writing paper, one for blotting paper, a pouch that held goose quill pens and a pen knife, even a strap that secured a bottle of ink. "You sit at the desk," he said. "I'll take the bed."

Feeling awkward and uncertain, I seated myself upon the trunk that contained the company's play books and handbills and pulled up my sleeves. "Um . . . an I'm to write swiftly, a plumbago pencil would be preferable to a quill pen."

"I don't have one."

"No matter. I do." I retrieved it from my wallet and tore

off some of the paper wrapping to expose a half inch or so of the graphite core. I glanced at the pages he had written out already. From copying out the actors' sides, I was used to reading Mr. Shakespeare's undisciplined scrawl; nevertheless, I found it hard to decipher these words. A good half of them had been crossed out. In addition, there were black blotches everywhere, as though an ink plague had struck the paper.

"They tell me," said Mr. Shakespeare, "there's a rumor about London to the effect that I never blot out a line. Obviously it isn't so." He sighed and added ruefully, "Would that it were."

One thing I could make out with ease was the title, for it was printed neatly in uppercase letters: LOVE'S LABOUR'S WON. I assumed it was to be a sequel to *Love's Labour's Lost* until I saw that, although it was set in France like that other play, the names of the characters were totally unfamiliar.

"Read to me what I wrote last, if you will."

"I'll try. 'I have seen a medicine that's able to breathe life into a scone—' "

"That's *stone.*"

"Ah. Sorry. 'Quicken a rock and make you dance . . . canary? . . . with sprightly fire and motion; whose simple torch—*touch*—is powerful to raise King Pepin, nay, to give great Charlemagne a pen in 's hand, and write to her a love-line.' " I looked up from the page. "It's a play about medicine?"

"No, no," said Mr. Shakespeare. "Only in part. The heroine's father was a physician, and she uses one of his nostrums to cure the king."

"Of what?"

"A fistula."

"Oh," I said. "But . . . I don't think a fistula may be cured wi' medicines. It needs to be cut away."

Mr. Shakespeare gave me a look that implied he'd just as soon I kept my opinions to myself. "This is a play, Widge, not a medical treatise."

"Sorry."

"Stop saying that. Let's proceed. 'And write to her a love-line.' 'And write to her a love-line.' " He squeezed his eyelids shut and pressed his fingers to his forehead as if trying to force the words from his brain. "All right. *King:* 'What *her* is this?' Ahh, too many syllables, I'll wager." He ticked the syllables off on his fingers. " 'And *write* to *her* a love-line. What *her* is *this*?' The meter limps a bit, but it'll have to do. You have that?"

"Aye."

"All right. *Lafeu:* 'Why, Doctor She. My lord, there's one arrived, if you will see her, by my faith I trow—' No, no. 'By my faith and honor' is better, though it doesn't scan. 'By my faith and honor, if seriously I may convey my thoughts, hath in her wisdom and her constancy amazed me.' Do you have that?"

"Aye, every word."

"Let me see."

I held up the paper and he peered at what I had written, which was

"Ah," he said. "You've used your . . . what is it called?"

"Charactery."

He handed the paper back to me with a quizzical smile on his face, altered by a wince of pain. "How will I ever know whether or not you've gotten it right?"

"Well, sir, I suppose you'll just have to trust me." The moment I said these words, I regretted them. After all, what cause did he have to put his trust in someone who had a history of stealing sermons and play scripts?

I feared he would say as much, but all he said was, "Yes, I suppose so. Anyway, you'll copy it all out in normal script later, I trust?"

"Aye."

He lay back on the bed with a slight groan, and continued. "Still *Lafeu:* 'Will you see her, sire, and know her business?' *King:* 'Bring her on, Lafeu.' Oh, God. That sounds as though she's a platter of meat. 'Bring her *hence,* Lafeu, that we may . . . that we may . . .' That we may *what*? That we may admire? That we may wonder? Damn!" He struck the bed a blow of frustration with his good arm, which jostled his injured limb; he at once cried out and pressed it to his chest. "That was stupid," he muttered brokenly.

"Can I get you something?"

"No, no . . . unless it's a new brain, one that works."

"It sounded well enough to me," I ventured.

"Yes, well, what do you know?" he snapped. Then he sighed, took a dose of brandy, and went on more kindly, "Go on to bed, Widge. I'm not accustomed to writing scripts in this second hand fashion, that's all. It'll go better next time."

"Aye, sir." I rose and closed up the portfolio. "Shall I blow out the candle, then?"

"What? No, leave it. I'll be awake for some time yet."

As I slipped from the room, I said softly, "Good night, sir." He made no reply. From the way he was staring at the candle flame, I judged that his thoughts were elsewhere—in France, perhaps . . . or in despair.

The room where the hired men and prentices slept was stifling. I longed to open the window and let in a bit of breeze, but I knew that I would be chastised if I did, for the others were, to a man, convinced that the night air was filled with ill humors. Jack was snoring with a sound like a dying pig, and I gave him a shove with my foot. He snorted, turned over on his side, and started in snoring once more, though at a more bearable level.

With a sigh, I sank down upon my wool mattress. Just as I was drifting off, I heard Sam whisper, close to my ear, "I've got it figured out!"

"What?" I murmured.

"I said, I've figured it out!"

"Figured *what* out?" I asked crossly.

"Why Sourpuss Pavy sleeps in the stable and uses it for a tiring-room."

"Oh. Well, are you going to tell me, so I can go to sleep?"

"I think it's because . . ." He put his mouth even nearer to my ear. "*He's* a *she*!"

I gave out with something that was half a gasp, half a burst of laughter, and muffled it with my hands. "You're daft!"

"No, no, think about it! We never suspected Julia was a girl, did we? But looking back on it, it was easy to recall things she did, things she said that if we'd added them up would have given her away. Well, this time I'm adding them up in advance. One: He doesn't sleep in the same room with us. Two: He doesn't change in the same room with us. Three: He's weak as water; he couldn't even lift one end of the arms trunk. Where am I? Four? Four: When he relieves himself, he always goes far back into the woods, out of everyone's sight. Five: He didn't take part in the scuffle yesterday afternoon, you notice."

"Nor did you," I pointed out. "As for how 'a relieves himself, I go out of sight meself. I like a bit of privacy."

"All right," Sam said defensively, "explain the stable business, then."

"I don't ken. Perhaps 'a's one of those wights who talks wi' horses. Ask him, why don't you, and let me sleep."

There was silence for a time, then Sam muttered, "I don't care what you say; I think Sal is a Sally." A moment later, he added, "Ow! You've no call to hit me!"

Sam was like a small dog who, once he has his teeth into something, will not let go no matter what. At least twice a day over the next week or so, he came up with some bit of "evidence" that supposedly added weight to his Sally Pavy theory. Most were pure foolishness, ranging from the fact that Sal Pavy scrubbed his teeth with salt rather than just a rag dipped in wine like everyone else, to the way he often sat with his legs crossed.

Though I scoffed at Sam's fancies to his face, I could not help regarding Sal Pavy in a new light, weighing his words and actions as an actor does those of his character, looking for the meaning that lies behind them. There was no denying that his manner was rather effeminate at times, but that was hardly surprising, considering he was given daily lessons in how to accurately impersonate a girl. I myself had grown so used to wearing a dress that occasionally I found myself reaching down to lift a hem that wasn't there. Besides, passing oneself off as another gender upon the stage was quite a different matter from keeping the pretense up all day, every day.

On the other hand, Sal Pavy had proven himself a master of deception. Whenever one of the sharers was about, he was the very picture of a willing, eager worker. But when we prentices were alone with any sort of task, from washing the muddy carewares to grooming the horses to airing out the mattresses, he always contrived to avoid actually contributing anything.

"At Blackfriars," he said, "we were taught how to act, not how to clean things."

"Yes," said Sam, with a meaningful glance at the sword Sal Pavy was supposed to be polishing. "I can see that. You know, Widge, when we return I believe we'd be wise to apply for a position at Blackfriars. It sounds as though it bears a striking resemblance to the land of Cockaigne." Cockaigne was, I had learned, a familiar fancy among Londoners—a mythical land of idleness and luxury.

I made no reply. Though I knew well enough that he was jesting, I found nothing amusing or appealing in the notion of leaving the Chamberlain's Men.

To Sal Pavy's credit, when it came to studying for his roles, he applied himself more assiduously than any of us. I thought myself an early riser, yet often I emerged from our room at some inn soon after sunrise to find Sal Pavy pacing about the courtyard, reciting his lines under his breath and practicing over and over the appropriate gestures to go with them.

He also worked harder than most at keeping himself and his attire clean and tidy. He bathed whenever the opportunity presented itself—in private, of course—paying from his own purse the two or three pence innkeepers customarily charged for such services. Naturally, Sam pointed to these habits as further indicators of a female nature.

We were working our way northward, now, traveling as quickly as we might and stopping at the smallest and shabbiest inns to conserve our dwindling funds. Lodging of any sort grew increasingly scarce and one night, finding ourselves between towns when darkness fell, we stopped alongside the road and spread our mattresses out upon canvas sheets beneath the carewares.

Though I welcomed the chance to sleep in the open air,

some of the other players griped about it, most notably Ned Shakespeare. I had noticed that he was not chary with his complaints at any time. The meals we ate were never to his taste; he grumbled over the fact that, though he was the famous playwright's brother, he must make the journey on foot; when the sun shone, he railed against the heat; when it rained, as it did almost daily, he cursed the damp.

It was a pity we were not farmers. Had we been, we could have put to use all the earth we turned up with the wheels of our carewares. And had we been growing crops, we might have welcomed the rain that made the roads into a morass of mud. Our definition of a good day became a day when the carewares bogged down no more than half a dozen times.

Sometimes the sharers could drag the wagons free by tying extra ropes to them and adding the pulling power of their mounts to that of the draft horses. Other times we prentices and hired men had to play the part of so many Atlases, taking onto our shoulders not the weight of the whole world but that of the wagons, which sometimes seemed nearly as great.

After one such dismal day we stopped at an inn outside Grantham, and several of the company paid for the privilege of a bath. Sam and I contented ourselves with scrubbing our clothing and shoes in the horse trough. When Sal Pavy crossed the courtyard from the stable to take his turn in the bathhouse, Sam sidled up next to me and announced gleefully, "I've a plan that will reveal the truth once and for all."

"The truth?" I echoed. "About what?"

"About whether it's Sal or Sally, you dunce."

"Sam," I said with a sigh, "must you always be harping on that same string?"

"Ah, Widge, you know you're consumed with curiosity about it."

"Nay, I'm not—truly."

He nudged me with his elbow. "Come, come, tell the truth and shame the devil. You admit, surely, that there's something suspicious about the boy—if he is, indeed, a boy."

"Well, aye, perhaps a bit, but—"

"Right. So let us find out what it is." So saying, he seized my shirtsleeve with one sopping hand and pulled me across the inn yard.

"Where are you taking me?" I demanded.

"Whist! Just over here." He led me to an alcove next to the bathhouse, where firewood was stacked. In the growing dusk, I could see a narrow shaft of light issuing from between the boards of the bathhouse and laying a yellow ribbon across the rough bark of the logs. "I discovered this earlier, when Mr. Phillips sent me to fetch firewood," Sam whispered. He knelt atop the woodpile and pressed his face to the crack in the wall.

"Stop it, you sot!" I said, and tugged at the back of his shirt, though not all that insistently, I admit. Some part of me, a part I did not much care to acknowledge, wanted to know if there was anything to Sam's theory.

Sam whispered from the side of his mouth, without taking his eye from the crack, "I can see him! He's starting to strip down! There goes the doublet . . . the breeches . . . the shirt . . . the hose . . ." There was a pause, then Sam exclaimed softly, "Gog's nowns!" and, without warning, jerked back away from the crack, nearly breaking my jaw with his pate, for I had leaned up close behind so as to hear him.

I could not see his face well in the fading light, but enough to read astonishment upon it. "What is it?" I demanded, still holding my jaw.

Sam slowly shook his head. "See for yourself," he said, and yielded his place to me.

Hesitantly, feeling uncomfortably like the fellow who peeped at Lady Godiva and was struck blind for it, I put my eye to the crack. The room was lighted by a candle I could not see; probably it was on the wall against which I leaned. In the center of the room was a wooden tub, like a half barrel, and Sal Pavy, naked as a nail, was just stepping into it.

His profile was to me, and I could see well enough that his appendages were appropriate to a boy. I was about to turn to Sam and say, "Did I not tell you so?" but then Sal Pavy shifted position, so that his back was to me, and I saw what had startled Sam so. A series of long, livid scars or welts descended his back like a ladder, continued across his buttocks, and down the backs of his thighs—the sort of marks left by a caning.

I knew the pattern well, for my own frame had been similarly decorated often enough by Dr. Bright's walking stick, when I had spilled some valuable medicine or was caught filching from the pantry. But my welts had always faded after a few days. I doubted that Sal had come by his so recently. For one thing, I could not imagine anyone in our company giving such a caning to a prentice. For another, these tracks did not look fresh. They looked, rather, like a permanent record of punishments long past.

I could only speculate about how severe the beatings must have been to have blistered the skin in such a manner, and how painful. Feeling suddenly queasy, I stepped back from the peephole and nearly lost my balance.

"Did you see it?" Sam asked in a soft, subdued voice.

"Aye," I replied. "And I would I had not."

"Who do you suppose might have given him such a smoking?"

I shook my head, unable to imagine. "You'll ha' to ask him that," I said, knowing that even Sam, with his rash tongue, would find that difficult to do.

I was still feeling shaken when I went up to Mr. Shakespeare's room. I found him at the folding desk, fighting valiantly to control his quill with his left hand, and losing. His hand, his sleeve, and his paper were all spotted and smeared with ink, and the words he had managed to set down were even more illegible than his normal script, a thing I would not have believed possible.

He laid the pen down and glanced up at me with an expression that put me in mind of the way Mr. Pope's boys looked when they were caught at some mischief. "Now I understand why the left hand is called sinister. It has a twisted will of its own and cannot be made to obey." He rose and gestured for me to take his place, then set about awkwardly trying to clean the ink from his hands using a rag soaked with brandy.

"When I was a schoolboy in Stratford," he said absently,

"I had a classmate—Laurence, his name was—who was left-handed. The schoolmaster believed this was contrary to nature and insisted that, for the purposes of penmanship at least, the boy must use his right hand. Laurence worked diligently at it, but was totally inept. The master, convinced that the boy was just being stubborn, tried to beat him into compliance."

I winced, thinking of the stripes on Sal Pavy's back. "Did 'a succeed?"

"He succeeded only in making an enemy of Laurence. When we grew bigger, one day Laurence wrested the rod from the master's hand and gave him a drubbing in return, using his right hand—just to show that he could, I suppose." Mr. Shakespeare sank onto the edge of the bed and cradled his bandaged arm. "Well. You see what I'm doing, don't you?"

"Easing your bad arm?"

He smiled wryly. "Yes, but I'm also delaying, trying to avoid setting to work."

"We need not, an you're in pain."

"The arm is not to blame. The swelling has gone down considerably, as you see." He held out the arm for my inspection. The flesh around the plaster bandage was no longer red and puffy, but nearly normal in appearance.

I smiled with relief. "I was afeared I'd done it wrong, and it wouldn't heal."

"No, you did as well as any surgeon, and I'm grateful."

"What does pain you, then?"

He frowned and lay back on the bed. "This play," he said.

I did not know how to respond. I had supposed that composing plays was an effortless task for a man of Mr. Shakespeare's gifts. But he was behaving as though it were something to be dreaded, as though it required a degree of fortitude or courage he was not sure he possessed. "Shall I . . . shall I read what I transcribed last night?"

"Yes, yes, read it all. God knows there's little enough of it."

It was true. I'd put down but half a dozen speeches the previous night, before Mr. Shakespeare grew frustrated and sent me away. The play's progress, in fact, closely resembled that of the tour as a whole—agonizingly slow, with much bogging down.

We were in the midst of what was meant to be a comic scene between the Countess and the Clown. Though Mr. Shakespeare's mood was anything but comical, he went on struggling with the scene, as his classmate must have struggled to write a satisfactory Italian-style script using the wrong hand. But Mr. Shakespeare had no master standing over him with a hickory rod. The only one driving him was himself.

He pressed his hand to his forehead in that fashion I had seen so often. "The Clown says . . . The Clown says . . . Ah! The Clown says, 'I have an answer that will fit all questions.' "

As I wrote down the line, I laughed. "An answer to fit all questions? It must be an answer of monstrous size."

"That's good!" said Mr. Shakespeare. "Write that down as well, for the Countess's line."

"Truly?" I said.

"Why not? I'm not above stealing a line when it suits."

I wrote down what I had said, happy to have been of some help, however small. "What is this answer to fit all questions, then?"

"Oh, Lord," groaned Mr. Shakespeare. "I've no idea." Then he paused and, to my surprise, smiled. "Wait. Perhaps that's it."

"What's it?"

" 'Oh, Lord.' That can be made to answer anything, depending on how you say it, can it not? Let's try it. Pose me a question."

"Pardon?"

"Pose me a question—any question."

Flustered, I asked the first thing that entered my mind. "How fares your arm, sir?"

"Oh, Lord, sir," he replied in a tone that implied it was in dreadful shape. "That works. Ask me another."

"Umm . . . ah . . . how goes the play you're composing?"

He rolled his eyes and replied in a tone of great dismay, "Oh, Lord, sir!" We both laughed at how apt the answer truly was. "Come, another," said Mr. Shakespeare. Suddenly the melancholy mood that had hung over us seemed to have lifted.

I thought of an old jest that could not well be answered with a yes or no. "Tell me, sir, do you still beat your wife?"

"Oh, Lord, sir!" This time the reply was laced with indignation. "Ha! You see, it works! Write it down! Rob will know how to make the most of it." He meant, of course,

Mr. Armin, who customarily played the broad comic parts.

Now that Mr. Shakespeare was in better spirits, he went on to dictate another scene and another, at such breakneck speed that I was hard-pressed to get it all down. It was an astounding feat, really. One might have thought the words were already fully formed in his head, and he was merely reading them off.

Though he was galloping along like a man on a fresh horse, I was fading fast. My eyelids drooped; my lines of charactery symbols, normally straight as a privy path, began to wander. I glanced at the watch that lay on the desk. It was past midnight.

Mr. Shakespeare seemed to notice neither the lateness of the hour nor my nodding head, so caught up in his creation was he. I pinched my leg mercilessly, to jar myself into wakefulness. Now that he was racing along at last, it would not be fair of me to bring him up short by pleading exhaustion. I kept up as best I could until, finally, he began to stumble and came to a halt.

"End of Act Two," he said with satisfaction. "A fair night's work."

"Fair?" I said, and yawned widely. "I doubt whether I could survive a *good* night's work, then." I looked about at the papers I had strewn this way and that in my haste.

"Go on to bed," said Mr. Shakespeare. "I'll clean up here. Did I work you too hard?"

"Oh, Lord, sir," I said, and we shared a final, fatigued laugh.

When I stretched out on my mattress in our sleeping room, Sam stirred and murmured, "How did it go?"

"Like the wheel of Fortune," I said. "Now up, now down."

"I don't see why he agonizes so over it. After all, it's only a play."

For a change, the room was not filled with Jack's snoring. "What's happened to Jack?" I whispered to Sam.

Jack's grumpy voice replied from the darkness, "You're keeping me awake with all your gabbling, that's what."

"Sorry."

After a moment, I heard Jack's voice again. "I know what you're up to," he said.

"How do you mean?" I asked.

"With all your extra work. You're trying to get in good with the sharers, so they'll keep you on."

I made no reply to this. In fact I said nothing until I heard him begin to snore. Then I poked Sam.

"What?"

"Jack says I'm trying to get in good wi' the sharers so they'll keep me on. Do you suppose there's some chance they *won't*?"

"Why wouldn't they?"

"Well, we're making no money at all. An this keeps up, perhaps they'll ha' to let some of us go."

"Who would they have to play girls' parts, then?"

"Sal Pavy, for one."

"Ahh, you're far better than he is."

"How do you ken?" I said. "You've not seen him perform yet."

"Ha! I see him perform every day for the sharers, in the role of the Good Prentice."

"Aye, and they seem to find him very convincing."

"Then perhaps it's our duty to enlighten them."

"Nay, it's not," I said. "Whatever his faults he's one of us."

Sam laughed ironically. "Just don't try to tell *him* that."

Sal Pavy soon had the chance to show the rest of the company how capable an actor he was. To our great relief, we were welcomed by the mayor of Newark. He did question us closely, though, to be sure none of the company had any symptoms of the plague. Though the contagion had not yet reached his town, rumors of it had.

In London, when we were to perform for the Queen, we first had to present our play to her Master of Revels. Here, though our audience would be nothing like royalty, we were expected to play first for the mayor and his aldermen, who would then pass judgment on whether or not we were fit for public consumption.

Since we had failed in our attempt to perform *Love's Labour's Lost* in Newbury, the sharers determined to do it now, assuming that a provincial audience would prefer comedy to tragedy. Perhaps, I thought, recalling what

Mr. Shakespeare had said about the Queen's taste, they were not so different from royalty after all.

We were all of us a bit rusty from not having exercised our skills for so long, but once the play was under way we performed smoothly enough. Sal Pavy's early-morning practices served him well; so did his naturally haughty manner. It was difficult for me to watch him play the Princess of France or to act alongside him. In truth, I suppose I was resentful, for always before, Sander had been the one to play the Princess. But even I had to admit that Sal Pavy brought to the role an uncommon dignity and grace.

After the performance, he had praise heaped upon him by the sharers. Sam and I, not wishing to seem poor sports, said a few complimentary and wholly unconvincing words. The mayor and his friends were enthusiastic, too, and a public performance was set for the following afternoon. Again, we prentices were given a sheaf of handbills to scatter through the town.

We split up, to make the task go more quickly. As I was returning to our inn, I spotted a troupe of a dozen or so men, some on horseback and some afoot, approaching on the highway. When they drew nearer, I noticed that they wore brown cloaks and orange caps—the livery of Lord Pembroke's Men.

I had seen Pembroke's company perform at the Swan, but not often enough so I could recognize the individual players, particularly without their makeup. One of their number—a stout fellow of perhaps twenty, with a ruddy complexion and a generous belly—did look somehow familiar at first, but as he drew nearer I saw that he wore a leather patch over his right eye. I didn't recall ever encountering anyone with such a distinctive feature.

I hurried to the inn, ran upstairs, and burst into Mr. Armin's room. He looked up in surprise from a sheet of paper he had filled with his neat, elegant script. "Remind me to add to your other instruction a class in courtesy," he said.

"I'm sorry," I said breathlessly, "but I thought you'd want to ken."

"Ken what?"

"The Earl of Pembroke's Men are coming."

He set paper and pen aside and rose. "Are you certain?"

"I recognized their livery—brown cloaks, orange caps."

"Shrew them! They've had the same idea we did, it seems. I didn't foresee having to compete with another London company."

"But we're here first. They'll have to be content wi' the leavings, will they not?"

Mr. Armin played idly with the handle of the dagger he always wore at his belt. "Perhaps," he said thoughtfully. Then he looked up and smiled slightly at me. "Thanks for the warning, at any rate. Next time knock, though."

"Aye. I will." I glanced at the sheet of paper. "Are you writing a letter home?"

"That? No, no. It's a—" He paused, as though unsure whether or not to go on. "Just between us, it's a play."

"Truly? I didn't ken you were a playwright."

"I'm not much of a one. Not of the same rank as Will,

certainly. I'm revising an old work of mine called *Fool Upon Fool, or A Nest of Ninnies*. I thought something mindless might appeal more to these Yorkshire wights. No offense. I'm Yorkshire born and bred meself, as you ken," he said, lapsing into the speech of the region. "I can't say I'm thrilled to be back. What about you?"

I shrugged. "It's nothing to me one way or the other. If there's time, though, I'd like to visit th' orphanage in York where I spent me early years."

"We'll make time," said Mr. Armin. "For now, let's go and see what Pembroke's Men are up to."

But it seemed that our rivals had not taken rooms at our inn, for we saw no sign of them, nor had the other members of the company. "P-perhaps they've no money for b-bed and b-board," said Mr. Heminges with concern in his voice.

"They did appear somewhat shabby," I said. "They had no carewares and no trunks, only packs slung over their saddles."

"My guess," said Will Sly, "is that they've been forced to sell or to pawn some of their gear. They may have to change their name to Pem's Broke Men."

"We ought to keep an eye on our own equipment, then," put in Jack.

"Oh, I hardly think they'd stoop t-to stealing," said Mr. Heminges. "They're a reputable c-company, after all."

"Well, if they do," said Sam, "Sally will surely stop 'em." This brought a laugh from some of the others and a kick under the table from me.

If we could have seen a few hours into the future, no one would have found Sam's jest the least amusing. Sometime after midnight, the door to our sleeping room burst open and a voice shocked us from our sleep with a single word: "Fire!"

I sat upright, rubbing at my eyes. Mr. Armin was stalking about among us, shaking the sleepers roughly. "Get up! The wagons are afire! Come! There's no time to dress!" He flung open the door that led to the gallery and ran outside. The hired men and prentices staggered after him, half asleep still, barefoot and clad only in our nightshirts.

We had brought the carewares into the inn yard and pulled them alongside the stable, assuming they would be safe there. We were wrong. The fronts of both wagon boxes were ablaze, and the flames were climbing the sides, threatening to set the canvas tops alight. In their flickering light, I spotted Sal Pavy shuffling across the inn yard, straining at the weight of a leather water bucket whose contents spilled onto the cobbles and onto the hem of his nightshirt.

Stunned, I stood clutching the railing of the gallery for a moment. "Gog's blood!" I heard Jack cry as he rushed past me. "Pembroke's Men are trying to burn us out!" Then Will Sly yanked at my nightshirt, setting me in motion. As I scrambled down the stairs, a splinter jammed into one bare foot, but I ran on.

Sal Pavy tossed what little remained of his bucket of water ineffectually at the burning wagon. Mr. Armin took the bucket from him and handed it to Jack. "Fill it at the horse trough! The rest of you, take hold of the wagon tongues! We've got to get them away from the stable! Widge! See if you can pull those canvas tops off!"

While the men hauled at one careware, trying to get it rolling, I clambered aboard the other and, clinging to the high wooden side, began fumbling with the loops of rope that held the canvas in place. "All together—heave!" shouted Mr. Armin, and their wagon lurched into mine, nearly dislodging me. My bare foot struck someone on the pate. I glanced down to see that it was Mr. Shakespeare, straining with his good arm at the spokes of one of the wheels.

I pulled the last of the ropes free, flung the canvas aside, out of the reach of the flames, and sprang for the other careware. I was too late. The canvas top on it was already burning. I believe we would have lost our battle with the flames had we not at that moment received reinforcements in the form of the innkeeper and his ostler. With their help, our men got the careware moving and pushed it across the cobbles to the horse trough.

While Jack and Sam and I doused the fire with bucket after bucket of water—Sal Pavy seemed to have disappeared—the rest of the men returned for the other careware. Within minutes, both fires were out. The players dragged our costume and property trunks from the wagon beds. Even in the pale light from the innkeeper's lantern, I could see that the wood was badly charred and, of course, soaked with water.

We carried the trunks into the stable and inspected their

contents. The armor and weapons and other properties were mostly undamaged, but the top layer of clothing was scorched, and all of it was wet. We spread the garments on the hay in the loft to dry and, leaving Jack and Will Sly to guard them, retired to our beds, grateful that our bedding, at least, had not been in the wagons.

We found Ned Shakespeare still in the room and still sound asleep. "The devil take him!" muttered Sam. "He's slept through the whole thing!"

"Mr. Shakespeare will be furious. Perhaps we'd best not tell him. 'A may not have noticed." But as I said this, I caught a movement in the corner of my eye and turned to see Mr. Shakespeare standing in the doorway. He clearly saw his brother's sleeping form, but he said nothing, only shook his head as though he had expected nothing more, and turned away.

After we washed up, I got Sam to draw the splinter—or at least most of it—from my foot. "How do you suppose the fire began?" he asked me.

"Mr. Armin said it looked as though someone had dropped burning bundles of straw into the front of the wagon beds."

"Who would do such a thing, and why?"

"Someone who dislikes players, I'd say. A fanatical Puritan, perhaps."

"Or maybe Jack was right. Maybe it was Pembroke's Men, trying to get rid of the competition."

After the night's exertions, we were all—with the exception of Ned and Sal Pavy—cross and tired the next day. Mr.

Phillips and Jack had suffered superficial burns. To my surprise, they came to me—grudgingly, in Jack's case—for medical advice. The best I could do for them was to smear on a salve of tallow mixed with comfrey, but it seemed to give them some relief.

Despite everything, we managed a passable performance that afternoon and took in a respectable box—most of which we promptly laid out again to have the damaged costumes repaired. The town councillors profited as much as we did, or more, for they had men passing through the crowd hawking bottles of ale.

As we stood behind the curtain waiting to go on, Sal Pavy, in his guise as the Princess, surveyed my dress, which was less elegant than the one I usually wore when playing Rosaline. "Why are you wearing *that*?" he asked distastefully.

"Because me better one has half the skirt burned away." This dress, too, had an unpleasant smoky odor to it, as did Sam's. Sal Pavy's costume had escaped the conflagration; dandy that he was, he had taken it from the trunk beforehand and hung it in the stable to air out.

"Well, you look more like a milkmaid than a maid in waiting," he said. I let his remark pass, but I suspected Sam would not, and I was right.

"Did you know you've a hole there?" Sam said innocently.

"Where?" Sal Pavy demanded, twisting his head around and feeling the fabric at his rear with both hands.

"Right in the middle of your bum!" Sam said, and went

into a fit of laughter that, though he muffled it with one hand, I was sure could be heard out front. Sal Pavy flushed angrily and, hiking up his skirts, stalked off—a short stalk, as the area behind the curtain was but one pace in depth and perhaps ten from side to side. "Oh, my," said Sam. "I've offended Her Majesty."

Halfway through the play, I caught a glimpse of one of Pembroke's Men, the paunchy fellow with the eye patch, standing just inside the door of the hall, watching the proceedings soberly—not like one who has come to enjoy himself but like one who is sizing up the competition. Somehow I suspected he had not bothered to pay his penny.

We could not depart the following day until the town's tailors had our costumes ready, and so we got only as far as Southwell before night fell. Though it was a far smaller town than Newark, the sharers decided to try a performance there, in the only enclosed space that was large enough—the wool market. Despite the stench, we drew an enthusiastic crowd that must have comprised two-thirds of the local population.

Buoyed by our success, we went on to perform in Mansfield, Sheffield, and Doncaster, where we were equally well received. By the time we reached York, we were ahead enough so that Mr. Heminges could pay the hired men six shillings apiece, and the prentices three—our regular weekly wage. But we had been on the road for nearly a month now, and these were the first wages we had seen. Still, it was certainly better than nothing.

I had hoped the company might send a share of our earnings home to Mr. Pope and Sander, but Mr. Heminges did not feel we could spare any yet. Mr. Burbage, he assured me, would see that they and the boys were provided for. All the same, upon our arrival at the Black Swan in York, I wrote a letter to Sander at once and enclosed a shilling to buy treats for the boys and Tetty.

Because we had changed our route, no letter from London had reached us yet. The sharers had by now a firmer notion of where our travels were likely to take us. Once we left York, we were to turn southwest and make a long loop that would take us through Leeds, Manchester, Chester, Shrewsbury, Coventry, and Mr. Shakespeare's home town of Stratford before we returned to London. I wrote out this itinerary for Sander, hoping he might send a reply in care of one of the towns along our route.

The sharers had expressed concern that, with the slow progress we'd made since leaving Newark, Pembroke's Men or some other company might have preceded us. We were gratified to learn that no London troupe had played here in years, only a few companies of lesser stature who hailed from the northern shires.

The city fathers examined our papers carefully and, satisfied that we were a renowned and reputable company, engaged us to play the Merchant Adventurers' Hall for an entire week. In addition, we were to receive our remuneration not from the audience but from the city treasury, to the tune of thirty shillings per performance.

At the inn that evening we celebrated our good fortune

with generous rounds of ale. Mr. Shakespeare even took a night off from struggling with *Love's Labour's Won,* for which I cannot say I was sorry. Despite the title, I had begun to wonder whether we would indeed win out as a result of all our labors, or whether the play would at some point simply fizzle out, like a firework with a faulty fuse.

Sal Pavy, wearing his cheerful face, condescended to join us in our festivities for a time. Before he retired to his stable I saw him draw Mr. Armin aside and engage him in a conversation that, from their expressions, appeared to be a serious one.

When we had drunk all we could hold—the ale they served us prentices was, of course, watered down, or my head could not have stood much of it—and were making for our beds, Mr. Armin beckoned to me. I stepped into his room. "I want your thoughts on something," he said.

I smiled amiably, in a mood to grant anyone anything. "Some ailment, no doubt," I said, and hiccoughed. "I seem to have become the company's unofficial physician—ah, there's a tongue twister you can use, sir, in our elocution lessons. Say it three times rapidly: unofficial physician, unafishy physician, unofficial position. I am most efficient in my unofficial position as a fisherman's physician."

Mr. Armin patted my shoulder lightly, but it was enough to unbalance me, and I sat down abruptly. "You've had too much ale," he said.

"Aye," I said, "that's me *ale-ment.*"

"Perhaps we should discuss this tomorrow."

"Nay, nay, I'm all right. What is 't? An upset stomach? A sore throat?"

"I'm not looking for medical advice. It's a theatre matter. Sal Pavy has asked that, when we do *Titus Andronicus*, he be given the part of Lavinia."

I blinked, taken aback. "But—but that's *me* part."

"I know. But you've been so busy helping Mr. Shakespeare, I thought you might be happy to have one less responsibility."

"So you promised it to him?"

"No. I told him I'd discuss it with you."

"Oh," I said. Though I tried not to show it, I was hurt by the proposal, for it implied that I could readily be replaced. I did not wish to seem temperamental, or unreasonable, but neither did I care to give up one of my best parts, especially to Sal Pavy. "Does 'a ken the part?"

Mr. Armin nodded. "He's been studying it."

So that was what he'd been up to in those early-morning solo sessions. I wondered what other parts he'd been committing to memory. Feeling as though I'd been wronged, I said sullenly, "An you think 'a can do it better, then I yield to him."

"Widge. It's not a question of who does it better, you know that. Sal feels we're not using him enough, that's all."

"Then let *him* play doctor and take dictation," I replied heatedly. Then I slumped forward and wearily hung my head. "I'm sorry. I didn't mean that. I'm tired and I've drunk too much."

"I know. I should not have brought this up now. Go on to bed. We'll take it up at a more opportune time."

I rose and walked unsteadily to the door. "Nay," I said with forced nonchalance, "an 'a wants the part, 'a may ha' 't. I've no claim on 't."

We were scheduled to play *Titus Andronicus* on Wednesday afternoon; as I now had no need to review my lines, I asked for that morning off, and Mr. Armin granted it. Sam begged to come with me, but I put him off. A journey into one's past must be made alone.

The orphanage was even more dismal than I had remembered it. The squat, square stone building had once been a prison, and, though the bars had been removed from the narrow windows and from the doorways and the interior walls had been whitewashed, there was no getting rid of the air of gloom that pervaded the place.

A clamor of children's voices came from the big room that served as classroom and dining hall, and it sounded so like always that I fancied for a moment I truly had gone back in time—until I saw the figure coming toward me down the hall. At first I did not recognize her, so changed was she. In my memory, she was a vigorous, imposing woman with a voice that any player would have envied. The eight years that had passed since I left the orphanage to apprentice to Dr. Bright had not been kind to her. She was still rotund as always, but no longer robust. Her hair had gone gray, and the spring had gone from her step.

"Mistress MacGregor?" I said uncertainly.

"Aye," she replied. "What is it?"

"You may not recall me," I said. "I'm Widge."

Her worn face brightened. "Not recall you? I should say I can!" To my surprise she put her arms about me and kissed both my cheeks, then stepped back to look me over, still gripping my arms. "You've grown!" she exclaimed, and then laughed. "Of course, 'twould be a wonder if you had not!"

I smiled. This was the Mistress MacGregor I remembered. "Well," I said, embarrassed, "I've not grown nearly as much as I'd like. I'm a player now, you know."

"Are you indeed?" she said enthusiastically. "A player? And what might that be?"

"You ken—an actor. In plays. In London."

She put a hand to her mouth in astonishment. "You're never!"

"Aye. And wi' the Lord Chamberlain's men, too. We're playing here in York this week, an you'd care to come."

She looked dubious. "Would a person have to dress up fine-like?"

"Oh, nay. Only th' actors."

"Then I'll do it, if I can get away." She squeezed my arm tightly. "Losh, I'm so happy to see you and to hear you've made something of yourself. Not that I ever doubted it."

"Do you ken what's become of th' other boys?"

She shook her head sadly. "The plague claimed many of them. Och, for a time this place was more like a pesthouse than an orphanage. Those who lived through it and left standing up seldom care to come back again."

I felt a painful pang of guilt. For some reason—or perhaps for none at all—Fortune had seen to it that I escaped the city before the plague struck in 1594.

"Have you been to see your old master . . . I dinna mind his name."

"Dr. Bright."

"Aye, that's him. I always thought it a poor name for him; he did not seem verra bright to me." She threw up her hands and exclaimed, "Och, bless me! Had his name not come up, I'd have forgotten, sure as sure. I've something for you."

"You ha'?"

"Aye." She led me into her office—not by the ear, for a change. "I'd have sent it to you, but you'd gone from Dr. Bright's and he could not, or would not, say where." With one of the jangling keys at her waist, she opened the top of a battered desk and fished some object from one of the compartments inside.

When she placed it in my hand, I saw that it was an ornate crucifix on a delicate chain. The figure of Christ was carved from ivory and set into a gold filigreed cross. I glanced up at Mistress MacGregor, bewildered. "What . . . why . . . ?"

"Bide a bit," she said, "and I'll tell you." Obediently I took a seat on a rickety stool, feeling seven again and about to be chastised for my misbehavior. Mistress MacGregor sat at the desk and went on.

"About a year ago, I was summoned to the poorhouse, to the bedside of a dying woman named Polly—not a resident of the poorhouse, you ken, but a housekeeper there."

I nodded, wondering where this could be leading.

"I kenned the woman but little, so I was surprised that she should ask for me in her last hours. I was even more surprised when she took that crucifix from a table beside the bed and pressed it into my hand. 'What's this, then?' says I, and she says, so low I could scarcely hear her, she says, 'I done a bad thing and I want to make amends.' 'Well,' says I, 'perhaps I should fetch a priest, then.' 'Nay,' says she, 'only you can help,' and she points to that crucifix. 'I took that off a woman as died in childbirth, years ago. I kenned 'twas wrong to do it, but I liked the look of it, and I told meself she'd have no use for it any longer. I've regretted it ever since,' she says. 'I couldn't even bring meself to wear it ever, or to tell anyone what I'd done.' 'Why tell me, then?' says I. 'Because,' says she, 'you ken who it rightly belongs to, for the child she bore was given over to you.' "

I waited for Mistress MacGregor to go on. Instead she gazed expectantly at me, as a player will at another whose turn it is to speak. Then the import of what she had said struck me so soundly that I seemed suddenly unable to catch my breath. Finally, I managed to respond. "You mean to say that . . . that the child was me? But—but how can you be sure? You must have taken in dozens of orphans whose mothers died in the poorhouse."

"Aye, but—" She tapped the worn record book that lay open on her desk. "I've checked me records for that year—

it was the year that Polly was first hired on at the poorhouse—and there were only two such cases. And in only one of them did the mother die afore she could even give the bairn a name."

The room fell silent save for the ticking of a clock on the mantel and the far-off sound of children's voices. I felt curiously displaced, detached and dreamlike, much the way I felt when I was playing a role upon the stage. With fingers that seemed not to belong to me I turned the crucifix over in my palm. On the reverse side someone had scratched some words, doubtless with the point of a knife. I had to wipe my eyes on my sleeve before I could make them out: FOR SARAH.

"Was that . . . was that her name, then? Sarah?"

"Aye. That was your mother."

"Me mother." I whispered the words, trying them out upon my tongue. "Me mother. After all this time." I raised my eyes beseechingly to Mistress MacGregor. "Did this Polly tell you aught about her, then? What she was like? What she looked like, even?"

Mistress MacGregor shook her head regretfully. "When they found your mother on the doorstep, she was near dead already; apparently she never spoke a single word. I had no chance to question Polly any further; not long after she gave me that cross, she drew her last paiching breath—without even being shriven by a priest." Mistress MacGregor learned toward me, as though to disclose some dire secret. "She was a Catholic."

"Me mother?" I said.

"Nay, I meant Polly. Though for all I ken your mother was as well. They're the ones as go in for the fancy crosses, mostly."

"A Catholic," I said. I knew little about Catholics, save that the Queen did not like them. Our enemy, Spain, was, after all, peopled by Catholics. So far as I knew, I had never met a Catholic. But then an allegiance to the Old Church was not, I gathered, the sort of thing one would confess at the drop of a hat.

"I only say she may have been. I canna say for certain. I did ask the other folk at the poorhouse if they minded your mother, but none had worked there more than a few years. I went through their records for that month and year, too, but they told me nothing, not even her name."

"Would there not be a grave?" I asked.

"Aye, but 'twould be a pauper's grave, all unmarked. I'm sorry."

I felt a pain in my hand, and realized I had been gripping the crucifix so tightly that Christ's crown of thorns had pierced my palm. I stared down at the drops of blood that welled from the wound and wondered if my mother, too, had clutched this cross for comfort as she lay dying—and giving birth to me. I wiped the crucifix on my breeches; traces of the blood remained in the deep scratches that made up her name. It was a pity that whoever had engraved the message had not seen fit to add her surname. It would have given me a stronger clue to her identity—and, after fifteen years of being known only as Widge, I would have had a real name at last, or half a one, at any rate.

"An she was a local lass," said Mistress MacGregor, "there must be someone here who kenned her."

"Aye," I said, a dell of hope rising up within me. "That's so. There must be someone who would recognize this cross, if I but kenned where to look."

"Well . . . an she did belong to the Old Church, then you might seek out others of that faith. Folk do say they stick together." She leaned forward again, with one hand alongside her mouth, for all the world like an actor signaling that he is about to reveal something slightly scandalous. "They also say that the Catholics are fonder of their drink than most. If I was you, I'd begin looking in the taverns."

The town's drinking establishments were easy enough to find. Whereas a tavern in London could be identified by the ivy or red lattice by its entrance, here in the north the sure sign was a large painted hand made of wood, projecting on a pole from the window. I started with the Hog's Head in Coney Street. No one in the place found the crucifix familiar, and the only Sarah any of them knew was a lady of ill repute who was very much alive. The story was the same at the next tavern and the next.

As I emerged from the Raven, I glanced at the clock on the steeple of the town hall. The afternoon's performance was but a little over an hour away, and I was expected to lend a hand with prompting and costume changes and the like. I dared not shirk my duties, lest the sharers decide they could do without me altogether.

I had begun to suspect that my quest was a hopeless one.

Still, I reasoned, it could do no harm to ask about in one or two more taverns, so I walked on to an unnamed alehouse that occupied the ground floor of a run-down house. Folk sometimes call the main room of a tippling house the "dark parlor"; this one certainly lived up to its name. It was so dim within that I had to stand inside the entrance for several minutes before I could see properly.

The benches that flanked the half-dozen trestle tables were mostly empty; clearly this was not one of the city's more popular drinking spots. I could see why. The rushes on the floor looked as though they'd not been changed since the Queen took the throne; the tops of the tables were chipped and gouged from years of being used as a sticking place for daggers; and the chinks in the wood had filled in with a putty composed of food remnants and dried-up puddles of ale.

The few patrons in the place turned hostile stares upon me, as did the tavern keeper, who was emerging from the taproom with a pint mug in each hand, the contents slopping over rims. "Good afternoon," I ventured. He gave me not so much as a nod in reply. I approached him, dangling the crucifix before me like some talisman to ward off danger. "I wonder if you've ever seen a cross of this sort before."

The tippler gave it a cursory glance, shook his head brusquely, and plunked the mugs down before his paltry pair of customers. One of them was a small, gnomelike fellow with but half an ear on one side—the rest of it had, I suspected, been clipped off as a punishment for thieving. He reached out one grimy hand and drew the crucifix nearer, to squint at it with rheumy eyes. Then he, too, shook his head and retreated with his drink into the dark recesses of the alehouse.

I tried to show the cross to the second man, but he waved me off. With a sigh, I sat down on the end of a bench, meaning to rest a few moments before heading back to our inn. "An you don't drink," said the tippler, "you don't sit."

I would, in truth, have welcomed a pint of ale, for I'd had neither drink nor food since early in the day. But I had only two shillings to my name and no notion of how long they'd have to last me. In any case, I would have been reluctant to drink a drop from any vessel in this unsanitary place.

Wearily, I got to my feet and headed for the door. Just as my hand fell upon the latch, a commanding voice from the gloomy depths at the rear of the room called out, as sharp and sudden as a cannon shot, "Hold!"

I was accustomed to doing as I was bid. I stopped in my tracks. "Come here, boy!" ordered the voice.

I turned slowly. "Me?"

"Of course, you. Do you see any other boys about?"

I moved hesitantly toward the rear of the room. The wight with half an ear sat at a table there, but I did not think his was the voice that had called me. "Come, come," said the voice, more kindly. "I'll not bite you." It came from a figure sitting in a dark alcove formed where the fireplace jutted into the room. "Sit down," the man said, and gestured to a bench that faced the fireplace. Once more I did as I was told. "Roger!" called the man, whose face I still could not see clearly. "A pint of ale for my young friend, if you please."

"Who's going to pay for 't?" asked the tippler.

"Ah, Roger," said the man reproachfully, "you know I'm good for it."

"I can't pay me bills wi' promises," grumbled the tippler, but he brought the pint all the same and thrust it into my hands.

"Fair 'chieve you," said the stranger, and clinked his mug against mine. "Drink up."

Obediently I put the earthenware mug to my mouth and did my best to drink without actually touching my lips to the vessel. Over its rim I studied my drinking companion as well as I could, given the little light that reached into the alcove.

The first thing that struck me about him was that he did not seem to belong here, in these shabby surroundings. Unlike the other patrons of the place, whose tattered and soiled tunics marked them as members of the laboring class—or, more likely, the thieving class—this fellow wore a gentleman's attire, a doublet and breeches that were, if not exactly new or stylish, at least presentable.

He leaned forward and, with a pair of tongs, fished a glowing ember from a clay pot on the hearth to light his long-stemmed clay pipe, giving me a better look at his features. He was about of an age with Mr. Shakespeare and Mr. Burbage—that is, thirty-five or so. His ginger-colored hair was unusually close-cropped. With the exception of Sal Pavy we prentices wore our hair short, finding it more convenient and comfortable when we donned the wigs that transformed us into women. But this man's hair was shorter still, and his beard was trimmed to within a quarter inch of his face. His long nose showed definite signs of having been broken, perhaps more than once. These features, plus his rather stiff-backed posture, put me in mind of a military man and, as I shortly learned, I had read him right.

The man puffed on his pipe and blew forth a billow of tobacco smoke that choked me. He laughed. "They say this weed is beneficial to the lungs—once you get used to it." After another few puffs, he added, "Forgive me for being so abrupt with you a moment ago. I was once a soldier, and have not yet lost the old habit of ordering folk about."

"What do you want?" I asked, impatient to be off to the Merchant Adventurers' Hall.

"I overheard you asking the others about a certain cross, and it piqued my curiosity." His speech, too, was more like that of a gentleman than of an ordinary workingman, and bore little trace of Yorkshire. "Might I have a look at it?"

I drew the crucifix from my wallet and held it by the chain before him. He bent forward, a bit awkwardly, as though the movement pained him, and laid the cross on his palm. I heard a sharp intake of breath, then he said softly, "By my fay! It's the very same!"

"Wh-what do you mean?" I asked, my voice suddenly shaky. "Do you recognize this?"

He let the cross go and glanced up at me, his eyes wide, their pupils like dark pools without a bottom. "Recognize it?" he said. "It's mine—or once was."

"Yours? Nay! How can that be? It belonged to me mother!"

He stared at me for a moment, with an expression I could not read. "It was I who gave it to her, and it was I who engraved the message on the back."

"The—the message?"

He nodded. " 'For Sarah.' "

I was stunned. He had not turned the cross over and, even had he done so, he could not have read the faint letters in this dim light. It took me a moment to respond. "You kenned her, then?"

He gave a small, rather rueful smile. "Better than anyone, I think. We would have wed, had not her family stood in our way." Again he took up the crucifix, which was twisting slowly about as it dangled from my trembling hand, and gently traced the ornate design with one finger, as though looking at it called up my mother's face. "My family were Catholics, hers Protestants. Though they forbade her to see me, we carried on a courtship for many months, at night, in secret. I would have wed her in secret, too, but she could not bring herself to defy her parents that far. So . . . " He shrugged. "So I became a soldier and went off to Ulster to fight Tyrone. When I returned from Ireland, I could find no trace of her or her family. Eventually I learned that her parents had died of the plague. I could only assume that she had met the same fate."

"Nay, she did not," I whispered. "She died i' the poorhouse . . . after giving birth to me."

When I was a child in the orphanage, I was convinced, like many of my fellow orphans, that a mistake had been made, that I had only been separated somehow from my mother and father. I felt certain that one day they would come for me, and I imagined our tearful reunion so clearly that it seemed inconceivable it would not come to pass.

Now, at last, it had, and it was nothing like I had imagined. We did not cry, we did not embrace, we did not even speak for some time. We only sat in silence, linked by the cross in his hand and the chain in mine. Finally he sat back, took a deep draught from his mug, and wiped his mouth. "Well. I don't often find myself at a loss for words." He laughed uncertainly and spread his hands. "What do we do now, then? Introduce ourselves?"

I gave a weak and awkward laugh as well. "It would be a start, I suppose."

He held out a large hand with short, broad fingers. "I'm Jamie Redshaw, lately of Her Majesty's musketeers."

Like an actor playing his part by rote I reached out and shook his hand. "And I'm Widge. Or at least that's what they call me. Me mother didn't live long enough to give me a proper name."

"I'm sorry," he said. "I didn't know. I didn't know what had become of her. I didn't even know she was with child. My child." He took another long drink, then sat gazing at me over the rim of his mug, appraising me as I had earlier been appraising him. "You must be thirteen or fourteen, then."

"Fifteen," I said.

He shook his head and ran a hand through his bristly hair. "It's been that long? It's difficult to believe. You've spent all those years here, in the orphanage?"

"Nay, I was apprenticed to Dr. Bright of Berwick for a time, then I went to London, and for the past year I've been a prentice wi' the Lord Chamberlain's Men."

He raised his eyebrows. "The Chamberlain's Men, is it? You've done well for yourself."

"You ken the company?"

"Of course. I saw them perform *Twelfth Night* only yesterday. I don't recall seeing you, though."

"Well, I looked rather different in me wig and makeup." I gasped then, and leaped to my feet. "Oh, gis! I nearly forgot! They'll be starting the performance! I ha' to leave!" I turned toward the door, then turned abruptly back again. "But—but I can't leave! There's so much . . . We haven't even . . . " I waved my hands in frustration, torn between my duty to the company and my desire to learn everything at once about a mother and father who had so suddenly and unexpectedly materialized.

Laughing, Jamie Redshaw rose to his feet and clapped me on the back, so soundly that it stung. "Don't fret, Widge. I'm not going to disappear. Why don't I come with you, and we can talk further after the performance."

"Oh, aye!" I said gratefully, and we made for the door.

"You've not paid for your drinks!" the scowling tippler reminded us.

Jamie Redshaw waved to him as blithely as though the man had wished us good fortune. "In due time, Roger. All in due time."

As we headed for the Merchant Adventurers' Hall, I glanced furtively at Jamie Redshaw again and again, trying to get my mind around the notion that this was my father walking next to me. It was difficult. As far as I could tell, our looks were as unlike as could be. My hair was dark; his was fair. My eyes were blue, his brown. My frame was small and slight; his was large and stout.

My mind was a mingle-mangle of thoughts and questions, each fighting to be spoken first. Some I had been wondering about for years; others had occurred to me but a moment before. Some were so trivial and foolish that I thrust them aside; others were so difficult that I felt I dared not put them to him just yet.

I began with the ones that had been with me longest. "Can you . . . can you tell me what me mother looked like?"

At first I thought he had not heard me, for he looked lost in his thoughts, too. Finally he raised his head, gazed at me a long moment, and then said, "Like you."

"And what was her surname?"

He scratched his short beard thoughtfully. "Hmm. It's been a long time; give me a moment. Rogers, that's it."

"Has she no kin left here?"

He shook his head. "None. If she had, I would have found them."

"Would you?" I said, more bitterly than I meant to. "You failed to find me."

He turned to me with a look that was half angry, half reproachful. "I had no idea you existed," he said.

We walked on in silence. Despite the fact that I was a head shorter, I found myself having to slow my pace so as not to get ahead of him. He did not limp, exactly; he seemed merely to favor his left side a little, to hesitate slightly each time he brought his left leg forward. Though he carried an impressive hardwood walking stick with a carving of a snarling lion's head on the handle, he did not lean on it but walked along rigidly upright, swinging the stick at his side.

"I'm sorry to slow you down," he said. "I've a wound that gives me a twinge now and again."

"A sword wound?" I asked.

"No, a fragment of an Irish cannonball. It went through my hip, the surgeon told me, and lodged near the base of my spine."

"Gog's blood!" I breathed. "All I've ever done is mock

fighting on the stage. I can scarcely imagine what it's like to be in the thick of a real battle."

"I hope you never have to learn," said Jamie Redshaw soberly.

I hoped so, too. Yet I couldn't help feeling, for the first time, a trifle ashamed of my profession, and wondering what a man who had truly known death and tragedy would make of our pale imitations.

"It's very odd," I said, "that you should be a soldier."

He frowned slightly. "Why? What do I look as though I'd be? A plowman?"

"Nay, nay," I replied hastily. "I only meant it's odd because not long ago someone asked about me father and, on a whim, I said 'a was a soldier. Ha' you always been, or were you a prentice, like me?"

"I apprenticed to a boatwright."

"A boatwright? Not in Yorkshire, surely?"

Laughing, Jamie Redshaw held up his stick as though to ward off my onslaught of questions. "Patience, boy, patience! We can't hope to make up for fifteen years in as many minutes, you know! As I said, I'll not disappear. There will be plenty of opportunity later for all your questions. For now, let us simply get to know one another, as new-made acquaintances do, shall we?"

I nodded, embarrassed. "Aye. I'm sorry."

By the time we reached the Merchant Adventurers' Hall, a long stream of playgoers were paying their pennies to Sam, who had a gatherer's box suspended by a thong around his neck. "Where have you been?" he wanted to know. "Everyone's been asking me."

"I've been—I was—" It was all too much to try to explain. "I'll tell you later," I mumbled, and squeezed past the paying folk.

" 'Here!" Sam called after Jamie Redshaw. "You've got to pay your penny, sir!"

" 'A's wi' me, Sam," I told him.

"Who is he?" asked Sam, never one to hold back a question, however difficult.

I glanced uncertainly at Jamie Redshaw, who gave me a conspiratorial wink. "A new-made acquaintance," he said.

At one end of the hall, the city had erected a stage for us nearly as large as the one at the Globe. I led Jamie Redshaw around the curtain to where the players, already in costume, were making up one another's faces in the absence of a decent mirror.

"Sorry I'm late," I blurted, before anyone could take me to task for it. "It won't happen again, I promise."

"It's not l-like you," said Mr. Heminges. "We thought you m-must have good reason."

"Actually," said Will Sly, "we were taking wagers. Mr. Shakespeare fancied that your old master had kidnapped you. Jack was sure you'd deserted and gone back to London. My contention was that you'd spent all your salary on strong drink and were out cold in a tavern somewhere."

"Well, you're all wrong," I said, "though I was in several taverns."

"Aha!" cried Will triumphantly. "I was nearest the mark!"

"Who's your friend?" asked Mr. Armin. "A would-be player?"

"Nay, 'a's . . . " I hesitated. The notion of having a father at hand was still so unfamiliar to me.

"I'm Jamie Redshaw," he volunteered. "And you have a performance to do, so I'd best let you get on with it. Widge, we'll talk later." He stepped down from the platform and disappeared behind the curtain.

Alarmed, I ran after him. "You're not leaving?"

"No, no," he assured me. "I'll just be out front here, watching the play."

I nodded and backed away, keeping an eye on him as long as possible, fearful still that he might vanish and, with him, the only link I had to my heritage.

The company were all too busy to question me further. I helped make up faces and pin together splitting seams; I made certain all the properties were in their places; I retrieved from the script trunk the plot of the play, which showed all the actors' entrances, and hung it on the back side of the curtain. It was fortunate that I had done all these things a hundred times before, for my mind was not on them.

In between tasks, I stole a look out into the audience to make certain Jamie Redshaw was still there. When I could not spot him at once, my heart seemed to stop; then I caught sight of him off to one side, perched upon one of the stools that were reserved for those who could afford an extra sixpence.

Once the performance began, I volunteered to hold the book and throw lines out to those actors who were floundering. Though Sal Pavy had never before played the part of Lavinia on the stage, he showed no sign of needing help. On the few occasions when he did lose his way a little, he managed to get his bearings again with no prompting from me.

I wished now, more than ever, that I had not been so obliging as to let him have the part. I longed to make my father proud of me, and I could not do that from behind the stage. And yet perhaps it was just as well this way; considering the state my mind was in, I would likely have forgotten half my lines.

I did my best to pick out flaws in Sal Pavy's performance and did, indeed, find two. When he came on at the end of Act II with his hands lopped off, I could see the tips of his fingers poking out of one sleeve; and when he tripped over the hem of his dress in Act III, I distinctly heard him mutter a curse, despite the fact that his tongue was supposedly cut out.

But as far as acting ability was concerned, I had to admit—difficult as it was for me to do so—that he played the part, as theatre folk say, to the life. All trace of the spoiled and self-important Sal Pavy had vanished, and in his place was a piteous young woman who had been "ravished and wronged." When I had played Lavinia, and was called upon to scratch out the names of the villains in the dirt, holding the staff in my teeth and guiding it with my stumps, my clumsiness sometimes elicited laughter, not pity, from the audience. When Sal Pavy did the scene, there was not a single snicker, not a sound except perhaps a sniffle or two from some softhearted member of the audience. I could not help it; I disliked him more than ever.

True to his word, Jamie Redshaw rejoined us after the play was done and returned with us to the inn. Though the situation was an awkward one for me, I should have known how to conduct myself. I had, after all, had dozens of fathers before this—Leonato in *Much Ado*, Shylock in *The Merchant of Venice*, Polonius in *Hamlet*. Yet I had always been a daughter, never a son. I felt as though I were living out that dream every actor dreads, the one in which he is unexpectedly called upon to play a role totally unfamiliar to him. I had no notion of what to say, or where the day's developments might lead.

Happily, Jamie Redshaw seemed more sure of himself than I. Over dinner, he revealed to the company what he had implied to me. I had expected my fellow players to react with surprise to this revelation, and they did. I had also expected them to be delighted for me. I had, after all, after fifteen years of thinking myself an orphan, discovered that I had a family, or at least part of one.

They were cordial enough, to be sure, and offered their congratulations, but I sensed a certain reserve, especially on the part of Mr. Armin and Mr. Shakespeare, as though they were taking Jamie Redshaw's measure. It put me in mind of the way they behaved toward the players who auditioned for temporary roles at the Globe. I had the feeling they were debating whether or not he was suited to the part.

As for me, I was, I suppose, more like a playwright who has waited year upon year for some actor to audition for a crucial role in his play and gotten not a single prospect. I would likely have taken anyone who happened along.

Not that I was disappointed in the player I got. Watching Jamie Redshaw converse with the members of the company, I felt an unexpected and unfamiliar swell of something that I could only identify as pride. Though he was a simple soldier, a man of action, and not a scholar, he seemed quite comfortable in the company of men as intelligent and witty as the sharers. In fact, he behaved as if they were not new-made acquaintances but the oldest of friends. If he was discomfited at all by their appraising manner he did not show it; indeed, he seemed not to notice. He proceeded to give a highly entertaining—and highly exaggerated—account of how he and I had met. When he recounted how I fell off my stool in astonishment, it drew a round of raucous laughter. Though I did not recall doing such a thing, I did not spoil the hilarity by saying so.

In the midst of Jamie Redshaw's story the innkeeper approached us and cleared his throat. "Begging your pardon, sirs, but there's a wight outside says 'a desires to speak wi' someone in your company."

"Well, h-have him c-come in," said Mr. Heminges.

" 'A says 'a wishes to talk out there."

The sharers glanced at one another. Mr. Armin got to his feet. "I'll go see what it's about."

When he was gone, Jamie Redshaw resumed his story,

but was interrupted again by a sudden loud snoring sound close at hand. I turned to see that Sam had put his head down on the table and was fast asleep. Several of the company laughed, but I did not, for I had taken note of how flushed Sam's face looked and how the sweat stood out on his brow. "I hope 'a's not ill."

"J-just tired, I expect," said Mr. Heminges. "That g-gathering box is a heavy b-burden for a boy."

"Especially considering how much money we took in," added Mr. Phillips. "Why don't you help him up to bed, Widge?"

I hesitated, reluctant yet to let Jamie Redshaw out of my sight. Seeming to sense my dilemma, he smiled and nodded. "Go on. I'll still be here when you get back."

As I assisted Sam in mounting the stairs, I heard Jamie Redshaw take up the thread of his story again. I could not make out the words; whatever they were, they drew more appreciative laughter from his audience. When I returned to the main room of the inn, however, no one was laughing, and Jamie Redshaw was no longer holding forth. Everyone was silent and sober-faced. "What's wrong?" I asked.

Mr. Armin, who had taken his place again at the table, looked up at me. "Our stay here has been cut short."

"For what reason?" I cried. "Did they not like us?"

"I'm afraid we've been upstaged," replied Mr. Armin. "By the plague."

The man Mr. Armin had gone to speak with was the town's bailiff. His message was that, since our company's arrival in York, there had been a rash of plague deaths. No one was accusing us of having brought them on, but the local officials thought it best to ban any public gatherings for a time, until the threat died down.

We had scheduled a shortened version of *The Taming of the Shrew* for the following morning, and we would be permitted to proceed with it, but we were not to finish out the week. Every member of our company was upset by the news, for it meant only half the profit we had anticipated. I had even more cause for distress; I would have to leave behind my newfound father without ever having gotten to know him. I did have an alternative, of course. I could drop out of the company and remain in York. But that prospect was even more painful than the first.

"I'm sorry, Widge," said Mr. Armin. "I know this creates a dilemma for you."

"If you f-feel you need to stay a few m-more days," said Mr. Heminges, "we c-could manage without you, I suppose." Though I knew he meant only to ease my mind, his words stung me. I would have preferred to hear that I was indispensable, that the company could not possibly spare me.

"No," Jamie Redshaw put in unexpectedly. "It would not be fair to the company for Widge to stay on here. You're having to double up parts as it is." I stared at him in dismay. Now I was being betrayed by both sides. Why was he so ready to let me go? Did I mean nothing to him?

"B-but you've only j-just found one another. We've no w-wish to wrench him from you so s-soon."

"Nor do I wish you to," said Jamie Redshaw calmly. "Fortunately I have a solution that I think will suit everyone."

"You do?" I said.

Smiling, he spread his hands palms upward. "It's simple," he said. "I'll come with you."

After only a few minutes' discussion among themselves, the sharers agreed to Jamie Redshaw's proposal. Mr. Heminges made it clear that they could not afford to pay him a hired man's wages; but, like every prentice's father, he was entitled to two shillings a week from the company in return for his son's services.

"Well," said Jamie Redshaw amiably, "it's more than I'm

receiving at the moment. By rights, I should be collecting an army pension, but they continually deny me it."

"Why?" I asked.

There was more than a trace of bitterness in his laugh. "Because," he said, "they're the army."

Through the night I heard Sam thrashing about restlessly and, when I put my hand on him to still him, I felt that he was soaked with perspiration; though the air in the room was close and warm, it did not account for such a surfeit of sweat.

In the morning he was too weak to come down to breakfast, so I took him up a bowl of porridge. Once he'd gotten it down he seemed stronger and in better spirits. Even so, when we set out for the Merchant Adventurers' Hall, he seemed hardly able to keep himself upright. "Are you going to be able to go on?" I asked.

"I'll manage," he said, his voice hoarse.

"After the performance, I'll tell them you need to see a physician."

"The company can't afford that," he said. "Can't you give me something?"

"How can I? I don't ken what's wrong wi' you."

He stopped and put a hand that trembled slightly on my arm. Softly he said, "It's not the contagion, is it, Widge?"

"Nay," I said, trying to sound confident and trying, too, not to shrink back from his touch. "Nay, I'm sure it's just some fever or other."

I took Sam's place at the entrance, collecting the patrons' pennies. I had expected, after what we learned the night before, to see our audience dwindle drastically. But either the news of the plague deaths had not yet reached everyone's ears or else they had all determined to take in one last performance before the privilege was denied them, for folk were flocking to the theatre in greater numbers than ever.

The box grew so heavy with coins that I had to set it at my feet and collect the money in my hand—until I came to think that someone in the throng might, in passing their money to me, also be passing on the plague. I opened the lid of the box, then, and asked each one to drop his money in.

Sam, who was playing several small roles, held up somehow through the first three acts. But in Act IV, he came on as Biondello, spoke his line—"O master, master, I have watched so long that I am dog-weary"—and collapsed upon the boards. I froze, unable to think of how to thribble my way out of this.

But Sal Pavy, in his guise as Bianca, was quicker-witted. "Ah, sir," he said to Ned Shakespeare as Lucentio, "you work your men too hard by far"—a clever bit of improvised pentameter. Then he paraphrased Sam's lines, still in perfect meter: "I spy a person coming down the hill will serve the turn."

I had presence of mind enough to change my line—"What is he, Biondello?"—to "What is he, Mistress, pray?" Sal Pavy replied with Biondello's part. When he and Ned left the stage, they dragged Sam's limp form with them. The audience must have thought it was all in the script, for it fetched a laugh.

Though we revived Sam with tincture of myrrh, he was too weak to go on, so we worked around his absence. He still refused to see a physician. "All I need is to rest a while," he assured us. The sharers, wanting to push on to the next town where we might perform, had him ride atop our rolled-up bedding in the careware, and this time no one objected, not even Jack.

The pace of the procession was more brisk than usual and I could see that Jamie Redshaw, with his stiff gait, was finding it difficult to keep up with the carewares. "There's no need to tax yourself," I told him confidentially. "We'll catch up wi' them on the hills."

When we fell a bit behind the others, I said, "Did you take in the morning's performance, then?"

He nodded but offered nothing further.

"Well?" I prompted. "How did you like it?"

He cast me an amused glance. "I suppose what you mean is, how did I like you?"

I felt myself go red. "I did not want it to seem as though I were angling for compliments."

"You did well," he said. I waited for him to go on, but he said nothing more on the matter. I tried to dull the disappointment I felt by telling myself that, of course, being a soldier he had likely had little experience with the theatre and did not know what to say. But I had used that same sort of reasoning over and over to excuse his lack of fatherly affection toward me, and it was wearing thin.

It was well before dark when we spied the town of Harrogate ahead of us. We were spied in turn by a man—a merchant, from the look of him—approaching on horseback. To my surprise, he at once wheeled his horse about and headed back toward town at a gallop.

"Now that's a bad sign," said Ned Shakespeare.

"Perhaps 'a merely forgot something," I suggested, "and had to go back for 't."

"Perhaps he's gone to get up a welcoming committee for us," said Jamie Redshaw.

We did indeed find a committee of a dozen or so men waiting for us, but they did not have a welcoming air about them. They stood blocking the road, their legs planted wide, their arms crossed, as though daring us to try and pass.

We pulled up the carewares, and Mr. Heminges and Mr. Armin rode forward to talk with the apparent leader of the group, a lanky man wearing the leather jerkin of a constable. The discussion appeared to be a heated one. Finally the blockade of bodies opened up and let our little troupe move on. The townsmen looked no more cordial than before, however, nor did they disperse. In fact they walked alongside us, as though escorting us.

Jamie Redshaw smiled in a friendly fashion and tried to exchange a few words with one of their number, but the man would not respond; he only stared straight ahead, with a scowl on his face. We came to an inn, but the sharers marched us on past it. We did not even pause until we were all the way through the town and into the countryside again. Then Mr. Heminges signaled us to halt, dismounted, and gathered us prentices and hired men about him.

"Why did they not let us stay?" demanded Ned Shakespeare.

"It's the contagion, isn't it?" I said.

He held up his hands to silence us. "P-please. G-give me a chance to tell you. We were p-preceded, it seems, by another troupe of p-players."

"Pembroke's Men!" cried Ned.

"No, apparently they were no legitimate c-company at all, only a company of thieves. They p-passed themselves off as players, of course. They'd had ill luck, they said, and asked the m-mayor for money for f-food and lodging, to be repaid out of the b-box from the next day's performance. They p-paid the innkeeper with promises as well, and then left in the m-morning with all the advance money and without g-giving a performance—save the one with which they d-duped the mayor. Naturally he was n-not anxious to be t-taken in again, by us."

"But we have papers!" protested Jack. "Did you show them our papers?"

"Of c-course. But these rogues had p-papers, too—very official looking, and very f-false."

"When were they here?" asked Jamie Redshaw.

"They left j-just this morning."

"Then we should not be wasting time," Jamie Redshaw declared, smacking his walking stick impatiently against his palm. "We've got to catch up with them."

Mr. Heminges smiled wryly. "We are not s-soldiers, Mr. Redshaw, looking to d-do battle with the enemy."

"But if we don't overtake them, they'll spoil every town for us before we get there!"

"I r-realize that," said Mr. Heminges, a trifle more sharply. "But we c-can assume they will stick to the smaller t-towns, where n-no one is likely to know the real P-Pembroke's Men. We'll t-try our luck in more p-populous places."

Jamie Redshaw shook his head disapprovingly. "Avoiding them will solve nothing. I'd confront them now, before they do more harm."

"Ah, but you see, you're n-not in charge of this c-company, Mr. Redshaw," said Mr. Heminges pointedly, and walked away.

I had watched the preceding scene with great discomfort. Though I felt my father's reasoning was sound and I wanted very much to ally myself with him, I was at the same time reluctant to speak out against the sharers.

While we were stopped, I got into our small stock of medicinal herbs and prepared for Sam an infusion of willow bark, a popular antidote for fever. But he no longer had a fever; he was trembling all over with chills. "How are you?" I asked as I covered him with my cloak.

"Oh, Lord, sir!" he said, and laughed shakily. Mr. Shakespeare's "answer to fit all questions" had by now become a familiar jest among the members of the company. "I heard what happened," he added. "Where will we go now?"

"Leeds, I expect. We should be there in a few hours, and then you'll have a proper bed."

"I'm all right," he murmured. "Don't fret about me."

Jamie Redshaw had taken advantage of the pause to light his pipe. As I jumped down from the careware, he asked, "How is your friend?"

"Not so good as I hoped, nor so bad as I feared." Softly, so Sam would not hear, I added, "Would that I could examine his legs for red marks; it would give me a better idea of what we're dealing wi'."

Jamie Redshaw puffed at his pipe a moment. "Whether or not it's the plague, you mean?"

"Aye. 'A's got his woolen hose on yet, from the play. An I ask him to remove them, 'a may guess that I'm looking for signs of the contagion. I've no wish to alarm him. It may be naught but the ague."

"He shows no other symptoms, then? No pustules?"

I shook my head. "Pray that 'a does not, for an 'a does, every one of us is in danger of being next."

Mr. Armin reined in his black mare and waited for us to come up alongside him. "This stretch of road between Harrogate and Leeds is a desolate one," he said, so all the hired men could hear. "Keep your weapons handy. No one is likely to try to rob a group of this size, but we can't be too careful."

"I ha' no weapon," I reminded him.

"How can you say that?" he replied in mock surprise. "Is the road not full of rocks?" He urged his mount on to the head of the procession again.

"Rocks?" said Jamie Redshaw.

"Aye," I said, embarrassed. "We had a skirmish back in

Newbury, and I pelted our attackers wi' stones. You'd think the company would trust me wi' a sword. I've been taking lessons in scriming for most of a year." Though I managed to sound resentful, secretly I was just as glad that no one expected me to exercise my sword-fighting skills except upon the stage. Sal Pavy, I noticed, had not called his lack of a weapon to anyone's attention. I glanced down at Jamie Redshaw's belt. "But . . . you've no weapon, either."

"Ah, that's where you're wrong." He shifted his walking stick to his left hand, gripped the carved lion's head in his right, and, in one swift sweeping motion, drew forth from the stick a thin blade two feet or more in length.

"That's clever," said Ned Shakespeare. "Where'd you come by that?"

"I won it in a game of primero."

Will Sly eyed the abbreviated blade. "I should hardly think it a match for a full-length weapon."

"Nor is it meant to be. It's the element of surprise that makes it effective."

"So, you're a fair hand at cards, then?" asked Ned.

"A bit better than fair, I should say."

Ned smiled slyly. "Shall we test your prowess when we reach our lodgings?"

Jamie Redshaw made an exaggerated bow. "At your service, sir. Presuming that we do, in fact, find lodgings."

As the afternoon waned, it began to look as if we might not. The sun approached the horizon, and still there was no habitation in sight, only vast stretches of deserted moorland on either side of the highway, dotted with clumps of furze. The only signs that any soul had ever passed this way before us were the wheel ruts, a few crumbling horse droppings, and a tilted, weathered stone cross beside the road, erected ages ago, I supposed, by some religious order to give comfort to weary travelers. Jack fumbled in his wallet for a penny and placed it atop the cross.

"What's that for?" asked Ned Shakespeare.

"Protection," said Jack.

Ned laughed and gestured at the bleak, treeless landscape around us. "From what? Do you really think it likely that a band of brigands will rise out of the ground and attack us?"

Jack scowled. "You never know."

For once Jack proved to be right about something. No more than ten minutes had passed when I heard a startled cry of "Ho!" from Mr. Armin at the head of the company. I jerked my head in that direction. To my astonishment, a dense patch of furze that lay near the road seemed to be opening up, unfolding like some huge drab and ravaged bud bursting into bloom. From its center emerged not a blossom but a group of five fierce-looking armed men. One of them held a wheel-lock pistol aimed directly at Mr. Armin's chest.

"Dismount!" ordered the bandit, a big-bellied fellow with a filthy, pockmarked face; his bushy black hair and beard were tangled and full of furze twigs. His leaner but equally grimy confederates spread out, swords drawn, to block the road.

Though I was taken aback, I was not as terrified as I would once have been. I had been with the ruthless

Falconer when, unaided, he dispatched or disabled half a dozen brigands with astonishing speed and skill. Mr. Armin had proven himself even more able with a sword than Falconer. I expected that, with the help of the others, he would make short work of these shabby thieves.

Sure enough, instead of swinging from his saddle as he had been commanded to, Mr. Armin spurred his horse forward, at the same time jerking back on the reins so that the animal reared up, front hooves flailing. But the man with the gun, instead of dropping it in panic, calmly took a step backward and fired. The pistol gave off a puff of smoke and a loud report. The black mare gave a sort of shriek and toppled sideways, blood spurting from her neck. Mr. Armin tried to throw himself free, but one foot must have caught in its stirrup, for his leg became pinned underneath his fallen mount.

Despite his bulk, the black-haired man moved swiftly. In an instant he was straddling the fallen rider and had the blade of a dagger pressed against Mr. Armin's throat-bole. "Now the lot of you," he shouted, "dismount and drop your weapons, or watch your friend bathe in his own blood!"

Our hired men's swords clattered onto the stony surface of the road—all except Ned Shakespeare's. "He's bluffing!" Ned whispered to the rest of us.

Jamie Redshaw gave him a look of disgust. With one flick of his walking stick, he knocked Ned's sword from his grasp. Then, wincing at the pain it caused him, he bent and laid the stick carefully on the ground.

"Gather them up!" the leader instructed his companions. When they had done so, he lifted the blade from Mr. Armin's throat and stepped away. "We meant only to relieve you of your money," he told us, "but as you've put me to so much trouble, I believe we'll have the horses as well."

Two of his men took hold of the sharers' mounts. The other two set about unharnessing the teams from the carewares. "Oh, gis!" I murmured. "They'll leave us stranded here!"

Jamie Redshaw nodded grimly. Part of me wanted to urge him to do something, to fight back. But I knew that if he had made a move to do so, I would have tried to hold him back. Now that we had found one another at last, I could not bear to risk losing him.

The leader of the bandits reloaded his pistol, cocked it, and surveyed us prentices and hired men a moment. Then he stepped forward and pressed the muzzle of the gun to Sal Pavy's head. "Which wagon has the money?" he demanded. Sal Pavy was rigid with terror. Tears streamed from his eyes. His chin quivered, but no sound came out.

"It's the rear one," growled Will Sly.

"Thank you," said the brigand, and showed his rotten teeth in a grin. "I didn't want any more trouble. I don't like trouble." He uncocked the pistol, thrust it in his belt, and strode to the back of the nearest careware. But as he reached inside to seize one of the trunks, his hands froze in midair. An unaccountable look of distress came over his pockmarked features. He gave a hoarse cry and took a stumbling step backward, as though his knees had suddenly gone weak.

I was momentarily bewildered by his unexpected reaction. Then Sam's head emerged from within the wagon, and I saw what had alarmed the bandit so. Sam's face had a bluish tinge and was blotched with what looked like open sores. There were dark circles about his reddened eyes; froth flecked the corners of his mouth.

"Water!" he pleaded in a desperate, rasping voice. "Please! I'm dying of thirst!" He reached one shaking hand toward the bandit, and I could see that the skin of it was spotted, too, with red marks surrounded by blue-black patches.

"Saints save us!" I breathed. " 'A's taken wi' the plague!"

Don't touch me!" cried the black-haired man. In his haste to distance himself from Sam, he collided with the cart wheel. The pistol fell from his belt, but he seemed not to notice. "Come away!" he shouted to his men. "Take nothing with you!" When they hesitated, he bellowed, "Now, you gawking gypes! It's the contagion!"

Sam had climbed out of the careware now, and was staggering about, begging for a drink of water. When he shuffled toward the bandits who were unhitching our horses, they bolted. The other two let go of the sharers' mounts and took to their heels as well.

Now that I could move without fear of being shot or stabbed, I hastened to draw a cup of water from the keg strapped to the side of the careware and held it out to Sam.

"Don't give him that cup!" protested Ned Shakespeare. "He'll contaminate it!"

"Then we'll get another," I said. "Go on, Sam; take it."

Sam turned his hollow eyes gratefully upon me and reached out for the cup. As his trembling hands closed over mine, I gave an involuntary shudder, wondering how much contact was required to transmit the plague from one person to another.

Instead of gulping down the contents of the cup, Sam upended it over his head. The water drenched his tousled, matted hair and coursed down his cheeks. The blotches and sores began to melt away and slough off, as though he had anointed them with water from the Grail. I blinked in astonishment. "What in heaven's name—?" And then the truth struck me like a fool's bladder, and I began to laugh. Sam gave a weak grin and abruptly collapsed in a heap on the ground.

"Help me get him back in the careware," I said to Jamie Redshaw.

He stepped forward uncertainly. "But is he not—"

"Nay, nay," I assured him, still laughing. "It's not the contagion. It's only face paint."

As we lifted him into the wagon, Sam came to and murmured, "I gave a good performance, didn't I?"

"You played the plague to the life," I replied. "Or should I say, to the death." I wet a rag and gently washed the rest of the makeup from his face. "How did you ha' time to do all this?"

He gave me a shamefaced smile. "The truth is, I started on it well before the bandits turned up. I had planned only to play a prank on you and the others."

"It would ha' been a cruel prank," I said. "We were all anxious about you."

"I just meant to give you all a good laugh and liven things up a bit. I'm sorry."

"Well, considering how things turned out, I expect everyone will forgive you." I put a hand on his forehead. "The fever seems to ha' broken. How do you feel?"

"As though my limbs were made of new cheese," he said.

"Rest, then. You'll feel stronger i' the morning."

The rest of the company had managed to lift the dead horse enough to pull Mr. Armin free. He was limping about, rubbing his bruised leg. "You're fortunate it's not broken," said Mr. Phillips.

Mr. Armin did not reply. Though it was too dark to see much, he was staring out across the moor in the direction the brigands had gone. "We should have pursued them," he said grimly, and put a hand to his throat as if feeling again the edge of the bandit's blade.

"How did they hide themselves so well?" asked Jack.

Jamie Redshaw, who was examining the clump of furze from which the thieves had emerged, flipped over one of the shrubs with his walking stick. "They cut some of the furze and covered themselves over with it. A clever tactic."

"Men disguised by bushes," mused Mr. Shakespeare. "I'll have to use it in a play."

"We m-may as well c-camp here for the night," said Mr. Heminges. "I d-doubt those brigands will b-be back."

We pulled the wagons off the road and then used one of

the teams to drag Mr. Armin's mare out of our sight. To my surprise, Mr. Shakespeare got out his travel desk and set it up next to one of the carewares. "You mean to work on the play?" I said. "Out here?"

"Ideas come to me as I ride along," he told me. "If I don't capture them soon, they'll be gone, like those bandits." He lit a horn lantern. "How is Sam?"

"On the mend, I think."

Mr. Shakespeare shook his head. "One hardly knows whether to fine the boy for playing such a stunt or reward him for saving our lives."

"Well, 'a did tell me 'a was sorry. Besides, as they say here in Yorkshire, all's well that ends well."

Mr. Shakespeare smiled and played thoughtfully with the ring in his earlobe. "That's what they say, is it?"

"Aye."

"It's a good line," he said. "Let's give it to Helena."

When we reached Leeds the next day, we were relieved to discover that neither the plague nor the mock players had been there before us. We were even more relieved to find a letter from Sander awaiting us. It did my heart good to hear his voice, which, even on paper, was good-natured and cheerful as a cricket. The letter was a long one, filled with anecdotes about what mischief the boys had been up to and with the latest news about events in London. He mentioned the plague only briefly, near the end of the missive.

> Though the death rate is rising, it has not yet reached the proportions everyone feared. Rest assured that all

of us here are in good health, aside from a touch of melancholy when we think of you, our absent friends. Mr. Burbage is providing well for us, but asks that you send a share of the box as soon as you are able. For my part, I value your letters more than any amount of money. Good fortune follow you or, even better, precede you.

Yrs. faithfully,
Alexander Cooke

I berated myself for not having written more often, and resolved to get a letter off to him that very evening if I could. Sander would, I knew, be nearly as pleased about my finding a father as I was myself.

My only cause for disappointment was that there seemed to be so little opportunity for Jamie Redshaw and me to discuss the dozens of questions, large and small, that still waited impatiently in the back of my mind, like some important role I had studied but had never been given the chance to perform.

More than anything else I wanted to know about my mother, but even in our rare moments of leisure I could not manage to pry more than a few sentences from him concerning her. It seemed painful for him, as though I were probing at his old war wound and not his memory. I concluded that he must have loved her a great deal, to be hurt so by the thought of her.

We spent a profitable three days in Leeds. Sam had recovered enough to play small parts, provided he rested between scenes. So he would not feel useless, I gave him the book to hold while I took care of the more strenuous stuff. Jamie Redshaw volunteered to take on the task of gatherer. Though the money box must have weighed heavily on his injured back, he bore it without complaint. He went beyond the bounds of duty, in fact, calling enthusiastically to passersby, "Come in and watch the show! Only a penny to see the best that London has to offer!"

One might have thought that Sal Pavy would pitch in and do his part, but, as always, he seemed to consider anything other than acting to be beneath him. In fact, several times he went so far as to chastise me when a property was out of place, as though I were there only to assist him. It was all I could do to keep from assisting him onto the stage with the end of my blunted sword.

I tried hard to be tolerant of him, partly because I wanted to keep peace within the company, and partly because I felt guilty yet about having spied on him. Each time I recalled that path of stripes down his back, I felt a pang of pity that I would not, I am sure, otherwise have had.

To make *King John* more concise and swift-moving, Mr. Shakespeare had pruned most of the female roles, so Sal Pavy and I were conscripted as soldiers for the battle scenes. I spent every spare moment, of which there were few, working on my scriming skills, determined that, if I could not impress Jamie Redshaw with my ability to say lines convincingly, I would at least make a good showing with a sword—something a former soldier could surely appreciate.

Sal Pavy apparently did not consider swordplay a part of acting; for all the pains he took to perfect his delivery of speeches and gestures, I never once saw him practice with a sword or a singlestick. Sam explained this in a hilarious parody of Sal Pavy's well-rounded tones: "It's becauwse at Blackfriahrs, you see, we were not expected to engaige in such uncouth displaiys of aggression."

Whatever instruction he had in scriming must have been minimal, for Sal Pavy's *stoccatas* and edgeblows were clumsy and tentative, not to mention badly aimed. Nor did he content himself with the moves we had rehearsed. When we were on the stage in the second act, locked in mock-mortal combat, he delivered an unexpected down-right blow that caught me unawares and struck my shoulder. It made both of us look foolish—me for dropping my sword, he for standing there looking like a ninny instead of skewering me, as any self-respecting soldier would have done.

The moment we made our exit I turned on him, hot with anger. "Who taught you to sword-fight? Your maiden aunt? You nearly broke me collarbone out there, and I don't think you're up to playing me part as well as your own!"

"Oh, I don't know," he said coolly. "It might be a considerable improvement." To my surprise, he stepped up close to me and peered at my face. "Do you know," he said, "I think you're starting to sprout a few whiskers." Despite myself, I put my hand self-consciously to my chin. Sal Pavy clucked his tongue in mock sympathy. "I wouldn't be surprised if your voice starts to go next."

Though my reason told me not to rise to his taunts, my anger spoke to me in a louder voice. Reaching out, I seized the neck of his leather breastplate and jerked him nearly off his feet. "You'd like it, wouldn't you, an me voice or me collarbone cracked? Because then you'd be able to take over all me best roles, not just a few! I'll wager that blow out there was no accident at all!"

"Boys?" said Mr. Armin as he came off the stage. "Is something amiss?"

Sal Pavy opened his mouth to answer, but I was quicker. "Nay, nay!" I assured him. I let go of Sal Pavy and thumped the front of his breastplate. "Just adjusting his armor. It was chafing him."

Mr. Armin nodded knowingly. "I see. You've taken care of it, then?"

"Oh, aye."

"Good. We wouldn't want any chafing. Would we, Mr. Pavy?"

"No, sir," said Sal Pavy, unable, for once, to quite get his cheerful-and-charming mask properly in place. When I was called upon to deal him a death blow in the next scene, I did it with more conviction than usual—in fact, with great relish. When I was alone behind the stage, I furtively examined myself in the mirror. To my dismay, I found that Sal Pavy was right. A few spindly hairs had made an appearance on my face. I plucked them out ruthlessly with a pair of tweezers.

Unlike most town halls, the one in Leeds had a separate room at one end that we put to use as our tiring-room. As we were changing out of our costumes, Mr. Armin noticed my mother's crucifix, which I had hung around my neck, and inspected it more closely. "That's a fine piece of work," he said. "This is the cross that Redshaw says he gave to your mother?"

Something about the way he put it seemed to suggest that what Jamie Redshaw said was not necessarily what had happened. "Aye," I said defensively. " 'A engraved her name on the back."

Mr. Armin turned over the crucifix. "Yes, I see. A bit of advice. I wouldn't wear that where it may be seen."

"Why not?"

"Folk may take you for a Papist."

"A what?"

"A Catholic. Now, you may be one for all I know, or for all I care. But it's not wise to advertise the fact. There may be no problem here in the north, where Catholics are said to be as common as cowpies, if not quite as visible. But the nearer we get to London, the more chance you'll run afoul of Papist-hating Protestants and bring trouble not only upon yourself but upon the company. We players are held in low enough regard already."

I held up the cross and gazed at it. "Perhaps I should not wear it at all, then."

"That's up to you. If you like, we can put it in the treasury trunk. It'll be safe there."

"All right. I worry about the chain breaking anyway," I said. "Sal Pavy nearly clove it in two out there."

He stepped closer and pulled aside the neck of my linen shirt. "And your collarbone as well, if I'm not mistaken. You'll want to put something on that welt."

"I will."

"If there's trouble between you two," he said, "I'd like to know about it."

"Nay, no trouble."

Smiling skeptically, Mr. Armin said, "I applaud your loyalty, Widge. But don't imagine that we sharers are fooled. We know well enough that Sal Pavy is not the model prentice he pretends to be. He shows a great deal of promise, though, as a player. All he needs is a bit more self-discipline."

I rubbed my shoulder. "And some serious scriming lessons."

Mr. Armin laughed. "I'll work on that. You work on being more tolerant. Bear with him, Widge. He's had a hard time of it."

"Not to hear him talk. 'A makes it sound as though at Blackfriars 'a was treated more like a prince than a prentice—a bedroom of his own, a private tiring-room, no chores of any sort—"

Mr. Armin shook his head soberly. "As I'm sure you realize, he's exaggerating . . . considerably. Come; let's head back, and I'll tell you something of his story." As we walked to the inn, he continued. "I learned what I know from Mr. Pearce, the choirmaster at St. Paul's. Sal was sent there at the age of eight, to be educated and to be trained for the choir. Mr. Pearce tells me he had an extraordinary voice, clear and pure as rain."

"That doesn't sound like such a terrible fate to me."

"It wasn't, of course. But when he was ten or eleven, Sal was forced into service by the Chapel company."

"How could they do that?"

"They kidnapped him, essentially. It's done all the time, and no one dares object, since the Children of the Chapel come under the Queen's direct protection. Theoretically the Chapel company is permitted to take boys only for its choir, but of course their choir doesn't turn a profit, and their acting company does, so you may guess where most of the boys end up—including Sal."

"Why did 'a not simply run off?"

"He did, I gather, several times—and was caught and punished."

I winced. Now I knew the source of those stripes that decorated his back.

"What's more, the masters of the Chapel company all but ruined his singing voice by constantly making him strain to speak his lines *vociferato* and to mimic an old man's voice. Apparently they know no more about vocal techniques than they do about sword techniques. The one good thing to come of all this is that, rather than giving up, Sal determined to be the best actor he could, to draw enough attention to himself to tempt some other company to take him on. And he's done that. We're trying to undo some of the damage that's been done, to his voice and to his . . . to his soul, if you will. If you and Sam can manage to treat him . . . sympathetically, it will help."

I sighed. "I've been trying. It's not easy."

"Nor is what he has been through. His saving grace, and the thing that makes him so gifted an actor, is that he's been able to make use of all those hardships and disappointments. He puts something of himself—his pain, his anger, his frustration, his desires—into every role he plays."

I nodded glumly. "And I do not."

As Sander so often had done, Mr. Armin put a hand on my shoulder, being careful to choose the uninjured one. "You will, Widge, in time. Perhaps you won't be able to truly put yourself into a part until you're a bit more certain who you are."

I had no immediate opportunity to practice being sympathetic to Sal Pavy for, as usual, he did not share our tiring-room, and he made short work of his supper. More unexpected was the absence at supper of two others of our company, Ned Shakespeare and Jamie Redshaw. I tried not to let myself worry over this. Most likely my father was having a drink in some tavern, that was all. But I could not dismiss the nagging notion that he might suddenly have decided he did not particularly want to have a son or to travel with a band of gypsy players, and had gone back to York and his old way of life. He was, after all, as unused to having a son as I was to having a father.

As casually as I could manage, I asked the others if they had noticed him about after the performance. Will Sly recalled seeing him and Ned outside the Golden Lion. There, you see, I told myself, it's just as you imagined; he's only tossing back a few, and will be along in due time.

But night came, and Jamie Redshaw did not. Mr. Shakespeare and I toiled on the third act of *Love's Labour's Won*, but I found it difficult to concentrate, and several times I had to ask Mr. Shakespeare to repeat himself, which galled him, for he was having difficulties of his own. This play was, he swore, the sorriest piece of work he had ever put his hand—or anyone else's—to, and had he not already promised it to the Queen, he'd have gleefully burned it, page by page, like the rubbish that it was.

"Nay," I said, trying to be helpful. "It's not so bad. I've seen any number of plays that were worse: *Fortune's Tennis*, for example, or *The Battle of Alcazar*."

Mr. Shakespeare stared at me as though I'd brought up some subject not fit for polite company. "If I thought for a moment that my work had sunk to the level of those . . . *abominations,"* he said acidly, "I would use my pen knife to open a vein and write a farewell note to the world in my own blood."

"Oh," I said. "I see. The world would not be able to read it, though, you ken, for you'd ha' to write it left-handed."

His look of exasperation gave way slowly, reluctantly, to a sort of smile. "Yes, well, when I reach that point," he said, "I'll be sure to call you in and have you write it for me."

When I returned to our common room, neither Ned nor Jamie Redshaw was there. Though it was late and I was weary, I left the inn and walked through the dark streets of Leeds to the Golden Lion. When I stepped inside the door I saw Jamie Redshaw at once. He and Ned sat at a table with two other men, playing at cards. A haze of pipe smoke hung in the air about their heads. In the center of the table was a pile of coins; smaller piles lay directly before each of the players—except for Jamie Redshaw, who seemed to have not so much as a gray groat.

I nearly turned and left the tavern. I was well aware that the sharers did not approve of gambling; in fact, there were pointed rules against it. Discovering Ned and Jamie Redshaw engaged in this forbidden pastime put me in an awkward position. Clearly it was my duty to report their transgression to the sharers. But if I did, the two would likely be slapped with a substantial fine, and I did not care to be the one responsible. I thought it even possible they might be dismissed—or at least Jamie Redshaw might be;

Mr. Shakespeare would likely be more lenient with his own brother.

As I stood there in the shadows near the doorway, debating with myself, one of the men playing at cards let out a startling whoop of triumph and, leaning across the table, gathered in the central pile of coins. Jamie Redshaw sat even more stiffly than usual, with an equally stiff smile upon his face. "Well," he said with a careless tone that was quite convincing, "easily gotten, easily gone, eh?" He rose carefully to his feet with the aid of his walking stick. "Shall we meet again tomorrow night, gentlemen?"

One of the strangers gave a crooked-toothed grin. "You mean we've not got to the bottom of your purse yet?"

Jamie Redshaw shrugged. "This one, perhaps, but I've several others. Coming, Ned?"

Ned glared grimly down at the pitiful few pennies before him. "Not as long as I've a farthing left."

That should have been my cue to exit, but I missed it. As Jamie Redshaw strode to the door, I shrank back farther in the shadows, not wishing him to know that I had been spying on him. My movement caught his eye, though, and he stopped and raised his cane. "Who's there?" He peered into the dim corner. "Widge?"

"Aye." I came hesitantly forward. "You weren't i' the sleeping room, so I came looking for you."

"Still afraid I'll run off?" He put an arm around my shoulder, making me flinch. "What's wrong?"

"I hurt meself i' the sword fight this afternoon. It's not much; only a bruise." When I thought of his awful war wound, I felt foolish for even mentioning my inconsequential injury. As we headed back to the inn, I said, "Did you watch the play this afternoon?"

"Some of it."

I waited for him to go on, perhaps even to praise me a bit for my performance. When he did not, I prompted him shamelessly. "Did our swordplay look at all real?" I winced again, recalling just how real it had been.

He laughed. "I didn't suppose it was meant to. It was a play."

I nodded glumly. "I suppose it didn't much resemble a real battle."

"No." Abruptly he changed the subject. "You should have joined us at cards."

I wanted to mention the rule against gambling, but I did not wish to seem prudish or chiding, so I said, "I ken naught about card games, and I've no money to wager."

"There were no vast sums involved, just a few pennies to keep the game interesting."

"What that man won looked like more than a few pennies."

"Well, a few shillings, then."

I couldn't help wondering where he'd come by his share of it. "Do you truly ha' several other purses full of money?" I asked.

He laughed. "Of course not. But I couldn't let them think they'd cleaned me out. A fellow has his pride."

I spent a restless night; my mind was still wrestling with the problem of where my loyalties lay. Jack's snoring did not help matters. To get some respite from it, I dragged my sleeping mat out onto the gallery of the inn. As I lay looking up at the stars, I heard a faint sound floating across the inn yard. At first I could not identify it. It blended with the chirping of the crickets and the croaking of frogs, and might have been mistaken for either of them but that it was more sustained and more musical.

Curious, I sat up and listened more closely. Still I could not be certain of its source. When I felt my way down the gallery stairs to the yard, I determined that the sound was coming from the stable. As I drew nearer, it became clear that what I was hearing was a high human voice, a slightly hoarse voice that sometimes wavered, sometimes cracked, but for all that had a haunting, moving quality to it.

It was Sal Pavy, singing.

Immediately after breakfast the next morning Mr. Armin gathered us prentices in the yard of the inn for a scriming session. Though the instruction was mainly for Sal Pavy's benefit, Mr. Armin did not say so, and did not spare Sam and me in the slightest.

While he worked with Sal Pavy on delivering and parrying edgeblows, Sam and I practiced thrusting, alternating rapidly between the *imbrocata*, which is delivered above the opponent's blade, and the *stoccata*, delivered beneath the opponent's blade. Though our rapiers were blunted, they were capable of inflicting a nasty bruise, so for protection we strapped on the light, boiled leather breastplates that passed for metal armor on the stage.

"Why do you smile, infidel," said Sam, "when you are about to die?"

"I was just recalling the time Nick stuck me wi' his

sword and we all thought 'a'd done me in—all except Sander. There I was, swooning and breathing what I thought were me last breaths, and Sander takes one look and says, 'You sot! He stuck your blood bag!' I didn't feel half a ninny."

Sam grinned and shook his head. "I wish Sander was here now," he said.

I merely nodded. As we were hotly engaged in mock battle, I heard a voice from the second floor gallery say, "It's fortunate that you're playing to townfolk and not to a company of infantrymen." I glanced up to see Jamie Redshaw leaning on the railing, watching our practice.

Mr. Armin and Sal Pavy left off swiping at one another. "Oh," said Mr. Armin coolly. "Why is that?"

Jamie Redshaw laughed a bit uncomfortably, like someone who's been put on the spot. "Well, because they'd hoot you off the stage." He descended the gallery stairs and crossed the cobbles toward us. "I mean, anyone who's ever fought in earnest knows it's nothing like what you're doing." He seemed to realize how condescending this sounded, for he added, "I don't mean to be critical; of course you can't be expected to recreate the feel of a real battle upon the stage."

"No, no," replied Mr. Armin in a tone that might have sounded cordial to someone who did not know him well. "We want to be as convincing as possible. Perhaps you'll give us a few pointers."

Jamie Redshaw shrugged. "If you like."

"Sal, give your sword to Mr. Redshaw, will you?" Sal

Pavy obliged and backed well out of the way. "Now," said Mr. Armin, raising his blade and his eyebrows, "what is it we should be doing, exactly?"

I had the distinct feeling that Mr. Armin was not so much interested in what Jamie Redshaw might teach us as in teaching a lesson of his own, something to do with not putting in one's seven eggs where they're not wanted. I only hoped he would not drive the point home too hard.

Jamie Redshaw seemed to suspect nothing amiss. He came on guard, not in the usual sidewise fencing posture but with his body facing Mr. Armin almost straight on. "First of all," he said confidently, "a fighting man does not waste much time in trading blows. That serves only to tire you out. The object is to put an opponent out of the way with as little ado as possible."

Before he had finished speaking the last word, his blade darted forward, like a striking snake. To my astonishment, Mr. Armin's weapon flew from his grasp and clattered onto the cobbles. Though Mr. Armin was surely as stunned as I, he managed not to show it. His eyes narrowed a little, and he flexed his hand a few times as though it pained him.

It took me a moment to realize what had happened. Jamie Redshaw, instead of engaging his opponent in the usual game of thrust and parry, had disregarded the rules and aimed his point directly at Mr. Armin's sword hand. "The secret, you see," said Jamie Redshaw, "is to do the unexpected."

"Ah," said Mr. Armin, his voice carefully controlled. "Thank you for that insight. Next time I'll know not to expect what I expected. Good day." Jamie Redshaw returned the sword to Sal Pavy and silently left the yard. Mr. Armin turned to us. "Remember that, gentlemen. If you wish to kill your opponent, do the unexpected. If you wish him to live until the next performance, stick to the script. Now, I imagine you're expecting me to assign you fifty *passatas.*" He paused. "Well, I'm afraid I'm just hopelessly predictable. Proceed."

As we lined up against the stable wall and began thrusting, Sam said, "Your da made Mr. Armin look a bit of a fool, didn't he?"

I made no reply. I could not make up my mind whether to be proud of Jamie Redshaw's actions, or ashamed.

Mr. Armin had finally finished his play, *Fool Upon Fool,* and our first performance of it did a brisk business. So did our presentation of *King John* in the afternoon. When Jamie Redshaw brought the box to the sharers, his shoulders were sagging under the weight of it. The company's treasury trunk had grown so weighty that it took two men to carry it to the town hall and back. We could not, of course, risk leaving it unattended in our rooms, nor could we spare a man to stay behind and guard it. I was glad to have it close at hand, for it contained not only my future wages but, more important, my mother's crucifix.

At supper that evening, to celebrate our good fortune, the sharers broke out a bottle of brandy from the small stock we carried with us and poured some for everyone—everyone, that is, save Ned Shakespeare and Jamie Redshaw, who were again conspicuously absent. I checked the common sleeping room, but without any real hope that they would be there. They were not. As I started for the stairs, Sam came pounding up them and dragged me back into the sleeping room.

"What's the matter?" I demanded.

"I just overheard Sal Pavy telling Mr. Armin that he saw your father filching money from the box! He says he arrived late for this afternoon's performance, after the entrance doors were opened, and he noticed your da dropping pennies in his purse instead of in the gathering box."

"The devil take him!" I cried. " 'A's lying! Why would 'a lie?"

Sam shrugged. "To make trouble for you?"

"Trouble for me? But why? I've done naught to him!"

"You play the parts he'd like to play," said Sam.

I was speechless with surprise for a moment. Then an alarming thought struck me. "Will they confront me father wi' this, do you think?"

"No doubt."

There was no doubt, either, about where they'd find him and what he'd be doing. "Oh, gis!" I grasped Sam's arm. "You're a good friend, to tell me this. Can you do one more thing? Can you keep them here a minute or two longer?"

"I can try." Sam dashed back downstairs. I exited the room by the gallery door, scrambled down the outer stairs, and ran all the way to the Golden Lion. When I burst through the tavern door, Jamie Redshaw and Ned were at the same table as before, this time with four other men.

As I strode up to them, one of the men rose, scooped up his small stock of money, and made a quick departure. Thanks to the haze of tobacco smoke, which made the dim interior of the tavern even dimmer, I did not get much of a look at the man, but his portly build and the eye patch he wore were familiar.

"Why are you dropping out so sudden?" called one of the other cardplayers, but the one-eyed fellow did not bother to reply, or even to look back.

I stopped at Jamie Redshaw's side and bent to whisper in his ear, "I think the sharers may be on their way here."

"Yes?" he said without looking up from his cards.

"You don't want them to find you gambling!" I said urgently.

"Why not?"

"There's a company rule against it!"

"Ah." He stood at once and gathered up the sizable pile of coins that lay before him. "Gentlemen, I must ask you to excuse me as well. Ned, I think you'll also want to depart."

"What?" protested one of their playing companions. "You've got to give us a chance to win some of our money back!"

"Another time, gentlemen, another time. Let's go out the back way," he said to me.

With Ned Shakespeare along, I did not feel I should bring up the matter of Sal Pavy's accusation. Instead, I said, "Who was that wight wi' th' eye patch?"

"He didn't mention his name," replied Jamie Redshaw. "Why?"

"I believe 'a's wi' Lord Pembroke's Men. I saw him in their company, back in Newark."

"Did you? Perhaps he's spying on us."

"If so," said Ned, "he learned little, and it cost him dearly. How much did you win from him and the others?"

Jamie Redshaw cupped his purse in one hand, as though weighing it. "A fair amount. How much did you lose?"

"A fair amount," said Ned sourly. He glanced over at me. "You'll say nothing to the others about . . . about what we were up to?"

I shook my head. "Nay. That is," I added, "an you promise to go and sin no more."

Jamie Redshaw laughed. "The boy drives a hard bargain. What do you say, Ned? Shall we forswear gambling?"

"If we must," Ned said grudgingly. "I don't care for all these petty rules of the company's. It's like being back in Stratford, but with four parents riding me rather than just two."

When we reached the inn Ned went inside, but I held Jamie Redshaw back. "I . . . I don't mean to pry, but you told me last night you'd been cleaned out."

"And so I was."

"Then what . . . I mean, where . . ."

"Where did I get the money to wager tonight?"

"Aye."

He raised his walking stick. For a moment I feared he

meant to strike me with it for my impudence and, from old habit, I ducked my head. But he only tossed it lightly into the air and caught it again. "I wagered this. In truth, I've made far more use of it as a gambling stake than as a sword."

I laughed, more with relief than amusement. "I was right, then. 'A was lying."

"Who?"

"Sal Pavy. 'A—'a accused you of taking money from the box."

"The little weasel! He needs a sound thrashing!"

"Nay, nay. Let it pass, please!"

"Let it pass? He's insulted my honor!"

"Aye, but it's not worth stirring up trouble i' the company over 't."

"Not worth it?" Jamie Redshaw shook his head. "If you think that, you have a good deal to learn about the importance of honor."

"No doubt. But I ken a lot already about th' importance of keeping peace wi'in the company."

"Then you need to teach it to your friend Master Pavy."

" 'A's no friend of mine. But I don't wish him to be an enemy, either."

"There is no middle ground. If you can't count a man your friend, then you must count him your enemy."

I stared at him, trying to read his face in the dark. "You truly believe that?"

"I've had to," he said, "in order to survive."

"In battle, you mean. But not in ordinary life, surely?"

He let the walking stick drop to his side, and its metal tip clanged on the cobbles. "All of life is a battle."

When we entered the main room of the inn, Mr. Armin still sat at our table, with a pint of ale in his hands. He glanced up at me. "Mr. Shakespeare's waiting for you," he said. "Mr. Redshaw, I'd like a word with you."

As I headed for the stairs, I caught Jamie Redshaw's eye and gave him a pleading glance that said, "Please don't make trouble for me."

Though I was distracted with wondering what went on downstairs, I managed to do a fair job of transcribing. We were into the fourth act of what Mr. Shakespeare was now calling *All's Well That Ends Well.* I was delighted to have made such a significant contribution to the play, but he was as unhappy as ever. In the past week or so, he had taken to muttering to himself, like a litany, "Something's missing; something's missing." But he seemed unable to hit upon just what the missing thing was.

I was anxious to cheer him up, but I knew that I must be cautious in what I said, lest I make his melancholy mood worse. "Perhaps you're being too harsh in your judgment of the play," I ventured. "It seems to me to ha' quite a number of good things in 't."

I half expected him to reply, as he had before, "What do

you know about it?" He did look peevish but instead of berating me he challenged me: "Name one."

"Well . . . there's Helena."

He rolled his earring about between thumb and finger meditatively. "You like her, do you?"

"Oh, aye. In truth, I admire her. She's loyal, she's clever, she's strong-willed. She kens exactly what she wants, and she'll not be deterred."

"Yes, yes, I grant you that. But however strong she may be, she cannot carry a play all by herself."

"Why not?"

He sighed. "I don't have the time just now to give you a course in how to construct a well-made play."

"I'm sorry. I was only trying to understand."

"I know, I know." He toyed with his earring again for a time and then went on. "A play is like a balance, you see. If, on one end of the arm, you place a certain quantity of loyalty and cleverness and strong will, on the other end you need an equal weight of something else, to offset it."

"Well, you ha' Bertram. 'A's selfish and haughty and rude." Though I did not say so, I was thinking what a pity it was that Sal Pavy had not yet graduated to men's roles, for he could have played Bertram to the life without any effort at all.

"But Bertram is no villain—nor can we let him be, or the audience will never accept the notion that Helena is in love with him so unswervingly."

"An you love someone," I said, "do you not overlook their faults?"

"Only to a point. No, we can't depend on Bertram to bring things into balance. Let's leave him in the middle, halfway between Helena on the one hand and, on the other hand, someone . . . someone truly despicable. But *what* someone?" He pressed a hand to his head and sighed again. "Never attempt to write a play, Widge," he said.

"I had no plans to."

"Good. They always betray you. When you're only imagining them, they seem so ideal, so full of promise and possibility. Then, when you try to get them down on paper, they turn on you and refuse to live up to your expectations."

One of the uncanny qualities about Mr. Shakespeare's words, I had learned, was that, however general they might seem, at the same time they somehow managed to speak directly to each individual who heard them, and to address his particular plight. "Perhaps the fault is ours," I said, "in hoping for too much. We cannot expect people to be flawless."

"People?" he said. "I thought we were speaking of plays."

I smiled sheepishly. "Of course. I was only—"

"I know." Wearily he closed his eyes and rubbed at his forehead. Then abruptly he stopped and raised his head, his eyes wide open. "I know," he repeatedly softly. "I know. I know who he is."

"Who *who* is?"

"The someone. The balancing someone. The despicable someone." As I had seen it do before, Mr. Shakespeare's mood transformed in the space of a few seconds from melancholy to manic. "He's a soldier—a friend of Bertram's, but not a true friend. He's a braggart. He's deceitful. He's a coward. Bertram, though, will not hear a word against him—like Helena, he's loyal—" Mr. Shakespeare waved his good hand at me. "Go back, go back," he commanded.

"Back?" I echoed.

"To Act One. We'll write him in."

I flipped frantically through the pages of the script. "What's his name to be, then?"

"I don't know. Something despicable. *Menteur. Poltron.* It doesn't matter. Just write."

And we were off, galloping once again. The demands of keeping up with the stampede of words that followed put all thought of Jamie Redshaw and Sal Pavy's accusation out of my mind for the moment. When Mr. Shakespeare was done with me at last and I hurried back down to the main room, I found Mr. Armin and Jamie Redshaw still there, and not at one another's throats but conversing amiably over their ale. "How did it go?" asked Mr. Armin—the very words I would have liked to ask.

"Quite well," I said. " 'A was a bit downcast at first, but that's naught of note."

Mr. Armin nodded. "He can hardly expect to write *Hamlet* every time. By the bye, he's told me he greatly appreciates your help and your patience."

"Has 'a, truly?" I said. " 'A seldom says so to me face."

"It's not his way." Mr. Armin turned to Jamie Redshaw. "Widge has been a valuable addition to our company, sir."

If I hoped to see some trace of fatherly pride, I was disappointed. Jamie Redshaw simply said, "I'm glad to hear it," then got stiffly to his feet. "I believe I'll retire." He waved a stack of handbills at me. "I've been given the job of posting these around town in the morning."

I would have left with him, for I hoped to learn what had been said in regard to Sal Pavy's charge. But Mr. Armin asked me to stay. It took him several minutes to get to what was on his mind. Finally he said, "How much do you know of this Redshaw?"

"Well . . . very little, I suppose," I admitted reluctantly. "I ken 'a's me father."

"Has he said so?"

"Not in as many words. But 'a was . . . well acquainted wi' me mother. They would ha' wed, 'a said, had it not been for her parents' objections."

"You're certain he knew her?"

" 'A kenned her name, and that it was engraved on the crucifix. Why? Do you doubt him?"

"I've no real reason to, just . . . just a feeling."

"What sort of feeling?"

"That not everything he says is so. For example, his statement that he and your mother were well acquainted implies that he grew up here in Yorkshire. Yet his speech says otherwise. I put him down as a Dorset man, or Somerset."

" 'A never said 'a grew up here. Besides, 'a's spent many years in other lands, as a soldier."

"So he says."

"You doubt that, too?" I tried to keep my tone calm and reasonable but did not entirely succeed.

Mr. Armin shrugged. "As I said, I've no real reason to, so let's let it drop for now. I can see it's upsetting you, and I can't blame you."

I was upset mainly because Mr. Armin was bringing into the light a shadowy something that I myself had secretly suspected but had always managed to dismiss. After all, I told myself, who was I to condemn a man for the occasional falsehood? Besides, even if Jamie Redshaw did stray from the truth from time to time, it did not mean that he had lied about everything. In any case, I felt it was my duty to defend him. "I suppose you have him down as a thief, too, on Sal Pavy's say-so?"

"No. Clearly not everything that Sal says can be counted on, either."

"Oh." My anger subsided a bit at this. "You did not accuse him, then?"

"I told him that Sal had accused him."

"And what did 'a do?"

"He laughed. And then he admitted that he had indeed taken several coins from the box."

My heart sank at his news. " 'A did?"

Mr. Armin nodded, then fished in his wallet and held out something for me to see. "They were these." In his hand were three circles the exact size of a penny but made of wood, with some silvery substance—quicksilver, perhaps—rubbed on the surface.

"Wooden coins?" I said.

"Coney-coins, some call them."

I shook my head in disgust. "What sort of wight would do such a thing?"

"A woodman?" suggested Mr. Armin slyly.

"Aye," I said, "a woodman would. Particularly a woodman who's wood," I added, certain that Mr. Armin would know that, hereabouts, *wood* was used to mean "insane."

He smiled appreciatively. "Aye, a wood woodman would, though I would 'a would not."

I could provide no further puns, only a prodigious yawn. In the street outside the inn a night watchman cried, "Ten o'clock, and all's well!"

"Holy mother," I said wearily. "I hope so."

When we headed for the town hall next afternoon, I noticed that many of the town's walls and fences still sported handbills for yesterday's *King John,* and only a very few held papers announcing that day's performance of *The Two Gentlemen of Verona.* In addition, most of the *Two Gentlemen* handbills had no date or time printed on them. "Oh, gis," I said to Sam. " 'A's not done his job!"

"Your da?" Sam said.

I nodded grimly. Even worse, when half past one came around, Jamie Redshaw did not turn up to act as gatherer. "I'll do it," Sam offered.

"Nay," I said, "you're still not strong. You help wi' makeup. I'll gather."

Sal Pavy arrived late, as was his habit lately. When he saw me holding the box, he smirked and shook a finger at me as if to say, "No filching, now." The gesture I gave him in return could not have been so readily translated, at least not by a person of good upbringing.

Jamie Redshaw did show up for supper, for a change. When Mr. Armin asked why he had not done his duty as gatherer, he said, with evident surprise and chagrin, "I assumed that, after yesterday, you would prefer that I not handle the money."

"If I implied that, I did not mean to," said Mr. Armin.

"There's the m-matter of the h-handbills, too," said Mr. Heminges. "You were t-to replace yesterday's with today's."

"I know, and I apologize. The truth is—" He paused, looking uncomfortable. "Well . . . it's difficult, as an old soldier, to admit this but . . . I was ambushed."

"Ambushed?" said Ned Shakespeare with an incredulous laugh.

Jamie Redshaw cast him a look sharp enough to sober him. "Attacked, if you will. I had posted but a few of the bills when I passed the mouth of a narrow alley. A moment later, someone struck me from behind with a cudgel or the like. When I fell to my knees, dazed, my assailant snatched the bills from my hand; before I could recover, he had vanished."

Mr. Armin frowned skeptically. "Why would anyone wish to steal our handbills?"

"You would know that better than I."

"For the same reason they'd set fire to our carts," said Jack resentfully. "To make life difficult for us." It was now Jack's lot to sleep in one of the carewares each night, lest they be molested again. Though it might be uncomfortable for him, it was a blessing for the rest of us, to be spared his snoring.

"Well," said Mr. Heminges, "they c-certainly succeeded. The audience was f-far smaller today; p-presumably folk thought we were d-doing *King John* again."

"It must be a rival company, then," said Mr. Phillips. "But whose?"

"Lord Pembroke's Men?" I suggested.

"We d-don't know that they're in the v-vicinity, Widge."

"But I—I think I saw one of them yesterday." I noticed Ned Shakespeare giving me a warning look, as though reminding me not to divulge under what circumstances I had seen the man. "The wight wi' th' eye patch."

"I don't recall anyone of that description among Pembroke's men," said Mr. Phillips.

"Nor do I," said Mr. Shakespeare. "But they may well have altered the company for touring purposes, as we have done."

"They were at Newark, too," I reminded them. "When the carewares were set afire."

"B-but what do they have to g-gain by harassing us?" said Mr. Heminges.

Will Sly shrugged. "Simple. If they run us off, they'll have that much less competition."

Mr. Armin still looked skeptical. "I find it hard to imagine them stooping to such base tactics, a respectable company like Pembroke's."

"In desperate straits," said Jamie Redshaw, "respectable men sometimes cease to be respectable." He rose from the table. "If you'll excuse me, I mean to go and lie down. My head is still throbbing."

"I'll bring you up some willow bark tea," I said.

He gave me a dubious look. "I'd prefer brandy."

"Nay, nay," I protested. "Spirits will only make your head ache worse."

"I'll vouch for that," said Will Sly, and the others laughed, for Will was known for his tendency to overindulge in drink from time to time.

When I brought the tea to the common room, Jamie Redshaw was not lying down, but standing in the open doorway to the gallery, looking out on the inn yard. He turned to me. "Your Mr. Armin seems suspicious of me, somehow. Has he said anything of the sort to you?"

"Nay," I lied. "I suppose 'a's just naturally a suspicious fellow." As soon as the words left my mouth, I felt guilty, for I well knew that Mr. Armin was a fair man, and that, if he seemed mistrustful or wary at times, it was only because he was concerned about my welfare, or that of the company.

We sat on our traveling trunks, and I poured some of the willow bark tea into an earthenware cup. Jamie Redshaw took a sip of it and made a face. "I still say it would be better with a dollop of brandy—a large one." He set the cup aside. "You seem to have taken on the duties of physician as well as clerk and actor. You should demand an increase in wages."

I shook my head emphatically. "I would never dare do that."

"Why not? You deserve it. You heard how highly Armin spoke of you. Shall I do the asking for you?"

I shook my head again, even more emphatically. "I've no wish to appear greedy. They might conclude they could do wi'out me."

"So? There are other companies. Perhaps one of them would better appreciate your worth."

The mere thought of leaving the Lord Chamberlain's Men sent a stab of dread through me, like the mention of the plague. "Nay! You can't ask me to give up me position here!"

Jamie Redshaw held up a hand to calm me. "I'm not asking that. It was but a suggestion. I've no right to tell you what to do."

"You're—you're me father," I said.

He looked uncomfortable, as though his head or his war wound were bothering him. "Well," he said, "you've done well enough without me up until now."

I gave a bitter laugh. "For the past year or so, aye," I said, more hotly than I intended. "For the fourteen years before that, I was not doing so well for meself. I could have used a father then."

Jamie Redshaw seemed taken aback by my outburst. "I'm sorry," he replied, though not very sympathetically. "As I've said, I had no idea you existed." He scowled and rubbed the back of his head. "I'm feeling a bit dizzy. I need to rest now." He stretched out on his mattress and closed his eyes.

Though he obviously meant for me to depart, I stubbornly lingered. "I was only wondering . . . that is . . . I ken how reluctant you are to speak of me mother, but . . . "

"But you want to know more about her."

"Aye," I said eagerly. "And about yourself as well."

He turned his head to me and opened his eyes. "Why?"

"Why? Well, so that . . . so that I ken something of where I come from, I suppose."

"That's not important," he said. "All that truly matters is where you end up." It was very nearly the same thing Mr. Armin had said to me a few weeks earlier, and it was not what I wanted to hear. "One thing I can tell you," he went on. "You don't want to end up like me." He turned away again. "I'll try to recall more about your mother, and we'll talk again. We've plenty of time."

But the right time seemed never to come. When the players were on the road, Jamie Redshaw and I were continually in the company of the other prentices and hired men, and though I could count Sam and Will Sly my friends, I could not say the same for Jack and Ned and Sal Pavy. Certainly I would not have cared to discuss so personal a matter before them.

When we were in residence in some town, our mornings were occupied with rehearsing and occasional lessons, and our afternoons with performing. In the evenings Jamie Redshaw was seldom at the inn with the rest of us. I suspected that he and Ned were, despite their pledge, still tarrying in the local alehouses, though heaven only knew what they found to wager with.

The sharers' plan—to play only the larger towns and thus avoid being associated with the company of thieves who were passing themselves off as players—proved to be flawed. The most populous places were, we found, also the ones most susceptible to the plague. Some of these contagion-racked cities turned away all travelers; others seemed to have a special dislike of theatre companies. The officials of some towns drove us off with threats; others paid us substantial sums not to perform.

When we reached Shrewsbury, which sat off the main road a little way, we found signs posted outside the town, forbidding anyone at all to enter. "That's unfortunate," said Mr. Heminges. "We're short on s-supplies."

"They can't keep us out," said Jamie Redshaw indignantly and, gripping his walking stick like a cudgel, strode forward, past the sign and up the broad main street. He had not gone fifty yards before the first men began to emerge from taverns and shops. Several had swords drawn. One—a tavern keeper, judging from his apron—carried a gun, a wide-barreled matchlock blunderbuss.

"In case you can't read," he called out, "the sign says no travelers allowed!"

Jamie Redshaw halted. "We need food and drink!"

"Go back beyond the sign, then. We'll bring it to you!"

When Jamie Redshaw rejoined the company, Mr. Armin said, "We would have handled the matter, Mr. Redshaw. It's not your concern."

Jamie Redshaw smiled, more smugly than apologetically, I thought. "My stomach is my concern," he said.

A short while later, a small group of men, led by the tavern keeper with the blunderbuss, approached us. One of the men carried a large basket of viands—cheese, bread, dried fish, apples—and another a small keg of ale. They set the provisions in the road. "That's seven shillings' worth," said the tavern keeper. "Put your coins in the plague stone."

"The p-plague stone?" repeated Mr. Heminges.

The man pointed to a limestone boulder that sat beside the road. A sort of bowl had been carved into the top of it, and this depression was filled with water. Mr. Heminges dropped a half-angel and two shillings into it.

I leaned over to whisper to Sam, "They must imagine that the water somehow drowns the infection."

"Doesn't it?" said Sam.

"I don't ken," I replied and, more irritably, added, "Why does everyone seem to think I'm a physician? I'm an actor."

"I can see that," Sam said calmly. "This is your impersonation of Sal Pavy, right?"

I tried to glare at him, but it somehow turned into a grin. "You sot."

In Telford we found that we had once again been preceded by the band of thieves posing as players. There was a new development in their deceit, now, though; this time they were calling themselves the Lord Chamberlain's Men.

The mayor pointed out to us one of the handbills the counterfeit company had posted, announcing a performance that the mayor paid for but never saw. The play it purported to advertise was none other than Mr. Shakespeare's *King John*.

"Gog's blood!" I said to Jamie Redshaw. "Now we ken who stole the bills from you, and why!"

I expected him to react with anger and vow to catch the culprits. Instead, he shook his head, tapped the handbill with the head of his walking stick, and said with something like admiration, "Well, there's no denying they're cheeky, clever rascals, is there?"

We moved on to Bridgnorth, where we played a single performance of *Fool Upon Fool,* then took ourselves to Kidderminster. Like most of the towns we had played since leaving Leeds, these were not on the itinerary I had sent to Sander. "An we play none of the places we planned to," I complained to Sam, "how can we ever hope for a letter from London to find us?"

Since few of these smaller towns had halls big enough to accommodate us, we often had to set up our wagon-bed stage in the courtyard of the inn where we were lodging. It was far from the ideal playing space; the boards sagged and swayed under our feet and, because the stage was so much smaller than we were used to, we were in constant danger of stepping off the edge.

In fact, I did just that during my *King John* sword-fighting scene with Sal Pavy. I was wary of his wild edgeblows still, and spent a good deal of my time retreating. He failed to warn me that I had run out of room, so off I went and landed, luckily, in the arms of one of the audience. For my pains, I got a round of laughter and applause.

As with the blow he'd delivered to my collarbone, I was

certain this had been no accident. Though I was furious, I neither confronted him nor complained to the sharers. Jamie Redshaw, who had seen me take the fall, urged me to retaliate in kind. "The next time you play the scene, let him have an 'accidental' thrust to the groin. He'll never expect it—and it's certain he'll never forget it."

I laughed weakly. " 'A deserves as much. But I cannot. I've promised Mr. Armin I'd be patient wi' him."

"It was a fool's promise. I know how boys like this Pavy work. If you don't strike back, he'll continue to push and push you until he's pushed you out of the picture." He gave me a searching glance. "You're not afraid of him, are you?"

"Of course not," I replied indignantly.

"Good. Then show him."

There would be no opportunity to exact revenge on Sal Pavy until we played *King John* again, which likely would not be for a week or so. Our next stop was Worcester—a town that was, for a change, actually on our itinerary. I was prepared to perform at an inn once more, but Worcester proved to have an actual theatre, built as a venue for gypsy companies like ours—one reason why our sharers had put it on their schedule. Several other companies, we learned, had been here before us, including a much-reduced Lord Admiral's Men and a scaled-down version of the Earl of Derby's Men.

When we emerged from the town hall, having secured permission to play two afternoon performances, we discovered a bedraggled troupe of players who had, presumably, come there for the same purpose. Every member of the company was afoot. Their single careware, which looked about to collapse, was pulled by two horses in much the same state. Though they wore no special livery, Mr. Armin recognized them as the Earl of Hertford's Men. He greeted the man who headed up the sorry-looking company, a tall, underfed fellow with crooked teeth, who would have looked more at home in a wheat field, chasing crows, than on a stage.

"Hello, Martin! You and your men look as though you're a bit down on your luck."

The man named Martin looked over our company, who were clad in our fine blue caps and capes. "And you look as though you've prospered."

"Only lately. We've had our share of hard times, too."

"I suppose you've gotten permission to play here already." At Mr. Armin's nod, Martin scowled. "We were counting on a brief engagement here to give us enough funds to limp back to London. We've already sold our livery, our best horses, and one of our wagons; we've nothing left to sell save our costumes and the clothes on our backs."

The sharers offered to let them perform in our place, but Hertford's Men refused. "That would be unfair," said Martin.

"Well, suppose we toss a coin," said Mr. Armin.

Martin shook his head. "Too arbitrary. I propose, instead, that we hold an acting competition. The players who acquit themselves best in the opinion of the audience will then get to perform for profit. What say you?"

After a moment's consultation, the sharers accepted the challenge. "Shall we say here, before the town hall, at four o'clock?" said Mr. Armin. "We'll send a crier around town to announce it."

That gave us a scant hour to decide what scene we would enact, with what actors, and to prepare ourselves. "It should b-be a scene with a m-man and a woman," said Mr. Heminges. "Those g-go over best."

"And a comic scene is most likely to win the audience over quickly," added Mr. Phillips.

"What about Viola and Feste's scene from *Twelfth Night*?" suggested Sam.

"Too insubstantial, I think," said Mr. Shakespeare. "We need something with more weight to it."

"Lavinia's scene with the staff, from *Titus*, then," said Mr. Armin.

Will Sly laughed. "Oh, yes, that's comical, that is. A ravaged girl reveals who it was that lopped off her hands and cut out her tongue. It'll have the audience rolling about on the ground."

"It's to be an acting contest," Mr. Armin reminded him, "not a jesting contest."

"Lord Hertford's Men are so d-defeated already," said Mr. Heminges, "p-perhaps we should let them win."

"Deliberately do our worst, you mean?" said Mr. Shakespeare. "No. I'm sure they'd prefer to lose, rather than to win that way."

Lord Hertford's Men did choose a comic scene, one from Peele's *The Old Wives' Tale*, and the audience responded with gales of laughter. By contrast, when Sal Pavy did his wordless turn as the unfortunate Lavinia, there was, as usual, scarcely a sound. But when we were done and those watching were asked to indicate their favorite, the applause given our scene was by far the heartier.

Though I had no right to be jealous, I was—fiercely so. I had been with the company far longer than Sal Pavy, after all, and the role had been mine before it was his. Why should I not be the one up there basking in the applause?

Lord Hertford's Men accepted their lot with good grace, consoled somewhat by the fact that our sharers offered to buy most of their wardrobe for considerably more than it was worth. We had no real need for the costumes, of course, nor any extra room in our carewares; it was a way of aiding a troupe of our fellows who were less fortunate than we, without wounding their pride.

In the morning Will Sly and I and Jamie Redshaw went about Worcester, putting up announcements for that afternoon's performance of *The Two Gentlemen of Verona*.

Since the whole town could be traversed in ten minutes' time, the job did not require three of us; we only wanted to be certain that our handbills did not fall into the hands of some rival company again.

As we toured the town, Jamie Redshaw made a note of where the alehouses were. "Care to join me for a drink after the play?" he asked Will Sly.

"Thanks, but I'd liefer do my drinking at the inn," said Will, "where I'm not so likely to be drawn into a game of chance."

"You have a weakness for gambling, then, do you?" asked Jamie Redshaw.

"I have a weakness for everything. I've learned that my only hope lies in staying in sight of the sharers. They have a way of keeping at bay anything that looks remotely like a vice or pleasure."

"Now, that's unfair," I said, though I could not help laughing a little. "They're only trying to keep the company respectable, and give the lie to th' image of players as disreputable wights."

"It seems to me," said Jamie Redshaw, "that they're trying a trifle too hard."

The sharers were cautious in other ways, too. After Sam's bout of ague, they had begun to insist that each of us learn several of our fellow players' parts, so that if one of the company was injured or fell ill, another could fill the breach. So it was that when Jack, against everyone's advice, ate some suspicious-looking brawn at lunch and came down with a gripe in his guts, Ned Shakespeare was able, if not exactly willing, to fill in for him.

Since Jack would be confined to our room anyway, we left the treasury trunk in his care, with instructions to keep both doors barred until our return. I gave him peppermint oil to settle his stomach, then set out for the theatre.

As I mounted the steps to the stage, I heard Ned's complaining voice say, "I don't see why you can't press Jamie Redshaw into service."

The voice that replied was his brother's. "Because we cannot afford to pay out another hired man's wages."

"Can't afford it?" exclaimed Ned. "The treasury trunk is near to overflowing!"

"And we've rents to pay upon our return, and new costumes to buy, and a hundred other expenses you know nothing of." Though Mr. Shakespeare's tone was reasonable enough, Ned was clearly rankled by it.

"Yes, well, Redshaw's paying himself a good wage, anyway," said Ned spitefully. "You may as well make him work for it." He emerged, scowling, from behind the curtain, gave me a quick and hostile glance, and then pushed past me.

I stepped through the curtain. Mr. Shakespeare sat before a polished metal mirror, trying without the use of his right hand to turn his features into those of Antonio. He glanced up at my reflection. "When did you say this plaster bandage can come off?"

"I didn't say. I'd only be guessing."

He sighed. "Well, if I can put up with it until we reach Stratford, I can consult the family's physician there. I presume he knows something about broken bones."

"I would not be too confident of it. Most physicians, I think, dislike the messier aspects of medicine. They prefer to dispense pills and nostrums."

"You may be right," he said.

I opened the costume trunk and dug out my dress for Silvia. "I . . . I overheard what Ned was saying."

"I'm sorry you did."

"Did 'a mean to say that me father is filching from the box?"

"Most likely." Mr. Shakespeare paused. "I mean that it's most likely what Ned was implying, not that your father is most likely stealing money."

"Oh. Do you think Ned may ha' seen it happen?"

"What I think is that Ned will say whatever suits his purpose at the moment." He flung his makeup brush down in frustration.

"Shall I help you?" I asked.

He shook his head. "I'd like to think I'm not totally helpless." He turned and gazed in the direction Ned had gone. "It was a mistake, bringing him along. He's been more of a hindrance than a help, I think." I made no reply, for I felt he was talking more to himself than to me. "But," he went on, "he is family, and we must make allowances for family."

To this I did reply, for the observation seemed to extend

to me and Jamie Redshaw. "Aye," I said. "They may not be as we'd have them be, so I suppose we must take them as they are, mustn't we?"

Mr. Shakespeare gave a rueful half smile. "Oh, Lord, sir," he said.

The other players arrived, one by one, and set about transforming themselves into their characters. Beyond the curtain, I could hear the audience filling up the hall, getting their coughs out of the way before the play began, talking to one another in curiously hushed tones, like people anticipating some momentous event. As always, it was both heady and at the same time humbling to think that we were that event.

Just before we were ready to go on, a small, nearly bald man poked his head tentatively around the curtain. "I'm the town clerk," he said. "Are you the Lord Chamberlain's Men?"

"Yes," said Mr. Heminges, "and we have p-papers to prove it."

"It's not that I doubted you," said the man, coming all the way around the curtain. "I only wanted to be sure I was putting this into the proper hands." He held out a folded paper sealed with wax. Mr. Heminges took it, read the back, and passed it on to me. "From S-Sander," he said.

My hand trembled with eagerness. "Dare I read it now?" I asked.

"Of c-course," said Mr. Heminges. "The audience c-can wait a few m-minutes more. B-but you must read it aloud."

"Aye." I broke the seal and unfolded the missive. I had expected another long, reassuring letter full of news and amusing anecdotes. It was, instead, succinct—two short paragraphs without even a greeting—and far from reassuring:

> This is but one of half a dozen letters sent to various towns along your route, in hopes that one of them will reach you. The situation here is growing grave. The contagion has become more of a threat. None of us has been afflicted so far. Mr. Burbage has departed for the country, though, to escape it.
>
> He left us a substantial sum, of course, but it has dwindled rapidly, for we have been obliged to pay a physician to tend Mr. Pope, who has fallen ill. The doctor calls it a stroke, and is bleeding him regularly. Goody Willingson and I are doing the best we can with the boys and Tetty, but I do not know how much longer our food and our funds will hold out. I know that the company may well be in reduced circumstances, too, but if there is any way you can send us even a pound or two, it would be a great relief.
>
> Your obt. svt.,
> Alexander Cooke

When I had finished reading, my fellow players stood in shocked silence a moment. Then Mr. Armin said, "What date did he put on the letter?"

"Twenty-four July."

"And this is the third of August. They must be in desperate straits by now."

"The quickest w-way would be for one of us t-take the money to them," said Mr. Heminges.

"I'll do it," I said at once. "Except for Sam, I'm the smallest and lightest."

Mr. Armin placed a hand on my shoulder. "Thanks for the offer. We really should have a more experienced rider, though—and a more experienced swordsman, I suspect, for there may be bandits along the way."

"I agree," said Mr. Heminges. Mr. Shakespeare and Mr. Phillips nodded.

"I'll depart immediately after the play, then," said Mr. Armin.

I stared at him incredulously. "*After* the play? Why not now?"

"Two hours cannot make much difference."

So distressed was I that I forgot all my resolve never to put my place with the company in peril by complaining or quarreling. "How do you ken that?" I said. "They may be starving even as we speak! Suppose they've run out of money to pay the physician?"

"We're players," said Mr. Armin. "We have a performance to give."

"Is a performance worth more than a life, then?" I cried. "We're merely to act, when we should be taking action?"

"That's enough, W-Widge," said Mr. Heminges.

I turned to him. "If none of you will go, then send me

father." Mr. Heminges shook his head. "Why not?" I demanded.

He seemed about to reply, and then Jamie Redshaw came around the curtain and set the gatherer's box down with a thump. "The audience is growing restless," he announced. He looked around at our solemn and strained expressions. "Is something wrong?"

"We'll explain later," said Mr. Heminges.

"Oh. Very well." Wincing, Jamie Redshaw hefted the box. "I'll take this back to the inn, then, and add it to the treasury trunk."

"G-good. Widge, g-go and get your play book, and we'll begin."

Though there was far more I wished to say about the matter, I feared I had said too much already. I clamped my mouth tight shut and, like a good prentice, did as I was told. I took my place in the wings as prompter until my time came to go on the stage. But tears of frustration stung my eyes so that, when Ned Shakespeare needed to be told his lines, I could not make out the words upon the page.

Though the actors said their speeches with unprecedented speed, the play seemed interminable. The moment Mr. Armin delivered his last line, he strode from the stage, tossed off his costume, and donned his street garb. I should have assisted him, I suppose, but I was too angry with him still.

As I was changing from my costume, it occurred to me that, if I could send a note of some sort with him, it might help cheer Sander and the others. Without even pausing to put away my wig and costume, I dashed from the theatre and down the street. I ran directly to the stable at the inn, supposing I would find Mr. Armin saddling one of the horses.

I supposed wrong. As I emerged into the yard, I saw that the door to our common sleeping room stood open, so I scrambled up the gallery stairs. When I burst through the doorway, I came upon a scene so unexpected that, despite my breathless condition, I gave a startled gasp.

Mr. Armin knelt on the floor next to the limp, sprawled form of Jack, who was clearly unconscious—or dead. My immediate thought was that his illness, which I had taken to be minor, had been worse than I suspected. And then I caught sight of the treasury trunk, which sat close at hand. Its hasp was twisted, its lid nearly torn from its hinges, and there was not a single coin within. Next to it sat the gatherer's box, every bit as empty.

"Gog's wounds!" I gasped. "What's happened?"

It was a foolish thing to say, for it was perfectly clear what had happened. Someone had assaulted Jack and made off with all our money. Mr. Armin did not bother to state the obvious, but said, "He's alive; I can feel a pulse in his neck. Help me lift him onto his bed."

As I hurried to take hold of Jack's legs, I got my first good look at his head as well. It lay in a pool of blood. When we had him laid out upon the mattress, I said, "I'll fetch some water and some bandages."

"Can you manage alone?" asked Mr. Armin. "If I'm quick, I may yet be able to catch the thief."

"Aye," I said, "go on. The others will be along shortly anyway." I ran down to the main room of the inn to fetch a ewer of water. As I was returning, Mr. Armin emerged from his room with a sword strapped to his side.

I was almost glad to have the duty of tending to Jack, for I did not care to think too much about the implications of what had happened. For one thing, if all the contents of the trunk were gone, that meant my mother's crucifix was gone as well. Even more troubling was the realization that, if the gatherer's box was here, then Jamie Redshaw must necessarily have been here, too.

I pushed these thoughts aside and forced myself to concentrate on Jack's wounds. He had been struck on the side of the skull with some blunt object—just one blow, as best I could determine. If it had been two inches lower, it would have hit his temple and most likely been the death of him. As it was, the effects were bad enough. The blow had torn loose a patch of his scalp, and the blood was welling steadily from the wound. If I was any judge of head injuries—which, in truth, I was not—the skull was surely fractured as well.

The first order of business was to staunch the bleeding. Gingerly, but rapidly, I clipped away the matted hair with a scissors from our medicine chest, plastered the flap of skin back in place, laid a pad of cloth on it, and bound the wound up tightly.

Before I had quite finished, Will Sly and Sam came trampling up the stairs, laughing over some incident from the afternoon's performance. They broke off abruptly when they saw the state of the room. "The devil take me!" said Will. "We've been robbed!" His eyes fell on Jack's unconscious form. "Is he dead?"

I shook my head. "Not yet, but near to 't, I'm afeared. 'A's leaked enough blood to fill a piggin."

"Have you any notion who did it?" asked Sam.

I did not wish to be the one to mention my father's name in connection with the crime. Nor, it seemed, did the others. Without a word, Will bent and examined the bare trunk and the gatherer's box. Then he stood and glanced at the doors to the room, both of which stood open. "The doors were this way when you arrived?"

"Nay. I unbarred the inside door to go downstairs. But the door to the gallery was wide open."

Will picked up the wooden bar, which was intact. "This door hasn't been forced. That means Jack must have unbarred it from in here. And that means—" He hesitated.

"It means," said Mr. Armin, who at that moment appeared in the doorway, "that whoever came to the door must have been someone well known to Jack."

I swallowed hard and said, "You—you saw no sign of the thief?"

"No," he replied quietly. His eyes met mine, and I saw something like pain in them, or pity. "But," he went on, his voice softer still, "I did find this, just outside the entrance to the inn yard." His right hand, which had been concealed by the doorframe, came forward, and in it was a wooden walking stick. The lion's head on the handle was barely visible, caked as it was with half-dried blood and tufts of human hair.

I shrank back from the sight, not wanting to look at it,

yet unable to take my eyes away. "Nay!" I cried. "It can't ha' been him, I'm certain of it!"

"I wish I could believe that," said Mr. Armin. "But look at the evidence."

"You look at it! You want it to be him! You've always disliked and distrusted him, from the day 'a joined the company!" I whirled and ran down the inside stairs, through the main room of the inn, and out into the street.

I stood there a moment, looking around frantically, for what I was uncertain—for some way out of this situation, perhaps. I wanted to run away, but there was nowhere for me to go. I wanted to find Jamie Redshaw, to ask him for an explanation, to warn him, but I had no notion where he might be. If he truly had played some role in the robbery—though I did not wish to consider that possibility, I must—then he would surely have fled or gone into hiding.

I began walking away from the inn with no destination in mind, only the desire to distance myself from Mr. Armin and from Jack's still form, from the empty money boxes and the bloody walking stick. I spotted the other sharers coming toward me, on their way back from the theatre. Abruptly I turned onto a side street. I could not bear to be the one to tell them all that had happened. Better to let Mr. Armin do it, I thought bitterly; he would get more satisfaction out of it.

As I turned another corner, I all but collided with Ned Shakespeare, who was emerging from an apothecary shop with a pouch of smoking tobacco. "You're in a hurry," he said. "Who's after you?"

"Ha' you seen me father?" I demanded.

"Not since before the performance. I wouldn't be surprised, though, if you found him at the sign of the Three Tuns." He gestured down the street. As I strode off in that direction, he called, "What's he done, robbed the box again?" I ignored him and broke into a run.

Ned was right. Jamie Redshaw sat at a table in the Three Tuns, intent on a game of primero. As I slid onto the bench beside him, he gave me a glance that did little to make me feel he was happy to see me. "Checking up on me, are you?"

"Nay," I said breathlessly. "I need to talk wi' you."

"Later, then." He laid two cards face down and was dealt two more.

I felt tears spring to my eyes and fought them back. "It's always later, isn't it?" I cried, my voice sounding choked and shaky. "This can't wait!"

He gave me a longer look now, his eyebrows raised. Then he turned back to his companions and laid his hand of cards on the table. "Prime, gentlemen. I'll collect my money in a moment." He took me aside. "What is it?"

Now that I had his attention, I was uncertain what to say. "The—the money," I managed. "It's gone. They think—they think you took it."

I had hoped for a reaction from him that would demonstrate his innocence—surprise, confusion, perhaps indignation at being falsely accused again. Instead, he scowled and muttered, "Damn! Are they on their way here?"

I shook my head slowly, but it was less a response to his

question than it was an attempt to clear the muddled thoughts in my mind, or perhaps to deny them. "I—I don't ken," I stammered. "I believe they think you've fled."

"And so I should, I suppose." He returned to the table and began to gather up his winnings.

I stood where I was a moment, dazed and dumb, and then tagged after him like a desperate beggar hoping against hope to be given some small bit of charity yet. "I can't believe—" I started to say. Then I broke off as the front door of the tavern was flung open and two men strode into the room. From his leather jerkin, I took one of them for a constable. The other was Mr. Armin.

Avoiding my gaze, he pointed an accusing finger directly at Jamie Redshaw. "That's the man."

The constable drew his sword and stepped forward. "You may as well come along peaceful, sir," he said, "and make it easy on yourself."

Jamie Redshaw hesitated, jiggling his coin-filled purse in his hand as if debating whether to turn and run or stay and fight. I watched him anxiously, uncertain which course I would have him choose. He chose neither. Instead, he shrugged and said, "This is poor timing, you know. I was winning for a change." Then he moved forward to meet the constable, who lowered the point of his rapier and smiled a little, obviously relieved that his prisoner did not mean to resist.

I felt a rush of relief as well, but with it came a sharp pang of disappointment that he would give himself up so meekly. Even if he was guilty, he might salvage some honor by putting up a fight or at least attempting to escape. But, I reminded myself, without his stick he had nothing with which to fight.

That situation changed abruptly. As the constable ushered his prisoner toward the door, Jamie Redshaw crowded him a bit. The officer knocked his knee against one of the benches. Before he could regain his balance, Jamie Redshaw swung his heavy purse upward in a swift arc. It caught the constable on the chin and sent him reeling backward. In an instant, Jamie Redshaw had seized the man's sword by its guard and brought the handle down across one knee, breaking its owner's grip.

Mr. Armin unsheathed his sword and came to the constable's aid, but a moment too late. Jamie Redshaw had turned to face him with the stolen rapier held at broad ward. "I've disarmed you before, and I'll do it again," warned Jamie Redshaw. "Let me pass."

Mr. Armin's reply consisted of a single word: "No." Then he closed in and their two rapiers clashed. Jamie Redshaw had no more to say, either; clearly, all of his concentration was taken up with turning aside Mr. Armin's blade as it darted in all directions, threatening first an edgeblow to the legs, then a *stoccata* to the stomach, a downright blow to the pate, an *imbrocata* to the chest.

"Stop!" I shouted, but of course they paid me no heed. I snatched up a heavy earthenware ale mug, meaning to launch it at someone's head, but I could not decide whose. If my aim was true and I managed to brain one of them, he would be at the mercy of the other. Though I did not wish to give Mr. Armin a chance to run Jamie Redshaw through, no more did I wish to let my father deal a deadly blow to my friend. In the end I could only stand gripping the handle of the mug, jerking it about this way and that in sympathetic movements, as though I were parrying phantom thrusts.

Under Mr. Armin's attack Jamie Redshaw gave ground again and again, unable to gain the offensive. Several times he tried the maneuver that had proven so successful in their previous bout, aiming the point of his rapier directly at Mr. Armin's sword hand. But now he did not have the element of surprise on his side. Each time Mr. Armin easily beat the blade aside and put him on the defensive again.

The constable had gotten to his feet, rubbing his jaw, but he made no move to interfere. I am sure it was as obvious to him as it was to me that Mr. Armin was the more skillful scrimer and would win out in the end. The grim look on Jamie Redshaw's face told me that he realized it, too. The stiff way in which he moved said something more to me—that the wound in his hip was causing him a good deal of pain. Yet he fought on so doggedly despite it all that it hurt my heart to see it.

When Mr. Armin at last left an opening—deliberately, I am sure—Jamie Redshaw lunged forward. Mr. Armin did a deft traverse to one side and delivered a *stramazone*, or slicing blow, to his opponent's unprotected forearm. The stolen rapier clattered to the floor and Jamie Redshaw took several staggering steps backward, clutching the wound.

Without stopping to consider the consequences, I sprang

forward, swept up the fallen weapon, and came on guard before Mr. Armin. "Widge!" he said as sharply as a sword thrust. "Stay out of this!"

"I will not!" I cried. "Whatever 'a may ha' done, 'a's still me father!" Over my shoulder I called to Jamie Redshaw, "Go! I'll buy you some time, at least!"

"Just see that you don't buy it with your life," he replied, and then I heard his retreating footsteps. The constable seemed about to pursue him, until I blocked his path with my sword point.

"Step aside!" Mr. Armin ordered. "I've no wish to fight you."

"Nor I you," I said, my voice as unsteady as my sword hand.

He swung his sword suddenly, meaning, I am sure, to catch me off guard and disarm me. But he had trained me too well for that. I turned the blow aside and automatically countered with one of the *passatas* I had practiced so interminably. The point of my sword nicked his doublet, and perhaps his ribs as well, for he drew in a sharp breath.

I had never meant for us to come to blows, only to give Jamie Redshaw time to escape. I am certain Mr. Armin did not wish it, either. But sometimes, I believe, our instincts override our intentions, and so it was now. There may have been other, less obvious elements at work as well. Mr. Armin surely resented being challenged by one of his pupils, and for my part I was still angry with him for being so suspicious of my father; the fact that his suspicions were well founded only made matters worse. I may even have felt compelled to prove that I could acquit myself well in a fight that did not involve stage swords and moves planned in advance.

Whatever our reasons, we found ourselves striking at one another in deadly earnest. Though my breath came in panicky gasps and my blood pounded in my ears, I do not recall feeling frightened, particularly. My brain seemed numb, in fact. But my body responded as it had been trained to. I held my ground and gave as good as I took.

Mr. Armin had taught me that a skillful scrimer always looks his opponent in the eyes, for in that way he can read what his opponent will do before he does it. At first, the look in his eyes was hard and determined, but that quickly gave way to puzzlement, as if he were wondering how we could have let this happen. Then, suddenly, he scowled, and made a move I could not have anticipated: he stepped back and disengaged. "Enough," he said. "This is foolishness. I am not your enemy." He spread his arms wide, offering himself as a target for my sword. "Here. Run me through, if you will."

When I made no move to do so, he turned and stalked from the room. The constable took his sword from my unresisting hand and followed, leaving me standing there alone, feeling bewildered and bereft. No longer was I torn between two forces pulling me in opposite directions. I had succeeded somehow in cutting myself loose from them both.

I had not the slightest notion what I should do next. I could hardly return to the company, after having taken Jamie Redshaw's side against them. But I could not very well join Jamie Redshaw, either. Even if I could have swallowed my scruples enough to take up with a thief—and, if Jack should die, a murderer as well—I still had no way of knowing where he could be found.

Though I was not thinking all that clearly, I realized I was probably not wise to stay where I was. Once the constable learned that I was Jamie Redshaw's son, he might decide to clap me in irons as an accessory to the crime, or possibly detain me as a sort of hostage, a means of keeping my father from fleeing the vicinity.

I wondered whether Jamie Redshaw would, indeed, leave town without knowing what had become of me. Surely not, after I had risked my life on his behalf. Besides, he was wounded, how seriously I did not know. He might require a surgeon to tend to the cut on his arm; heaven knew he had plenty of money now to pay for such services.

The money itself might hold him here as well, at least for a time. There was a good deal of it, and all in small coins—too much for him to carry about comfortably, at least on foot. More likely he would look around for a horse to buy before he went anywhere.

These thoughts reassured me a little and set me in motion. I had somewhere to begin looking for him, anyway. When and if I found him, perhaps I could somehow convince him to make amends. Though he might be impulsive, I was certain he was not a bad man at heart. If I told him how urgently the money was needed to aid Sander and the boys, I might persuade him to give it up, or at least some of it. If nothing else, I would surely be able to retrieve my mother's crucifix.

But I was getting ahead of myself. My first task was to locate Jamie Redshaw, and my most immediate concern was that, if I had guessed where he was likely to be, then Mr. Armin would surely have done the same.

Keeping to the back streets and snickleways to avoid Chamberlain's Men and constables, I sought out the few local physicians and surgeons. None had treated a man with a sword cut recently. Late in the day, I inquired at the town's sole stables and was told that no one matching my description of Jamie Redshaw had purchased or hired a mount. In hopes that he might yet do so, I asked leave to lodge in the hayloft. The stable owner, a short, bandy-legged fellow, agreed to this; he even provided me with supper, in the form of one of his wife's meat pies. I would have offered to pay for it but that I had only a bit more than a shilling left from my wages, and no notion of how long it might have to last me.

The feeling of being all alone in the world was threatening to overwhelm me; to keep it at bay I engaged the man in conversation, asking if the plague had been a problem hereabouts. He said that, God be thanked, only a few townfolk had contracted the contagion, and those had been immediately confined in a pesthouse, thus preventing the spread of the disease.

We went on to talk of other things, including the performance of *Two Gentlemen* the stable owner had taken in that afternoon. Though I thought it best not to reveal my connection with the company, I asked him how they had acquitted themselves, in his opinion. "Quite well, overall," he said. "Not so good as the Admiral's Men, who were here a month ago, mind you. Not near enough laughs for my taste."

I nodded, and held my tongue, with some effort. According to Mr. Shakespeare, all the world's a stage; it seemed to me, rather, that all the world was a critic. "I can't fault the acting, though," the stable owner went on, "particularly the fellow who played the main bloke—Protocol, was it?"

"Proteus," I said.

"That's the one. I liked his lady friend as well—I disremember her name."

"Julia," I said—Sal Pavy's part, of course.

"You saw the play, too, then?" he said.

"Aye. Tell me, what did you think of Silvia—th' other lady friend?"

"Oh, she was good as well. Very natural."

Though it was hardly high praise, I was gratified all the same. I had not been overwhelmed with favorable comments on my acting lately. In truth, since we had set out on tour several months earlier, I had begun to feel that my command of charactery and my rudimentary skills in the healing arts were of more consequence to the company than my ability as a player. Yet with me gone and Jack out of commission for a good while—if, indeed, he lived—they would surely have trouble filling all the roles.

I wondered whether they would miss me. I was certain Sam would, and equally certain that Sal Pavy would not. The others would, I imagined, be regretful, but I had no doubt that, being practical men, they would not hesitate to fill my place with the first suitable candidate.

I forced myself to think no more on the matter. I could not bear it.

Jamie Redshaw did not turn up that evening, or the next morning, either. It would be a waste of time, I was sure, to look for him in the alehouses. But time was one thing I had a surfeit of, so I squandered it. Not surprisingly, no one had seen him since the previous afternoon.

I slept in the stable again that night. When I woke in the morning, it was with the certainty that Jamie Redshaw had departed, and so must I. If I could not salve my conscience by helping remedy the ills he had caused, I might at least return to London and do what I could to aid Sander and Tetty, Mr. Pope and the boys.

The stable owner pointed out the proper route, which led straight south. "When you get to Cheltenham," he instructed me, "turn east. That'll take you to Oxford and thence to London." He also sent me off with a full stomach, and another meat pie for the road.

I got as far as Upton before night fell, slept once more in a stable loft, and set out southward again in the morning. The miles went by slowly, with no companions to talk to. At first, out of old habit, I went over my lines in my head for the roles I was least sure of. But after a time I gave up on it. What was the use, when I had so little hope of ever playing those parts again?

I tried to pull myself out of the bog of despair into which I was slowly sinking by telling myself that perhaps I was better off this way. Perhaps I should think about finding a new career. There was no denying that acting was a tough and a thankless profession. It required so much hard work for so little return. It afforded not a groat's worth of security or stability. One could easily see why the sharers disliked and discouraged gambling; the everyday existence of a player was gamble enough without adding to it.

It occurred to me, then, that all these same things were true of life in general. Yet folk were not ordinarily eager to abandon it in hopes of finding some better alternative. To my knowledge there was but one other option, and not a very satisfactory one at that.

As tiresome as it is to travel in solitude, it is even worse on an empty stomach. I had had nothing to eat since the previous afternoon, save a little cracked corn I had filched from the horse trough at the stable in Upton. To make my misery complete, the skies, which had been as gray as my mood all day long, decided that since there was not a tree or any other shelter in sight, now was a good time to let loose with a deluge.

When I reached Gloucester at last, I was as wet and weary as I had ever been, with no prospect of anything better ahead of me than another night of sleeping on straw and a handful of horse feed to eat. So desperate was I that I might have turned my hand to begging, had there not been strict rules against it. Beggars were, like players, required to show the proper papers.

As I shuffled on my last legs down the street, looking for a place to lodge for free, I passed one of the thick upright posts that towns often provide for displaying public announcements. A familiar handbill tacked to it caught my eye.

A Performance of
the Pleasant Conceited Comedie
called
LOVES LABOURS LOST
by Wm. Shakesper

Plaide by the Right Honourable
the Lord Chamberlain his Servants
Lately of the Globe Playhouse, London

TO-MORROW 2 O'CLOCK

I am certain my mouth must have fallen open in surprise. The Lord Chamberlain's Men? Here? I had understood that, upon leaving Worcester, they would proceed directly east, to Mr. Shakespeare's home at Stratford. Perhaps the theft of the money had altered their plans. Perhaps they had decided, as I had, to return at once to London. Apparently they still were not overly concerned about Mr. Pope's plight, if they meant to waste a day in performing.

The stable owner in Worcester had said that I would come to a fork in the road here. I already knew which route to choose. I had not been prepared for this figurative fork in the road, though, and had no notion how to proceed. Should I seek out the company and ask their forgiveness? Or should I go on my way, making no attempt to reconcile with my friends—if indeed I could still count them my friends?

If I took the first course, would it mean I was somehow betraying my father? I was not sure it mattered; had he not betrayed me, after all, by using me as a means to insinuate his way into the company, and then making off with all our money?

After living most of my life without family or friends, I had only lately begun to learn about loyalty, so I did not yet know all it entailed. I wished to be faithful to my father, but if he had committed a crime I was not sure I still owed him any loyalty. Besides, what about my obligation to the Chamberlain's Men? In the hierarchy of loyalties, which came first—family or friends?

Though I knew little about the demands of honor or of

duty, I was well acquainted with the demands of the body and, unprincipled as it may seem, these were what finally swayed me. If the company took me back, I would at least have decent food to fill my stomach and a soft place to lay my head. Besides, if I did not rejoin them soon, Sal Pavy would surely usurp all my old roles.

All that remained was to find the players. If they had managed to put on a performance in Worcester, as scheduled, they might have made enough to pay for lodgings, so I checked at the first inn I came to. My friends were not there, but the host directed me to another inn, the Wheatsheaf. By the time I found the place, I was faint with hunger and fatigue and, despite the warmth of the evening, shivering in my wet clothing.

As I stepped from the dark outdoors into the main room of the inn, the light of the candles fairly blinded me. The smell of roasting meat filled my nostrils. Supporting myself against the doorframe, I surveyed the room, hoping to see a familiar and welcome face. To my painful disappointment, I recognized no one there.

Or nearly no one.

As I turned to leave, I caught sight of a figure that made me stop and stare: a fat-bellied man with an eye patch. Though he had his back to me, I was certain it was the same familiar-looking fellow I had seen weeks before, with Lord Pembroke's Men, and again at the tavern in Leeds, playing cards with Jamie Redshaw.

He was engaged in a game of cards now, with three other men. Piles of coins on the table told me that there was gambling involved. Apparently the one-eyed man was not faring well, for there was not a single coin in front of him. As I watched, he pulled something from his wallet and dangled it before the others, evidently offering it as a wager, in lieu of money. In the light of the small chandelier that hung over the table, the object in his hand glinted gold, and I gave a gasp of surprise, for even at that distance, I knew at once what it was—my mother's crucifix.

For a moment I stood transfixed while my brain, muddled by exhaustion, tried to work out what this meant. The cross had been in the company's treasury trunk; when Jamie Redshaw had stolen the contents of the trunk, he must have taken it, too. That meant he was here somewhere, or had been recently, long enough to lose the cross to the one-eyed fellow.

This realization set me in motion. I strode unsteadily across the room to the quartet of cardplayers and leaned over to get a closer look at the crucifix. There was no mistaking the ornate design. "Where did you come by that?" I demanded.

The man turned to me and, though his face was shadowed by his hat brim, I saw his one good eye widen in an expression I could not quite read. "What business is it of yours?" he said, between teeth that were clenched around a pipe stem. His voice was not the sort I expected from an actor. It had a rough, hoarse quality, as though he'd strained his vocal cords by shouting or was suffering from the grippe.

I knew I had heard that voice before, but it wasn't until he removed the pipe from his mouth and turned his head further, so the candles illuminated his face and neck, that I realized with a shock who it was that sat before me.

The eye patch and the amount of weight he had put on had fooled me. But the long, livid scar on his throat gave him away, for I myself had bound up the wound that caused it. "Nick?" My voice, too, came out sounding husky and uncertain.

He pushed back his chair and stood. "So, you haven't forgotten me, eh, Horse?" The grin on his face was not the sort that said he was happy to see me.

Hearing the old name with which Nick used to taunt me banished any doubt that it was, indeed, him.

"I—I heard you were dead."

"Well, that just goes to show, you can't believe everything you hear."

He pulled the eye patch aside. The eye beneath it was cloudy white, and the skin around it embedded with small, scablike flecks of black that I took to be grains of powder from the pistol that had backfired in his face. "Needless to say, I'm no longer playing girls, with this face . . . and this figure." He patted his expansive belly.

"But you're acting, still? Wi' Pembroke's Men?"

He laughed unpleasantly, and the other men at the table

joined in. "Sometimes we call ourselves that. This week, however, we're the Lord Chamberlain's Men, right, fellows?"

"That's right," said one of his companions, a bald fellow with a red, bulbous nose. He raised his mug of ale. "Don't you recognize us? I'm Will Shakespeare, and this here's Burbage."

"And this"—Nick stepped nearer me and clapped a rough hand on the back of my neck—"this is Horse. He's with a company who also call themselves the Chamberlain's Men. Isn't that a coincidence?" He seized a clump of hair on the nape of my neck and pulled my head back. "Where are your friends now, Horse?"

"I—I don't ken," I said.

"What do you *ken*, exactly?"

I jerked my hair painfully from his grasp. "I ken that crucifix belongs to me. How did you come by 't?"

Nick glanced at his companions, then shrugged. "Dishonestly," he said. "Would you like it back?"

I swallowed hard and nodded. "Aye."

"Well, then." His hand went to his waist and came up with a dagger. "You'll have to take it from me." He thrust the dagger at me, and I stumbled backward. "What's wrong, Horse? You don't want it after all?" He dangled the crucifix before me, daring me to reach for it. I glanced toward the door, gauging my chances of escape. "You want to leave, instead, is that it?"

"Aye."

"You want to return to the Chamberlain's Men, no doubt, and spill your guts about what you've learned. Well, I have a better idea." He advanced on me, the blade of his dagger moving in a slow circle that held my terrified gaze. "I believe I'll just go ahead and spill them right now. And this time, Horse, it won't be sheep's blood."

I kept retreating from the threat of the dagger and the menacing grin, until the backs of my knees came up against a bench. I lost my balance and sat down hard on my hucklebones. Before I could scramble to my feet again, Nick was leaning over me, with the blade at my throat-bole. "No, no," he said, "I've just had an even better idea. Remember *Titus Andronicus*?" He jabbed the point of the dagger against my chin. "Stick out your tongue."

"Nay!" I choked.

"Neigh all you want, Horse. It won't save you. Come now, let's have your tongue."

Though my vision was blurred with pain and panic, I could see an indistinct shape move up behind Nick. Then the dagger jerked to one side; I felt it slice my skin and, though there was no pain at first, I cried out in alarm.

Nick was pulled backward, struggling and cursing. I slumped forward, holding my bleeding chin. I had to wipe away the tears that filled my eyes before I could discover who had dragged Nick off me.

It was Jamie Redshaw. He had seized Nick's right arm by the wrist and twisted it up behind his back so far that the point of the dagger threatened to puncture the back of

Nick's skull. With a bellow of pain and rage, Nick let the weapon drop. I had presence of mind enough to snatch it up and put it in Jamie Redshaw's hand.

He pressed the edge of the blade to Nick's throat and turned his hostage around so they faced the rest of the Mock Chamberlain's Men. "Stay where you are, gentlemen," he said calmly. "If we all keep our heads, then your comrade will get to keep his."

The bald, red-nosed man laughed. "In truth, we'd just as soon you did the blighter in." Casually he got to his feet and drew his rapier. "All the more money for the rest of us, you see." At his cue, the other men of the thieves' company closed in, too, with their weapons before them.

"Run, Widge!" Jamie Redshaw called over his shoulder.

"Nay!" I replied. "Not wi'out you!"

"I'll be right behind you! Now go!"

I turned to flee and then, remembering the crucifix, turned back and yanked it from Nick's grasp, snapping the delicate chain. As I headed for the door, I saw Jamie Redshaw plant a foot in Nick's back and send him reeling forward into his companions, who very considerately turned their swords aside to avoid impaling him.

With Jamie Redshaw at my heels, I dashed across the highway, nearly breaking an ankle in the deep ruts, and into the safety of the dark woods. "Hold!" called Jamie Redshaw softly. I slowed, and he caught up with me. "They'll not pursue us, I'm certain, for they're a lazy lot of louts. Let's sit down a while." Groaning slightly, he sank to the ground next to a broad beech, and I sat beside him, on a cushion of dead leaves that had escaped the rain under shelter of the tree.

"Are you hurt?" I asked.

"No, it's just the old wound acting up. What about you?"

"It's not a bad cut; I've stopped the bleeding. It would have been much worse, had you not come along. I should have done more to save meself, but I was too frightened."

"It's good to be frightened. It keeps you from being over confident."

"That's exactly the same thing Mr. Phillips told me about acting. You didn't seem frightened."

"I didn't have a knife at my throat. You acquitted yourself well enough—and even better back in Worcester."

It was the first word of praise I had ever heard from him and I held on to it as tightly as I held the crucifix. "How did you happen to be here, at the same inn wi' those miscreants?"

"I thought it might be worth my while to join their company—just temporarily, until some better opportunity should present itself."

"Join them? But . . . they're thieves!"

"Well," he said nonchalantly, "no one is without faults."

"How long ha' you been in league wi' them?"

"Just since your Mr. Armin chased me off. Oh, I had made their acquaintance before that and, as you may have guessed, sold them a few of your handbills."

"Oh." I had hoped he might reveal that the robbery was all their idea, that he had been only an unwilling accomplice. "What will you do about the money?" I said.

"The money?"

"What you took from the Chamberlain's Men."

"Oh. I'm afraid that's all gone."

"Gone?"

"I had a streak of ill fortune with the cards."

"You gambled it all away?" I said incredulously. "There must have been twenty pounds in that trunk!"

"The trunk? I never touched the trunk. I took no more than a few shillings from the gatherer's box."

"But . . . you brained Jack! We found your stick!"

"It's no longer my stick. Three or four days ago I wagered it on a hand of cards, and lost."

"To whom?" I asked, though I was sure I knew the answer.

"Richard."

"Richard?" I echoed in surprise. "Who is Richard?"

"Why, the very villain who so nearly cut your tongue out."

"Oh. That's not his true name. It's Nick. He was once wi' the Chamberlain's Men."

"And now he's taken to robbing them and burning their wagons? Nice fellow. I expect he deliberately left the stick behind to divert suspicion from him and his companions."

"No doubt. Tell me, in your time wi' them, did the name Simon Bass ever come up?"

"It did. I gathered that most of them were once players in a company run by Bass. How did you know that?"

"I'll tell you sometime," I said. "In the meanwhile, is there aught we can do to recover the money?"

"We might try asking very politely. Or, on the other hand, we might kill the lot of them."

Irked by his lack of concern, I said, "What about your honor? Do you not wish to clear your name?"

He laughed. "I'm afraid my only hope of having a clear name lies in taking a new one. Besides, you can tell your fellow players that I'm not the culprit. They'll believe you."

"I can't go back to the Chamberlain's Men," I said glumly. "Not after all that's happened."

"Of course you'll go back. What else can you do?"

I hesitated, like a player who is reluctant to say a line he has been given because he is uncertain how the audience will react to it. Finally I forced myself to say it. "I might go wi' you."

In the darkness I could not make out Jamie Redshaw's face, to read his reaction. I could only wait anxiously for his reply. It was a long time coming. At last he said, "No. You would not care for the sort of life I lead. I go where my whims or the whims of Fortune take me, and when I've overstayed my welcome, I leave. I get my living by whatever means I may. I cannot afford to concern myself with how honest it is. And I have as many ways of losing money as I have of making it. No," he said again. "It's no life for a lad like you, who can amount to something."

Though I listened to his words, I did not hear them. What I heard was that he did not want me. "But," I said, my voice trembling now, "even an I could return to the company, I could never go wi'out you. You're me father."

Jamie Redshaw blew out a long, heavy sigh, as though he had come face-to-face with something he had been making every effort to avoid. "As I said, honesty is not always my first concern."

If I had been stunned when he first claimed kinship with me, I was stricken now. "You—you lied to me, then?" I managed to say.

"Let us say, rather, that I misled you."

"But—" I held up the crucifix, which I still clutched in one hand. "You kenned me mother's name. You kenned it was carved on the back of this."

"A cozener's trick, nothing more."

"A trick? How—?"

"You recall the little man with half an ear? He and I were confederates, helping one another to relieve coneys of their excess coins."

"Coneys?"

"Gulls. Marks. Victims. He saw in you an opportunity for us to ally ourselves with a renowned—and profitable—company of players. I don't think he expected me to leave town with them."

"Nay!" I cried. "I don't believe you! You didn't lie to me then; you're lying to me now, so I'll go back to the Chamberlain's Men! You want to be rid of me!"

Jamie Redshaw did not reply at once. He got stiffly to his feet and brushed himself off. I could barely make out his dark form, silhouetted against the stars. "Well," he said, "as I've told you, I use whatever means I may." He turned away, then, and I heard his footsteps moving off through the damp, dead leaves, heading toward the highway.

I wanted to call out to him, to go after him, but I was afraid that, if I did, Nick and his friends might find us. In any case, I could not have found the words. There were so many questions tumbling through my mind, I could never have hoped to choose just one. Even if I had, and even if he had answered it, I would have had no way of knowing whether or not the answer was true.

Perhaps he had told me one true thing, at least. It was no doubt best to let him go back to his life, and I to mine. Whether or not we had the same blood in our veins, it was clear that we were cut from different cloth, he and I. If I stayed with him, I knew he would expect me to live by his rules, to behave and believe as he did, and I was not certain that I could, or would even wish to. But the heart does not always want what is best.

In the end I stayed where I was, curled up in the leaves at the base of the beech tree, partly because I was too exhausted to go on, partly because I feared that, if I came out of hiding, I might encounter the company of thieves, and partly, I think, because I still harbored some faint hope that Jamie Redshaw might return for me.

When it grew light enough to see, I found the road that would take me to Oxford and London. I was not certain how much help I could be to Sander and the boys. What they needed mostly was money, after all, and I had next to none. But I thought I might manage to find some sort of work. And in any case, I had nowhere else to go.

After I had walked along for an hour or so, a cart came by, loaded with casks of ale. "Going to Oxford?" asked the driver. I nodded. "There's room on behind if you care to ride—and if you care to help me deliver these kegs when we get there."

In Oxford I got a ride with another carrier, under the same conditions—that I help him unload his freight. By the time we reached London, three days after I left Cheltenham, I was so stiff and sore from being jostled about in wagons that I felt as though I'd been beaten soundly.

I took my leave of the driver at St. Paul's. I was shocked to see how quiet the courtyard of the cathedral was. Ordinarily the space was filled to overflowing with the booths of booksellers, stationers, and other vendors, and with folk come to buy their wares or just to mingle. Today there were perhaps half the usual number of sellers. The few folk who patronized them were not standing about casually, looking over the goods, as they normally did. Their movements were much more deliberate. They headed straight for a particular booth, made a hasty purchase, and departed again, avoiding as much as possible any contact with other customers.

Most of the business was at the booths of the apothecaries, and the liveliest trade was in plague remedies and preventatives—amulets filled with arsenic and mercury, tonics made of borage and sorrel juice, salves of egg yolk and swine grease. So far as I knew, no one at Mr. Pope's was in need of such nostrums. All the boys did, however, suffer from a chronic case of sweet tooth, so I stopped at a candy seller's stand and parted with a few of my own pennies in exchange for a bag of marchpane. I was so starved, it was all I could do to keep from eating the candies myself.

As I headed south toward the Thames, I noted that the traffic in the streets, too, was unusually sparse for such a pleasant summer's day. Many of those I passed were holding wadded kerchiefs up to their mouths and noses, like folk downwind of a dung heap; others wore twigs of rosemary in their hair. Though I put little trust in such measures, at the same time I felt uneasy, vulnerable, going about as I was with no means at all of countering the contagion.

Every so often I came upon a house that had been boarded up, and a cross nailed to the door, often with the words LORD HAVE MERCY UPON US scrawled beneath it. I hurried past these with a shudder, as though expecting some dread demon to spring from them.

At the embankment by Blackfriars, where ordinarily a dozen wherry boats were gathered, awaiting passengers, there were now but four. The wherryman who took me across instructed me to toss my penny into an iron pot that, he said, he would later place over a fire, to drive off the venom.

"The venom?" I said.

"That's how the plague is passed on, you know—through a poison, like snake venom, that seeps through a person's skin."

"Nay," I said, "I didn't ken that."

He leaned forward, but not too close. "Here's another tip for you," he said confidentially. "Don't bathe."

"Ever?" I said.

He shook his head emphatically. "It opens up the pores, you see, makes it easier for the venom to get in."

"Ah. Thanks for sharing that." I stifled a cough. It was obvious the man was following his own advice religiously.

After all the signs I had seen of the plague's presence, I was half afraid to arrive at Mr. Pope's lest I find a cross and a plea to God upon the door. I was relieved to see that the place looked the same as always—from the outside, at least.

When I stepped through the doorway, the boys, who were playing in the main hall, spotted me at once and descended on me like wild Irishmen, crowing with delight. As I fought to keep my balance under their onslaught, Goodwife Willingson came trotting from the kitchen, calling, "Whist, boys, whist! You'll disturb the master!"

I drew the bag of sweets from my wallet and dangled it over their heads. "This is for those who are quiet!"

When they had returned to their play, their mouths full of marchpane, Goody Willingson came to me and, seemingly about to break into tears, clasped both my hands in hers. "Thank the Lord you've come at last, Widge. I've been at my wit's end these past several days, what with Mr. Pope being ill, and scarcely a morsel of food to put on the table, and—oh, that's not the worst of it." She bit her lip and hung her head, as though she couldn't bear to go on.

"What?" I urged her. "What is it?"

"It's . . . it's Sander," she said. "He's gone."

I could scarcely believe I'd heard her right. "Gone?" I said. "How do you mean?"

"He went off a week or more ago, and he's not returned since."

"Did 'a not leave a message of any sort?"

"No, nothing."

"Did 'a take aught wi' him? Clothing? Food?"

"Not that I could tell."

I put a hand to my head, which had begun to throb. "Perhaps . . . perhaps 'a went out to try and find work."

"Well, he'd found something already, that's the thing. For a week at least he'd been going out several hours each day, but he was always home by dinnertime, bringing with him a few shillings or some food."

"Do you ken where 'a was working?"

She shook her head. "He never said. I suspect it was some lowly task he didn't care to admit to."

"That's not like Sander, though, to be so secretive."

"He's not been himself, lately. He's been distracted, like. To tell the truth, I believe he was hurt and disappointed that the company didn't respond to the letter he sent asking for help. I told him it might well have failed to reach you."

"It reached us, all right, but at the worst possible time. You see . . . every bit of money the company had was stolen."

She put a hand to her mouth in distress. "Oh, Law! They've sent nothing with you, then?"

"Nay. In truth, they did not even send *me*. I . . . I had a falling-out wi' them."

"Oh, Widge, no! What was the cause of it?"

"I'll tell you about it later." I dug from my purse the few coins that remained to me. "Here. That may buy a little food at least. Is Mr. Pope still under a physician's care?" Goody Willingson nodded. "How is 'a?"

"Up and down, like Fortune's wheel. For a time he seems

to be getting his strength back, and then Dr. Harvey comes and bleeds him, and he takes another turn for the worse."

I frowned. "How often is 'a bled?"

"Every few days."

"Gog's malt! It's a wonder the poor man has a drop of blood left to let! Has either of you asked this Dr. Harvey to leave off the bloodletting?"

Goody Willingson's look of surprise was as profound as if I'd asked whether they'd renounced their allegiance to the Queen. "Why, no! I'm sure the doctor knows what's best for him."

"Perhaps. I'll go up and see him."

"Yes, do. But mind you don't say a word about Sander. I've not told him yet. It might be best, too, if you don't mention the stolen money. We don't want him to fret."

When I looked in on Mr. Pope, I found him so weak he could scarcely talk. He had been such a vigorous man, despite his age, that it was shocking to see him so helpless. I sat by his bedside and, to spare him the effort of asking, told him all the things I was sure he would want to know about how the company was faring.

He reached out unsteadily to pat my hand. "I'm glad you're back," he whispered. He closed his eyes, then, and I thought he had gone to sleep. But as I rose to leave I heard him say, "Widge. Where is Sander?"

" 'A's just . . . gone out," I said, casually. "When 'a returns, I'll send him up."

As I stepped out into the hallway, I saw Tetty's slight

figure sitting on the top step of the stairs, looking down through the balustrade at the boys playing in the hall below. I sat down next to her. Without turning, she said somberly, "You came back."

"Aye," I said. "I had your picture to remind me."

"Good. You won't leave again, will you?"

I hesitated. I was not sure myself what I would or should do next. Finally I said, "Not for a while, anyway." I fished from my wallet some sweets I had saved for her. She accepted them as gravely as though they had been physicking pills.

Around a mouthful of marchpane, she asked, "Why did Sander leave?"

"I don't ken, exactly."

"Was it because we were bad? Some of the boys complained when there wasn't enough food."

"No, no," I assured her. " 'A would never stay away over such a trifling thing. There must be some more drastic reason."

In the morning I went looking for work, and found nothing. With the rising death toll had come a corresponding drop in business for the city's merchants and tradesmen. They were more inclined to let help go than to hire more. As I went about Southwark, I inquired of every familiar face I encountered whether they had seen Sander recently. No one had.

That afternoon, on a whim, I went by the Globe Theatre. All the entrances were locked. The only windows at ground level were those in the tiring-room. I grabbed the sill and hoisted myself up to peer inside. The place was, of course, as empty as a granary in May. Through the open tiring-room door, I could just catch a glimpse of one of the stage entrances and, beyond it, a small section of the stage itself.

The sight sent a stab of something through me—I was not certain what, but it was akin to the feeling I had experienced upon seeing again the orphanage in York where I had spent my early years. It was, I think, the curious sensation one gets when seeing a familiar place from a new perspective—from the outside, as it were, rather than the inside.

I had had no desire, of course, to be inside the walls of the orphanage again. But the sight of the stage filled me with a fierce longing. I dropped to the ground, wishing that I had not taken that look within. I knew that, in a month or so, when cool weather reduced the threat of the plague, the company would return and the theatre would reopen. What I did not know was whether or not I would be with them.

I sat on the steps outside the rear door of the theatre for a long time, hoping without much conviction that Sander might somehow be drawn back here. Finally, fearing that Goody Willingson and Tetty and the others would think that I had deserted them, too, I rose and, heavy-hearted, made my way back to Mr. Pope's.

The following day the physician returned to see to his patient. Dr. Harvey was a gaunt man with pasty skin. In truth, he looked as though he had been administering his bloodletting cure to himself, and had overdone it. Goody Willingson obviously knew the procedure well; she had already fetched a bowl. Dr. Harvey laid his patient's right arm across the rim of the bowl. Both Mr. Pope's forearms were dotted with small scars from previous bloodlettings. As the doctor opened his medical case, I got up the nerve to open my mouth. "Excuse me, sir," I said.

He gave me a cursory glance. "Who are you?"

"Widge, sir."

He selected a narrow-bladed scalpel from the case. "What's happened to the other boy, the tall one?"

"Sander." I glanced at Mr. Pope. "We . . . we don't ken, sir."

"What do you mean, you don't *ken*?"

"I mean, 'a's been gone a week; we don't *know* where."

"Hmm." The doctor took out a tourniquet and tied it about Mr. Pope's upper arm to make the veins stand out.

"I ha' a question," I said. "I understand that Mr. Pope's condition seems to grow worse after 'a's been bled."

"That's not a question," said Dr. Harvey.

"All right, then. *Should* his condition grow worse after 'a's been bled?"

"Yes, yes, that's to be expected. The patient always feels a bit weak at first from loss of blood. It's only temporary."

"But . . . well, is there not some other treatment you could try? One that would build him up, rather than making him weaker?"

Dr. Harvey sighed heavily. "The patient has suffered a stroke. That means there's a surfeit of blood, and *that* means it must be let out." He took hold of Mr. Pope's wrist and searched for a suitable vein to open.

I stepped closer to him. "But it would do him no dare, would it, an you left off bleeding for a week or so, to see what happens?"

The doctor turned to glare at me over the tops of his spectacles. "Do you have a university degree in medicine?" he demanded.

"Nay, of course not. I was only—"

"Well, I do. So stop trying to tell me how to do my job!"

Mr. Pope, who had lain quietly until now, somehow summoned the strength to sit up a little. His arm fell off the rim of the bowl. "Here," he said, his voice thick, as though he had drunk too much ale, "you've no call to be harsh with the boy. He's simply asking."

"Asking? What he is doing, sir, is questioning my ability."

"Nay," I said. "Only your methods."

"You must admit," said Mr. Pope, "the bleeding hasn't exactly been a great success. In fact, you might say it's been a bloody failure."

Dr. Harvey stood rigid a moment, looking as though he were contemplating letting blood from both our jugulars. Then he nodded brusquely and threw the scalpel carelessly back into its case. "Very well," he said, and untied the tourniquet so roughly that Mr. Pope winced. "Obviously, you don't want the care and advice of a physician. Go see an apothecary; he'll mix you up some fancy-sounding and foul-tasting concoction that is guaranteed to make you well. The catch is, you see, you can't ask for your money back if you're dead!"

"I wasn't—" I started to protest, but the doctor was already stalking from the room. I scrambled down the stairs after him. "I wasn't saying we should consult an apothecary. I only thought you might know of some other treatment."

"Well, I don't!" the doctor said sharply over his shoulder.

Angry and ashamed in equal parts, I trudged back up to Mr. Pope's room. "I'm sorry," I said. "I'll find another physician."

Mr. Pope waved a hand weakly, dismissively. "Sometimes common sense is the best doctor—and the cheapest, as well. Better we should spend what little money remains on food."

"But what an 'a's right? What an you've a surfeit of blood and something bursts?"

"Do I look to you as though I've a surfeit of blood?"

As I plumped up the pillows behind him, I studied his face, which was, as they say in Yorkshire, all peely-wally. "Nay. You look as though you're made up to play the ghost in *Hamlet*."

"Well, I'm not a ghost," he said. "Not just yet. Is there any meat in the house?"

"A little, I think."

"Then have Goody Willingson make me a cullis of beef broth, will you? Suddenly I'm starving."

The next afternoon, I went about the Bankside neighborhood again, asking after work and after Sander; I returned with little hope of finding either. To my dismay, I encountered Dr. Harvey coming from the opposite direction. I would have gone on by him without a word or a glance, but he stopped me. "I've something to tell you."

"An it's about yesterday," I said hastily, "I'm sorry I was—"

He held a hand up to silence me. "No, no," he said impatiently, "I'm not here looking for an apology. I wanted to let you know that I've found your friend."

"Me friend? Sander, you mean?"

Dr. Harvey nodded.

"Well . . . where is 'a?"

"In the pesthouse in Kent Street."

All the breath seemed to go out of me. With what little was left, I said, "The pesthouse? Where they take folk wi' the plague?"

"Yes. I look in there from time to time, and do what I may to ease their suffering. There's little anyone can do, except God."

Though the weakest parts of me, of which there were many, cried out against it, some small courageous part said, "I've got to go see him."

"If you do, you'll be in grave danger of infection yourself."

"So are you," I said. "Yet you go there regularly."

"I take precautions."

"Then so will I."

Dr. Harvey gave me a cloth bag filled with arsenic and instructed me to bind it to myself beneath my shirt and doublet, next to my heart. The theory behind this was that one venom repels another.

Folk fall prey to all manner of illness, of course, and as we made our way to the pesthouse I held on to the hope that Sander might not have the plague at all, but some other disease of similar symptoms. Perhaps, like Sam, he only suffered from the ague.

But when we entered the pesthouse and I saw him, that hope vanished. It took several moments for my eyes to find him, among the dozens of patients who lay about the room on straw mats. Even then, I was not certain it was he, so altered was his appearance.

The attendants at the pesthouse had burned his garments; he was covered only by a linen sheet pulled up to his chest. His arms were spread out at right angles to his body, like those of Jesus on the cross, so as to keep any pressure off the grotesque black pustules on their undersides. There would be similar painful swellings, I knew, on the insides of his thighs. His face was not pale and drawn like Mr. Pope's, but dark and contorted, as though he were slowly strangling.

"He's experiencing severe cramps," said Dr. Harvey dispassionately. "That's a mortal sign."

I gave him an angry glance, as though, by speaking of Sander's approaching death, he were helping to hasten it.

"I'll leave you alone with him," said the doctor. "It's best if you don't get too close."

What would have been best, I thought, was never to have gotten close to Sander to begin with. If I had not let myself come to regard him as my nearest friend, perhaps I would not feel now as though the arsenic in the bag I had bound to me were eating away at my chest and at the heart within it.

I knelt down next to his mat; the bay leaves and lavender and rose petals that were strewn about to purify the air gave off a scent that was spicy and sweet but not nearly strong enough to overcome the sour smell of sickness. "Sander?" I said.

He turned his head to the side with obvious effort; when his dull gaze fell upon me, he gave me a faint semblance of his old smile. "Widge," he said in a hoarse whisper. "You came."

I swallowed hard. "Aye." Though I had given up lying, I made an exception, knowing that it would ease his mind. "I've brought money wi' me—enough to provide for the household."

"Good. Good. I knew you'd manage it somehow. I hoped you wouldn't manage to find me, though."

"Why?"

"I didn't want you to see me like this. I wanted you to remember me as I was."

"I will, I swear." I fought back tears, wanting him to remember me, too, as I was in better times. I tried to think of something cheerful to say, but the question that was in my mind forced itself to the fore. "How did this happen? No one else in the household has come down wi' the contagion."

So faintly that I could scarcely hear, he said, "I had to get work, to keep the boys fed. It was all I could find."

"What was?"

"Carting the dead away for burial."

"Oh, Sander," I said.

He shrugged slightly, apologetically. "I followed your advice. I kept a kerchief soaked in wine over my face."

"Nay, nay, I never said it was certain proof against the plague!" I cried. "You should not ha' listened to me!"

With much effort he raised one hand, as though to clap me on the shoulder in his old familiar fashion, but then stopped himself. "It's not your fault, Widge. It was my choice. I'm certain that all of them"—he waved his hand weakly to indicate the other patients in the pesthouse—"tried the best they knew how to ward off the plague, and it claimed them anyway. There's nothing anyone can do. There are no rules to follow. It's all a game of chance."

I did not dispute him. I had heard other folk say the same thing about the plague and about other sorts of ill fortune. I think it gave them some comfort to believe it was so. It is far easier to accept one's lot in life as inevitable, a whim of fate, than it is to struggle and rail against it.

But I was not certain it was so. I suspected that, like every other disease, the contagion had a cause, and if that cause could be discovered the plague could be contained, perhaps even cured. Surely, someday someone would uncover its secrets. But it would be too late for Sander.

I longed to do something to ease his suffering but, as Dr. Harvey had said, there was nothing to be done. I had seen Dr. Bright drain the pustules of plague victims and apply ashes and quicklime to them, but the treatment had seemed only to cause the patient more pain, and it made no difference in the end.

I took my mother's crucifix from about my neck and placed it in his outstretched palm. His hand closed tightly about it, and he smiled faintly one last time. I fetched water to slake his constant thirst, but beyond that all I could do was to sit by and watch him fade farther and farther from me, as gradually and as surely as the evening sun was fading from the sky.

I could not even arrange for a funeral, for at sunset all the day's dead were carted away at once and buried in hastily dug graves outside the city. I went along so that Sander would have someone to mourn him, and I marked the site with a small pile of stones, vowing to replace it someday soon with a proper headstone.

After the burial, I hurried home, knowing that Mr. Pope and Goody Willingson would be worried about me. To lessen the chance that I might carry the plague with me, I stripped off my clothing and burned it, and scrubbed myself all over with lye soap before I went inside. There was, unfortunately, no way I could avoid carrying to the others the sad news about Sander. I waited until the boys had gone to bed, wanting to spare them a while yet. I had hoped that, in telling Mr. Pope and Goody Willingson, some of the weight would be lifted from me, but it was not.

"I suppose I must let his parents know as well," I said. "Can you tell me where to find them?"

Mr. Pope shook his head. "In one of the shabby tenements along the south bank, I believe. Sander never told us much about them. It was my feeling that he was rather ashamed of them."

"I do recall him saying once," put in Goody Willingson, "that his mother made a bit of money taking in washing, and that his father turned around and spent it all again on drink." She clucked her tongue disapprovingly. "Imagine such a good boy as Sander coming from such sorry stock."

"Mr. Armin said to me not long since that it mattered naught what sort of heritage a wight had; the important thing, 'a said, was what you did wi' 't." I thought of Jamie Redshaw, and of my still unknown mother, and of myself. "Perhaps 'a was right," I said.

I had not yet spoken to them of Jamie Redshaw or of my reasons for leaving the Chamberlain's Men. I knew that, soon or late, I must, just as I must reveal to Mr. Pope that I had come to them almost empty-handed. But it would have to wait. We had all had enough dreary news for one day.

As I left Mr. Pope's room, I heard the sound of footsteps retreating along the darkened hall, and a door latch clicking shut. Someone had been listening in as I told of Sander's sad end. I had a strong suspicion who it was.

I opened the door to the room that Goody Willingson shared with Tetty. Though the young girl lay still in her bed, I could hear how harsh and rapid was her breathing. I sat on the edge of the bed and hesitantly laid a hand on her shoulder. "You overheard."

After a pause, she nodded. "I told you," she said.

"Told me? Told me what?"

"Every time I come to like someone, they die."

I shook her shoulder firmly, as though to dislodge this

notion. "Nay. Don't think that. You had naught to do wi' Sander dying, I promise you."

She turned to face me, her dark eyes accusing. "You're a good doctor. Could you not have done something to make him well?"

"Nay. There was naught that could be done."

"I suppose you'll be leaving us now, too."

"I—I don't ken," I said.

"If you do stay, I won't like you. I'm never going to like anyone again. It hurts too much."

I could not come up with a reassuring reply to this, for the truth was at that moment I felt much the same way. Yet I had to say something. I could not bear to sit helplessly by as I had with Sander. I cleared my throat. "It doesn't matter," I said softly. "I'll still like you."

Beneath my hand the tense muscles of her thin back slowly relaxed. It seemed to me that for once I had managed to say the right thing. Perhaps it was not just what Sander would have said, or Julia, or Mr. Armin, or any of the others by whom I had measured myself in the past, but it was what I felt and that, I supposed, made it the right thing.

In the morning Goodwife Willingson sent me off to the market in Long Southwark to see if I could prevail upon one of the vendors there to let me have a bit of food on the promise of future payment. She had exhausted her own credit with them, she said. She hoped, however, that they might be open to an appeal from a new face. But the merchants were no fools; they knew me as a member of Mr. Pope's household, and knew that we were not likely to settle our account with them anytime soon. A fishwife did suggest that, if I returned late in the day, she might let me have those fish that had grown too fragrant to sell.

I shuffled home, feeling myself an utter failure. I had done nothing at all to aid Mr. Pope and the boys. All I had given them was yet another mouth to feed. I told myself that it would surely be better for everyone if I did not return to Mr. Pope's and, in fact, when I came to the house I walked on by it—to test myself, I suppose, to see if I could bring myself to leave.

I could not.

And a moment later I was extremely grateful for that fact. At the table in the kitchen sat a figure so unexpected and so welcome that I actually cried out, "Oh!" I had thought until that moment that crying out such things as "Oh!" was something that occurred only in plays.

Smiling, Mr. Armin rose and took my hand in both of his. "I hoped I would find you here," he said.

Finding me had not, of course, been Mr. Armin's sole purpose in coming. When the Chamberlain's Men reached Stratford, Mr. Shakespeare had raised fifteen pounds by collecting on some old debts, and Mr. Armin had been dispatched at once to London with the money.

"I'm to meet up with the company again at Bristol in four days' time," he said. "I hope you'll come with me."

"Truly? You've no sore feelings, then, over what happened?"

"Not any longer." He rubbed gingerly at his ribs. "I've a bruise the size of a sovereign where you stuck me, but my feelings are scarcely sore at all. It was natural that you should come to your father's defense."

I winced, for he had found a sore spot on me as well. "I'm not certain that 'a was me father."

"I always had doubts about it. One thing is certain, though—he was not the one who robbed us."

"I ken that. But how did you?"

"Ned Shakespeare told us how Jamie Redshaw lost the walking stick in a game of cards."

"Aye," I said, "and wait until you hear who 'a lost it *to*."

Now that he was not being bled dry on a regular basis, Mr. Pope improved rapidly. Mr. Armin hired Goody Willingson's niece to help run the household until our return, and then we set off on Mr. Armin's new mount, to rejoin the company. By the time we reached Bristol I had recounted all that had happened to me since we parted ways, and Mr. Armin had managed to convince me that the company would welcome me with open arms and without reservations. Of the two undertakings, I believe the latter occupied the greater amount of time.

Mr. Armin had not deceived me, though. With the exception of Sal Pavy, who glared at me from afar, all the players seemed quite pleased to have me back. Even my old nemesis Jack greeted me with something resembling goodwill—a tribute, apparently, to the effort I had put into patching up his pate.

Sam seemed particularly glad to see me. Taking me aside, he whispered, "Since you left, Princess Pavy has been more unbearable than ever, and Toby is no help at all against him."

"Toby?" I said.

Sam nodded toward the other end of the inn's main hall, where a chubby-faced lad of thirteen or fourteen sat talking with Mr. Phillips. I had assumed he was the innkeeper's son or the stable boy or some such, but now that I looked more closely I recognized him as one of the prentices from the Earl of Hertford's Men, the company we had bested in the acting competition.

"Oh, gis!" I muttered. "It's just as I feared! They've replaced me!"

Sam laughed. "You needn't fret. He's as wooden as a well bucket, and twice as thick. They took him on only out of necessity. We had no idea, after all, whether or when you would return."

Sam's assessment of the new boy proved sound. Toby was suited to play only the smallest and most undemanding parts. However, Sal Pavy had laid claim during my absence to yet another of my customary roles, that of Blanche in *King John*. Though I resented this liberty, I let it pass, not wishing to seem ungrateful after the company had so generously taken me back. But I could not help recalling what Jamie Redshaw had said to me about Sal Pavy—that he was the sort who would push and push until he pushed me out of the picture.

With his arm now free of the plaster cast, Mr. Shakespeare had no more need of my services; he could write the final scenes of *All's Well* on his own. Though I knew it was unfair of me, I resented this a little, too, feeling as though another of my old roles had been wrested from me.

My skills with a pen were still in some demand, for I had to translate into ordinary writing all the parts of the play I had set down in charactery, so the actors might decipher them. I had to rush the task a bit. The sharers wished to begin rehearsing the play immediately upon our return to the Globe, so that when we performed it before the Queen at Yuletide, it would be as polished as possible.

Now that the script was all but completed, Mr. Shakespeare seemed content enough with it, or at least resigned to it, as he was resigned to having an idle slouch for a brother. Though he trusted me, I think, to transcribe his work accurately, he was not above looking over my shoulder and goading me good-naturedly.

"I don't recall composing that line," he said. " 'He wears his honor in a box unseen that hugs his kicky-wicky here at home'? That's an abominable line. Are you sure you got it down properly?"

"Oh, Lord, sir!" I replied, pretending to be offended. "An 't sounds abominable, I take no responsibility for 't. I wrote down only what you told me to."

"But *'kicky-wicky'*? What was I thinking of?"

"Nicky-nacky?" I suggested.

"Oh, certainly," he said. "That's so much better." Shaking his head, he turned to go, then turned back. "By the bye, Widge, when you copy out the sides, could you begin with Helena's? It's a demanding part, and I'd like to give him as much time as possible to study it."

"Him?" I echoed.

"Yes. Sal Pavy."

So stricken was I by his words that I lost control of my pen. It went skating across the paper, leaving a trail of ink like an open wound from which black blood welled. "Sal Pavy? You don't mean 'a's to play Helena?"

Mr. Shakespeare avoided my gaze. "We felt that he was best suited to the part."

"But . . . but I supposed that I would . . . " I trailed off.

Mr. Shakespeare spread his palms in a gesture of helplessness or apology or both. "I'm sorry, Widge. We have you down for Diana. It's a substantial role."

"But it's not Helena." The moment I said this I wished I had not, for I realized how petulant it sounded. I realized, too, that Mr. Shakespeare was likely to reply, "And you are not Sal Pavy."

He was not that unkind. He simply said again, "I'm sorry," and walked away.

It was difficult for me not to go after him. I wanted to remind him that, had it not been for me, the play would never have been put down on paper. I wanted to explain that I *knew* Helena, as surely as though I had watched her grow from infancy—which, in a way, I had. I had even been the source of some of the words she spoke.

But more than that, I felt a kind of kinship with her. Like me, she was an orphan; like me, she had been taught the rudiments of medicine; like me, she had offered her loyalty to a soldier and been rejected. She was plagued by the boastful and deceitful character now called Parolles, I by the boastful and deceitful character known as Sal Pavy.

There was one obvious difference between us, though. Helena had the courage and determination to pursue what she wanted until she got it. I, on the other hand, had stood by and let Sal Pavy steal from me, one by one, the roles that I had worked so hard to make mine, in the same way that Mr. Pope had let the doctor drain his life's blood from him a little at a time, without making a move to stop it, without even a word of protest.

Though I was as uncertain of my origins as I had been when we set out on the tour, I had not gone through all the trials of the past few months without learning something about who I was and what I was capable of. I had learned that, when the occasion demanded it, I could speak out against something I knew was wrong, that I could push aside my fears in order to aid a friend, that I could mend a broken arm or a broken head, that I could take up a sword in defense of someone I cared for. If I could do all that, then certainly I could stand up to Sal Pavy.

It was not Sal Pavy himself that I feared, of course; it was the possibility that if I upset the balance of the company, I might lose my place in it. But the fact was that, because I had failed to fight back, I was losing my place just as surely—not in one sudden fall from grace, but inch by inch, role by role. It had made the process more gradual, as being bled by a scalpel is more gradual than being skewered by a sword. If I was to be cut loose, I would just as soon it were done quickly.

Besides, unlike the subtle slice of a scalpel, a sword thrust may be parried. Jamie Redshaw had suggested that I counter Sal Pavy's attack by using similar tactics, by seeing to it that he met with a well-planned accident. But that was Jamie Redshaw's method, not mine. There were other, more civilized ways of fighting back.

That evening, while the rest of the company were gathering for dinner in the main room of the inn, I was searching through the costume trunk for a pair of long linen gloves that I had worn in the wedding scene of *Much Ado.* Then I waited, concealed upon the stairs that led to our bedrooms, listening for some line that would serve well as my cue. It came when Mr. Armin said, "Has anyone seen Widge lately?"

I made my entrance. I strode across the room and straight up to Sal Pavy, who sat as near to the sharers and as far from the prentices and hired men as he could get. Without a word, I flung down one of the linen gloves before him; it very nearly landed in bowl of stew.

Sal Pavy stared at me as though I'd taken leave of my senses—and he was not the only one in the room to do so. "What's this?" he demanded.

"Me gage," I replied.

"Your *gage*?"

"Me gauntlet, an you will."

He lifted the cuff of the glove distastefully, as though it were a worm, and gave an incredulous laugh. "You're challenging me to a duel?"

"Aye," I said. "An acting duel—to determine who will play Helena."

He gave another laugh, a rather uncertain one this time, and glanced around at the rest of the company. "Is this another jest? I'm afraid I don't see the humor in it."

Mr. Armin gazed curiously at me. "No, I'd say he's quite serious—resolute, in fact." He turned to the other sharers. "What do you make of this challenge, gentlemen?"

"Well," said Mr. Heminges, "if two c-companies may decide who will p-perform by m-means of a competition, I s-see no reason why two individuals should not."

"August?" said Mr. Armin.

Mr. Phillips shrugged. "It's bound to be more interesting than watching them shoot pistols at each other."

"Will?"

Mr. Shakespeare played thoughtfully with his earring. "We did tell Mr. Pavy that the part was his. If he does not feel he's up to the challenge, we can't very well force him to accept it."

All eyes were upon Sal Pavy now. His features remained so carefully composed that I could not guess what went on behind them. I was fairly certain he would not refuse me.

There was no way he could do so without looking foolish or white-livered. Besides, if I knew him he had every expectation of winning such a duel. He did not disappoint me. Putting on his most disdainful look, he tossed the glove back to me and said, "Name the time and place."

We settled on two days hence, at the Guild Hall in Salisbury, where we expected to be performing. Since we could not hope to con the entire part in that short a time, we limited ourselves to the final scene of Act I, between Helena and the Countess.

After Sal Pavy had retired to his stable, Mr. Armin came and sat down next to me. "So," he said soberly, "you've decided, as Hamlet says, to take arms against a sea of troubles and, by opposing, end them."

"Aye," I replied a bit defiantly. "I thought it was time I stopped retreating from Sal Pavy and took the offensive."

He nodded. "Well, I've only one thing to say in the matter."

"What's that?" I asked anxiously.

Mr. Armin leaned close to me and said sotto voce, "Why in all halidom did you wait so long?"

"Well, because . . . because I feared that, an I complained about Sal Pavy or quarreled wi' him, you and the others might—"

"Might what?"

"Might give me the chuck."

He patted my shoulder and said confidentially, "If we dismissed every member of the company who's ever been guilty of complaining or quarreling there would be no one left."

When I had been chosen the previous summer to play Ophelia before the royal court, I had had but one week to prepare for the part. It had been a trying week, filled with anxiety and self-doubt and sleepless nights. I believe I agonized every bit as much over this single scene from *All's Well*; the difference was, it was all of it crammed into two days.

Though I had never seen an actual duel, I doubted that the two combatants were expected to load their weapons and prepare themselves to kill or be killed while sitting within ten feet of one another. Sal Pavy and I, however, were forced to share the same small space behind the stage in the Guild Hall as we dressed ourselves and painted our faces and chanted our lines over and over like a paternoster under our breath.

I put my back to him and tried to ignore his presence, knowing that, if I gave him the opportunity, he would attempt to undermine my confidence or break my concentration. He did not wait for an opportunity. "You've put far too much cochineal on your cheeks," he said.

"Mind your own concerns," I muttered.

"Only trying to be helpful," he said innocently. "I didn't suppose you'd want to go out there looking like a fool." He glanced into the mirror and fluffed up his wig. "Or should I say *more* of a fool?"

I clenched my teeth. Let it pass, I told myself, and tried to think only of my lines.

"If you're determined to make a fool of yourself anyway, why not ask for the part of Lavatch? He's *supposed* to be a fool. And they're as likely to give it to you as they are to give you Helena."

I might have managed to let even this pass had I been striving still to be the good prentice, but I was not. I was striving to be Helena. I took the time to put the final touches on my makeup—and to count to ten—and then I turned to face him. "I suspect," I said evenly, "that your opinion of me acting ability is not nearly as low as you'd have me believe."

"Oh?" said Sal Pavy, clearly taken aback a bit. I am sure he expected me to respond with anger to his goading.

"An you truly felt I was no match for you, you would never have gone to so much trouble to try to get rid of me. It's only because you ken how capable I am that you consider me a threat."

"A threat?" He laughed, not entirely convincingly. "The only thing I've ever feared from you was that you would forget your lines and I would be forced to cover for you."

"You're lying. They say that no one may spot a lie like another liar. Well, I've been a liar most of me life. It's only lately that I've given it up."

"You may as well give up trying to compete with me as well, because you'll never win."

"We should not be competing at all, you and I. Theatre is

supposed to be a cooperative effort. Did they never teach you that at Blackfriars?"

For the first time his mask of superiority began to slip, giving me a glimpse of something darker and more vulnerable behind it. "No," he said. "But they taught me many other things, and one of them was that if I ever managed to get free of them I would not go back. I would do anything to avoid going back."

I nodded. I understood better than anyone the fierce determination he felt to keep his place within the company, at any cost. "I am certain that you want no advice of any sort from me, but I'll give 't to you all the same. An you truly wish to stay wi' the Chamberlain's Men, you'll never do 't through trickery and deceit; I ken that well, for I tried it meself. The only way you will ever belong is by being a hard and willing worker, and by being honest and loyal, so that you earn the trust and respect of the company."

"Trust and respect?" Sal Pavy sounded as though he were unfamiliar with the terms.

"You don't mean to tell me," I said, "that there was something you did not have at Blackfriars?"

Since he was the challenged party in the duel, Sal Pavy dictated the order in which we would perform. He chose to let me go first. As I stood by the curtain, waiting to go on, I felt unaccountably calm and confident. Mr. Heminges, who was playing the Countess to both our Helenas, came up next to me, adjusting his gown and wig. "Ready?"

I took a deep breath. "Aye."

He nodded encouragingly. "I b-believe you are."

Ordinarily when I made an entrance I was careful not to take much notice of the audience. It was easier for me to imagine, then, that I was living the scene, and not merely making a show of it. This time, though, I took a long look out into the hall. I was not playing to some mingle-mangle of strangers, come to lose themselves for a couple of hours in a world that was more interesting and exciting than their own. These were my fellow players, my friends.

An ordinary audience knew nothing about us actors, and cared less. Their only concern was for the fate of the characters in the play. But to these men—to Mr. Shakespeare and Mr. Armin and Mr. Phillips and Will Sly and even to Jack—I was not merely a player; I was a person. It was not enough, then, for me just to give them Helena. I had to give them something more. I had to give them me.

Always before, when I got well into a part, my awareness of everything outside the boundaries of the stage faded away. The only thing real to me was the world of the play. It was like slipping into a two-hour dream.

This time was different. I felt more the way one feels when he is just on the threshold of waking. Although he is still within the imaginary world conjured up by his sleeping mind, sounds and such from the real world intrude and influence the course of the dream.

So it was that, when I as Helena spoke of my father, images of Jamie Redshaw came into my mind. When I as Helena told the Countess, "You are my mother, madam; would you were—" I thought for a moment of my own mother, whom I never had known and never would. And when Mr. Heminges as the Countess remarked upon the tears that filled my eyes, he did not have to imagine them; they were there.

At the conclusion of our scene, we received an enthusiastic round of applause from the company. Under cover of it, Mr. Heminges said to me, "Well done, Widge." I could not help but agree.

Now that I had taken my shot, it was Sal Pavy's turn. I was not certain I wanted to watch. It would be like watching an opponent in a duel level his pistol at you, and wondering whether or not you would survive. In the end, I sat close behind the curtain and listened.

He made a strong beginning. His Helena was more forceful and vibrant than mine, who, though strong-willed, was soft-spoken. He was clearly determined to make my portrayal seem pale and anemic—and he seemed to be succeeding.

But a few minutes into the scene he lost momentum somehow. It was as though some part of his mind was occupied with something besides the role—perhaps with the conversation we had had not long before. Well, I had meant to give him something to think about, but not necessarily now. When he came to the line "My friends were poor but honest," he seemed to falter and forget where to go.

Out of old habit, I threw him the next line, but he failed to take it. Thinking he had not heard, I repeated it, more loudly. Still there was only silence from the stage. I peered through the opening in the curtain. To my surprise, Sal

Pavy was not facing his partner in the scene but had turned to look out at the members of the company who formed the audience. "The lines seem to have left my head," he told them. His voice was steady; his head was held high. "I could do a bit of thribbling, but you would know. I prefer instead to concede." He made a dignified bow, turned, and walked off the stage. A generous burst of applause followed him.

Suspecting that Sal Pavy would prefer to be alone, I ducked around the curtain and joined my friends, all of whom congratulated me warmly. Actually, Jack's comment could probably not be considered warm. What he said was, "I could never con that many lines in two days." It was, I supposed, the best I could expect from him.

Mr. Shakespeare said, "With you as Helena, perhaps this will not be such a poor play after all."

Mr. Armin gripped my hand almost painfully hard. "Don't think for a moment," he said, "that you won only because Sal Pavy conceded defeat. It was your performance and nothing else. It was astute, it was assured, it was affecting."

I did not know what to say. Fortunately Mr. Armin covered for me. "You know," he said, "when an actor truly shines in a role for the first time, we say that he's found himself. Well, it seems to me that you've found yourself. How does it feel?"

I thought of a line at last, one that would fit any situation. "Oh, Lord, sir," I said.

SHAKESPEARE'S SPY

Also by
GARY BLACKWOOD:

Shakespeare's Scribe

The Shakespeare Stealer

The Year of the Hangman

Moonshine

Wild Timothy

SHAKESPEARE'S SPY

~

Gary Blackwood

DUTTON CHILDREN'S BOOKS
New York

This book is a work of fiction. Names, characters, places, and incidents are either the product of the author's imagination or are used fictitiously, and any resemblance to actual persons, living or dead, business establishments, events, or locales is entirely coincidental.

CIP Data is available.

Published in the United States by Dutton Children's Books,
a division of Penguin Young Readers Group
345 Hudson Street, New York, New York 10014

www.penguin.com

Printed in USA First Edition
1 3 5 7 9 10 8 6 4 2
ISBN 0-525-47145-6

For Emily, who is partly insane
and totally great

SHAKESPEARE'S SPY

Of all the dozens of tasks a fledgling actor is called upon to perform, surely the two most difficult are dying and falling in love.

As a prentice with the Lord Chamberlain's Men, I was called upon to do both, sometimes on a daily basis. Not in earnest, of course; I was expected only to approximate them. This is not as simple as it may sound. I could feign sadness well enough, or fear, or loneliness, for growing up an orphan as I did, I had known more than my share of such things. But my experience with love and death was more limited. Though I did my best to persuade the audience that my groans of mortal agony and my melancholy, heartbroken sighs were real, they always seemed to me to lack a certain conviction.

Most of the stories we acted out were rife with romance, but in our ordinary lives it was sadly absent, and no wonder. Since women were not permitted to appear upon the stage, all the parts were played by men and boys. As a result, I seldom came in contact with anyone of the fairer gender, aside from Goodwife Willingson—who kept house for my mentor, Mr. Pope—and Tetty, a young orphan girl who lived with us.

Foul murders and duels to the death were also an important part of our repertoire. But, though we spent several hours each day hacking at one another with stage swords, either in practice or in performance, our lives were seldom truly in peril. Unless he fell victim to the plague, the worst a player could ordinarily expect was that he would misjudge his position and tumble off the edge of the stage, into the arms of the groundlings.

But Fate cares little about our expectations. In the winter of 1602, the Lord Admiral's company were performing *Palamon and Arcyte* at the royal court when the stage, hastily built and loaded down with heavy scenery, suddenly collapsed. Five of the actors were injured and three were crushed to death.

Now, if the truth be told, there was no love lost between our company and theirs; in fact, in the ongoing struggle for ascendancy in the world of London theatre, the Admiral's Men were our chief rivals. Still, not one of us would have wished such a calamity upon them. Though they might be the enemy, they were also fellow players, and we were saddened and sobered by the tragedy—especially when we considered that we might easily have been its victims, instead. Only a week before, we had presented Mr. Shakespeare's play *The Merry Wives of Windsor* upon those same treacherous boards.

Fortunately for the Admiral's Men—though not for us—all their principal players were spared, and within a fortnight they were once again competing with us for the playgoers' pennies—and there were far fewer pennies than usual to go around that winter.

Ordinarily we played outdoors at the Globe Theatre right up until Yuletide, when we peformed at Whitehall for the queen and her court. But this year, winter had forgotten its cue and come on early. The groundlings were a hardy lot, willing to stand uncomplaining in the drizzling rain and the baking sun for hours on end, asking only to be rewarded with a bit of fine ranting, a reasonable number of laughs, and, from time to time, a limb or two being lopped off and a few guts spilled upon the stage. But we could hardly expect them to risk having their ears and toes bitten by frost for the sake of art.

So in the middle of December we had forsaken the Globe and begun performing indoors, in the long gallery at the Cross Keys Inn. Though the audience was grateful, we players were not. The Cross Keys lay on the north side of the Thames, a long, cold walk from Southwark, where most of the company lived. The smaller confines of the inn meant smaller profits as well; no matter how tightly we packed them in, we could accommodate only half the number of playgoers that the Globe held.

In January, the royal court made a move of its own, from the damp, drafty palace at Whitehall to warmer quarters upriver at Richmond. It was there that we gave our second command performance of the season for the queen.

We were always a bit anxious when appearing before Her Majesty. After all, it was mainly thanks to her that the London theatre managed to flourish as it did. Without her support and protection, we would be at the mercy of the Puritans, who insisted that the stage was a breeding ground of sin. If something about the play displeased her—and, according to her master of revels, she had lately become even more difficult to please than usual—she might be more inclined to listen to the mounting protests of the Square Toes, and let them close us down.

We had worried very little about how *Merry Wives* would be received, for it was an old favorite of Her Majesty's. In fact, Mr. Shakespeare once told me that he had written it at her behest. After seeing *Henry IV*, she was so taken with the character of Sir John Falstaff that she insisted he must have a play of his own.

Our second show, *All's Well That Ends Well*, had no such favorable history. Mr. Shakespeare had composed it only the previous summer, while we were on tour to escape the plague. Thanks to a broken arm, he had been forced to dictate most of it; I had put the words on paper for him, using my system of swift writing. Though the script had been approved by Mr. Tilney, the master of revels, and given a trial run at the Globe, the queen would be seeing it for the first time.

For my part, I was seeing the palace at Richmond for the first time. A year earlier, I had performed in the banquet room at Whitehall, playing Ophelia in *Hamlet*, and been awed by its magnificence. The great hall at Richmond was even larger and more lavish. When we entered, Sam, the youngest of the prentices, gave a low whistle. My other companion, Sal Pavy, glanced about with a rather bored expression, as though he were wholly accustomed to playing such places.

"Widge." Sam elbowed me and pointed upward. I followed his gaze. The entire ceiling was covered in great billows of muslin, painted with fanciful figures representing the constellations of the night sky. "I hope they fastened that up there really well," said Sam. "If it lets go, we'll all be smothered."

"Perhaps," I said. "But I'm more concerned about the stage." Mr. Tilney's men had constructed a platform for us at one end of the hall. The three-foot-high trestles that supported it looked far too flimsy and widely spaced to suit me, especially considering the amount of furniture, properties, and painted backdrops the Office of Revels felt was necessary for the production. "I don't ken why we must ha' so much stuff. We did well enough at the Globe wi' naught but a few chairs."

Sam shrugged. "Perhaps royal folk don't have much imagination."

"Well, I like it," put in Sal Pavy, rather haughtily. "We always had elaborate sets at Blackfriars."

Sam groaned and rolled his eyes. Sal Pavy had said this same sort of thing so often about the theatre at Blackfriars, where he had belonged to the company called the Children of the Chapel, that it had become a standard jest. Sam would surely have had some choice comment to offer had not Mr. Armin, our fencing master, called out just then, "If you're quite done gawking, gentlemen, there are costume trunks to be carried in."

One thing I had learned about royalty, in my few brief encounters with them, was that they kept later hours than us ordinary wights. Because our stage was in the banquet hall, we could not begin our performance until after supper—a meal that did not commence until eight o'clock or so, and might drag on for hours.

While the queen and her court dined, we players donned our costumes, wigs, and face paint in an anteroom, then waited about anxiously for our summons. When Mr. Tilney, the master of revels, strode into the room, we all got to our feet, but he motioned for us to sit again. "Not yet, gentlemen, not yet," he said brusquely. "Where is Mr. Shakespeare?"

"P-pacing back and f-forth in the hallway, most like," replied Mr. Heminges, our business manager. "I'll f-fetch him."

When he returned with our playwright in tow, the master of revels approached them hesitantly, clearly embarrassed about something. "Ah, Will. I . . . I meant to tell you this earlier, but . . . you see, I've been so busy with—"

"Tell me *what?*" interrupted Mr. Shakespeare.

Mr. Tilney shifted about uncomfortably and cleared his throat. "Well, just that . . . that you must . . . or, rather, that it would be in your best *interests* if you were to delete from the play any reference to the King of France's illness."

Our entire company stared at him incredulously. Mr. Armin was the first to find his voice. "For what reason?" he demanded.

Mr. Tilney glanced about, as though afraid of being overheard, and then explained, almost in a whisper, "Since you performed for her at Yuletide, Her Majesty's health has declined considerably. The last thing she will wish to see is a monarch with a mortal disease."

Mr. Heminges, who played the king, scowled and shook his head. "I'm n-not sure it c-can be done, it's such an essential p-part of the play. After all, if I'm not d-dying, Helena can hardly g-go to Paris to c-cure me, can she?"

"How long before we go on?" asked Mr. Shakespeare.

"Oh, half an hour, at least," Mr. Tilney said blithley, as though that should be ample time to compose a whole new play.

Mr. Shakespeare nodded grimly. "We'll manage it somehow."

When Mr. Tilney was gone, Mr. Heminges cried, "We'll *m-manage* it? How?"

"I don't know, exactly. But if I hadn't said so, we'd never have gotten rid of him." Mr. Shakespeare turned away and began toying with his earring, as he habitually did when deep in thought.

Sam could be counted upon to offer some harebrained solution to nearly any problem, and he did not disappoint us now.

"I have it! The king has really bad hair, and so he sends for the best hairdresser in all of France—Helena!" He clapped me on the shoulder. The role of Helena, of course, belonged to me.

Mr. Shakespeare either did not hear Sam's proposal, or chose to ignore it. Finally he looked up and said, "Here's what we'll do. We'll keep the illness, but instead of the king, it will be Lafeu, the king's lifelong friend, who is dying. Can you reword your lines accordingly, Widge?"

"Aye, I wis." There was a time when such a request would have sent me into a panic, but in my year and a half with the company, I had become quite adept at thribbling—that is, improvising new lines when something went awry on the stage. It took a fairly serious calamity to throw me out of square.

One was not long in coming. The first two scenes of *All's Well* did, indeed, go well enough—except that the most important member of our audience seemed to be missing. Then, halfway through the third scene, Her Majesty made her entrance. We actors might as well have stopped speaking altogether, for the attention of everyone in the room turned to her.

Had it not been for the red wig and the dozen or so maids of honor who clustered about her, I might not have recognized her, so changed was she. I knew well enough that Her Majesty was getting on in years; after all, Mr. Pope, who was nearing sixty himself, told me that he had been a mere boy when she took the throne. But never before had I seen the years hang so heavy on her.

When we performed *Merry Wives* for her, she had looked remarkably well preserved. This was due in part, of course, to the thick mask of white lead and cochineal with which she concealed the ravages of time and to the well-made wig, which was far more natural looking than those we prentices wore. But her behavior, too, had belied her age. She had laughed at Sir John's antics, flirted with her male courtiers, and consumed a prodigious amount of ale.

Though she still wore the makeup and the wig, she seemed to have forgotten how to play the part expected of her, that of the ever-youthful Gloriana. Mr. Tilney had warned us that her health was poor, but I had not expected to see her shuffling along, head bowed, like an old woman. In one hand she carried a rusty sword, which she used as a cane to support herself. When she reached her chair, she had trouble gathering in her skirts so she could sit properly. One of the maids of honor rushed forward to help, but she brushed the young woman irritably aside.

So taken aback was I by Her Majesty's condition that I dropped my lines, forcing Sal Pavy, who was playing the countess, to repeat his: "'Her eye is sick on 't; I observe her now.'"

"'What is your pleasure, madam?'" I replied.

Before Sal Pavy could get out his next line, he was interrupted by the queen's voice; despite her illness, it had lost little of its power or its sting. "It is our *pleasure,*" she said, "that you speak up! We can scarcely make out the words!"

Though we put on our best Pilate's voices, we got no more than twenty lines in before she berated us again. So exasperated was she that she neglected to use the royal *we.* "Can you hear me up there?"

Sal Pavy and I glanced at each other. Though it was considered bad form for a player to break character, he turned to the queen and bowed. "Yes, Your Majesty."

"Then why can *I* not hear *you?*"

"I beg Your Majesty's humble pardon. We will try harder."

But try as we might, we could not speak loudly enough to suit her. Finally she rose and, grumbling, laboriously dragged her heavy chair forward, fending off all attempts to assist her, until she sat only a few feet from the stage. I wished she had not. At that distance, no amount of paint or dye or elegant clothing could conceal the painful truth: the queen was wasting away.

A blow that is struck without warning is always the most telling, and at that moment it struck me for the first time that Her Majesty was mortal, the same as ordinary folk—that she might not, in fact, live through the winter.

I shuddered to think what effect her passing might have on England, which had known no other monarch for nearly half a century, and on our professsion in particular. What would become of us poor players when we no longer had her powerful presence standing like a breakwater between us and the swelling tide of Puritans? At that moment I had an inkling of how the Admiral's Men must have felt when the stage gave way beneath their feet.

Every member of the company was, I think, unnerved by having Her Majesty so close at hand. But we were accustomed to adversity. After all, we had acted in inn yards while the ostlers led horses back and forth; we had put up with conceited wights who took seats upon the stage in order to be seen; we had been pelted by hazelnuts and leather beer bottles when we failed to please our audience.

Though our performance before the queen was not the best we had ever given, neither was it the worst. We recalled a reasonable percentage of our lines, and for those we forgot, we usually substituted something fairly sensible. We even managed to remove the king's deadly fistula and give it to poor Lafeu.

By the time we took our bows, it was past midnight, and we were, to a man, exhausted. Luckily the next day was Sunday, which meant we could sleep late. Ordinarily I went to morning services at St. Saviour's, along with Mr. Pope and the orphaned children who shared our household. All Her Majesty's subjects were, in fact, required to attend church, or risk paying a substantial fine. But when I woke, it was nearly noon. Mr. Pope, as I later learned, had taken pity on me and told the priest that I was indisposed.

I scarcely had time to eat before Sam and Sal Pavy came to fetch me for our Sunday outing. In truth, after six long days in the constant company of my fellow players, I would have welcomed a bit of solitude. But I also welcomed the opportunity to see something new, and it was not the best idea to go wandering about London alone, especially those parts of London that appealed most to us.

Though Sam was not the most reliable or the most responsible member of the Chamberlain's Men, he could be a good companion—provided he was expected to be neither serious nor silent. I had even learned to like Sal Pavy to some degree. Well, perhaps *like* is too strong a word. There were things I liked about him: he was talented; he was dedicated; he was determined. He was also vain, quarrelous, and ungrateful. But one of our many duties as prentices was to keep peace among ourselves. So I did my best to overlook his numerous and glaring faults and appreciate his few feeble virtues.

He and Sam and I got along well enough. Still, I could not imagine us ever truly being friends, in the way that I had been friends with our other prentices, Sander and Julia. It had been six months since the plague claimed Sander, but the thought of his death still made me feel as though I had been struck soundly in the ribs with a blunted sword, and not a day passed that I did not think of it.

Julia had not gone to paradise, only to Paris, where she could fulfill her desire to be a player. But there was little hope that she would return, unless the queen suddenly declared that women would henceforth be allowed to act upon the London stage.

Her Majesty was as likely to do that as a gib-cat was to sing sweetly. Though she might ignore the protests of the Puritans, she listened closely to the voice of the common people. And their voice said unmistakably that though any woman was free to watch a criminal get his neck stretched on Tyburn Tree or a toothless bruin be savaged by dogs in the bear-baiting ring, or to dress in rags and beg for alms in the street, or to sell her favors to men for a farthing, she must not be corrupted by taking part in a play.

I had not lost touch with Julia altogether. Every few months a French sailor turned up bearing a letter from her. These were usually brief and disappointingly impersonal, devoted mainly to what roles she was playing at the Théâtre de Marais. But now and again she let slip some line that made me suspect she was not as happy with her lot as she would have us think. The letters I sent in return were as carefully cheerful as hers; if she was pining for home, I had no wish to make her burden heavier by reminding her of how much she was missed.

Though the premature winter had hurt our company's profits, in the city as a whole commerce seemed unaffected. Shopkeepers went on displaying their goods in the street before their shops; St. Paul's churchyard still swarmed with vendors and buyers; beggars still pleaded with passersby on every corner; ballad-mongers and sellers of broadsheets still waved their printed wares aloft and called or sang out enough of their contents to whet the appetite for more; and we prentices, on the one day of the week that we could call our own, still strolled through the streets, looking for an excuse to part with a bit of our weekly wage of three shillings.

Sam, the most daring among us, usually led the way, and Sal Pavy and I were content to follow after. On most Sundays, he led us first to the area of St. Paul's churchyard where the agents of the royal lottery had their booths. And on most Sundays I tried to talk him out of it.

"You ken, do you not, that these wights must sell half a million chances at the least. That means the likelihood of you winning even one of the fourteen-shilling prizes is . . . um . . ."

"One in fifty," put in Sal Pavy.

I cast him a peevish look. "I was about to say that."

"No," said Sam, "it's one in twenty-five."

"How's that?"

"Because I intend to buy two chances."

"At a shilling each? You noddy! If you kept the two shillings instead, you could save up the same amount in—" I held up a restraining hand in front of Sal Pavy's smirking face. "Don't tell me. Seven weeks."

"Very good, young man," said Sal Pavy, in a schoolmaster-ish voice.

Sam made a scoffing sound. "You don't really imagine that I'd be content with fourteen shillings, do you? I've got my eye on the *big* prize." He leaned forward, his eyes wide, and whispered as though it were a secret known only to him, "Five . . . thousand . . . pounds!" Sal Pavy and I burst into laughter, but Sam was unperturbed. "Go ahead and laugh, like the clap-brained coystrels that you are; I care not a quinch. You know what they say: Let him laugh that wins the prize. You see, I've been told that I am to win, and very soon."

"Ah!" Sal Pavy said. "He's been *told!* That's different!"

"Told?" I said. "By whom?"

"By a soothsayer."

"You mean"—I lowered my voice—"a *witch?*" Where I came from, witches were not openly discussed, for fear one of them might overhear.

"No, just a cunning woman."

"What's that?"

"You know," Sal Pavy said. "Someone who finds lost valuables, and tells your future, and so on."

"Oh. I thought the city had a law against practicing that sort of thing."

"It does. It also has laws against cutpurses and moneylenders—and, if it comes to that, against performing plays within the city limits."

"How does it work, then?" I asked Sam, still half whispering.

"What?"

"How does she tell your future?"

He shrugged. " I don't know, exactly. She has this ball, made of something black and shiny, and she stares into it."

"And it tells her the future? I'd like to see that."

"Well, come on, then." Sam strode off abruptly, heading west on Fleet Street.

Sal Pavy was staring at me rather contemptuously. "Surely you don't believe in all that?"

"Not really," I replied softly. "But it's got him away from the lottery, hasn't it?" I hurried after Sam, calling, "You might wait for us!" The last word, though it was but one syllable, covered two octaves, for my voice broke, as it had been doing lately with alarming frequency.

Sam turned back with a mischievous grin on his face. "Was that your voice cracking, or were you attempting to yodel?"

"Neither," I said sourly. "I'm—I'm coming down wi' something, I wis." To support my contention, I coughed a few times, the same pitiful cough I sometimes used on the stage when dying of a chest wound.

"A likely tale," put in Sal Pavy. "I can spot a cracked voice as easily as a cracked coin." He directed an aside to Sam. "Have you noticed he has little hairs sprouting from his chin as well?"

"Nay!" I protested, feeling my jaw. "I got them all, I'm sure—"

Sam snickered. "So, you've been doing a bit of plucking, have you?" He reached out and gave my face a pat in supposed sympathy. "Poor babby. Did it hurt?"

I knocked his hand aside. "You two striplings are envious of me manliness, that's all."

"Envious, is it?" Sam said. "Much!"

"Striplings, is it?" Sal Pavy stood next to me and pulled himself up to his maximum height. "I'm nearer to fully grown than you by a good three inches!"

"Oh, aye," I replied. "Only most of it is hair." Sam and I had taken to cropping our costards closely so that the wigs we donned for our female roles would go on and off more easily. But Sal Pavy refused to part with his golden locks, which were so abundant that he could scarcely contain them beneath his woolen prentice's cap.

"You know, I do believe Widge is gaining on you, though," said Sam. "And small wonder. Did you notice how many helpings of beans he shoveled in last night at supper?"

"No," said Sal Pavy, "but I noticed them later." He pinched his nose and made a face.

I gave him a look of mock reproach and clucked my tongue. "Master Pavy, I seem to recall when you were too refined to speak of such vulgar matters."

His cheeks, already ruddy from the cold, turned a brighter shade of red. "That was before I fell under such bad influences," he murmured.

"Talking of food," I said, "I'm hungry as a hawk. Let's find a sweetmeat seller."

Sam rubbed his gloveless hands together. "A roasted-potato seller, more like. Anyway, you've got to wait until we've seen the cunning woman."

As we continued along Fleet Street and passed through Ludgate, Sam and Sal Pavy went on talking, but I was occupied with my own thoughts. Though I had managed to brush off their jests concerning my chin hairs and my uncertain voice, secretly I considered them no laughing matter. Rather, they seemed to me an unsettling omen, a reminder that I could not go on playing girls' parts forever.

In terms of physical development, I had always lagged well behind most boys my age—thanks, no doubt, to a lack of proper nourishment. Now that I was provided with good food and all I cared to eat of it, my body seemed bent on making up for lost time. For an ordinary wight, this was a source of pride, a sign of approaching manhood. But I was no ordinary wight; I was a player, and any pride I felt was overshadowed by a sense of apprehension.

I had been assured by other members of the company—and even by the queen herself—that I was a capable actor. In most of the parts I was praised for, though, I was impersonating a girl. It wasn't that I minded doing female roles; I was only acting, after all. But I could not shake the nagging fear that once my voice deepened and my beard began to show, the company might no longer have any use for me.

I half hoped that the cunning woman truly could see into

the future. Perhaps she could give me some hint of what lay in store for me so that I might either put my mind at ease or else prepare for the worst—and I could not imagine a fate much worse than being turned out of the only family I knew, or had ever known.

Sal Pavy was asking Sam what he meant to do with the five thousand pounds he had been assured of winning. Sam ignored the snide quality of the question. "Actually," he said, "I've given that a good deal of thought. I believe I'll buy a ship."

"A *ship?*" I said.

He nodded smugly. "A big three-master. I'll sail her to India and return with a hold full of spices and silk. I've always wanted to go to sea."

"Oh, aye," I said. "That's why you prenticed to an acting company."

"Well, I wasn't old enough to be a sailor, and it seemed like more fun than sweeping chimneys or tanning hides."

Sal Pavy gave him a disparaging look. "What a good reason to go into the theatre."

"Is there a better reason?"

I thought of Julia, and how desperate she had been to be a player. "Because you love it?" I suggested.

He shrugged. "It's all right. But doesn't it ever strike you that there's something a bit odd about what we're doing? I mean, if you think about it, we're not really *doing* anything, are we? We're just *pretending* to do things. Sometimes I could do with a bit less acting and a bit more action, that's all."

We crossed the stone bridge that spanned Fleet Ditch. Though it lay outside the walls, Salisbury Court was still part of the city proper, and it had its share of legitimate businesses—

taverns, printers, booksellers. But it was also headquarters for a considerable number of less respectable concerns—bawdy puppet shows, sleight-of-hand artists, palm readers, astrologers, and the like.

Sam led us to a tattered, grimy tent set back a few yards from the edge of the road. Before it stood a folding wooden sign that bore no words, only a crude and rather unsettling painting of a huge eye, with rays of what was presumably meant to be light shooting out from it in all directions.

I had rarely seen Sam appear anything but cheerful and cocky, even in those moments when we stood behind the stage waiting to go on, and when I was trying hard to hold down my dinner. But now he was clearly a bit out of square. He seemed to find it necessary to screw up his courage a bit before he called, in a voice that might have been more steady, "Madame La Voisin?"

There was no reply. Sam glanced at us rather sheepishly, shrugged, and called out more loudly, "Madame La Voisin!"

A low, hoarse voice from within commanded, "Be silent, fool!"

Clearly startled, Sam took a step backward, treading on my foot. "Sorry. She—she must be in the midst of a reading already."

"Perhaps we should just go," I suggested, feeling not a little uneasy myself now.

"No, no!" Sam said heartily, and then, glancing toward the tent, spoke more softly. "It's all right. It'll be worth the wait, you'll see."

We stood shivering in the cold for several minutes before the flap of the tent lifted and a woman emerged. She looked utterly out of place here, with her richly embroidered gown, her starched neck ruff, and her elegantly coiffured hair. Lifting her skirts a little, she brushed past us, leaving a sweet scent from her pomander hanging in her wake.

"I take it," said Sal Pavy, "that was not Madame La Voisin."

"No." Sam lifted the flap and motioned us inside. The interior of the tent was dim, and so thick with acrid smoke that I could scarcely see, let alone breathe.

"Be seated," said the same rasping voice we had heard before. Stifling a cough, I eased myself onto a rickety three-legged stool. Sam sat on the one remaining stool. Sal Pavy stood just inside the tent flap, shifting about restlessly, as though ready to make a run for it if necessary.

When my eyes adjusted to the lack of light, I could make out a hunched figure whose head was swathed in a number of dirty, moth-eaten scarves. On her hands were a pair of equally soiled kid gloves with the fingertips cut off, allowing the ends of her fingers to protrude. When I wiped my stinging eyes, I could see that her knuckles were clustered with a multitude of small warts.

On the wooden table before her, cradled between her palms, was a surprisingly clean cloth that concealed something spherical. On the ground next to her sat a black iron kettle—the source of the smoke that threatened to suffocate me. I leaned forward and peered into the cauldron, half expecting to find some eldritch brew of newts' eyes and adders' tongues, but saw only glowing chunks of Newcastle coal, with no purpose more sinister than to warm the tent.

La Voisin's hoarse voice issued again from the folds of her several scarves. "And what do you young ladies wish of me?"

Sam gave a feeble laugh. "Ladies? We're no ladies, madame."

"Perhaps not today," she replied slyly. "But sometimes, yes?"

Sam glanced my way and lifted his eyebrows slightly. "How did you know?"

"It is my business to know things."

"Could you—could you tell our futures, then?" When La Voisin made no answer, Sam shifted uncomfortably in his seat and seemed about to repeat the question. Then the soothsayer laid one of her hands on the table, palm up. "Oh." Sam dug in his purse for a penny, which he dropped into her worn glove.

"I have told your fate before," La Voisin said. Then she pointed a finger in my direction. "I will tell *his*." She laid aside the cloth, revealing a globe perhaps six inches across, fashioned from some substance that was black as coal; it had been polished until it gleamed darkly, like the pupil of an enormous eye.

She stared into the ball for a long while. Finally she spoke, in a tone so bleak and ominous that it made me shudder. "I see," she said, "that you will come into a fortune."

Sam's face took on a look of surprise and indignation. "That's the same thing you told *me!*"

"Not so," said La Voisin. "What I said was, 'You will receive more money than you imagine.' "

"That's the same thing, isn't it?" When the cunning woman made no reply, he fished out another coin and clapped it into her palm. "Tell mine again."

"As you wish." While she peered into the ball, I sat weighing the words she had directed at me. A fortune? How could I possibly come into a fortune? I could hardly inherit it. My mother had died in the poorhouse, and I had no notion who my father was. Perhaps, as Sam implied, the cunning woman gave more or less the same prediction to everyone. After all, folk were more likely to come back, and to bring their friends, if she told them what they wanted to hear.

La Voisin lifted her head but said nothing. "Well?" Sam prompted her.

"You are certain you wish to hear it?"

"Of course. What is it? What did you see?"

The cunning woman turned toward him, and I caught for the first time a glimpse of her visage. The skin of her face was as thickly covered with warts as a pox victim's is with scars. "I see that you will turn traitor."

Sam gaped at her for a moment before he found his voice. "That's not a prediction! That's an accusation!"

"You said you wished to hear it."

"And now I wish to have my penny back! I didn't pay good money to be insulted!"

"I am not responsible for what the future holds; I merely say what I see."

Sam got to his feet, grumbling under his breath, "Yes, well, if you ask me, you need spectacles." He waved Sal Pavy toward the stool. "It's your turn."

"I—I don't believe I—" Sal Pavy started to say.

Sam cut him off. "Come, now, stop your whingeing and take it like a man. Your future couldn't possibly be any worse than mine." Reluctantly, Sal Pavy perched on the edge of the stool. "You've got to give her a penny," Sam reminded him. "Though perhaps you'd do well to make it tuppence; you might get a better reading." He turned to me. "Not to forget, you owe me a penny. You can well afford it," he added, with a secret wink, "seeing as how you're coming into a fortune, and all."

"Silence!" hissed La Voisin. She gazed into the ball even longer than before. I nearly strangled, trying to keep from coughing as the coal smoke wafted about me. When the cunning woman spoke at last, she sounded puzzled. "I see . . . I see *nothing*."

Sal Pavy laughed. "What does that mean? That I have no future?"

La Voisin gave him a look that erased his skeptical smile. "Perhaps," she said. "I will look again."

"That's not necessary." Sal Pavy started to rise. "You may keep the penny."

"*Sit,*" said the woman. Sal Pavy's knees seemed to bend of their own accord. "I will look again." She hunched over the ball, her nose nearly pressed against it. After a long minute or two, her voice broke the silence, but only barely. She seemed to breathe the words, rather than speak them, as though they came forth without her willing them to, or even wishing them to. "I see . . . a rough hand gripping you . . . a knife . . . at your neck . . . " She sat back abruptly and, snatching up the cloth, draped it over the globe. "It has gone dark."

"But . . . what did all that mean?" Sal Pavy demanded.

"I do not interpret. I only see."

Sal Pavy got to his feet, obviously angry, but just as obviously shaken. "What a lot of bilk! I know what you're trying to do! You believe that if you make only half a prediction, I'll give you money to hear the rest! Well, you're not as good at seeing the future as you imagine for, by my troth, you'll have not so much as a brass farthing from me!" He spun about and pushed through the tent flap.

Sam cleared his throat and, with uncharacteristic meekness, said, "I—um—I'd like to apologize for our friend's behavior. He's a bit of a hothead, is all. While I'm at it, I apologize for anything I might have said that . . . that might have . . . "

"You need not bother with your false contrition," said La Voisin. "I am not going to call down a curse upon your heads. That is Fate's task, not mine." She pointed toward the flap of the tent. "Go now."

We did not need to be told twice. There was no sign of Sal Pavy outside. "Now, where do you suppose 'a's got to?" I said as we walked back toward Ludgate.

"If I was him, I'd go find another soothsayer, and get a second opinion."

"So should you, I wis. What could she have meant by that—turning traitor?"

Sam waved a hand dismissively. "Who knows? Who cares? Obviously she's just making it all up."

"When she predicted you'd win the lottery, you believed her."

"Well, wouldn't you like to believe that you're going to come into a fortune, the way she said? Speaking of which, where's my penny?"

I gave him a hurt look. "Don't you trust me to pay you back? I thought we were friends."

Sam hung his head. "Of course we are," he said. "That's why I'd really hate to have to pound you to a pudding if you don't give me the bleeding penny."

With a sigh, I tossed him a coin from my purse. "We'd best find Sal Pavy now, afore some scanderbag pounds *him* into a pudding and takes all his money."

"Some *scanderbag*?"

"Aye. What's wrong wi' that?"

Sam shook his head. "How long have you been in London?"

"Nearly two years. Why?"

"You still sound as though you'd arrived from Yorkshire yesterday. How do you manage to keep from sounding like such a lob when you're on the stage?"

"I don't ken, exactly. The same way Mr. Heminges manages not to stammer, I suppose."

Sam laughed. "One of these days you're going to forget your lines and have to thribble, and it's going to come out in Yorkshire-ese." He put a hand to his brow, in a parody of the way I played Ophelia in *Hamlet*. "'Gog's blood! I wis some scanderbag has brast his noble costard wi' a waster!'" He yodeled the last word in imitation of my uncertain voice.

I tried to scowl at him, but my features kept wanting to break into a grin. "You sot! I'll never again be able to do that scene wi' a straight face!"

Unexpectedly, Sam's own expression turned from silly to sober. "Whist! Did you hear that?"

I halted in my tracks and listened. From a dark, narrow alleyway between two buildings came the sounds of a struggle, then a frantic cry that was cut off abruptly.

"Oh, gis!" I breathed. "That's Sal Pavy's voice. I'm certain of it!"

Like all prentices, Sam and I were armed only with short daggers that were designed for dining, not for defense. But we drew them and hastened to the mouth of the alleyway.

Within its gloomy confines I could make out three figures, bunched together. One was, as I had suspected, Sal Pavy. A bald, burly wight with a wooden leg had Sal's arms pinned behind him with one huge hand; the other was clamped over the boy's mouth. The scoundrel's scrawny companion was clutching Sal's long blond locks and sawing at them with a knife twice the size of ours.

"Let him loose, you dog-bolts," I shouted, "or we'll carve you into collops!" My voice chose that moment to break like a biscuit.

The underfed fellow laughed. "With those toothpicks? Law, I'm so afeared, I'm trembling!"

"Stay back now, the both of you," warned his one-legged friend. "We've no wish to harm anyone."

"Nay, nor do we," I said.

I picked up a good-sized cobblestone, and was set to launch it at him when Sam cried, "Let it be! All they want is his hair!"

"Smart lad." The skinny brigand severed the last of Sal Pavy's golden hair and held it aloft, like Jason holding the Golden Fleece. "Some grand lady will pay a pretty price for this, to make up for what nature failed to give her."

The one-legged fellow released Sal Pavy and gave him a shove. The boy stumbled toward us, holding his shorn head between his hands and sobbing. As the two thieves sauntered off down the alley, the burly man said, "Perhaps we should have taken his leg as well. I could have used it."

"You'd have more use for a wig," replied the other man, and cackling with laughter, draped Sal Pavy's curls across his companion's bald head.

I tossed the stone aside. "Stupid sots. We shouldn't let them get away wi' this."

"There's no point in getting ourselves killed over it," Sam said. "There's little point in calling a constable, either. Those two will get rid of the hair at the nearest wig shop, and even if we found it, we can't very well put it back, can we?" He retrieved Sal Pavy's cap and carefully covered the ragged remnants of the boy's hair with it. "I don't see any wounds. Did they hurt you?"

Sal Pavy had ceased sobbing and was fiercely wiping away his tears with the hem of his cloak. "You might have done more to try and chase them off!"

"What would you have us do? If we'd come any closer, they'd have cut your throat, not just your hair. Besides, we didn't dare let them get a look at *our* luxurious locks." Sam pretended to stroke his nonexistent tresses. "They surely would have cast you aside and snatched us instead."

This attempt to coax Sal Pavy out of his foul mood failed miserably. "I might have expected you to make a jest of it! You've always made fun of my hair, both of you! I suppose you think it serves me right, getting it chopped off!"

"Well, you know," Sam replied, "if you'd had it cut sooner, you could have sold it for a good price yourself. As it is, you've neither the currency nor the curls."

I took Sam's arm and drew him aside. "Can't you see how upset 'a is? Don't make it worse."

"Well, he behaves as though it's *our* fault, for not saving his wretched hair!"

"Perhaps it was. Perhaps we should have done more. In any case, it's not *his* fault. Let's get him home now."

"Home? It's not even nones yet! We have half the afternoon ahead of us!"

"Well, do as you like. I'm taking him home."

"When did you become so concerned about his welfare?"

"When 'a became a part of our acting company," I said.

He scowled. "You're beginning to sound the way Sander used to—like an older brother."

"I consider that a compliment. Now, are you coming wi' us or not?"

Sam sighed heavily. "All right, all right. It's no fun going about by myself."

Sal Pavy walked well ahead of us, his cloak pulled tightly about him, his shoulders hunched to shelter his newly bare neck from the cold.

I said softly to Sam, "Did you notice that things happened back there just as the cunning woman said they would?"

"Of course I noticed."

"Can she truly see into the future, then, do you wis?"

He sniffed skeptically. "More likely she was in league with those two louts, and she let them know somehow that there was a good head of hair to be had."

"I suppose you're right." I couldn't help wondering, all the same. I was not so naive as to suppose that everything La Voisin said could be counted on to come true. Even so, was it not possible that occasionally she got a genuine glimpse of things to come?

Sam tried his best to talk me into taking a shortcut home, across the Thames. Ordinarily, that would have been a sensible enough suggestion; we need only have paid a wherryman to row us across. But the winter had been so unusually cold that the river was frozen over from London Bridge to Whitehall, so solidly that folk had begun to venture out upon it to skate or to fish through the ice. Some parts were less solid than others, though, and the unfortunate souls who found them often ended up in the land of Rumbelow—that is to say, a watery grave.

Though Sam seemed to think that it would be a great lark to cross on the ice, I insisted on using the bridge. "Ha' you never heard the saying: Wise men go over London Bridge; fools go under?"

"I had no intention of going under the bridge," Sam grumbled, "only across the ice."

We came to the spot on Cheapside where the public pillory stood. Despite the cold, the authorities had sentenced some poor wight to stand there with his arms and neck imprisoned. He appeared more prosperous and respectable than the usual occupant of the pillory. He twisted his stiff neck to give us a beseeching look. "I don't suppose I could prevail upon you to do me a small favor?"

"Such as setting you free?" Sam suggested.

The man tried to grin, but it was more in the way of a grimace. "I wouldn't refuse. But what I'd really like is for someone to wipe my nose. There's a kerchief in the pocket of my cloak."

Sam retrieved the kerchief and then swiped the man's cold-reddened nose several times. "You don't look like a vagrant to me. What did you do to earn this?"

"Nothing wicked, I assure you. I'd move on now, if I were you. You don't want to be seen talking to me. They may think I'm attempting to convert you."

"What do you mean?" I asked.

Sal Pavy spoke up unexpectedly, and his voice still carried a load of spite. "He means he's a Papist."

"A Catholic? I didn't ken they punished a wight just for that."

Sam leaned in close to him and whispered, "You're not a *priest,* are you?"

"Hardly. Only a printer who was unwise enough to publish a few rather harmless pamphlets defending the old faith."

Sam gave the man's nose a last wipe and returned the kerchief to him. As we turned down Fenchurch Street, Sam said, "It doesn't seem right, does it, him being put in the stocks just for printing a few pamphlets?"

"Not just any pamphlets," Sal Pavy pointed out. "*Papist* pamphlets."

Sam snickered. "I'll wager you can't say that quickly three times in a row."

"Yes, yes, make a jest of it, as always. You've not been exposed to Catholics, as I have."

"Oh, you've *exposed* yourself to them, have you?"

"Stop it, Sam," I put in. "Can't you tell when you've touched a sore spot?" I turned to Sal Pavy. "What crow do you have to pull wi' them, then?"

He scowled at me. "*What?*"

"I mean, what's given you such a poor opinion of them?"

"I'll say no more. You'll only mock me." Yanking his cloak tightly about him, he again put several paces between himself and us.

I had no strong feelings about Papists, one way or another. In truth, I knew very little about the old faith except that it had fallen out of favor many years before, when Queen Mary, a staunch Catholic, died and left the throne to her half sister Elizabeth, the present queen.

My personal experience with Catholics was limited as well. In fact, I had known but two. One was Jamie Redshaw, who for a time had claimed to be my father. He had later done his best to convince me otherwise. As with La Voisin's predictions, I was left wondering what the truth was. Reason told me to believe one way; hope inclined me in the other.

My other Catholic acquaintance was the playwright Ben Jonson. Mr. Jonson had been working mainly for the Admiral's Men, but the company's manager, Philip Henslowe, had refused to produce his latest play, *Sejanus,* on the grounds that it was full of pro-Catholic sentiments. Mr. Jonson had proceeded to offer the play to the Lord Chamberlain's Men. Our company's sharers had agreed to perform it, provided that he tone down the Papist propaganda. Mr. Jonson had spent the past week or so resentfully revising it.

When we set out for the Cross Keys on Monday morning, Sam tried again to talk me into crossing on the ice, and again I insisted on going by way of the bridge. He shook his head in disgust. "You know what your trouble is? You've no sense of adventure."

As we entered the courtyard of the inn and climbed the stairs to the rooms our company rented, Will Sly leaned over the railing above us. Will was one of our hired men—a step above us prentices, and a step below those who owned shares in the company. "Widge, Mr. Shakespeare's been asking after you. He's in the dark parlor."

"Oh, law!" Sam exclaimed in mock dismay. "What have you done now?"

"Naught that I ken."

"I wouldn't fret," said Will Sly. "He didn't seem angry, just out of sorts. Where's your friend Sal Pavy, by the by? I hear he got his curls cropped."

"Sulking somewhere, I expect." Sam stopped at the door of our makeshift tiring-room. "Ah! I know why Mr. Shakespeare wants you!"

"Why?"

"He means to give you that fortune you've got coming!" Laughing, Sam ducked inside the room before I could assist him with the sole of my boot.

I descended to the main room of the inn. Though it was by tradition called the dark parlor, it was in fact well lighted by a bank of windows that looked out upon the street. Along one wall was a row of tables with wooden dividers between them, providing a degree of privacy for those who desired it.

I discovered Mr. Shakespeare in one of these booths. Before him sat several sheets of paper filled with scribbles. At the moment he was adding nothing to them, only gazing out at the traffic on Gracechurch Street. I stood there, still and silent, for a passing while, unwilling to interrupt his reverie lest I put to flight some idea or snatch of dialogue that he was attempting to lure into the net of his thoughts.

When two or three minutes went by and he still took no notice of me, I cleared my throat softly. Absently, he lifted his earthernware tankard and set it at the edge of the table, as though to be refilled with ale. "Um," I said. "You wished to see me?"

"What?" He turned to me with a puzzled frown. "Oh, it's you, Widge. I thought you were the tippler."

"Nay. But I can fetch you more ale, an you like."

"No, no, sit down. I have a more demanding task for you."

I noticed that he was rubbing his right forearm, the one that had been cracked by a catchpoll's club the previous summer. As I had been the one to mend the arm, I took a sort of proprietary interest in it. "It looks as though your arm is paining you."

He nodded and flexed his hand. "It doesn't like the cold, and when I work it for any length of time, it begins to complain. Actually, it reminds me a good deal of my brother Ned."

I couldn't help laughing at the apt comparison, though in truth Ned's habits were more annoying than amusing. If he had been anyone but Mr. Shakespeare's brother, the company would surely have given him the chuck long ago. As an actor, he was competent enough, even engaging given the right role; it was the way he acted off the stage that kept him in constant trouble.

"However," Mr. Shakespeare went on, "I did not bring you down to listen to me rail about Ned. I'd like your help."

I glanced at the papers spread before him. "Transcribing, I wis."

"Do you mind? It'll give my arm a rest."

"Nay, I don't mind." I pulled the pages to me and peered at his unruly handwriting. "What's this play about, then?"

"An excellent question. Would that I had as good an answer for you."

"You might reply, 'Oh, Lord, sir,'" I suggested. This was an all-purpose answer Mr. Shakespeare had devised for the clown in *All's Well That Ends Well.*

He smiled faintly. "Perhaps I should." He toyed with the ring in his ear. "The truth is, I'm not at all certain what the play is about. So far, it appears to be about a wealthy man who is overly generous with his wealth, and when he loses his money he finds that all the friends he imagined he had are no longer his friends."

"Does 't ha' a name? The play, I mean."

He gave me a rather peevish glance. "I did not bring you here to ply me with questions."

"I'm—I'm sorry. I'll just . . . get me pencil, then." I dug into my wallet for the plumbago pencil I used when I needed to write rapidly.

Mr. Shakespeare sighed. "You needn't apologize, Widge. I'm not upset with you, only with the play."

"Oh. It's not going well, then?" Realizing I'd asked yet another question, I added quickly, "An you don't mind me asking."

"If 'not going well' is the Yorkshire way of saying 'a total shambles,' then yes, I'd say that's an accurate assessment." He lifted his tankard and, finding it empty, rapped it on the table. When the innkeeper had filled it, Mr. Shakespeare took a long draught of ale and then sighed again. "At this point the play has no title. I suppose I could name it after the main character, Timon, but that seems a bit dull."

"You called *Hamlet* after the main character," I pointed out.

"Yes, well, this is not *Hamlet*. More's the pity."

"Most of the wights seem to ha' Roman names: Lucius, Sempronius, Flaminius. Is that where it's set, then?"

"That was my plan, originally. But considering how cold the climate is these days for Catholics, I thought it would be wiser to choose some non-Papist country."

At a nearby table, a quartet of well-dressed wights who had clearly swallowed too many tokens, as they say, had been trading drunken insults for some little while. Now their dispute suddenly turned physical. It might have escalated into a duel with rapiers and daggers had not one of their number suddenly been seized by the urge to bring up all the ale he had consumed, even more quickly than it had gone down.

When the cursing innkeeper had chased them out and set about mopping up the mess, I said, "I don't ken how you manage to write anything down here, wi' all the hurly-burly."

"I seem to work better where there's life going on about me. It's far too quiet in my lodgings—not to mention cold. Besides, I like to read the dialogue aloud. My landlord disapproves of theatre folk enough as it is; if he were to catch me ranting to an empty room, he'd likely call a constable and have me evicted. But here"—he gestured at a table across the room, where a grizzled man in a dyer's apron was apparently having a spirited discussion with a meat pie—"no one even notices." Mr. Shakespeare took another swig of ale. "All right, then. Where did I leave off?"

I did my best to read his scrawl. "*Flavius:* 'The greatest of your having lacks a half to pay your present . . . belts'?"

"*Belts?*" echoed Mr. Shakespeare. "Where does it say 'belts'?" I pointed to the word in question. "Oh. It's *debts*. Go on."

"*Timon:* 'Let all my land be solid—*sold*.' That's where you stopped."

He stared out the window again, fingering his earring. "*Flavius:* ''Tis all engaged, some forfeited, some . . . ' No. 'Some forfeited and gone. And what remains . . . and what remains will hardly stop the mouth of present dues; the future comes apace.'" He glanced at the paper. "Am I going too rapidly?"

"Nay, I've got it. See?" Though Mr. Shakespeare's hand was difficult for anyone but himself to decipher, mine was impossible, for I had used the system of swift writing taught to me by Dr. Bright, my first master. The passage I had put down looked like this:

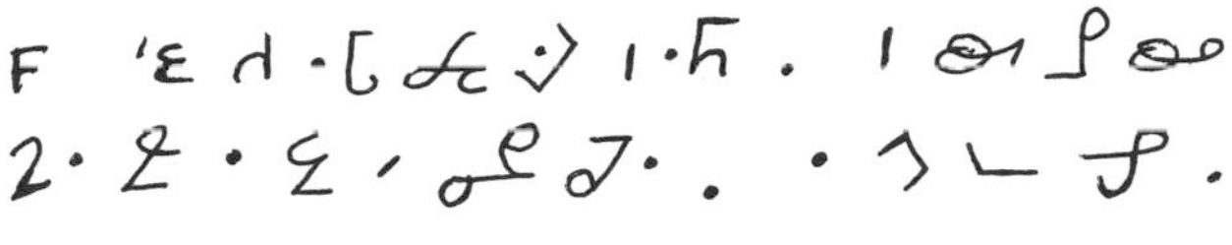

Mr. Shakespeare waved the paper away. "I'll take your word on it, Widge. Let's proceed." But before he could dictate another word, a slim, beardless fellow with black hair that was pulled back into a horse's tail strode up to the table and, without a by-your-leave, blurted out, "Will! I must speak to you! At once!"

Mr. Shakespeare turned to his brother with a look that would have made anyone with an ounce of tact apologize and return at some better time. Instead, Ned glared accusingly at me, as though I were the intruder. "Don't you have something else to do, Widge?"

I, in turn, looked to Mr. Shakespeare. "Shall I . . . ?"

"Yes, yes, go on," he said. "We'll work some more this afternoon."

I slid from the booth and Ned took my place, so impatiently that he trod on my foot. As I headed upstairs, I heard Mr. Shakespeare say wearily, "What is it *this* time, Ned?"

I did not linger to listen to Ned's reply. I was already more familiar with his troubles than I cared to be. They were predictable, in any case, nearly always involving either a game of chance, a drunken brawl, or an insult to someone's honor—very often a woman's. Occasionally he managed to combine all three. The most predictable thing was that Ned himself was never at fault. He was, he insisted, a mere victim of circumstances, condemned by Fate forever to be in the wrong place at the wrong time and in the wrong company.

I made for the tiring-room, meaning to unpack and examine my costume for that night's performance of *The Two Gentlemen of Verona*. I found Sam rummaging through a costume trunk like a badger digging a den. The floor was strewn ankle-deep with gowns and cloaks, doublets and breeches. There was no sign of our tiring-man. "Where's Richard, then?" I asked.

"At home," Sam replied without looking up from his task. "Sick with the ague."

"Oh," I said. "That's good. I was afeared 'a might be buried under all this. I thought you were supposed to be straightening up this room."

"I am!"

"Well, an this is your notion of straightening up, I'd hate to see you make a mess."

He paused from his pawing to wave his arms about despairingly. "I can't find my costume for tonight! I've looked everywhere!"

I placed a hand on his shoulder. "Calm yourself, Sam. It's certain to be here somewhere—beneath all this, no doubt." I picked up several items of clothing, smoothed them out, and hung them on one of the many hooks that lined the walls. "You've made a mingle-mangle of these. Help me sort them out."

Grumpily, Sam left off digging and set about separating the costumes into lots, according to the name tags that were sewn inside them. "This gown says *Julia*. Does that mean Julia the character, or Julia the real person?"

"Julia the character." I picked up the dress labeled *Silvia* and held it up near the window to catch the dull winter daylight.

There was a ragged hole under one arm. "Oh, gis. A rat's been gnawing at me gown. It'll ha' to be mended."

"Never mind that now," Sam said. "Help me find Lucetta's costume. If it doesn't turn up, they'll take it out of my pay."

"Surely they wouldn't blame *you,* would they?"

"That's the rule. We're each of us responsible for our own stuff."

"Oh. I thought it was up to the tiring-man to take care of the costumes."

Sam shook his head. "The sharers made the rule several years ago, when costumes started disappearing. As it turned out, one of the hired men was making off with them and selling them for several pounds apiece."

"Gog's nowns! They're worth that much?"

"Why do you think I'm so frantic to find mine? Even if they held back my whole wages, it would take me months to pay it off."

"Unless, of course, you win the lottery," I said.

"Well, I was hoping you'd help me out, once you come into that fortune."

"I might. For now, let's keep looking."

Between us, we shook out and hung up every piece of clothing from the trunk. There was no sign of Sam's costume for *Two Gentlemen.* Sighing, he sat on the trunk and put his head in his hands. "It's no use. I'm in the briars."

"Perhaps it got put i' some other trunk by mistake?"

"Well, we don't have the time to go through them all. I'll just have to wear something else." He eyed my gown, which was spread out on the windowsill. "Perhaps I'll wear yours. As much as you've grown in the past year, I'll wager it no longer fits you."

"I'll wager it does."

"A penny?"

"A penny." I began unhooking the front of my doublet.

Sam picked up Sal Pavy's gown and studied the tag that read *Julia*. "What do you hear from the real Julia, then?"

I tossed my doublet aside and started on my linen shirt. "Naught, for three months or more. I hope she's not fallen ill or something."

"It's possible. I hear the plague took nearly as many lives in Paris as it did here."

The mere suggestion that Julia might have met the same dismal fate as Sander sent a shudder of dread through me.

"I'm sorry, Widge," Sam murmured. "I wasn't thinking."

I forced a smile. "It's all right. I'm sure there's naught amiss wi' her. Most likely she's busy, that's all." I was down to my underclothing and about to slip into the gown when the door to the tiring-room swung inward and a face appeared in the opening. To my surprise and dismay it was not one of the men from the company. It was, in fact, not a man at all, but a very attractive young woman.

I quickly covered myself with the gown, my face hot with embarrassment. The intruder, however, was apparently neither very embarrassed nor very apologetic. More than anything else, she seemed amused. Her eyes, which were strikingly blue in contrast to her milk-white skin, gave my gown an appraising glance, as though I had held it up for her approval. "Very fetching," she said. "But the hem is several inches too short."

"There, I told you!" crowed Sam. "You owe me a penny!"

I was having some difficulty finding my voice. When I finally did, it betrayed me by breaking dramatically. "What—" I cleared my throat, and blushed even more deeply. "What did you want then, mistress?"

Her only difficulty seemed to lie in keeping a laugh from escaping her. She succeeded by biting her lower lip—which, I could not help noticing, despite my discomposure, was red as a rose petal. "I was looking for my father, actually."

"Oh." It was all I seemed able to come up with.

Luckily, Sam was not so tongue-tied. "If you tell us *who* he is, perhaps we may tell you *where* he is."

"Mr. Shakespeare."

"Which one? Ned or Will?"

She laughed a very charming laugh. "Does it seem likely to you that Ned Shakespeare would have a daughter of seventeen?"

Sam shrugged. "He may have gotten an early start."

"I'm sure he did. But not *that* early."

The tiring-room had no heat save what little crept in from adjacent rooms, and in my scantily clad state I had begun to shiver. "An you gi' me a moment," I said pointedly, "I'll be happy to take you to your father."

"All right." She added mischievously, "I suppose you'd like me to wait outside."

"Aye."

She had started to leave, but this brought her back. "*Aye?* You're not from London, are you?"

"Nay. No. Yorkshire."

"Really? How did you happen to come to London?"

My teeth were fairly chattering now. "Do you mind an we discuss this another time?"

"*An* you insist." She closed the door at last. I scrambled into my breeches, shirt, and doublet.

"I never knew Mr. Shakespeare had a daughter," Sam said. "He so seldom speaks about his family. She's a lot better looking than he is, don't you think?"

"I can't say that I noticed," I lied.

Sam laughed. "Much! That's why you were gaping at her so dumbly, as though she were some Gorgon whose gaze turns men to stone."

"I was embarrassed, that's all." I sat on the trunk and put my hand to my chest.

"What's wrong?"

"I—I don't ken, exactly. Me heart's pounding and I'm—I'm all out of breath, as though I'd been dancing the Spanish panic. And just feel me forehead." Despite the chill in the room, my face felt like a live coal.

Sam's face grew grave. "I've seen these same symptoms before, Widge. They're unmistakable."

I tried to swallow a rising sense of fear, but my throat was dry and tight. "What do you wis it is, then? It can't be—it can't be the plague, surely. I've shown none of th' other signs."

"I'm afraid it's even worse than that. Unless I'm sorely mistaken, you've a bad case of lovesickness."

For a moment I stared incredulously into his face, which now wore a broad grin. Then I shoved him away. "You huddypeak!" I got to my feet and straightened my doublet. "Love's not an illness!"

As I exited the tiring-room, Sam called after me, "I wouldn't be so sure!"

Mr. Shakespeare's daughter was waiting just outside the door. I suspected, in fact, that she had been eavesdropping. If so, she showed no sign of shame. "Well, at last!" she said. She turned to her companion, a tall, fashionably dressed fellow with a curly black beard, a swarthy complexion, bushy eyebrows that nearly met over a nose like a hawk's beak, and eyes as dark as lumps of coal—or Madame La Voisin's scrying ball. "And I thought," the girl went on, "that it was only women who were so slow in dressing themselves."

"I—I was only—" I stammered.

"Instead of trying so hard to embarrass the lad," said the stranger, "you might introduce us."

"I can't," the girl said, a bit petulantly. "I don't know his name."

"It's Widge," I offered.

"*Widge?* What sort of name—?"

"My name is Garrett," the man interrupted, and offered his hand to me. His grip was so firm that my finger bones ached for some time afterward. "And this is Mistress Judith Shakespeare. You'll have to pardon her if she seems a bit lacking in the social graces. She's from Warwickshire, you know, and doesn't get out much."

I was accustomed to such good-humored jesting, but the indignant look on Judith's face told me that she was not. Though I was not schooled in the social graces myself, I knew how well-bred folk sounded from having played them so often. "As Aristotle says, 'Beauty is a greater recommendation than any letter of introduction.'"

The man named Garrett laughed heartily. "Well-spoken, lad."

A smile stole across Judith's face, making it even more striking. "You know, I think I'm going to like you, Widge."

Even had I had another suitable line at the ready, I could not have found the breath to utter it. All I could manage to do was look at my feet.

"You promised to take me to my father," Judith reminded me.

"Oh. Aye. Yes. This way." I led them down to the dark parlor, where Mr. Shakespeare and Ned were still engaged in a heated discussion.

"Our father would have helped me out readily enough!" Ned was saying.

"Perhaps so. Unfortunately, he's dead." When Mr. Shakespeare saw us approaching, his face took on a curious expression that seemed composed equally of astonishment, delight, and disapproval. "Judith! What in heaven's name brings you here?"

"Why, a horse, Father." She curtsied to Ned. "God you good day, Uncle."

"Yes, hello." Ned seemed to be not so much pleased to see his niece as he was peeved by the intrusion.

Judith gave her father a kiss on the cheek. Mr. Shakespeare smiled rather wanly and patted his daughter's hand. "What an unexpected surprise."

"You don't seem very happy about it."

"Of course I am; of course," Mr. Shakespeare said, not very convincingly. Clearly, her sudden appearance had put him out of square, and thinking about it later, I could see why. Mr. Shakespeare's world was divided into two hemispheres. One centered around his hometown of Stratford and his family, the other around London and the theatre, and the two seldom intersected. To have someone arrive unannounced from his other life must have been jarring, as though he had been performing in *Hamlet* and a character from *The Comedy of Errors* had suddenly strolled onto the stage.

Though Judith pretended to be put out, I had the feeling that she rather enjoyed seeing her father so disconcerted, just as she had enjoyed catching me unclothed. "As you see, I've brought someone with me. This is Father—" She broke off and cast a sidelong glance at Mr. Garrett. She appeared flustered, as though she had said something improper. "That is . . . I mean . . . Father, this is John. John Garrett. He was kind enough to accompany me all the way from Warwickshire, providing me with both companionship and protection."

Mr. Shakespeare shook the man's hand. "My thanks, sir." He turned back to Judith. "But why—"

"Have we met before, sir?" Ned interrupted. "I don't recognize the name, but your face seems familiar to me."

"It's possible," said Mr. Garrett. "I travel about a good deal."

"Do you? For what purpose?"

"Uncle!" Judith said. "You're being rude!"

"Why?" Ned asked innocently. "Does he have something to hide?"

"Ned!" Mr. Shakespeare put in. "A gentleman's business is his own."

Ned glanced irritably at his brother, then made a slight, ironic bow in Mr. Garrett's direction. "My apologies, sir. And now I must take my leave. I have business to attend to."

"Do you?" said Mr. Garrett. "What sort?"

Ned gave a quick, sharp laugh. "Touché. Your point."

"Will you not stop and talk awhile, Uncle?" Judith said. "I've only just arrived."

"You'll be here a few days, won't you?"

Judith turned to her father with a look that seemed to carry a subtle challenge. "Longer than that, I hope."

"Then we'll talk later." He placed a swift kiss on her pale cheek and departed.

"Now," said Mr. Shakespeare. "We will all sit down and have a drink, and you will tell me why you came to London."

"I—I'd best see to me costume," I said. "I'm afeared it will ha' to be let out."

"You're keeping it prisoner?" said Mr. Garrett.

"Nay. It will need altering, I mean. It's grown too small."

"I suspect it's you who have done the growing," said Mr. Shakespeare.

"Oh, don't you rush off as well, Widge." Judith patted the seat next to her. "Come. Sit with me." She gave Mr. Shakespeare that challenging look again. "My father is about to chide me, I suspect, for being so impulsive, and he may go easier on me if I've a friend at my side."

"You've Mr. Garrett," I pointed out.

"Oh, he's an *adult*. He'll side with Father."

"You may as well sit, Widge," said Mr. Shakespeare. "If we don't let her have her way, she's liable not to speak to me at all."

Judith clucked her tongue. "You make me sound as though I were a spoiled child!"

"I'm sorry. It's—it's difficult sometimes for me to realize that you've become a young woman."

"Perhaps," she said, "that's because you see me so seldom." There was an awkward silence, then Judith went on, more brightly, "Anyway, that's one reason I've come to London—so that we may spend some time together."

"Oh. Of course. I'd like that. Unfortunately, I don't have a great deal of time, what with the demands of putting on existing plays, and the constant need to turn out new ones, and . . . "

Judith nodded, as though this was precisely what she'd expected to hear. "That's just what Mother said. But I don't ask for much—an hour or so in the evenings, that's all, and I could come to the plays and see you perform. That would be all right, wouldn't it?"

"I suppose so . . ."

"And Widge could show me around the city, couldn't you, Widge?" When she turned to me, I caught the scent of cloves, which ladies sometimes chew to sweeten their breath. It worked.

I looked to Mr. Shakespeare for my cue; he shrugged rather helplessly. "I—I don't ken," I said. "We prentices don't have many hours free, either . . ."

"Well, it's time you did, then."

"Have you given any thought to where you'll stay?" said Mr. Shakespeare.

"Wherever you lodge, I suppose."

"Oh. Well. The Mountjoys do have a daughter near your age. Perhaps she would be willing to share her room . . . for a *short* while."

Judith clapped her hands. "Good! It's all settled, then! Now. I believe that Mr. . . . Garrett"—she stumbled over the name like an actor who is uncertain of his lines—"would like to speak with you in private. I'll just go help Widge with his costume. I'm not a bad hand with a needle, you know." She slid sideways, nudging me out of the booth. The fleeting contact between our bodies turned my knees so weak that I could scarcely stand.

"Wait one moment," said Mr. Shakespeare. "You said that a desire to spend time together was *one* reason you came to London. What was the other?"

"Oh. I'm to try and persuade you to send more money home."

Sam had managed to put the tiring-room in order, or as near as one could expect from a wight who once cleaned the sheep's blood from his costume by giving it to a dog to lick. "Did you find your gown for tonight?" I asked him.

He shook his head in disgust. "I suppose I can say farewell to my wages for the next several months."

"Not to worry; I'll lend you half of mine."

"Thanks. And don't forget—you owe me a penny."

"Nay! I paid you back!"

He held up the gown that no longer fit me. "Our wager, remember?"

I drew a penny from my purse and threw it to him. "I'm surprised you haven't asked for interest on 't."

He grinned. "Well, now that you bring it up—"

"Don't you have something else to do?" I suggested.

"Yes, and so do you. It's called rehearsal."

"Aye, all right. I'll be along."

"Take your time. I'll just tell Mr. Lowin that you're already busy rehearsing . . . " In a sugary, fluttering voice, he added, "A looovvve scene!" At that moment I longed for something far larger and more dangerous than a penny to throw at him. As he went out the door, he could not resist a parting shot—a line from *Two Gentlemen:* "'I think the boy hath grace in him; he blushes!'"

"I'm sorry," I murmured in Judith's direction. "'A's such a swad."

"Oh, he's young, that's all. He'll fall in love himself one day, and then he'll sing a different tune." Taking my gown by the sleeves, she held it up against my shoulders and surveyed it critically. She seemed wholly unaware that, only a few inches from her right hand, my heart was doing its utmost to leap out of my chest. "If we let down the hem a bit and move the hooks and eyes out, you may get by with it—provided you don't make any sudden movements. Where can I find a needle and thread?"

"I'll—I'll just get them." Reluctantly, I pulled away and went to seek out the sewing box.

"Sam mentioned someone named Mr. Lowin. I don't recall my father ever speaking of him."

"'A's new to the company. When Mr. Pope retired, John Lowin took his place."

"Oh? When did Mr. Pope retire?"

"Well, when we toured last summer, 'a stayed behind, and 'a's never performed since." I handed her the sewing box. "It's his health, you ken. 'A no longer has the strength for it."

She set about threading a needle. "That's a pity. He must miss being on the stage."

"No more than we miss him, I wis. I've naught against Mr. Lowin, but it's just not the same. Of course, I still see a good deal of Mr. Pope, as I lodge wi' him." I stole a glance at Judith, to find that she was regarding me with open amusement. "What?"

"Your speech." She proceeded to mimic me. "'I wis.' 'I've naught against him.' 'I lodge wi' him.'"

I felt my face flush again. "And I suppose in Warwickshire they all sound like princes, do they?"

She laughed. "Far from it." She laid her hand—the one not holding the needle—on mine. "I'm sorry, Widge. I wasn't trying to hurt your feelings. I just find it . . . quaint."

I had been called many things in my life—a poor pigwidgeon, a lazy lout, a liar and a thief, even a horse—but no one had ever considered me *quaint* before. I was not certain how I felt about it. I would have preferred to be thought of as courageous or clever or handsome. Still, I supposed that being quaint was better than being a liar or a thief.

I would also have preferred that Judith go on resting her hand on mine for the foreseeable future. But at that moment the door of the tiring-room opened and Sal Pavy entered. It was clear that he had been to a barber. His hair, which had been ragged and unsightly after his encounter with the hair bandits, was now evenly cropped. He still seemed self-conscious, though, tugging at the back of his cap as though to conceal as much of his head as possible.

"You're missing rehearsal," I said, not very cordially.

"So are you." He looked Judith over rather suspiciously, eyeing her yellow tresses in particular, as though he suspected her of being the receiver of his stolen hair. "Have we hired a seamstress?"

Judith gave him a swift, sarcastic glance and then said to me, "Have you hired a new fool?"

I suppressed a smile. "Nay. Sal has been wi' us for some time now. Sal Pavy, this is Judith, Mr. Shakespeare's daughter."

"Oh?" Sal Pavy's manner changed at once. "Well, that explains how the lady came by such a sharp wit. It certainly served to cut me down to size. Mistress Shakespeare." He bowed to her, and she half rose from her stool to perform a cursory curtsy.

Though Sal Pavy was often disagreeable, he could put on the trappings of charm, like a new suit of clothes when it suited him. The other members of the company had long since ceased to be fooled by his performance, but Judith was seeing it for the first time, and she was an appreciative audience.

"Never fear." Smiling, she held up the rat-chewed sleeve of my gown, which she had nearly mended. "I am also very good at making a*mends*."

I got to my feet. "We'd best get ourselves upstairs." Though I had no wish to quit Judith's company, I wished even less to quit the Lord Chamberlain's company. I was not likely to get thc chuck merely for being late to a rehearsal, of course. But I had worked hard to earn a reputation for being trustworthy and conscientious, and I didn't mean to compromise it.

Judith looked hurt. "You're not going to leave me here all alone, are you?"

"I'm certain no one will mind if you attend the rehearsal," said Sal Pavy, and offered her his hand.

"What a good idea!" Judith tossed aside my gown and slipped her arm through Sal Pavy's. "Coming, Widge?"

"Aye," I replied miserably—but quaintly.

For the past week, our morning rehearsals had been devoted to getting that ancient, creaking vehicle called *The Spanish*

Tragedy into suitable shape to go on. Like my gown, it needed extensive alterations. But rather than letting it out, we were taking it in, so that it would fit into the two hours between evening prayers and curfew—the only time of day when the city fathers grudgingly permitted us to present our plays.

Though *The Spanish Tragedy* was set in a Catholic country, of course, our audience loved it so that we were obliged to resurrect it at least once a year. Perhaps its appeal lay in the fact that so many of its Popish characters were killed off. Despite the script's many flaws, I had a certain fondness for it; it was the first play in which I appeared at the Globe. I had played a messenger, with a total of three lines to say. Now I had the part of Bel-Imperia, and two hundred and twelve lines—as every aspiring player does, I had counted them. I had made a good deal of progress in less than two years.

No one would have guessed it from the performance I gave that morning. I had long since grown accustomed to spouting speeches before a crowd of several hundred rowdy playgoers. Aside from the irrational fear that always seized me just before I stepped onto the stage, it no longer bothered me. Yet I found myself reduced to a blethering, nowt-headed noddy by an audience of one well-mannered girl who neither offered her opinions of my acting at the top of her voice nor pelted me with hazelnuts.

Though I prided myself on my excellent memory, I could not say two sentences together without consulting the side, or partial script, I had tucked in my wallet. Despite daily lessons in graceful footwork, I found myself stumbling over the other players' feet, and occasionally my own. To make my mortification complete, my voice reminded me regularly of how unreliable it had become.

My one consolation was that none of the sharers was there to witness the debacle. They customarily went over their lines on their own, while the prentices and hired men practiced under the eye of a seasoned player such as Mr. Lowin. Very often our first performance before an audience was also the first time the entire ensemble was on the stage together.

From the the way the company clustered about Judith after rehearsal, anyone would have thought that she had been the one performing and that we were all complimenting her. I knew that, with all the attention being paid her, she would pay none to me. Heaving a melancholy sigh, I slunk off to the tiring-room.

Just as I reached the door, it opened and a tall, unfamiliar figure emerged, dressed in the apothecary's robe from *Romeo and Juliet*. "Here!" I cried, my voice breaking yet again. "Who are you, and where are you going wi' that costume?"

The man raised his hands, as if to show that he was unarmed and harmless. "It's only me, Widge. John Garrett, remember?"

"Mr. Garrett?" He looked very different from the man I had met a few hours earlier. His hair was cut nearly as short as my own, and it was now an odd brownish hue. So were his mustache, his beard, and his eyebrows, which no longer met in the middle. His beard had been trimmed into a neat spade shape. The only feature I recognized was the coal-black eyes. Even his swarthy complexion seemed to have grown several shades lighter.

There was one other peculiar thing about him—he gave off a rank smell that I could not quite identify but that put me in mind of a stable somehow, one that had not been cleaned lately. Grimacing, I stepped back. "What—why are you wearing one of our costumes?"

"Mr. Armin will explain. Do you by any chance know where I might find Mr. Jonson?"

"Try Mr. Heminges's office, two doors down. 'A may be there, working on his script."

"Thank you. And thank you for being so polite as to not mention my offensive odor. Mr. Armin will explain that as well."

In the confines of the tiring-room, the awful odor was so strong that I could scarcely keep from gagging. Mr. Armin seemed not to notice. He was busy gathering up barber's tools, sponges, and jars of makeup. "What reeks so badly?" I demanded.

"Horse urine," Mr. Armin said matter-of-factly. He handed me an earthenware mug—clearly the source of the smell. "Will you empty that outside for me, please?"

"Horse urine?"

"Yes. You know, the yellow liquid sometimes known as—"

"Aye, I ken what it is well enough. What I don't ken is why you'd want a mug of 't."

"For bleaching purposes."

"Oh. Mr. Garrett's hair and beard, I wis."

"Exactly."

"I don't suppose 'a will be performing in a play wi' us?"

"No."

"So it's a disguise?" I took Mr. Armin's silence as an affirmative. "I expect that Garrett is not his true name, either." Mr. Armin remained silent. "Has 'a done something wrong, then, that 'a must conceal his identity?"

"That's a matter of opinion," Mr. Armin said. "I happen to think not. Still, it would be best if you do not inquire further into the matter. Can I depend on you?"

"Aye."

"Good. Now empty that mug, will you?"

I dumped the horse urine into the ditch that ran down the center of Gracechurch Street. The ditch had been designed to carry rainwater—and, along with it, household wastes and the contents of slop jars—downhill into the Thames. It did not fulfill its function very well, mainly because home owners tossed into it all sorts of inappropriate objects, some too large to be washed away by anything short of a flood—animal hides and guts, dead dogs, broken crockery, moldy straw from bed ticks, and the like.

Some folk felt that the plague was caused by corrupted air; if they were correct, then the city's gutters must be the prime breeding ground for the disease. But the corrupted air theory was only one of many. Astrologers blamed some particular alignment of the stars. Others, depending upon their own religious convictions, claimed that the contagion was part of a Popish plot, or a Jewish one, or even a Protestant one.

I had my own tentative theory about the plague and how it spread. I had noticed how often the illness was preceded by a rash of tiny red marks on the victim's limbs, like so many insect bites. My old master Dr. Bright believed that the contagion passed from person to person by means of invisible "plague seeds"; though he was not a particularly good physician, I suspected that, for once, he had stumbled upon the truth. Perhaps, then, the seeds could be conveyed not only through the air, but also through the bites of mosquitoes, fleas, bedbugs, and the like, that carried the seeds within them. After all, these insects were at their worst in the summer months, when the plague was also at its peak.

I had converted our housekeeper, Goodwife Willingson, to my way of thinking, and she had begun a crusade against all manner of bugs. So far her tactics had worked; since Sander's death, no one in Mr. Pope's household had been stricken. It remained to be seen whether or not they continued to work once the hot weather returned.

Just to be safe, Goody Willingson insisted that we have our daily spoonful of sage, rue, and ginger steeped in wine, and that we take the time-honored precaution of wearing about our necks small pomanders filled with wormwood and rosemary. I wondered whether she might know of some such measure one might take to avoid being stricken by love.

But perhaps it was too late for that. Perhaps I needed not a preventive but a cure. Each time Judith's face entered my mind—though, in truth, I don't believe it ever quite left—a curious feeling came over me, not unlike the one that always gripped me just before I was due on the stage. It was impossible to define, it was such a mingle-mangle of conflicting emotions—anticipation and uncertainty, eagerness and dread, pleasure and pain.

A rapping sound brought me out of my reverie. I turned to see Mr. Shakespeare beckoning me from within the dark parlor. I scoured out the mug with snow and went inside.

Mr. Shakespeare had obviously continued working on his unnamed play—or at least had attempted to. The booth was littered with wads of crumpled paper. The stack of completed pages, though, seemed no thicker than before. He was not writing now, only staring into his ale pot as though, like Madame La Voisin's scrying ball, it might tell him how to proceed.

"Did you want me to transcribe for you, then?" I asked.

"Not really." His voice echoed a little in the empty tankard. "Unless you can think of something yourself to set down. I certainly can't—nothing that isn't a pile of putrid tripe, at any rate."

I perused the few uncrumpled pages. "Perhaps . . . perhaps an you found somewhere quiet . . ."

"What I *need,*" he replied sharply, "is not somewhere quiet. What I *need* is a decent story to work with—something with a bit of life to it. Plays should not be about *money.*" He flicked the pages contemptuously with one finger. "They should be about . . . about madness and betrayal, about love and death."

"Like *Hamlet.*"

"Yes. Like *Hamlet.*" He rubbed his high forehead as though it pained him. "Unfortunately, money is the thing that is uppermost in my mind these days. Perhaps I was trying to purge myself by writing about it." He gathered up the wadded papers. "But that's not your concern. The reason I called you in was to ask another sort of favor."

"Gladly. What is 't?"

"I want you to escort my daughter to my lodgings. You know where I live?"

"Aye. The corner of Silver and Monkswell Street in Cripplegate."

"I've sent her trunk on ahead, along with a note to the—" Mr. Shakespeare broke off as someone approached the booth. The scent of cloves infused the air around us.

Judith slid in next to me. I kept my eyes on the table, certain that the expression on my face must be a foolish one. "You were saying, Father?" she prompted.

"I was saying that I've sent your trunk to my lodgings, along with a note to Madam Mountjoy, asking if she will kindly put you up for a few days."

"I would rather you had said a few weeks." Judith picked up his tankard and peered into it to see whether any ale remained. I snatched up the mug that had held the horse urine, lest she decide to examine it, too. "In fact," she said, "I'm not at all sure that I won't decide to stay in London indefinitely."

Mr. Shakespeare appeared alarmed by this prospect. "Oh? Have you discussed this with your mother?"

"Of course not. She'd have had a seizure." Judith gave a long-suffering sigh. "Oh, Father, you know what Stratford is like. Aside from mother, there's absolutely no one and nothing there that holds the slightest interest for me." She gave an impish smile. "And, honestly, sometimes even Mother can be a bit tiresome."

Mr. Shakespeare did his best not to look amused. "All the same, I don't think it would be wise to stay in London. What would you do with yourself?"

"I don't know. Be a gatherer for the Globe, perhaps. I'm good at managing money. On what you send us, I've had to be."

"That's enough of that!" Mr. Shakespeare snapped. Judith's smile faded and she looked down at her lap as though a trifle ashamed of her impudence—but only a trifle. "Now," her father continued, "I've asked Widge to accompany you to the Mountjoys'."

Judith's gaze met his again, and it seemed puzzled, reproachful. "You've asked Widge? I thought that *you* would . . ."

Now Mr. Shakespeare was the one to look away. "I'm sorry. As I've told you, I'm very busy just now. We have a sharers' meeting shortly. We must come to a decison on whether or not to raise the admission price of the plays."

"Oh. Well. I can see how that would be more important than squiring me about." She slid from the booth and held out a hand to me. "Come, then, Widge. You'll no doubt be better company, anyway."

Though Mr. Shakespeare pretended to ignore his daughter's barbed remark, I could tell from the way he stiffened slightly that it had struck its mark. As I got to my feet, Judith said to her father in a voice as cool as a cowcumber, "I trust you were able to make some arrangements for Mr. . . . Garrett?"

"Yes. Ben Jonson has volunteered to take him in."

"Good." She slipped her arm through mine. "I suppose I'll see you after the performance this evening, Father?"

"Yes. You needn't wait up for me, though. I may be late."

"Of course." She swept out of the parlor, hauling me with her. After fetching our cloaks, we passed through the courtyard and onto Fenchurch Street. Judith drew in a deep breath of the cold air and put on the semblance of a smile. "Parents can be so vexing. Particularly fathers. Don't you agree?"

"I . . . I wouldn't ken," I murmered.

"What do you mean?"

I was not anxious to reveal how little I knew of my mother and father and their station in life. Mistress MacGregor, who ran the orphanage where I grew up, had given me a crucifix my mother once wore, inscribed with the name Sarah. Jamie Redshaw had told me a few more things about my mother, but whether or not any of them were true I could not say, any more than I could say whether anything he had said about himself was true.

Judith peered into my downturned face, making me so flustered that I missed my footing and very nearly sent us stumbling into the path of a costermonger's cart. "Sorry," I mumbled.

"Never mind. I want to know what you meant when you said you wouldn't ken."

"It means I wouldn't *know*."

"I ken that. But why would you not know?"

"Because." I would have left it at that, but the way her bright blue eyes were fixed upon me somehow made me wish to tell her everything that was in my mind and in my heart, all in one great rush. "Because me mother died borning me, and me father . . . well, I'm not exactly certain who me father was."

She bit her lip. "I see. You're an orphan, then?"

"Aye," I admitted mournfully, half expecting her to pull away, as though I'd confessed to being the bearer of some dread disease.

To my surprise, she drew even closer and patted my arm. "But that's not such a bad thing, is it? I mean, if you don't know who your parents are, then they might be anyone, mightn't they? Who knows, perhaps you're the illegitimate son of some great lord with piles and piles of money."

"Would that were so," I said fervently. "Then I might hope to—" My voice broke then, and perhaps it was just as well, for I had been about to say something I had no business saying, or even thinking: that if I were rich and of noble birth, and not a poor prentice with no prospects beyond my next role, then there would be some chance, however small, that I might win her affections.

"What?" she urged. "What would you hope for?"

"Nothing," I said. But the knowing smile on her face led me to suspect that she had guessed my thoughts.

She tossed her yellow curls. "Well, in any case, I believe it doesn't matter whether a man is born high or low, not in this day and age. If you work hard and use your wits, you can make of yourself what you will. Look at my father, or Mr. Jonson. They're the sons of tradesmen, both of them, and yet they've earned both renown and respect."

"I didn't ken that anyone had much respect for theatre folk—even for playwrights."

"Of course they do. My father's name and work are well regarded all over England."

"It sounds as though you're very proud of him."

"I am. I may not always show it, I grant you. Even though he's a genius and all that, he can be a bit of a dolt sometimes. My mother says that it's not just him, it's men in general." She shook my arm playfully. "Tell me, Widge, are you a dolt sometimes?"

"Aye. More often than not, I expect," I said glumly.

Suddenly aware of how dismal her image of me must be, I rummaged through myself, as Sam had rummaged through the costume trunk, searching for some admirable quality or uncommon skill that I might bring to her attention. My acting? No, she had seen a sample of that this afternoon, and I did not care to remind her. In my desperation I resorted to a deplorable habit I had foolishly thought I was rid of: I lied. "I am writing a play, though."

A lie is like an arrow: once you've let it fly, there's no calling it back; the damage is done. And telling a single lie is like loosing a single arrow at an angry bear: one is seldom enough; it must be followed by another, and another.

"You're not!" she said.

"You doubt me?" I managed to sound indignant.

"No, of course not. What's this play of yours called, then?"

I pulled a title out of the air, a phrase I had once heard. "It's called *The Mad Men of Gotham*." There was a certain perverse satisfaction in finding that my talent for fabling had not grown rusty from disuse.

"And what is it about?"

I had asked Mr. Shakespeare the very same thing that morning, and, like a good player, I recalled the line he had given me in reply. "An excellent question. Would that I had as good an answer for you."

"Oh." She smiled slyly. "I see what you're doing."

I swallowed hard, fearing my lie was so transparent that she had seen through it. "You do?"

"Yes. You're putting me off, because you don't want to discuss it. Father does the same thing. I think he's afraid that if he talks too much about a play in progress, it will put a curse on it somehow, and he'll never complete it."

"That's it exactly. I don't wish to put a curse on 't."

"Well, will you let me read it, at least?"

I wanted to say, *Aye, at the last Lammas*—meaning never. Instead I shrugged and said, "I might. When I'm further along wi' 't."

"I can't wait." She shook my arm again. "Perhaps it'll be performed, and become wildly popular, and make a fortune for you!"

Her words brought to mind Madame La Voisin's prediction that I would come into a fortune. I let out a nervous laugh. "Much! I've never heard of a play making its author rich."

"Oh, I don't know. Father does well enough with his."

"'A does?"

She nodded. "He never lets on to Mother and me how much he makes, of course; he doesn't want us demanding more of it. But"—she leaned in close to me, nearly stopping my poor heart—"it's enough to allow him to buy a hundred acres of land in Stratford, and the largest house in town—three stories, it is, with ten fireplaces!"

"Gog's blood! I never would ha' thought it. 'A lives so modest a life here, and 'a's always fretting about money."

"I know. To tell the truth, he's a bit of a miser. He won't even consent to loan money to his nearest friends. I think he's afraid of ending up like his father—my grandfather."

"How's that?"

"When Grandfather died, he was up to his ears in debt. Father says it's because he was too trusting, too ready to loan money to anyone who asked. But Mother says there's more to it than that. She says it's because . . . " She stood on tiptoe to whisper in my ear. "Because he was a *recusant*."

"A what?"

"A Catholic who refuses to attend the Anglican services."

"Oh. So 'a paid all his money out in fines, then?"

"That was part of it. But his business suffered because of it, too. No one but his fellow Catholics would buy wool or gloves from him, or rent his properties from him. He lost a good deal of property as well, in the rash of fires that Stratford suffered several years ago. Grandfather always claimed that the fires were set deliberately by Puritans. My mother has always staunchly denied it, but of course she would, being a Puritan herself."

"I take it you're not, then?"

"Not really. I suppose that when it comes to religion, I take more after my father. He says that the world is so full of ideas and customs and beliefs, each with its own merit, it seems a shame to place our faith in only one and rule out all the others." She turned her face up to me. "And what about you, Widge?"

"What about me?"

"Well, I assume you're not a Puritan, or you wouldn't be a player. But what are you? A good Protestant? A Church Papist? A skeptic? An atheist?"

"I don't ken, exactly. Is there a name for folk who can't make up their minds?"

"Yes," she said. "They're called women." Though she clearly expected a laugh from me, I was not in a laughing mood. In fact, my heart had suddenly turned as heavy as horse-bread.

My face must have given me away, for Judith said, "What is it, Widge? What's wrong?"

I nodded toward the house that lay just ahead of us. "We're here," I said grimly.

She laughed. "You needn't sound as though you're delivering me to the Tower."

"I'm sorry. It's just that—" I faltered, unable to give voice to the feeling that rose up in me—the feeling that, despite the cold, despite the fact that my shoes were soaked through with slush, I would willingly have gone on walking—in circles, if necessary—for another several days at least, as long as I had her company.

Once again she seemed to read my thoughts and, patting my arm, said, "Don't worry, Widge. We'll have lots more time together."

"Truly?"

"Of course. After all, we'll have to, won't we, if you're to read me your play?"

I left Judith in the care of Mary Mountjoy, a plump, rose-cheeked girl I had met several times before, when I carried some message to Mr. Shakespeare. I had always thought her attractive enough, but put up against Judith, she seemed as plain as porridge.

Reluctantly, I turned my steps again toward Cheapside, the most direct route back to the Cross Keys. My head was as full of thoughts as a hive is of bees. Like a player committing a new part to memory, I went over and over every word that had passed between Judith and me, relishing hers, deploring my own. My conversational skills were on much the same level as my acting skills had been earlier in the day. At least at rehearsal my lines had been written out for me, and so my speeches, when I could get them out, had consisted of something a bit less plodding and obvious than "I'm sorry" and "How's that?" and "'A does?"

I had often wondered why the wights in plays were forever composing songs or sonnets to their ladies, and not just saying straight out what was in their hearts. Now I understood. But, thanks to my lying tongue, Judith would never be content with a mere stanza or two of maudlin verse. She expected an entire play. When it came to stupid behavior, the Mad Men of Gotham—whoever they might be—could not possibly hope to compete with me.

And yet, as I mulled it over in my mind, the notion of writing a play was not really so preposterous as it seemed on the face of it. I had some little knowledge, after all, of how the deed was done, from transcribing Mr. Shakespeare's *All's Well That Ends Well* for him. I had even made a few modest contributions of my own, including the title.

Though I might be stupid, I was not so stupid as to imagine that I could come within hailing distance of a gifted poet such as Mr. Shakespeare, even at his worst. But not all the plays we performed were as accomplished as his. In fact, there were times, as I was mouthing some silly, stilted speech from *The Dead Man's Fortune* or *Frederick and Basilea,* when I swore that I could do far better without even breaking a sweat.

In truth, the notion of composing a play held a certain appeal for me. Though I found acting more gratifying than anything else I had ever done, I sometimes felt less like a player than like an instrument, a mouthpiece for someone else's words. The feeling was not an unfamiliar one; I had experienced it years before, when I was forced to copy down other rectors' sermons for Dr. Bright in the swift writing he taught me, and again when I was hired to set down the words of

Hamlet as it was being performed. All my life I had been compelled to do and say as others instructed me to. I wondered what it would be like, for once, to be the one telling others what to say and do, to be the craftsman, not the tool.

What I had told Judith might not be altogether a lie, then. Perhaps it was like one of La Voisin's predictions, instead. Sam had said that she was only telling her clients what they wished to hear. Perhaps I had merely been expressing some secret wish.

I was startled to my senses by the sound of the bells at St. Paul's tolling nones. For the first time I took a good look about me. Not only had I lost track of time, I had lost my way. I had come out not on West Cheap as I had meant to, but a good deal farther to the south and west, where Ludgate Street passed through the city wall. After two years of navigating London's crooked streets, I still had not fully mastered the maze, just as I had not completely mastered London speech.

I was but two or three minutes' walk from Salisbury Court, where we had visited Madame La Voisin the day before. I had missed dinner already and, if I did not hurry, I would miss scriming practice as well and be obliged to pay a fine. But such mundane concerns as food and fines seemed of little consequence at the moment. I had more weighty matters on my mind—my future, for example.

Folk who are contented with their lot in life tend not to give much thought to the future. Ever since I joined the Lord Chamberlain's Men, I had been more or less contented. My thoughts about the future had been limited mostly to wondering what would become of me if I lost my position with them. Now, suddenly, like a sailor who spies some green and welcome land on the horizon, I had been given a glimpse of new and unfamiliar territory, and I longed to know whether or not I had any hope of reaching it.

It took me some time to find the cunning woman's tattered tent, for the sign with the enormous eye no longer stood before it. I paused at the flap, uncertain whether or not to call out to her. To my surprise, a rough voice within said, "You may enter, young lady." When Sam and Sal and I came here together, she had called us young ladies. Did she know it was me waiting outside, then? Or was it simply that most of her clients were young ladies?

I ducked through the opening. The interior was even more smoky than I remembered. When my eyes adjusted to the gloom, I saw why. Instead of coal, she was burning a chunk of the wooden sign in her kettle.

"Sit," said La Voisin, and I obeyed. She peered at me from beneath the layers of woolen scarves. "I have already read your future."

"Aye. But I—I'd like to know more."

"Hmm. It is not wise to try to learn too much of what lies in store."

"I don't wish to know *everything* . . . "

She gave a hoarse, humorless laugh. "Only the good things, eh?" When I had placed a penny gingerly in her grimy hand, she unveiled her scrying ball and gazed into it, but only for a few seconds. Then she said matter-of-factly, "I see that you will make a name for yourself."

Though I suppose this should have pleased me, I was disappointed. It seemed to me a sort of all-purpose prediction, designed to appeal to anyone and everyone. "That's all?"

"It seems quite enough to me."

"Can't you tell me something more . . . well, *specific?*"

"Just what did you have in mind?"

"Perhaps something about . . . " I had no desire to discuss with this odd old woman anything as awkward and intimate as love. " . . . about other people?"

"Other people," she muttered. "I can try. But I see only what I see." She held out her hand and I dropped another penny into it. This time she stared into the ball, motionless, for so long that I feared she had drifted into some sort of daze, or fallen asleep with her eyes open. As surreptitiously as I could, I waved the wood smoke away from my face. The motion seemed to bring her out of her trance. When she spoke, it was in a monotone, without inflection, without emotion. "Because of you," she said, "someone will die." Before I had quite gotten my mind around this ominous prediction, she made a second that was even more startling: "But another will return to life."

"Return to life?" I said. "How is that possible?"

"I do not interpret. I only—"

"Aye, I ken. You only see." I leaned forward to get a closer look at the scrying ball. "I don't suppose you saw aught about someone . . . " I hesitated, embarrassed. " . . . someone named Judith?"

She pulled the cloth protectively over the black ball. "No." Then on her shrouded, wart-speckled face, I saw something approaching a smile. "But if you were to send this Judith to me, I could tell her future . . . and perhaps make certain that you appeared in it."

"For a price, of course."

"Of course."

So, not only did she tell her clients what they wished to hear, she would also tell them what someone else wanted them to hear. She was clearly a fake. And yet . . . and yet she had revealed to each of us one thing that we could not conceivably have wished to hear—that Sam would turn traitor, that Sal Pavy would lose his hair, that I would be the cause of another person's death. Those were hardly the sorts of predictions that were calculated to keep us coming back for more.

I got unsteadily to my feet, dizzy from breathing in the smoke—or from too many confusing thoughts buzzing in my brain. "I must go. God you good day."

"A good day," she said, "would be a warm one."

I glanced at the smoldering sign. "You've run out of fuel, then?" She nodded and pulled her scarves more tightly about her. Impulsively I reached into my purse, brought out my last shilling, and laid it on the table. "To buy coal with." As I left the tent, I thought I heard her murmur something in reply; I could not be sure of the words, but they might have been "May Fate be kind to you."

Only when I was halfway back to the Cross Keys did I realize how foolish I had been to give her that shilling. What would I use now to pay the fine Mr. Armin was sure to demand of me for missing scriming practice? And, as I soon discovered, that was not the only penalty I would be expected to pay.

In my preoccupation with Judith, I had forgotten all about my costume for that night's performance, and the fact that it had not yet been let out to fit me. With our tiring-man home ill and but two hours remaining before performance, it would have to wait. Perhaps no one would notice if I pressed into service my costume from *The Spanish Tragedy*.

But when I dug through the trunk of clothing for that play, there was no sign of Bel-Imperia's gown. Alarmed, I went through the lot again, piece by piece, and still failed to turn it up. "Oh, gis!" I sank to the floor, my head in my hands.

"S-something wrong?" said a voice behind me.

"Aye," I groaned. "Me gown for *The Spanish Tragedy* has come up missing."

Mr. Heminges crouched down next to me. "I hate to t-tell you this, W-Widge, but we're not d-doing *The Spanish Tragedy* this evening."

"I ken that. But me dress for *Two Gentlemen* no longer fits, and I thought I'd substitute this one, only it's gone."

Mr. Heminges sighed heavily, as though he'd heard this same tale before and was weary of it. "That's unf-fortunate. But I'm n-not surprised. It's the f-fourth item that's d-disappeared in as m-many weeks."

"Is someone stealing them, do you wis?"

"I'm afraid it's a p-possibility. Of course, it's also p-possible that they're st-still at the Globe somewhere, though I d-doubt it. Richard is always very c-careful in p-packing the costumes."

"I suppose it'll come out of me wages, then?"

"I'm s-sorry, but that's the r-rule. We c-can't make an exception for you. If we f-find out who the th-thief is—assuming th-there is one—we'll return the m-money to you." He got stiffly to his feet. "N-now, let's see about that other g-gown."

When I tried it on, the hem proved to be, as Judith had guessed, several inches too short, and no matter how Mr. Heminges tugged at the back of my bodice, the hooks and eyes could not be made to meet. "Well, we d-don't have much t-time. If you'll s-see to the hooks and eyes, I'll l-let down the hem—pr-provided you thread the n-needle for me; my eyes are n-not what they were."

Though, like all prentices, I had made my share of emergency repairs, I was no great hand with a needle. Before I had managed to move all two dozen hooks and eyes to their new positions, I must have dropped each of them at least twice; several were never seen again. Mr. Heminges's needlework, however, was swift and sure. When I commented upon this, he laughed. "When you have b-been on the road as many t-times as I have, without b-benefit of a seamstress or t-tiring-man, you learn to d-do for yourself."

"Will we go on the road again this summer, do you wis?"

He paused and rubbed thoughtfully at his graying beard. "It's hard to s-say, at this p-point. What we d-do will depend largely upon what the p-plague does. I hope it will not c-come to that. Our p-position is precarious enough as it is. If we had to c-close down the theatre for several m-months, it could be—" He broke off, then, as though he had said too much, and went back to his stitching. "Well, as I s-said, I hope not."

Though I did not wish to pry into matters that did not concern me, I had the uneasy feeling that this *did* concern me. "Are we—is the company in difficulty, then?"

Mr. Heminges considered for several moments before replying. "A bit. But we'll w-weather it. We always have." He gave me a rather worn smile. "In any c-case, there's n-no need for you or the other pr-prentices to worry. L-let us sharers do the w-worrying, all right?"

I would willingly have obeyed him; I had more than enough on my mind already. But worry is like the plague—or, it seemed, like love. It's no good at all ignoring or denying it; once the seed has found its way inside you, you are doomed.

Even had I succeeded in casting aside my concern, it would not have been for long. As we players stood in the cramped space behind the stage, listening to the audience arrive and trying to judge from the sound of them what mood they were in, Mr. Shakespeare, still dressed in his street clothes, burst through the door that led to the outside stairway, bringing with him a gust of frigid air. "Widge!" he called above the din of the playgoers.

"Aye!" I made my way toward him through the shifting mass of actors applying their face paint, adjusting their costumes, mumbling their lines to themselves, making all sorts of curious sounds meant to limber up their voices.

When I was within his reach, Mr. Shakespeare drew me to him. "The master of revels sends word that some men from the queen's Privy Council are out there tonight, checking up on us."

"Is there something amiss wi' our privy?"

He laughed. "The Privy Council is a body of Her Majesty's closest advisers. No doubt they hope to catch us feeding the masses some morsel of Papist propaganda, as a priest gives out morsels of the host at Communion. I imagine Henslowe has put them up to it."

Our sharers had long suspected the manager of the Admiral's Men of mounting various strategies to injure our reputation or our box—that is, the amount of money we took in—including attaching Mr. Shakespeare's well-known name to plays written by Henslowe's own committee of hacks, inciting Puritan preachers to stand outside the Globe railing at the playgoers, even planting his men in our audience, where they shouted insults at the actors.

"You have a line about confession, do you not?"

"Aye. Eglamour says, 'Where shall we meet?' and I say, 'At Friar Patrick's cell, where I intend holy confession.'"

"Yes, yes. I want you to replace that line."

"Wi' what?"

"You'll think of something. Are there any other Popish sorts of speeches that you can recall?"

"Nay. But—"

The sound of Mr. Phillips's hautboy signaled that the play was about to commence. Mr. Shakespeare glanced down at his everyday doublet and breeches. "By the matt!" he whispered. "I nearly forgot; I'm playing the duke!" He left as precipitously as he had come, leaving me to invent some new bit of dialogue for myself. Well, if I had any hope at all of living up to my boast of writing a play, surely I could conjure up a line and a half of passable iambic pentameter. If nothing else, the effort would give me something to do besides fret, which is what I was ordinarily doing at this point in the performance.

Mr. Pope had assured me that a certain amount of fear before going on was a good thing. "Without frets," he was fond of saying, "there is no music." But none of the other actors, not even the prentices, looked as though they were going to face the hangman, as I had been told I did. Sal Pavy was examining himself in a looking glass, touching the locks of his blond wig as though wishing they were his own. Sam, dressed in a gown borrowed from the *As You Like It* trunk, stood next to me at the stage-right curtain, whistling a tune under his breath and practicing a little jig step Mr. Phillips had taught him.

I took a deep breath—or as deep as I could manage, considering how tightly my ribs were bound by the bodice of my dress—and tried to compose a line to replace the censored one. *Where shall we meet? Ta tumpty-tumpty tum. Behind the abbey wall?* No. *Some nonreligious place?* When I glanced again at Sal Pavy, who played my romantic adversary, Julia, a clever though totally unsuitable possibility entered my head: *Let's meet in Julia's room, where I intend to strangle her with her wig.*

"What are you sniggering about?" Sam asked softly.

"Oh, nothing. I was just thinking of strangling Julia."

Sam nodded, as though this were a perfectly reasonable proposal. "May I help?" This set me laughing again, so violently that I had to cover my mouth to avoid being heard on the other side of the curtain. "Careful," Sam said. "You'll burst your bodice." When I had gotten my mirth under control, he said, "I hear you've lost a costume, too."

"Aye. Between that and the fine for missing scriming practice, I'm afraid I'll ha' no money to help you out."

"No matter. Mr. Heminges has promised to withhold only a shilling each week."

"We'll still receive two shillings, then? That's good. That's more than you imagined." Something about those words struck me as odd, or perhaps familiar. I had to mull it over for a moment before I realized where I had heard them before. "Sam!" I whispered. "The cunning woman's prediction!"

"What about it?"

"She said, 'You will receive more money than you imagine.'"

He stared at me. "No. That can't be what she meant. Can it?"

Out on the stage, Will Sly, our Proteus, delivered the last line of the scene: "I fear my Julia would not deign my lines, receiving them from such a worthless post."

Sal Pavy appeared beside us. "That's our cue!" he told Sam.

But Sam seemed not to hear. He was shaking his head in disbelief. "That can't be what she meant," he repeated. I had to plant my foot on his nether end and propel him onto the stage.

Though Mr. Shakespeare was disturbed at having members of the Privy Council in the audience, I much preferred their presence to Judith's. I was distracted enough just thinking about her in the abstract; to have her there in the flesh would certainly have undone me completely.

Just in case I should happen to forget my infatuation with her for a second or so, the play seemed specially designed to make certain I would not, from Sal Pavy's first speech—"But say, Lucetta, now we are alone, wouldst thou then counsel me to fall in love?"—to the end, when Mr. Shakespeare spoke the line with which Sam had teased me earlier in the day: "I think the boy hath grace in him; he blushes."

The one thing I did manage to forget was the need to think up a new line, until the very scene was upon me. When Mr. Armin, as Eglamour, asked, "Where shall we meet?" I froze. Seeing that I was speechless, he did as any good player would—he prompted me. "Shall we meet at Friar—" he began.

"No!" I interrupted frantically, my voice cracking. "Let's not! Let's meet . . . somewhere else! In the forest!"

Mr. Armin was too seasoned an actor to let this throw him. "An excellent idea, your ladyship," he said. When we met behind the stage later, he gave me a look of mock disparagement. "In the *forest?*"

"It was all I could think of," I protested. "At least I said *no* rather than *nay*."

"Why did you say it at all? I was about to cover for you."

"Mr. Shakespeare told me to cut the line about Friar Patrick. 'A says there's a wight from the Privy Council out there."

"A pox on the Privy Council!" muttered Mr. Armin. "They were here last week as well, for *Romeo and Juliet*. John Lowin had to amend his line about going to confession. No doubt they would have been even happier had we made Friar Laurence an Anglican priest." He smacked a fist into his palm. "They've never bothered us before. Why now? And why would they pick the very plays that happen to have references to Catholic rites in them?"

"Perhaps because the plays are set in Italy?"

"Perhaps," Mr. Armin said. "Or perhaps someone is keeping the Privy Council apprised of everything we do."

"You mean . . . "

"I mean," he said, "a spy."

By the time I returned home that evening, I was as bone weary as I had ever been, even the previous summer, when we sometimes slogged along a muddy road in the rain from dawn until dusk. Though for a prentice every day is a hectic one, this day had been without equal or precedent, as full of alarums and excursions and general hurly-burly as both parts of *Henry VI* put together.

As was their custom, the dozen or so orphan boys who lodged with Mr. Pope were waiting to pounce on me the moment I came through the door, yelling like wild Irishmen, rifling my wallet in search of the sweetmeats I sometimes brought them, begging me to play a game of Barley-Break or Rise Pig and Go. But when Goody Willingson saw how haggard I looked, she chased them off to bed and brought me a cup of what she called clary—warm wine with honey, pepper, and ginger—and a bowl of frumety—wheat kernels boiled in milk—which she had kept hot for me on the back of the cast-iron heating stove.

I was too exhausted to eat more than a few mouthfuls. "Has Mr. Pope retired for the night?" I asked.

"He's in the library."

I sighed, knowing that he was waiting for me, too—not so that I might play a game, but so that I might tell him all the day's news. I did not like to disappoint him, for I knew how much he missed being a part of the company, and how eager he was to hear what we were up to.

In warmer weather, Mr. Pope frequently made the short journey to the Globe, sometimes to watch a performance from behind the stage, sometimes simply to share conversation and a drink with his old comrades. But the combination of cold weather, ill health, and distance kept him from coming to the Cross Keys, so he relied on me to keep him abreast of things. We had a running jest about my being his informant, his spy within the company. Now, in light of Mr. Armin's deadly serious remark, it did not seem so amusing.

Mr. Pope had his feet propped up before the fire, a mug of clary in one hand and a woolen blanket draped over his ample belly. "Come in, Widge, come in. Sit down. You look as though you've had a long, hard day."

"Good. I'm glad I've something to show for it." Like the messenger in a play, who describes for the other characters and for the audience some action that took place off the stage, I proceeded to give him an account of all that had happened that day, in as few words as I reasonably could.

In truth, I did not include everything. I did not tell of my visit to La Voisin and what she saw in her scrying ball. Nor did I repeat what Mr. Armin had said about a spy, or what Mr. Heminges had said about the company being in difficult circumstances. The physican who attended Mr. Pope had cautioned us that any undue strain or stress could worsen his patient's condition, and I had no wish to fulfill the cunning woman's prediction that I would bring about another person's death, least of all his. I did describe for him the mysterious Mr. Garrett, thinking that they might have crossed paths before. But Mr. Pope had no notion who or what the man might be, or why he would feel compelled to disguise himself.

When I introduced Judith into my story, I did my best to sound nonchalant, but I was not a good-enough actor to carry it off. Though I confined myself to facts, carefully avoiding any mention of feelings, Mr. Pope was not fooled for a moment.

"I believe you neglected to clean all the rouge off your cheeks, my boy," he said mischievously. "Either that, or the frost has nipped them a bit."

I ducked my head sheepishly. "Aye, I expect that's it."

"I've met Will's daughters a time or two. Judith is the fair one, is she?"

"Aye."

"She is a pretty thing. I'm not surprised that you'd be smitten with her."

"I never said I was."

Mr. Pope laughed. "There's no need to say it. It's written all over your face." His smile slowly faded then, to be replaced by a look of concern, and he leaned forward in his chair. "Widge. I hope you don't mind my saying this. I know you haven't asked for my advice, but . . . well, I think of you almost as a . . . as a son, and . . . while I don't wish to meddle, or to say anything against Judith, I think you'd do well to be . . . careful."

"Careful?"

"Yes. I wouldn't like to see you hurt."

"What do you mean?"

"I mean that . . . On occasion Will has spoken to me about . . . about his family, and from what he's told me, I gather that Judith is . . . " He shifted uncomfortably in his seat. "How shall I put it? Well, you recall the duke's description of his daughter in *Two Gentlemen*?

"No, trust me: she is peevish, sullen, forward,
Proud, disobedient, stubborn, lacking duty;
Neither regarding that she is my child,
Nor fearing me as if I were her father."

I stared at him, unable to quite grasp what he was getting at. "Aye?"

Mr. Pope sighed. "Never mind, Widge. You're tired. We'll talk more in the morning."

"Aye, all right." On the last word, my weary voice broke.

Mr. Pope winced. "It sounds as though your pipes can't decide which octave to play in. Has that been happening often?"

I nodded despondently. "No one i' the company has mentioned it yet—except Sam and Sal Pavy, of course—but I'm certain they've noticed."

"Well, don't let it worry you. It doesn't mean you're through playing girls' parts; it just means we'll have to work a bit more to keep you sounding sweet. We'll get some oil of almond for you to gargle with daily, and I'll show you some vocal exercises that will keep your throat strings in tune. For now, go on to bed."

I got to my feet. "Before I do, can I fetch aught for you?"

"No, no." He lifted the blanket to reveal a thick book wedged in next to him. "I've a cup of clary and a volume of Rabelais. What more could a man want?"

My brain was not so befogged that I failed to hear the wistful tone behind his words. What he wanted, I suspected, was not to sit before a fire with a book in his lap, but to strut before an audience with a speech in his mouth. In the doorway of the library, I turned back. "Mr. Pope?"

"Yes, lad?"

"Ha' you ever tried writing a play?"

"Me?" He laughed heartily, as though the notion were ludicrous. "No, I'm happy to leave that task to Will. What makes you ask such a thing?"

"I—I only thought it might gi' you something to do," I lied.

"Thank you, but I believe I'd prefer to dig a ditch. Dirt is far more agreeable to work with than words."

As I started up the stairs, I discovered Tetty sitting halfway up them, clad only in her nightshirt, her thin arms wrapped about her knees. "Tetty!" I whispered. "Why are you sitting here? You'll catch a chill!"

"I was waiting for you to tuck me into bed."

"And not eavesdropping at all on me conversation wi' Mr. Pope, I suppose?" I led her down the hall to the room she shared with Goody Willingson, who was still cleaning up in the kitchen.

"Only a little," she said. "Who's Judith?"

Here it was dark enough to hide my blushes. "Mr. Shakespeare's daughter." I turned back the covers, and when she was done snuggling into her spot, I tucked them around her.

"Is she very beautiful?"

If neglecting to tell the whole truth counts as a lie, I was guilty once more. Instead of confessing that Judith was the most comely creature I had ever set eyes upon, I simply said, "I suppose so."

"Are you going to marry her?" Clearly Tetty was no more fooled by my show of indifference than Mr. Pope had been.

"Marry her? I've kenned her but a single afternoon!"

"After Romeo talks to Juliet for only five minutes they're exchanging their love's faithful vows."

"How is it you ken so much about Romeo and Juliet?"

"Mr. Pope told me. He acted out all the parts." She gave a soft, sleepy giggle. "He doesn't make a very good Juliet."

"No, I expect not."

Tetty yawned. "You mustn't marry her, you know." Her voice was growing drowsy now.

"Why not?"

"Because," she murmured, "you must wait for me."

Despite my exhaustion, I spent a restless night. I woke well before dawn, and as I could not force myself back to sleep, I rose and lit a candle. Then, wrapping my blankets about me, I sat at the small table by my bed and took up my plumbago pencil, determined to write something resembling a play—or at any rate enough of one to make the lie I had told Judith seem more credible.

It was more than just a matter of making good my boast, though. I wished desperately to do something that would impress her favorably. Heaven knew I had done little enough in that line thus far. I was very much afraid that if I remained in her eyes—her bright blue eyes—nothing more than Widge, the quaint prentice, she would have little time for me. If, on the other hand, I were Widge, the quaint playwright . . .

Well, she had said herself that she was more than willing to spend time with me in order to hear my play. The main problem, as I saw it, was that I had no play, not even the ghost of an idea for one—nothing more than a title, in fact, and a rather stupid one at that.

The *ghost* of an idea . . . Well, there was a possibility. The groundlings went wild over anything with a ghost in it. The only thing they relished more—as the undying popularity of *The Spanish Tragedy* attested—was revenge. Something about a ghost who demands revenge, then? It wasn't exactly clear where the Mad Men of Gotham would fit in, but I could always tell Judith I had decided to change the title. After all, it was a practice her father routinely indulged in; *All's Well That Ends Well,* for example, had begun life as *Love's Labour's Won.* I could redub mine something on the order of *The Madman's Revenge.* I rolled the title on my tongue: *The Madman's Revenge.* That wasn't bad; in fact it was quite good. Using my swift writing, I scribbled it down on the back of a broadsheet.

I rubbed my hands together, partly in anticipation, partly to warm them up a bit. This was beginning to look less like a chore and more like a lark. All right; I had a ghost. Whose ghost was it, then? Someone who had been foully and treacherously murdered, no doubt, since it was demanding revenge. A prince, perhaps, or a king—the penny payers liked to see royalty up there on the stage, not dull, ordinary wights like themselves. So, let us say that this prince—or king, if you will—is poisoned by some villain who covets the throne, only the prince's ghost—or king's, if you will—comes back, all mangled and bloody—let's have him hacked to death, then, instead of poisoned—and torments his brother, or his son, or someone, and . . .

I stopped scribbling. Wait a moment, I thought. This all sounds awfully familiar. It sounded, in fact, very much like *Hamlet.* Disgusted, I held the broadsheet over the candle flame and watched it burn. Then I snatched up another sheet of paper and smoothed it out before me.

What else would the stinkards flock to see, then? A rollicking comedy, of course, full of puns and pratfalls, misunderstandings and mistaken identities. But, though I knew next to nothing about composing a play, I knew enough to realize that a script of that sort would demand a wit keener than mine; even worse, it would require an involved and intricate story. I was better off sticking with something simple and straightforward, like death. Or perhaps love. If there was anything that appealed to the general playgoer as much as a tragic tale of murder and revenge, it was a tragic tale of star-crossed lovers.

Again, it was best if they were royalty, or at least nobility. What maiden in her right mind, after all, would waste her time pining away after a cob carrier, or a rat catcher—or an apprentice player? If the romance was to end tragically, there must be some obstacle, something to keep them apart. If they were both of noble birth, it could not be a difference in station. Or could it? What if one of the lovers—the boy, let us say—discovers that the man and woman he believes to be his parents are, in fact, not? What if they reveal to him that he was a foundling whom they took in and raised as their own? What if his true parents were, say, a cowherd and a milkmaid?

I groaned. That was not tragic; it was merely pathetic. What about the other way 'round, then? The lovers are simple country lobs—the groundlings might not mind that; they always cheered the rustics in *Midsummer Night's Dream,* and besides, I knew far more about rustics than I did about royalty—but then one of them—the girl, let's say—discovers somehow that she's actually the daughter of a duke or earl or something, who gave her to this cowherd and this milkmaid to raise, and . . .

As Sam was fond of saying: "Much!" What reason in the world would a duke or an earl have to hand his daughter over to a couple of poor peasants that way? Our audiences were often asked to accept the unlikely, but there were limits to what one could ask of them. When I was growing up in the orphanage, I imagined—as did most of my fellow orphans, I am certain—that I had been sent there by mistake, that someday my parents would come and claim me, and they would prove to be wealthy folk of high degree—or at least wealthy. But that was a child's dream, not the sort of thing that ever actually occurred.

The second sheet of paper went the way of the first. Though as a premise for a play it was hopeless, at least it served to warm my hands a little. I took up a third sheet and stared at it. There was something intimidating, almost mocking, about its blankness, as though it were daring me to fill the void with something of consequence. I was tempted to burn it as well, just for spite. Instead I pinned it roughly to the table with one hand and with the other held my pencil poised over it. Now. What else might keep these hypothetical lovers apart? Money? Religion?

When I first met Jamie Redshaw he told me a touching tale of how my mother's parents had forbidden her to have anything to do with him because they were Protestants and his family were Catholics. Though I now suspected that the whole thing had been a fabrication, a ploy to win my trust, at the time I had been utterly convinced by it. Might it not, then, convince an audience as well?

I had the page nearly covered with scribbled notes—names for the characters, possible titles *(The Mad Monk of Gotham; The Revenge of the Rosary),* thoughts on how I might work in a ghost of some sort—before it occurred to me how foolish, even dangerous, it would be to compose a play in which one of the protagonists was a flagrant Papist.

As I sat watching yet another idea go up in smoke, the bells of St. Bennet, directly across the river from us, began to ring prime. I sprang to my feet and flung off the blankets. I was due at the Cross Keys in half an hour. I pulled on my clothing as quickly as I could and sprinted downstairs. Before I had taken two bites of my porridge, Sam came to call for me.

As I hurried out the door, Goodwife Willingson snatched me by the cloak and thrust into my hand two thick slabs of bread with slices of cold beef packed between them.

"Overslept, did you?" said Sam, casting an envious eye at the bread and beef.

I broke it in two and handed half to him. "Nay, as a matter of fact I've been up for hours."

"Doing what?" he asked around a monstrous mouthful of food.

I was not about to tell him what I had truly been up to; then I would have two people pestering mc for a look at my nonexistent play—and very likely far more than that, for Sam was not known for keeping his tongue in his purse, as they say. So, to avoid compounding the trouble my first lie had gotten me into, I was forced to come up with a totally ncw onc. Was there no end to it? "I was working on improving me charactery."

"Improving your character? I don't see that getting up a bit early is all that virtuous."

"Nay, nay, not me *character*; me *charactery*—you ken, me swift writing." Well, that was not altogether untrue. Dr. Bright's system was, to put it kindly, imperfect. There were times when I grew so frustrated with its shortcomings that I swore I would devise my own set of symbols. One day I might even get around to it—when I was finished writing my play, perhaps, or at the last Lammas, whichever came first.

At the start of each day, it was the job of us prentices to put the tiring-room and property room in order again, after the two hours of disorder they had suffered the night before. When Sam and I arrived in the property room, Sal Pavy was already hard at work—at least until he saw that it was only us and not one of the sharers who had entered, at which point he reverted to his normal practice of doing as little as possible.

Sam cast him a look of disgust. A moment later, as he was putting a leather breastplate into its proper trunk, Sam suddenly stood stock-still, his eyes squeezed shut as though in concentration, a hand clapped to his forehead. "I've just had a vision of the future," he intoned, in a voice very like Madame La Voisin's. "I predict . . . I predict that Master Pavy is about to say—" He switched to a wicked imitation of Sal Pavy's rather nasal tenor. "'At Blackfriahs we were not obliged to pick up propahteeahs.'"

It was Sal Pavy's turn to express disgust. "If I sounded remotely the way your parody of me sounds, I'd quit the stage at once and become a hermit."

"Promise?" Sam said.

"Stop it, you two," I said. "We've work to do."

Sam picked up the rope ladder used by Valentine in *Two Gentlemen* and began winding it into a neat bundle. "I mean no offense, Sal, but if you had it so easy at Blackfriars, why didn't you stay there?"

I had a good idea what the reason was, for I had seen the stripes that decorated Sal Pavy's back—the result, I did not doubt, of frequent and severe beatings. Sam had seen them, too. But Sal Pavy, for all his talk of Blackfriars, had never talked of this. "You may tell us," I said. "We're all friends here."

Sal Pavy glanced warily at me, then at Sam. "He'll only make another jest of it."

"Not I," Sam vowed, and drew a cross over his heart.

"Don't do that!" Sal Pavy's tone was unexpectedly harsh. "It puts me in mind of *them*."

"Who do you mean by *them?*" I asked.

"Mr. Giles and Mr. Evans."

I recognized the names. "They're the wights i' charge o' the Chapel Children?"

Sal Pavy nodded. He looked about furtively, as if fearing that one of them might have infiltrated our theatre. Then he said, in a voice so low that I could scarcely hear him, "They're also Papists."

"Papists?" Sam said incredulously. "Running the queen's own company?"

"You sound as though you don't believe me!"

"I believe you, Sal, I believe you. It just seems a bit . . . risky, doesn't it?"

"Well, obviously they don't go about telling everyone. But we Children all knew. It would have been impossible for us not to. Every week we had to make a confession to one of them."

"A confession?" I said. "Were they priests, then?"

Sal Pavy shook his head. "They insisted we confess our sins to them, all the same. If we couldn't think of anything we'd done that was sinful enough to suit them, they accused us of holding out on them, so we'd have to make something up. Sometimes a number of us would get together the night before and share ideas for despicable things we could confess to."

"Why didn't you just refuse to do it?" Sam asked.

"I did," Sal Pavy replied defensively. "Several times. And then I got tired of being beaten, and decided it was better just to do what they wanted."

"Gog's nowns," I murmured. "Could you not simply leave?"

"I tried that as well, but my—" His voice faltered and he looked down at the floor as though ashamed.

"It's all right," I said. "Go on."

"My parents always sent me back. When I tried to tell them what went on there, they wouldn't listen. All they could think of was what a great honor it was for me to be one of the Chapel Children."

"They didn't object when you joined the Chamberlain's Men?"

He gave a thin, bitter smile. "They were willing to sacrifice a bit of honor in favor of the fee the company pays them for my services."

I placed a sympathetic hand on his shoulder. "Now I ken why you were so desperate to stay on wi' us."

He shrugged off my hand. "I didn't tell you all that in order to get your *pity*."

Sam gave him a peevish look. "Why did you tell us, then?"

"A few days ago you asked me why I had such a poor opinion of Papists. Now you know." With that, he stalked out of the property room.

"Well," said Sam. "Just when I was starting to think that perhaps he wasn't a complete ass after all, he began to bray again."

"Don't be too hard on him. 'A let down his guard for a moment, and now 'a's feeling a bit vulnerable, I expect."

"That may be. But I expect he's also feeling a bit smug."

"Why is that?"

"Well," Sam said, looking about at the still-cluttered room, "you'll notice that he's left us to clean up the properties without him."

We did not see Sal Pavy again until rehearsal. He seemed resentful toward us, as though, like his former masters, we had forced him to confess to us against his will.

I prayed that Judith would not turn up to torment me again and cause me to turn our Spanish tragedy into a French farce, with me as the principal clown. But then, when she did not appear, instead of being grateful, I was sorely disappointed, even desolate, as though I had been forsaken.

Fortunately my mood was perfectly suited to playing Bel-Imperia, whose lover, Don Andrea, has been slain in battle. Mr. Lowin even commended me on how convincingly wretched I sounded. If I had said a word to Sam about how I felt—which I did not—he would surely have seen it as yet another sign that I had contracted a severe case of lovesickness. There was one classic symptom, though, that I had not yet suffered—a lack of appetite. I had not had much in the way of food that morning, and by the time our midday break came around, I was ravenous.

For most of the company, going home for dinner would have meant a walk of a quarter hour or more in the cold, so we customarily dined downstairs, at a long trestle table set up specially for us by the innkeeper. As we would not have the leisure for another bona fide meal until after the evening performance, we made a feast of this one, often lingering at the table until nearly nones.

It was my favorite part of the day—a time for companionship, conversation, a congenial game of cards. Today we had even more companionship than usual, for Mr. Garrett had joined us. Before sitting next to him, Mr. Armin sniffed him warily, like a dog. "Just checking, to make certain you'd gotten the smell out."

"And have I?" asked Mr. Garrett.

"For the most part. You smell less like a stable now, and more like a brewery."

"That's because I rinsed myself with ale, at Ben Jonson's suggestion."

"Well, you have it from an expert, then," said Will Sly. "No one knows more about ale and its uses than Ben."

"Are you a c-cardplayer, sir?" asked Mr. Heminges. "We n-normally engage in a r-rousing round of whist after d-dinner."

"Thank you, sir. I'd be delighted to join you."

Mr. Garrett proved an entertaining dinner companion. Though he seemed to know little enough about the theatre, he had something intelligent, and often witty, to say about nearly every other topic on which we touched.

I watched him closely and listened to him carefully, looking for some clue to his identity and why he chose—or was compelled—to conceal it. He spoke with a slight lisp, but not the precious sort so often affected by fops. His seemed, rather, to be the result of some injury to his upper lip, where a thin scar was still visible beneath his newly bleached mustache. When he turned toward me, I could see traces of other old wounds on his neck and on his forehead. Whatever else his past life might have been, it had certainly been dangerous.

I was, I noticed, not the only one in the company who was taking Mr. Garrett's measure. Ned Shakespeare was regarding him with narrowed eyes and a furrowed brow, as though still trying to recall where he had seen the man before. Ordinarily Sam paid far more attention to the food and drink than to the conversation, but when Mr. Garrett began to speak of all the countries he'd traveled to and all the strange things he had seen, Sam hung on his every word, as though he hungered far more for adventure than for the mackerel and the parsnip fritters on his plate.

Mr. Garrett could also hold his own when the talk turned to such popular pursuits as hunting, falconry, and gardening. And, although he had been in London but two days, he was already knowledgeable on the subject of most concern to us all—the state of the queen's health.

"This morning," he said, "I spoke with . . . with someone in a position to know. He tells me that Her Majesty grows weaker with each day that passes. She often seems confused and forgetful, and will seldom speak except to complain that her limbs are cold. Yet she adamantly refuses to take any of the medicines prescribed by her physicians, apparently because she fears being poisoned."

The sharers glanced solemnly at one another. "What I fear, gentlemen," said Mr. Armin, "is that we players will not have Her Majesty's protection much longer." He turned to Mr. Garrett. "Do you know whether or not she has given any indication of who she wants to succeed her?"

"According to the man I spoke with, she has not. Everyone expects, of course, that her choice will be the Scottish king."

"Lord help us," said Mr. Shakespeare.

"Is that bad?" I asked. I knew nearly nothing about King James, except that he was the son of Mary, Queen of Scots, who once tried to claim the English throne and had her costard chopped off for it.

"Well," Mr. Shakespeare said, "let me put it this way: How many Scottish theatres have you heard of?"

I thought for a moment. "None."

"And how many famous Scottish playwrights are there?"

"None?"

He nodded grimly. "How well do suppose we players are likely to fare, then, under James's rule?"

"I understand, though," said Mr. Garrett, "that his queen, Anne of Denmark, often presents elaborate masques at court, and even performs in them."

"Oh, good," said Mr. Armin. "We'll all become courtiers, then, and prance about before a lot of fake scenery, pretending to be gods and goddesses, and spouting doggerel."

"P-perhaps it won't be as b-bad as you imagine," put in Mr. Heminges, always the optimist.

"And perhaps it will be a good deal worse," said Ned Shakespeare. "After all, His Royal Scottishness was raised by Puritans, and most, if not all, of his advisers are Puritans." He took a great gulp of ale and wiped his mouth on his sleeve. "If you ask me, we'd better all pray very hard that Her Majesty makes a miraculous recovery."

15

The congenial, companionable mood had vanished. It was as though a sneaping southerly wind had swept into the room, bringing on its wings a load of melancholy, which hung over the company like a dark and dreary cloud.

There was a long stretch during which no one spoke very much and everyone drank a lot. Then Mr. Heminges cleared his throat. "I w-was reluctant to bring this up b-before, but as we're all in a f-foul humor anyway, I m-may as well." He glanced at the other sharers as though for moral support, and then went on. "A short wh-while ago, it was discovered that yet another c-costume has d-disappeared from its trunk."

Murmured complaints and curses went up from one end of the table to the other. Mr. Heminges's voice rose above them. "Now, one or two m-missing garments may be chalked up to c-carelessness, but when the t-toll reaches half a dozen, we c-cannot help suspecting . . . " He paused and cleared his throat again. "Well, n-naturally we do not w-wish to accuse anyone, but—"

"If you're looking for someone to blame," put in Ned Shakespeare, "I'd begin with the tiring-man. He has the most ready access to the costumes, after all."

"P-perhaps. But R-Richard has always been v-very reliable. Besides, the trunk I m-mentioned was sent over from the Globe only t-two days ago, and Richard has b-been laid up for n-nearly a week. In any c-case, as I said, we d-do not wish to accuse anyone, so we've decided to t-take the following m-measure: From n-now on, the t-tiring-room and property room will be kept locked d-during the day, until an hour b-before the performance. That should leave sufficient t-time for all of you to dress and c-collect your properties."

There was another round of discontented murmurs. Mr. Heminges held up his hands for silence. "I would j-just like to add that the n-necessity of replacing the costumes p-puts rather a severe b-burden on the company's finances. As you've n-no doubt noticed, the s-size of the audience has been gr-gradually diminishing these l-last few weeks."

"Yes, I have noticed that," said Sam. "It's gotten so that they can scarcely see over the edge of the stage."

The jest drew a few halfhearted chuckles from the company at large, and a faint smile from Mr. Heminges. "Thank you, S-Sam, f-for that attempt to introduce a b-bit of levity into the proceedings. But I'm afraid there's n-nothing very amusing about the s-situation. Once we've m-met our expenses, gentlemen"—he lowered his voice a little—"including the p-percentage we g-give to the Cross Keys, there's b-barely enough left over to p-pay your wages. Now, as you m-may also be aware,

M-Mr. Henslowe has raised the pr-price of admission to the F-Fortune Theatre, by a p-penny."

Will Sly gave a low whistle. "That means it'll cost the groundlings twice as much to get in."

"V-very good, Will. We considered f-following his example, but we c-concluded that we would be in d-danger of pricing ourselves out of b-business. I suspect that a g-good half of our audience s-simply could not afford to hand over an extra p-penny just to see a p-play. They have b-better uses for the m-money—such as buying f-food, for example."

"How will we manage, then?" asked Sam.

Mr. Shakespeare answered. "We sharers have agreed to put some of our past profits back into the company, to keep it afloat until warmer weather, when, we trust, the playgoers will return to the Globe in great flocks, like so many swallows."

"An it will help," I said, "I'm willing to forgo me wages for a while."

Sam gave me a sharp poke in the ribs, and a look that said, *Have you gone mad?*

"Thank you, W-Widge," said Mr. Heminges, "but that won't be n-necessary." I thought I heard him add, under his breath, "I hope." I could not be certain, though, for the noise level in the room had escalated as the players began talking animatedly among themselves.

"You nupson!" Sam whispered. "Don't offer to give up money that way! They might ask us all to do the same!"

"I'm sorry. I only wanted to do me part." In truth, I would have given nearly anything—though heaven knew I had little enough to my name, and not even a proper name for that matter—to keep the Lord Chamberlain's Men from ruin. Julia had once said to me, soon after I joined the company, that she would gladly forgo her wages as long as she was allowed to perform. At the time I did not see how a person could want something so much. Now I understood. It was not just about performing; it was about belonging.

It had puzzled me, too, when Julia said that she and I were birds of a feather. I knew now what she meant: that neither of us had ever belonged anywhere before. Though she was not technically an orphan, she might as well have been, for her mother was dead and her father was a common thief with no interest in her beyond what money she could bring in.

Like me, she had found a family in the theatre. Unfortunately membership in that family was limited to men and boys, at least in England. I only hoped that, across the Channel in France, she had managed to make a more permanent place for herself.

Even as I was turning all this over in my mind, our all-male province was invaded by two fair and fashionably dressed young ladies. So finely turned out were they, in fact, that I almost failed to recognize them. But my heart did not; it leaped in my chest. "Judith!" I exclaimed softly.

Sam elbowed me again. "Come now, if you want her attention, you'll have to speak up." But even had I been brave enough to call out to her, I could not have done so, for my breath had deserted me. The company rose as one to greet the girls. "Who's the wench with her?" Sam whispered.

"Mary Mountjoy, the daughter of Mr. Shakespeare's landlord."

Sam pursed his lips appraisingly. "She's even better looking than Mistress Shakespeare."

I stared at him in disbelief. "You truly think so?"

He grinned. "No. I was just trying to get a rise out of you."

"I'm sorry," Judith was saying, "that we couldn't join you all for dinner. We were too busy buying things."

"What sort of things?" Mr. Shakespeare asked, apprehensively.

"Why, our dresses, Father!" Judith lifted the hem of her gown and turned in a slow circle so we might admire it, then gestured to Mistress Mountjoy, who giggled and made a cursory twirl. "And our shoes!" Judith gave us a glimpse of a pair of chopines with soles a good six inches high, designed to keep her skirts from dragging through the mud and slush. "And our billiments!" She patted the satin band, garnished with jewels, that adorned her hair.

Radiating disapproval as a stove does heat, Mr. Shakespeare led his daughter over near the window. But, though the rest of us did our best not to notice them, it was impossible. Over Mr. Armin's voice inviting Mistress Mountjoy to have some fruit and cheese, I could hear Mr. Shakespeare asking how much all their finery had cost, and Judith replying nonchalantly that she wasn't certain but it might have been seven or eight pounds. I nearly choked on my cheese; that was a full year's wages for a prentice.

Mr. Shakespeare sounded nearly as astonished as I was, and considerably more upset. "And how did you manage to pay for it?"

"I asked them to send the bill to you," she said, as though the answer should have been obvious. "They said they were happy to, and were certain you were good for it."

"Then they're far more certain than I am," growled Mr. Shakespeare.

"Oh, Father, you can't expect me to come to London and not buy a few new things for myself."

"I didn't expect you to come to London at all."

Mr. Armin, who had been patiently listening to Mary Mountjoy prattle on, saw that we were eavesdropping. "I'm sorry to cut short our delightful conversation, my dear, but it's time I took these wag-pasties upstairs and put them through their paces."

"Paces?"

Mr. Armin pretended to run her through with an invisible sword, eliciting a burst of giggles. "Sword practice, mademoiselle."

"Oh!" cried Judith from directly behind me. "May we watch, sir?"

I had seldom seen Mr. Armin taken off guard, either by sword or by speech. "Well, I—I—" He looked to Mr. Shakespeare for help. "What do you think, Will?"

Mr. Shakespeare took half a step back, as though he meant to stay out of it. "It's up to you, Rob."

Mr. Armin frowned. "I'm not certain it's such a—"

"We won't be any bother," Judith assured him. "Will we, Mary?"

"No! Not a bit!"

With obvious reluctance, Mr. Armin said, "All right—provided you're quiet and stay out of the way."

Since none of the chambers at the Cross Keys was spacious enough for swordplay, we held our practice sessions in the long gallery, before the stage. As we mounted the stairs, Judith called over her shoulder, "How is your play progressing, Widge?"

I groaned inwardly, knowing what was coming next. Sure enough, Sam spoke up. "His *play?* You're writing a play, Widge?"

I murmured something noncommittal, hoping they would let the subject drop. It was a vain hope. "Hasn't he told you?" Judith said.

"No, he hasn't." Sam gave me a reproachful look, as though hurt that I should tell Judith before him. "What's it about, then?"

"So far, it's about two pages."

"Pages? The sort that wait on nobles, you mean?"

"Nay, the sort you write on."

To my relief, Mr. Armin cut the conversation short by handing us our wooden singlesticks. "Sam, you and Sal square off. Widge, you'll work with me."

Judith and Mary were as good as their word, sitting far up in the two-penny seats, well out of reach of even the most wayward sword thrust. But perhaps it was too much to ask them to be silent as well. No sooner had we begun our practice than they began whispering and tittering behind their hands. I suspected, from their sidelong glances, that we were the source of their amusement.

We did not mean to be amusing. Under Mr. Armin's unforgiving eye, even Sam was on his best behavior—for a time, at least. We prentices had more or less mastered the basic cuts and thrusts—the *stoccata,* the *passata,* the *imbrocata,* the *stramazone,* the *dritta* and *riversa*—and had lately been working on a new move. The *montano* was an underhanded sweep of the sword, designed to catch the opponent's blade from beneath, where his wrist is weakest.

At first, I was painfully self-conscious, afraid of embarrassing myself before Judith. But serious swordplay requires such concentration, such precision, that after half a dozen blows I lost all awareness of being watched—until I heard the sounds of stifled laughter coming from the two-penny seats. I glanced toward the girls, and saw at once the reason for their merriment: Sam's last *montano* had not been quite according to

Caranza, as they say. It ended up not beneath his opponent's sword but between his opponent's legs. Sal Pavy was standing practically on tiptoe, with an extremely worried expression on his face. Sam was giving his singlestick little jerks upward and snarling, "Yield, varlet!"

Something struck my left shoulder painfully, making me cry out. "That is what happens," Mr. Armin said, lowering his weapon, "when you allow yourself to be distracted." He turned to the other two scrimers. "That's enough, Sam."

Sam hung his head. "I was only having a bit of fun."

"Oh? Well, I like a bit of fun myself. Why don't you and I have an amusing bout or two while Widge and Sal blade it out?"

Sam looked as though Mr. Armin had proposed a round of shin-kicking with hobnailed boots. Reluctantly he took my place and I took his.

The girls had gone back to merely whispering. I did my best to ignore them and concentrate on Sal Pavy. He wasted no time in striking the first blow. No doubt he was humiliated by Sam's horseplay and anxious to redeem himself, for he swung his stick much harder than he should have. My weapon went flying.

Angry, I snatched up the stick and delivered a blow that made Sal Pavy draw back. He replied with an edgeblow aimed at my knees. I knocked it aside and, without thinking, gave him a *stoccata* that would have knocked the wind out of him had he not dodged. Even so, it scraped his ribs. He cursed under his breath and swung at me again, harder than before. Without our really meaning it to, our friendly practice had degenerated into a hostile duel.

When Sal Pavy first joined the Chamberlain's Men, I had regarded him as a rival for the choicest roles and had naturally resented him. Though I had come to accept him as one of us, there were times when that old enmity welled up unexpectedly, like some intermittent fever that, just when you think you've rid yourself of it, makes you sweat again.

This was one of those times. Though I am not ordinarily a violent sort, I laid on as though I meant to disembowel him at the very least. In truth, I had no wish to harm him, only to show him up, to make him look bad and myself look good.

I was very much aware of the audience now. Judith and Mary called out words of encouragement, though which of us they were aimed at, I could not tell. Mr. Armin was shouting at us, too, and I suspected that his were not words of encouragement. We were too intent on each other to heed him.

Though I hated to admit it, Sal Pavy put up a good defense. Not only did he turn aside my every blow, he answered with several that nearly found their mark. For the first time, I began to wonder whether he might be the one to show me up.

But I knew his weakness. For all his skill at convincing folk that he was charming and a hard worker, when it came to scriming he was a poor deceiver. Each time he made a move, you could see it coming, in his eyes and in the way he set his body. I, on the other hand, was quite good at falsifying—feigning one sort of blow and delivering another.

I started what seemed to be a right edgeblow, deliberately leaving myself open. When Sal Pavy lunged at me, I stepped aside and swung a downright blow that would sorely have cracked his collarbone if it had connected. Luckily for both of us, it did not. It met Mr. Armin's singlestick instead, with a resounding clunk that numbed my forearm.

"If you two wish to kill each other," he said, "there are more efficient ways than with dull wooden swords."

"I'm sorry," I mumbled, rubbing my tingling arm. "I got carried away."

"So I noticed. And if that blow had landed, Sal might have been carried away as well."

I recalled La Voisin's prediction—that I would cause another's death—and a shudder went through me. "I'm sorry," I repeated, so earnestly that my voice cracked.

"I know. It was not entirely your fault."

"Well, it certainly wasn't mine!" put in Sal Pavy.

Mr. Armin gave him a look that said he'd be wise to put his tongue in his purse. Then he turned to Judith and Mary. "Ladies, I must ask you to leave."

Judith bit her lip and folded her hands demurely in her lap. "We'll behave, sir. I promise."

"The problem is not so much *your* behavior as the way you make these poor wights behave. Go on now, before I give you swords and set you to scriming."

"Oh, would you?" Judith exclaimed. "It looks like great fun!"

When they left, I was both disappointed and relieved. I apologized to Sal Pavy for attacking him so fiercely.

"Oh, were you?" he said. "I thought you were going easy on me, so I did the same." One thing about Sal Pavy; he was reliable. If I should ever forget exactly why I had once disliked him so, I could count on him to remind me.

After scriming practice, Sam did a bit more prying about the play. I dared not confess that the whole thing was a fabrication; however solemnly he might swear not to, he would surely let the secret slip out, and then Judith would know me for the liar I was. Besides, I might yet produce a play as promised, if only I could come up with a sensible story.

"So," Sam said, "what's this play of yours called, then?"

My original title, *The Mad Men of Gotham,* had begun to seem irredeemably stupid. I replaced it with the first thing that came to mind: *"Let the World Wag."*

Sam nodded thoughtfully. "Not bad. A comedy, is it?"

"Aye. But not your usual comedy. It's got ghosts, and revenge, and star-crossed lovers."

"Ah," said Sam. "Sounds hilarious."

As the company stood behind the stage that evening, waiting to go on in *The Spanish Tragedy,* Will Sly said, "I hear you're writing a play."

Thanks to the hubbub from the audience, he probably did not hear the curse I uttered under my breath. "I'm trying," I said.

"I hope there's a part in it for me?"

"Of course." Knowing how fond he was of dashing, romantic roles, I added, "You get to play a leprous beggar."

To my surprise, he replied, "Excellent!" and rubbed his hands together gleefully. "Will I be horribly disfigured, with appendages falling off and such?"

"I was only jesting, Will. There's no leper." I did not bother to mention that neither were there any other characters of any description.

His face fell. "Oh. But you could put in a leper if you wanted, couldn't you? I mean, it's your play."

I sighed. This play was already getting out of hand, and I had yet to write a single word of it. "I'll do me best. I can't promise anything." I took out the small table-book I carried with me and jotted down a new title possibility: *The Leper's Revenge.* What audience could resist that? Well, in one way at least I had the advantage of Mr. Shakespeare—I had no shortage of compelling titles. Perhaps he and I should become collaborators; I could supply the titles, and he could write the scripts to go with them.

Though I was tempted to peek around the curtain to see whether or not Judith was in the audience, I talked myself out of it. I was better off not knowing. That way, I would have no call to be either disappointed or self-conscious.

As it turned out, I was wise to restrain myself. After the performance, Judith came clomping onto the stage in her chopines to congratulate us. She clasped one of my hands in hers; I would have expected them to be warm, but they were cold as a key. "You were very good, Widge. So convincing. If I hadn't known, I never would have suspected you were a boy."

Before I could compose a reply that did not sound half-witted, she had let go of me and latched onto Sal Pavy. "Master Pavy! You were . . . Oh, how shall I put it?"

"Superb?" he suggested.

She laughed. "I was about to say magnificent."

"That's even better." He swept off his wig as though it were a cap and made a small bow. "I thank you for your kind words, and will endeavor to be worthy of them."

"Oh, you are, I assure you! When you were lamenting Horatio's death, I nearly cried."

I could bear no more. I flung open the door and took the outside stairs two at a time, avoiding a broken neck only by grace of the fortune that protects fools, for the steps were coated with ice. I changed quickly and left without waiting for Sam; I had no desire to talk to anyone. Though I had forgotten my cloak, I was so hot with spite and shame that I scarcely noticed the cold.

By the time I reached Mr. Pope's, I had cooled down a bit. When Goody Willingson asked how my day had been, instead of shouting "Utterly miserable!" I replied in a relatively calm voice, "I've had worse." And it was true; I had had worse days—the day my mother died giving birth to me, for instance. The difference was, I couldn't remember that one.

Though I was hardly in a playful mood, I dutifully gave each of the younger boys a ride off to bed on my back, and consented to a game of One Penny Follow Me with the older ones. They seemed not to notice how distracted I was. But Tetty's dark eyes did not miss a thing. "What's wrong, Widge?" she asked as I tucked her in.

"What makes you think there's something wrong?"

"Your face."

"What about it?"

"You know how, when you've twisted your back, you hold it all stiff to keep it from hurting?"

"Aye?"

"That's the way your face looks."

"I'm tired. That's all." And, though it was not all that ailed me, I was indeed weary. But before I could give myself up to sleep, I had to make my nightly report to Mr. Pope.

Once again I skipped over certain selected portions of the day. I said nothing about the play that I was supposed to be writing but was not. Nor did I mention how Judith had been able to spare but a few bland morsels of praise for me, while Sal Pavy received a far more sweet and generous helping than he deserved. Though I was still secretly stewing over the incident, I did not wish to bring it up; it would only make Judith sound heartless and me sound foolish.

I did not expect Mr. Pope to let me off so easily, though, and I was right. When I finished, he said, with a trace of mischief in his voice, "So tell me, how is the fair Judith faring?"

I did my best to sound neutral. "Well enough, I suppose."

He gazed at me over the rim of his wine cup. "You certainly are taken with her, aren't you?"

"What makes you think so?"

"The expression on your face."

This conversation seemed familiar somehow. "What sort of expression?"

"Woeful, for want of a better word. Rather like a puppy who's been chastised for leaving a puddle on the floor."

"There's no call to make fun of me."

"I'm not, lad; I'm not. I'm only commiserating. I remember well enough what it's like to be lovestruck."

"You do?"

Mr. Pope laughed. "You sound as though you don't believe me."

"I didn't mean to. It's just . . . "

"I know. You find it hard to credit, a fat old fulmart like me, eh? But I was young once, and hot-blooded—and not bad to look at, either, if I say so myself."

I narrowed my eyes, trying to see him as he must have been. "You had a lady friend, then?"

"Oh, several. But one in particular. A stout, spirited girl with a smile that could stop your heart—or start it."

"What became of her?"

The wistful smile faded from his broad face. "She and her family disapproved of my profession. They gave me a choice: I could give up acting, or give up her." He sighed. "It was a difficult choice, and there are times when I ask myself whether I chose rightly. Especially now . . . now that I no longer have the company of the audience or of my fellow players to console me."

I had seldom seen him so melancholy. I searched for something to say that might lighten his mood. Before I found it, he drained his cup of clary and pushed his heavy frame from the chair. "Well, that's enough feeling sorry for myself. A fellow has to do a little of it now and again, just to keep from getting too complacent." He made a move to rumple my hair, as I had so often seen him do with the younger boys, but with my crown so closely cropped it did not rumple so much as bristle. "If you want my advice, Widge—and perhaps you do not—I'd advise you not to get too attached to the young lady; I have a feeling she'll be going back to Stratford soon."

I turned to look at him in dismay. "But—but she told her father that she despises it. She said there was no one and nothing there that held the slightest interest for her."

Mr. Pope smiled. "You know, Will once told me the very same thing. But I rather suspect that Judith is less her father's daughter than she is her mother's."

In my room, in the few minutes I had left before sleep claimed me, I tried to put my mind to work on the problem of the play, but it stubbornly insisted on bringing up again and again the same unanswered questions: Would Judith stay or go? Who was spying on the Chamberlain's Men, and who was stealing from us, and were they one and the same person? Would the queen recover, and if not, what would become of us?

I shook my head hard. What was the use in dwelling on such questions? They could not be answered, at least not by me. I could only wait and see. With the play, I had more control. I could make the story come out however I wished—provided I had a story—and could decide the fates of all the characters—provided I had characters.

Perhaps where I'd made my mistake was in attempting to write about highborn wights and ladies. Though I had impersonated them enough times upon the stage, what did I truly know about them or their problems? I might do better to people my play with the sort of folk I knew at first hand.

Let us say, for example, that the hero is an orphan, and that he's taken in by . . . by a band of players? No, not exciting enough. As Sam said, actors never actually *do* anything; they only pretend to. What, then? A band of lepers? No, too much of a good thing. A band of madmen? Or thieves? Yes, thieves were exciting. And then suppose he falls in love with . . . with someone. With the head thief's beautiful daughter, let us say. Only she's not interested in him, because she's in love with . . . with whom? A poet? No. A soldier? Yes! A soldier who has sworn to bring the band of thieves to justice. The hero knows, then, that he must kill the soldier, not only in order to save his friends, but also in order to get rid of his rival for the girl's affections.

Wait a moment. This was the *hero?* What sort of character would fall in with a lot of thieves in the first place, let alone wish to kill a wight just because he's jealous of him? He didn't sound much like a hero. He sounded, in fact, a good deal like me.

My previous master had been a thief, after all, and had made me into one as well. And I had more than once imagined various unpleasant fates befalling Sal Pavy, my rival for roles and now, it seemed, for Judith's attentions. Though I had never actually tried to kill him—at least not consciously—there was no denying that I was jealous of him.

Well, audiences did not come to the theatre to see the likes of me up there on the stage. I laid my pencil aside and once more fed my efforts to the candle flame. I lulled myself to sleep with promises that I would try again in the morning, when I was more alert.

• • •

But in the light of day—or rather the half-light before dawn—the notion of my writing anything worth reading seemed even more absurd than it had the night before. I made a few half-hearted attempts at ideas, only because I had promised myself I would and did not like to lie to myself. But I came up with nothing very useful, only a couple of new titles: *The Mad Monarch* and *Gamaliel Ratsey, the Masked Highwayman*—the latter inspired by one of the ballad sheets I was using for writing paper.

As I was up anyway, I thought I might as well get an early start at the theatre. After a quick breakfast, I set out for the Cross Keys alone. Sam would only have plagued me with questions I was in no mood to answer, such as how the play was going, or whether I had come into that fortune yet. Even worse, he might propose some harebrained scheme from his seemingly inexhaustible supply—an infallible method of winning the lottery, perhaps, or a plan for me to make Judith jealous by pretending to be in love with Mistress Mountjoy, or a method by which we might snare the costume thief.

It occurred to me then, for the first time, that Sam himself might conceivably be the culprit. No, surely not. Though he might be impudent and unreliable, he was no thief, I was certain of it. And yet . . . and yet, Madame La Voisin had said that he would turn traitor. Was this what she meant? Suppose he truly did have a scheme to win the lottery? Suppose he sold the stolen costumes and bought dozens of chances, meaning to pay the theatre back once he won the big prize?

I laughed aloud at my own folly. Such a story deserved to be burned, along with all the other implausible ones I had concocted. My suspicions had made me feel ashamed, and I quickened my pace, as though to leave them behind. I had another reason for making haste, of course: I had left my cloak at the Cross Keys, and though it was the second week of March, winter was stubbornly hanging on.

I meant to set to work on the property room, but I had forgotten the sharers' decision to keep it locked. I went looking for someone to let me in, and found Mr. Shakespeare in the office he shared with Mr. Heminges, hard at work on his script. Knowing now how much concentration the task required, I would have slipped away without disturbing him. But just then he put down his pen, sat back on his stool, and rubbed at his old injury.

"Shall I do some transcribing for you?" I asked.

He glanced up and, for a change, smiled; the play must be going well for him . . . the lucky wight. "God you good morning, Widge. Thank you for offering, but I'm not composing any lines just yet, only making some notes."

"Oh? I thought you were well into the play by now."

He laughed. "I may be quick, but I'm not *that* quick. I came up with the idea only last night."

"But . . . But two days ago you had half a dozen pages done."

"Oh, you mean the unnamed Roman play. I've given up on that. This is something new, and far more promising." He toyed with his earring reflectively. "But then they all seem that way at first blush, don't they?"

Ordinarily I was comfortable enough around Mr. Shakespeare, but the subject I wished to broach now made me shy as a suitor. "An I might interrupt you for a moment, sir," I said, my voice doing some of its octave shifting, "there's something I'd like to ask."

He gave me a rather suspicious glance. "Does it have anything to do with my daughter?"

"Nay! That is, not directly."

"Good. What is it?"

"Well, I was wondering . . . where do you get your ideas?"

His eyebrows lifted. "My ideas? For plays, you mean?"

"Aye."

He considered the question a moment, then leaned forward and said, in a low voice, "Well, you're not to tell this to anyone, but there's a certain stall at St. Paul's where you can buy them for half a crown—five shillings for really good ones."

I gaped at him. "Truly? Someone *sells* them?" Then I saw the hint of amusement hiding in his eyes, and my face went red. "Oh. You're tweaking me."

"Of course. Would that it were that simple. The truth is, I have no idea where they come from, or why. Sometimes they seem to rain down upon you from out of the ether. Other times, it's as though a drought has descended, and everything dries up, including your brain. When that happens . . . " He shrugged. "The only thing left to do is to steal from someone else."

I was taken aback for a moment, before I concluded that he was jesting again. "Nay, you'll not fool me again. I ken you don't mean that."

"But I do, Widge." He gestured at the pages of his abandoned script, which were crammed into a compartment at the back of the desk. "Take the story of Timon, for example. I found it in Plutarch's 'Life of Antony.' Come, now; you needn't look so dismayed. Don't you know that there are no new ideas in the world? Every story has been told—and lived—a hundred times before. The best we can hope for is to find some new way of telling them." He rubbed at his forearm again. "Now it's my turn to ask you something."

"All right."

"What do you care where I get my ideas?"

I had known from the moment I broached the subject that I would end up telling him about my own poor efforts at play-writing. But how could I, without sounding hopelessly naive and foolish? "I, um . . . that is . . . I'm attempting to, um . . . "

"To write a play?" he suggested.

"Aye. How did you ken?"

"It's no secret. You seem to have told everyone else in the company. I was wondering when you would get around to telling me."

"Actually, I told but one person."

He nodded knowingly. "Sam, I've no doubt."

"Nay. I told your daughter."

Mr. Shakespeare's expression changed from merely knowing to truly understanding. "Ah. I see. And now that you've told her, she insists upon reading it."

"Aye."

"Is there anything for her to read?"

I grimaced. "Oh, Lord, sir."

"Nothing at all?"

"Does a title count?"

"Well, it's a start. In fact, it's more than I ordinarily have to work with. What is it?"

"In truth," I said, "I've quite a number of them."

"Oh. Do you have a story or a premise of any sort in mind?"

"I've a number of those, too, all of them equally . . . what was the word you used? Putrid, that's it."

Mr. Shakespeare twisted his earring between his fingers. "Well, you know, Widge, if all you really need is something to show Judith, I have approximately two-fifths of a play I'd be happy to give you, just to be rid of it."

"You mean . . . the play wi'out a name?"

"Yes. The Roman play, that is. Not this one." He picked up the pages he'd been working on, and waved them. "This one has no name yet, either."

"You'd truly be willing to let me ha' what you've written?"

He shrugged. "I'm certain I'll never finish it. Perhaps you will, eh? Besides . . . " He leaned toward me again and said, sotto voce, "We men must stick together and help one another, else the ladies will always have the advantage of us." Mr. Shakespeare plucked the abandoned script from its compartment. "There you are. Do with it what you will." Before I could even thank him, he went on. "By the by, Ben Jonson informs me that he's finished censoring *Sejanus*, and will have it to us in a day or two. I'd like you to make a clean draft of it and write out the sides for the actors. I'm sure Sal and Sam can manage without your help for a few mornings."

"Aye, all right. That reminds me—I came to ask for the key to the property room so I might get started on 't."

Mr. Shakespeare looked uncomfortable. "I'm sorry, Widge. I'm afraid we'll have to wait until someone is here to oversee you. You mustn't think that I mistrust you. It's just that . . . "

I nodded. "I ken. It's the rule."

"Yes. Unfortunately." He took a ring of keys from his wallet. "I would like you to have a key to this room, though, so you have a place to work on Mr. Jonson's script." He gave me the key, and a conspiratorial smile. "And your own, of course. I wouldn't show it to Judith in its present form; she would recognize my abominable hand at once."

"Will she not recognize your words as well?"

"I doubt it. It's hardly my best writing. She'll probably just think you're imitating me."

All through the morning and the afternoon I was so occupied with the usual round of tasks that I had no chance to begin disguising Mr. Shakespeare's words as my own. It hardly mattered, though. Judith did not appear until dinner, and then she was too busy bcing the center of everyone's attention to say much to me, let alone inquire about my play.

Sam was one of the few members of the company who did not seem to care much what Judith had been up to all day. He was more interested in conversing with Mr. Garrett. I was concentrating on Judith and did not hear much of what Mr. Garrett was saying. Whatever it was, it held Sam spellbound. As we reluctantly followed Mr. Armin upstairs for scriming practice, I said, "What were you and Mr. Garrett going on about?"

"He was telling me more of his adventures in France, and Holland, and elsewhere."

"'A's certainly been a lot of places. Was 'a a soldier, do you wis?"

"No, I don't think so. He was just traveling about, having adventures, I guess." Sam caught me by the sleeve and whispered eagerly, "He says that perhaps one day, if he returns to the Continent, he'll take me with him."

I stared at him. "You'd truly be willing to give up the theatre?"

"Wouldn't you, if it meant a chance to see the world?"

I considered this for all of several seconds. "Nay," I said. "This is world enough for me."

Mr. Garrett continued to join us regularly for meals and card-playing. But, though he contributed much to the conversation, it was always information of a general sort; he seldom revealed anything of any consequence about himself. Aside from his own past, the one topic he carefully avoided was religion. When Ned Shakespeare asked his opinon on the question of whether Walter Ralegh, once the queen's favorite, was an atheist or merely a skeptic, Mr. Garrett replied, "My opinion, sir, is that gentlemen should not discuss matters of theology."

Though the man's tone was perfectly cordial, Ned reacted as though he'd been rebuked. "And it is *my* opinion, sir, that a gentleman should not be afraid to speak his mind on any matter, unless he has something to conceal."

Mr. Garrett seemed unperturbed. "Do you not suppose that everyone at this table—perhaps everyone everywhere—has some topic he would just as soon not touch upon?" He regarded Ned steadily with those unnerving coal-black eyes. "You, for example. Is there not some part of your life that you would prefer to keep to yourself?"

Ned could not meet the man's gaze. "That is not your business."

Mr. Garrett turned his palms upward as though to say he had proven his point. "You're quite right. As I believe your brother put it, a gentleman's business is his own."

Later, as the troupe was dispersing, each man to his own task, Judith approached me and Sam. "Master Pavy has graciously offered to show me the city this Sunday, after church services. I was hoping you two would come along. We could have a fine time, the four of us."

"It sounds good to me," said Sam.

It did not to me. It sounded like the worst idea I had ever heard. Though I wanted to protest that we could have a far finer time if there were but two of us, I kept sullenly silent.

"Widge?" said Judith. "You'll come with us, will you not?"

As an actor, I had learned that if you cannot play the leading role, the next best thing is to be a martyr—some character who faces his or her tragic fate with such dignity as to wring a tear from the audience's eye. "I'm sorry," I replied, in my most dignified voice, "I must work on my play, you know." The artist who suffers for his art—there was a role guaranteed to win her sympathy. I had even remembered to say "my" and "know," and thus avoided sounding quaint.

My speech did not have quite the effect I had intended. Judith pressed her petal-like lips together in a look of exasperation. "I might have known."

"What's wrong?"

"Oh, nothing. Nothing at all." She turned to Sam, suddenly smiling again. "We're meeting outside St. Olave's as soon as services are over."

As we headed upstairs, Sam said to me, "Don't think I don't know why you're not coming."

"I explained why."

"Much! That's not the reason. The reason is, you'd rather have her all to yourself. Am I right?"

"Nay! It's as I said—I need the time to work on me play."

"Well, even if that's true, I don't believe I'd have told her so."

"Why not?"

"Because, you noddy, I'll wager she's heard that very excuse from her father a hundred times, at least."

Though I longed to return to Judith's good graces, I knew I would never accomplish it by tramping about London with her in the company of Sam and Sal Pavy. I did not need Madame La Voisin to predict what would happen. I would be sulky and resentful, and then Sam would poke fun at me, and then I would grow angry. Though playing the martyr had not worked so well, it was better than playing the fool.

I made up my mind then that I would show them. I would make good on what had, until now, been no more than an empty boast: I would write a play, and it would be good, and it would be produced, and profitable, and praised, and then let them dare to make fun of me.

It should not be such a difficult task. After all, I had two-fifths of the script written already, and I hadn't even begun. As far as I knew, there were no ghosts or lepers in it, or even lovers, but it did have folk ranting about their money problems, and that surely was something everyone could relate to. So fierce was my resolve that if I could have, I would have set to work at once. But of course there was scriming practice, and then singing practice, and then a performance.

By the time I reached my room that night, after playing with the boys, tucking Tetty in, and reporting to Mr. Pope, my eagerness to work on the play had faded considerably. Nevertheless, I forced myself to the table and not the bed. I unrolled the script, set various objects upon it to keep it flat, and began to copy it in my own hand on a clean sheet of paper.

ACT I

Scene I: Rome. A Hall in Timon's House

Well, that was no good. Setting the play in Italy was like sending an engraved invitation to the queen's Privy Council, begging to be investigated. I crossed out *Rome* and, after a moment's thought, wrote in *Athens*. That was innocuous enough. The Greeks didn't even have a God, let alone a pope. I would have to find replacements for all those Roman-sounding names as well, but that could wait.

The first scene was a bit slow compared to *Hamlet,* which starts right out with a ghost. But there were several speeches that were worthy of Mr. Shakespeare, particularly those of Apemantus, a sarcastic, unpleasant wight who rather put me in mind of Sal Pavy. Well, I'd have to see to it that he was given the role. Buoyed by a wave of optimism, I transcribed the entire first scene. I changed almost nothing, aside from substituting *Athenian* wherever it said *Roman*.

When I reached Scene Two, however, my heart sank. I didn't know what acting company Mr. Shakespeare had in mind, but it must have been one considerably larger than the Lord Chamberlain's Men. There were at least eight Roman nobles—make that *Athenian* nobles—in the scene, each with several attendants. As though that wasn't impossible enough, an actor playing Cupid came on, accompanied by "a masque of Ladies as Amazons, with lutes in their hands, dancing and playing." Of course, we often met the demands of a large cast by playing several roles apiece—but generally not all at the same time.

I sighed wearily. Obviously I would have to do more with this scene than just copy it out. It would have to wait, however, until I could hold my eyes open.

In the morning, I set to work afresh and managed to dispense with about half the original cast before Sam called for me. "You look as though you've hardly slept a wink," he said. "I've heard that's a common plight among those tormented by love."

"It was the Muse that tormented me," I replied haughtily.

"Mews?" said Sam, feigning puzzlement. "Has Mr. Pope begun taking in orphaned cats as well?"

I gave him a disdainful look. "I would not expect you to understand. You have never experienced the throes of poetic creation."

"You're right. And if it turns a person into a total goosecap, I hope I never do." I pretended to ignore his unkind remark. After a while he said casually, "So, is there a good role for me in this play of yours?"

"Oh, aye. In fact, I've written a part especially for you."

"Really? What sort of part is it?"

"Cupid."

He stared at me incredulously. "*Cupid?*"

"Well, I thought it only fitting," I said, "as you seem to ken so much about love."

When we entered the courtyard of the Cross Keys, I caught sight of an unsavory-looking man in a dirty, seam-rent tunic standing outside the dark parlor with his face pressed to the window. Despite the cold, he wore no cloak, only a woolen scarf wrapped about his neck. All the talk I had heard of late about theft and spying had made me uneasy, and my hand went to the handle of my dagger. "Do you ken that wight?" I whispered to Sam.

"No. And I don't think I care to."

The stranger did not appear to be armed, which gave me the courage to call sternly to him, "You, there!"

He whirled about, a startled scowl upon his face. One hand reached inside his tunic, as though to retrieve a weapon. Then, apparently seeing no threat in us, he relaxed and his manner changed abruptly from menacing to ingratiating. "Good morning to you, young sirs. Might you by any chance be associated with the folk that put on the plays here?" His lower-class London accent was so thick that I understood only about half the words, but it was enough to catch his meaning.

"Ha' you some sort of business wi' them?"

"I do. Could you tell me where to find the gentleman in charge?"

Still wary, I replied, "I can carry a message to him, and ask whether or not 'a wishes to see you."

The man's friendly facade slipped a little. "Oh, he'll wish to, right enough. Tell him . . . " The stranger paused and, eyes narrowed, searched my face carefully. "Here, I know you. You're the lad that was so thick with Julia, ain't you?"

For a moment I was struck speechless by this unexpected reference to my old friend. "You—you ken Julia?"

He grinned, revealing a row of rotten teeth. "I should think I do," he said. "I'm her da."

19

Julia had mentioned her father a time or two, in rather contemptuous terms, but until now I had not set eyes upon the man. I saw no hint of a family resemblance. Though Julia had been gone more than a year, I could picture her perfectly. She was tall for a girl, with auburn hair, brown eyes, and the ruddy coloring common to folk of a sanguine humor. This fellow looked more like the choleric sort, with his sallow, yellowish skin and his blue eyes, so pale as to be nearly colorless. His hair and beard, had they been washed, might have proven to be a light brown. He was short of stature, and his frame was as slight as mine.

"Is she well, do you ken?" I asked. "I haven't heard from her in some time."

"Oh, she's healthy enough, if that's what you mean. But she's in a bit of a whipper just now."

"A *whipper?*" said Sam.

"You know, a plight. A tight spot. That's what I've come to see your masters about."

"What sort of plight?" I asked anxiously.

"Well, now, why don't you just take me to whoever's in charge here, eh? That way I won't have to say it all twice."

"Aye, all right. Sam, go ahead and start on the tiring-room."

"I want to hear about Julia's whipper," he protested.

"I'll gi' you all the details later." As I led Julia's father up the outer stairs, I said, "How is 't that you kenned who I was?"

"I seen you and her together. I never said nothing. She didn't fancy me coming 'round the theatre, or talking to any of her actor friends. She wouldn't want me coming here even now, I expect. She's always hated asking anybody for aught." He gave me that rotten grin again. "I don't know where she gets that. It's never bothered me."

"No, I suppose not." From what Julia had told me, he certainly did not hesitate to accept anything from anyone—usually without their knowledge or permission. Both Mr. Heminges and Mr. Shakespeare were in the office, one setting down columns of figures, the other lines of dialogue. "Excuse me, sir," I said softly to Mr. Heminges. "There's a wight here to see you."

"Oh? Wh-what sort of wight?"

"Julia's father, actually."

Mr. Heminges rose to greet the stranger. "I d-don't believe we've m-met, sir. John Heminges, the c-company manager."

Julia's father ignored the hand that Mr. Heminges offered. He pulled his scarf up under his chin, even though the room was warm, and looked about rather furtively; obviously he was not used to such surroundings, modest though they were. His manner was a curious mixture of sullen and obsequious, as though he recognized that he was not on the same social level as these men, but at the same time resented it.

"And your n-name, sir?" Mr. Heminges prompted him.

"It's Cogan. Tom Cogan."

"Of c-course. W-would you like to sit down?"

"No. This won't take much time. The long and short of it is, the girl's in trouble over there in France, and needs money to get home."

"Tr-trouble? N-nothing serious, I hope?"

Cogan drew a worn leather pouch from his grimy tunic and fished from it a sheet of paper folded into a small square. "Here's what she sent. I had a fellow read it to me, but I don't recollect it all." As he passed the paper to Mr. Heminges, he held the scarf in place with his other hand, as though afraid of catching a chill. "Read it for yourself."

"Aloud, if you will," said Mr. Shakespeare.

Mr. Heminges unfolded the paper and read its contents in the same way he spoke upon the stage—with no trace of a stutter. "She writes, 'Father. You will no doubt be astonished to hear anything of any sort from me, least of all a plea for help. However, I have no one else to turn to, and whatever our feelings toward each other, we are bound together by blood. For reasons I cannot go into here, I have had to leave Monsieur Lefèvre's acting company, and quit my lodgings as well.

"'I have found a shabby sleeping room that costs only a few francs, and is worth far less, but I have been unable to find any sort of work that is respectable, and the little money I have saved is quickly disappearing.

"'I know that it is unfair of me, after having nothing to do with you for so long, to ask you now for aid, but if there is any way you can send me three pounds to pay my passage home, I would be most grateful. If you cannot . . . Well, at the risk of sounding overly dramatic, I honestly do not know what will become of me.'" Mr. Heminges returned the paper to Cogan. "I assume th-that you intend to send her the m-money?"

"O' course I do! What do you take me for?"

"I m-meant no insult. Three p-pounds is a substantial sum, though. How m-much have you r-raised?"

"Not a gray groat," Cogan cheerfully admitted. "I'm out of work myself just now, you see. I was hoping you gentlemen might see your way clear to put up the money, considering she was a prentice here, and all."

Mr. Heminges exchanged glances with Mr. Shakespeare. "We will need to discuss this privately," said Mr. Shakespeare. "Widge, will you wait outside with Mr. Cogan, please?"

I wanted to ask them what there was to discuss. I wanted to point out that the amount neeeded to rescue Julia was less than half of what Judith had so casually spent on a gown and a pair of shoes. But I said nothing, only showed Tom Cogan into the hallway.

Once he was out of the room, all trace of obsequiousness vanished, and the sullenness took over. "You'd think they'd just hand it over. Three pounds is nothing for the likes of them."

I was inclined to agree. Though the company was having financial troubles of late, I was certain that most of the sharers were well-off, if not wealthy. Mr. Pope, with all the mouths he had to feed, was the exception.

After only a minute or so, Mr. Heminges called us in. "W-we would like to help J-Julia, of course," he said. "If she tr-truly is in trouble."

"What d'you mean *if?*" Cogan said. "You seen the letter!"

"But how can we be sure it's genuine?" said Mr. Shakespeare.

Cogan gave a derisive laugh. "D'you suppose I wrote it myself?"

"Of course not. But you might have had someone write it for you."

"For what purpose?"

"For the purpose of prying money out of us, perhaps."

Cogan stepped toward him, a threatening look on his face. "Here! Are you calling me a thief?"

"I don't believe I need to," Mr. Shakespeare said calmly. "*That* says it plainly enough." I followed his gaze. The scarf Cogan had kept wrapped so carefully around his neck had loosened, revealing a vivid patch of scar tissue in the shape of a *T*—the mark of a man who has been branded by the law.

Cogan pushed the scarf back into place. "That happened a long while ago. All I took was some bread, to feed my wife and my daughter."

"Really?" said Mr. Shakespeare. "I've never heard of a man being branded for stealing bread."

"Might I look at the letter?" I put in. "I've seen Julia's hand enough times to recognize it." Cogan held out the paper. "It's from her, right enough," I said.

"There, you see?" said Cogan triumphantly.

"All the same," said Mr. Shakespeare, "if we turned over three pounds to you, what reason do we have to believe that it would ever reach her?"

"She's my *daughter,* that's what reason!"

"You've n-never shown m-much concern for her welfare in the p-past," Mr. Heminges pointed out.

"So you'll not give me the money, is that it?" Neither man replied. Cogan stared at them fiercely for a moment, as though he were considering demanding the money at the point of a knife. Then he said disdainfully, "I might have known I'd get no help from you lot. It was you that brought this on her to begin with. If you'd let her stay on here, she'd never have had to go to France." He strode to the door and flung it open. "You know, if I'd been smart, I wouldn't have come here; I'd have met you in a dark alley somewhere. You'd have handed over the money then, I'll wager."

Dismayed, I watched him leave, then turned to Mr. Shakespeare. "You're not going to help Julia at all, then?"

"You know as well as I that if we handed the money over to her father, she would never see a penny of it."

No doubt he was right; Cogan was a thief, after all. But I couldn't help feeling that the sharers were more concerned about the fate of their money than about Julia's fate.

"P-perhaps we can f-find some other way of helping her," Mr. Heminges said. He tried to put a comforting hand on my shoulder, but I pulled away.

"How *can* we, when we don't even know where to find her?" I hurried out, hoping to catch up with Cogan and learn where Julia could be reached. I scrambled down the stairs, across the courtyard, and into the street. There was no sign of him in any direction. I started walking west at a rapid pace, thinking he might be headed for Alsatia, the foul and fearsome precinct that was claimed by the city's criminal class as a sort of sanctuary. I knew that Julia had once lived there; perhaps her father still did.

After a quarter of an hour I was forced to conclude that either he walked far faster than I or he had gone some other way. As I reluctantly headed back to the Cross Keys, I set myself to thinking about how I might help Julia.

It was clear that, for whatever reason, she had not wanted me or the company to know of her plight. Otherwise she would surely have written to us, not to her father. But now that we did know, we could not sit by and do nothing—or at least I could not. Though she was far off in France, I still considered her my nearest friend. If the sharers would not rescue her, then it was up to me.

The problem was, of course, that I hadn't three shillings, let alone three pounds. If only I had saved my wages all these months, instead of throwing so much away on things of no consequence. Some of my purchases, such as sweetmeats and stockings for Mr. Pope's orphan boys, I did not regret. But why had I wasted one penny after another having my future read while Julia's future hung in the balance?

There must be some way I could raise the money. I could not ask Mr. Pope for it, at least not all of it. The cost of running so large a household left him with little to spare, even in the best of times.

Sam would no doubt advise me to buy a chance in the lottery, but that was about as reliable as one of La Voisin's predictions. Though there was a slim possibility that I might win something eventually, there was no way of knowing how much, or when. I needed three pounds, and I needed it now.

There were always dishonest means, of course. According to Sam, one costume from the company's trunks might be worth several pounds. But the tiring-room was closely guarded these days. In any case, however angry I might be at the sharers, I could not have brought myself to steal from them.

I was certain that Tom Cogan had no such scruples. Why had he not simply gotten the money through his usual methods, then, instead of coming to us? Perhaps it was just too large a sum. No ordinary tradesman, and few gentlemen, carried about a purse that fat. Cogan would have had to hold up the lord mayor himself.

I would gladly have sold everything I owned to help Julia, but there was nothing among my paltry possessions that would fetch more than a farthing. Or was there?

A good play was a fairly valuable commodity. After all, I had been brought to London for the express purpose of stealing one. I wasn't certain just how much a playwright could expect for his work. Sam once told me that Mr. Shakespeare got twenty pounds per script, but then Sam was known to exaggerate.

In any case, no one in his right mind would pay twenty pounds for a script by an unknown apprentice player, no matter how good it was, unless . . . unless perhaps I put Mr. Shakespeare's name on it as coauthor. No, it would be unfair to trade on his reputation that way. But when he gave me the play, he clearly said that I might do with it as I wished. So I could in good conscience claim it as my own. With any luck, I might sell it for a couple of pounds—provided, of course, I could finish it.

As Hamlet would say, "Aye, there's the rub." I vowed that I would renew and redouble my efforts that evening, and make as quick work of it as I could. Then all that would remain was to find Cogan. Ah, well; compared to writing a decent play, venturing into a den of desperate criminals and convincing them to reveal the whereabouts of one of their own should be a lark. In the meantime, I was wanted at rehearsal.

To my relief, Judith did not attend. She had not been at our performance the night before, either. Whatever interest the theatre had held for her seemed to be fading.

Though I tried hard to give my full attention to my lines, Julia's plight weighed heavily on my mind, and I made nearly as many blunders as I had with Judith watching. The rehearsal seemed interminable.

When Mr. Heminges entered the room, I gave a silent sigh of relief, thinking that he had come to summon us to dinner. Then I saw that he was not alone. Four unfamiliar figures appeared at the top of the stairs. Three of them were guardsmen, clad in metal breastplates and helmets and armed with the combination of ax and spear that is called a halberd. The fourth was a tall, gaunt fellow who wore the garb of a gentleman. The man's eyes surveyed the room, searching the face of each player in turn, as though he was seeking someone in particular. Clearly, whoever he sought was not among us. He scowled and, turning abruptly, headed back down the stairs with the guards close behind him.

When they were gone, we gathered around Mr. Heminges, who looked uncharacteristically grim. "What did that lot want?" asked Sam.

"They were p-pursuivants," said Mr. Heminges.

"I beg your pardon?" said Sam.

"Pr-priest hunters."

Sam laughed. "And they expected to find one in a company of players?"

"Ap-parently so. It would s-seem that the man who calls himself G-Garrett is, in fact, F-Father Gerard—a J-Jesuit priest."

We were all of us momentarily struck dumb by this revelation. Though it had been clear all along that Garrett was hiding something, I doubt that anyone suspected what it was. Neither his appearance nor his behavior was the sort one expected from a priest. There was nothing remotely spiritual about him; on the contrary, he was clearly well versed in the ways of the world. And yet someone must have guessed his secret, in order to give it away.

Sam broke the stunned silence. "God precious potstick!" he breathed. "A priest!"

"Ha' the priest hunters looked downstairs?" I asked.

Mr. Heminges nodded. "G-Garrett—or sh-should I say Gerard?—has not t-turned up yet. He m-may be on his way, however."

"We must warn him!" said Sam.

"Why?" put in Sal Pavy. "Let them catch the mass-monger."

Sam cast him a venomous look. "Do you know what they *do* to priests?"

"I'll try to head him off," I said.

"G-good lad. You kn-know where he's staying?"

"Aye."

"Well, what are you waiting for?" exclaimed Sam. "Move your bones!"

I slipped down the outer stairs and hurried along Gracechurch Street, toward the river. Mr. Shakespeare had said that Garrett—that is, Gerard—was lodging with Ben Jonson, and I knew that the playwright had lately taken up residence in the palatial house of his patron and fellow Papist, Sir Thomas Townshend, on the Strand.

I was nearly to Sir Thomas's house when I saw Gerard approaching along the Strand. I called to him and he raised a hand in greeting. Then he reached inside his cloak, produced a sheaf of papers bound with string, and waved it at me. "Jonson's play. He's laid up with a cough and a fever, and asked me to—"

"Never mind that! I've come to warn you! There's a band of priest hunters at the Cross Keys!"

He did not seem distressed by this, only resigned, as though he had expected it. "So you know my secret, then?"

"Aye."

Taking my arm, he led me across the street and down a narrow alley. "We'd best stay out of sight. They may come here looking for me."

"No one will tell them where to find you."

"I wouldn't think so. But then I wouldn't have thought that anyone would betray me to the pursuivants in the first place."

"It could not ha' been one of the Chamberlain's Men, surely; none of us kenned you were a priest."

"Judith knew, and she may have let it slip. It's also possible that Ned Shakespeare knew."

"How could he?"

"For the past several years I've been traveling about the Midlands, saying Mass in secret for those of the old faith and ministering to the dying. One of those to whom I gave the last rites was John Shakespeare—Ned and Will's father."

"And Ned was still in Stratford then?"

Father Gerard nodded. "Well, there's little use in speculating about who's responsible. I knew I'd be found out sooner or later."

"Why did you come to London, then? Why did you not stay up north?"

"There are priest hunters there as well. Besides, my superiors felt I was needed here."

"To do what?"

"I have two missions. One is to convince young men to join the Society of Jesus." He gave me a sly look. "Interested?"

I laughed. "I mean to be a player, not a priest."

"Well, you can't fault me for trying. My other mission is to save the souls of prisoners."

"You actually go into *prisons?* Isn't that like sticking your costard i' the lion's mouth?"

"It is risky, yes. But I pose as a physician, and I pay the warders enough so they're willing to look the other way." He halted and placed a hand on my shoulder. "I want to thank you for coming to warn me. It was a brave thing."

"I couldn't let you be caught. You haven't done anything wrong." A bit uncertainly, I added, "Ha' you?"

"No." He smiled wryly. "Aside from being a traitor to the Crown, of course."

"Well, I should be getting back." I glanced about me. We had made several turns, and I was not entirely sure where the Cross Keys lay. "Assuming I can find me way, that is."

Gerard pointed to his left. "You'll want to head in that direction. But before you go, there's something I must tell you. I'm sorry for not bringing it up sooner, but I had to be certain I could trust you."

"Trust me?"

"As you will see, I couldn't very well reveal this without also revealing my profession." He paused, as though to collect his thoughts, then went on. "Several months ago, when I was holding services in Leicester, I was called to a tavern outside the town, to give the last rites to a thief who had been shot while trying to rob a wealthy merchant. Before he died, we had a chance to talk. When I mentioned that I was going to London soon, he asked if I would contact his son, who, he said, was a player . . . with Mr. Shakespeare's company." Gerard fixed his black eyes on me. "He seemed quite proud of the fact."

With the little breath I could muster, I said, "What . . . what was this fellow's name, then?"

I suspected what his reply would be, and I was right. "Jamie Redshaw," he said.

From time to time, some small-minded critic took Mr. Shakespeare to task because so many of his plays were neither strictly tragedy nor strictly comedy, but a mingle-mangle of the two. Mr. Shakespeare seemed unperturbed by such accusations. He was, he said, merely trying to reflect the nature of real life, which was invariably a mixture of the awful and the absurd—hilarity one moment, heartbreak the next, and sometimes both at once.

My situation proved his point. All my life I had longed to know who my parents were. Now that I had been given the final piece of the puzzle, I should have been overjoyed. But how could I be, when, at the very moment I learned at last who my father was, I also discovered that he was dead?

I was stricken not so much by grief as by a sad sense of regret. As the circumstances of his death showed, Jamie Redshaw had not been the most admirable of men. Yet he had possessed admirable qualities—among them courage and cleverness. Who could say what he might have become had Fortune dealt him a better hand? If he and my mother had not been kept apart by her parents, his life would no doubt have been quite different. And so, of course, would mine.

"I'm sorry," said Father Gerard, "that I was unable to save his life. The wound was too grave. But the fate of our earthly body matters little when compared to the fate of the soul. Be assured that he has gone to a better life."

"I hope so, for the one 'a had here was naught to boast of."

Gerard placed the script of *Sejanus* in my hands. "You should go. If they do find me, I don't want you implicated."

"You'll leave London now, surely?"

He shook his head. "Not for a while yet."

"But where will you stay?"

"I'll find a place. There are a number of the faithful here who are willing to put their lives in jeopardy by sheltering us. Go now."

When I returned to the Cross Keys, dinner was over, but the sharers were still sitting about the table with grim looks on their faces, talking in low, somber voices. They all seemed relieved to see me. "Widge!" said Mr. Armin. "Thank heaven you're all right. I was afraid the pursuivants might catch Gerard, and you with him."

"Nay. We saw no sign of 'em." I took a seat and scavenged what few morsels were left.

"G-good," said Mr. Heminges. "I wish the m-man no ill, even though he has c-caused us a good d-deal of trouble."

"Will they shut us down for harboring a priest, do you wis?"

"It's doubtful," said Mr. Shakespeare, "at least as long as we have the queen's protection." He sighed heavily and put his head in his hands. "I apologize to you all for my part in this. If I had known he was a priest, I would not have agreed to help him. Judith led me to believe that he was a recusant from Warwickshire who had refused to pay his fines and was forced to flee to avoid being imprisoned. She also said that he had been a friend to my father, at a time when my father had few others."

"Well, that much was true," I said. "'A told me that when your father was ill, 'a tended him and gave him the last rites." I glanced about the room. "Where is Judith now?"

Mr. Shakespeare sighed again. "I'm not certain. We . . . we had words, and she ran off." He glanced down at the script of *Sejanus,* which lay on the bench next to me. "Where did that come from?"

"Father Gerard was on his way to deliver 't to us. Mr. Jonson is laid up wi' th' ague."

"You may as well set to work on it, then. For the moment, anyway, we're still in business."

I popped a boiled egg in my mouth and headed upstairs. When I entered the office, I found Judith sitting on the floor next to the windows, her legs drawn up, her face buried in the folds of her gown, weeping as though she had lost her only friend. I had experienced that sort of grief once, when Sander died, and feared that I might again, if I could not bring Julia home.

Judith had not actually lost a friend, of course; she was upset because Mr. Shakespeare had reprimanded her—rather harshly, no doubt, and in front of the entire company. I knew how that felt as well. Though I had little experience in comforting folk, I did my best. I knelt and laid a hand gently on her arm. "Please don't cry. It's not so bad, really."

She turned her tear-streaked face toward me; though her eyes were red and swollen from weeping, her fair skin mottled, she somehow contrived to look more appealing than ever. Mr. Pope had known a lady, he said, who could stop a man's heart with her smile. Here was one who could do it with her tears. "Yes, it is," she said, her words broken by sobs. "It *is* bad. I'm being sent home."

Stricken, I sank to the floor next to Judith. "Oh, gis! I suppose 'a has a right to be angry wi' you, but to send you home . . . Is there any chance 'a will change his mind, do you wis?"

Judith gave a trembling, bitter laugh. "You don't know my father very well. Once he's made up his mind to something, there's no changing it. He never wanted me here to begin with."

"I'm sure that's not so," I lied. "Anyway, surely 'a won't just pack you off on your own. 'A will ha' to find someone to travel wi' you." Had it not been for the unfinished business with Julia, I would have volunteered my services.

She wiped her eyes with the hem of her gown. "Yes, I suppose you're right. Perhaps it will be a while, then, before he can make the arrangements."

"Aye, it might be weeks—months, even." I did my best to sound confident and cheerful, though I felt quite the contrary. It was not enough that I must see to it that Julia got home; now I had to try to make certain that Judith did not.

I suddenly felt quite overwhelmed by it all. If love was difficult to play upon the stage, it was even harder to manage in earnest. I needed a respite from it; I needed to throw myself into some task that would make no demands on my mind or my emotions. "Listen. I really must get to work on this play."

"Oh. Well. If you'd rather do that than talk to me."

"It's not that, it's just—"

"I know, I know. I've heard it all before." She rose and straightened her gown. "You did promise to read some of it to me, though."

"Nay, it's not *that* play. It's Mr. Jonson's. Your father's asked me to copy it out."

"Well, then, of course you must do it. We must all do as Father says, mustn't we?" She examined her face in the small looking glass Mr. Shakespeare used for his makeup and rubbed at her cheeks with a kerchief. "You needn't feel too sorry for yourself, Widge, for never having had a father. They're a mixed blessing at best." As she went out the door, she whispered archly, "Havc fun with your *play*." Her tone made it clear that she considered it just that—play, not work. Whatever it was, I was grateful to occupy myself with such an undemanding task.

According to rumor, one of the priest hunters' favorite methods of extracting a confession was a procedure known as *peine forte et dure,* in which a slab of stone is placed upon the chest of the reclining victim; the next day a second slab is added, then a third, and so on, until the subject either gives up the desired information or gives up the ghost.

Though I had so far been spared the slabs of stone, for the past week or so Fortune had been busy laying troubles upon me, one by one, until I felt at times as though I could not breathe. I had no notion, however, what I was expected to confess. All I could do was try to ignore the growing pressure by turning my mind to other things.

I had copied out no more than half a dozen pages of *Sejanus* before I was interrupted by a breathless, perspiring Sam, fresh from scriming practice. "Well?" he demanded.

I glanced up irritably. "Well, what?"

"Did you manage to warn Mr. Garrett in time?"

"Father Gerard, you mean."

"Yes, yes. Did you?"

"Aye."

Sam gave a relieved grin. "Thank heaven."

"You might wish to thank *me* as well."

"Thanks. He's not leaving London, is he?"

"Not for a while yet, 'a says. But 'a's not likely to come around here again."

"Oh, bones. I suppose not. Do you know where he's staying?"

"Nay. And I wouldn't go looking for him an I were you. Priests are dangerous company."

Sam scowled at me. "Will you stop it?"

"Stop what?"

"Playing the older brother." He rose and started from the room, then turned back to say, "Mr. Garrett's my friend, Widge; I'm not going to forget about him just because he happens to be a Papist."

That evening we performed *All's Well That Ends Well* again. I knew the play backward and forward and so was able to lose myself in it, as in a dream, and give no thought to anything. Julia had never acted in the play, so there was nothing in it to remind me of her, and since Judith did not turn up, I was even able to forget about her for moments at a time.

Ordinarily I looked forward to my time with Mr. Pope at the end of each day. But tonight I felt rather as though I were headed for a session of *peine forte et dure,* in which all the doubts and worries I had tried so hard to suppress would be squeezed out of me. Though it would have been a relief to unburden myself to someone, I dared not make Mr. Pope my confessor; we had been instructed not to bring up anything that might upset him.

When I reached the library, I found Mr. Pope asleep in his chair. I stole silently out again, grateful that I had neither to reveal nor to conceal the news that Father Gerard had given me concerning Jamie Redshaw. I needed to digest it myself first, to mull over what it might mean to me.

Though I knew now where I came from, did it really change anything? I had no notion whether any of Jamie Redshaw's relations—or my mother's—were still alive or, if they were, where to find them. And even if I did manage to uncover them, how likely was it that they would welcome some long-lost, illegitimate child who claimed to be their kin? And even if they did accept me, could I bear to leave London and the world of the theatre for some other world I knew nothing of?

Once again I was thankful to have something less confusing to turn my mind to, something more within my control. I retreated to my room, lit a candle, and sat down at my desk with Mr. Shakespeare's script—no, *my* script—before me. In a quarter hour or so, I had finished copying into my own hand all that Mr. Shakespeare had written, up until the end of the second act. After that, there were no complete scenes, only scraps of speeches, plus some notes he had made concerning the mechanics of the story.

Well, he had given me the bare bones; it was up to me to put flesh upon them. I took a deep breath and wrote on a fresh sheet of paper *Act III.* Then I sat staring into space for a very long time. I had only now begun to realize that being in control might prove to be more of a curse than a blessing. With perhaps ten thousand possible words at my disposal, how did I settle on just the right one, and then one to follow it, and so on?

And yet, was it really so impossible? After all, in real life we managed to speak to one another well enough without agonizing over every word. Well, then, perhaps what I must do was not write the lines but speak them, say whatever came into my head, as folk do in conversation. Sometimes, admittedly, the results were unfortunate. But I had the luxury of taking mine back.

Mr. Shakespeare had already established that Timon was in financial trouble. What I needed now was a scene in which he sends his servant, Flaminius, to ask one of the nobles—Lucullus, let us say—for a loan. So. *Scene I. A Room in Lucullus's House. Flaminius waiting. A servant enters* and says . . . says what? Well, I ought to know; I had played the part of a servant often enough. "I have told my lord you are here," I said aloud, under my breath. "He is coming down." Hardly inspired, but believable, at least, and certainly far better than a blank page. I wrote it down. And Flavius replies . . . "Tell him to hurry"? No, too cheeky. "I'll just sit down here"? No, that would require a chair. "Thank you"? Good enough. Now to bring Lucullus on. *Servant:* "Here's my lord." A bit obvious, but never mind. Lucullus is a greedy wight, so . . . *Lucullus (aside):* "One of Lord Timon's men? Bringing me another gift, no doubt."

As though I had broken through a barrier of some sort, the words began to flow from me, through my pencil, and onto the paper—only a trickle at first, but then such a steady stream that I was forced to switch from Italian script to my system of swift writing in order to keep up. I felt almost as if someone were dictating the lines to me—not Mr. Shakespeare, certainly; he would have dictated better ones.

Well, no matter that it was not deathless prose; I could always go back later and liven it up a bit. I made no attempt at meter. As with most of his plays, Mr. Shakespeare had begun writing this one in fairly regular iambic pentameter. But by the middle of Act II he was, for no apparent reason, putting in long passages of prose. If it was good enough for him, it was good enough for me.

For nearly two years, however, I had been spouting verse for several hours every day. It was bound to affect me. I found myself unconsciously composing ten-syllable lines, with the stress on the even-numbered syllables:

> Has friendship such a faint and milky heart
> It turns in less than two nights? Oh, you gods!

Sometimes the meter limped a little, but then Mr. Shakespeare's lines did not always glide as smoothly as swans, either.

Just when I grew used to the words pouring onto the page, without warning the source—whatever it was—dried up, and I was back to squeezing lines out of my brain, drop by drop. But even at its most frustrating, the task held a sort of perverse satisfaction. While everyone else in our household—and in other households all over the city—were in their beds, here was I at my desk, slaving away, creating a work of art. I felt noble, righteous, a martyr in the service of Melpomene, the muse of tragedy. Like those who slept, I was spinning out a sort of dream. But, whereas theirs would fade even before they awoke, mine would be written down and perhaps acted out, for others to hear and to see, again and again.

I did not feel nearly so righteous in the morning. I felt, in fact, less like a noble playwright than like a noddy who has slept half the night in a hard chair, with a pile of papers for a pillow, and who has wax in his hair from a melting candle. Well, I reminded myself, a martyr is expected to suffer for his cause, otherwise he would not be a martyr, only an ordinary wight doing an ordinary job that anyone might do as well. As I tried to get my stiff limbs in working order, I consoled myself with the knowledge that I was now nearly one act nearer to having a completed play and the money to rescue Julia.

Sam could not, of course, resist commenting upon my haggard appearance. "Don't tell me. The cats of creativity kept you up until all hours again with their infernal mewing."

"As a matter of fact, I was hard at work writing posies for the lottery." I had learned from Sam that when you bought a chance in the lottery, you gave the agent a slip of paper with some distinctive motto or verse upon it; when the winners were announced, their posies were read aloud.

"*You're* going to enter the lottery?"

I nodded soberly. "Not the royal one, though. This lottery is only for the Lord Chamberlain's Men, to determine which of us will get his wages this week."

Sam gaped at me. "Truly?"

"Nay. I was only jesting."

He swatted my arm. "That's nothing to jest about." As we entered the courtyard of the Cross Keys, he said, "I suppose you won't be favoring us with your company again today?"

"Nay. I'll be another two days, at least, copying Mr. Jonson's script—or should I say *deciphering* it. His hand is so poor, the whole thing looks as though it's in some sort of code that only remotely resembles th' alphabet."

"Perhaps it is!" Sam whispered dramatically. "Perhaps it's a secret means of communication known only to Catholics!" When I looked dubious, he said, "Well, it's possible. They have a whole mysterious language of their own, you know."

"Aye. It's called Latin. And it's not all that mysterious." I peered through the window of the office; there was no one inside. I dug from my purse the key Mr. Shakespeare had given me.

"It's mysterious if you've never studied it," Sam said.

"I ha', a bit."

"Have you? Say something in it, then."

"Umm . . . *Totus mundus agit histrionem*."

"Ahh, I know that one already. It's on the front of the Globe. 'All the world's a stage.' Say something else."

I rolled my eyes long-sufferingly. "*Carpe diem, tempus fugit.*"

"What does that mean?"

"It means 'Get to work.'"

I was tempted to tell Sam the news about Jamie Redshaw. But if I told him, it would be the same as telling everyone, and I was not eager for Judith to know. As long as my heritage remained a mystery, there was always the possibility, however unlikely, that I was the son of some great lord, and not of a common brigand.

I found it harder than ever that morning to make sense of Mr. Jonson's scribbles—perhaps because my eyes were closed so much of the time. It was not only my lack of sleep that was to blame; no matter how well rested I was, Mr. Jonson's script would surely have sent me into a stupor.

How could such a coarse and colorful wight, I wondered, write such insipid stuff? Considered purely as poetry, there was nothing wrong with it. It was dignified, evocative, and eloquent. But as dialogue for the stage, it was, to use Mr. Shakespeare's term again, putrid—hopelessly stilted and unnatural. I wondered whether I should introduce Mr. Jonson to my method of speaking the lines aloud before I wrote them down. Probably not. If I did, he would no doubt speak aloud a few choice lines himself. They would not be suitable for use upon the stage, of course, but at least they would have some life in them.

Though copying the script was a struggle, it did teach me a valuable lesson. I still did not know much about how to write a play, but at least I knew a good deal about how *not* to write one. That night, I sat down at my own desk with a new determination. For the first time I actually believed that if I worked hard enough at it, I might write something worth reading, and worth acting—if not with this play then with the next one, or the next.

Perhaps, in the process, I might even manage to make something of myself—unlike my father. But, though Jamie Redshaw had done little enough for me, there was one thing I might thank him for: Like Mr. Jonson, he had instilled in me a fierce resolve not to follow in his footsteps.

To my surprise, I had no trouble staying awake to work on my play. It was as though, after so many hours of plodding along in a sort of daze, I had at last passed beyond the boundaries of weariness and into some other realm, where the body gives up trying to have its way, and the mind becomes master.

In the morning, of course, my body came to its senses again, and it was all I could do to drag myself to the theatre. But I had another half an act to show for it. I tucked several pages of the script into my wallet, meaning to read them to Judith if the opportunity presented itself.

It did not. In fact, Judith did not present herself, even at the midday meal. Though I longed to know where she was and how she was, I was not inclined to ask Mr. Shakespeare. I was still angry with him and with Mr. Heminges over their seeming lack of concern for Julia, and was doing my best to avoid them.

Sam, who never hesitated to ask anyone about anything, reported that Judith had been banished from the Cross Keys as punishment for putting the whole company in jeopardy. This only added to my resentment. If she could not come to the theatre, and I could not leave it, how would we ever meet?

There was, of course, tomorrow afternoon, when she had arranged for Sal Pavy and Sam to show her about the city after church. Though it would be hard to be content with one-third of her attention, perhaps it would be better than not seeing her at all. If Mr. Shakespeare made good his threat to send her home, there was no telling how many more chances I might have.

The weather had been so miserable of late that I feared it might spoil our plans. But for once Sunday lived up to its name, dawning bright and clear. By the time we set out for St. Saviour's, it was almost too warm for a cloak. Sam, who lodged with Mr. Phillips but a few streets away from us, ordinarily accompanied us to church, to the delight of Mr. Pope's orphan boys; they laughed at all his jests, however inane, and were awed by his simpleminded sleight-of-hand tricks, such as pulling pennies from their mouths.

When he failed to join us, the boys were sorely disappointed. As we filed into the church, I spotted Mr. Phillips; Sam was not with him, either. Before I could ask him what had become of the boy, Mr. Phillips asked me the same thing. I had no answer for him. I only hoped that Sam's absence would not be noted by the priest or the deacons.

It was possible, of course, that he was only late, and would show up at some point in the services. To my shame, I found myself wishing he would not; then I would have to share Judith only with Sal Pavy—who was, unfortunately, sitting in his usual spot at the end of our pew, alongside Mr. Armin.

The priest began by asking us all to join him in a prayer for the queen's health. Apparently there was some small hope that Her Majesty would yet recover. Though her body might be weak, her will was not; she was as stubborn and independent as ever. She had refused to take to her bed, for to do so would be to concede that she was near the end. Instead, she spent all her time sitting upright on cushions placed upon the floor.

After the services, I searched for Sam, but there was still no sign of him. I caught Sal Pavy coming out of the church and let him know that I intended to join him and Judith. To my surprise, he seemed agreeable, or at least as agreeable as Sal Pavy ever got. "What about Sam?" he asked.

"Whist!" I said softly. After making certain no one would overhear, I whispered, "'A never turned up."

"Oh. He won't be happy if we go without him."

"Then 'a should ha' been here. Besides, 'a would only ha' pestered us to cross over on th' ice."

"It would be a good deal quicker than going by way of the bridge."

"Aye, and perhaps a good deal wetter as well. Now that the weather's changed, th' ice may begin breaking up at any time."

Sal Pavy gave me a smirking smile. "You sound a bit white-livered to me."

"I'm not afeared, an that's what you mean. I'm cautious, that's all."

"Caution is but another name for fear."

"And daring is but another name for stupid."

"Well, I'll tell you what. You cross the bridge, and I'll cross the ice, and we'll see which of us gets to Judith first."

I searched his face for some sign that he was jesting, and failed to find any. "You mean it?"

"Of course."

He was clearly issuing a challenge, like the one I had issued several months earlier when I proposed an acting duel to determine who would play the part of Helena in *All's Well.* If I ignored his dare and took the bridge, he would most likely follow. But suppose he did not? Even if I ran all the way to St. Olave's, I might arrive to find him and Judith gone or, even worse, sharing a laugh over my foolish caution, which they would take for fear.

Whether he was truly serious or only bluffing, I had no choice but to take up the gauntlet he had thrown. "All right, then," I said, with a nonchalance that was badly damaged by my voice breaking. "Let's be stupid—I mean, daring."

"Good." Sal Pavy gestured toward the steps that led to the river. "After you."

"It was your idea," I reminded him.

He could not deny it. With his head held high, rather like a condemned man determined to make a good show on his way to the scaffold, he descended the stairs and, with a reluctance that was hardly visible, stepped onto the ice. He turned to me with a smug look, tinged with relief. "There, you see? It's perfectly safe."

I had no doubt it would be, this close to shore, where the water was still. It was the part farther out, where the current flowed fastest beneath its frozen shell, that worried me. As we shuffled toward the middle of the river, I took some heart in the fact that a dozen or so wights were out there already, fishing through holes they had cut in the ice. Of course, we had no notion how many more had made holes through it without meaning to, and were now down there with the fish.

"Sam will really be angry with us now, for going without him," said Sal Pavy.

"Assuming we survive, you mean."

When we had gone perhaps fifty yards, I began to notice dark patches here and there, where a pocket of air or a mass of floating debris had been trapped in the ice. Though I carefully detoured around these spots, Sal Pavy seemed to pay no attention to them—until he put his weight on one and the ice gave way like the trapdoor in our stage at the Globe, which could be used to send an evil villain plunging into the pit of hell.

Sal Pavy's cry of dismay was cut off as he dropped into the river and the water closed over his head. My instinct was to run headlong to his rescue; then my reason took over and told me that if I did, I might well join him instead. I flung myself onto my stomach and scuttled along like a crab until I reached the spot where he had fallen through. Sal Pavy had fought his way to the surface—within the circle of open water, luckily, and not beneath the ice—and was clinging with both hands to the crumbling edge of the hole, choking and coughing up water. Between spasms, he called out in a faint and trembling voice, "Widge! Help me!"

I crept several inches nearer. I could hear the ice creaking under my weight, and expected a new chunk to break loose at any moment. "I'm here! Take my hand!"

"I can't! I daren't let go!"

"All right," I said, as calmly as I could. "I'll take yours, then." I groped about until I located what I took to be one of his hands; it was hard to be sure, for it was as cold as the ice. I pushed myself forward another few inches and wrapped my fingers around his wrist. It was impossible to pull him to me, though; I could get no purchase on the slick ice. "You'll ha' to climb up me arm."

"I can't!" he gasped. "My cloak. Too heavy."

"Unfasten it wi' one hand, then. I'll keep hold of th' other."

"Don't let go!" he begged. For what seemed like a full minute or more I heard him thrashing about, trying to free himself from the waterlogged cloak. At last I felt his fingers clutch the sleeve of my shirt.

"Get a good grip," I said. "I'm going to let go of your other hand now."

"No!" he cried.

"I must, Sal. You'll need it to pull yourself out. The moment I let go, you grasp me arm. All right?"

"I'll try," he said weakly.

"Good." I released my hold on his wrist. He slumped down in the water, and for a moment I thought I'd lost him. Then his other hand slithered forward and seized the fabric of my sleeve. With painful slowness, using me as his ladder, he dragged himself from the river and onto the ice.

I let him lie there and recover a moment. Then I bent, draped one of his arms around my neck, and hoisted him to his feet. "Come along. We must get you indoors." As soon as he could support himself, I took off my cloak and fastened it around him. "That may help a little."

Through chattering teeth, he murmured something I could not quite make out, but I believe it may have been "Thank you." By the time we reached the stairs, he had warmed up a bit and was walking and speaking in a more or less normal fashion. He had also resumed his normal haughty attitude. "I can manage on my own from here," he said.

"Are you certain?"

He waved a shaky hand at me. "Yes, yes. Besides, you need to meet Judith. She'll be wondering what's become of us." He fumbled with the cords that tied the cloak together.

"You may keep that for now," I told him. "I'll be warm enough."

He gave me a slight, stiff smile. "That may depend," he said, "on what sort of mood she's in."

I soon discovered that the air was not as warm as I had imagined. There was a stiff breeze off the river. To make matters worse, my doublet and breeches were wet from lying on the ice. Even though I walked briskly—across the bridge, this time—I was cold as a cellar stone before I reached St. Olave's Church. The place was deserted—which was not surprising, considering how late I was.

Wrapping my arms about myself, I hurried on to Mr. Shakespeare's lodgings. I nearly wore the knocker out before anyone answered the door. To my disappointment, it was Mary Mountjoy. She regarded me quizzically, as though she felt she should know me but couldn't think from where. "Yes? What is it?"

So flustered was I at the prospect of seeing Judith, I could scarcely get the words out. "I—that is, we—that is, Mistress Shakespeare was to meet us. Me. At the church. But there's no one at the church. So. Is she here?"

"No, I'm afraid she's gone."

"Gone?" I echoed dumbly. "Gone where?"

"Why, to Stratford. She left half an hour ago."

In a week so full of distressing developments, I should not have been surprised, I suppose, to be struck by yet one more. I had known, after all, that Judith was likely to leave at some point. I just never imagined it would be this soon. So out of square was I that I thought perhaps I had not heard Mistress Mountjoy properly. "You mean . . . you mean *home?* To Warwickshire?"

"Yes," the girl replied, pouting a little. "And we were getting to be such good friends, too."

"But . . . but surely her father didn't pack her off all alone?"

"Of course not. An old acquaintance of his—a Mr. Quiney, I believe; or was it Quincy? Something with a *Q*, anyway—was going to Stratford on business, and let her travel with him. Mr. Shakespeare is accompanying them as far as Uxbridge."

"Can you tell me, did she leave any sort of . . . message, or anything?"

"For whom?"

"Well . . . for me."

She gave me that quizzical look again. "I'm sorry, which one are you?"

"Widge."

"Oh, yes."

"She *did?*" I said eagerly.

"No, I only meant, 'Oh, yes, now I remember you.' She left no message. In fact, she didn't say much of anything when she left, not even to me, she was that upset and angry. She did say she'd write back, though, if I wrote her. Is there anything you'd like me to pass on to her?"

"Nay. What's the use? As she told me herself, she's heard it all before, and from better wights than me, I wis."

"You look cold," she said. "Would you like to come in and warm up?"

I shook my head and turned away. If I was to be miserable, I might as well make a good job of it. It would not be difficult. A whole long afternoon and evening stretched ahead of me, and nothing better to do with it than to sit about feeling sorry for myself. I had neither money nor friends, and even if I had had both, I would have had no appetite for the frivolous pastimes with which we ordinarily occupied our Sundays.

I might as well go home and work on my play. I had reached the point in the script at which Timon, a destitute and friendless outcast, declares that he hates all mankind. It fit my mood and my circumstances exactly.

There is nothing like spite to motivate a person. Though my room was nearly as cold as the outdoors, I shrouded myself in blankets and sat scribbling away for the next several hours, giving voice to all the insulting and reproachful remarks that I could not say myself by putting them in Timon's mouth:

"Away, thou issue of a mangy dog!" "Would thou wert clean enough to spit upon." "I am sick of this false world, and will love naught."

But, as gratifying as this was, I knew that if I confined my hero to mere curses, he would not seem heroic, only hateful. I must provide him with some means of avenging himself. Besides, our audience loved revenge. According to Mr. Shakespeare's notes, he planned to have Timon raise an army and lay waste to Rome—now Athens. But that seemed unlikely. Soldiers don't fight unless you pay them, and Timon was so poor that he was reduced to living in a cave in the woods and eating roots.

Well, suppose he gets some money, somehow. Suppose he comes into a fortune, and suddenly all his former friends want to be his friends again, and he just laughs at them. Yes, that was good. But where would he get a fortune, living in a cave in the woods? Steal it? Inherit it? Write a successful play? Dig up gold nuggets while he's grubbing for roots to eat?

When this notion first struck me, I didn't take it seriously; it seemed rather silly, in fact. But the more I thought about it, the more the irony of it appealed to me. I knew it would delight the penny playgoers as well; if there was anything they loved more than guts and gore, it was gold. Certainly it would hold their attention better than watching Timon write a play, or read his uncle's will.

Though I had said little to Goody Willingson or Mr. Pope about the play, they seemed to sense my need for privacy and somehow kept the boys from pestering me for much of the afternoon. But boys, like spirited horses, may be kept in check only so long.

I was just bringing a band of thieves into the script when the boys burst into the room, surrounded me, and took me captive.

Though I showered them with curses only slightly less vile than Timon's, they merely laughed and vowed not to release me until I had played Banks's Horse with them—a favorite game they had invented in which I impersonated a celebrated gelding who could dance, do sums, and answer questions.

When I had had my fill of neighing and pawing the floor, they pressed me into a game of Barley Break that lasted until supper. As I was stuffing my mouth with mutton pie, anxious to return to my desk before the Muse grew tired of waiting for me, Goody Willingson said, "Is your writing going well, then, Widge?"

In trying to clear my mouth enough to answer, I nearly choked.

"Just paw the table," said a boy named Walter. "Once for yes, twice for no." This sent the others into fits of laughter. With a grin made lopsided by my mouthful of food, I gave the table a single swipe.

"Have you let Judith look at the script?" asked Mr. Pope.

My grin faded. "Nay. She's gone home."

"Oh. I'm sorry, lad. Though I'm certain you won't agree just now, I assure you it is for the best."

I wondered whether, if I had said I was struck soundly on the brain-pan and robbed, he would have told me that it was for the best. In truth, I believe I would have preferred to be beaten and robbed; it would surely have hurt less, and I would have lost nothing but my purse. I wiped my mouth and rose from the table. "An you'll excuse me, I'd like to get back to me play."

"Oh, good!" shouted Walter. "What shall we play this time?"

I worked uninterrupted until the bells at St. Bennet rang compline. I was in the midst of a scene in which the poet and painter come to ask Timon for some of his gold when I heard a faint knock at my door. I did my best to ignore it, but a moment later the door swung open a crack and a soft voice said, "Widge?"

I turned to see Tetty peering through the opening. "I'm sorry," I said. "I forgot to tuck you in."

"It's all right, you needn't. I only wished to bid you good night." When I held out my arms, she scurried barefoot across the cold floor and, standing on tiptoe, gave me a quick hug. "I'm sorry about Judith." After considering a moment, she added, "But not very."

"Oh? Why is that?"

"I told you, you must wait for me. I'm growing as quickly as I can."

I groaned as I lifted her onto my knee and wrapped my blanket about her bare legs. "You certainly are. You must weigh nine or ten stone, at least."

She snickered. "I'm not growing *that* quickly." She examined the papers spread before me. "Is this your play?"

"Aye."

"What's it called?"

"It doesn't have a proper name yet."

"Then it's like you, isn't it?"

"I suppose it is."

"Will you read it to me when it's done?"

"I don't ken whether you'd fancy it. It's not like *Romeo and Juliet;* it hasn't a dell of romance in it."

"Oh. Well, that's all right," she said. "I expect you've had enough of romance for a while."

I was reluctant to stop writing, not caring to be alone with my thoughts. But when the words ceased to make sense, I put my pencil down and crawled into bed, resigned to a night of fretting and tossing about. To my surprise, I fell swiftly to sleep and awoke feeling more rested and cheerful than I had for some time.

Sam, on the other hand, seemed unusually subdued and thoughtful as we walked to the theatre. Even when I recounted our near-fatal adventure upon the ice the previous day, he had little to say. "By the by," I said, "why were you not at church services yesterday?"

"I was," Sam replied.

"Nay, you never! I looked all over for you."

"I didn't say I was at St. Saviour's, did I?"

"Where, then?"

He gave me a haughty look. "As Father Gerard would say, a gentleman's business is his own."

"Tell that to the deacons when they fine you for missing church."

"A pox on the deacons," he said.

At the Cross Keys, as we were climbing the stairs to the second-floor balcony, the door to Mr. Shakespeare's office flew open with a crash that rattled the windows. A hefty, hairy wight who rather resembled a bear burst forth and came thundering down the steps, causing them to shudder and us to fling ourselves to one side, lest we be trampled. Though I had been too busy saving my skin to get a good look at him, I knew that I had seen that bearlike build before, and those bulging eyes, which made him look as though he were choking on something.

"Who was that unmannerly swad?" Sam asked loudly, before the fellow was quite out of earshot. The man cast us a glowering look.

When he had exited the courtyard, I said, "Mr. Henslowe, from th' Admiral's Men."

"Oh. That explains why he was trying so hard to wreck the place."

"I believe 'a was angry about something—the script of *Sejanus,* unless I miss me guess."

Mr. Heminges and Mr. Shakespeare confirmed my suspicions. Henslowe had come to demand Mr. Jonson's play. It was his by right, he reminded them, as he had paid the playwright ten pounds for it, in advance. "Then *I* r-reminded *him,*" said Mr. Heminges, "that he had r-refused to perform it, on the gr-grounds that it was full of P-Papist propaganda. 'And so it was,' he replied. 'But I understand that Ben has succeeded in reforming it.'"

"Will 'a come back, do you wis?"

"I doubt it," said Mr. Shakespeare. "But if he does, he had best be armed."

I went at Mr. Jonson's script with a vengeance, determined to be done with it as quickly as possible, in case Mr. Henslowe did decide to return with reinforcements. I was well into the last act when the door to the hallway opened and Ned Shakespeare strolled in. I gave him a cursory nod, assuming he was seeking his brother—probably in order to ask for money.

"What's that you're copying?" he asked.

"*Sejanus.*"

He leaned over the desk. "It looks as though you're about done, eh?"

"Aye. I'll start on the sides tomorrow."

"Hmm. That's too bad."

"It is?"

"Of course." He slapped me playfully—and rather painfully—on the shoulder. "That means we'll have to perform it, doesn't it?"

"That's so. Perhaps I should write more slowly."

"Well, this will put it off a bit, at least: the sharers have called a meeting of the entire company upstairs."

"Oh? When is 't to be, then?"

"Now."

When Ned and I entered the long gallery, everyone else was there, with the exception of Sal Pavy. Mr. Heminges wasted no time in telling us the reason for the gathering. "The qu-queen has t-taken a turn for the worse. Ac-c-cording to her physician, she m-may have but a few more d-days. The Privy C-Council has asked that, out of r-respect for Her M-Majesty, all p-public performances be suspended for the t-time being."

"*Asked?*" said Ned. "Ordered, you mean."

"C-call it what you w-will; the r-result is the same."

"And what does 'for the time being' mean?"

"It means," said Mr. Shakespeare, "that we don't know. Her Majesty still has not named her successor, but I think we can assume it will be James. What *that* will mean, we can only guess."

"In the m-meantime," said Mr. Heminges, "we have d-decided to go on as always, re-rehearsing and l-learning lines, and so on, with one d-difference—you w-will all have your evenings free."

Though Sam was more subdued than usual, he was still Sam. "Speaking of free," he said, "will we still get our wages?"

Mr. Heminges smiled, a bit wanly. "F-for the time being."

When the meeting ended, I caught Mr. Armin and asked after Sal Pavy. "He's at home—his parents' home, I mean—

in bed. He's come down with a bad case of the coughs and sniffles—brought on by his swim in the river yesterday, no doubt."

"Oh, gis. Will 'a be all right, do you wis?"

"Most likely. He's being well cared for by his mother."

I shook my head. "I should never ha' let him cross on th' ice."

"Don't go feeling responsible now. After all, you were the one who saved him."

"Aye, I helped a bit. But 'a would not ha' needed saving had I not been so stupid as to accept his challenge i' the first place."

Mr. Armin shrugged. "You didn't wish to seem a coward; that's natural."

"Perhaps," I said. "And perhaps I would ha' shown more courage by refusing."

24

The prospect of the queen's death sobered us all. Though we went about our duties as usual, and even traded a bit of good-natured banter from time to time, we seemed less like comrades bound together by a common goal than like shipmates aboard a sinking vessel.

That evening, with several more hours than usual at my disposal, I brought my play to an end. I had performed in enough tragedies to know that the hero is expected to die. Mr. Shakespeare had jotted down three alternative fates for Timon: "Killed by thieves?" "Angry senators slay him?" and "Takes his own life?" As Timon was so disgusted with the world and everything in it, the last possibility seemed the most fitting. After giving him one last malediction to utter—"What is amiss, let plague and infection mend! Graves only be men's works, and death their gain!"—I had him hang himself from a tree—off the stage, of course. Though the audience would no doubt have perferred to actually see him dangling, I feared that the actor playing the part might object.

I had supposed that when I set down the final line, I would experience a great sense of satisfaction, of accomplishment. Instead I felt rather the way I did when awaking from a particularly vivid dream—a bit dismayed by the dreariness and the demands of the real world, and half longing to slip back into the world of my imagining.

I had another reason as well to regret having completed the script. Now I would have to show it to someone—at least if I hoped to make any money with it. Unless I wished to hire a hall and a troupe of players and present the play myself, I must submit it to one of the city's existing theatre companies. And the logical place to begin was with the Lord Chamberlain's Men. The notion should not have bothered me, I suppose. After all, I had grown accustomed to being criticized by them—for my acting, for my singing, for my dancing, for my scriming. But those were all external things, mere skills to be mastered. The play was personal, a product not of my muscles or my vocal cords but of my mind. If they found flaws in it, the flaws were mine; if they judged it foolish, I would be the fool.

Thoughts and events that seem plausible enough, or even profound, within the context of a dream often seem, upon waking, like so much nonsense. It was the same with my play. While I was caught up in composing it, the story had been sensible, the characters clear, the lines lyrical. But when I looked it over in the light of day, it seemed to have undergone a hideous transformation. The situations were now contrived, the characters shallow, the dialogue lame: "Now breathless wrong shall sit and pant in your great chairs of ease, and pursy insolence shall break his wind with fear, and horrid flight"? Had I really written such a hopeless line? I must have been not only dreaming, but delirious.

It was fortunate that I did not have a lighted candle at hand; I was so overcome with loathing for my creation that I would surely have sentenced it to the fiery death it deserved. Instead, I folded it haphazardly and crammed it into my wallet, to get it out of my sight. I must indeed have been dreaming or delirious to imagine that I, a paltry prentice player and offspring of an outlaw, might produce something remotely worth praising, or paying for.

As I was in no mood for conversation, I set out for the Cross Keys without waiting for Sam. The day was bright, almost balmy. Spring seemed to have remembered its cue at last. But I was in no mood for it, either. To my surprise, I found Ned Shakespeare, who ordinarily arrived half an hour later than everyone else, waiting outside the office. "What brings you here so early?" I asked.

"I wanted a word with you."

"Wi' me?" I dug out my key and turned it in the lock. "What about?"

He glanced this way and that, then pulled me abruptly inside the room. "Do you have the sides for *Sejanus* yet?"

Puzzled by his furtive behavior, I pulled my sleeve from his grasp. "Nay; as I told you, I'll get to them today."

"Oh, yes. Well, I was wondering whether you might copy out my part first."

"I suppose. But why?"

He looked uncomfortable. "I wouldn't want this to get out, but the truth is . . . I'm having difficulty remembering my lines."

"That's not exactly a secret."

"No, and I 'm sure you all think it's because I put off learning them. But it isn't." He thumped his forehead with his knuckles. "I just seem to have trouble getting them to stick in my head, no matter how many times I go over them. I thought perhaps if I got started on them before anyone else, it might help."

"All right. I can ha' your side for you afore the morning rehearsal."

"Excellent. Thank you. I'll let you get to work, then." He slipped out the door and pulled it softly shut behind him.

As I wrote out Ned's speeches and the cues that led into them, it struck me again how lifeless the lines were. I began to wonder whether I had been too critical of my own efforts. I took the crumpled script from my wallet, smoothed it out on Mr. Shakespeare's desk, and tried my best to examine it with an objective, unbiased eye. It was impossible, like trying to see my own face the way others saw it, or to hear my own voice as it sounded to someone else.

As a person may be aware that his nose is too long or his chin too short, I was aware that there were awkward spots in the play. But it seemed to me there were also some passages that Mr. Shakespeare himself would not have been ashamed to admit to—though he might not wish to boast about them, either.

So absorbed was I in studying the script that I did not hear the inner door of the office open. It wasn't until Mr. Heminges cleared his throat loudly that I noticed him standing over me. "G-God you good morning, Widge. Hard at w-work already, I see."

"Aye," I said, feeling a bit guilty for being occupied with my own script and not Mr. Jonson's.

"Well, I'll tr-try not to disturb you. I m-must go over the b-books and see how long we m-may hope to survive w-with no income." He sat at his desk and opened the ledger in which he kept track of the company's finances. "Oh, b-by the by, has Will t-told you that we m-may have hit upon a way of helping J-Julia?"

"Nay! Truly?"

"Mountjoy, his landlord, is a f-former Frenchman who does a g-good deal of business with c-companies in Paris. He c-can arrange for one of them to loan Julia the m-money she needs for her p-passage. A b-bill of exchange, I believe it's c-called."

"Gog's nowns! That's good news! You ken where she may be reached, then?"

He turned to me with an anxious frown. "N-no. I th-thought *you* did."

"I ha' th' address of her old lodgings, but she's no longer there, remember?"

"Sh-shrew me! I hadn't th-thought of that. W-was there an address on the l-letter her f-father showed us?"

"I didn't notice."

"N-nor did I. There m-must have been, though, otherwise C-Cogan would have had n-no notion where to send the m-money—pr-presuming he m-meant to send it at all, wh-which I doubt. D-do you know where he m-may be found?"

"Somewhere in Alsatia, I expect. I've been meaning to seek him out. I thought that . . . I thought that you and Mr. Shakespeare were not willing to help Julia, so I planned to raise the money meself."

He gave me a look that was half reproachful, half astonished. "D-did you truly imagine that we w-would leave her stranded over there?"

"I . . . I didn't ken."

"Well, you sh-should have," he said sternly. Then, in a gentler tone, he added, "And how, m-may I ask, did you propose to c-come up with three p-pounds?"

I hung my head, embarrassed. "By selling me play," I murmured.

"What p-play is that?"

I patted the script. "This one."

"M-may I see it?" He scanned the first several pages. "This is the script W-Will gave up on, is it not?"

"Aye. 'A said I might do wi' it as I wished."

"And so you c-completed it?"

"Aye."

"Th-that's quite an accomplishment. Does it have a n-name?"

"Not yet. I've been thinking, though, that it should ha' something to do wi' revenge or retaliation—*An Eye for an Eye,* or *Like for Like,* or perhaps *Measure for Measure.*"

"*M-Measure for Measure,* eh? That has a r-ring to it. T-tell me, to whom d-did you expect to sell this?"

I shrugged. "Whoever was interested."

"Have you sh-shown it to Will?"

"Nay. I was afeared 'a would think it . . . well, putrid. Besides, I've been—" I broke off.

"You've b-been angry with him," Mr. Heminges finished.

"Aye."

"For s-sending Judith home, I expect."

"Aye."

"Well, it is a p-pity it had to c-come to that, but she br-brought it upon herself."

"I ken that. But 'a might ha' been kinder to her while she was here. 'A might ha' spent more time wi' her."

"That's so." Mr. Heminges leaned toward me and said softly, "B-but just between the t-two of us, I believe he was af-f-fraid to."

"Afeared? Why?"

"He t-told me that he never kn-knows what to say to her."

I laughed. "Sorry. It's just that it's hard to imagine the likes of Mr. Shakespeare being at a loss for words. I thought it was only me."

"N-no, I suspect that p-particular problem is a universal one. In f-fact, I'm convinced that m-men and women actually speak t-two separate languages, in which the w-words happen to s-sound alike but have t-totally different meanings."

"I never had any trouble talking to Julia."

"Ah, but you see, that was b-because she was pr-pretending to be a boy." He glanced at the script in his hand. "If you don't m-mind, I'll r-read through this, and then p-pass it on to the other sh-sharers."

"Including Mr. Shakespeare?" I asked apprehensively.

"Of c-course. He w-won't scoff at it, if that's what w-worrics you. R-remember, he was once a n-novice playwright himself." Mr. Heminges leaned toward me confidentially again. "Well, you've d-done *Two Gentlemen,* so you kn-know well enough that his w-words are not always g-golden, and his structure s-sometimes creaks a bit, eh?"

I sighed. "Aye, all right, show it to him, then."

"G-good lad. And d-don't worry about Julia, either. We'll tr-track her father down somehow."

Despite Mr. Heminges's assurances, I could not help fretting about Julia's fate. In her letter, she had said that her funds were fading fast; by now she might well be wandering the streets of Paris, starving. Nor could I help wondering how my first faltering efforts at playwriting would be received by men who had been performing plays half their lives.

With these matters occupying my mind, I had little to spare for Mr. Jonson's script. I did manage to copy all of Ned Shakespeare's lines before rehearsal, as I had promised, but not much else. As we assembled downstairs for dinner, I spotted my script changing hands, from Mr. Armin's to Mr. Shakespeare's. I cornered Mr. Heminges and asked anxiously, "Has Mr. Armin read it, do you wis?"

"Ap-p-parently so," said Mr. Heminges.

"And you? You've read it as well?"

He smiled at my expectant, insistent manner. "I have."

"Well?" I prompted him. "What did you think?"

"I th-think that you show a g-good deal of promise. We'll t-talk about it this evening, after the others have had a ch-chance to look at it, eh?"

I nodded without enthusiasm. I didn't like the sound of that word, *promise*. It was the very term that had been applied to me by various members of the company, back when I first began acting with them in insignificant roles. Now that I was more experienced, I realized that it had been a euphemism, a kind way of saying that I was hopelessly incompetent, but might have a faint hope of someday becoming adequate.

Though I had never considered myself a glutton for punishment, I went begging for it that afternoon at scriming practice by asking Mr. Armin his opinion of my play. He clapped a hand on my shoulder, as he sometimes did after I had shown unusual skill with the sword. "Very promising," he said.

As I had given such short shrift to *Sejanus* that morning, I did my penance by returning to the office to copy another side or two before I headed home. The door that opened into the office from the hallway was locked. I drew my purse from within my doublet and dug into it. My fingers encountered nothing but the few coins—mostly pennies and farthings—that made up my enire fortune.

Puzzled, I turned the purse upside down, shook its contents into my hand, and examined them incredulously. Perhaps someone had replaced my purse with one of those trick purses used by sleight-of-hand artists, for the key had unaccountably disappeared. I searched my wallet and found only my table-book, my plumbago pencil, and a petrified sweetmeat that Mr. Pope's boys had somehow missed.

I extended the search to my brain. When had I last seen the

key? Earlier that morning, I was sure, when I let myself and Ned in through the outer door. Ned had distracted me by asking for his side; perhaps without thinking I had tossed the key onto the desk. Or had I left it in the lock? Surely I had not been that much of a harecop.

Well, there was but one way to find out. I descended to the dark parlor, meaning to go into the courtyard and up the outside steps to the balcony. As I headed for the door, I heard my name called. I turned to see four of the company's sharers sharing a booth and a round of ale.

Mr. Armin beckoned to me. "We were wondering what had become of you."

"I was about to copy some more of *Sejanus*." I carefully avoided any mention of the missing key.

"Well, come and sit with us a moment, first." While I pulled a chair up to the end of the table, Mr. Armin summoned the tapster and ordered an ale for me.

"We've j-just been discussing *M-Measure for Measure*," said Mr. Heminges.

I stared at him, momentarily baffled. "What's that, then?"

"Your play?"

"Oh? Oh, aye! I've considered so many titles, I'd forgotten that one."

"It's a good title," said Mr. Phillips.

"Yes," said Mr. Shakespeare. "I wish I'd thought of it."

"Well, you may ha' 't, an you like. I can easily call mine something else. I've no shortage of titles."

"Thank you," he said.

"It's naught." I glanced nervously about at the four of them in turn. "So . . . is that all you liked about it, then? The title?"

"No, no," said Mr. Shakespeare. "In fact, it has quite a number of good qualities."

I waited for him to go on, to cite some of its good qualities. When he did not, I swallowed hard and said, "But it's not good enough, is it?"

Mr. Shakespeare cast a beseeching glance at Mr. Heminges, as though asking for help from a more tactful quarter. "N-not as it stands," said Mr. Heminges gently. "P-perhaps if you were to w-work on it a b-bit more, and then sh-show it to us again."

Unaccountably, I found myself fighting back tears. I felt nearly as forlorn as I had when Judith left, or when I learned that my father had died. Though none of the sharers had said, or even suggested, that my work was worthless, it was what I heard—or at least what that part of me that was governed by emotion heard. Yet, at the same time, some more reasonable part acknowledged that they were right, of course, that I could not possibly expect to turn out a well-made play on the first try, any more than a scrimer could expect to defeat the first opponent he ever faced. It was just that I had worked so hard on it, and hoped for so much from it.

"You mustn't be discouraged, Widge," said Mr. Shakespeare. "We're all agreed, I think, that the play shows—"

"Aye, I ken. It shows *promise.*"

"I was about to say that it shows considerable skill, and a good ear for dialogue. There were several speeches in there that I would have sworn I wrote myself."

"You d-did," Mr. Heminges reminded him.

Mr. Shakespeare laughed. "I meant in the parts that Widge composed." He turned to me. "You know, if you intend to be a playwright, you may wish to take a *nom de plume,* one that will look a bit more distinguished on a playbill."

"And with your talent for titles," said Mr. Phillips, "you should have no trouble coining a good name for yourself."

It struck me, then, that none of them knew yet about Jamie Redshaw. I had not meant to keep it from them, only from Judith, and now that she was gone, what did it matter? "Actually," I said, "I do ha' a name—or the nether end of one, at least."

Half my audience seemed astonished by my news; the other half were not. Mr. Phillips and Mr. Armin confessed that they had never really believed Jamie Redshaw's story. Mr. Shakespeare and Mr. Heminges said that though they had not completely trusted the man, they had never doubted that he was my father.

"Will you take his name, then?" asked Mr. Armin.

I stared thoughtfully into my pot of ale. "I've not made up me mind."

"Redshaw never indicated what your Christian name might be?" said Mr. Phillips.

"Nay. 'A was not around when I was born, and me mother didn't live long enough to name me. I do recall Mistress MacGregor saying once that the priest who baptized me gave me his own name, for want of any other. No one has ever called me by it, though."

"Do you know what it was?"

"William, I believe."

"That's an excellent name," said Mr. Shakespeare.

Mr. Heminges nodded approvingly. "W-William Redshaw. That would not l-look amiss on a playbill."

I gave a skeptical sniff. "Assuming I ever manage to write a decent play."

"Oh, you w-will." He turned to Mr. Shakespeare. "Will he n-not, Will?"

Mr. Shakespeare shrugged and gave me a rather sly smile. "If he has the will, he will."

I refused to be coaxed out of my sour mood by their banter. "Well, i' the meanwhile, will you gi' me back the putrid one?"

Though I wanted nothing less than to look at another play just then, I forced myself to return to the office, this time by way of the outside stairs. Even if I did not work on *Sejanus*, I must at least determine what I had done with the key. The sky was nearly dark now, and even before I reached the second-floor balcony, I noticed a faint glow of light issuing from the small window of the office.

Someone must be working within. But who? All the sharers had either gone home or were gathered in the dark parlor. Curious and a little alarmed, I crept along the balcony, crouched down next to the window, and peered inside.

A single lighted candle sat atop Mr. Shakespeare's desk. Bent over it, one large hand cupped about the flame as though to keep its light contained, was a hulking figure that I did not recognize at once. Only when the man's face moved from the shadows and into the candle's light, revealing thick, unruly eyebrows set above bulging eyes, did I realize who the intruder was—Henslowe, from the Admiral's Men. It was easy enough to guess why he was here; he wanted the script of *Sejanus*.

If I had had a dell of sense, I would have run and fetched the sharers. What prevented me was the thought that had I not left the key in the lock, the man could not have gotten into the room. If I handled this myself, perhaps no one need know of my blunder.

I was not foolish enough to try to subdue Henslowe; he was roughly twice my size. I would do better to trust my wits. I took a deep breath, stood, and flung open the door. Henslowe spun about with a quickness surprising in such a bulky wight. In one hand he clutched the script of *Sejanus*. "I wouldn't take that an I were you," I said. Despite my efforts to keep my voice calm and confident, it cracked a little.

Henslowe looked me up and down, as though assessing how much of a threat I might pose. He seemed to conclude that it was very little. "And why is that?"

"Because. That's th' old script, the one wi' all the Papist propaganda. The new version is locked in a trunk i' the property room."

Scowling, he glanced at the script, then back at me. "No. It can't be." But it was clear that if my lie had not convinced him, it had at least given him pause. With a look that warned me to keep my distance, he turned and held the script to the light. "You're lying. This is not in Jonson's hand; someone has copied it. Who would bother to copy out a script they couldn't use?" He stuffed the papers into his wallet and headed for the door.

I blocked his way with my body. "I won't let you—" I managed to say before his fist knocked all the breath out of me. I doubled over and fell to my knees. Henslowe shoved me out of the doorway and was gone.

Gasping, I struggled to my feet and stumbled after him. When I reached the top of the stairs, I halted, taken aback by the scene below me. Henslowe lay sprawled upon the steps, with the point of Mr. Armin's rapier at his throat. Mr. Shakespeare was bent over Henslowe, digging through the man's wallet.

Mr. Armin glanced up at me. "We've caught the culprit. Are you all right?"

"Aye," I groaned. "More or less." I slowly descended the stairs, holding the railing with one hand and my aching gut with the other. "Shall I fetch a constable?"

"No," said Mr. Shakespeare. "We may as well let him go; we have what we want." In one hand he brandished the purloined pages; in the other, the key to the office.

Mr. Armin lowered his blade and Henslowe got to his feet, straightening his doublet. "It's I who should call the constables," he growled. "I was only taking what already belonged to me."

"Well, you may as well bring on the catchpolls," said Mr. Armin. "Heaven knows you've tried everything else to shut us down."

To my surprise, there was very little real rancor in either man's voice. In truth, they sounded less like enemies than like members of opposing teams engaged in some rough-and-tumble sport, a sort of grown-up version of King of the Hill that would decide once and for all which was the premier theatre company in London.

"I've no idea what you mean," replied Henslowe.

"Why, Henslowe," said Mr. Armin. "I do believe you've missed your calling. You feign innocence and indignation so well, you should have been a player."

"And you two should have been thieves." Henslowe scowled at his empty wallet, then at the bundle of pages in Mr. Shakespeare's hand. "You have a paper there that's not part of the script. I'll have it back."

Mr. Shakespeare held up a sheet that had been folded several times. "Is this what you mean?"

"Yes." Henslowe reached for it.

Mr. Shakespeare drew it back. "No, I believe we'll keep this for now. If you want it so badly, there must be some reason."

Henslowe glared at him a moment, then shrugged. "Well, it doesn't matter; you won't be able to read it, anyway." He turned to me. "How can you bear to be part of this band of thieves?"

"At least they don't go about walloping folk i' the gut," I said.

Henslowe gave a short laugh. "I like your spirit, lad. If you ever decide you'd prefer to work for a reputable company, come and see me." Pushing roughly past the sharers, he stalked off into the night.

"I tried me best to stop him," I said.

"Well, it looks as though you stopped his fist, at least," said Mr. Armin. "Come, let's lock up and go home. You've done enough work for one day."

As we climbed the stairs, Mr. Shakespeare said, "What I wonder is, how did Henslowe come by this key?"

"Um . . . I can answer that," I said reluctantly. "I left it i' the lock this morning, I wis."

Though Mr. Shakespeare did not exactly look happy, he did not chide me. "Well, there's no harm done, I suppose, except perhaps to your stomach—assuming that the play is all here, that is." He held the crumpled pages up to the light and examined them.

I peered over his shoulder. "That looks like all of it."

He unfolded the sheet that Henslowe had said was not a part of the script. "Well, he was right. I can't begin to read this." Mr. Shakespeare handed the paper to me. It was smaller than the script pages, and contained neither Mr. Jonson's handwriting nor mine, but several rows of curious symbols that might have been some foreign alphabet:

"It's some of your scribble hand, is it not?" said Mr. Armin.

I shook my head emphatically. "Nay. A few of the characters are similar to ones I use, and a couple of them look like numerals, but most I've never set eyes on afore. It's obviously a message of some sort, though."

"Obviously. The question is, from whom?"

Mr. Shakespeare was looking at me in an odd fashion, not unlike the way Henslowe had looked when I told him he had the wrong script. He took the paper from me, refolded it, and tucked it into his wallet. "I have no doubt," he said, "that it's from our spy."

Mr. Armin looked thoughtful. "You know, perhaps we should give Henslowe a dose of his own poison—hire someone in *his* company to be *our* informant."

"Do you have anyone in mind?" asked Mr. Shakespeare.

"No," admitted Mr. Armin. "I'm sure Henslowe has convinced them all that we're Satan's minions." He held up a hand. "Ah, I have it! One of us will cleverly disguise himself and convince the Admiral's Men to hire him!"

Mr. Shakespeare laughed. "That's the worst idea I ever heard."

"Oh, I don't know," said Mr. Armin. "It always seems to work in your plays."

Neither of the men had paid Mr. Pope a visit for some time, and they decided to make up for it now. In fact, as Mr. Armin revealed, that was the very reason they happened to meet Henslowe on the stairs—they had been on their way to fetch me and accompany me home.

Mr. Pope greeted them with such enthusiasm that I feared his health might suffer. "This calls for a round of brandy!"

"I'll fetch it," I said, not wishing him to overtax himself.

"Thank you, Widge."

Mr. Armin held up an admonishing hand. "Tut, tut, Thomas. You must address the boy properly. From now on it's to be William Redshaw, Esquire."

Mr. Pope gave me a baffled look. "Redshaw?"

"Aye. 'A was me father after all, it seems."

"How long have you known?"

"A few days, is all."

"Why did you not tell me sooner?"

"I—I don't ken. I suppose I was waiting for the right moment."

"I'm sorry, Widge," said Mr. Armin. "I assumed he knew."

"You called me Widge," I said.

"I'm sorry. William, then."

"Nay. I'll not be William, either. That was no more a real name than Widge was, only a sort of expedient. If I'm to have another name, I'll choose it meself." I turned and left the library. I had nearly forgotten about La Voisin's predictions, but one of them came back to me now: *You will make a name for yourself.*

When I returned with the brandy, the three sharers were huddled together like conspirators, talking in low tones. "Thank you, Wi—" Mr. Pope broke off. "Well, whoever you may be. Why don't you find Goody Willingson and ask her for something to eat? The three of us have business matters to discuss."

The manner in which he dismissed me seemed brusque and impersonal, not like Mr. Pope at all. I supposed that he was cross with me, for not telling him about Jamie Redshaw. I felt almost as though I had been cast out, like Timon. But instead of retreating to the woods, I went only as far as the kitchen, where, as I had no roots at hand, I cut a slice of bread and buttered it, then sat nibbling halfheartedly at it while I mulled over what my name should be.

• • •

I could not work on the sides for *Sejanus* the next morning; Mr. Shakespeare had kept both the script and the key to his office, as though he no longer trusted me with them. Instead, I helped Sam in the property room. As there had been no performance the night before, there was little for us to do. Nevertheless, in the time-honored tradition of prentices everywhere, we managed to make it look as though we were hard at work.

"It's a pity Sal Pavy isn't here," said Sam. "He's so good at pretending to be busy. He could give us a few pointers."

"Ha' you looked in on him?"

Sam reacted as though I'd asked whether he had looked in on the inmates of Bedlam, the asylum for the insane. "Don't you know that the grippe may be passed on, like the plague?"

"That may be. But it's not quite as likely to kill you."

"I prefer not to take the chance. Besides, he'd only tell us how they never had the grippe at Blackfriars."

The prentices and hired men gathered for rehearsal, just as though we had every expectation of performing again soon. We were attempting to revive Mr. Shakespeare's *Much Ado About Nothing,* which had lain buried in the book-keeper's trunk for at least a year. It was not responding.

As we were making much ado ourselves about who should read Hero's part in Sal Pavy's absence, Mr. Shakespeare and Mr. Armin appeared and asked to speak to me privately. "Can't it wait?" asked Mr. Lowin, who was conducting the rehearsal.

"I'm afraid not," said Mr. Armin.

They took me aside, scarcely out of earshot of the other players. Mr. Shakespeare drew two sheets of paper from his wallet and held them up, side by side. "This is the coded message we took from Henslowe. This is a page from *All's Well,* written in your charactery. We've compared them, and find a number of similarities—too many, in our opinion, to be the result of coincidence."

I stared at him incredulously. "What are you saying? That *I* wrote this? That I'm in league wi' Henslowe?"

"Soft," said Mr. Armin, "unless you wish the others to hear."

"Let them! I've nothing to hide!"

"We believe you do. How could Henslowe have gotten the key, unless you gave it to him?"

"It's as I told you—I left it i' the lock!"

"Deliberately, perhaps."

"Nay! What would I ha' to gain from Henslowe stealing the script?"

"Money?" suggested Mr. Shakespeare.

"Money?" I fairly shouted. "For what?"

"For Julia, perhaps. You said yourself that you didn't think we would help her."

The rest of the company had given up any pretense of minding their own business and were gaping at the scene unfolding before them, which must have been as compelling as any play ever acted. Tears had sprung to my eyes, and I made no effort to stay them. "I would never do such a thing, so help me God and halidom!" My voice broke like thin ice.

"Not even to save Julia?" said Mr. Shakespeare.

I could not deny that the idea had occurred to me. Though I had not acted upon it, I could hardly blame them for believing that I had, especially in view of my past record as a thief and a liar—and, of course, the even worse record of my father. Still, I was innocent, and I must not let myself appear otherwise. With all the dignity I could muster, I looked Mr. Shakespeare in the eye and said, "An you and the other sharers truly believe that I would betray you, then I can no longer consider meself a part of this company."

"Under the circumstances," said Mr. Shakespeare, "I think that would be best. But you needn't give up acting altogether; remember, Henslowe has promised to take you in."

So it was that the thing I had feared the most—more than the death of the queen, more than the plague itself—had come to pass.

We prentices had been taught always to exit the stage as swiftly as possible so as not to draw the audience's attention away from the next scene. Accordingly, I made my exit from the Cross Keys a quick one, not wishing to be a part of the scene that I knew would follow. I could not bear to face my fellow players and their questions, their disbelief, their doubts, perhaps their derision. I should have known that no matter how nimble I was, I could not escape Sam.

Just as I left the courtyard I heard him calling behind me, "Widge! Wait!" Though I hurried on, heedless, this did not discourage him in the least. He came trotting up alongside me to ask breathlessly, "Where are you going?"

"To see whether the Admiral's Men ha' room for another prentice."

"You can't!"

"What do you suggest, then? I'm too old for the Chapel Children, and too young to be a hired man wi' one of the small companies."

"Come back to the Cross Keys. The sharers will change their minds. The rest of us will stand up for you. No one believes that you're a traitor. I *know* you're not."

Another of La Voisin's forgotten predictions came bobbing to the surface of my mind. *You will turn traitor,* she had told Sam. "What makes you so certain?"

"Because. I know you."

"So do the sharers. They ken that I tried to steal a script from them once before. They also ken that me father was a thief—and, as they say, the seedling bears the same fruit as the tree."

"But perhaps they were just uncertain; perhaps they were testing you, making accusations to see whether you would confess."

"The way the pursuivants do wi' the Jesuit priests, you mean? An the sharers would stoop to that, I don't care to be part of their company."

Sam scowled. "All right, then. If you're set on leaving, I'm going, too. Without you there to hold me back, I'm certain to strangle Sal Pavy within a week."

"Nay, you won't. Wi'out me there, you two will ha' to become friends. Besides, Henslowe would never hire you. 'A would suspect you of being a spy for the Chamberlain's Men."

"And what makes you think he won't suspect you?"

"Why would 'a, when the Chamberlain's Men ha' given me the chuck?"

"How will he know that?"

"The real spy will tell him."

"If you can get Henslowe to trust you, perhaps he'll reveal who it is."

"Oh, aye. And perhaps 'a will gi' all of Mr. Alleyn's roles to me as well."

This notion was so ludicrous that it drew a halfhearted laugh from Sam. Next to our own Mr. Burbage, Edward Alleyn was the most celebrated player in London. We walked on in silence for a while. Finally Sam said, "How will you break this to Mr. Pope?"

I groaned. "Oh, gis. I dare not tell him at all. It would upset him too much. You're not to say a word about it, either. Promise me."

"All right. But he's sure to find out sooner or later."

"Let it be later, then."

Though Sam seemed to have given up on bringing me back, he went on walking with me, all the way across the city and through the wall to the parish of St. Giles Cripplegate, where Henslowe's theatre lay.

Unlike the Globe, which was eight-sided, the Fortune playhouse had been built in the shape of a square. Each side was eighty or ninety feet in length. On the side that faced Golding Street was an elaborate carving of Dame Fortune, wearing a cloth over her eyes to show that she was blind. She held one hand poised next to a wheel, as though about to give it a spin.

Four small figures rode upon the wheel, like prentices riding the roundabout at Bartholomew Fair, except that not all these fellows looked happy with their lot. The one who sat at the top of the wheel was clearly pleased with himself, and the one who appeared to be on his way up looked hopeful. But the upside-down face of the man on his way down was a mask of dread and dismay—and small wonder, for the figure below him, at the lowest spot on the wheel, was roasting over carved wooden flames. His mouth was wide open in a soundless scream.

"You see that wight at the bottom?" I said. "I ken how 'a feels."

Adjacent to the playhouse was a tavern, also owned by Henslowe and also called the Fortune, where the Lord Admiral's Men played during the coldest months. Now that the weather was becoming more springlike with each day that passed, their company and ours would soon be performing upon our outdoor stages—provided, of course, that we were permitted to perform at all. Once we were deprived of the queen's influence, we might all find ourselves cast out and falling to the foot of Fortune's wheel.

Sam surveyed the alehouse, then the playhouse. "Which Fortune will you choose?"

"Neither," I said. "But as I've come this far, I may as well go inside." Sam turned slowly to face me, a look of astonishment, or perhaps revelation, upon his face.

"What is it?" I asked.

"You will come into a fortune," he said.

"What?"

"Madame La Voisin's prediction: You will come into a *fortune*." He gestured at the buildings before us.

I made a scoffing sound. "She said *a* fortune, not *the* Fortune."

"Well, there's more than one, isn't there?"

"Oh, gis," I said. Could she truly have been referring to a tavern or a theatre, and not to a treasure, as I had imagined? Of course she could. She had also predicted that I would make a name for myself, and I had foolishly supposed she was talking about my reputation, when in fact she was using the phrase in a very literal sense.

"You're certain I can't come with you?" said Sam.

"I'm certain."

He looked down at his feet. "Well, then, I suppose I should get back to the Cross Keys. No doubt I'll have to pay a fine to Mr. Armin as it is."

"Aye, go on. You needn't worry about me."

Sam shook his head. "I don't see how you can just accept all this so calmly."

"What choice do I ha' ? It's Fate." I held out a hand and he grasped it. "We will still see each other, in church and elsewhere."

"Well," he said, "perhaps not in church."

"What do you mean?"

He seemed about to reply, then apparently thought better of it. "Nothing." He raised a hand in farewell and started off down Golding Lane. But he was not the sort to leave without an exit line, so I waited for it. Sure enough, he turned back and called to me, "Break a limb—preferably one of Henslowe's."

I tried the dark parlor of the Fortune tavern first, but saw no one there I recognized. Aside from my painful introduction to Henslowe the night before, I had not met any of the Admiral's Men in person, but I had seen them all act more than once. The Lord Chamberlain's Men sometimes sent us prentices here to spy upon the performances of their rivals, particularly when the play they were doing was one of ours, or purported to be. Several of Mr. Shakespeare's works had been published in the form of playbooks, and any company was free to perform these. But Henslowe had also been known to present his own slipshod versions of our more popular plays, or to falsely advertise Mr. Shakespeare as the author of some script composed by one of Henslowe's own hacks.

Unless you counted *Sejanus,* our sharers did not steal Henslowe's plays. That would have been like stealing jewelry made of paste or glass when you already owned genuine diamonds and pearls. They were not above copying a good bit of stage business, though, or borrowing an idea and improving upon it. Some said that the story of *Hamlet* was based upon a far inferior script that the Admiral's Men had presented many years before.

According to the tapster, the company had just finished moving all their properties and costumes from the tavern to the playhouse. I went next door and, finding the main entrance to the theatre open, stepped inside. The interior looked much like the Globe's, with three covered galleries for those playgoers who could afford them, and an open yard for those who could not.

Their stage was nearly identical to ours—perhaps forty feet square and three feet off the ground. At the moment it was occupied by only one actor, who was performing an odd sort of jig, skipping sideways across the boards, then forward, then back. But it was not one of their clowns rehearsing his dance steps; it was none other than the famous Edward Alleyn, a tall, broad-shouldered wight with rugged features framed by a curly black beard.

When he spotted me, he broke off his curious dance in midstep and came forward to the brink of the stage. "I was testing the boards," he explained a bit sheepishly, "to see whether any are rotten. So far the only thing I've discovered that's rotten is my dancing."

Despite my gloomy mood, I had to laugh. "I must admit, your acting is considerably better."

"You've seen me upon the stage, then—other than just now, I mean?" Mr. Alleyn sat on the edge of the platform; his long limbs almost reached the ground.

"Aye. Several times. You're nearly as good as Mr. Burbage." I had meant it to be a compliment, but it sounded more as though I were calling him second-rate. "That is—"

"No, no, don't apologize. I value an honest opinion. So, I take it you've seen the Chamberlain's Men perform as well?"

"I'm a—I *was* a prentice wi' them . . . until today."

"What happened today?"

"They gave me the chuck."

"Oh. I'm sorry." There was genuine sympathy in his voice. Clearly he understood what a dismal fate it was for a player to lose his position. After years of hearing our company speak badly of the Admiral's Men, I had expected to find them a rather loathsome lot. But Mr. Alleyn seemed quite amiable. In that respect, at least, he had the advantage of Mr. Burbage, who was aloof and conceited.

"They suspected me of being a spy for you and Mr. Henslowe," I said.

"Really? You're not, are you?"

"Nay!"

"Sorry. Philip doesn't keep me very well informed about his various schemes. I knew he was getting inside information from the Globe, but I had no idea who his source was. So, now that your old company has—what was it? Given you the chuck?—you've come to see whether we'll take you on, is that it?"

"Aye."

"Can you act?"

"Ha' you seen any of our—*their* plays?"

"Recently? Only *Hamlet*."

"I played Ophelia i' that."

"That was *you?* Well, that answers my question; you can act, all right." He held out a hand to me. "Jump up here, and we'll go talk to Philip about you." As we headed for the rooms behind the stage, he said, "You haven't told me your name."

Out of old habit, I nearly said, "Widge," but I stopped myself. I had made up my mind to choose a new name, and what better time could there be than now, when I was entering upon a new stage, quite literally, of my career?

I had never really considered taking Jamie Redshaw's family name, for I didn't care to be identified with him. Yet there was no escaping the fact that he was my father. Though he himself had done his best to deny it, in the last moments of his life he had acknowledged it and made certain that I would know. It was his attempt, I supposed, to ensure that someone in this world would remember him when he was gone. Though I did not feel that I owed him much, I could at least see that some small part of him survived, even if no one realized it but me.

"James," I said. "It's James."

The area behind the stage was very like that at the Globe, too—so much so that I would not have been surprised had Sam or Mr. Armin emerged from the tiring-room or the property room and greeted me. The Fortune was a good deal newer than our theatre, though, and less worn and weathered. I felt almost as though I had been transported back in time, to the Globe as it was when I first joined the company—before Julia left, before Sander died, before I knew Judith or Jamie Redshaw, before I was so burdened by ambitions and responsibilities, when I was still just Widge.

The sudden sense of loss that swept over me was so powerful that it staggered me, like an attack of vertigo, and I had to stop and steady myself. "Is anything wrong?" asked Mr. Alleyn.

"Nay," I murmured. "Just gi' me a moment."

"You're feeling a bit homesick for your old company, I expect."

I nodded. "Aye."

"Perhaps they'd take you back if Philip were to go to them and plead your case, tell them that you're not his informant."

"They'd never believe him. They'd only think 'a was trying to get me back i' their good graces so I could resume me spying."

He placed a hand on my shoulder, much the way Mr. Heminges was accustomed to do, or Mr. Pope. I wished it had been them. "Well, I think you'll find our company as cordial as the Chamberlain's Men, once you get to know us."

"I've not been accepted into it yet."

"You will be, though, if I have my way." He smiled a bit smugly. "And I usually do."

We found Henslowe in his office, writing in a bound journal. When he saw me, his bulging eyes fairly started out of his head. "Well, well! When I invited you to come and see me, I never imagined it would be so soon. How's your belly?" Before I could reply, he addressed Mr. Alleyn. "The lad tried valiantly to keep me from snatching *Sejanus,* and I was forced to resort to violence."

"You have the script, then?" asked Mr. Alleyn.

Henslowe scowled. "Regrettably, no. I ran into Armin and Shakespeare, who took it from me at the point of a sword, like the pirates that they are." He glanced at me. "I see you're not bothering to defend them. Have you some grudge against them, too?"

"Aye. They've cast me out."

"Why, the ungrateful wretches! After you practically risked your life trying to save their precious play?"

"They think I'm i' league wi' you—that I told you where to find the script, and gave you the key."

Henslowe shook his head. "They're even bigger fools than I

thought. You're better off without them. I suppose you've come to ask me for a position."

"You did offer me one."

"Now, I didn't promise anything. I merely said to come and see me. In any case, I didn't expect you to take me up on it right away. We've been shut down, the same as every other company, and without money coming in, we can barely meet the expenses we already have."

Mr. Alleyn laughed. "Oh, don't go playing the pauper, Philip. With all your various enterprises, you have more money than you can count. The boy's a fine actor; I've seen him. He'd be an asset to the company."

"That may be. But we don't need another actor, no matter how good he is, if they won't let him act."

"The theatres will open again eventually."

"Then let him come back eventually."

"And what do you expect him to do in the meanwhile? Starve?"

For all his skill as a player, Mr. Alleyn was playing this scene all wrong. I knew that Henslowe cared no more about whether or not I starved than he did about whether or not I could act. He was a man of business and was likely to be swayed only by the promise of a profit.

Luckily I had kept a trump card in reserve that I might play if the game was not going my way. "Oh, I don't expect I'll starve," I said calmly. "I have more to offer to a company than just me acting ability."

"Oh?" said Henslowe. "And what might that be?"

"Two things, actually. One is me skill at swift writing." I opened my wallet, drew out a sheaf of papers, and laid it on the desk before him. "This is the other."

"A script?" He picked up the first page, read it over rapidly, and gave me an incredulous look. "Unless I miss my guess, this is Shakespeare's work."

I did not reply, only sat there with what I hoped was a mysterious smile on my face.

Henslowe handed the page to Mr. Alleyn, who, after perusing it but a moment, said, "If it's not his, then it's a very good imitation. Where did you get this?"

"Mr. Shakespeare gave it to me." Even though this was perfectly true, I had a notion that it would not sound that way to Henslowe.

I was right. He smiled skeptically. "*Gave* it to you, eh?"

"Aye. 'A said I might do wi' it as I wished."

At this, Henslowe laughed outright. "Did he, indeed?" He shook his head. "I suspect that you're a better thief than you are a player, lad. I don't believe your story for a moment." He examined several more pages of the script. "So, I'm supposed to want this enough to hire you as a prentice, is that it?"

"Nay. You're supposed to want it enough to hire me *and* to pay me eight pounds for the script."

Henslowe's bulging eyes went wide. "Eight pounds? Are you mad? What's to prevent me from simply tossing you out on your ear and keeping the script?"

"Well, for one thing, you wouldn't be able to read it."

"And why is that?"

"See for yourself."

He shuffled through the pages until he came upon the scenes that I had written in charactery. "What's this?"

"The swift writing I mentioned."

"You transcribed this for Shakespeare, then?" He scowled at the strings of symbols. "You know, this looks very much like the . . . " He trailed off.

"Like the code you and your spy use to communicate," I finished.

"Yes. But it's not, is it?"

"Nay."

Henslowe leaned back in his chair and regarded me with a mixture of amusement and respect. "You're a clever lad. I believe you're right, Edward. He would be an asset to the company." He drummed his fingers together thoughtfully. "I will pay you," he said finally, "six pounds for the play—three pounds now and three more when you've put it into a form we can read."

"And you'll take me on as a prentice?"

"Yes."

"Done," I said. And, like two merchants concluding a business transaction, we shook hands on it.

My first task as a member of the Admiral's Men was agreeable enough: to adjourn to the tavern for dinner. I'd had little to eat that morning and was growing light-headed from hunger, yet I was not at all eager to join the others. In fact, I felt as apprehensive as I did just before a performance.

Though playgoers might be raucous and hard to please, seldom were they downright hostile, as these wights were sure to be, considering I had come to them from the company that was their fiercest rival. Still, I could not refuse to appear before them, any more than I could refuse to make my entrance in a play.

To my surprise they welcomed me, as members of a congregation might welcome into their church a convert from some other, less enlightened faith. A few of the faces around the table regarded me with disapproval or suspicion, but those sorts were to be found everywhere, even within the Chamberlain's Men. For the most part they were, as Mr. Alleyn had promised, a cordial and companionable lot—except when the conversation turned to the Chamberlain's Men.

The Admiral's Men held as low an opinion of my old company as the Chamberlain's Men did of them. Their ill will was founded upon more than mere jealousy, though. They voiced several complaints that, even had I been in a position to defend my comrades, I would have been hard-pressed to answer satisfactorily.

They seemed to resent most the fact that Mr. Shakespeare was so closefisted with his plays. Most playwrights, they said, sold their works to a printer after a dozen or so performances so that other companies might have a chance at them. Only a handful of Mr. Shakespeare's plays were in print, and those were pirated versions, scribbled down during a peformance, or recited, usually inaccurately, by some cast member in exchange for a few shillings.

They were also out of square over their rivals' refusal to raise the price of admission. Mr. Henslowe was more than just out of square; he was fairly furious. "The amount we pay for costumes has nearly doubled in the past several years, as has the amount we pay for properties and scripts, and for hired men and musicians, and for meals, and for coal, and for renting rooms. How can we hope to survive, let alone make a profit, if we do not increase our prices as well?"

• • •

After dinner, he and Mr. Alleyn escorted me back to the office, where I was to begin writing out in a normal hand the indecipherable passages of my script. "If I were you," Mr. Alleyn said to me in a stage whisper, "I would not set down a word of it until I'd seen the color of his money."

Mr. Henslowe shook a huge fist at him. "I've given the boy my word; that should be good enough."

"Not quite as good as gold, however," I said.

The big man cast me a dark look, but he also cast three sovereigns upon the table, which I promptly put into my purse. "It's just as I said," he growled. "I have to pay twice as much for scripts as they're worth. What's this one called, by the by?"

I had been giving so much thought to my own name lately that I had neglected to christen the play. "*Timon of Athens,*" I said blithely, as though that had been in my mind all along.

"Hmm. Not much of a title. But at least Shakespeare had the sense not to set it in a Papist country. Although, once the queen is gone, who knows what will be acceptable and what will not? In six months it may be the Catholics who are taking us to task for sounding too Puritan."

They went to deal with other matters, leaving me alone in the office. I copied out one page of the play as rapidly as I could. Then, after taking a quick look out the door to make certain no one was about, I began a systematic search through the various papers and ledgers on the shelf above the desk. Before I could discover anything of use, I heard footsteps approaching. I thrust the journal I was examining back into place and bent over the script.

One of the company's clowns stuck his head into the room. Seeing how absorbed I appeared to be in my task, he murmured, "Pardon me," and moved on. It went that way the rest of the afternoon. Each time I tried to resume my search, one of the players passed by, forcing me to scramble back to the script.

In spite of myself, I had nearly all the play in a readable form by the end of the day. I did not reveal this to Mr. Henslowe, however. Instead, I complained that with all the interruptions, I was having trouble concentrating. I suggested that I might make better progress early in the morning, when the place was quieter.

"You'll be here early, right enough," he said. "We expect all our prentices to be in the theatre by prime. No doubt you were accustomed to sleeping late when you were with the Chamber Pot's Men, but we run this company like a business, not a midsummer fair."

That evening, after supper and a round of shove-penny with the orphan boys, I was summoned to the library to give my daily report. "So, how is Fortune treating you?" asked Mr. Pope.

I smiled in appreciation of his wordplay. "Well enough." I pulled out my purse and jingled it. "They gave me three pounds for the play, wi' three more to come."

Mr. Pope gave a low whistle. "Not bad, for a novice playwright."

"Well, they assumed it was all Mr. Shakespeare's work, of course, and though I didn't actually say it was, neither did I say that it wasn't. Unfortunately, I wasn't able to find the key to their code. I'll try again tomorrow."

"They weren't suspicious of you, then?"

"Not that I could tell. They considered the Chamberlain's Men a bunch of blackguards already, so when I told them I'd been sacked unjustly, it only served to confirm their opinion.

What about our company? Did anyone suspect that it was all a sham, do you wis?"

"Not according to Will. He says you played your part very convincingly."

"It wasn't difficult. I just imagined how I would feel an I were truly given the chuck. It's not as bad as I feared, though, being a member of the Admiral's Men. They actually treated me quite kindly, except for Mr. Henslowe—and even 'a was not altogether a swad. I' truth, I feel a bit guilty for deceiving them."

"They've never had any such qualms, you may be sure."

"Perhaps not. All the same, it's a pity the two companies can't be on better terms. They're not blackguards, either. They're just players, like us." I got wearily to my feet. "Me throat's parched. I'm going to ha' a drink of ale. Shall I fetch some for you?"

"No, thank you. I'm off to bed."

"You don't look as well as you might. I wish Mr. Armin and Mr. Shakespeare had not made you a part of their scheme. The doctor said you were not to be upset."

He shrugged. "They didn't want to send you off behind enemy lines, as it were, without my approval. Besides, I'm not upset, only tired. It's something that happens when you get old, you know."

I yawned. "Then I must be getting old."

Goody Willingson was in the kitchen, wiping clean the supper dishes. As I drew a mug of ale from the keg, she sidled up to me and said softly, "You know, if you're looking for a new name, you could do worse than take Mr. Pope's. He's been far more of a father to you than that Redshaw fellow ever was or ever would have been."

"That's so. I'm not certain 'a would care to ha' the son of an outlaw using his name, though."

"Do you really suppose that matters to him? You once said yourself, it's not your heritage that matters, it's what you do with it."

"Aye, well, so far I haven't done much of anything, have I?"

I woke well before dawn the next morning but still had to hasten, for the walk to St. Giles was a long one and I could not abbreviate it by taking a wherry boat across the Thames. Though the ice in the middle of the river had broken up, there was still a wide border of it along the banks, too rotten to set foot upon.

By the time I neared St. Olave's, its bells were already ringing prime. Yet even though I was late, and even though it meant going out of my way to do so, I could not resist passing by the church and pausing a moment to gaze at the steps where Judith was to have met me several days before. It was as though I hoped to find some trace of her still there—some small item that she might heedlessly have dropped, perhaps, or the faint scent of cloves lingering in the air. But of course there was nothing, not even the memory of a fond parting to console me. I hurried on.

I need not have worried about my tardiness. For all Mr. Henslowe's talk of running the Fortune like a business, neither he nor any of the other players had arrived yet, only the tiring-man, who, fortunately, had been instructed to let me into Mr. Henslowe's office.

Certain that I would not have the place to myself for long, I set to work at once—not on the script of *Timon,* but on the assortment of books and papers that lay upon the shelf. After a few minutes of frantic searching, I found what I was looking for, at the back of the journal in which Mr. Henslowe had been writing the previous afternoon. So much the methodical man of business was he that he had labeled the page in a clerk's precise hand so there could be no doubt about what it contained: *Cypher Key.* Beneath this heading he had set down in neat rows, as though he were doing accounts, the following:

I considered copying the symbols, but it would take so long that I risked being discovered. Instead I drew my dagger and ran the point of it down the left margin of the page; then I tore the cypher key from the book, tucked it inside my doublet, and returned the journal to its place.

Within half an hour I had finished translating *Timon*'s passages of charactery into the queen's English. After straightening up the pages and stacking them neatly on the desk, I dipped Mr. Henslowe's pen into the inkwell and wrote carefully at the top of the first page:

Timon of Athens: A Lamentable Tragedie. By James . . .

I hesitated only a moment before setting down the latter half of the rightful author's name: *Pope.*

I was halfway back to the Cross Keys before the irony of what I had written occurred to me. Mr. Henslowe was so fearful of performing anything that smacked of Catholic sympathies. Imagine how distressed he would be, then, to discover that he had paid good money for a play composed by a Pope.

At least he could console himself with the fact that it had cost him only three pounds instead of the six we had agreed upon. No doubt I could have collected the other three if I had gone on pretending that the work was Mr. Shakespeare's. But that would have been unfair, both to Mr. Henslowe and to Mr. Shakespeare. I had no qualms about keeping the three sovereigns I already had, however. Surely, even with all its faults, my play was worth that much.

The courtyard of the Cross Keys was the scene of more frenzied action than a French farce. The company's two-wheeled carts sat in the yard, piled high with trunks full of costumes and properties. Ned Shakespeare stood in the bed of one of the carts, shifting the trunks a few inches this way or that, with an intent look upon his face, as though he were performing some essential task. When he spied me, his expression changed to one of astonishment. "What the devil are *you* doing here? I thought they'd given you the sack."

"And so they did. But I've some unfinished business. Ha' you any notion where I might find your brother?"

He jerked his head toward the second-floor balcony. "Up there—fetching all the stuff that doesn't weigh much, I'll wager."

Mr. Shakespeare was, in fact, stuggling to drag his desk across the floor of the office. When I entered he gave a sigh of relief. "Ah, Widge; it seems you have the one quality essential to a player."

"What's that?"

"Good timing. Give me a hand with this infernal furniture, will you?"

"We're moving back to the Globe, I take it?"

"Very perceptive. Take hold." As we manuevered the desk out of the door and onto the balcony, he said softly, between grunts of effort, "Any success?"

"Aye. I've got the code."

"Excellent." He stood erect and rubbed at his old injury. "Let's leave this for someone larger to wrestle with, shall we? Come." We went down to the dark parlor, where Mr. Shakespeare, after ordering ale for both of us, drew from his wallet the coded message he had found on Mr. Henslowe. I, in turn, produced the cypher key and placed it before him. "Where did you find this?" he asked.

"I' Mr. Henslowe's journal."

"He actually left you alone with it?"

"Aye. 'A seemed to trust me. So did most of the Admiral's Men. I feel a bit as though I've betrayed them."

"Yes. I can see how you would. You also have that other quality that makes a good player—the ability to identify with others, to see things through their eyes. Unfortunately, you can't very well be loyal both to them and to us."

"I ken that. But why does being loyal to this company mean that I ha' to hate th' Admiral's Men? Why must we be rivals, and not simply fellow players?"

"All the theatre companies in London want the same thing—as large an audience as possible. That means we're in competition."

"Isn't there enough audiencc to go around? Besides, an all the theatres close down, *none* of us will have an audience.

Would it not be better an we all formed an alliance or something, to try and prevent that? Even oxen ha' sense enough to pull together, instead of always trying to outdo one another."

Mr. Shakespeare was regarding me with a rather startled look. Prentices did not ordinarily speak their minds quite so forcefully. "I'm sorry," I murmured. "It's just . . . well, it puts me i' mind o' the way the Catholics and Anglicans are at each other's throats, while the Puritans despise them both. How can they be such deadly enemies, when they all serve the same god? It seems to me that it's the same wi' us theatre folk: we all serve the same god. Do we not?"

Mr. Shakespeare was twisting his earring between thumb and finger, and staring thoughtfully—but no longer at me. His gaze seemed fixed on something far off, as though he were trying to see all the way to St. Giles and into the hearts of the Admiral's Men. There was a long stretch of silence, during which the tapster brought our ale and I began to regret that I had been so outspoken. Finally, Mr. Shakespeare said, "You're very persuasive with words, Widge. Perhaps you'll make a playwright after all."

"I hope to try. But not under the name of Widge."

"William, then?"

"Nay. James."

"Oh? Very well. I still favor William, myself, but James is a perfectly respectable name—especially as there's likely to be one on the throne. I hope you didn't choose it for that reason."

I laughed. "Hardly. It's after me father."

"You're taking his surname, too, I suppose?"

"Nay. I've decided—" I broke off. I had not yet told Mr. Pope of my decision, and he should certainly be the first to know.

"I understand," said Mr. Shakespeare, even though I had not attempted to explain. "Now. Let us see if we can determine who our spy is, shall we?"

Because Mr. Henslowe's code provided more than one symbol for each letter of the alphabet, it took some effort to decipher the message. As I completed each group of words, Mr. Shakespeare read it aloud. "Script of *Sejanus* finished . . . Company gone by vespers . . . I enclose key to . . . "

As the last few words emerged, letter by letter, Mr. Shakespeare trailed off, unable to speak them. I went back over the symbols, thinking perhaps I had translated them wrong. But there was no mistake. The final sentence read, "I enclose key to my brother's office."

Mr. Shakespeare sat motionless for a long while, staring at the words as though waiting for me to translate them yet again, into some form that he could comprehend. At last he said, so softly that I could scarcely hear, "Ned. I should have known."

"So should I, after 'a cornered me i' th' office that morning so early, wi' so flimsy a reason. I *did* leave the key i' the lock, then, and Ned made off wi' it."

Mr. Shakespeare nodded grimly. "I have no doubt that it was he who betrayed Father Gerard, as well."

"But why would 'a do such a thing?"

"For the same reason he served as Henslowe's spy, and the same reason he stole costumes from the company. He needed the money—to pay off gambling debts, and bribe his way out of trouble with the law, and God knows what else." He buried his face in his hands and sighed heavily. "*Money,*" he said, in the tone one uses for uttering a curse. "Would that it had never been invented."

"Folk would only ha' found something else to covet. Salted herrings, perhaps, or fern seeds."

Despite his melancholy mood, there was a hint of amusement in the glance Mr. Shakespeare gave me. "Fern seeds?"

"Aye. Up Yorkshire way folk say that an you eat enough of them, they make you invisible. The problem is, they also make you puke."

"I know the feeling." He took several long swallows of his ale. "Would you be so kind as to send Ned in here? I may as well have done with it; it's not likely to get any easier."

Ned was still pretending to rearrange the load on one of the carts. When I told him that Mr. Shakespeare wanted to see him, he scowled. "What about?"

"Something about fern seeds, I believe."

He gave me an incredulous look. "Fern seeds?"

I grinned. "That's exactly what Mr. Shakespeare said."

Ned stalked off, shaking his head, and nearly collided with Sam, who was hurrying across the courtyard toward me. "Widge! Gog's blood! What brings you back here?"

"Shank's mare," I said, meaning my feet. "I've done meself out of a Fortune, you see."

"You've quit already? Are you going to rejoin us, then?"

"I never actually left. It was all a sham, designed to get me into the Admiral's Men so I might do a bit of spying."

He aimed a blow at me, which I dodged. "You sot! You let me believe you'd been sacked!"

"I had to. We dared not let the truth be known lest Henslowe get wind of it, by way of his informant." I did not let on, of course, that I had half suspected Sam of being that informant.

"Did you find the culprit out, then?"

I hesitated, unwilling to be the one to break the news, and then merely nodded.

"It's Sal Pavy, isn't it?"

"I can't say. You'll learn soon enough, I expect."

"It's him, though, isn't it?" Sam insisted, but I would not be moved.

I surveyed the courtyard. "Where *is* Sal Pavy, by the by?"

"Still home in bed, being waited on hand and foot, and enjoying every moment of it, no doubt, while the rest of us are here working our arses off."

"You don't appear to be working very hard just now," I observed.

"I'm trying to pry an answer out of you. I call that hard. Come now, you may tell me; it's Sal Pavy, right?"

When we gathered for dinner, Mr. Shakespeare announced that Ned had quit the company. Though he did not specify the reason, it was clear that everyone knew, and that no one was surprised—except Sam, who shook his head and muttered, "I would have sworn it was Sal Pavy."

"I would appreciate it," said Mr. Shakespeare, "if the circumstances of Ned's departure were kept among ourselves. I don't wish to harm his chances of finding a position with another company."

"I w-wonder whether there's any th-theatre left in London that hasn't already had a t-taste of him," said Mr. Heminges.

"Probably not," Mr. Shakespeare admitted. "He may have to go farther afield."

"I ken a company i' Leicester that may be able to use him," I said. This drew a laugh from the others. They knew well enough what company I meant—the very one that had sent me here to steal the script of *Hamlet,* and the one that had caused us so many problems the previous summer, when we toured the northern shires.

Thinking of *Hamlet* had brought Julia, who had once been our Ophelia, to the forefront of my mind again. As we went back to loading the carts, I caught Mr. Heminges and asked whether he had tried to locate Tom Cogan. "R-Rob has," he said. "I'll let him t-tell you about it."

Mr. Armin had been to Alsatia, Cogan's home ground, to make inquiries. "Which," he said, "was rather like climbing into a pit of snakes to inquire about one viper in particular. I got a lot of hisses and venomous looks and very little information. Eventually, though, I found a beggar who was willing to talk to me—for a price. According to him, Tom Cogan was placed under arrest several days ago, for stealing a gold bracelet from the queen's treasury."

"The queen's treasury?"

"Well, that part may have been only a rumor. He seemed certain, though, that Cogan had been arrested for *something,* which means we may have to look for him in prison."

"Oh, gis. Which one, do you suppose?"

"There's no telling. I've sent word to Father Gerard asking him to keep an eye out for our man when he's ministering to his Papist prisoners."

I felt inside my doublet for my purse, to reassure myself that I still had the three pounds Julia would need for her passage home. The money was there, right enough. What good was it, though, if I had no way of getting it to her?

"Oh, before I forget," said Mr. Armin, "Sal has asked that you come by to see him."

"Me?" I hardly considered myself a close friend of his. But perhaps I was the closest thing to it. "How is he?"

Mr. Armin shook his head soberly. "Not good. The grippe has infected his lungs."

By the time we carted all our possessions across the bridge to the Globe and unloaded them, it was all but dark, and I was all but dead. I would have put off visiting Sal Pavy until another day had it not been for the guilt that was still lodged inside me, like a sliver, reminding me that I had been responsible, at least in part, for his near drowning.

Sal Pavy's mother, a small, grim-looking woman, showed me to her son's room. "You mustn't stay long, and you mustn't let him do much talking. He's very weak."

"Ha' you brought in a physician?"

She nodded. "He says the boy should recover in time, if he's kept quiet."

In truth, Sal Pavy did not appear to be very near to death's door. Perhaps it was only an effect of the fever, but his face was flushed and his eyes were bright. Propped up in his bed by a multitude of down pillows, he looked rather smug and pampered. Then I glimpsed the kerchief that lay crumpled between his hands. It was covered with rust-colored stains.

"We've missed you," I said, which was not altogether a lie. Sal Pavy was like one of those obnoxious secondary characters that playwrights so often create—Parolles, for example, or Polonius, or Apemantus. Though their main function seems to be to irk the other characters, the play would be poorer without them. He seemed about to reply, but was seized by a fit of coughing that imprinted the kerchief with a fresh stain. "Perhaps . . . perhaps I should come back another time, when you're stronger."

He shook his head and motioned for me to sit on the end of the bed. After struggling for several moments to find enough breath, he got out a few words. "Mr. Armin . . . says that . . . you blame yourself . . . for what happened to me."

"Aye. I should ha' had more sense. You never would ha' gone out on the ice had I refused to."

He shook his head again. "You're wrong. I would have . . . done it anyway. Only you . . . would not have . . . been there . . . to pull me out."

I gazed at him curiously. "Why are you telling me this?"

"Because. You've always tried . . . to be . . . a friend. When I die . . . I don't want you . . . feeling responsible."

I forced a feeble laugh. "What makes you think you're going to die?"

"What makes you . . . think I'm not?"

"The doctor. He says you'll be good as new in a week or so."

He pressed the kerchief to his lips and stifled a cough. "Well . . . if I do die . . . I won't mind so much . . . really. This way, you see . . . I'll be remembered as a . . . talented youth . . . full of promise. If I'd lived . . . to be sixty . . . I'd have been . . . just another old actor."

I arrived home so weary and downcast that even the boys noticed. They let me forgo the usual games and settled for hearing a story instead. Though it was a rousing one, replete with ghosts and magic and bloody deeds, it was far less taxing than being Banks's horse.

Mr. Pope suggested that my daily report could wait until morning, but I had one matter to discuss that would not wait. "I was wondering," I said hesitantly, "whether you would mind me taking your last name as me own?"

He stared at me for a moment, as though I'd asked his permission to sprout wings and fly. Then he laughed and, seizing both my arms, shook them so hard that my teeth rattled. "Mind? I'd be honored, Widge!"

"Umm . . . I've decided on a new first name as well. I'd like to be called James."

"James it is, then!" He tested the words on his tongue. "James Pope. James Pope. I like it! We must christen you, like a ship, with a bottle of brandy!" He called for Goody Willingson and sent her to the cellar to fetch the spirits.

When she returned, she announced, "That same gentleman is here as was here a week ago, and is asking for you, Widge—or James, should I say?" She shook her head. "That will take some getting used to."

"Show him in," said Mr. Pope. "I'll take myself off to bed."

"There's no need," I told him. "Perhaps it's time I began letting you in on things, instead of keeping them from you."

Father Gerard had altered his appearance yet again. He wore the sort of linen robe favored by physicians, and he had dyed his beard a shade of red that matched his wig.

"Can I offer you a nip of brandy?" said Mr. Pope.

"No, thank you. I mustn't linger. I have a message for Widge. From Tom Cogan."

"You've found him, then?" I said.

Gerard nodded grimly. "He's in Newgate."

"Gog's blood! That's where they take wights that are to be hanged!"

"Yes. He's been convicted of theft, and it's his second offense. I was told to ask Cogan for a letter of some sort—something to do with his daughter?"

"Aye. Did 'a give it to you?"

"No. He'd scarcely even talk to me. He said he didn't trust me. When I told him I was a priest, he said that was all the more reason to distrust me. The only person he will speak to is you, Widge. He says you were his daughter's friend."

"All right. Should I go now?"

"No. Meet me outside the prison tomorrow at nones. The warder on duty then is a good Catholic—and an even better one since I slipped him a sovereign. We can tell him you're Cogan's son. That'll get you in."

The moment Gerard was gone, Mr. Pope began unexpectedly to chuckle.

"What is 't?" I asked.

"Sorry. I know this is serious business. It's just that up until a week ago, you had no father at all. Now, suddenly, you've got three of 'em—Redshaw, Cogan, and me." He poured an inch or so of brandy into a glass and handed it to me. "Now. Tell me about Julia."

Ordinarily I did my best to avoid Newgate. No doubt it had once been an attractive edifice, especially the stone gatehouse. But over the course of nearly two centuries, the soot from the city's chimneys had given the walls a dark and forbidding aspect that hinted at what lay inside them.

Mr. Henslowe would no doubt have found the prison admirable, for it was run like a business. Those prisoners who could afford it were put in well-lighted, airy quarters, with reasonably comfortable furnishings, and given decent food and drink. Those who could not were thrown together in dark, damp cells that reeked of human waste. They slept on straw—if they were lucky—and dined on gruel and water. The only consolation for these poor wretches was the thought that they might cheat the hangman by dying of jail fever before their execution day arrived.

Tom Cogan was, of course, one of the unfortunate ones, as he had been all his life. Unlike his fellow prisoners, who lounged about playing at cards or dice, or simply sat hunched hoplessly in a corner of the cell, Cogan was pacing restlessly back and forth, back and forth, like a caged lion I had once seen on display at the Tower. Like that beast, he seemed oblivious to everything around him, including the curses of one of the dice players, who threatened to break his kneecaps if he didn't stop his infernal pacing.

When the warder let us into the cell, Cogan descended upon me like a lion upon its prey. "Good lad! I knew I could count on you!"

"You could have trusted Father Gerard."

Cogan gave the priest a dismissive glance. "Ahh, all he's interested in is saving my soul, which ain't worth the trouble. It's my neck I'm worried about." He sank his fingers painfully into my arm and drew me to the far end of the cell. "And you," he whispered, "are going to help me save it."

"Me?" I said. "What can *I* do?"

"Julia never told me nothing much about her actor friends, but she did say once that you was prenticed to a physician."

"Aye. But what—?"

Cogan's fingernails sank more deeply into my arm. "This wight I once met—a bid-stand, he was"—this, I had learned, was the London term for a highwayman—"told me that he'd got himself out of prison by taking some stuff that put him into a sort of trance, so they mistook him for dead. As they were hauling him off to the graveyard, he came to and made his escape. Now, have you ever heard of a root or a plant or the like that would do such as that?"

I pried his fingers from my arm. "As a matter of fact, I ha'. But not as a physician's prentice; as a player. When I'm acting the part of Juliet, Friar Laurence gives me a vial of distilled liquor. An I drink it, 'a says, it will bring on a cold and drowsy humor that has the appearance of death: 'No warmth, no breath, shall testify thou livest.'"

"That's but a play!" Cogan scoffed. "Anything may happen in a play!"

"I ken that. But I asked Mr. Shakespeare what was supposed to be i' the vial, and 'a said the juice of mandrake root. According to him, it truly works. 'A learned about it from an apothecary."

Cogan considered this a moment, then leaned in to me and whispered, "I want you to get me some of it."

"Mandrake?"

"Whist! Keep your voice down!"

"Sorry. But how would I manage to get it past the warder? 'A searched us on the way in."

"Tell him I'm sick, and you're bringing me medicine."

"You don't look very sick."

He grinned, disclosing his rotten teeth. "You're not the only wight that can act, you know."

His scheme sounded doubtful at best and, at worst, risky. But if we did nothing, there was no doubt about what the outcome would be: he would hang. I must at least try—if not for him, then for Julia. "All right. I'll do 't. But you must do something for me first."

"What's that?"

"Gi' me the letter wi' Julia's address so I may send her money to get home."

He gave me another unpleasant grin and shook his head. "No, no. First you bring me the mandrake." He clapped a hand on my shoulder. "It's not that I don't trust you, lad. It's just that I've learned a wight is more likely to do what you want if you've got something *he* wants."

• • •

As we passed from the gloomy, stinking interior of Newgate into sunlight and fresh air again, I told the warder, "I'll be back in a little while. Me da's feeling poorly, and I'm to fetch him some wormwood, to settle his stomach."

The man nodded sympathetically. "I expect I'd feel poorly, too, if I was to be hanged in a few days."

When we were well away from the prison, Father Gerard asked, "Is Cogan really ill?"

I shook my head. "'A wants me to bring him mandrake, not wormwood."

Gerard stared at me. "Does he mean to take his own life?"

"Nay, only to feign death, in order to escape."

"He may do more than just feign it; mandrake is a deadly poison."

The apothecary we called upon agreed that in a large enough quantity, mandrake would surely prove fatal. "However, a drop or two of the diluted juice is often used to deaden pain."

"What about half a dozen drops, then?" I asked.

"I'm not certain. It might cause temporary paralysis and unconsciousness."

Father Gerard did his best to convince me that Cogan's plan was foolish, and that I must not be party to it. "Suppose you give him too large a dose? Do you wish to be responsible for a man's death?"

His words brought another of La Voisin's predictions back into my mind, where it rang like a death knell: *Because of you, someone will die. Someone will die.* "But suppose I do naught, and they hang him? Will I not still be responsible? Besides, 'a refuses to tell me Julia's whereabouts unless I do as 'a says."

"There are other ways of escaping. I gained my freedom from the Tower of London by sliding down a rope."

"Truly? I've heard folk say that no one has ever escaped from the Tower."

"Well, they're wrong. Some six or seven years ago, during my first assignment to London, the pursuivant's men brought me in for *questioning,* as they called it—which meant stringing me up by the arms and beating me, in an effort to make me tell them who my superiors were and where they could be found. That's how I came by these." He touched the several scars on his face. "When I refused to cooperate, they locked me in the Salt Tower. No doubt they would have executed me eventually, as they did so many of my fellow priests, had my friends not managed to smuggle a rope in to me."

"But how did you get out of your cell?"

"I wasn't confined to a cell. I was free to walk about on the battlements."

"Is Tom Cogan permitted out of his cell?"

"Probably not," Gerard admitted.

"Then a rope would not do him much good, would it?"

When we came within sight of Newgate, the priest halted. "I'm sorry, Widge. Go on, if you must, but I'll have no part of it. It's my duty to save souls, not to damn them." He turned and walked away.

I called after him, "Would his soul be saved, then, an he met his end on the scaffold?" He did not reply.

The warder took me to the condemned cell at once. "Your da's gotten worse since you left," he said. "I think he's going to need something stronger than wormwood."

Cogan was no longer pacing back and forth. He was curled up in a corner of the cell, twitching and groaning pitifully. A communal water keg sat against one wall, with a metal cup next to it. I dipped out a cup of water and knelt next to him. He gave a cry so startling that I nearly dropped the cup. "Don't you think you're overdoing it just a bit?" I whispered.

He opened one eye and peered at me. "I'm supposed to be dying, ain't I?"

"Most folk don't make such a fuss about it." I took out the apothecary's vial and eyed the dark liquid within. "Perhaps this is not such a good idea. What an I gi' you too much? Th' apothecary says that a large dose is fatal."

Cogan shrugged. "In any case, I'll be no worse off than I would have been at the end of a rope, will I?"

"I suppose not." Feeling that it was better to err on the side of caution, I put only four drops into the water and stirred it with my finger. I was about to hand the cup to him when I remembered his end of the bargain. "Where's the letter?"

His mask of make-believe agony slipped a little, and a look of genuine discomfort showed through. "Ah," he said. "The letter."

"Aye, from Julia. You ha' it, do you not?"

"Actually . . . no. The constables who nabbed me took it, along with the bracelet."

"Oh, gis! So you've no idea, either, where to find Julia?"

"Well, I wouldn't say *no* idea at all. I mind that the name of the woman who runs the lodging house was Hardy. I remembered it particularly because it don't sound French."

I sighed. "That's all very well, but I can scarcely send a package i' care of Madame Hardy, Paris, France, can I?"

"I could take it there."

"Then we'd need another three pounds for *your* passage. In any case, you can't go anywhere until we get you out of here." I handed him the cup.

He raised it to his lips, then lowered it. "If I take this, there's a chance I won't wake up again?"

I nodded glumly.

"It ain't that I'm afeared, you understand. It's just that . . . well, I've a confession to make first."

"You should ha' spoken to Father Gerard, then."

"It ain't that sort of confession. It has to do with Julia. I know I can trust you to pass it on to her, in case I should hop the twig."

"Hop the twig?"

"Knock off. You know—die."

I pointed out that he was supposed to be dying even now, or at least should appear to be. He ignored me, and launched into a long and complicated narrative that was every bit as astounding and unlikely as any I had concocted in my fevered attempts to compose a play. Yet he related it all in such a matter-of-fact manner and provided so many convincing details that I did not doubt for a moment that it was true.

When it came to lengthy parting speeches, Cogan managed to outdo even Hamlet—who, after saying, "I am dead, Horatio," goes on for another twenty lines or so. Cogan spoke without pause for a good quarter of an hour. When his tale finally reached its end, it left me as stunned as I had been at the conclusion of the first play I ever saw performed. It took me several moments to collect myself enough to speak. "Does—does Julia ken any o' this?"

Cogan shook his head. "Not a bit."

"Why did you never tell her?"

With one hand he gestured at the dismal prison cell that surrounded us. "You see where knowing it has gotten me." He lifted the cup and stirred the contents with his finger. "Well, one way or another, I won't be here much longer." He threw back his head and downed the mandrake potion in two great gulps, then gave a shudder. "Aggh! That's nasty stuff. I only hope it does its job." He waved a dismissive hand at me. "You go on now. I can die well enough by myself."

"Aye, but can you come back to life by yourself? An you stay unconscious for long, they may bury you."

He scratched his beard thoughtfully. "Good point. Then it's up to you to get my corpse off the meat wagon—the cart that takes away the dead prisoners. It comes around every day, just after dark. Revive me if you can. If not . . . " He shrugged. "Well, give me a decent burial, will you? It's more than I'd have got if they'd strung me up."

I considered returning to the Globe and enlisting Mr. Armin's help. After all, someone might well object to my carrying off a body. And even if no one did, I wasn't certain I could carry Cogan by myself.

An hour or two of daylight remained. I could probably make it to the theatre and back before the meat wagon arrived. But what if I did not? When Cogan came to, he might find himself locked inside a charnel house, in the middle of a pile of stiff, staring corpses—or, worse yet, under the ground.

I had chosen, against Father's Gerard's advice, to be an accomplice in Cogan's cock-brained scheme; it was up to me to see it through. I concealed myself in the shadows at the mouth of a narrow alleyway and waited.

When at last a one-horse cart bearing a few bodies rumbled up Newgate Street and stopped before the prison, I sorely regretted not having gone for reinforcements. Instead of the single, shambling carter I had expected, the meat wagon was escorted by two guards in breastplates and helmets, with rapiers at their sides.

"Gog's nowns!" I breathed. If I had had a sword of my own—which I did not—I might conceivably have overcome a single guard, provided he was not too good a swordsman; against two of them, I stood no chance at all.

Something tapped me lightly upon the shoulder. With a gasp, I spun about. A tall robed figure loomed over me, indistinct in the shadows. "Soft!" said a familiar voice. "They'll hear you!"

"Father Gerard?" I whispered. "Why are you here?"

"To help."

"But—you said you wanted no part of our plan."

"I said I would not be a party to poisoning a man. I have no objection to resurrecting him."

"Ha' you a weapon?" I asked hopefully.

"I'm no more willing to stab or to shoot a man than I am to poison him."

"Then how i' the name of halidom will we deal wi' those wights?"

"Well," said the priest, "we might try trickery."

Tom Cogan, as I soon learned, had no monopoly on cock-brained schemes. But any action we might take, however ill-conceived, would be better than none at all. For the next several minutes, all I did was hide there in the alleyway, watching as the warder and his helper carried three bodies, one at a time, from the prison and tossed them onto the cart. From where I stood, it was impossible to tell whether or not one of the corpses was Cogan's.

"That's the lot," the warder told the guards. The moment he and his helper went inside, I dashed out of the alleyway and up the street toward the wagon, calling in the same pitiful voice

I used for playing Lavinia—before her tongue is cut out, of course—"Help me, sirs! Please help me!"

"What is it, lad?" asked the smaller of the guards.

"It's me da! 'A's being robbed and beaten!" I pointed to the alley. "I' there! Hurry!" I seized the man's sleeve and began dragging him along. When his companion hesitated and glanced toward the meat wagon, I cried, "There's three of 'em! Come quickly, afore they murder him!"

Newgate Street was not entirely dark; every twenty or thirty yards, a lanthorn on the front of a house cast a feeble glow. But once we were within the narrow confines of the alley, the sole source of light was the thin strip of stars overhead.

"Where's your da, then?" demanded the larger guard. "I don't see nothing."

"At th' end of th' alley! Come!" Though they were clearly reluctant to advance into the unknown, I might have lured them a little farther along. But at that moment the horse that hauled the meat wagon let out a startled whinny. The guards headed back toward the mouth of the alley, drawing their swords as they ran.

I scrambled after them. "Wait! What about me poor da?"

They ignored me, for they had caught sight of the tall figure pulling at the horse's harness in an attempt to calm the rearing, neighing animal. "You there!" shouted one of the guards. "What are you up to?"

I expected Gerard to run. Instead he snatched the horsewhip from its socket on the side of the cart and turned to confront the two armed men. Though the whip was not a long one—perhaps six feet from handle to tip—it was longer than a rapier blade, and Gerard used this fact to his advantage. By snapping the whip this way and that, he kept the guards at a distance—

for a few moments, anyway. Unfortunately they had enough sense to separate and come at him from opposite directions. Gerard could not face them both. If I did not come to his aid, one of the guards would find an opening soon, and skewer him.

Since joining the Chamberlain's Men, I had spent a good deal of time honing my sword-fighting skills. But I had not forgotten altogether the skills I had learned in the orphanage, defending myself against boys who were considerably larger than I.

Apparently my mock distress had been so convincing that the guards still did not suspect me of being in league with Gerard, so I played the part for all it was worth. I descended upon the smaller guard, wringing my hands and sobbing, "Oh, please, sir! You must save me da! Please, sir!"

"Get away, lad!" the man growled, never taking his eyes off the madman with the whip.

I let out a wail of distress and tugged frantically at the back of his breastplate, pulling him off balance. "You can't let him die!"

The man's patience broke, and he swung the hilt of his rapier about, meaning to club me with it. I ducked under the blow and flung myself at the backs of his legs, which folded under my weight. The guard pitched forward; his sword flew from his grasp and clattered across the cobbles.

I dived headlong for it. The instant my hand closed around the hilt, I rolled onto my back—but too late. The guard was already upon me, with his dagger drawn. He thrust the tip of it against my throat-bole. "Don't move, boy!" Keeping the dagger painfully in place, he turned his head to check on his comrade. From the corner of my eye, I could see that Father Gerard had disarmed his adversary and was advancing toward mine, swinging the whip before him.

"Stay where you are," called the guard, "or the lad will have a new breathing hole!" The priest halted uncertainly.

"Get Cogan!" I managed to shout, before the guard's dagger cut off my words and very nearly my windpipe as well.

"Drop the whip!" the man ordered. After a moment's hesitation, Gerard obeyed. "Jack?" said the guard. "Are you all right?"

"I believe my arm's broken," came the reply.

"Well, see if you can manage to tie up that fellow while I take care of this—" He was interrupted by the sound of spectral moaning somewhere nearby. "What the devil was that?"

"It's—it's coming from . . . in *there,*" said Jack in a voice that trembled.

Something moved within the wagon, making the horse snort and shuffle about nervously. Then a groping hand emerged from between the wooden slats. "God's bloody bones!" gasped the guard who stood over me. "They're coming to life!"

"It's sorcery!" cried Jack. He stumbled backward a few steps, then turned and fled, clutching his broken limb. His comrade, unwilling to face the undead alone, followed as fast as his feet could carry him.

I got unsteadily to my feet, holding the spot where the dagger had pricked my neck, and regarded the hand that projected from the cart, fluttering feebly. "I trust that belongs to Cogan," I said hoarsely.

Gerard peered over the side of the cart. "I think so. Help me get these other bodies off him."

We lifted the two dead prisoners from the top of the pile and laid them gently on the cobblestones. "I hope these wights did not die o' the plague."

"Plague victims are taken out separately," said Gerard, "and not by armed guards. No one wants to steal their bodies."

"You mean someone *would* want these poor wretches?"

"Medical students—for studying anatomy."

The corpse that showed signs of life was, to my relief, Tom Cogan's. His head bobbed about as though he had St. Vitus's dance, and he was making guttural, half-intelligible noises—the sort that Sander used to make in his sleep when he was dreaming something unpleasant.

Though I had bought a vial of smelling salts from the apothecary to revive Cogan, this did not seem the proper time to use it. It was more important just now to get him well away from Newgate. Gerard hoisted the man's twitching form almost effortlessly and draped it across his shoulders. "Let's find a tavern," he said. "A fellow who's staggering and babbling incoherently will not seem out of place there."

Keeping to the backstreets and snickleways, we got safely to the Warwick Inn, where we installed ourselves in a private chamber. Even with the help of the smelling salts, it took Cogan some time to come around. "It's fortunate that I gave him such a small dose," I said. "'A came back to life at just the right moment." I paused and gave a short, ironic laugh. "La Voisin was right yet again."

"La Voisin?"

"A cunning woman. She said that someone would return to life because of me." Though one-half of her prediction had come to pass, the other half still troubled me. "She also said that . . . that I would be the cause of someone's death."

"Well, Cogan was mistaken for dead; perhaps that was what she saw."

"Perhaps." After all, none of the other things she predicted had come true in the way I imagined; there was no reason to believe that this one would, either.

"Did you get the letter you were after?" asked Gerard.

I shook my head despondently. "It was taken from him. All 'a remembers is the name of the woman Julia is lodging wi'—Madame Hardy."

"That may be enough information to let you find the place."

"It might be—provided I was i' Paris."

"Well," said Gerard, "it may be that I can find it for you."

Gerard's superiors, he said, had ordered all Jesuit priests to return to the seminaries in France. The queen's death now seemed certain and imminent, and if history was any indication, it would be followed by a period of dismay and disorder. Elizabeth had been beloved, even revered, by most of her subjects; the bitter truth—that she was but a frail mortal—would not go down easily with them. They would look for a scapegoat, and their blame would fall on those same groups that they had always suspected—sometimes rightly—of conspiring against Her Majesty: the Jews, the atheists, and the Papists.

Most Catholics, it seemed, believed that if James took the throne he would usher in a new and better era for the faith; his mother had been a Catholic, after all, and so was Anne, his queen. But in the meantime, Papists were likely to be more persecuted and reviled than ever. Gerard planned to leave England soon, taking with him the small contingent of future priests he had recruited. "I don't suppose," he said, "that Sam has told you yet."

I stared at him, uncomprehending. "Told me what?"

"That he is one of my recruits."

"'A means to be a *priest?*"

Gerard nodded. "He's spent a good deal of time with me lately, learning about the faith."

"Shrew me," I murmured. "'A's turned traitor after all."

He gave me a startled glance. "You consider Catholics to be traitors?"

"Nay, not I. It's another of La Voisin's predictions." Though I suspected that Sam's interest in religion was not nearly so strong as his admiration for Gerard, I did not say so. I did not need to. The priest seemed to have read my mind.

"I am not so naive," he said, "as to think that it was my lectures on the Trinity and original sin that won Sam over. More likely it was my accounts of exotic places and hairbreadth escapes. But the Church is not particular about our reasons for joining." He gave a wry smile. "If it were, I would be a gentleman farmer now, managing my father's lands, trying to save sick sheep and not souls. Like Sam, I was attracted more by the prospect of travel and adventure than by the faith itself. That came later."

"Aye, well, don't expect too much of Sam. 'A's not a bad sort, but a bit of a scamp." I drew my purse from inside my doublet and shook the three sovereigns from it. "An you find Julia, will you give her these, to pay her passage home?"

The priest closed one hand around the money and the other around my arm. "I'll find her," he said.

With the aid of the smelling salts and a bit of brandy, we brought Tom Cogan fully back to life at last. But, as Gerard pointed out, that life would be worth very little if he remained in London, for he would surely be apprehended again.

"I don't know where else I'd go," Cogan said sullenly.

"I can take you to France with me," Gerard offered. "Of course," he added, "you'd have to agree to join the Society of Jesus."

Cogan snorted. "I'd as soon join the Society of Satan." He poured himself another drink of brandy and downed it. "No, gentlemen, I'll take my chances here in London. If I keep to Alsatia, the authorities can't touch me. Where I made my mistake was in stepping outside it, and mixing with well-bred folk." He shook his head and gave a bitter laugh. "It's funny, though, isn't it? If I'd just gone ahead and stole the money to send to Julia, instead of humbly asking folk for it, none of this would have happened." He fingered the T-shaped scar on his neck. "I guess it's best just to be what's expected of you."

His words sounded familiar, but it took me a moment to recall where I had heard them before: Julia had said something almost identical, when she was forced to quit the company because she was a girl.

In the morning, I woke to the sound of church bells. They were not the gentle treble bells, though, that rang prime each dawn; these were deep-voiced bells with melancholy tones, and they were tolling slowly, rhythmically, without ceasing.

I sat up and peered through my window. Across the river, in the vicinity of St. Paul's, a shifting tower of gray smoke was climbing into the sky. To the east, somewhere near the Cross Keys, rose another. I sighted a third far to the northeast, where Finsbury Fields lay, and a fourth in the northwest—at St. Bartholomew's, no doubt.

My first muddleheaded thought was that we were being invaded by some foreign army—from Spain, perhaps, or France—and that its soldiers were setting fire to the city. But it was not an alarm that the bells were ringing, either; it was a death knell. Once I realized that, it was easy enough to guess what the source of the smoke was: It came from the bonfires that, by tradition, were lighted to signal the passing of the Crown from one monarch to another.

33

The queen's was not the only death we mourned that day. When I reached the Globe I learned that Sal Pavy had passed away during the night. So La Voisin's last unfulfilled prophecy had come true: someone had died because of me—because I had not had sense enough, or courage enough, to ignore a foolish dare.

I had hoped to say farewell to Sam. But soon after the news of Her Majesty's death spread through the city, Father Gerard and his recruits boarded a ship bound for France. I knew that the priest would do his best to locate Julia and send her home, as he had promised; what I did not know was whether his best would be good enough. I could only wait and see.

The fate of the Chamberlain's Men was equally uncertain. In her final hours, Elizabeth had indicated at last, through the use of signs—for her voice had deserted her entirely—that her successor would be James, the current King of Scotland. We had all expected that, of course. But we had no idea what else to expect of him; no one seemed even to know when he might arrive in London, let alone what he might do once he got there.

Nearly a week passed without news from any quarter, aside from a rumor that the Admiral's Men had hired Ned Shakespeare as a player, not merely an informant. It seemed that, like us, they had determined to go on as though the future of the London theatre were assured.

We could not truly go on the same as always, though. With Ned and Sam and Sal Pavy all gone, the company was as sparse as it had been on tour the previous summer. There were not enough actors left to cast any of our usual plays, and yet we could ill afford to take on new prentices or hired men until we knew where we stood.

The weather had grown so warm that on the afternoons when it did not rain, we held our rehearsals upon the stage. The long winter had been hard on the boards; many were warped and a few were rotten, so that treading on them was nearly as risky as walking on the river ice had been. We were willing to put up with it, though; we all longed to play to an audience again, and when we were on the stage we could at least have the illusion of performing.

Occasionally some tradesman or truant prentice passed by and, hearing our voices declaiming and our swords clashing, peered in through the entrance and perhaps lingered for a while to watch. No one attempted to chase off these interlopers. Any audience was better than none.

As the weather improved, so did Mr. Pope's health. Several days a week he joined us for dinner at the Globe, or sat in on a rehearsal and read all the unfilled parts. He had already grown accustomed to calling me James. The rest of the company was just as quick to adjust. It was nothing new to them, after all, having to address a fellow player by a different name; every one of us changed his identity, sometimes even his age and gender, from performance to performance.

On the days when Mr. Pope did not visit, I made my nightly report to him as usual. One evening as we sat talking over mugs of ale, Goody Willingson entered the library with a curious look on her broad face—half eager, half guarded, as though she had received some delicious bit of news but had been forbidden to tell it. "There's a young gentleman here to see you," she said solemnly.

"What sort of young gentleman?" asked Mr. Pope.

Goody Willingson lowered her voice almost to a whisper. "A rather scruffy-looking one, sir, to tell the truth."

"Did he say what he wanted?"

"No, sir."

Mr. Pope sighed. "Well, I suppose you may as well send him in." When the housekeeper departed, he turned to me. "Collecting for some charity, no doubt." A few moments later the boy appeared in the doorway—a slight lad, dressed in a shabby tunic and trousers, with a woolen prentice's cap pulled low over his ears. His face was liberally smudged with coal dust.

"Begging your pardon, sirs." He had the same thick, working-class accent as Tom Cogan. "I was wondering whether your acting company might have room for another prentice."

"They may, in a few weeks." Mr. Pope looked the lad over. "Can you act?"

"Apparently so," said the boy. Laughing, he yanked off the cap, revealing a wealth of auburn hair.

"Gog's blood!" I cried. "Julia!"

Mr. Pope was even more astonished than I. Clutching his chest, he staggered backward and slumped into his chair.

"Oh, gis! The shock was too much for his heart, I wis!"

Julia ran to the old man's side and seized one of his limp hands in hers. "I'm sorry, Mr. Pope! I'm sorry! Are you all right?"

His lolling head suddenly popped upright and he beamed at her triumphantly. "Apparently so!"

She flung down his hand. "You were *pretending?*"

"No, my dear, I was *acting.*"

"Whatever you call it, it was cruel. I thought you were dying."

"And I thought you were a lad, so we're even."

Julia could not suppress a smile. "I suppose we are, at that." She turned to me with a mischievous look. "I had you fooled as well, didn't I?"

"Only for a moment," I said indignantly. "It was the dirt on your face that did it. It hid your features."

She wiped one cheek with the sleeve of her tunic. "That's the idea. I thought I'd be safer among all those sailors if they didn't suspect I was a girl."

"Gerard gave you the money I sent, then?"

"Gerard?"

"The priest."

She shook her head. "I talked to no priest."

"Then how did you pay for your passage?" asked Mr. Pope.

"Well, after a week or so I despaired of ever hearing from my da, so I did the only thing I could think of: I sold my clothing."

"Your *clothing?*"

"Two very elegant gowns, given to me by—" She paused, clearly embarrassed. "Well, at any rate, they fetched a good price, enough so that I could pay the rent I owed and purchase these rags—" She plucked distastefully at the worn tunic and trousers. "—and still have enough left over to buy my passage."

"You needn't ha' done that," I said. I went on to recount the whole story of how Tom Cogan had come to us, and everything that ensued—or nearly everything. I made no mention of the things Cogan had confessed to me prior to taking the mandrake potion. He had asked me to reveal them to Julia if he died. But since he had survived, he could do it himself, if he chose.

"There," said Mr. Pope. "James has told you what went on here; now we'd like to hear your side of the tale."

Julia gave me a puzzled glance. "*James?*"

"It's me new name. I'll explain later—after you've told us why you had to leave France."

Julia lowered her gaze. "I'm afraid it's not a pretty story."

"Well, you needn't tell us if you'd rather not," said Mr. Pope. "But you're among friends now, my dear."

She smiled faintly. "I know. And I'm grateful to be. I've missed you all, very much." She wiped at her face again, this time leaving damp, pale streaks in the coal dust. Then, in a voice so soft at first that I could scarcely hear, she gave us a brief account of all that had befallen her during her fifteen months in Paris.

I knew many of the details already, from her letters. She had had the good luck to arrive in France at a time when the notion of women acting upon the stage was just beginning to gain acceptance. Because there were so few experienced actresses, Julia had found a position at once with one of the most successful companies in Paris.

What she had never revealed in her letters was that most of the public still regarded female players as degraded and immoral, little better than women of the streets, and treated them as such. And, as the companies themselves did not consider actresses the equal of actors, they were paid a pittance. In an attempt to improve their social and financial status, most of the women players found a patron, some wealthy lord who would offer them protection, money, and a measure of respectability in return for their favors.

Julia flatly declared that she would be no man's mistress. For a time she managed well enough, lodging with the company manager and his wife and discouraging the amorous advances of male players and playgoers with the help of a concealed dagger.

As her popularity and the number of roles she played increased, she caught the eye of the Comte de Belin, who was well known for his many affairs. At first he expressed his admiration only with gifts—including the two gowns she had later sold for passage money. But with each month that passed his attentions grew more and more ardent, and the more she resisted them the more insistent he became, until at last he declared that if she would not come to him willingly, he would take her against her will. That same day, she quit the company and found a room in a seedy section of the city where the count could not find her.

When she had finished her story, she bowed her head, as if in contrition. "You've nothing to be ashamed of, my dear," said Mr. Pope. "You behaved courageously and virtuously."

"Oh, yes, I know," she replied. "I was not very shrewd, though, was I? In being so courageous and so virtuous, I lost my one remaining chance to be a player."

Though Julia could never have brought herself to ask for charity of any sort, when Mr. Pope insisted that she stay with us for the time being, she was clearly relieved. For the next several nights, she and I sat up long past the time when the rest of the household had retired. Mostly, we talked; it had been an eventful year for both of us, and there was much to tell. But sometimes we sat silent for long stretches, lost in our own thoughts yet always aware of each other—not separated by the silence so much as sharing it, the way folk may share a warm and satisfying meal.

During one of these times, I caught Julia gazing at me in a peculiar fashion, as though I had done something amusing or unexpected—let go a belch, perhaps, or torn a hole in my hose. "What?" I said.

"You've changed."

I ran a hand self-consciously over my close-cropped head.

"It's me hair, no doubt, or the lack of it. No more pudding basin."

"I noticed. But that's not it."

"I'm an inch or two taller than when you saw me last."

"I noticed that as well. But it's not that, either. I think it's your manner."

"Me manners?" I thought perhaps I had belched after all, or passed wind without knowing it.

She laughed. "Your *manner*. The way you speak and act."

"Well, me acting's got a bit better, but me speech has stayed the same. Folk still make fun of 't."

"You sot. That's not what I meant, and you know it."

"Aye," I admitted. "I suppose I have changed. I could hardly help it, given all that's happened in the past year—or even the past few weeks. I lost one father and gained another, wrote a play, did a bit of spying and a bit of fighting, fell in—" I broke off. Like Tom Cogan concealing the brand upon his neck, I had no wish to reveal how badly I had been burned.

"Yes?" Julia prompted me. "Fell in what? A well? The space beneath the stage?"

"No," I said sullenly.

"In love?" she suggested, in that same bantering tone. Though I made no reply, I was certain that my face answered for me. "Oh. I'm sorry, Widge. I didn't mean to make light of it."

I shrugged. "It doesn't matter. I'm over it now."

"Yes, I can see that." There was another silence, more awkward this time, and then she said softly, "You're fortunate, you know."

"Fortunate? Like those wights who survive the pox or the plague, you mean, and carry the scars all their lives?"

"Yes. The only love I've ever felt is for the theatre, and it was not returned."

"Nor was mine."

She smiled and laid a hand on my arm. "Perhaps not. But there will be others."

In the second week of April, the Privy Council announced that the king had begun his progress south from Scotland at last. There seemed to be some doubt over whether or not His Majesty would actually come to London, for with the return of warm weather the plague had begun to make its presence felt again in the city.

In the past, when the death toll from the contagion rose, the queen and her retinue had taken refuge at Hampton Court or Windsor, both of which lay far upriver, where the air was less corrupted. James would undoubtedly do the same.

We ordinary wights did not have the luxury of moving to healthier surroundings, unless we wished to emulate those townfolk who followed in the queen's wake, bearing bundles of straw with which they constructed makeshift shelters on the riverbank. The only measure we could take, aside from wearing pomanders filled with marjoram and rosemary, was to keep the household as free as possible of vermin—lice, fleas, bedbugs, rats, and the like.

Julia had always been a willing worker, and she lent her efforts to the cause. She also cooked meals and cared for the younger orphans, who found her nearly as entertaining as they had Sam. Though I urged her almost daily to pay a visit to the Globe, she refused. It would be, she said, like my paying a visit to Judith; she did not wish to be reminded of what she could not have. She showed little inclination to visit Tom Cogan, either. "I don't need him," she said shortly. "The one time when I did, he failed me."

"'A tried to raise the money," I said.

"Yes, the same way he always does—dishonestly."

I had told her how he was arrested and imprisoned for stealing a bracelet; I had not, however, revealed the whole truth—that he was not, in fact, guilty. I did not see how I could, without also revealing a good deal more. Tom Cogan should be the one to do that. But how could he, if they never spoke? "Julia. 'A never stole that bracelet. It was planted on him."

"Planted? By whom?"

"I can't tell you."

"Why not?"

"I can't tell you that, either. Just go and see him, will you?"

After several days of delaying, she set off at last to seek out Cogan. When dusk came and she had not returned, I began to regret that I had talked her into going. Alsatia was a dangerous place, and even though Julia had grown up there, she might not be immune from its dangers.

I resolved finally that if she did not turn up by compline, I would fetch Mr. Armin and try to find her, even though it would mean breaking the curfew. Ordinarily a wight could do so with relative impunity, but since the queen's death the mayor had doubled or trebled the number of night watchmen in an attempt to quell the riots that had been flaring up, in protest of one thing or another.

Many of the demonstrators were denouncing the new king, even though they had no notion of what he looked like, let alone how he would rule the country. They claimed that this latest outbreak of the plague was an omen, a clear sign from God that James was not meant to wear the Crown. Who *was* meant to wear it was apparently not so clear.

As I was putting Tetty to bed, she said, "I've decided that you may marry Julia, if you like."

"Oh? You said before that I was to wait for you."

"I know. But perhaps you won't want to wait that long, and I wouldn't really mind very much your choosing someone else, if it was Julia."

A few weeks earlier, such a notion would have seemed to me quite odd, even ludicrous. I had always thought of Julia as a close friend, like Sander or Sam, nothing more. In truth, I believe I still had not quite gotten over thinking of her as a boy. But in the weeks since she had joined our household, I had begun to see her with new eyes—the eyes of James Pope, I suppose, and not Widge—and to feel toward her something more than mere friendship. I could not have given a name to it; I did not seem to be experiencing any of the startling symptoms that Judith Shakespeare had inspired in me. When Julia and I were together, I was comfortable and contented, not dumb and desperate. When we were apart, my thoughts of her were pleasant, not painful—except for now, when I was anxiously wondering what had become of her.

I was just about to ask Mr. Pope's permission to go after her when the front door opened and Julia hurried in, wide-eyed and breathless. I was so overcome with relief that I came very near to throwing my arms about her.

"I'm sorry, James," she said, for she had finally broken the habit of calling me Widge. "I know you must have been worried."

"Oh, I wasn't worried," I said.

"You weren't?"

"Nay. *Frantic* would be a better word, I wis."

She stared at me. "Truly?"

"Of course. I was afeared you'd been . . . Well, I don't ken what, exactly, but something dreadful."

She took hold of my hand. "I'm glad."

"*Glad?* That I was half out of me wits?"

"No. That you should care so much what happens to me."

"Did you doubt it?"

She smiled. "I suppose not. Come, let's sit. I'm exhausted from outrunning the night watchmen." I led her to the library, where Mr. Pope, in his delight at seeing her safe and sound, actually did embrace her. "I have a good reason for being so late, I assure you," Julia said. She paused and lowered her eyes. "Well, I should not say a *good* reason. In fact, it was rather a tragic reason. I was attending my father's funeral—such as it was. His body, and perhaps a dozen others, were all dumped into a single grave."

"Oh, dear," said Mr. Pope. "The contagion claimed him."

She nodded. "It's even worse in Alsatia than in the rest of the city." With a weary sigh, she sank into a chair. "It's odd. The thing that distresses me most about his death, I think, is how little sorrow I seem to feel."

"That's natural, my dear. It hasn't quite struck you yet, that's all."

"I don't know. As heartless as it may sound, I'm not certain that I'll ever mourn him very much. The truth is, I never felt as though . . . " She trailed off.

"As though 'a was truly your father," I said.

Julia turned her sad gaze upon me. "Is that how you felt? When Jamie Redshaw died?"

"Aye, more or less. But you ha' more reason than I to feel that way."

"What do you mean?"

"What I mean is . . . " I paused, drew a deep breath, and began again. "What I mean is that Tom Cogan was not your father."

Thanks to my actor's memory, I had no trouble recalling every detail of the confession Cogan had made to me in his prison cell. The difficult part was bringing myself to reveal it to Julia. I feared that once I had, nothing would ever be quite the same between us. Yet neither could I bring myself to keep it from her.

The story was so intricate that I could not tell but one piece of it, any more than I could have recounted a single scene from *Hamlet* or *Comedy of Errors* and expected my audience to make any sense of it. I had to begin, as a play does, at the beginning.

Several years before Julia was born, Tom Cogan married a childless widow named Alice—not so much for love, he admitted, as for the wages she made as a charwoman at Whitehall. Like every other female who worked or lived in the palace, Alice was smitten with the queen's dashing young master of the horse, Robert Devereux, Earl of Essex. Not content with being the queen's favorite, Essex seemed bent on seducing, one by one, all of Her Majesty's ladies-in-waiting. Each time the jealous queen got wind of such an affair she was furious, and sent the unfortunate girl home in disgrace.

One of Essex's conquests was Frances Vavasour, the daughter of an impoverished nobleman. When Frances learned that she was carrying Essex's child, she became frantic. Unable to trust the other ladies, who were envious of her, she confided in a friendly servant—Alice Cogan. They managed to hide her condition until the queen departed on her annual progress from one great lord's house to another. While Her Majesty was gone, Frances gave birth to the baby, attended only by Alice. Her motherly instincts proved less powerful than her fear of the queen's wrath. She offered to pay Alice a small sum yearly if she would raise the baby as her own, and the childless charwoman readily agreed.

Alice died of a fever three years later, leaving her husband to raise the child—and, of course, collect the stipend—on his own. By this time, Her Majesty had arranged a very favorable match for Frances; she was to wed Thomas Shirley, the son of the royal treasurer. Now she had even more reason to want her affair with Essex kept a secret. When Essex tried to stir up a rebellion and was beheaded, it became downright dangerous to admit any association with him.

For nearly thirteen years, Tom Cogan's only contact with Frances Shirley was through a servant, who brought him the annual payment that ensured his silence. But the time came at last when he needed a far larger sum, in order to pay Julia's passage home from France. After Mr. Shakespeare and Mr. Heminges turned him down, he went to call on Madame Shirley, confident that though she might not claim Julia as her daughter, she would not let the girl starve.

When she refused to give him the money, he foolishly threatened to speak to her husband. She seemed to change her mind, then, and offered him a gold bracelet that would, she said, easily fetch three pounds from a moneylender. He had not gone half a dozen blocks before the constables caught him and charged him with stealing the bracelet.

I had supposed that Julia's reaction to these revelations would be much the same as mine. But I saw no sign of astonishment on her face, only skepticism. "My da told you all this?"

"Aye. Well, not your *real* da. Tom Cogan."

"And you believed him?"

"What reason would 'a ha' to lie?"

"I don't know. To make you believe that he wasn't a thief, perhaps. Besides, he didn't need a reason to lie; it was a habit. Right now, I'll wager, he's trying to convince the Devil that it's all a mistake, that he merely got on the wrong coach."

I shook my head emphatically. "'A told me those things only because 'a thought 'a might not survive the mandrake potion. Folk don't tell lies when they're about to die."

"You don't know my da. What do you think the last thing was that anyone heard him say before the plague took him? He said that . . . that he loved me." She gave a bitter laugh that was very like a sob. "What a lie *that* was."

"Well, perhaps he did, though," put in Mr. Pope. "After all, he raised you as though you were his own daughter."

"His own daughter? Don't tell me *you* believe his story as well?"

"I believe that when a man is looking death in the face, he tends to tell the truth about things."

She stared at him incredulously. "You don't really suppose that I'm the illegitimate child of the Earl of Essex?"

Mr. Pope smiled. "You would not be the only one, my dear, I assure you. It's well known that he had a son by another of the queen's ladies-in-waiting. The boy was raised by Essex's mother." He studied Julia's face. "Besides, I met Essex a number of times, and I can see the resemblance. You have the same hair, the same eyes . . . and the same impetuous nature."

Julia considered this for a long moment. "Well," she said finally, "there is one way of settling the matter for certain."

"What's that?" I said.

"I'll pay a visit to Madame Shirley, my supposed mother."

"Nay!" I cried. "You can't! An she's as desperate to hide the truth as Cogan says, she may ha' you tossed i' prison as well!"

"Or she might simply laugh in my face. In any case, she's not likely to throw her arms about me and invite me in, is she?" Julia got to her feet. "Well, thank you for such an entertaining tale, James. I wish I could believe it." She started from the room, then turned back to us with a faint, melancholy smile. "You know, when I was a young girl, I used to console myself by imagining that my da was not truly my da, that I'd been abducted as an infant from some respectable family. But then . . . " She shrugged. "Then I grew up."

When she was gone, I moved over next to Mr. Pope and said softly, "I'm certain that Tom Cogan was telling the truth. Why does she doubt it?"

Mr. Pope scratched thoughtfully at the bald spot atop his head. "I expect that the idea frightens her a bit. She grew up among thieves and beggars, after all. The notion that she has noble blood in her veins will take some getting used to."

"Why should it? She's played fine gentlemen and ladies a hundred times on the stage."

"That's so. But playing at something is not the same as *being* it. You've feigned death a hundred times; it's a good deal different, actually being dead. Or so I would imagine."

"In truth," I said, "I almost hope that she goes on doubting it."

"Why is that?"

"Because. An she begins to think of herself as one of the . . . the *better sort,* as they say, perhaps she'll no longer ha' any use for us."

Though Julia gradually accepted the possibility that she was the daughter of a lord, it did not seem to affect her much. She went on as always, helping with the chores and with the children. She behaved no differently toward me, either, except perhaps that she was a bit more quiet and somber than usual.

When I asked whether I might tell my fellow players the news, she made no objection. The company reacted much the way they had when I told them of my true father. Half of them were astounded; the other half declared that her likeness to Essex was so unmistakable that they should have seen it before.

I returned from the theatre late that afternoon to find Julia gone and Goody Willingson growing anxious. "She said she'd be back in time to help with supper. I don't mind that she's not; I'm just wondering what's become of her."

"Did she say where she was going?"

"To see a friend. Someone named . . . Frances, I believe."

"Oh, gis!" Without pausing to explain, I dashed out of the house and down to the river, where I paid a wherryman sixpence to make the quickest crossing he could.

I knew well enough where Sir Thomas Shirley's mansion lay. It was one of the grandest in a string of grand houses that stretched out along the north bank of the river, their red tile roofs glowing like great gems in the light of the sinking sun. The moment the boat touched shore, I leaped from it and scrambled up the stairs. When I reached Thames Street, I hurried down it, scanning both sides of the thoroughfare, praying that I might see Julia heading home, safe and sound.

Instead I found her sitting on a low stone wall across the street from Shirley House, gazing at the imposing structure. "What are you *doing?*" I demanded breathlessly.

She gave me a startled look. "I might well ask the same of you."

I sank down next to her. "Trying to keep you from doing something foolish."

"You needn't have bothered. I wasn't planning to burst in and declare myself the rightful heir, or anything."

"You told Goody Willingson you were going to see Frances."

"And so I did. She came out not a quarter of an hour ago. She crossed the street and passed by me, so near that I might have reached out and touched her."

"But you didn't."

"No. Nor did I speak to her. I only wanted to have a look at her, to see . . . "

"To see whether you resembled her. I ken. I did the same wi' Jamie Redshaw. And do you?"

She gave a small, self-conscious laugh. "No. She's very beautiful."

I shrugged. "Oh, well, wi' enough face paint and a costly gown and the right wig, anyone can look beautiful—even me. Besides, I think you're quite comely."

"Do you?"

"Aye."

"Well. Thank you."

"You're welcome. Can we go now, or do you want to have a look at Sir Thomas as well?"

"No. I'm done." As we headed toward the river, she said, "That's one of the things I miss most about acting—getting to wear those elegant gowns." She sighed. "I suppose it's caps and aprons for me from now on."

"There may yet be hope. I've heard that the new queen enjoys performing in plays and masques and such. Perhaps she'll talk her husband into letting women appear upon the stage."

Julia laughed humorlessly. "He'd have to get rid of all the Puritans first."

"That's not a bad idea," I said. "He could send them all off to colonize the New World."

Though Julia and I had by now discussed in great detail nearly all that had befallen us in the year we were apart, there were two subjects I had carefully avoided. One was my infatuation with Judith; the other was my pitiful attempt to compose a play. I had been foolish to imagine that either was within my limited reach. The most I hoped for now was that I might manage to forget about them both.

Unexpectedly, Judith proved easier to get out of my head than did the notion of writing a play. Ideas and characters and titles came to me unbidden at the most inconvenient times—often in the dead of night—and I found that the only way to stop them plaguing me was to write them down. Once I had done that, I refused to have anything more to do with them. They could sit at the back of my desk until they moldered into dust for all I cared.

One of my titles, however, had found a place for itself. Mr. Shakespeare was calling his latest play *Measure for Measure.*

Without the demands of a nightly performance to occupy his time, he had finished the script in record time, and even though it was still uncertain whether or not we would ever perform again, he instructed me to begin copying out the players' sides.

By the time the new king arrived at last in London, the plague was claiming nearly a thousand lives each week. His Majesty remained in the city scarcely long enough for the Crown to settle on his royal costard, and then he retreated to Hampton Court, some ten or fifteen miles upriver.

Our sharers had concluded that if we hoped to win the king over to our cause, we must get to him before the Puritans did. To my surprise, they also concluded that it would be far wiser if, instead of each company pleading its case alone, we combined our forces. What was even more surprising was that Mr. Henslowe agreed. The less renowned companies were only too eager to join this unlikely, uneasy alliance.

So it was that, toward the end of June, a delegation made up of members of all the London companies, from the largest to the smallest, set out for Hampton Court, determined to convince the new monarch that the theatre was not an evil influence upon his subjects, as the Square Toes claimed, but an innocent source of entertainment and enlightenment.

The half dozen of us who remained were given the day off. It was just as well; we were all so distracted with worry over the company's fate that it would have been useless to try to rehearse. I was unaccustomed to being idle, though. By midday I had grown so restless that I decided I would be better off at the theatre, copying out sides.

"I'll go with you," said Julia.

I stared at her. "Truly? But you said—"

"I know what I said. I've decided I was being silly. After all, I can't very well refuse ever to enter a theatre again, can I?"

"I suppose not. None of the company will be there, though, except for me."

"Good. This will be hard enough without having to face them as well."

As we neared the Globe, Julia halted and stood gazing at it, in the same wistful way she had regarded Shirley House—as though she would have liked to feel she belonged there, but knew that she never could. When we entered the area behind the stage, her face took on an expression of such longing that I had to look away. "Perhaps you were right to begin wi'," I said. "Perhaps you should not ha' come."

"No, it's all right." Though her voice was a bit unsteady, it was calm and determined. "You go on and do your work. I'll just . . . have a look about."

By now I had done so much transcribing for the company that I scarcely needed to give any thought to what I was copying; my hand seemed almost to have a mind of its own. But ever since I began struggling to write a play, I had been paying closer attention to Mr. Shakespeare's verse. In truth, I believe I was looking for flaws in it. As petty and mean-spirited as it may seem, I found it curiously comforting to be reminded that even the most accomplished and highly regarded of playwrights sets down his share of putrid passages.

I had, in fact, just copied one: "Go to your bosom; knock there and ask your heart what it doth know." Had I composed such a line myself, I would have burned it. Though I gloated each time the script struck a sour note, the truth was that they were few and far between. For every awkward speech, there were a score of others so graceful and well made that I found myself speaking them under my breath, just to savor the sound of them.

As I was finishing up Isabella's part, which I thought of as mine, I heard a clamor of voices outside and rose from the desk to investigate. Before I reached the rear door of the theatre, it burst open, revealing Mr. Heminges and Mr. Shakespeare. They were clearly in good spirits—and, from the looks of them, they had gotten some of those spirits in an alehouse along the way. It took them a while to actually come inside, for each of them was loudly insisting that the other enter first. "Age before beauty, " said Mr. Shakespeare.

"N-no," protested Mr. Heminges. "William the C-Conqueror always goes before K-King John." He spotted me, then, and, pushing Mr. Shakespeare aside, sprang through the doorway, lost his balance, and used me to steady himself. "James! W-we succeeded! Your n-namesake has proclaimed that all the th-theatres in London are to resume b-business as usual!"

"Gog's blood! How soon?"

"Well," said Mr. Shakespeare, "we can't actually reopen the Globe until the plague deaths decline a bit. In the meantime we'll be presenting our performances at the court." He shifted his gaze to something behind me, and I turned to see Julia coming through one of the curtained entrances that led to the stage.

She curtsied slightly to the sharers. "God you good day, gentlemen." Her manner was a bit guilty, as though she'd been caught trespassing. "I was just seeing whether anything had changed."

"Well, I'm glad you're here," said Mr. Shakespeare. "We've some good news for you."

"Yes, I heard." Though she wore a smile, it seemed a bit forced. "I'm happy for you all."

"Thank you. But that's not the news I meant. This concerns you directly."

"Oh?"

Mr. Heminges wiped his brow. "Let's sit d-down to discuss it, shall we? I'm f-feeling rather light-headed, and there's a s-sort of humming in my ears."

"I believe it's the hum in your belly that's the problem," said Mr. Shakespeare. *Hum* was the London term for a mixture of ale and spirits. Mr. Shakespeare stepped into the alcove at the rear of the stage and dragged forth the two chairs that served as our royal thrones. He helped Mr. Heminges into one and seated himself in the other. "If we're to be the King's Men we should begin behaving accordingly."

I gaped at him. "The *King's* Men? His Majesty himself is to be our patron?"

Mr. Heminges nodded enthusiastically; his head appeared a bit wobbly. "It seems he's quite f-fond of the theatre after all. His son, Pr-Prince Henry, is to be H-Henslowe's new patron, and Worcester's c-company are henceforth the Queen's M-Men. And speaking of the creen— the queem—" He turned unsteadily to Mr. Shakespeare. "P-perhaps you'd best tell it, Will. My t-tongue has t-turned trader. Traitor."

Mr. Shakespeare gestured at the book-keeper's bench. "You two may as well sit; this will take some explanation. You see, after our audience with the king, Queen Anne summoned me to her chambers, to discuss the possibility of my writing a masque for her court to perform."

"And did you agree to?" I asked. I knew how contemptuous he was of those stilted, stylized spectacles, which, he said, were no more like a real play than a plate of marchpane is like a meal.

"Not exactly. I told Her Majesty that a good masque—if indeed there is such a thing—required a lighter touch than mine, and I recommended Ben Jonson as the best man for the job. But the point is, during this discussion, Julia, your name came up. As a woman with acting ambitions of her own, I thought Her Majesty would appreciate your plight. I also took the liberty of mentioning that you were Essex's daughter. Well, it was as though I had told her you were the daughter of Zeus. It seems that Essex visited the Scottish court several times—no doubt plotting with James to seize the English throne—and, like most women, Anne found him irresistible. She insisted that you come to court at once, to join her retinue of young ladies."

Julia gave an astonished laugh. "*Me?* I know nothing about waiting upon a queen!"

"I don't believe it's your waiting ability she's interested in; it's your acting ability. She wants you to perform in her plays and masques."

For a day or two, I fooled myself into believing that Julia would not accept the queen's offer—which in truth sounded less like an offer than like a command. Though she would not have admitted it, Julia was clearly intimidated by the prospect of mingling with royalty. But she had never before let a little fear prevent her from getting what she wanted. The main thing that seemed to be holding her back was a reluctance to leave Mr. Pope and Goody Willingson and the children—and, perhaps not least of all, me.

Had the lot of us implored her to stay, I suspect she would have done so. I also suspect that she would have been miserable. However strong her wish to remain with us might be, I knew that her desire to be a player was stronger. Of course, if she left, then I would be the miserable one. But given the choice between her happiness and mine, I preferred hers. Perhaps that is the true measure of love.

If the country's Catholics had imagined that a new monarch would mean a new era of religious tolerance, they were sorely disappointed. Those who converted to the Old Faith, or preached it, were still considered traitors, and those who failed to attend Anglican services on the Sabbath still risked paying a substantial fine. I was content enough to spend my Sunday mornings in church; at least it was something to do. Now that Julia was at court, playing the part of a maid of honor, I no longer had any companions my own age, and the one afternoon I had to myself seemed empty and endless, more of a burden than a boon.

For all the grief the contagion had caused, it had one benefit: the streets of the city and its public places were practically deserted. I had never grown quite used to the hurly-burly here, and though I would have welcomed the company of a friend or two, I rather relished not having to rub shoulders with a thousand strangers.

Even the churchyard of St. Paul's, which was ordinarily as crowded as a cheap coffin, had no more than twenty or thirty folk wandering about like lost souls. Most were purchasing herbs and infusions that were guaranteed to guard against the plague. Should the herbs fail, of course, the buyer was seldom in a position to demand his money back.

I had little faith in such nostrums. I was drawn, instead, to the rows of sixpenny playbooks displayed at the printers' stalls. As I was leafing idly through them—looking, I suppose, for putrid passages at which I might scoff—a particular title caught my eye. I picked it up and stared at the cover. *Timon of Athens,* it read. *A Lamentable Tragedie. By Wm. Shakspear.* I waved it at the printer. "Who sold you this script?"

"Mr. Henslowe, from the Lord Admiral's Men."

"Do you mind telling me how much you paid for 't? I'm a beginning playwright meself, you see, and I was wondering how much a good play might fetch."

"I gave him ten pounds for it—but only because it's Shakespeare's work. If it had been anyone else, I wouldn't have paid more than six."

So I need not have bothered feeling guilty because I had taken three pounds for the play under false pretenses. I might have known Henslowe would manage somehow to turn a profit on it. "Is it a good play, then?" I asked nonchalantly.

He shrugged. "I read no more than half an act—just to be sure it sounded like Shakespeare."

"Oh." I tried to put myself in the role of someone who had never encountered the script before, to see how it would strike me. I opened the playbook at random and silently scanned the first passage that met my eye:

O, the fierce wretchedness that glory brings us!
Who would not wish to be from wealth exempt
Since riches point to misery and contempt?

Not bad, really. I turned the page and sampled another speech:

The sun's a thief, and with his great attraction
Robs the vast sea; the moon's an arrant thief,
And her pale fire she snatches from the sun.

If I had not recalled writing those lines myself, I might have taken them for Mr. Shakespeare's. Perhaps I was not so poor a playwright as I had imagined. I could string words together well enough, if only I could find a thread strong enough to support them. I recalled Mr. Shakespeare's reply when I asked how he came up with the stories for his plays. "You wouldn't happen to have any ideas for sale, would you?"

The man looked at me blankly. "Ideas?"

"Never mind." I tossed the playbook aside and turned away. What was the use in dredging up that foolish ambition again? It was no more likely to succeed than anything else I had attempted lately. If the experiences of these last few months had taught me anything, it was that the efforts we mortals make to determine our own fates are as feeble and fruitless as trying to change the course of the wind by blowing against it.

Nothing I had put my hand to had turned out as I planned. I had hoped I might win Judith's affections; instead, she had gone home. I had dreamed of becoming a great playwright and discovered that I was merely promising. I had dragged Sal Pavy from the cold clutches of the Thames, only to have him succumb to the grippe. Fate had mocked me yet again by letting me rescue Tom Cogan from the hangman's rope and then striking him down with the plague. All my scheming to save Julia had come to naught; she had ended up saving herself.

I had been walking west, with no particular destination in mind, and now found myself at the wall. If I went on through Ludgate I would wind up in Salisbury Court—hardly the best neighborhood to explore on one's own. But I had been here before and come to no harm. Besides, what was the use in being cautious? If Fate had it in for me, I was not safe anywhere, and if I was in her good graces, then I had nothing to fear.

If only a person could know in advance what Fate had planned for him, he might save himself a good deal of trouble and worry. Had I known that Tom Cogan would die anyway, I need not have put myself and Father Gerard in danger. Had Julia foreseen that she would end up performing at the royal court, she could have forgone her ill-fated trip to France.

The ability to anticipate Fate would let a wight prepare a bit, too. Julia could have been practicing her maid-of-honor skills. The Chamberlain's Men could have hired half a dozen new players. Had I been forewarned that Judith and Julia would leave, or that Sander would die, I might have been more careful not to grow so fond of them.

The cunning woman had seen some of what lay in store for Sam and Sal Pavy and me. Perhaps there was more. Though she had warned me that it was not wise to examine the future too closely, I was willing to take the chance. I was sick of being tossed about by the winds of chance. I wanted some star to steer by, however faint.

When I found La Voisin, she was taking down her tent. Though she had shed most of her woolen scarves, she kept one wrapped about her head and face—to conceal the warts that disfigured her, no doubt. She gave me a suspicous glance. "I suppose you've come to complain."

"Nay. To ha' me fortune told."

"Again? Most of my customers find that once is quite enough. In fact, a number of them have come to demand their money back. That's why I'm leaving."

"Your predictions for them didn't come true, then?"

"Oh, they came true right enough—just not in the way they may have expected."

I grinned ruefully. "I ken how that is."

"Yet you've come back for more?"

"Aye. I'm weary of being Fortune's fool. It seems to me that any glimpse of what's ahead, no matter how brief or how blurry it is, must be better than fumbling along blindly."

La Voisin sighed. "Well, I suppose I must oblige you, after you gave me money for coal." She sat at the table and drew her scrying ball from a pouch at her waist. "Had you not, I might have been forced to burn this, to keep warm."

"It would burn?"

"Of course. Though it may be carved and polished, it's still a lump of coal." She uncovered the black ball and peered into it.

"I was hoping you might tell me—" I began, but she cut me off.

"I do not make fortunes to order. I see only what I see. Now be silent."

Meekly, I took a seat on the other stool and waited, scarcely moving a muscle, until she finally spoke again in that ominous, otherworldly voice. "You will tell a great many lies," she said.

I blinked at her, then at the ball. "What sort of prediction is *that?*"

She spread her wart-speckled hands, palms up. "I do not interpret, I only see."

"But—but I've been doing me best *not* to lie. Now you tell me that I must keep on?"

The cunning woman wrapped up her scrying ball and returned it to its pouch. "I never said you *must*. I said you *would*."

"Oh. Well, that's certainly a comfort." I rose from the stool. "Perhaps I was wrong. Perhaps it's best to fumble along blindly after all. God buy you."

As I walked away, La Voisin called after me, "We are not truly Fortune's fools, you know."

"Nay? What are we, then?"

"Her instruments. You imagine that there's no use struggling against Fate, that she will always have her way, no matter what we do. But don't you see? It's our very efforts to cheat Fate, or to change it, that make things come to pass in the way they were meant to."

At first, this explanation of hers seemed to me as baffling as the prediction she had made. But the more I mulled it over, the more I came to see the sense in it. It was easy to conclude that since we could not hope to alter Fate, we might as well not try. But that was like saying that since the plague struck down whomever it chose, there was no use trying to prevent it. It was like saying that we players should not bother rehearsing so hard, since the audience would either like the play or not.

It was true that most of my own efforts of late had failed. But what might have happened had I not made them at all?

Pulling Sal Pavy from the river had not prevented his death, only delayed it—but long enough for him to say farewell, and to forgive me. If I had not helped Tom Cogan arrange his escape from prison, he would have taken the truth about Julia's parentage with him to the grave. If I had not been so eager to impress Judith and to raise money for Julia's passage, I would never have written my play.

Of course, the world would have been no worse off without *Timon of Athens*. Still, creating it had been satisfying, in a perverse sort of way. It was rather like the satisfaction I had once gotten from being able to lie so convincingly. It was very much like it, in fact. I had always thought of acting as a form of lying; after all, we players habitually posed as someone we were not, and spouted sentiments that were not our own. But, though we were not the people we pretended to be, we were at least people. Plays were nothing but a lot of words on paper, attempting to give the illusion of life. What more outrageous lie could there be than that?

Though I was well out of sight of La Voisin's tent by now, I turned and gazed thoughtfully in that direction. Perhaps I was making the same mistake I had made before, the very mistake that the cunning woman's other clients had made—taking her predictions at face value. She had said that I would tell a great many lies. But might she not have meant the sort of lie that players and playwrights tell, the sort that the audience knows is untrue but chooses to believe anyway?

Well, even if that was not what she had meant, I could choose to believe that it was. If it was my fate to be a liar, then I would revel in it. I would write the most real and riveting lies I could concoct, lies that theatre companies would delight in telling and that folk would pay to hear, again and again.

I quickened my pace. Before long the sun would be down and I would need to head home, where the boys would be waiting eagerly to harness me and turn me into Banks's horse, and Mr. Pope would want to hear about all I had seen and done that day, and Tetty would ask me to tuck her into bed. And I would not, for all the world, have had it otherwise.

But for the next few hours my time was my own, and I meant to spend it in a quiet booth at the nearest tavern, where no one could find me, writing down as many lies as I could think of, in hopes that one of them might turn into a play. I would need paper, of course. I reached into my wallet and drew forth a dozen or so sheets. Though the fronts were filled with my lines from *Measure for Measure,* the back sides were invitingly empty.

I glanced at my part, feeling a bit guilty. We were to start rehearsing the play the following afternoon, and I had not yet learned a single line. Well, perhaps I could go over them for half an hour or so that evening, before sleep claimed me. After all, none of the other players would have their parts down yet, either, particularly not the new prentices and hired men the company had taken on. They would be as uncertain as I where they were to stand and what they were to say.

It occurred to me, then, how nearly real life resembles the first rehearsal of a play. We are all of us stumbling through it, doing our best to say the proper lines and make the proper moves, but not quite comfortable yet in the parts we've been given. Still, like players who trust that—despite all evidence to the contrary—the whole mess will make sense eventually, we keep on going, hoping that somehow things will work out for the best.

I could not be certain what sort of part Fortune had written for me; all I could do was to play it out to the best of my ability. I had the feeling that it would prove to be rather like the script for *Timon of Athens*—far from perfect, but full of promise.

AUTHOR'S NOTE

Though *Shakespeare's Spy* is obviously a novel and not a history text, I did my best to make it as accurate as I could. Sometimes, for the sake of the story, I did take a few liberties with the facts, or indulged in a bit of speculation. For example, I'm not certain that the Thames actually froze over in the winter of 1602–1603. But the river did freeze several times during Queen Elizabeth's reign, so solidly that celebrations called Frost Fairs were held on the ice.

I also put in a number of people who, as far as I know, didn't exist. Widge is my own invention, of course; so are Jamie Redshaw, Julia, Tetty, and Tom Cogan. Nearly everyone else in the story is based on a real historical character—though again, I did sometimes fudge the facts a little. La Voisin, the cunning woman, practiced her art in the 1660s and '70s, so, unless she lived to an unusually ripe age, she probably wasn't around in 1603.

Frances Vavasour was one of the queen's ladies-in-waiting, and she did marry Thomas Shirley; there's no evidence that she had an affair with the Earl of Essex, but it's not at all unlikely, considering how numerous his conquests were. Sal Pavy may never have acted with the Chamberlain's Men, but he did act at Blackfriars. And, though there's no record of the cause, he did die at the age of thirteen.

Shakespeare had not just one daughter, but two—Susanna and Judith. In 1603, Judith would have been seventeen or eighteen. At the age of thirty-one, she married Thomas Quiney, the shiftless, alcoholic son of one of Shakespeare's friends.

Father John Gerard's career contained far more danger and daring than I could fit into this book. Luckily he wrote his own, *The Autobiography of a Hunted Priest,* which was reprinted in the 1950s.

King James's wife, Anne, really did fancy herself an actress. She and her ladies-in-waiting regularly performed in expensive, elaborate masques at the court. But it wasn't until 1660, when King Charles II took the throne, that women were allowed at last to appear on the stages of public playhouses in England.

The cast of characters is not the only thing based on historical fact, of course. Most of the big events—the plague, the queen's death, the closing of the theatres, James's accession to the throne—happened more or less the way I've presented them. Some of the smaller elements in the book are true as well. As you know if you've read *Shakespeare's Scribe,* Widge's "swift writing" was an actual system of shorthand invented by Dr. Timothy Bright in the 1580s. And the cyphers Henslowe uses to communicate with his spy are part of a code devised by Queen Elizabeth's secret service, whose job it was to uncover Papist plots against Her Majesty.

Like all the other plays mentioned, *Timon of Athens* is the real thing. It's even still staged occasionally. But because the script is, if not exactly putrid, at least not top-notch, many Shakespearean scholars think that someone besides the Bard had a hand in writing it.